Thoughtless

Thoughtless

S. C. STEPHENS

**SIMON &
SCHUSTER**

London · New York · Sydney · Toronto · New Delhi

A CBS COMPANY

First published in Great Britain in 2012 by Simon & Schuster UK Ltd
A CBS COMPANY

Copyright © 2012 by S.C. Stephens

1 3 5 7 9 10 8 6 4 2

Simon & Schuster UK Ltd
1st Floor
222 Gray's Inn Road
London
WC1X 8HB

www.simonandschuster.co.uk

Simon & Schuster Australia, Sydney
Simon & Schuster India, New Delhi

A CIP catalogue copy for this book is available
from the British Library.

ISBN: 978-1-47112-607-9
eBook ISBN: 978-1-47112-601-7

Printed and bound by CPI Group (UK) Ltd, Croydon, CR0 4YY

Thank you to everyone who has supported

me and the publication of this story.

I couldn't have done it without you!

Thoughtless

Chapter 1
MEETINGS

It was the longest drive I had ever been on. That really wasn't saying a whole lot, since I had never driven more than sixty miles away from my hometown. Still, by anyone's standards, the drive was absurdly long. According to MapQuest, it was roughly thirty-seven hours and eleven minutes long. I'm assuming that's if you're superhuman and never need a pit stop, of course.

My boyfriend and I were driving away from Athens, Ohio. I had been born and raised there, along with every other member of my family. It was never discussed among our little foursome, but it was a known-from-birth fact, that my sister and I would be attending and graduating from Ohio University. Therefore, it had been a terrible family tragedy when, a few months ago, during my second year there, I'd made plans to transfer out in the fall. What had shocked them even more, if that were possible, was the fact that I was transferring nearly twenty-five hundred miles away to Washington—more specifically, the University of Washington in Seattle. I had landed a pretty nice scholarship, though, and that had definitely helped to sway my parents. Helped, but only a little. Family gatherings were going to be . . . colorful from now on.

The reason for my transfer was sitting beside me, driving us away in his beat-up Honda. I looked over at him and smiled. Denny

Harris. He was beautiful. I know, it's not the manliest way to describe a guy, but in my head, it was the adjective I used most often and it fit him to a tee. He was originally from a small town in Queensland, Australia, and a lifetime spent in the water at that exotic locale had left him tanned and muscular, but not in a beefy kind of way. No, in a more natural, proportioned, athletic way. He wasn't overly tall for a guy, but he was taller than me, even when I wore heels, and that was enough. His hair was a dark, dark brown, and he liked to have it lightly styled into chunky but orderly pieces. I loved to do this for him, and he adoringly let me, sighing and complaining the whole while that he was just going to shave it off one day. He loved it though.

His eyes were warm and a deep, dark brown and were currently turned in my direction to sparkle at me. "Hey, babe. Not too much longer now, maybe a couple of hours." The way his accent slid over his words was curiously intoxicating to me. It never ceased to bring me some small sliver of joy, as weird as that was.

Luckily for me, Denny had an aunt who, three years ago, had been offered a position at Ohio University and moved over here. Denny, being the sweetheart that he is, had decided to come with her and help her get settled. Having loved being in the States for a year back in high school, it didn't take him long to decide to transfer to Ohio U, which to my parents, up until he had swept me away that is, made him the ideal candidate for my affections. I sighed and hoped they got over this college thing quickly.

Thinking I was sighing at his statement, Denny added, "I know you're tired, Kiera. We'll just be a minute at Pete's and then we can go home and crash."

I nodded and closed my eyes.

Pete's was apparently the name of the popular bar where our new roommate, Kellan Kyle, was a local rock star. Though we were heading off to be his new permanent houseguests, I didn't know much about him. I knew that while doing his junior year of high school abroad, Denny had stayed with Kellan and his parents, and I knew that Kellan played in a band. Yep, I knew two whole facts about our mysterious new roomie.

I opened my eyes and stared out the window, watching the thick, green trees blur past me. The numerous streetlamps on the freeway cast an odd orange glow upon them. We had finally made it over the last mountain pass; I had been worried for a moment there that Denny's old car wouldn't be able to make it. We were currently zig-zagging past lush forests, rocky waterfalls, and vast lakes sparkling in the moonlight. Even in the dark of night, I could tell it was beautiful here. I could already see a new life opening up for me in this pictur-esque state.

Our departure from my comfortable life in Athens had started several months ago, with Denny's impending graduation from Ohio U. He was brilliant, and I wasn't the only one who thought so. "Gifted" is how his professors commonly referred to him. They had written him numerous letters of recommendation, and Denny had started applying for jobs everywhere.

I couldn't bear the thought of being away from him, even if it was only for two years until I finished school, so I applied to uni-versities and colleges everywhere that Denny applied for a job or internship. My sister, Anna, thought that was odd. She wasn't exactly the type to go traipsing around the country after a guy, not even an attractive one like Denny. But I couldn't stop myself. I could not bear to be without that boy's goofy grin.

Of course, being so brilliant, he landed his dream internship in Seattle. He was going to work for a company that, according to Denny, was one of the leading advertising agencies in the world, and was responsible for coming up with a certain golden-arched fast-food chain's world renowned jingle. He would repeat that fact to any-one who would listen, and he said it with an odd look of reverence, like they had invented air or something. Apparently, their internships are really rare. And not just in how many a year they offer, but also in how involved they allow their interns to be with projects. Denny would immediately be a member of the team, not just a fetching boy.

He had been practically giddy in his excitement to leave for Seattle.

I had been a panicky mess. I had downed a half bottle of Pepto daily, until I'd finally received my acceptance for transfer to the University of Washington. Perfect! Then, I somehow managed to swing a scholarship that paid for nearly all of my tuition. I wasn't Denny's level of brilliance, but I wasn't a dummy either. Double perfect! The fact that Denny actually knew people in Seattle, and that one of them had an extra room for us at a fraction of what we were expecting to pay . . . well, it made the whole affair seem like it was fated to be.

I smiled as I watched the names of roads, parks, and small towns fly by us. We were coming upon towns more frequently now, starting to move away from the majestic mountains that I could no longer see behind us in the darkness. Rain spattered our window as we approached a larger city with a sign directing us toward Seattle. We were getting closer. Our new life would start soon. I knew virtually nothing of our new city, but I would get to figure it all out with Denny by my side. I reached over to grab his hand and he smiled softly at me.

Denny had graduated a week ago with a double major in business economics and marketing—the hunky dork—and we'd packed up to leave. His new job required him to be there this coming Monday. My parents had not been thrilled about the all-too-soon separation. Once they had grudgingly accepted my decision to leave, they had been looking forward to having me for one last summer. While I would miss them terribly, Denny and I had been living apart, he at his aunt's and I at my parents', for nearly two achingly *long* years, and I was eager to advance our relationship. I had tried to keep a solemn face while kissing them all goodbye, but on the inside, I had been glowing with the thought of finally being on our own.

The only part of the move I had protested, vehemently, was driving there. A few hours in a plane versus days in a cramped car . . . it really was a no-brainer to me. But Denny had some odd attachment to his vehicle and refused to leave it behind. I supposed it would be convenient to have a car in Seattle, but I got a good half day of sulking out of it anyway. After that, Denny had just made the trip too much fun for me to complain anymore, and of course, he had found numerous ways to make his car quite . . . comfortable. There were a couple of rest stops that are now forever etched in my fondest memories.

I smiled widely at that thought and bit my lip, once again excited at the very idea of a place of our own. The ride had been entertaining and full of many happy memories, but we had driven straight through. Even in my happiness, I was bone-tired. And even though Denny had managed to make his car surprisingly cozy, it was still a car, and I was dreaming of an actual bed. My smile turned into a contented sigh when the lights of Seattle finally showed themselves to us.

Denny had gotten directions on the way over, and we easily found Pete's Bar. He managed to find an empty space in the it's-Friday-night-let's-go-drink jammed-full parking lot and nimbly pulled the car in. The second the engine shut off, I practically jumped out of the door and stretched for a solid minute. Denny chuckled at me, but did the same. Grabbing each other's hands, we made our way to the open front doors. We were later than we had expected to be, and the band was already playing, their music drifting out to us in the lot. We walked inside the doors and Denny quickly scanned the room. He pointed out a really big guy leaning against the side wall, watching the audience, who were mostly watching the band, and we started making our way through the packed room to him.

On the way over, I looked up at the stage to the four guys performing there. They all looked to be around my age, in their early twenties. Their music was fast, driving rock, and the singer's voice was perfectly matched to the style, rough, yet really sexy. *Huh, they're pretty good,* I thought, while Denny expertly navigated us through a sea of feet and elbows.

I couldn't help but notice the lead singer first. No one would be able to overlook him—he was drop-dead gorgeous. He had intense eyes that were busy scanning the crowd of adoring women clustered around the front of the stage. His light, sandy-brown hair was a thick, wild mess. It was longer on the top with shorter, shaggy layers all the way around, and he was running his hand through it in a rather adorable way. As Anna would say, he had "bedroom hair." Well, okay, she would use a cruder adjective—my sister could be a little crass—but it *was* the kind of style that looked like he had just been ravished in the back room. I blushed as it occurred to me that maybe he had been. . . . Anyway, it was alarmingly attractive on him. Not everyone could pull off that kind of look.

His clothes were surprisingly basic, like he knew he didn't have to accessorize his looks. His shirt was just a gray tee, with the long sleeves pushed back to the elbow. It was just tight enough to hint at what was most definitely a fabulous body underneath. He wore perfectly lived-in black jeans with black, heavy boots. Simple, yet stunning. He looked like a rock-god.

Even with all that, the most amazing part of him, besides his alluring voice, was his unbelievably sexy smile. He only showed glimpses of it through the words he was singing, but it was enough. A smooth half-smile here and there—flirting with the crowd. Utterly charming.

He was downright sexy. Unfortunately, he knew it.

He met eyes with every one of his adoring fans. They went crazy as his gaze passed over them. Now that I was looking closer, his half-smiles were disconcertingly seductive. His eyes were practically undressing each and every one of the women around the stage. My sister also had a choice turn of phrase for those kinds of eyes.

Watching him seduce the entire cluster of female groupies was making me uncomfortable, and I shifted my focus to the remaining three members.

The two guys on either side of the singer were so similar that they had to be related, probably brothers. They seemed about the same size, slightly shorter than the singer, and thinner, not quite as . . . well built. They had the exact same slim nose and thin lips. One played lead guitar, one played bass guitar, and they were both passably cute. Possibly, if I had seen them first instead of the singer, I would have thought them more attractive.

The lead guitarist wore khaki shorts and a black T-shirt featuring the name and logo of a band I didn't know. His hair was blond, short, and spiky. He played the difficult-sounding piece with a look of concentration on his face, his light eyes flicking over the crowd every once in a while, then back down to his hands.

His equally light-eyed, blond-haired relative wore his hair longer, down to his chin and tucked behind his ears. He was also wearing shorts, and his T-shirt made me chuckle a little. It simply read, "I'm with the band." He played the bass with an almost bored expression on his face and kept looking over to the guitarist, who could so easily be his twin. I got the impression he would rather be playing that instrument.

The final guy was tucked behind the drums, so I couldn't see much of him. I was just thankful that he had clothes on at all, since many drummers seem to feel the need to be nearly naked when they play. But he had the kindest face in the world, with big, dark eyes and buzz-cut brown hair. He had gauges in his ears, maybe half-inch ones. I wasn't too big a fan of those, but on him, they looked oddly attractive. His arms were covered in bright, colorful tattoos, like an art mural, and he flew through the complicated drum patterns effortlessly, scanning the crowd with a big grin on his face.

Denny had only mentioned that our new roommate, Kellan, was in this band. He had never elaborated on which member he might be. I hoped it was the big, teddy-bear-looking guy in the back. He seemed like he'd be easygoing.

Denny had finally worked us through the crowd to the burly man. He'd noticed us approaching and was smiling broadly at Denny. "G'day, mate! Glad to see ya again," he yelled over the music, trying to mimic Denny's accent and butchering it horribly.

I smiled to myself. Everyone always tried to sound like him, once they heard him speak. Usually, nobody pulled it off. It was just one of those accents that sounded phony unless you had lived in Australia. Denny was always trying to get me to use it, because it highly amused him when people tried. I knew I couldn't, so I didn't give him the satisfaction. No point in making myself look stupid.

"Hey, Sam, long time no see." Denny's year in Seattle as an exchange student back in high school had introduced him to Kellan. Since Sam looked about Denny's age, I assumed that was how he knew him too. I smiled wider as they gave each other a swift "guy" hug.

Sam was a big guy. He definitely had a beefcake body and wore a red shirt that barely contained his muscles. His head was completely shaved, and if he hadn't been grinning, I would never have dared to approach him. There was just an air of menace about him, which, now that I noticed the name of the bar across his shirt, seemed appropriate. He obviously worked as a bouncer here.

Sam leaned in closer to us, so he didn't have to talk quite so loud. "Kellan told me you were coming in tonight. Staying with him, huh?" He looked over at me standing beside Denny. "This your girl?" he asked, before Denny could answer his first question.

"Yeah, this is Kiera, Kiera Allen." Denny smiled over at me. I loved the way his accent slid over my name. "Kiera, this is Sam. He and I were mates in school."

"Hello." I smiled at him, not knowing what else to do.

I hated meeting people for the first time. It always made me a little uncomfortable and very self-conscious. I didn't feel like I was anything special to look at. Not that I was unattractive, just nothing special. My brown hair was long and, thankfully, thick, with a slight curl to it. My eyes were hazel and I'd been told expressive, which in my mind always translated to overly large. My height was in the middle for a girl, 5'5", and I was pretty lean, thanks to running track in school. But overall, I felt very average.

Sam nodded back at me and looked over to talk to Denny again. "Anyway, Kellan had to start his set, but he left your key with me in case you guys didn't want to stay . . . . you know, long drive and all." He reached in his jeans pocket and handed the key over to Denny.

That was sure nice of Kellan. I was dead tired, and really just wanted to get settled in, then sleep for about two days straight. I didn't want to have to wait for who-knows-how-long a set lasted to get our key.

I glanced back at the band again. The singer was still mentally undressing every woman he spotted. Occasionally, he would suck in a breath through his teeth, exaggerating the sound in a way that was almost intimate. He leaned over the microphone and reached out a hand to get closer to his adoring fans, making them squeal in delight. Most of the men in the bar were farther back, but some boyfriends had stuck close to their girls. Those men eyed the singer with decided distaste. I couldn't help but think that some day he was going to get his ass seriously kicked.

More and more, I believed the nice-looking guy in the back was Denny's "mate." The drummer just seemed like the good-natured, carefree type of person that he would easily bond with. Denny was taking a minute to chat with Sam, asking him what he was up to now. When they were finished catching up, we said our goodbyes.

"Ready to go?" Denny asked, knowing how tired I was.

"Oh, yes," I said, aching for an actual bed. Thankfully, Kellan had told Denny that the last tenant had left some furniture behind.

Denny laughed a little and then looked over to the band. I watched him waiting to catch his friend's eye. Denny liked having light facial hair along his jawline and upper lip. Not a lot, and not heavy; he just looked like someone who had been on a long camping trip. It made his could-be baby face seem older and more rugged. It was soft, though, and felt nice when he nuzzled my neck. It was also incredibly sexy. I realized I was ready to leave for more than one reason.

Still intently watching Denny, I noticed him raise the hand clutching the key and nod his chin up. Apparently he had finally gotten Kellan's eye, and signaled to him that we were heading home. I was so lost in my dreamy thoughts that I'd forgotten to watch who he signaled. I still wasn't entirely sure which one Kellan was. I glanced over, but none of the four were looking our way.

As we started to make our way back to the door, I looked over to Denny. "Which one is Kellan anyway?"

"Huh? Oh, I guess I never really explained that, did I?" He nodded back to the band. "He's the singer."

My heart dropped a little. Of course he was. I stopped and looked back, and Denny stopped with me, watching the band as well. Sometime while we had been walking away, the song had changed. The beat was slower, and Kellan's voice was lower and smoother, sexier, if that were possible. But that wasn't what made me stop and listen.

It was the words. They were beautiful, heartbreaking even. It was a poetic declaration of love and loss, insecurity and even death. Of wanting someone left behind to remember him as a good person, a person worthy of being missed. The insipid girls, whose number had doubled, were still clamoring for his attention. They didn't even seem to recognize the change of the music's tone. Kellan was completely different though.

Both hands were now curled around the microphone, and he looked out over the crowd, his eyes unfocused, absorbed in the music. His whole body was lost to the words; they seemed to come from deep in his soul. Where the other song had just been fun, this one was personal. It obviously meant something to him. He stopped my breath.

"Wow," I stated when my breathing started back up. "He's . . . amazing."

Denny nodded over to the stage. "Yeah, he's always been really good at this. Even his band in school was good."

I suddenly wished we could stay all night, but Denny was every bit as tired as I was, maybe more so, since he had done the majority of the driving. "Let's go home." I smiled up at him, loving the way that sounded.

He grabbed my hand and pulled me through the rest of the crowd. I glanced back at Kellan one last time before we stepped out the door. Surprisingly, he was looking straight at me. That perfect face focused solely on me was making me shiver a little. His powerful song still played on. Again, I wished I could stay to hear the end.

He was so different now from the first time I had noticed him. In that first glance he had just seemed so . . . sensual. Everything about him had screamed, *I'm going to take you right here and make you for-*

get your own name. But now he appeared deep, soulful even. Maybe my first impression was wrong? Maybe Kellan was someone worth getting to know better?

Living with him was going to be . . . interesting.

Denny found our new place easily; it wasn't terribly far from the bar. It was on a smaller side street that was crammed with houses. The street itself was so completely lined with vehicles, it was practically a one-way street. The driveway looked just big enough for two cars, so Denny pulled into the spot farthest from the front door.

He grabbed three of our bags from the backseat while I grabbed the remaining two; then we made our way inside. It was small, but charming. The entrance had hooks for jackets, all of them empty, and a half-moon table, where Denny tossed his keys. To our left was a short hallway ending in a door. A bathroom maybe? Off that hallway, I could just make out a countertop. Must be the kitchen. Directly in front of us was the living room. An overly large television set was its most prominent feature. *Boys will be boys,* I thought. To our right was a set of stairs that curled around to the top floor.

We followed the stairs up and stopped at a set of three doors. Denny opened the right door—the exceedingly messy bed and an older-looking guitar propped in the corner gave it away as Kellan's room. He shut the door and tried the middle one, laughing a little at our guessing game. Ah, he had found the bathroom. That left door number three. Smiling, he opened it wide for us. I started to look around, but didn't get much further than the impressively large, queen-sized bed in the middle of the wall. Not one to miss an opportunity, I grabbed Denny's shirt and pulled him suggestively to that bed.

Alone time didn't happen very often. We were usually surrounded by so many people—his aunt, my sister, or, ugh, my parents. It was cherished, and one thing I had quickly realized upon inspecting our tiny new home was that we weren't going to be quite as alone here as I had hoped, especially upstairs; I could tell the walls were very thin, not much in the way of privacy. So we threw our bags

in the corner of the small room and took advantage of the fact that
our roommate had a night job. The rest of our stuff could wait to be
brought into the house. Some things were just too important.

I awoke early the next morning, still groggy from days of traveling,
but refreshed. Denny was stretched out on his side of the bed and
looked entirely too peaceful to wake. A small thrill passed through
me at waking up next to him. We rarely were able to spend an entire
night together, but now we would get to every night. Careful not to
disturb him, I stood and made my way to the hall.

Our door looked directly across to Kellan's room and his door
was slightly cracked. The bathroom was in between the two small
rooms and the door was shut. My family had never closed the bathroom door unless someone was in there. I couldn't see a light under
the door, but it was bright enough outside now that no light would
be needed.

Should I knock? I didn't want to feel like an idiot, knocking on
my own door, but I hadn't been introduced to Kellan yet, and walking in on him was not the way I wanted to meet him . . . not that I
ever did want to walk in on him. I glanced over to his door and listened until I thought a vein might burst. I thought I could hear light
breathing coming from his room, but really, I could have been hearing my own. I hadn't heard him come in last night, but he seemed
like the type to stay out 'til four and sleep in 'til two, so I took a
chance and turned the knob.

Relief washed through me that the bathroom was empty. Relief,
and the intense desire to wash the travel grime from my body. Making sure the door was securely locked—I didn't need Kellan walking
in on me either—I turned on the shower.

Last night, I had hastily scrounged through my stuff for my pajamas before passing out from exhaustion. Now, I stripped off my
sleep pants and tank top and stepped into the near-scalding water. It
was heaven. I suddenly wished Denny were awake. I wished he were
in here with me. He had the nicest body and it was even more so

streaming with water. But then I remembered how dreadfully tired he'd looked last night. Hmmm . . . maybe another time.

I relaxed into the hot water and sighed. I hadn't remembered shampoo in my hurry to the bathroom, but luckily there was a bar of soap in the shower. Not the greatest way to wash my hair, but I wasn't comfortable using Kellan's expensive-looking stuff. I luxuriated under the hot steam for a lot longer than I should have, considering the other people who probably wanted a tiny bit of warm water for themselves. I couldn't help it though—it just felt so good to be clean again.

Finally, I shut the water off and dried away the droplets with the only available towel. It was dreadfully thin and slightly too small; I would need to remember my big, comfy towel next time. Hastily wrapping the small towel around me, I braced myself for the cooler air in the hallway and opened the door. I had forgotten all of my toiletries, not to mention a change of clothes, in my desire to be clean. I was concentrating on remembering which bag in our chaotic pile held my stuff, when I noticed that Kellan's door was now open . . . and occupied.

He was standing in his doorway, yawning lazily and scratching his bare chest. Apparently, he preferred sleeping in just his boxer shorts. I couldn't help but be momentarily distracted by the sight of him. A night's rest hadn't affected his messy hair negatively at all; it looked downright delicious, going every which way. His body took up most of my attention however. It was as fabulous as I had suspected. Where Denny's body was great, Kellan's was just ridiculous. He was tall, maybe a good half foot taller than Denny, and his muscles were long and lean, like a runner's. And they were very clearly defined. I could have taken a marker and etched every single line.

He was, well . . . hot.

His eyes, an impossibly deep shade of blue, sparkled at me as he cocked his head to the side in a distractingly charming way. "You must be Kiera." His voice was low and slightly husky from just waking up.

Embarrassment flashed through me as I realized that our first meeting wasn't that far from how I'd feared it would be. At least we were both dressed, sort of. Mentally chastising myself for not putting the tank top and lounge pants I had slept in back on before leaving the bathroom, I awkwardly extended a hand to him in some feeble attempt at formality.

I mumbled, "Yes . . . hi."

An adorable half-smile appeared on his face as he shook my hand. He seemed to find great humor in my reaction. He also didn't seem bothered in the slightest that neither one of us was dressed decently. I felt a blush coming and desperately wanted to flee to my room, but I had no idea how to politely get out of this odd meeting.

"You're Kellan?" I asked. Dumb question. Obviously he was— only three of us were living here.

"Mmmm . . ." He nodded in acknowledgment, still watching me closely. A little closer than I was comfortable having a strange man stare at me while I was half-naked.

"Sorry about the water. I think I used all of the hot side." I turned to find our doorknob, hoping he would take the hint.

"No problem. I'll just use it tonight, before I leave."

I wondered briefly where he was going, but instead mumbled, "See you later then," and dashed back into my room. I thought I heard a soft chuckle behind me as I closed the door.

Well, that was mortifying. I guess it could have been worse. Ugh, that's exactly why I hated meeting people for the first time. I tended to come out of those meetings looking like an idiot, and today was no exception. Denny claimed our first meeting had been endearing. My memory attached a different word to it. I dreaded just how often I was going to have to do this in the coming months. At least for those future meetings, I would have more clothes on . . . I hoped.

I laid my head back against the closed door and waited for the embarrassment to fade.

"You okay?" Denny's clear, accented voice poked through my thoughts. I cracked my eyes open and saw him propped up on his elbow, watching me curiously. He still looked tired and I hoped I hadn't woken him.

"Just meeting our new roommate," I explained sullenly.

Denny knew me so well that he wasn't too surprised at my reaction over something so small. He knew how embarrassed I would be, running into someone I didn't know in only a thin towel.

"Ah, come here." He opened his arms to me and I eagerly crawled back into bed.

I snuggled my back into his warm, comforting embrace and his arms tightly cinched around me, pulling me close. He tenderly kissed my damp head and then let out a long sigh. "Are you sure about this, Kiera?"

I reached back and playfully smacked him on the shoulder. "We're already here. Isn't it a little late for that?" I moved so I could look at his face. "I am *not* driving back," I teased him.

He smiled a little, but his face was serious. "I know what you gave up for me by coming here—your family, your home. I'm not blind; I know you miss it. I just want to make sure that this is worth it for you."

I placed my hand on his cheek. "Don't. Don't ever question that. Of course I miss my family, miss them terribly. But you *are* worth it, you're worth anything." My fingers gently stroked his cheek. "I love you. I want to be where you are."

He smiled in earnest. "Forgive me for being a little sappy here, but . . . you are my heart. I love you too." And then he kissed me deeply and started to unwrap the suddenly bulky towel from around my waist.

I had to remind myself over and over that the walls were very thin. . . .

Chapter 2
D-Bags

After a while, Denny and I came down the stairs holding hands. It was almost like we were teenagers in puppy love. We were both thoroughly enjoying finally living together. I told Denny what we looked like, and we were both laughing as we rounded the corner into the kitchen.

The second thing I'd noticed about this house, right after taking in the small size of it, was how sparse on decorations it was. It was clearly evident that it was simply a place to sleep at night. A guy's pad. I was definitely going to have to do some shopping soon. It was just way too barren for any girl, even me, to leave alone for long.

The kitchen was decently sized, considering. The far wall had a long counter ending in a refrigerator. The opposite wall was half the length, with a stove, above which a microwave sat. On the left of the stove was another short counter with a coffeepot full of freshly brewed coffee. The smell emanating from it made my mouth water. The back portion of the room had a moderately sized table with four chairs and a large window that overlooked the postage-stamp backyard.

The space in between the short wall and the windowed wall opened up to the living room, and Kellan was walking through it. He was holding the morning paper and reading the folded front page.

He was already dressed for the day in shorts and a short-sleeve tee. His wavy hair was still messy, but more orderly than earlier . . . perfect. Even though Kellan was simply dressed, I suddenly felt very plain in my basic jeans and T-shirt. I tightened my hand in Denny's and dealt with it, though.

"Hey, man." Denny smiled and went over to Kellan, who looked up at his voice.

"Hey, glad you guys made it!" Kellan smiled back and clasped Denny's shoulder in a quick hug. I smiled too. Guys could be so cute.

With a warm smile in my direction, Denny said, "You already met Kiera, I hear." My smile left me at the memory.

"Yes." Kellan's eyes sparkled . . . a little too mischievously. "But nice to see you again." At least he was being polite about it. Still smiling, Kellan walked over to the fresh pot and grabbed some mugs from the cupboard above it. "Coffee?"

"Not for me, no. I don't see how you guys can drink that stuff," Denny said, making a disgusted face. "Kiera loves it though." I nodded in agreement and smiled up at Denny. He didn't even like the smell of coffee. He was more of a tea guy, which I found completely amusing and adorable.

Denny looked down at me. "Hungry? I think there's still some food in the car."

"Starving." I bit my lip and looked at his beautiful face for a second, then lightly kissed him and playfully smacked him in the stomach. Yeah, we were definitely teenagers in love again.

He gave me a brief peck and then turned to leave. As he moved away, I noticed Kellan behind him, watching us with an amused expression on his face.

"Okay, be right back." Denny left the kitchen and I heard him grab his keys from the entryway table, where he'd tossed them the night before. The door closed a second later, and I marveled at how he wasn't even fazed that he was only wearing the T-shirt and boxers he had slept in.

Smiling, I went to the table to sit and wait for him. Kellan came over a few moments later with two cups of coffee. I made a move to stand up and put cream and sugar in mine, but looking at the coffee more closely, I could see that he already had. How did he know that I liked it that way?

Noticing my puzzled expression, he said, "I brought mine black. I can switch you, if you don't like cream."

"No, actually I do like it this way." I smiled at him as he sat down. "I thought maybe you could read minds or something."

"I wish," he chuckled, taking a sip of his black coffee.

"Well, thank you." I raised my cup a little and took a sip. . . . Heaven.

Kellan looked across the table at me, his head tilted. "So, Ohio, huh? Buckeyes and fireflies, right?"

I smiled and mentally rolled my eyes at his limited knowledge of my home state. I didn't press him though. "Yep, that's about it."

He looked at me quizzically. "Do you miss it?"

I paused for a moment before answering him. "Well, I miss my parents and my sister, of course." I paused again and sighed a little. "But I don't know . . . a place is just a place. Besides, it's not like I won't ever see it again," I finished, smiling.

He frowned at me. "Don't take this the wrong way, but why did you come all the way out here?"

I was a little annoyed at the question, but I tried to ignore it. I didn't know Kellan well enough to judge him. "Denny," I stated, as if that were the most obvious thing in the world.

"Huh." He didn't elaborate, just sipped his coffee.

Needing to switch subjects, I blurted out the first thing that popped into my head. "Why do you sing like that?" I instantly realized how horribly offensive that must have sounded and regretted saying it. I didn't intend it that way. I was just curious about why he was so . . . flirtatious . . . on stage.

His blue eyes narrowed at me. "What do you mean?" he asked. I got the feeling that his singing was something people usually didn't question him about. I couldn't tell if he was angry, but I didn't want to steer him that way. This was not how to make a good impression on the person I now shared a home with.

Pausing for time, I took a slow sip of coffee. "You were great," I started, hoping to mollify him. "But sometimes you were just so . . ." I cringed mentally, but knew I needed to just be a grown-up and say it. ". . . sexual," I whispered.

His expression softened and then he laughed for what felt like five minutes.

Irritation flared in me full force. I wasn't trying to be funny and I was getting really embarrassed, not to mention uncomfortable. Why did I have to open my big mouth? I stared down into my coffee cup, wanting to crawl inside it and disappear.

Kellan finally noticed my expression had changed and worked at regaining his composure. "Sorry . . . It's just, that's not what I thought you were going to say." I wondered for a moment what he had expected me to say and looked back up at him. Still slightly chuckling, he thought for a moment. "I don't know. People just tend to respond to it." He shrugged his shoulders.

By "people," I inferred that he meant women.

"Did I offend you?" he asked with a twinkle in his eye.

Great, now he thought I was this prudish person who couldn't handle him. "Nooo." I overly stressed the word and glared at him. "It just seemed excessive. Besides, you don't need it—your songs are great."

He seemed a little taken aback by that. He sat back in his chair and watched me in a way that made my heart beat quicker. Seriously, he was just absurdly good-looking. I looked down at the table uncomfortably.

"Thank you. I'll try to keep that in mind." I looked back up at him again. He was smiling softly at me and he seemed to genuinely mean it. Changing topics, he asked me, "How did you and Denny meet?"

I smiled as I remembered it. "College. He was a teaching assistant in one of my classes. It was my first year, his third. I thought he was the most beautiful person I had ever seen." I blushed a little bit over calling him beautiful out loud, and to a guy. I generally tried to not use that word in everyday conversation. People tended to look at me strangely. Kellan was just smiling peacefully at me however. I supposed he was used to hearing a wide variety of glowing adjectives.

"Anyway, we just hit it off and have been together ever since." I couldn't help but smile at the flood of memories we had together. "What about you? How did you meet Denny?" I knew the basics of the story, but not much more.

He thought a moment, a smile on his lips that matched mine. "Well, my parents thought it would be a good idea to host an exchange student. I think their friends were impressed with that. " His smile faded a bit before instantly returning. "But Denny and I hit it off right away too. He's a cool guy."

He turned his face away and a look passed over him that I couldn't comprehend . . . almost grief. "I owe him a lot," he said softly. He turned back to me, his charming grin back in place, and shrugged. "Anyway, I'd do anything for the guy, so when he called and said he needed a place to stay, it was the least I could do."

"Oh." I was curious about his sudden sadness, but he seemed back to normal now and I didn't want to press him. Anyway, Denny came back into the kitchen at that point.

He looked very apologetic. "Sorry, all I could find were these." He held up a bag of Cheetos and a bag of pretzels.

Kellan softly laughed while I held my hand out and gave Denny a sweet smile. "Cheetos, please." Denny frowned but gave them to me, and Kellan laughed harder.

We finished our "nutritious" breakfast, and then I called my parents (collect, no less) to let them know we were here and we were safe. Denny and Kellan caught up on their years apart while I chatted with my family. The only phone in the house was an olive-green, corded, seventies-looking contraption in the kitchen, and Denny and Kellan's stories were getting louder and funnier as they sat at the table and reminisced. I had to glare over at them a couple of times, nonverbally asking them to be quiet so I could hear my parents. Of course, they thought that was hilarious, and it only seemed to make them laugh even louder. Eventually, I turned my back on them and ignored their happy conversation. It wasn't as if my mom and dad were saying anything other than "Ready to come home now?" anyway.

After my too-long conversation, Denny and I headed back upstairs. He quickly showered while I rummaged through his bag for some clothes. Choosing his favorite, faded blue jeans and a light beige Henley shirt for him, I started setting out the rest of our things on the bed.

The person who had rented this room before us had been kind enough to leave the bed (sheets and all), a dresser, a small television, and a nightstand, complete with an alarm clock. I wasn't sure why, but I was extremely grateful, since Denny and I had absolutely no furniture. In Athens, we had lived with our relatives to save on cash. I had tried on numerous occasions to get Denny into an apartment of our own, but, ever the money-savvy one, he hadn't seen the logic in wasting all that cash when our families were only a few minutes from school. In my head, I had a very long list of reasons why . . . most involving a bed, sheets and all.

And of course my parents, although they adored him, weren't keen on him moving into my bedroom. They hadn't even been okay with me moving into his aunt's place, and since they were paying for my pricey education, I hadn't pressed the issue too far. But now we sort of had to live together to save on money, so I guess, in the end, I had won the argument. I smiled at that thought as I began putting our clothes into the small double dresser—his on one side, mine on the other. We didn't have a whole lot of clothes, and I was finished by the time Denny came back from his shower.

Seeing him wrapped only in a towel greatly pleased me, and I sat on the bed with my arms around my legs, head resting on my knees, to watch him get dressed. He laughed at my rapt attention, but was comfortable enough that he had no problem dropping his towel and dressing. I would have made him turn around, or close his eyes or something, if our roles had been reversed.

Once finished, he sat on the bed beside me. I couldn't resist running my fingers through his damp hair, rustling it around a little bit, and styling chunky pieces. He waited patiently, a warm glow in his eyes, a soft smile on his lips.

When it appeared that I was finished, he kissed me on the forehead, and we made our way back downstairs to get the rest of our boxes from the car. It only took two trips—we really didn't have a whole lot of stuff. We were, however, completely out of food. We put the boxes on our bed and decided to brave our way through the city streets in a quest for sustenance. Denny had lived here for an entire year, but that had been several years ago and he hadn't been driving then. So we got some directions from Kellan and made our attempt.

We easily made our way down to the pier and Pike Place Market to look around and get some fresh food. It truly was a beautiful city. We strolled hand in hand down the pier, watching the sunlight sparkle off the Sound. It was a warm, clear day and we stopped and watched the ferries shuttle back and forth while the seagulls flew low over the water. Like us, they were scrounging for food. A light, cool breeze brought the smell of salt water with it and, perfectly content, I leaned my head back on Denny's chest as he wrapped his arms around me.

"Happy?" he asked me, rubbing his jaw along my neck, the light hair along it making me giggle.

"Deliriously," I answered, turning my head to give him a soft kiss.

We did all the touristy things in the area—went through all the quaint shops, listened to the street musicians, sat on a cute little merry-go-round, and watched the fishmongers chuck huge salmon to each other while the packed crowd cheered. Eventually we picked up some fresh fruits, vegetables, and other edibles and made our way back to the car.

One unfortunate thing about Seattle that was quickly apparent to us on the drive home was the roller-coaster-steep hills. Driving a stick shift on them was next to impossible. By the third near-accidental rear-ending, we were both laughing so hard that I couldn't stop the tears. We eventually made it back home in one piece after getting lost twice.

We were still laughing about our little adventure as we walked back into the kitchen carrying a couple canvas bags of groceries. Kellan looked up at us from where he was sitting at the table, writing notes on a spiral pad of paper. Lyrics, maybe? He gave us an amused grin and went back to his work.

Denny put our food away while I went upstairs and began sorting through our few boxes of stuff. It went pretty quickly. Knowing we weren't moving into a huge place, we had only brought the essentials with us. We had left the majority of the stuff that a person accumulates over any given period of time in my mom's attic. It didn't take nearly as long as I thought it would before I had put away all of our books, Denny's work clothes, my school stuff, and a few pictures and other mementoes. I finished by putting our toiletries in the bathroom. Seeing our dollar store shampoo next to Kellan's expensive stuff made me smile. There. I was done.

Heading back downstairs, I turned into the living room to find Kellan and Denny watching ESPN. The space was like the rest of the house—barely decorated. I really was going to have to do something about that soon.

The room consisted of a large TV against the back wall, next to a slider that led out to the backyard. A long, ratty-looking couch took up the far wall, with a seemingly comfy looking chair catty-corner to it. A round table with an old lamp on it was tucked between the two. Kellan appeared to live as simply as he dressed.

Denny was sprawled across the long couch, looking like he might fall asleep at any moment; he probably was still dreadfully tired. I was beginning to feel the long trip, combined with walking around the pier all afternoon, catch up with me as well, so I walked over to Denny and crawled on top of him. He shifted so I could sink in between him and the couch, my leg over his, my arm across his chest, and my head nestled in his shoulder. He sighed contently and pulled me tight, softly kissing my head. His heartbeat was slow and steady and was gently pulling me into sleep. Before I closed my eyes, I glanced over at Kellan, who was sitting in the chair. He seemed to be watching us curiously. I could do no more than wonder about it, before my eyes slipped closed and sleep washed over me.

I woke up a while later when Denny shifted beneath me. "Sorry, I didn't mean to wake you," he said, his accent warm and delightful around the words.

Stretching luxuriously, I yawned and pushed myself up a little to look at his face. "It's okay," I mumbled, giving him a light kiss. "I suppose I should wake up anyway, if I want to sleep tonight." I looked around but we were alone in the room.

Alone.

The thought made me instantly aware of how close Denny and I were snuggling on the couch. Grinning mischievously, I kissed him again, but harder. He laughed a little, but kissed me back eagerly. It didn't take long for my breath and my heartbeat to quicken. Desire filled me for this warm, beautiful man beneath me, and I ran my fingers down his chest and slipped them under his shirt to feel his smooth skin.

He gripped my hips with his strong hands and shifted me over, until I was directly on top of him. I sighed happily and pressed into him. Somewhere in the corner of my mind, I registered a door closing, but Denny's hands pulling me even harder against him quickly drove any other thought from my head.

I was happily kissing his jaw and moving to his neck, when a faint, amused chuckle woke me from my reveling. I sat bolt upright on Denny's lap, causing him to grunt in surprise. I hadn't realized Kellan was still here, and I was pretty sure the color on my cheeks made that painfully obvious to him.

"Sorry." Kellan was laughing a little harder now. He stood in the entryway and grabbed his jacket from a hook by the front door. "I'll be out of your hair in a minute . . . if you want to wait." He seemed to ponder that for a moment. "Or don't. It really doesn't bother me." He shrugged, still chuckling.

It bothered me. I immediately flew to the other side of the couch, too embarrassed to say anything. I looked over at Denny, hoping he could somehow rewind time a few minutes. He just lay there with an amused smile that matched Kellan's on his face. Irritation flowed through me. *Men!*

Needing to change the focus somehow, I blurted out, "Where are you going?" It came out more harshly than I meant it to, but it was too late to change that.

Kellan blinked at me, a little surprised by the angry outburst. I got the feeling we really could have been having sex on the couch and he wouldn't have cared. Apparently he was very open about that sort of thing. He probably had only meant to tease me, not embarrass me. My irritation cooled slightly.

"Pete's. We've got another gig there tonight."

"Oh." Now that I was paying more attention to anything but my mortification, he did seem dressed differently than this morning—a brilliant red, long-sleeved shirt and perfectly faded blue jeans. He looked freshly washed too, his hair fabulously messy, but still slightly damp. He looked like the rock-god that I remembered from the night before.

"Do you guys want to go . . ." he paused and grinned devilishly, ". . . or stay here?"

"No, we'll go. Sure," I blurted out, more from remembered embarrassment and irritation than any real desire to see him perform.

Denny blinked at me in confusion, and what looked a little like disappointment. "Really?"

Trying to find a way to recover from my unthinking pronouncement, I came up with, "Yeah, they sounded really good last night. I was hoping to hear a little more."

Denny slowly sat up on the couch. "All right. I'll get my keys."

Kellan shook his head at me, an amused grin on his face. "Okay, I'll see you there then."

On the car ride there, I tried to cover my earlier embarrassment by asking Denny about the odd conversation in the kitchen with Kellan. I looked over at him. "Kellan seems . . . nice?" I didn't mean for it to come out like a question, but it kind of did.

Denny looked across at me. "No, he is. You kind of have to get used to him. He can seem like a real figjam, but he's a really great guy."

I raised my eyebrow at his weird Australian slang and smiled, waiting for him to explain. Every once in a while, he would throw words out at me and I had no idea what they meant.

He smiled, knowing what I was waiting for. "Fuck I'm Good, Just Ask Me," he explained.

I blushed a little, thinking I preferred the shortened version, and then laughed. "You never really talked about him before. I hadn't realized you guys were so close." I tried to think back over the few times he had mentioned his friend in Washington, but nothing jumped out in my head.

He looked back to the road and shrugged. "I guess we kind of lost contact when I went back home. I talked with him once or twice when I came back to the States . . . but we never really kept in touch. Busy, you know."

Puzzled I said, "I got the feeling from him that you were closer. He kind of seems to love you?" I felt a little weird saying that; guys weren't usually so blunt with their feelings. It wasn't as if Kellan had been writing him sonnets or anything. It was just a feeling I got from him. His comments about "owing Denny" and "doing anything for him"—in the guy-verse, that equaled love.

Denny seemed to understand what I was talking about and looked down for a second, a little embarrassed. "It's nothing. I don't know why he makes such a fuss over it. Really, it was no big deal." He looked back to the road, biting his lip.

Insanely curious now, I asked, "What?"

He paused. "Well, you know I lived with him and his parents for a year?"

"Yeah . . . ?"

"Well, he and his dad had a . . . strained relationship, I guess you could say. Anyway, one day his dad took it too far, knocked him around a little. I didn't really think about it, I just wanted it to stop. I guess I kind of stepped in front of him, took a blow for him." He looked over at my reaction for a second, before turning back to his driving.

I stared at him, shocked. I hadn't heard this story before. It sounded exactly like something Denny would do, though. My heart squeezed a little for Kellan.

Denny shook his head, his brow creased. "That seemed to wake his dad up a little. He didn't bother him again, at least not while I was there." He shook his head. "I don't know about after though. . . ." Looking over at me, he gave me his goofy grin. "Anyway, Kellan just kind of felt . . . like we were more a family than his real family after that." He laughed and looked back to the road. "I think he's more thrilled that I'm back than I am."

When we arrived at the bar, Kellan was already there, sitting with his three other bandmates at a table in the back near the stage. He sat on the end, looking relaxed and comfortable with one foot propped on his knee. He was sipping a beer. To his left sat the longer-haired blonde that I remembered as the bassist. Across from him was the teddy-bear drummer who I'd hoped was our new roommate, and finishing the circle, to the drummer's left, was the last member of the group, the blond guitarist. I was a little surprised that they weren't hidden away somewhere, getting ready to play. But they looked completely confident that they were going to be great, and were simply relaxing with a few beers before going up there.

Two women sitting at the table across from them were openly watching their every move. One was clearly gaping at Kellan. She looked drunk enough, and intrigued enough, that I thought at any moment she was going to lunge across the aisle and plop right down in his lap. While Kellan paid her absolutely no attention, I wasn't sure if he wouldn't mind if she decided to do just that.

Kellan's attention, however, was currently being held by the bassist sitting next to him. From the door I couldn't tell what they were talking about, but all of the guys were listening to his story with smiles on their faces.

Denny noticed them as well. Turning to smile at me, he led us over to their table. As we got close enough to hear the bassist's words, I decided that coming here had been a bad idea. I wished that I had kept my mouth shut, and that we were warm and comfortable, snuggling on the couch again. Denny pulled me steadily forward though, so I glumly followed.

". . . this girl, damn, she had the best rack I've ever seen." The bassist paused to make a crude gesture with his hands, as if the guys would need that statement clarified. "And the shortest skirt too. Everybody around us was completely wasted, so I ducked under the table and shoved that skirt as high as it would go. Then I grabbed my beer bottle and stuck—"

Kellan smacked him on the chest, noticing Denny's and my arrival. We stopped at the end of the table before him. Denny chuckled a little. I was sure I was bright red, and tried to keep my face as smooth as possible.

"Dude . . . I'm getting to the good part, hold on." The bassist look mildly confused.

"Griff . . ." Kellan pointed over to me. "My new roommates are here."

He looked up to glance at Denny and me. "Oh yeah . . . roommates." He looked over at Kellan again. "I miss Joey, man . . . she was hot! Seriously, why did you have to tap that? Not that I blame you, but—"

He cut off as Kellan smacked him in the chest again, even harder. Ignoring the bassist's irritation, Kellan pointed up to us. "Guys, this is my friend Denny and his girlfriend, Kiera."

I tried to fix my face into a smile. I hadn't known why his old roommate had left, and I was a little shocked and a little embarrassed at the crude conversation we'd walked into. Denny smiled and smoothly said, "Hello."

I managed to mumble out a "Hi."

"Hey." The bassist nodded his chin up in greeting. "Griffin." He eyed me up and down, making me extremely uncomfortable. I squeezed Denny's hand harder and moved slightly behind him.

The bassist's could-be twin, across the table from Kellan, stuck his hand out in a more polite greeting. "Matt. Hi."

"The guitarist, right?" Denny asked him while he shook his hand. "You're really good!"

"Yeah, thanks, man." He seemed genuinely pleased that Denny had remembered what he played. Griffin however, snorted, and Matt threw him a look. "Oh, get over it, Griffin."

Griffin shot him a look right back. "All I'm saying is that you totally messed up that last riff. I rock that song; I should totally play it."

Ignoring what sounded like an ongoing argument, the big teddy-bear-looking guy beside Matt stood up and extended his hand to us. "Evan. Drummer. Nice to meet you."

We shook his hand while Kellan stood up. He walked across the aisle to the drunken women. I thought the one who had been gaping at him earlier might pass out at his nearness. He leaned over the back of her chair, brushed aside a lock of her hair, and whispered something very closely in her ear. She nodded, flushing slightly, and then he stood and grabbed a couple of empty chairs from beside them. The women were giggling like schoolgirls as he walked away.

He set the chairs down for us at the end of the table, a slight smile on his face. "Here, have a seat."

Feeling odd about that whole exchange, and not entirely comfortable with our new companions, I sat down with a small frown on my face. Kellan's smile widened. He seemed to really enjoy it when I was uncomfortable.

Griffin was turning his attention to Denny as we sat down. "What's your accent . . . you British?"

Denny smiled politely at him. "Australian."

Griffin nodded, like he had known that all along. "Ahhhh. Ahoy, mate."

Kellan and Evan laughed. Matt looked over at him like he was the world's biggest idiot. "Dude, he's Australian . . . not a pirate."

Griffin sniffed haughtily. "Whatever." He took a swig of his beer.

Laughing a little, Denny asked, "What's the name of your band anyway?"

Griffin sniggered while Kellan stated, "D-Bags."

I looked over at him incredulously. "Seriously?"

Griffin, surprisingly, frowned a little. "They made me condense it, the pussies. I wanted the full thing. State it loud, state it proud!" He smacked the table.

Matt rolled his eyes. "If we ever want to play somewhere bigger than Pete's, then we need a name they can put on the marquee." At least one of them seemed to have goals for a bigger future.

Griffin shot an irritated look over to Matt, while Kellan and Evan laughed. "Dude, I made T-shirts. . . ."

"No one is stopping you from wearing them," Matt muttered, rolling his eyes again.

Kellan and Evan laughed harder, and even Denny chuckled a little. I couldn't help but smile at them. "Are you guys brothers?"

Griffin looked at me in horror. "Absolutely not!"

Surprised, I looked back at Matt and then to him again. They really could have been twins. "Oh, sorry it's just you look so—"

"We're cousins," Matt explained. "Our dads are twins, so the resemblance is . . . unfortunate." He frowned.

Griffin snorted again. "Unfortunate for you . . . that I'm hotter." The rest of the guys at the table laughed while Matt rolled his eyes again.

Abruptly, Kellan lifted two fingers in the air, raised his chin, and motioned the fingers down at Denny and me. I looked across the room to where he was focused. An older woman, who gave him an odd smile, was running the bar at the far end of the long room. She seemed to know exactly what he meant, because she handed two beer bottles to a waitress and pointed her in our direction.

I looked back over at Kellan, but he was already talking with Denny about Denny's new job. Kellan was curious about what an internship in advertising entailed. Having heard the story a million times before, I tuned it out and took a look around the bar.

Pete's was warm and comfortable looking. The floors were oak and worn with years of use. The walls were a pleasant cream and red, with nearly every square inch covered with signs, advertising various brands of beers. Dozens of tables, in varying sizes and styles, dotted the wooden floor, cram-packed wherever they could fit, except for a twenty-foot area in front of the stage that took up one of the shorter walls.

The stage was oak as well. The wall behind it was painted black and covered with hanging guitars in different styles and colors. Huge speakers sat on either side of the stage, pointing out toward the crowd. The lights above the stage were currently off. The microphones, guitars, and drums sat on the darkened stage, waiting for their owners.

I looked over to the other side of the large rectangular room while the guys chatted around me. The other short wall was one long bar. The mirror behind the bar was lined with shelves, all filled with every kind of liquor bottle you could imagine. The bartender was now busy filling drink orders for the crowd that was starting to pour in from the double doors along the front wall. Large windows dotted that wall, letting in the glow of various neon bar signs.

A pretty blond waitress approached and handed Denny and me our beers. We thanked her and Kellan gave her a friendly nod, which made me curious for a second. The waitress only smiled politely at him, however, so I figured they were just friends.

I sipped my beer and watched the waitress walk through some double doors along the other long wall of the bar. I could see steel and movement and hear the clatter of food being prepared. That must be the kitchen. A large archway, not far from the kitchen doors, led to a decent-sized room that appeared to have a couple pool tables in it. Continuing down the rest of the wall, I noticed a hallway close to the stage that receded around a corner. Signs indicated that restrooms were in that direction.

As I was looking at the hallway, my eyes fell upon the two women who had been watching the guys earlier. Denny and I were now partially blocking their view, since we were sitting on the end of the table. The one who openly wanted Kellan did not look happy that I was sitting right next to him. In fact, she looked downright pissed. I quickly turned back around.

A moment later, I felt someone approaching me from behind. My body involuntarily tensed as I looked over my shoulder. Surely that woman wasn't going to try to start something with me? I sighed softly with relief at the sight of an older man approaching our table.

He was dressed nicely, in khaki slacks and a red collared shirt with the name of the bar in the upper corner. He looked to be in his midfifties with graying hair and a weathered face. He did not look happy at all.

"Guys ready? You're up in five," he sighed heavily.

"You all right, Pete?" Kellan asked him, frowning a little.

I blinked. Pete must be the owner of Pete's. How cute.

"No . . . Traci quit over the phone, she's not coming back. I had to have Kate pull a double so we were covered tonight." He glared, rather angrily, at Kellan. That made me curious, until I remembered that the ex-roommate, Joey, had left abruptly because of Kellan. Maybe it was a pattern with him?

Kellan, in turn, glared over at Griffin. Griffin looked a little sheepish and took a long swig of his beer before muttering, "Sorry, Pete."

Pete sighed and shook his head. I guessed there were just some occupational hazards that Pete was accustomed to involving this particular band. I couldn't help feeling sorry for him.

Surprising myself, I said, "I was a waitress. I need to get a job, and working nights would be perfect when school starts."

Pete looked over at me curiously and then back to Kellan. Kellan smiled and pointed to us with his bottle in turn. "Pete, these are my new roommates, Denny, Kiera."

Pete nodded and looked me over. "You twenty-one?"

I smiled nervously. "Yeah, since May." I wondered briefly what he would do if I said no while sipping on a beer.

He nodded again. "All right. I could use the help, and soon. Can you start Monday, six p.m.?"

I looked over at Denny, wondering if I should have talked this over with him first. With his internship during the day, nights would be all we had together. He was smiling at me though, and as I raised my eyebrows, he nodded almost imperceptibly.

"Yeah, that would be fine. Thank you," I said quietly. And just like that, after less than one full day of being in this new city, I had a job.

Chapter 3
New Job

Listening to the band play their full set was amazing. They really were good at what they did. Kellan was unbelievable. I was a little surprised that someone hadn't scooped him up yet. He was the poster child for a bankable rock star—talented, seductive, and smoking hot. And the band already had quite the fan base. Almost immediately after they started their set, the floor around the stage was crowded with people.

Denny pulled me out to the floor near the edge of the pack, where we had more room to dance and move about. The song the band was playing was extremely catchy and easy to dance to, and Denny twirled me around, then brought me tight to him as we danced close together. I laughed and slung my arms around his neck. Then he dipped me, and I laughed harder. Most of the D-Bags' songs were fast, but Denny and I were comfortable with each other and danced together easily.

Occasionally, I glanced up at the group onstage. Kellan gently kept time to the music with his body as he smiled flirtatiously through his words. He was captivating to watch and I found myself staring at him more and more frequently as the night went on.

Watching the way his body swayed while he sang, I happened to notice Griffin look over at Matt and scowl. Somehow, without ever

looking at him or missing a note on his guitar, Matt managed to flip
him off, making Denny and me giggle and Griffin roll his eyes. Evan
watched over the group, slowly shaking his head and laughing as
well. Kellan either didn't witness the exchange, or he ignored it. He
kept his eyes focused on the adoring crowd instead.

For some of the songs, Kellan picked up his guitar and played
along with Matt. Kellan's guitar wasn't amplified like Matt's, and the
different sounds blended together nicely. He started off an intro to
a slower song by himself, and I couldn't help but notice how good
he was on the guitar, probably as good as Matt. Most of the people
around the front of the stage were still cavorting and dancing, even
though the song was slower, but some of the couples near Denny and
me were starting to slow dance.

Denny pulled me close, slipping his arms around my waist. He
grinned at me goofily, in a way that I immensely loved, and pulled me
tight against him. I sighed happily and brought my arms around his
neck again. Running my fingers through his dark hair, I gave him a
soft kiss. As the music swelled and picked up intensity, I hugged him
tight, laid my head on his shoulder, and breathed in his wonderful,
familiar scent. Looking over Denny's shoulder, I watched Kellan on
stage. He was smiling sweetly at me during a break in the vocals, and I
smiled back. Then he winked at me. I blinked in surprise. He laughed.

They played one more fast-paced song after that. Most of the
couples returned to regular dancing. Denny and I chose to stay
locked together, smiling at each other and softly kissing. When that
song finished, Kellan's voice—speaking, this time, not singing—
broke through the noise of the crowd.

"Thank you for coming out tonight." He paused, waiting for the
crowd's sudden eruption of screams to die down. After a minute, he
smiled charmingly and held up a finger. "I want to take a second to
introduce you all to my new roommates."

His finger pointed right at Denny and me. I wanted to run, but
Denny laughed and moved to my side, his arms still around my
waist. I looked over at Denny, biting my lip and wishing we had left

after the slow song. He grinned and kissed my cheek while Kellan
told the whole bar our names.

I buried my head in Denny's shoulder, mortified, when Kellan
cheerily said, "Now, you'll all be happy to know that Kiera is joining
the happy little family here at Pete's, starting Monday night."

The crowd screamed again. . . . I had no idea why, and I blushed
and glared up at Kellan, wishing he would be quiet. He laughed at
my look. "I want you all to be nice to her." He looked over to the
D-Bag beside him who was grinning indecently at me. "Especially
you, Griffin."

Kellan said good night to the crowd, which hollered yet again.
Then he sat down on the edge of the stage. My embarrassment fading, now that the attention was no longer focused on me, I thought
to go up and tell him how great he was. It apparently wasn't necessary
though. Almost instantly, at least five girls hovered around him. One
brought him a beer, one played with his hair, and one even made herself quite comfortable on his lap. I'm pretty sure I saw her lick his neck.
After witnessing that, I figured he didn't need any encouraging words
from me tonight. I could just tell him something nice in the morning.

Denny and I left soon after the band finished, and practically
stumbled to bed in our tiredness. I don't know exactly when I heard
Kellan get home, but it was much later than us. So naturally, I was
pretty surprised when I groggily made my way down to the kitchen
the next morning, and there he was, already sitting at the table, fully
dressed, looking annoyingly perfect while sipping his coffee and
reading the paper.

"Mornin'," he said, a little too cheerfully.

"Uh," I replied grumpily. So, not only was he talented and ridiculously attractive, he was also one of those people who can run
smoothly on very little sleep.

I grabbed a mug and poured some coffee while he finished his
paper. Upstairs, I could hear the water start running as Denny prepared for his shower. I finished making my coffee and went over to
sit across the table from Kellan.

He smiled at me as I sat down. For a second, I felt really self-conscious in the lounge pants and tank top I had slept in. Irritation at his all-too-perfect face swept through me. Really, did one person need to be so blessed? It didn't seem cosmically fair. Then I remembered Denny's conversation with me in the car about Kellan and his dad. That cooled my anger. Things hadn't always been easy for this attractive boy.

"Well, what did you think?" he asked, smiling, like he already knew my answer.

I tried to frown, like I was going to say it sucked, but I couldn't and laughed a little instead. "You guys are amazing. Really, it was unbelievable."

He smiled and nodded, sipping his coffee again. Not a great shock to him, then. "Thanks. I'll tell the guys you liked it." He looked up at me with the corner of his eye. "Less offensive?"

I started to blush, remembering our conversation yesterday, but then his performance started replaying in my head. With mild surprise, I realized that he *had* toned down the sensuality. He had certainly still been flirty and charming, but less . . . obvious. I smiled over at him. "Yes, much better . . . thank you."

He laughed at my comment, and it pleased me a little that he had actually listened to something I had, rather rudely, criticized him for.

We sipped our coffees in silence for a few minutes, and then something said in conversation last night suddenly popped into my head and slipped out of my mouth before I could stop it. "Joey was the roommate before us?" Really, what was wrong with my loose tongue around him? I was going to have to work on that.

He slowly set his coffee mug down. "Yeah . . . she left a while before Denny called about the room."

Curious at the odd look in his eyes, I said, "She left a lot of her stuff here. Is she going to come back for it?"

He looked down at the table for a second, then back up to my eyes. "No . . . I'm pretty sure she left town."

Surprise loosened my tongue again, "What happened?" I really had had no intention of asking him that question. I wondered if he would answer me.

He looked thoughtful for a second, like he was wondering as well. "A . . . misunderstanding," he finally said.

Firmly, I shut my thoughts off and focused on my coffee. I was *not* going to pry anymore. It was not my business and I didn't want to ruffle my new roommate. It didn't matter anyway. Her situation and mine and Denny's were so vastly different. I just hoped that, if she did come back, she would leave the bed. It was incredibly comfortable.

Denny and I spent the remainder of that lazy Sunday resting and preparing for the jobs that we would start the next day. Denny's internship paid next to nothing, so we were both relieved that I had found a job so quickly. I thanked Kellan for his small part in introducing us to Pete and mentally thanked Griffin for not being able to keep it in his pants, the thought of which, of course, made me blush a little.

I *was* nervous about it though. I had never waitressed at a bar before. Denny and Kellan had a great couple of hours quizzing me on different drinks and what was in them. I protested at first, since my knowledge really wasn't that stellar, and told them repeatedly that the bartender was making the drinks. I only had to repeat the orders. But after some amusingly suggestive drinks, some of which I'm sure Kellan completely made up, I started having fun playing their little game. I supposed it would help me to know everything I could.

By that evening, Denny was starting to get nervous about his first day as well. He picked out three different sets of clothes, flipped through all his old schoolbooks, organized his briefcase four times, and eventually sat on the couch and tapped his feet. Kellan excused himself to meet with the band—apparently they met nearly every day to rehearse. That was probably why they felt so comfortable before a show. I took the opportunity of our aloneness to do everything in my power to get Denny's mind off of his nerves.

After the second time, I think he finally relaxed. . . .

• • •

Monday morning came quicker than expected. I made my way downstairs for my morning cup of coffee while Denny got ready for his first day. Kellan was at his usual spot at the table, casually leaning back in his chair, drinking his coffee, and reading the paper. I had to chuckle at his shirt. He was wearing a black T-shirt with "Douche-bags" printed boldly in white across the front. He noticed my laugh and my gaze and crooked a smile.

"Like it? I can hook you up." He winked at me. "I know people." I smiled and nodded back at him as he went back to drinking his coffee.

Denny came down a little while later, looking very handsome in a nice, light-blue button-up dress shirt and khaki slacks. He looked over at Kellan and pointed to his shirt. "Nice, man . . . Score me one of those."

Kellan laughed and nodded while Denny came up and slipped his arms around me. I frowned at him as he gave me a kiss on the cheek. "What?" he asked, looking himself over quickly.

I smoothed out the front of his shirt, then ran my hand along his jaw. "You . . . are entirely too attractive. Some perky blonde is going to snatch you away from me."

He raised an eyebrow and smiled. "You silly nong."

Kellan popped up from the table. "No, she's right, man." He seriously shook his head at him. "You're hot." Then, grinning, he went back to drinking his coffee.

Rolling my eyes at Kellan, I gave Denny a long kiss and wished him a good day at work. Kellan playfully came up and gave him a peck on the cheek as well. Denny laughed, and, still looking rather nervous, made his way out the door.

I didn't have a whole lot to do during the day since I wasn't starting school for another two and a half months, so I called my mom again and told her I already missed everyone terribly. She immediately offered me a plane ticket back home, of course. I assured her that in spite of being homesick, everything was going great here, and that I even had a job already. Sighing repeatedly, she wished me luck and lots of love. I told her to give Dad and Anna kisses for me.

I spent the rest of the day watching TV and watching Kellan write lyrics at the table. He seemed to be constantly jotting down some notes or thoughts, scratching them out, moving things around, and chewing on his pencil, thinking. Occasionally he asked my opinion about a verse. I tried to give him as insightful an answer as possible, but music theory was not one of my strong points. It was fascinating to watch him work though, and the time passed quickly. Before I knew it, I needed to get ready for my shift.

I showered, dressed, fixed my makeup, and pulled my hair back into a ponytail. Looking into the mirror, I sighed. Not great, but presentable, I guessed. I made my way downstairs to grab my jacket from the hook at the front door.

"Kellan?"

He looked over at me from the living room where he was watching TV. "Yeah?"

"Is there a bus schedule around here? I want to look at the route again." Denny, with our only vehicle, wasn't home from work yet, and I wanted to leave early since I didn't know how long the bus ride would take.

He looked at me quizzically before he understood. "No. . . . I'll take you, though."

"No, no. You don't have to do that." I really didn't want to be a burden on him.

"No problem. I'll grab a beer, chat with Sam." He threw a charming half-smile at me. "I'll be your first customer."

Great. I hoped I didn't spill beer in his lap. "Okay. Thanks." I sat with him on the couch to watch TV for a while, since I didn't need to leave right away after all.

"Here, I wasn't really watching anything," he said, casually handing the remote over to me.

"Oh, thanks." It wasn't necessary, but it was a sweet gesture. I started flicking through channels and stopped on what I thought was HBO. "Oh, do you get the premium channels?" It seemed odd to me that he would splurge on the extra ones when he didn't really seem to watch anything.

He grinned mischievously over at me. "Griffin. He likes to have . . . everything . . . available to him when he visits. I guess he knows some girl at the cable company."

"Oh," I said. I was thinking about what Griffin might want to watch on our TV, when I finally noticed what was currently playing. I had stopped on an erotic scene involving a naked man and woman, clearly in the throes of passion. Either the man was a vampire or had a severe biting fetish. He was giving the woman a passionate nibble to her neck, which resulted in lots of blood and lots of extremely suggestive licking and sucking. Blushing furiously, I turned back to Kellan's original show and threw the remote back to him.

I tried to ignore the look he gave me as he laughed softly beside me.

When it got late enough, Kellan turned off the TV and looked over at me. "Ready?"

I tried to smile. "Sure"

He chuckled at me. "Don't worry, you'll be fine."

We grabbed our coats and made our way out the door. I had hoped that Denny would be home in time to take me. I'd really missed him all day, but I guessed he was still at work. I hoped his first day had gone well. I hoped my first day went well.

We walked out to Kellan's car and I had to smile. It was an older, sixties-looking muscle car—a Chevy Chevelle Malibu, according to the logo on the side panel. Shiny black with polished chrome everywhere, it was sleek and impossibly sexy; it matched its driver perfectly. I rolled my eyes a little at the extremeness of his attractiveness, which the car oddly seemed to accentuate.

The inside was surprisingly spacious, with black leather bench seats in the front and the back. I had to suppress a laugh at the old-fashioned-looking tape deck. Aside from the living room TV, Kellan was a little behind on technology. Not that I was really up on it either—Denny and I didn't even have cell phones. Obviously enjoying his vehicle, Kellan smiled when he slid behind the wheel. What was it with guys being so attached to their cars?

We were both quiet on the ride over, and I quickly started getting nervous butterflies in my stomach. The first day on a new job always made me feel like getting sick. I stared out the window and started counting the street lights to distract myself.

Upon arrival at Pete's—just beyond the twenty-fifth light—I suddenly realized that I had no idea what to do or where to go. Luckily, the pretty blond girl who had brought us the beers the other night met me at the door, introduced herself as Jenny, and, waving at Kellan, led me to the hallway. The hallway led to a back room across from the bathrooms.

The back room was a large storage area, with multiple shelves along one wall that held boxes of liquor and beer, napkins, salt, pepper, and other random bar supplies. A couple of extra tables were propped up on their sides against another wall, with stacks of chairs beside them, and another wall had a group of lockers for the staff. Jenny grabbed me a shirt from one of the boxes on a shelf. She showed me which locker was mine and where to clock in. I took my very own red Pete's T-shirt and changed in the bathroom. I immediately felt a little more relaxed. Something about looking like everyone else who worked at the bar made me feel like I belonged.

When I had told Pete I had been a waitress, I was exaggerating a tiny bit. I had filled in for my sister one summer while she went off to "discover herself," whatever that meant. The tiny diner where she had worked got maybe half the amount of traffic that Pete's got on a typical night. I was a little terrified.

Coming out of the hallway a few moments later, I noticed Kellan sipping a beer and leaning against the long bar. The bartender was leaning over the bar and eyeing Kellan seductively. She had cut her red Pete's shirt so it was obscenely low in the front. Kellan, ignoring her, sipped his beer casually and smiled when he saw me.

I frowned a little bit at his beer. He noticed my glance. "Sorry, Rita beat you to it." He smiled. "Next time."

The bartender, Rita, was an older blond woman—though I highly doubted that was her natural color—with skin that had been faked 'n' baked one too many times, and was now a little leathery. Maybe at some point in her life she had been attractive, but time had not been kind. In her eyes though, she was still gorgeous, and she was outrageously flirtatious. And, as I learned throughout the night, she thoroughly enjoyed her job, and seemed to enjoy relaying all the juicy gossip customers told her even more. I blushed several times during my shift while she repeated their stories and mentally reminded myself never (not that I ever would) to confide in a bartender . . . especially not this one.

Throughout the night, I shadowed Jenny as she took customers' orders. It was a little confusing, since most of the people who came in were regulars who always ordered the same thing. She would simply walk up to the table and say, "Hi-ya, Bill, same for you today?" He would nod and she would smile and head to the bar or the kitchen to relay an order that I'd never actually heard. It was intimidating.

She noticed my worried expression. "Don't worry, you'll get it. Weeknights are pretty easy with the regulars. . . . They'll be nice to you." She frowned a little. "Well, most of them will be nice to you. I'll help you with the rest." She smiled warmly and I was very grateful for her kindness. Her looks perfectly matched her sparkling personality. She was, as the phrase went, cute as a button—petite, with flowing, silky blond hair, pale blue eyes, and just enough curves to get more than a few appreciative glances from some of the customers. I couldn't be jealous of her, though—she was just too sweet. Besides, I instantly felt a connection with her.

Sometime during the night, Kellan came up to me and tipped me for the drink I never actually gave him. He smiled as he excused himself for the evening. "I have a gig at another bar." He pointed with his thumb over his shoulder. "I gotta go meet the guys . . . give them a hand with all our stuff."

"Thank you so much for the ride, Kellan." I gave him a light kiss on the cheek, which, for some reason, made me blush and caused Rita to speculatively raise her eyebrows.

Kellan looked down, smiled, and muttered something about not mentioning it. He left the bar shortly after, tossing a "Have fun" over his shoulder on the way out the doors.

Later in the evening, Denny stopped in to see how I was doing. He gave me a long hug and a sweet kiss, also to the delight of Rita, who looked at him a little too seductively for my taste. He only stayed for a few minutes, though. He had a project he wanted to start working on at home. He was insanely happy, and that happiness infected me. I found myself smiling widely for a long time after he left.

When I wasn't shadowing Jenny, they had me clean up. I spent a good chunk of the night wiping tables, washing glasses, helping in the kitchen, and, when things got slow at the tail end of the night, cleaning the graffiti from the bathroom stalls. Pete gave me some gray paint and a little brush and left me to it. Rita gave me instructions to let her know anything juicy written up there. Jenny smiled and wished me good luck. I sighed.

I started with the women's bathroom, thinking it would be less offensive than the men's. I didn't really want to walk into the men's room anyway. There were three stalls in the women's room, and all of them had pen and Sharpie scribbles on the inside and the outside. I sighed again and wished they had just given me a roller. This was going to take a while.

Some of the stuff was innocent enough: *I love Chris, A.M + T.L, Sara was here, TLF, I hate vodka, go home, you're drunk* (I had to laugh at that one). But a lot of them were less innocent: *I'm horny, I wanna screw tonight, my boyfriend gives it good,* random swear words. And then there were some directed at people I knew: *Sam makes me hot, I love Jenny* (hmmm, I wondered about that one, since I *was* in the women's room), *Rita's a skank* (I chuckled, wondering if that was the juicy gossip she wanted to hear).

And finally, a huge portion of the graffiti was directed at the four band members. It surprised me at first, but then I thought it made sense, since they played here so often . . . and they were attractive, I guessed.

The notes about Griffin were the most explicit. I couldn't even stand to read them fully. Blushing, I covered up the extremely graphic words detailing what girls had either done to him, or wanted to do with him, as quickly as I could. There was even an exceptionally vivid drawing of an act so absurdly crude that I worried about how long it would stick in my head. I sighed, knowing I was going to turn bright red the next time I saw Griffin. He would probably love that.

Matt's and Evan's tributes were more subtle. Girls wrote in adoration for Evan: *I love him, I want him, marry me.* Girls wrote with praise for Matt: *Damn, he's hot, he can pluck me any day, Matt rocks me.*

But of course, the largest portion of all the graffiti was directed toward Kellan. From the sweet: *Kellan loves me, Kellan Forever, future Mrs. Kyle* to the . . . not so sweet. Apparently, Kellan had been right when he said that women responded to his sexual nature. The remarks were quite graphic, almost as graphic as Griffin's, and described just what different girls wanted to do with him.

There was also a section of comments from women who seemed to already have intimate knowledge of him. Whether real or not, theirs were the most explicit: *Kellan licked my* . . . (I brushed out the near paragraph on exactly what had been licked), *I blew Kellan's* . . . (whoa, really now), *for a good time call* . . . (I blinked; that was actually our phone number. I quickly brushed it out), *Kellan shoved his* . . .

Ugh, I didn't even bother reading that one. I was already going to have horrid visions of Griffin. I didn't need them about my roommate too.

I finally finished with the women's room and made my way over to the men's, no longer worried about it. There was no way it was cruder than the stuff the girls had come up with.

Jenny sweetly gave me a ride home after work and, even though I tried to be quiet, Denny woke up when I entered our room. He patiently listened to stories of my first day and then regaled me for at least an hour with tales of his new job. He was in heaven, and I couldn't have been happier for him.

Denny, Kellan, and I quickly fell into an easy routine at home. Kellan was almost always the first one awake, and there was usually a fresh pot of coffee waiting for me when I finally shuffled into the kitchen. We chatted companionably, sipping our java as Denny showered and got ready for his day at work.

Denny insisted that I didn't have to wake up with him, since I got home so late on nights I worked, but I loved seeing him off every morning. He was all smiles when he left. He was having way too much fun at his new job, and I was elated for him. After he was gone, I had a lot of time to myself, and even though I was getting anxious at the thought of school beginning in a couple months, I was really starting to want something to do during the day. As it was, I mainly just napped and lounged.

Kellan didn't seem to have any job other than the band. He would leave for a few hours in the afternoon or early evening to meet with the guys; they played a couple of other smaller bars during the week and Pete's every Friday and almost every Saturday. He would sometimes go for a run during the day. He even invited me to go with him a couple times, but I wasn't quite comfortable enough to say yes. The rest of his time was spent resting, reading, writing, singing, or playing his guitar. He did his own laundry, made his own food, and, aside from his messy bed, cleaned up after himself. He was pretty easygoing, as far as roommates go.

I also fell into a fluid rhythm at my new job at Pete's. My limited waitressing skills were starting to kick back in. That first week, Denny came in every night after work and let me "practice" on him. He would order different things from the menu, and make it as complicated as possible, to see if I could get it right. It made me laugh every time, but it helped. By the third night, I finally got him the food he actually ordered, which was good, because the guys in the kitchen were getting a little irritated with us.

I was surprised at how often Kellan and his band came into the bar during the week. They always sat at the same table, back by the stage. I don't think it would have mattered to them if people were already sitting there or not. It was just known in the bar that that table was theirs, and when they came in, you better plan on sitting with them or you better move.

Weeknights were busy, but nowhere near as packed as the weekends, and while women still watched Kellan openly, the weeknight people were regulars and generally left the guys alone. Generally. There were still pockets of adoring fans here and there. The guys came in after rehearsal or, if they had a show that night, they came in before their gig. They were there practically every day.

Their claimed table happened to be in my section. On my second night, they had all come in together. I'd had to grit my teeth to approach them. Luckily, Denny had been with them too. That had definitely made it easier to talk to them. They were just way too intimidating all grouped together like that, especially with the bathroom homages still fresh in my mind. And, as predicted, I had blushed furiously at Griffin, and he had found that immensely entertaining.

By the following Monday, after a hectic weekend of waitressing for the throngs of people the guys had brought in on both Friday and Saturday nights (that first weekend was so crazy-busy, I couldn't even remember it), I was finally comfortable approaching the group. Unfortunately, they were all too comfortable with me by that point as well. Except for Evan, who was just a big sweetie, they all seemed to delight in teasing me.

Watching them walk in, I sighed and rolled my eyes. *Here we go again*. Evan came in first and gave me a great big bear hug. I laughed when I could breathe again. Matt and Griffin seemed lost in some disagreement, but Griffin still managed to smack my ass on the way to his chair. I sighed at him and glanced over at Sam, who was paying no attention to the quartet whatsoever. Anyone else would have been kicked out on their rump for that, but apparently, these four owned the place.

Kellan came in last, looking perfect as usual. He had his guitar slung over his shoulder tonight; he brought it in sometimes when he was working on new stuff. He nodded at me with a small, adorable smile on his face and took his seat.

"Usual tonight, boys?" I said, trying my best to sound as confident as sweet Jenny did.

"Yeah, thank you, Kiera," Evan replied politely for the group.

Griffin was not so polite. "Fuck, yeah, of course, sweetheart." He grinned at me mischievously. He seemed to know how his crudeness irritated me, and he played it up whenever I was around. I ignored him the best I could, and worked on keeping my expression even.

Apparently, I hadn't worked hard enough, and he noticed my irritation. "You're so sweet, Kiera. You're like an innocent schoolgirl." He shook his head in open delight. "I just want to . . . deflower you." He winked at me.

I blanched and stared at him, totally speechless.

Kellan chuckled softly, watching my face, and Matt, beside Griffin, snorted. "Dude, she's been with Denny forever. I'm pretty sure you missed that opportunity."

My mouth dropped open as I listened to them in mortification. Were they really discussing my virginity . . . right in front of me? I was too stunned to move away from the table.

Griffin turned to face Matt. "Too bad . . . I could have shown her the world."

Evan and Kellan laughed at him while Matt, barely containing his own laughter, said, "When have you ever shown any woman . . . the world?"

Griffin scowled at them. "I have skills—you guys just don't know. I've had no complaints."

Kellan grinned. "No repeats either."

"Fuck you, man. I'll show you right now! Grab a girl . . ." He looked around the bar, like he was searching for a volunteer. His eyes eventually rested on me, and I paled even more and backed up a step.

"Noooooo," all the guys loudly said at the same time, backing away from Griffin a bit and holding their hands out, as if to physically restrain him if necessary.

Regaining my composure, since the conversation had moved away from my experience level, I thought now was as good a time as any to slip away from them. I started sliding slowly to the side, but Griffin's eyes were still on me. He grinned widely as he ignored the laughing going on around him.

"Kiera, if you've already been deflowered"—he threw an irritated glance at the guys—"by a tool, I'm sure"—he looked back to me while they laughed harder—"then let's hear something naughty." His pale eyes sparkled with playfulness and he started playing with the barbell pierced through his tongue. My stomach turned a bit at the sensuality of the move. I really didn't want to answer his stupid request.

I grimaced and made to walk away. "I have to go back to work, Griffin."

"Oh, come on . . . just one little curse. Don't you ever swear?" He reached out and grabbed my arm as I tried to walk by him.

More focused on pulling my arm away from his grasp than what I was saying, I sighed. "Yes, Griffin, I swear." I immediately regretted saying that.

"Really? Let's hear it." He seemed genuinely amused at the idea of me trying to be as crude as he was. Evan looked embarrassed by his persistence and rolled his eyes. Matt put a hand on his chin and leaned forward, and Kellan ran a hand through his hair and leaned back, both looking at me curiously. I was starting to get uncomfortable under their scrutiny.

I glared at Griffin. "Damn."

Both Matt and Kellan chuckled. Griffin tucked his blond hair behind his ears and pouted. "Oooh, vicious. Now let's hear a real one."

"That *is* a real one." I just wanted to walk back to the bar, but I felt trapped by the odd conversation. Kellan was openly laughing at my discomfort now, and my irritation toward him, specifically, was growing.

"Okay, how about a little more colorful one . . . an easy one. How about . . . bitch?" He grinned devilishly at me as he crossed his arms over his chest.

"You're such a child, Griffin." I rolled my eyes and looked over at Evan, silently begging him to end this conversation, since he was the only one besides me who looked mildly uncomfortable.

Griffin laughed at my obvious plea. "You really can't say it, can you?"

"I don't need to." It wasn't that I never swore . . . it was just usually safe in my head, where it wasn't quite so offensive. I wasn't about to do anything just to please Griffin, anyway. I considered simply walking away from the table to end his stupid game, but I could just imagine how hard that would make him laugh.

He leaned across the table, hands held together. "Come on. Something, anything, I don't care . . . just say somethin' dirty," he begged.

I shifted uneasily, still thinking of an escape. Could I just slap him? That would definitely take the focus off of me . . . but I didn't know him well enough to know how he would react to that. I really didn't need him mad at me . . . or turned on by it.

Kellan butted in at that point. "She called me sexual once."

Griffin just about fell off of his chair laughing.

I glared over at Kellan, who looked at me with an adorably innocent look on his face, hands raised in an expression that clearly said, *What?* Seeing my break to get away—and really, the whole table was laughing now, even my ally, Evan—I headed back to the bar.

Hoping my face wasn't too red, I walked over to where Rita was already getting the guys' drinks ready. I cautiously looked back at the table. Griffin and Matt were still laughing over Kellan's stupid comment. Evan was looking at me apologetically; at least he felt bad about laughing. Kellan, still chuckling a little, had grabbed his guitar from the floor and was idly strumming a rhythm.

He lightly started singing a song that I thought was a new one. I couldn't make out the lyrics from this distance, but the melody trickled over to me and was quite pretty. Instinctively, I started moving back to the guys so I could hear him better.

"I wouldn't bother," Rita said roughly.

THOUGHTLESS 51

"What?"

"That one." She pointed at Kellan. "Don't waste your time."

Not knowing quite what she meant, I forgot to tell her that I was just interested in his song and instead asked, "What do you mean?"

She leaned in conspiratorially, happy for the chance to tell her little story. "Oh, he's deadly attractive for sure, but he'll just rip your heart out. Loves 'em and leaves 'em, that one."

"Oh." I supposed that wasn't too big a shock, considering the swarm of rabid fans who seemed to attack him at every show, and the numerous comments he'd gathered on the stall walls. "We're not like that. He's my roommate . . . nothing else. I was just listening to—"

She cut me off. "I don't know how you live with that." She looked over at him, biting her lip seductively. "*That* would drive me crazy, day in, day out." She set a couple of beer bottles on the counter.

I was beginning to get a little irritated at her looking at him like she was, and continuing to call him "that," like he wasn't a fully formed person or something.

"Well, having my boyfriend there helps, of course." It came out a little sarcastically, but honestly, what did she think we were doing at our house?

She laughed a little. "Oh, sweetie . . . do you think that matters to him? Baby, I was married and that didn't seem to faze him in the slightest." She put the last two bottles on the counter with a small smile on her lips. "Well worth it, though." She winked.

I dropped my mouth in shock. Rita was at least twice his age and, from what I'd heard, was currently on husband number four. Apparently Kellan wasn't too choosy about whom he brought home, and I was starting to get the feeling that that was everybody. It was just kind of odd that I hadn't seen any girls at the house yet.

Gathering my composure, I muttered, "Well, it matters to me." I grabbed the bottles and walked back to the guys' table, slightly agitated . . . and not sure why.

Chapter 4
Changes

Denny quickly impressed the people at his work, just like I knew he would, and we didn't have nearly as much time together as I would have liked. I still tried to see him off every morning, but as I started getting into the routine of going to bed later and later, it became harder and harder to wake up with him. Eventually, he got a "see-ya" kiss out of me in bed, and that was about it. Wanting to make a good impression with his bosses, he usually stayed past the time I had to leave for work as well. That made it pretty evident early on that the only time we'd have together was the weekend afternoons before my shift and the night or two I had off during the week.

Denny did what he could to spend time with me, though. He'd come into the bar after work to see me, sometimes staying for dinner or a drink with Kellan and the guys. We would hug and kiss tenderly, and the regulars at the bar would groan in mock exasperation. Some-one even threw a crumpled-up napkin at us once. I had a sneaking suspicion it was Griffin, and I was glad it had only been a napkin.

The month of June sped by in our easy routine, and before I knew it, it was July. Denny had to go into the office on Fourth of July afternoon. I had been a bit perturbed over that, since we had planned on spending the day at Denny's favorite beach here—a little sun and water for my water-loving boy—but he promised he would come into Pete's that night and spend the entire evening there, even though I'd be working, and that cooled my ire a bit.

I ended up spending most of the day reading a book and tanning in the small, sunny backyard. Well, tanning implies that my skin was the type that would darken into a beautiful sun-kissed color like Denny's. My alabaster skin did not. My skin went bright pink, then right back to pale white. So I popped on a two-piece swimsuit, slathered on the sunscreen to at least avoid the bright pink part, and enjoyed the warmth of the sun, if not the color-changing side effects.

I read my book and basked in the warmth tickling my thighs and lower back. I looked up and spotted a dainty dragonfly resting on a long blade of grass just inches in front of my face. Its body and the very tip of its tail were the same bright turquoise as some of the Native American jewelry I'd seen displayed in the local shops. It seemed completely happy, resting on its little perch and enjoying the perfectly sunny day, just like me. I smiled at it and then went back to my book. It was nice to not be completely alone back here.

Eventually, my body absorbed its daily quota of vitamin D, and I stumbled into the house in a sun-drunken state, almost instantly falling asleep on the couch. I awoke a half hour before my shift was to start and hurried to change and get ready. I made it to the bus and to the bar just in the nick of time. Well, at least I wouldn't be tired during my shift.

True to his word, as he always was, Denny came into the bar that evening, when he was done with work. It was oddly packed, considering it was a holiday, and he had to sit on a stool at the bar. Rita's appealing glances at him were starting to really irritate me, when suddenly Kellan and the band appeared. They confiscated their usual table and happily squeezed in an extra chair for Denny. Even in the packed bar, the laughter at that table was loud the whole night.

A bit before the band's evening performance, Denny and Kellan went over to shoot some pool. I stopped and leaned against the archway on my way to the kitchen. I couldn't help the smile on my face as I watched their easy friendship. They joked around and talked while they played as if they'd been best friends for years and had never spent any time apart.

I also couldn't help smiling at how bad at pool Kellan was. Denny would chuckle at his missed shots and try and teach him how to do it properly, but Kellan only laughed and shrugged his shoulders, like he knew he was never going to get it. I wasn't that great either, and Denny, who was actually really good, had tried to teach me a time or two. He had patiently told me on several occasions, "It's just physics, Kiera," as if just by knowing that, somehow the shot would magically become easier. Denny noticed me watching the two of them play and gave me a wink as I sighed happily and went back to my work.

They had just finished their game, and Kellan was starting to make his way over to the stage, when we heard the city's fireworks display from outside. Matt and Griffin got goofy grins on their faces and ducked out the front door—half a dozen girls following them. Grinning, Evan and Jenny followed a moment later, with another half-dozen people. Kellan approached Denny and me with a short girl whose blond hair had an interesting mix of bright red and bright blue streaks. He threw his arm around the girl's shoulders and, smiling, motioned for us to follow him. We shrugged at each other and left the bar with about a dozen people following us.

So about half the people from the bar were in the parking lot, looking up at the sky over Lake Union, where the city was lighting off explosion after explosion. Fireworks in breathtaking colors and beautiful designs lit the city skyline. Griffin and Matt were off to one side, watching the display. Well, Matt was watching. Griffin had grabbed a girl inappropriately and was being assaulted—and loving every minute of it. Jenny had her arms around Evan's waist and, leaning against him cozily, was watching the show on the other side of the lot.

Denny slipped his arms around me, hugging me tight to his chest, and I relaxed back into him and laid my head against his shoulder. Kellan was in front of us, one arm slung casually around the girl, his hand in her back pocket. He had brought his beer out with him. Turning his head away from the girl to take a swig, he noticed Denny and me behind him. He swallowed his drink, then gave me a warm smile when he caught my eye. I gave him a shy smile in return as Denny sighed contentedly, kissing my head.

The woman with Kellan must have spoken to him; he turned back around to her and quietly said something. She leaned up and kissed his neck, slipping her hand into his jeans pocket. He smiled and hugged her tight. I wondered if I would see her in the morning.

I was turning my attention back up to the show, when I heard, quite loudly, from behind us, "Hey! I don't pay you guys to stargaze."

Turning, I saw Pete standing near the front doors, eyeing Kellan with an unhappy expression. The band was already supposed to be onstage. "Go play," he muttered, pointing inside the bar. He looked up at the display for a brief moment while Kellan chuckled, and then he brought his attention down to Jenny and me. "And you two. Go . . . waitress. There are still thirsty people in there."

Jenny released herself from Evan and gingerly bounced over to Pete. "Sorry, Pete," she said brightly, as she kissed him on the cheek and darted into the bar.

Kellan followed immediately after her, his red-and-blue-striped girl in hand. "Yeah . . . sorry, Pete." Then, grinning crookedly, he gave Pete a quick peck on the cheek as well. He jumped back as Pete made a move to smack him. The girl at his side giggled uncontrollably as he ducked back into the bar after Jenny.

Denny and I lingered for a second in each other's arms, watching the dazzling display, and then followed the rest of the crowd back into the bar. The band was particularly good that night, and Denny stayed for the entire show. We even snuck in a couple dances together. By the end of my shift, I was ready to go home and snuggle in bed with him. As I was finishing up my duties, I happened to catch sight of Kellan as he left the bar. Surprisingly enough, he was alone. Denny grabbed my hand as I came out of the back room a few moments later and, smiling at each other, we went home too.

I sighed as I snuggled in bed with him later, happy and loving my little life here, finding enormous contentment in the fact that nothing about it would be changing for at least the next two years.

It was only two weeks later, on a Friday evening at work, when something did change. . . .

The guys were at their regular table in the back, relaxing before their show. To the delight of several nearby females, Griffin was shirtless. He was showing Sam a new tattoo on his shoulder that he had gotten sometime during the last week. It was a snake wrapping itself seductively around a naked woman. Sam was grinning. He seemed to really like it. I thought it was a little tasteless. The snake was just a bit too sensual and the woman was outrageously disproportionate. Seriously, a real woman shaped like that would not be able to stand up straight. I had to smile though; the tasteless tattoo did match its owner perfectly.

Matt was also showing Sam his new tattoo, a symbol on his inner wrist. I didn't know what it was, or what it meant, but I highly preferred it to Griffin's. Sam nodded at him, then looked back at the naked woman tattoo. I was ready for Griffin to put his shirt back on. Evan, who had tattoos all up and down his arms, was ignoring the show-and-tell. He was too busy sitting on the edge of the stage and flirting with a group of girls.

Kellan sat backwards on his chair and watched me. He motioned me over.

"Hey. Beer?" I asked.

He smiled warmly and nodded. "Yeah, thanks, Kiera." I suddenly wondered if Kellan had any tattoos, like the rest of them. Realizing I had seen him nearly naked before, I blushed. If he did have one, it was well hidden. He noticed my embarrassment. "What?"

Knowing it would just be easier to ask him, I said, "Do you have one?" and pointed at Griffin's shoulder.

He looked over at a still half-naked Griffin. "Tattoo?" he asked, shifting back around to face me. He shook his head. "No, I can't think of anything I'd want permanently etched on my skin." He smiled crookedly at me. "You?"

I blushed again at his charming smile. "Nope . . . virgin skin here." I instantly regretted saying that, as my face surely went bright red. He chuckled, enjoying my reaction, and I muttered, "I'll be right back with your beer. . . ."

I hurried away as quickly as I could, murmuring softly about how I really needed to think before I spoke, and almost collided into Denny as he was entering the bar. "Oh, hey! Guess what!" Denny grabbed my shoulders, beaming.

Smiling at his enthusiasm, I said, "I have no idea."

"Mark from the office pulled me aside today. They want me to go with them to set up the new office in Tucson!" He seemed really excited at this prospect, but my heart sank.

"Tucson? Really? For how long?" I tried not to deflate his excitement, but I was already not thrilled over this idea.

"I don't know . . . couple of months, maybe?" He shrugged his shoulders.

My mouth dropped open. "A couple months! But we just got here! I start school in a little over a month. I need to get registered, get my schedule, books. . . . I can't go to Tucson right now."

He looked at me, a little confused. "You wouldn't need to come. It's just for a couple months, Kiera."

Now I didn't care about his enthusiasm. Now I was mad. "What?" I said loudly, and people around us turned to look. Denny gently grabbed my arm and pulled me outside.

Once in the cooler air of the parking lot, he grabbed both of my shoulders again and forced me to look at him. "It's my job, Kiera . . . our future. I need to do this." His accent was thick over the words, as concern filled him.

I could feel tears welling. "Two months, Denny . . . that's so long." In all our time together, the longest we had ever been apart was the two weeks when he had gone home to visit his parents after his grandfather had died. I had hated every minute of those two weeks.

He brushed aside a tear that had fallen. "Hey . . . it's okay. Maybe it won't be that long. I'm not really sure." He pulled me in for a hug. "This is for us, Kiera. Okay?"

"No," I said brokenly. Two months sounded like an eternity. "When would you leave?" I whispered.

"Monday," he whispered back. I couldn't stop the tears then. After a while, Denny released me. "I'm sorry. I didn't mean to upset you. I thought you'd be happy for me." He frowned a little. "Sorry, I should have waited until after work to tell you."

Sniffling a little, I felt the guilt coming on. "No, it's fine. You just surprised me, that's all. I'm overreacting. It will be fine, really."

He hugged me again for a few minutes. "I'm sorry. . . . I can't stay." He looked at me sheepishly. "They want me to come back to the office, get some details hammered out. I have to go, I'm sorry. I just really wanted to tell you."

I blinked back tears. "Go, it's fine. I have to get back to work anyway. . . ."

He held my cheeks in his hands. "I love you."

"I love you too," I muttered back.

He kissed my forehead and sprinted back to his car. He sure seemed peppy to ditch me. I sighed and waved as he drove away. Sullenly, I walked back into the bar. The first thing I noticed was Kellan talking to Rita and sipping on a beer as he leaned against the counter. Oh, yeah. He'd wanted a beer before . . . Denny. The thought brought fresh tears to my eyes and I quickly swiped them away, but not before Kellan noticed.

He frowned at me and walked over to where I was standing by the door. "Are you okay?"

I stared over his shoulder, knowing that if I saw the concern in his eyes, the tears would start in full force. "Yep."

"Kiera . . ." He lightly put his hand on my arm and I instinctively looked up at his face.

The concern in his eyes and the unexpected tender touch set me right off, and the tears started streaming. Without hesitation, he pulled me to him in a tight embrace. He lightly rubbed my back and rested his cheek on my head. It was very comforting, but I sobbed anyway, while the people around us stared. He ignored the stares and questioning looks (he did have quite a reputation, after all) and held me without comment or complaint until my tears stopped.

At some point Sam came up to him, probably to let him know they were up, but before Sam could say anything, I felt Kellan shake his head at him. I pulled back from him a little and wiped some tears from my cheeks. "I'm fine. Thank you. Go, go be a rock star."

He looked at me, concerned. "Are you sure? These guys can wait a few more minutes."

Touched by his offer, I shook my head. "No, really, I'm fine. I should get back to work anyway. I missed getting you your beer again."

He released me and laughed a little bit. "Next time." He rubbed my arm and, with a half-grin, turned to join his bandmates, who were already starting to take the stage.

Kellan's band was amazing, of course, but I couldn't help but notice that Kellan's eyes drifted to mine more than usual. Sometimes he frowned a little at me, and I found myself smiling back reassuringly. Honestly, I was fine. He didn't need to worry over me, sweet as that was.

I hung out later than usual after the bar closed, refusing Jenny's polite offer of a ride home. I just wasn't ready to go there yet. The thought of talking to Denny again about him leaving hurt. The thought of Denny not being home from work yet hurt too. I wasn't sure which one would hurt worse, and I didn't want to find out just yet.

I sat backwards in a chair near the bar, dangled my arms over the back, and rested my chin on my arms. Monday. Everything had been going so smoothly, and now I only had one weekend before Denny was gone for two whole months. I pondered what I was going to do while he was gone. It all felt too soon to think about. We would have tomorrow afternoon, then all day Sunday, then . . . I really wasn't sure when I'd see him again.

I could feel the tears start again and I angrily wiped them away. Seriously, it was probably just a month or two, nothing to get so worked up over. *Calm down,* I ordered my body.

I felt Kellan sit beside me before I saw him. "Hey." He smiled softly at me. "Want to talk about it?"

I looked over to the stage, where the band was still hanging out. Evan was preoccupied with Sam, but Griffin and Matt were staring at Kellan and me. Griffin muttered something to Matt with a twisted grin on his lips. Matt rolled his eyes and laughed. I could only imagine what they were talking about. No, I did not want to talk here. I'd surely break out into embarrassing blubbering, and I didn't need the D-Bags to see that. They teased me enough already. I shook my head.

Kellan noticed my eyes glued to the band and seemed to understand. "Want a ride home?"

I looked back at him gratefully and nodded. My options for getting back home this late were quickly dwindling. "Yes, thank you."

"Sure, just let me get my stuff and we'll head out." He smiled charmingly at me and for some reason, I blushed. He walked over to the guys, who were indulging in an after-hours drink with Sam, and said a couple words. They nodded. Griffin poked Matt in the ribs and smirked. Kellan shook his head at them and grabbed his guitar. He was turning to head back to me when Evan grabbed his arm. He said something to Kellan. Kellan gave him an irritated look and shook his head. Evan seemed satisfied with his answer and let go of his arm.

Kellan walked back over to me and gave me a warm smile. "Ready?"

Nodding and standing, I sighed and mentally prepared myself to either see or not see Denny. I waved sheepishly at Rita as we left the bar. She raised her eyebrow at me and smiled knowingly, winking in a way that made me blush again. She seemed to think I was going to jump Kellan every time we were alone together. Her provocative nature made me very uneasy.

The car ride home was comfortably silent. Kellan never once pressed me to speak. His kindness, and the memory of his sweet embrace earlier, made me *want* to open up to him, though. "Denny is leaving," I said quietly.

He looked over at me shocked. "But . . . ?"

I stopped his train of thought, once I realized how ominous that statement had sounded. "No, just for a few months . . . just for his job."

He relaxed and smiled a little. "Oh, I thought maybe . . ."

I sighed. "No, I'm just overreacting. Everything is fine. It's just . . ."

"You've never been apart," he said softly.

I smiled, relieved that he understood. "Yeah. I mean, we have, but not for that long. I guess I'm just used to seeing him every day, and, well . . . we waited so long to live together, and things have been going so perfectly, and now . . ."

"Now he's leaving."

"Yeah." I turned my head to gaze at Kellan. He had turned back to the road and seemed deep in thought. The streetlamps splashed light across his face at regular intervals. The effect heightened his attractiveness. The contrast between his lightened and darkened face was hypnotic, and I couldn't look away. I wondered what he was thinking.

"Nothing. . . ." He turned to look over at me. I startled a bit, not realizing I had said that last part out loud. He smiled at me. "I was just hoping things work out for you guys. You're both . . ." He didn't finish that thought, just smiled and looked back to the road.

I blushed and thought, once again, that I needed to be more careful about what I said around him. Apparently, I needed to watch what I thought around him as well, since even my thoughts seemed to slip out without permission.

Shortly after that, we pulled up to the drive. I sighed and relaxed a little. Denny's battered old Honda was already parked there. I guess I *had* been hoping he would be home. Twisting to face Kellan, I warmly said, "Thank you . . . for everything."

He looked down, almost shyly. "Not a problem, Kiera."

We got out and made our way inside and up the stairs. I paused at my door, hand on the doorknob, suddenly too nervous to go inside. "It will be fine, Kiera," Kellan said from where he had paused at his door, watching me.

I smiled and whispered good night, then steeled myself and entered the dark room. It took a few moments for my eyes to adjust after I closed the door. I heard Denny stirring in bed before I could finally see him. He was propped up on his elbows, watching me. "Hi . . . you're late." His accent curled thickly on the words in his sleepiness.

I didn't say anything. I still wasn't sure how I felt about this new situation, other than sad, anyway. I sat on the end of the bed and changed into my pajamas while he silently watched me. When I finished, he finally broke the silence.

"Kiera," he said softly, "talk to me."

I sighed and crawled under the covers with him, watching as he rolled over onto his side to face me. He ran his fingers though my hair, then stroked my cheek. "What's going on up there, huh?" He lightly tapped my temple.

I smiled over at him. "Just wondering what I'll do without you . . ." My smile faltered.

He kissed my forehead. "Home . . . work . . . home . . . work. . . . Probably the same stuff that you would do if I were here."

"Yes, but now I won't enjoy any of it," I muttered sullenly and stared at his pillow.

He laughed. "I'll miss you too."

I looked back up to his eyes. "Really?"

He blinked at me, surprised. "Of course. Wait . . . do you think I want to leave? That this is easy for me? That I won't miss you terribly, every day?"

"Yes." Those exact thoughts had crossed my mind once or twice this evening.

Now he sighed. "Kiera, that is really absurd." He grinned at me with my favorite goofy grin. "You are going to get sick of how often I call you."

I managed a smile. "Not a chance." My tone turned serious on me. "You really have to go . . . you really have to do this?"

Recognizing my tone, he stopped smiling. "Yes." He nodded once.

I cocked my head at him. "And you'll be back when you're done?"

He smiled again. "The instant I'm done."

"Well . . ." I paused for a moment. "I guess there's only one thing left to talk about. . . ."

He looked at me curiously. "What's that?"

I put my hand on his cheek and kissed him tenderly. "How are we going to spend your last two days?"

He smiled and leaned over to whisper in my ear everything we could do in the next two days. I smiled, I laughed, I smacked him on the shoulder, I laughed again, I blushed, and finally I kissed him very deeply. And for just a moment I forgot that things were about to change. . . .

Monday morning came faster than I could possibly have imagined. We had spent every minute that we could of the last two days together. Denny was excruciatingly patient with my clinginess. He knew how hard this was going to be for me. I silently hoped that it was going to be equally difficult for him. A part of me wanted him to do great, to impress his bosses, and to have a marvelous time. The majority of me wanted the whole experience to suck so much that he wouldn't ever leave me again. I may have been a little bitter.

Kellan graciously offered to drive us to the airport to see Denny off. I was so grateful to him for that. I knew I was too anxious to drive, and I didn't think I could do a cab-goodbye. I needed every last possible second with Denny, and I needed to see the plane take off, needed the closure of that.

But when the plane finally did take off, and Kellan and I were standing alone in the airport, I suddenly wished I was back at home, sobbing into my pillow. Kellan, seeing the tears start to form, sweetly put his arm around my shoulders and silently guided me back to his car.

I was only vaguely aware of walking with him, of getting back in the car and driving home. My mind was busy dreaming up a host of horrible situations, all the bad things that could happen so that I would never see my beautiful boy again. The sobs finally hit on the freeway.

Being very sweet and, surprisingly, not negatively affected by my tears as most guys would be, Kellan sat me on the couch and brought me some water and tissues. He plopped down in the chair beside me and found some stupid comedy for us both to watch. It worked; half-way through the mindless show we were both laughing. Somewhere near the end, I started falling asleep, and I felt Kellan wrap a light blanket around me before I succumbed.

I awoke alone in the living room, hours later, and replayed the last few moments that Denny and I had had together in the airport, both hating and savoring the tender exchange. . . .

Denny had pulled me in for a tight goodbye hug. I had grabbed his face and kissed him as deeply and as passionately as I could—let him think about that while he was gone. He had finally pulled away from me, breathless, but smiling softly.

"I love you. . . . I'll be back soon, okay? No worries." He had kissed me on the cheek and I could only nod, having lost the ability to speak over the lump in my throat.

He had then walked over to Kellan, who had been standing a re-spectable distance away, watching our exchange. Denny looked back at me oddly, then leaned over to whisper something to Kellan. Kellan blanched and flicked a glance at my direction. Denny had pulled away from him, a serious look on his face, and extended his hand to Kellan. Face pale and slightly confused, Kellan had nodded once, taken Den-ny's hand, shaken it, and mumbled something back. I had watched them, wondering what Denny had said. Then Denny turned back to me a final time, blew me a kiss, and boarded the plane. Leaving me.

I sighed miserably as I replayed the memory, yet again. Suddenly the phone rang, and I rushed to answer it. Denny's sweet voice filled my mind and my heart. I'd only been apart from him for half a day and already his absence was excruciating. He filled me in on how his trip had gone so far and where he was staying. I made him stay on the phone with me long after he said he needed to hang up. Finally, he told me he really had to go, but he would call me that evening before bed. Grudgingly, I agreed.

I had to go into work that night and I hated every second of it. Knowing that I could be missing Denny's phone call was physically painful. He hadn't clarified exactly when he would call, just that it would be before bed. But was that his bedtime, or mine? I was irritated all night. I ended up snapping at Rita, who had made an exceedingly inappropriate remark about me being alone with Kellan now. I messed up a few customers' orders and didn't even bother apologizing. I even ended up smacking Griffin across the head when he grabbed my ass. Actually, I enjoyed that part of the evening.

Kellan stayed late at the bar that night and very sweetly gave me a ride home again. I was an anxious mess the whole car ride, hoping that I hadn't missed Denny's call, that he was still awake and I could talk to him, hopefully for hours. Maybe I'd just lie down on the counter in the kitchen and sleep there, so I could talk with him until I passed out. I sighed. I really needed to get control over myself.

Kellan smiled at my sigh. "I'm sure Denny is still awake if you want to call him."

I smiled back. "Thank you for driving me all over the place today."

He laughed softly. "It's not a problem, Kiera," he whispered. I watched him for a second, then let my mind drift back to Denny's last sweet embrace.

The phone rang just moments after we got home, and, grinning like a schoolgirl, I answered it on the first ring. Denny had known I was working, and had timed his call perfectly. I relaxed, realizing I hadn't needed to be so anxious all night. Denny wanted to talk to me too. He would make it happen, one way or another.

Kellan came in and, smiling, grabbed the phone. "Good night, Denny." Handing the phone back to me, he winked and then headed off to bed.

Denny and I talked and laughed . . . for hours.

Chapter 5
Lonely

That first week was the longest of my life. With school not started yet and me still not having anything to do all day, I had started to dwell. I felt every single second of every single minute of every single hour of every single day tick slowly by.

Kellan did his part to try to entertain me. He chatted with me over coffee, he tried to teach me to play the guitar (which I was astoundingly bad at), and he eventually did drag me out on one of his runs. I quickly developed a dislike for Seattle; a beautiful city—yes, but friendly to runners who prefer a flat, oval track to leg-cramping hills—no. I had to stop halfway through the run and turn around to walk home. Kellan laughed a little, but offered to walk with me. Feeling weak and rather stupid, I shooed him off to finish his run and went back home to wallow.

Kellan went with me to the grocery store when my supplies started running dangerously low. That was a fun but completely embarrassing outing. Thankfully, I was fully stocked on feminine products—which would have been way too blush-inducing to buy with him there. Although he made me blush anyway, by casually tossing a box of condoms into the cart. Grabbing the box while I looked around discreetly with, I'm sure, a horrified look on my face, I gingerly handed it back to him like it was on fire. At first he wouldn't take it, and he only looked at me with a wry grin on his lips. But as my face and gestures became more frantic, he finally took the box from me and slipped it back onto the shelf, all the while laughing at my embarrassment.

Quickly getting over the incident, I pushed the cart down the aisle while Kellan, softly singing along to the cheesy background songs (he knew every single one), tossed things in—and only things I approved first. I smiled as I watched his attractive, grinning face. We were halfway through the store and entering the cereal aisle when suddenly the song he was singing along to became a duet. He looked over at me expectantly on the girl part and I could feel the heat creep up my face. I was not a singer.

He laughed, amused at my unwilling expression, and sang his next part louder, walking backwards and gesturing like he was serenading me. It was highly embarrassing, and a few people who walked by us smiled and laughed at him. He ignored them and continued singing to me, watching my face turn a bright red as my blush deepened. His eyes practically sparkled with enjoyment over my discomfort.

Hands splayed out in a "go ahead" gesture and eyebrow cocked, he again waited for me to sing the girl part. I stubbornly shook my head and smacked him on the arm, hoping he would stop mortifying me. He laughed and grabbed my hand, spinning me around right there in the middle of the aisle. He whirled me away and then back to him. He even dipped me, never once stopping his serenade. An older couple smiled as they scooted around us.

Laughing as he stood me back up, I finally, and very softly, sang the girl part for him. He smiled charmingly at me and then, chuckling, released me. We finished our shopping . . . and the song. After that, I just sang back whatever he wanted me to. Defying him was just too darn embarrassing.

More to pass the time than anything, I grudgingly called my parents. I'd had no intention of telling them that Denny had left their baby girl all alone in a strange city, but somehow it slipped out, and

I had to endure an hour-long "I knew he was no good, get your butt back here" speech. For the millionth time, I told them that I was staying in Seattle, that I was happy here. At least, I would be when Denny came back. I repeatedly assured them that they didn't need to worry so much.

Denny did call me two to three times a day, which became the highlights of my day. I found myself hanging around the kitchen, waiting for the phone to ring so I could talk to him. Eventually, that really started to irritate me. I was my own person. I could get through the day without talking to him, if I happened to miss a call. Well, I could make it a few hours at least. I tried not to obsess so much after that . . . but of course, I still did, and I cherished every phone call that I did get.

"Hey, babe."

I knew I was grinning like an idiot into the phone, but I couldn't help it. I missed his voice. "Hi . . ." I practically sighed the word. "How are you doing? Ready to come home yet?" I cringed, knowing I sounded exactly like my parents.

Denny laughed into the phone, like he realized that too. "I'm great, tired . . . but great. We're not nearly done yet though . . . sorry." His voice reflected true remorse and I couldn't help but smile.

"It's all right . . . I guess. I miss you like crazy though."

He chuckled again. "I miss you too."

This was practically our daily routine. *Are you coming home? No. I miss you. I miss you too.* I smiled at how much I loved that goofy boy.

"I was just about to grab something to eat and then crash. What are you up to on your night off?" He let out a soft grunt like he had sat down, completely exhausted.

I sighed. "Absolutely nothing, and Kellan's band is playing at Razors tonight, so I'm going to be completely alone here. . . ." I said that last part quietly as I looked around the suddenly huge house. How could I ever have thought it was tiny?

"Why don't you go?" he said, yawning a little.

I looked at the phone, confused. "Huh?"

"With Kellan . . . why don't you go listen to the band? It will at least give you something to do. . . ." He yawned again, softly, and made a sound like he had flopped onto his bed.

"You're really tired, aren't you?" I asked. I felt bad for keeping him awake, but I didn't want to get off the phone yet.

"Yeah, it's all right though." I could hear his smile through the phone. "I'll stay up to talk to you."

I felt stubborn tears brewing. I missed him so achingly bad. "I don't want to wear you out even more. I can talk to you in the morning, before your work. We'll have breakfast together." I tried to make my voice happy at that prospect when, really, I just wanted to sob at him to come home already.

He yawned again. "Are you sure? I really don't mind. . . ."

No, I wanted to talk to him all night. "Yes . . . eat, get some sleep, and hurry home to me."

"I love you, Kiera."

"I love you too. . . . Good night."

"Good night." He yawned a final time as he hung up the phone.

I stared at the receiver for a full minute while the stubborn tear dripped down my cheek. It had only been nine days, and here I was, already crying with loneliness. That didn't sit well with me. Maybe he was right and I should go out? It would, at the very least, make the evening go by faster. Breakfast would be here before I knew it. That thought perked me up. I brushed aside the tear and walked upstairs to Kellan's room.

I knocked on his closed door and he immediately said, "Come on in."

I immediately blushed upon entering; he hadn't exactly been decent yet. He was standing by the bed, facing the door and buttoning his jeans. His fresh T-shirt was still lying on the bed and his absurdly defined body was still slightly damp from the shower he had just gotten out of.

He looked up at me curiously. "What's up?"

I realized I was standing in the doorway and gaping at him stupidly. I made myself close my mouth. "Um . . . I was wondering . . . if I could go with you . . . to Razors . . . listen to the band. . . ." I was feeling more and more like an idiot with every word escaping my lips. I suddenly wished I had opened my door, for a night of sulking, instead of his door.

Grinning broadly, he grabbed his shirt from the bed. "Really? You're not sick of listening to me yet?" He winked as he pulled the T-shirt over his fabulous body.

I swallowed a little. I couldn't help openly watching him. I made myself shut my mouth again. "No . . . not yet. It will give me something to do, anyway." I immediately regretted saying that, as it probably sounded horribly rude.

He chuckled delightfully as he ran his fingers through his thick, damp hair and then, grabbing something from his dresser, tousled it up into a wonderfully shaggy mess. I watched him, curious. I'd never seen anyone style their hair that way before. He never even looked in a mirror; he just instinctively knew how to make it look perfectly styled in a completely unstyled way—fabulously sexy.

I blinked when he spoke to me. "Sure, I'm almost ready to go." He sat on the bed to put his work boots on, and patted the space beside him. I sat and watched him, feeling silly for even coming in here. "Was that Denny on the phone?"

"Yeah . . ."

Kellan paused and watched me for a moment. "Any idea when he'll come home?" he asked, grabbing for his other boot.

"No," I sighed.

He half-grinned at me charmingly. "I'm sure it won't be too much longer." He stood up and grabbed the newer of his two guitars, shoving it in an open case on his bed. "It will fly by . . . really." He smiled at me so encouragingly that I smiled too. "Ready?" he asked, shutting the case and pulling the strap over his shoulder.

I nodded and we made our way downstairs. He grabbed his keys, and I grabbed my ID and some cash from tips, and we were off.

The night at Razors was surprisingly fun. Razors was a much smaller bar than Pete's. It was a long, narrow rectangle of a building with a small area for the band at the front, a long bar against one wall, and tables and chairs occupying the rest of the space. Kellan plopped me down at the closest table, for a front-row seat to the intimate show.

The band played astoundingly well, of course, but they sounded more subdued. It was almost like a private performance for me and twenty of my closest friends. Kellan sat on a stool while he sang and strummed his guitar, his flirty behavior nearly cut in half with his adoring flock of females all but gone. Not that the girls here weren't shouting for him and the rest of the guys, but these people were mainly bar patrons who'd happened to come in tonight, not the zealous stalkers who seemed to hang out at Pete's, where the band was based.

I found myself absorbed in Kellan's performance, really listening to the lyrics and the timbre of his voice, and even softly singing along to a few songs, which made him smile gloriously when he noticed. Denny's suggestion was brilliant, and the night did fly by. Before I knew it, the guys were packing up their stuff and Kellan was saying goodbye to a few people he knew there . . . and obliging a few forward women with kisses on their cheeks. Then we were back in his car and heading home.

On the ride back, Kellan smiled and softly sang the last song the band had played, thumping a rhythm with his thumbs on the steering wheel. It happened to be the song that had moved me so much my very first night in Seattle, the song that had really made me notice the inner Kellan. I leaned my head back on the seat and turned to watch him. He looked over at my rapt attention and smiled wider through his words.

"I love that one." I smiled back and he nodded, still singing it. "It seems important to you. Does it mean something?" I hadn't meant to ask that. Oh well, too late now.

He stopped singing and looked at me curiously. "Huh," he said, pausing his fingers and returning his attention to the road.

"What?" I asked timidly, hoping I hadn't somehow offended him.

He only half-grinned at me though, not looking at all slighted. "No one's ever asked me that before. Well, no one outside the band, that is." He shrugged as he looked over my face. I blushed and looked away, wondering if he thought I was an idiot for asking.

"Yes . . ." he said softly.

I blinked and turned back to look at him, thinking maybe, once again, I had spoken my thoughts out loud and he had just agreed that I was an idiot. But smiling warmly at me, he only added, "It means a lot to me. . . ."

He said nothing further. I bit my lip and made the conscious decision to not ask him any more about it, even though I desperately wanted to. I could tell from the way he too-carefully watched the road, and from the way he occasionally flicked me quick glances from the corner of his eye, that he didn't want to elaborate on it. It took great effort on my part, but I was respectful and didn't ask him anything else.

I relayed my evening to Denny over our phone-breakfast the next morning, and he seemed pleased that I had been able to have a fun night without him. I wasn't too thrilled at that thought—I wanted to be having fun *with* him, but I supposed he was right. I did need to get out more and enjoy myself while he was gone. Dwelling was getting me nowhere.

So I started hanging out with Jenny more. In fact, the very next Sunday afternoon, she came over to our dreary house. She was as shocked as I had been that it was so barren. We spent the entire afternoon hitting every consignment shop and thrift store in town, looking for the cheapest yet nicest stuff we could find to spruce up the place.

We managed to find a couple of nice art-deco pieces for the living room, a couple scenic prints for my room, some coffee-themed pictures and, of course, one tea-themed picture for the kitchen, and an interesting water-drop photo for the bathroom. I even happened across an old Ramones poster that I thought Kellan would like, since his room was as barren as the rest of the house.

I scooped up a whole bunch of empty photo frames and got some pictures developed that we'd taken with Denny's camera that first week we'd moved in. Some were of Denny and me, a couple were just of the boys, and a few, including my very favorite one that I planned on sharing with my family, had all three of us together. Of course, we found a whole bunch of girlier items, too: baskets, decorative plants, nice towels for the bathroom. I even managed to find a cheap answering machine, so I wouldn't have to stress quite so much about missing a phone call.

I wasn't sure how thrilled Kellan was going to be about us girlifying his house, but he wasn't home when we got back from our trip. We hurried, giggling the entire time, to get everything up before he got back. We were just finishing up in the kitchen when he finally did get home.

He looked over at Jenny and me putting up the last coffee print in the kitchen and, smiling, shook his head a little. Laughing softly, he turned and headed upstairs to his room. Jenny and I figured that his response was as much of a "looks good" as we were going to get, so, laughing a little ourselves, we quickly finished the decorating project.

When Jenny had to leave shortly afterwards to start her shift, I thanked her for occupying my mind and beautifying our house. She shouted a goodbye up the stairs to Kellan and, upon his "bye" response, waved to me and headed out the door. Thinking that maybe Kellan wasn't thrilled about the new look, I quietly made my way upstairs.

His door was cracked, and I could just make him out, sitting on the edge of his bed, staring at the floor with a strange expression on his face. Curious, I knocked on his door. He looked up as I opened the door wider and waved me in.

"Hey . . . sorry about the stuff. If you don't like it, I can take it down." I smiled at him apologetically and sat on the edge of the bed beside him.

He smiled and shook his head. "No, it's fine. I guess it was a little . . . empty." He pointed over his shoulder, to the poster I had hung on his wall. "I do like that . . . thanks."

I smiled back at him. "Yeah, I thought you might . . . you're welcome." Wondering what he had been thinking about earlier, I blurted out, "You okay?"

He looked at me, confused. "Yeah, I'm fine . . . why?"

Suddenly embarrassed, I wasn't sure what to say. "Nothing, you just looked . . . nothing, sorry."

He looked at me thoughtfully for a moment, and I thought he was deciding whether or not to tell me something. I started holding my breath under the intensity of his deep-blue eyes. Suddenly, he smiled at me and, shaking his head a little, asked instead, "Hungry? How about Pete's?" He smiled brilliantly. "It's been so long since we've been there."

The bar was pretty packed, even though it was early. Kellan and I sat at his usual table, and Jenny smiled at us as she came over to take our orders. We picked out a couple burgers and a couple beers, and I watched the crowd while we waited for our drinks. It felt a little odd to sit alone in public with Kellan, especially at the place where I worked. Rita watched us curiously, and I tried to avoid eye contact with her. She tended to think the worst about us.

Kellan seemed completely comfortable, however. He sat laid-back in his chair, foot propped up on his knee, watching me. It suddenly occurred to me that I had spent the whole day out with Jenny, and then I'd been busy decorating, and now I was out at Pete's. I hadn't talked to Denny today. That thought made me frown. We hadn't gone a whole day without talking to each other. It bothered me enough that I almost asked Kellan to take me home.

He noticed. "You okay?"

Realizing I was being silly, and that I could listen to Denny's voice on our new machine over and over if he did call while I was gone, I smiled and shrugged. "Yeah, just Denny-sick. I'm fine, though."

He seemed to consider that for a minute, then nodded.

Jenny brought us our beers and he sipped his in silence, still watching me intently. Starting to feel slightly uncomfortable, I was glad when she brought our food out a few minutes later. The weirdness between us quickly passed, and we ate and talked companionably. We sat and ate and talked and drank our beers for, well, I'm not sure how long, but, eventually, we weren't alone at the table.

The rest of the D-Bags had finally made their almost-nightly appearance at Pete's. They joined our table without even considering that they weren't invited. I didn't mind. The guys were entertaining to hang out with. Well, maybe not so much Griffin, but as long as he kept his hands off of me, I could tolerate him.

Luckily, he sat over by Kellan on the far side of the table from me. Of course, he had to smack Kellan on the shoulder and say, "Nice, man," while leering at me suggestively. I rolled my eyes while Kellan chuckled at him. Matt sat next to me, while Evan pulled a chair up to the end and sat down.

Jenny quickly brought everybody beers and, just like that, I was the fifth member of the band for the night. The guys were interesting to watch in action this close, and with the bar so busy, there were plenty of opportunities to watch them interact with people. Okay, mostly with women. I found the differences in how the guys interacted with their fans interesting. Of course, they all did it, even quiet Matt and sweet Evan. They all seemed to enjoy their pseudo-stardom, just in different ways and to different degrees.

On the extreme end was Griffin, who, I think, if he ever had the idea, would keep a running tally of his conquests on his arms. He ceaselessly reiterated his adventures to anyone who would stop and listen. I found it disgusting and tuned him out as much as I possibly could. Being typical guys, the rest of the band seemed to find it all amusing. Even some women stopped and practically drooled on themselves over his crude stories. I could almost see them mentally replacing themselves with the random woman in his tale.

Griffin also seemed to be in some weird competition with Kellan. He was always asking him if he'd been with this or that girl. To his credit, Kellan was surprisingly quiet about his dalliances. He never answered Griffin directly. He tactfully changed the subject, without ever actually saying if he did or didn't "do" said girl. In fact, thinking back over our time here, if he'd been with someone, or more than one someone, I had never seen it. Nothing beyond flirting. Tons of flirting actually. The boy did enjoy a good snuggle. I had heard plenty about his conquests, but mostly from the women around the bar, or the guys in the band, or, ugh, on the bathroom walls. Finding it hard to believe that someone as good-looking as he was wasn't "getting some" regularly, I wondered where he went.

Even now, Kellan was chatting with some brunette, brushing her hair away from her shoulder and leaning in to whisper in her ear while she giggled and ran a hand down his chest. Turning my head, I watched Evan sitting on the edge of the stage.

Evan was boisterous and fun . . . and a flirt. From what I'd heard, he tended to focus on one woman for a short period of time and then, when it was almost beginning to get serious, he would shift his focus to someone else. When he was in love, he was deeply in love, but it never held his interest for long. He was "in love" a lot. Currently, he was pledging devotion to some buxom blonde in hot pants.

I smiled and turned to look over at Matt, the only band member just people watching, like me. He smiled back at me and sipped his beer in comfortable silence.

Matt was almost shy around girls. I never saw him approach anyone. They always approached him first. Even then, he usually let them do most, if not all, of the talking and flirting. I could completely understand Matt and his shyness. In some ways, we were a lot alike. But before the end of the night, even Matt had caught the interest of a pretty girl, who brought over a chair to sit beside him.

I rolled my eyes, sipped my beer, and continued my people—well, band—watching. The superfluous flirting going on around me suddenly made me miss Denny very, very much. I was staring sadly at my beer bottle when I felt someone approach. I looked up at Kellan, smiling at me and holding his hand out. Confused, I took it and he pulled me up.

"We're going to play some pool . . . join us?" He motioned back at Griffin, who was downing the rest of his beer.

I wasn't eager to hang out closer to Griffin, but Kellan was warmly smiling at me, and I found myself nodding. He put his hand on my back and we made our way to the pool room. I noticed the woman he'd been flirting with earlier following us with a couple of her friends. Griffin followed them, with a highly inappropriate look in his light blue eyes.

Griffin shot first while Kellan stood beside me, a stick upright in his hands. He grinned at me when Griffin didn't make anything on the break. Then he leaned over the pool table and, watching me with a cocky half-smile on his lips, he made his shot. I laughed softly when his ball completely missed every other ball. He looked back at the table and frowned, then looked back up at me and laughed, shrugging his shoulders as he straightened back up. His woman put a hand over his stomach consolingly, but he didn't look over at her.

Griffin smacked him on the back as he walked by. "Nice! Thanks."

Griffin sank the next two balls while Kellan sat on a stool beside me, his flirty friend standing close beside him and looking down at him like she was considering plopping herself onto his lap. He unconsciously rubbed the skin behind her knee with his thumb, his fingers drifting up her short skirt a little, while he watched Griffin shoot.

Ignoring the flirting, which was making me slightly uncomfortable, I commented on his playing instead. "You really aren't good at pool, are you?" I smiled widely at the thought.

Laughing, he looked over at me. "No, thanks for noticing." He looked back at Griffin while the brunette ran a hand through his hair above his ear. "I think that's why Griffin likes to play me." He laughed again and smiled up at the girl, making her giggle.

I rolled my eyes at him. "Maybe if you concentrated more . . ." He looked back at me, mock offended, and I laughed.

He stared at me for a second, his eyes oddly serious, and then laughed as well, shaking his head. "Yeah . . . maybe."

I looked away from him and watched Griffin make another two shots. He actually wasn't bad. Kellan started chuckling again, highly amused at something, and I peered over at him. He was watching me watch Griffin play, a wry smile on his lips. "You get to play the winner," he said, touching my knee lightly with the hand holding his pool stick.

My eyes widened at that. I really was not good at pool . . . and apparently he wasn't either. Even more alarmed, I looked over at Griffin, who, in between his shots, was attempting to lift up some girl's skirt with his stick. There was no way in hell I was playing pool with him! Kellan laughed harder as my face apparently made that clear to him.

Kellan finished up his game (okay, he lost terribly to Griffin and then called it quits) and gave his suddenly very sad brunette a kiss on the cheek. Then we said our goodbyes to Jenny, the rest of the band, and an amused Rita, and he took me home. Even with my loneliness, the evening was surprisingly a lot of fun. But fun or not, the first thing I did when Kellan and I got home was check the answering machine for a missed message from Denny.

Nothing . . . nothing at all. I sighed brokenly and shuffled off to bed.

After not hearing from him at all the evening before, Denny's phone call the next night sparked my irritation. He apologized profusely, swearing up and down that work was crazy busy, and he hadn't had a chance to stop and eat, much less call me. He invented a couple of creative ways to make it up to me, which eventually made me laugh and cooled my anger, somewhat. But a few nights later it happened again, and then a few nights later, again.

On top of worrying and wondering about that, the time was up for me to register for school. Denny had been the one who was going to show me around the new campus. Not that he knew it any better than I did—he didn't. But we'd planned on making a day of it: going on a Sunday and registering for my classes (he was a pro at creating the perfect schedule), checking out the bookstore, taking the self-guided campus tour and figuring it all out . . . together. But now he was away, indefinitely, and I was going to have to figure it out on my own.

I was scowling at brochures, course catalogs, and a map of the massive campus when Kellan came into the kitchen one Wednesday afternoon. Angry again at Denny's absence, I finally swept my arm across the table and, cursing rather dramatically, knocked everything to the floor. Of course, I hadn't realized that Kellan was standing right behind me, or I wouldn't have been so theatrical. I just wasn't looking forward to walking aimlessly around the school alone, looking like a lost idiot.

Kellan laughed at my outburst and, startled, I spun to face him. "I can't wait to tell Griff about that one." He smiled broadly, enjoying the moment a little too much. Blushing furiously, I groaned at the pictured amusement on Griffin's face. Great.

"School starting, huh?" He nodded over to the brochures on the floor.

Sighing, I bent over to pick them up. "Yeah, and I still haven't really been on the campus. I have no idea where everything is." I straightened to look at him. "I just . . . Denny was supposed to be here for this." I hated how that sounded, like I couldn't function like a normal human being with him away. It was going to be embarrassing, figuring all this out on my own. . . . But I should be able to do stuff on my own. I frowned at my dark thoughts. "He's been gone almost a month."

Kellan watched me intently, too intently, and I looked away. "The D-Bags play the campus every once in a while." I looked back and he smiled oddly. "I actually know it pretty well. I can show you around if you like."

Relief washed through me at the idea of having a guide. "Oh, please, yes." Struggling to regain my composure, I added, "I mean, if you don't mind."

He half-smiled adorably at me. "No, Kiera, I don't mind. . . ."

Ignoring the oddity in his voice at the tail end of that sentence,

I added, "There's a registration thing tomorrow. Could you take me, and then Sunday we could look around?"

He smiled broadly again. "Sounds great."

The next day, Kellan rather cheerily took me to school and walked me to the admissions office, since he seemed to know exactly where it was. "Thank you, thank you, thank you, Kellan."

He brushed off my gratitude with his hand. "It's no big deal."

"Well, I appreciate it . . . and I have no idea how long I'll have to wait for my turn, so don't worry about picking me up. I can take the bus back home."

He looked at me funny, then smiled. "Good luck."

I stood with other nervous-looking students in the waiting area. I stared at my hands, mentally going over what classes I should take, until a woman came up to me and motioned me to an open door leading to the registration office.

The office was warm and inviting, which relaxed me a little bit. Two incredibly large bookcases were crammed full of thick, hard-bound books. Multiple file cabinets and a large, clean desk in front of the window overlooking the quad were all in a deep, dark cherry color that coordinated with the beige walls perfectly. Plants were everywhere around the room. The person who occupied this office must have had a green thumb; I couldn't keep anything alive for more than three days.

A woman sitting at the desk looked up at me as her college-age assistant motioned me through the open door. She was very professional looking, and I suddenly felt very dowdy and uncomfortable. I had an odd desire for Kellan to still be here. I knew that he would be completely comfortable walking up to this woman, giving her a sly half-smile, and getting whatever he wanted from her. She would be putty in his hands. A twinge of jealousy passed through me. Life must be so much easier when you know that you're absurdly attractive.

I sighed internally and straightened myself as I approached her. I might not have been anything special to look at, I told myself, but I was smart, and in a place such as this, smart counted more. I held out my hand, trying to picture what Denny would do in this situation. "Hello. I'm Kiera Allen. I'm transferring in this year and need to register." I smiled, thinking that had come out okay.

She smiled and took my hand. "Nice to meet you, Kiera. Welcome to U-Dub. What can I help you with?"

I smiled and sat down. That had gone much better than I'd thought it would. We sat and talked about what I had already taken at Ohio U and what I still needed to graduate. We debated my schedule and went over the open classes, finding a few that fit together perfectly. I only needed three this semester, which worked out great, leaving me time to study . . . and, quite frankly, sleep, since I was working so late most nights.

By the end of the meeting, I had my three classes lined up. European Lit, with all the great classics: the Brontë sisters, Austen, Dickens. I was really looking forward to that class. Microeconomics, which Denny had suggested I take, insisting that he could help me study. I'd told him that I could handle it, but he had been so excited to teach me. And finally, a psych class. I had really wanted to take psychology, but the only open course that fit into my schedule was Human Sexuality. Already embarrassed, I signed up for it. I could take a seat in the very back of the room and not say a word. Besides, when Denny got home, he could help me study for that one too. . . .

When I left the admissions office, quite a bit later, I blinked in surprise at seeing Kellan leaning against the wall across from the door, one foot propped up, and an espresso in each hand. Upon seeing me, he lifted one up and raised an eyebrow. I couldn't help the huge smile as I walked over to him.

"What are you doing here?" I asked, gleefully taking the coffee he offered me. "I said you didn't have to come back for me."

"Well, I thought you might prefer a ride home . . . and a pick-me-up." He lifted his own coffee and took a sip.

I could only stare at him, dumbfounded for a second, before I finally gave him a kiss on the cheek. "Thank you, Kellan . . . for everything."

He looked down and, smiling, shook his head. "Come on," he said softly. "Let's go home. You can tell me all about your classes." He looked back at me and grinned.

Thinking of my psych class, I felt my cheeks heat. Kellan laughed.

That Sunday, Kellan took me on a tour around the campus. There were a surprising number of people walking around, either getting ready to reenter the school, or, like me, checking it out for the first time. The campus was massive, more like a small city than a school. Of course, the first place Kellan showed me was a small bar across the way from the university bookstore. Smiling at him, and shaking my head a little, I went inside with him for a quick lunch and a beer before our little adventure. Next, we went to the bookstore, where I found all the books I needed. I got most of them used, which saved me a bundle—books are dang expensive. I had to smile at Kellan while I was in line; he was flipping through a thick book on human anatomy and talking to two giggling college-age girls . . . always the flirt.

Then we crossed the street to enter the campus. It was breath-takingly beautiful. Paths leading to imposing brick buildings criss-crossed the expertly landscaped and maintained lawns. Dormant cherry blossoms were everywhere in the quad; the campus would be truly stunning in the spring. People of various ages and ethnicities were lounging around the grass, enjoying the sunny day.

Smiling at me, Kellan led me past the stately buildings. He not only knew the name of each one, he knew what was taught there: Gowen Hall—Asian literature and political science; Smith Hall—history and geography; Savery Hall—philosophy, sociology and economics (where my Microeconomics class would be); Miller Hall—the admin hall, which was the only place on campus I'd already been; Raitt Hall—speech communications and nutritional sciences . . .

He went on and on with the detailed explanations of what and where everything was. I had brochures, but he barely looked at them. He just seemed to know everything by heart. He was the best guide I could have asked for, and I found myself more and more appreciative of him and his kind offer, and not only because he seemed to know every nook and cranny of the campus, which seemed really odd to me, since he'd made it sound like he'd only visited a couple of times for some shows.

No, mostly I was grateful for the fact that walking beside him down the paths and the halls of the school caused me to be practically invisible. He drew almost every eye to him like a flame. Women—and even a few men—openly stared. The guys who weren't staring at him watched the women with puzzled looks on their faces, like they didn't get it. Either way was fine with me, as long as *he* was the one being looked at. Since Denny's departure, I'd been feeling really lonely, and more than a little depressed. We were walking through swarms of people I didn't know, that I didn't feel like getting to know today, and I was more than happy to disappear.

Kellan was pleasant company and chatted politely with me. He made eye contact with several of the girls in the hall, and surprisingly avoided eye contact with others. I had suspicions about that. We walked through a lot of the campus and through some of the various buildings and hallways. He made sure to go through the buildings where my classes would be held and pointed out which rooms were mine and what routes would get me there most quickly.

The afternoon had been pretty uneventful, aside from the stares he drew, when suddenly we came across someone who surprised us both. We were walking down the hallway to where my European Lit class would be, when from behind us we heard . . . "Oh! My! God! Kellan Kyle!"

Kellan looked puzzled as a petite redhead with springy hair and a face full of freckles bounded down the hall toward us. Then panic crossed his features, and I thought for a second he might try and run for it. Before he could do anything though, the tiny girl had flung her arms around his neck and was kissing him voraciously.

I blinked in shock and sudden discomfort. Taking a break from his lips, she sighed ecstatically. "I can't believe you're visiting me at school."

Kellan blinked, his mouth open in surprise, but he remained quiet.

The girl glanced over at me and frowned. "Oh, I can see you're busy." She reached in her small purse for a piece of paper and a pen, scribbled something on it, and shoved it, rather seductively, in Kellan's front pocket. He fidgeted slightly, an odd look on his face.

"Call me," she breathed, kissing him passionately again before taking off back down the hall.

And just like that, she was gone.

Kellan started walking again, like nothing even remotely weird had just happened, and I hurried to catch up with him. I couldn't help but stare at him in disbelief. He acted like being mauled was commonplace. Eventually, he turned to look over at me.

"Who was that?" I asked.

He scrunched his face adorably, in confusion and concentration. "I really have no idea." He reached in his pocket and took out the note. "Hmmm . . . that was Candy." His eyes snapped up as recognition flared. He grinned and looked back to where she had disappeared. I rolled my eyes, a little irritated. My earlier suspicions were pretty much confirmed at that point.

He surprised me by crumpling the note and tossing it into a wastebasket as we walked by. I wondered about that, my irritation cooling. I'd kind of figured Candy had been about to get a phone call later. I couldn't hold back the smile. Poor girl. And she had been so excited too.

A week later, on a bright and cheery Sunday morning, I was aimlessly flipping through channels on the television. I wasn't really watching anything, too lost in thought. Denny hadn't called again last night. It was starting to become a more frequent thing, and I was really beginning to lose patience. I tried to remind myself, over and over, that he would be home in a few weeks, that this purgatory would eventually end. But nothing was lifting my mood, not today. Today I was wallowing in self-pity. That was my plan, anyway.

I was on my thousandth sigh when Kellan abruptly appeared in the living room and stepped between me and the TV.

"Come on." He held his hand out to me.

I looked up at him, confused. "Huh?"

"You're not spending yet another day moping on the couch." He smiled. "You're coming with me."

Not moving, and frowning at his cheeriness, I sullenly asked, "And where are we going?"

He smiled his charming half-smile. "Bumbershoot."

"Bumper-what?"

He laughed a little and smiled wider. "Bumbershoot. Don't worry, you'll love it."

I had no idea what that was, and I smiled mockingly. "But that will ruin a perfectly good day of wallowing."

"Exactly." He beamed at me and his sudden handsomeness caught my breath. Hmmm, this could be interesting. . . .

"Fine," I sighed, and ignoring his still outstretched hand, I stood myself up and, exaggerating my irritation, headed upstairs to change while he laughed at me.

He was dressed casually in shorts and a T-shirt, so I copied him and picked out my shorty-shorts and a tight tank top. He watched me as I came down the stairs, and then looked away, smiling to himself.

"Ready?" he asked, grabbing his keys and wallet.

"Sure." I still had no idea what I'd just gotten myself into.

Surprisingly, Kellan drove us to Pete's. "Bumbershoot is at Pete's?" I asked mockingly.

Kellan smiled at me and rolled his eyes. "No, the guys are at Pete's."

My heart unexpectedly dropped a little. "Oh, they're coming too?"

He put the car in park and frowned at me, noticing my disappointment. "Yeah. . . . Is that okay?"

Wondering why that had bothered me, I shook my head. "No, of course that's fine. I'm intruding on your day anyway."

He cocked his head in the cutest way. "You're not intruding on anything, Kiera."

I smiled and looked out the window, and my heart sank again. There was one thing that hanging out with the guys entailed that I wasn't all too fond of, and it was currently walking right toward me. Griffin. I sighed and Kellan noticed what had my attention. He laughed and leaned over to whisper in my ear, "Don't worry. I'll protect you from Griffin."

I blushed a little at his unexpected nearness, but threw him a smile in response. Griffin banged on the window, startling me, and then pressed his lips against the glass, making obscene movements with his tongue, his piercing clicking on the glass. I grimaced and looked away.

Matt opened the rear door from Kellan's side and smiled over at me, his pale blue eyes looking genuinely pleased to see me. "Hey, Kiera, coming with us, huh? Cool." He hopped in and shut the door behind him while I nodded.

"Hi, Matt."

Evan opened the rear door on my side and waved for Griffin to get into the middle seat. "Uh-uh. No, I'm not taking the bitch seat. You take it." Griffin stated indignantly, shaking his head at Evan.

"No way, man. I have to sit by a window, or I'll get carsick." Evan sighed, giving him a just-do-it face, and indicated the seat again. Griffin rolled his eyes and looked over at Matt. Matt smiled back, clearly not moving. Griffin put his arms across his chest, clearly not moving either. Evan and Kellan both sighed.

"Oh, for Pete's sake," I muttered, then carefully crawled over the front seat to sit in the "bitch seat," as Griffin so charmingly put it.

"Sweet!" Griffin quickly slid onto the seat next to me and shut the door in Evan's face. I immediately regretted my decision and looked over at Kellan, who shrugged at me. I sighed again and scooted over toward Matt, while Griffin got as close to me as physically possible in the big backseat.

Evan got in the front seat, waved hello at me, and we took off for wherever we were going. Luckily, the trip didn't take too long. I only had to smack Griffin's hand from my thigh three times and push him away from my neck once. Kellan watched us periodically from the rearview mirror, but I couldn't quite see enough of his face to know if he was irritated or amused.

Bumbershoot turned out to be a music and art festival at the Seattle Center. Kellan parked us in the lot across the street and waited to take my hand, which I thought was very sweet of him. As we entered the Center, I could see it was also very practical, since the place was packed. Kellan bought my ticket, insisting that he had invited me along so he would pay, and we made our way inside the massive campus.

It was amazing. There were art exhibits and performers everywhere. We walked near the Space Needle on the way in, and Kellan pulled me close, telling me we could go up later if I wanted. As we got farther inside, the place was overwhelming. There were a dozen or so stages outside, and almost another dozen enclosed theaters, all with different types of bands. Every music style was accounted for, from reggae to rock. There were even some comedy shows going on as well. There were a ton of food and merchandise booths, and even an amusement park. I had no idea where to go first.

Luckily, Griffin and Matt seemed to know exactly where they wanted to go, so we followed them through the mob of people. As we got closer to one of the outdoor stages, the crowds got even thicker. I squeezed Kellan's hand and he smiled and pulled me close to him. I was still missing Denny, but hanging onto Kellan was nice. It made me feel kind of . . . content.

Griffin, Matt, and Evan were moving toward the front of a particularly rowdy group of fans, who were listening to some rock group that I hadn't ever heard of before. It looked a little violent for me, so I was relieved when Kellan stopped a distance from the chaos. We listened, and Kellan sang along to some of the songs, never dropping my hand. I pressed into his side as people behind us roughly pushed into me, trying to get by. Seeing I was being jostled, Kellan slipped his arms around my waist, and pulled me safely in front of him. Unlike with Griffin, I didn't smack him away. His arms were warm, comforting.

I watched the band for a while—personally, I thought Kellan's group was better—and then I watched the rowdy crowd. I didn't see the other D-Bags (the band's name still made me chuckle). I looked around and finally found them off to the side, standing with a small circle of people all passing around cigarettes. Only, I had the feeling that wasn't really what they were.

Kellan noticed my attention and looked over. I looked up and watched him watch his friends. I was curious if he would go over there or not. His blue eyes sparkled as the sunlight hit them and, after a moment, he looked back down to my curious eyes and shrugged, smiling a little at me. Then he turned his attention back to the show.

I was relieved that he was happy to stay over by me. I started to wonder over that, but then decided he was pleasant to be around, and not too bad to look at, and that was a good enough answer for right now. Besides, I had been so lonely lately and, right or wrong, his closeness was making that feeling fade.

Relaxing for the first time in what felt like weeks, I turned and slipped my arms around his waist, resting my head against his chest. I felt him stiffen a little at how closely we were connected, and then he relaxed, too, his thumb lightly stroking my back. I wasn't sure why I did that, but I sighed contentedly at the warmth of his embrace.

We spent the majority of the day that way, making our way to all the different styles of music on all the different stages. Griffin and Matt would lead us through the crowd—Griffin hooting at cute girls that would pass by—some responded, some looked affronted. Matt would occasionally smack him to get his attention and change the direction we were going. Evan strolled alongside Kellan and me, watching the crowds and curiously eyeing Kellan, who was still holding my hand. Once up to a stage, the guys would disappear, getting as close as possible to the front, with the more aggressive people, while Kellan would stay by me, seemingly happy and content farther back.

I felt a little guilty that he was missing out on what guys considered "fun," but I liked having him near, so I didn't say anything.

Around midday we stopped at one of the numerous food stands and got some burgers and fries. Kellan grabbed my food and, smiling, nodded over to an empty spot on a nearby lawn. Matt and Evan sat down and Matt grabbed a water bottle and started pouring something into their sodas. Griffin squatted down in front of him and handed him his drink for a fill-up. I wasn't sure exactly what it was, but I was pretty sure it was alcoholic. I frowned, then sighed. Boys will be boys.

Matt held the bottle up to me politely. I sat down next to him and shook my head no. He shrugged and looked up at Kellan, who also, surprisingly, shook his head no. I smiled into my straw as I took a sip of pure soda. I was happy that Kellan didn't feel the need to "enhance" his fun. Matt shrugged again and, taking a quick swig, put the bottle back in his bag.

Griffin stood up from in front of Matt and made a move like he was going to sit next to me, but Kellan sat down right beside me before he could, sitting close enough that we were touching. I nestled gratefully into Kellan's side and he nudged me playfully with his shoulder. Throwing Kellan a look, Griffin stalked off to sit over by Evan, on the far side of Matt.

I laughed at his frustration, and at the fact that we were all sitting in a line on the lawn instead of bunched together. But as words from the story Griffin started telling Evan drifted down to me, I was mostly grateful. Matt turned to listen to him, but on the words "freaky" and "un-fucking-believable," I quickly turned my head to Kellan, who grinned and rolled his eyes. Tuning Griffin out, I concentrated on having a conversation with Kellan.

Of course, the women here were no different than everywhere else I went with Kellan. Even just sitting on the lawn, eating and chatting with me, he attracted them. But for the first time that I had ever seen, Kellan ignored them. Usually he would, at the very least, smile and make eye contact, but today he just seemed to be happy to sit by my side and talk with me. The guys were more than happy to make up for his lack of attention to the females, and several women were only too eager to move their affections over to the other boys when Kellan appeared indifferent. Our straight line ended up a strange, lopsided oval of flirty girls. It made me feel oddly wonderful that, at least for today, I seemed to have Kellan's full attention.

After lunch, the guys decided to hit the small amusement park. Evan, Matt, and Griffin, all obviously feeling no pain, decided to go on a ride that looked terrifying to me. It wasn't just the fact that the ride swung rapidly back and forth while rising higher and higher into the air; it was that once it reached the top, it held you upside down. I didn't like that at all. I clenched Kellan's hand as we approached it, and he looked down at me thoughtfully. He stopped a little way back as the guys got in line. I looked up at him questioningly, but he only smiled calmly back at me. I nestled close to his arm and put my head on his shoulder, grateful that we were, apparently, not going anywhere near the ride.

The other three guys, all with girls scrunched close to their sides, thoroughly enjoyed the crazy thing. I had to look away as they reached the very top. Kellan chuckled at me, then turned and pulled me toward some less terrifying entertainment. Smiling and laughing, we attempted some of the carnival games. Eventually, he won me a stuffed animal at a ball toss, and I gave him a swift kiss on the cheek in thanks.

As we were leaving the games section, a little girl in front of us started crying as her ice cream cone hit the hot pavement. Her mother tried consoling her, but the girl was having none of it. Kellan watched the exasperated mom and her red-faced child as we walked around them. He looked back once at them, then over to me. I eyed him curiously as he glanced down at the bear he had won for me. "Do you mind?" he asked, nodding his head at the child who was still crying over her puddle of ice cream.

I smiled warmly at his thoughtfulness and handed the bear to him. "No. Go ahead."

He excused himself and walked over to the little girl. With an *Is this okay?* glance at her mother, who smiled and nodded, he squatted to the girl's level and handed her the stuffed animal. She immediately hugged it and stopped crying. Clutching her mother's leg shyly with one arm and her new prize with the other, she thanked Kellan quietly and started giggling. Kellan ruffled her hair and stood to face her mother, who sincerely thanked him. Kellan nodded and, smiling kindly at them, said it was no problem. My heart warmed as I watched him walk back to me.

Reaching out for his hand, I smiled a half-grin as he took it and interlaced our fingers. "You're just a big softy, aren't you?"

He looked around discreetly. "Shhh, don't tell anyone." Then he grinned and laughed. Looking down at me he said, "Do you want me to win you another one?"

Thinking that no toy could replace the sweet memory he had just imprinted on my brain, I smiled and shook my head. "No, I'm fine." He smiled sweetly at me and then led me back to where we had left the guys.

When it started getting dark and I could barely keep walking I was so exhausted, we headed back to the car. Deciding I was not going to put up with Griffin again, I crawled into the middle of the front seat, between Kellan and Evan. I couldn't help but smile as Griffin pouted in the backseat.

The rocking of the car was slowly pulling my body toward sleep, and I laid my head on Kellan's shoulder. A full day of holding hands and having his arms around me had made me feel really comfortable around him. And it was oddly appealing to me to touch him. I was nearly asleep when I felt the car stop and heard the doors open. I wanted to open my eyes and say good night to the guys, but I just couldn't get my body to respond.

"Hey, Kellan, we're gonna stay at Pete's. You comin'?" I couldn't tell which one had asked it . . . maybe Evan.

I felt Kellan move a little, like he had looked down at me, nearly asleep on his shoulder. "No, I'll pass tonight. I think I'll get her to bed."

There was a long pause from the still open door. "Be careful, Kellan. You don't need another Joey and . . . Denny is a friend, man." I wanted to say something to that; my irritation tried to rise, but my tired brain couldn't focus long enough to respond.

An even longer pause came from Kellan. "Evan, it's not like that. I wouldn't . . ." He didn't finish that thought, and I was really curious where it had been going. "Don't worry. Yeah, maybe I'll drop in later."

"Alright, see ya." The door closed softly.

Kellan sighed deeply and then drove the car out of the parking lot. I faded in and out of consciousness as we drove home. I really wanted to lie down in his lap but thought that might be pushing the limits of our friendship. After what felt like only a few seconds of driving, the car stopped again.

Kellan waited in the dark, silent car for a moment, and I could feel his eyes on me. I wondered if I should get up now and go inside, so he could leave for Pete's, but I was really curious as to what he would do, and honestly, I was quite relaxed. The silence grew while we sat in the car. It started to make my heart beat faster, which started to make me uncomfortable, so I yawned and stretched a little.

I lifted my head to find his beautiful blue eyes watching me. "Hey, sleepy," he whispered. "I was beginning to think I'd have to carry you."

"Oh . . . sorry." I blushed at the thought.

He laughed a little. "It's all right. I wouldn't have minded." He paused for a second. "Did you have fun?"

I thought back over the day and realized that I had. "Yes, a lot. Thank you for inviting me."

He half-smiled and looked away, almost shyly. "You're welcome."

"Sorry you had to hang back with me and miss all the moshing," I laughed.

He laughed once and then looked back over at me. "Don't be. I'd rather hold a beautiful girl than be all bruised tomorrow." He smiled, looking a little embarrassed. I looked down. Someone as good-looking as him calling *me* beautiful was beyond ridiculous, but sweet, anyway. "Well, come on. I'll get you inside."

I shook my head at him. "No, you don't have to do that. I can manage. You can go on to Pete's."

He looked over at me, suddenly alarmed. I realized then that he'd assumed I was sleeping through that whole conversation with Evan.

I tried to cover with, "I'm guessing that's where the other D-Bags went off to?"

He visibly relaxed. "Yeah, I don't have to go though. I mean, if you don't want to be alone. We could order pizza, watch a movie, or something."

Suddenly starving, I thought pizza sounded like a great idea. My stomach noisily agreed. I laughed, slightly embarrassed. "Okay, apparently my stomach votes for option two."

"All right, then." He smiled.

We ordered our large pepperoni pizza and ate it standing in the kitchen, laughing over some of the absurdly goofy things Griffin and the guys had done throughout the day. Afterwards, I snuggled up on the chair while he sprawled across the couch and turned on *The Princess Bride*. I vaguely remembered the little boy talking to his grandfather before I was sound asleep. I woke up when Kellan laid me down on my bed and started pulling the covers over me.

"Kellan . . ." I whispered.

His hands stopped moving. "Yeah?"

I looked over to what little of him I could see in the darkness. "We forgot the Space Needle."

He smiled at me and finished tucking me in. "Next time."

When he was done, he paused, still leaning over me. His eyes were unreadable in the darkness, but, weirdly enough, he was giving me butterflies, looking at me like he was. After another second, he smiled, then whispered, "Good night, Kiera," and left. My stomach settling, I smiled at remembering the day and how, for almost the entirety of it, I hadn't missed Denny . . . too much.

Chapter 6
Coming Together, Breaking Apart

After that day, I was more aware of Kellan. I couldn't help but notice how sweet he was. His cute little nods hello when he entered the bar, how he would look at me and smile sometimes when he sang, how we chatted every morning over our coffees, how much I loved it when he would sing just for me at home. Every day I felt closer to him, which delighted me and worried me. But, wrong as it might have been, noticing him distracted me from missing Denny. I still craved his phone calls, but if we went a day or two without one, I could satisfy my loneliness by spending time with Kellan. Kellan never seemed to mind me hanging around him. In fact, he seemed to encourage it.

We continued our friendly flirting that had started at Bumbershoot. On nice days, we sat outside in the backyard and lay down on the grass to read and enjoy the sunshine. He would usually take his shirt off to sunbathe and, lying close beside him, I usually felt my heartbeat spike a bit. He would eventually fall asleep and I'd roll on my side to watch his perfect face in slumber. Once, when I'd been doing that, he hadn't really been asleep yet and he'd smiled and cracked an eye open, making me blush furiously and roll onto my stomach to hide my head while he softly laughed at me.

On nights that I had off, he sometimes came back home after rehearsal instead of going to Pete's with the guys, and we'd have dinner together and then snuggle close to watch a movie. Sometimes he'd put his arm around me and lightly rub mine with his fingertips. Sometimes he would hold my hand, playing with my fingers and smiling that amazingly sexy half-smile.

On the nights I did have to go in, we'd sit together and cuddle on the couch, reading or watching TV before work. He let me relax into him and put my head on his shoulder. Once, when I'd been exhausted after a sleepless night of missing Denny, we'd snuggled on the couch and he'd gently pulled me down to rest my head on his lap. I had fallen asleep that way, turned slightly into him, with his arm over me protectively and his other hand running through my hair. Somewhere in the back of my head, I knew it was probably more than Denny would be okay with, but it was comforting, it was nice. It concerned me a little, how much I enjoyed being close to him . . . and yet, I couldn't seem to stop doing it.

One weeknight, someone put a particularly dancey song on the jukebox and Griffin, proudly wearing his Douchebags T-shirt, felt the need to grab every available girl at every nearby table and pull her to the dance floor. Of course, they all went willingly. But then he spotted me and started moving suggestively in my direction. Not relishing his roaming hands anywhere near my body, I put my hands out in front of me and started backing up. Evan laughed and grabbed Jenny for a quick dip, making her giggle. Matt sat on the table, chuckling at everyone.

Griffin was almost within my reach when I was suddenly pulled away and twirled a few times on the floor. Laughing at Griffin's disappointed face, Kellan spun me a few more times to the other side of the room. I smiled at him as he twirled me out and, kissing my hand, released me. Within seconds he was surrounded by a half-dozen women wanting to dance with their rock-god. He spent the remainder of the night dancing rather sexily with a rotating group of females. He moved effortlessly to the music and was exceedingly enticing to watch. I found my eyes roaming to him more than a few times during my shift.

I was still thinking of Kellan's body moving to the music when I opened our front door after work. I was greeted by a ringing phone. Smiling, and thinking it could only be Denny calling me this late at night, I received a small shock when I recognized the voice on the other line.

"Hey, sis."

"Anna! Long time no hear . . . what are you up to? Why are you calling so late?"

"Well, I received your care package today. . . ." I had sent my parents and Anna some pictures of the city—my school, the bar, and a picture of Kellan, Denny, and me. "Oh my God . . . Who is the hottie and why didn't you tell me about him the minute you got there?"

I should have realized earlier that Kellan would pique my sister's interest. "That's my roommate, Kellan."

"Damn! Now I'm coming to visit for sure."

My sister and Kellan in the same room together. Now *that* would be interesting. I suddenly did not want my sister anywhere near him. "Well, now really isn't . . . Wait, what about Phil?"

"Pfffttt . . . Phil, please. Compared with your hottie roommate? Sorry, no contest." Mom had told me that Anna had known Phil for a whole two weeks before moving in with him. Apparently the honeymoon was over.

"Well, now really isn't a good time. School's about to start and Denny's still away. . . ."

"Denny's gone?"

"Geez, Anna, don't you ever talk to Mom and Dad?" I sighed, not really wanting to have that conversation with another family member.

"Not if I can help it. What happened?"

"It's a work thing. He had to go to Tucson for a while." An "a while" that was feeling like an eternity, and he hadn't called again today. . . .

"Ahhh, so he's traipsing about the desert and he left you home alone with Hot-Bod?" I could hear the smirk through the phone line.

"God, Anna . . . it's not like that." I sighed. We were a little more . . . friendly . . . with each other than before, but it most definitely was not what my sister was thinking.

She laughed. "So, fill me in. . . . It was Kellan, right? What's he like?"

"He's, well . . ." How did one sum up Kellan? "He's . . . nice." I glanced upstairs hoping that "he" was also asleep. He had ducked out of Pete's a few hours ago after yawning three times in a row while talking to Jenny. I guess being an early bird and a night owl eventually catches up with you.

"Oh, God . . . he's gay, isn't he? All the really hot ones are." She sighed, rather dramatically.

I laughed. No, from all I'd seen and heard so far, Kellan was most definitely straight. "No, I'm pretty sure he's not."

"Good! So when can I come up?" Her voice brightened at the prospect.

Mentally I sighed. She wasn't going to let this one go. "Okay, how about during winter break? We could all go clubbing or something." I guess the image of Kellan dancing was still in my head. It *was* a good activity for all of us to do, though.

"Ohhh . . . I love that. All hot and sweaty on the dance floor with him. Of course, I could rip off his shirt, just to help him out, you know. Then, later, we could snuggle in his bed to keep warm during the long, hard winter night."

"Jesus, Anna! I do have to live with the guy." I really didn't like the picture she had just put in my head. Mentally laughing, a different version came to mind. "You know, if you think *he's* hot, you should see his friend Griffin."

"*Really?*"

"Oh, yeah!"

I spent the remainder of our conversation convincing her of Griffin's many virtues. I had never lied so much in my life.

The next afternoon, Denny finally called me after a two-day absence. I felt like I hadn't talked to him, *really* talked to him, in forever. I ached to actually see him, hold him. The conversation was brief, and he seemed distracted, like the call was an obligation and not something he really wanted to be doing. He excused himself a few minutes into the conversation, saying he was getting called away for a meeting. Ice flooded my stomach and my heart sank as I said goodbye and hung up the phone. I stared at it for twenty minutes, wondering if he would call back . . . wondering why he was talking to me less and less.

Later that same night, I woke up in a panic, heart fluttering wildly. I had been having a nightmare, I was sure of it. I couldn't remember the dream, just the underlying terror behind it. I wanted to cry. I wanted to scream, and I had no idea why. I sat up in bed and clutched my knees, trying to stabilize my breathing and my heart rate. I didn't want to close my eyes again. I looked around the darkened room, trying to get a bearing on what was real. Dresser, TV, nightstand, Denny's empty side of the bed . . . Yep, all real, painfully real.

I had an overwhelming urge to talk to Denny. I wasn't sure, but I felt like my dream had been about him. I wondered if it was too late to call his hotel room. I sat on the edge of the bed and looked at the clock—3:30. Ugh, that was too late to call, too early to wake him up. I'd have to wait a few more hours and see if I could catch him before work.

Oddly, I could hear sounds coming from downstairs. Someone was flicking between channels on the television. Thinking Kellan was awake, and maybe I could talk to him instead, I got up and made my way down the stairs. I realized Kellan wasn't alone as I rounded the corner and the living room came into view. I wanted to turn around and head right back to my room, but it was too late.

"Kiera! Hey, sex kitty!" Griffin was standing in the living room sipping a beer, TV remote in hand. "Nice PJs." He winked at me and I flushed with color.

Kellan looked over from the couch apologetically as I finished walking down the steps. "Hey, sorry. We didn't mean to wake you."

Matt looked over from the comfortable chair and smiled at me. I didn't see Evan anywhere.

"You didn't . . . bad dream." I shrugged my shoulders.

He half-smiled at me. "Beer?" he asked, holding up his own a little.

"Sure." I didn't want to go back to sleep for a while anyway.

He left to get me one from the kitchen, while I stood awkwardly behind Matt in the chair. Griffin went back to flipping channels on the TV. Matt turned to watch as well. Kellan reappeared a minute later and, handing me a beer, nodded over to the couch. I followed him.

Griffin sat on the end of the couch, near the table. He set his beer down, frowning slightly. He didn't seem to be finding whatever he was looking for. I quickly passed Kellan and sat on the opposite side of the couch. Smiling at me and shaking his head, Kellan took the middle, sitting close to me, which made me grin. I scooted over to him and pressed against his side, pulling my feet up to the couch, my knees angled in, toward him. I had gotten so used to snuggling with him that it was just a habit now. He smiled down at me, put an arm around my thighs, and nudged me playfully with his shoulder. I rested my head against his shoulder and smiled back.

Still looking frustrated, Griffin said, "You know, I've been think-ing." Matt groaned loudly, and I laughed at him. Griffin ignored us both. "When this band breaks up . . ." I raised my head and my eye-brows at that, and Kellan grinned at me. "I think I'll do God-rock."

Involuntarily, I spat out the sip of beer I had just taken. Most made it back in the bottle, but I choked on the rest. Kellan smiled at me around his mouthful of beer. He shook his head at Griffin and rolled his eyes.

Matt turned his spiky blond head to stare at Griffin incredu-lously. "God-rock . . . you? Really."

Griffin smiled, still flipping through channels. "Yeah! All those hot, horny virgins. Are you kidding me?" He grinned devilishly while I continued choking on my beer.

Finally, he smiled and stopped flipping through channels, apparently finding whatever it was he had been looking for. I swallowed a few times and took a long draw of beer to soothe my throat.

Griffin said the oddest things sometimes. He really was kind of perfect for Anna. Sighing at that thought, I looked over at the television and finally noticed what he had stopped on. It looked like porn . . . or some cable show that was close enough to it. I could feel my cheeks flushing and I stared down at my bottle. Matt and Griffin settled back to watch while Kellan looked over at me curiously.

I tried to stay composed. If I got up and left, Griffin would have a field day the next time I saw him at the bar. If I just sat here and pretended to watch with them for a while, he would probably just let it go. The noises from the TV weren't helping with my blush, however. Really, why did guys watch this stuff? And why was Kellan watching *me*?

Eventually, he leaned over and whispered in my ear, "Are you uncomfortable?"

I shook my head no. I didn't want him thinking me any more prudish than he probably already did. In fact, if he could just ignore me and watch his smut, that would be great. I wondered how long I would need to sit here until I could slip out unnoticed by the guys. Accepting my answer, Kellan leaned forward slightly, blocking my view of Griffin and Griffin's view of me. Grateful, I smiled and looked up at his face. He was intently watching the television set, and I found the look on his face interesting. I had no desire to watch the movie, but watching Kellan watch it was fascinating.

At first he simply watched, but after a while his eyes started changing, started burning with an alluring intensity. He took a sip of his beer and swallowed, his mouth lingering on the bottle for an extra few seconds. His lips parted slightly; his breathing seemed to just fractionally increase. Still intently watching the screen, he brought his tongue slowly over his lower lip and then dragged his teeth even more slowly across them.

The move was so distractingly sexy that a soft noise escaped my throat and my breath caught. The sound of the TV drowned me out, but Kellan, being so close to me, noticed. His smoldering blue eyes slid to mine. I could see why no woman resisted him with a gaze like that. I could feel my breath quicken in response. I couldn't imagine anyone telling that look no. Would I, if he did anything? What was he thinking right now? I had no idea. . . .

His breath noticeably quickened in response to mine. Suddenly his gaze flicked down to my lips and I knew. I knew exactly what he was thinking. He shouldn't be thinking that. I shouldn't want him to think that. He touched his bottom lip with his tongue again and his gaze flicked back up to mine for a second. His eyes burned even deeper. He looked back down to my lips and started moving toward me. My heart raced. I knew I needed to push him back, I just couldn't think straight enough to remember *why*. I couldn't move.

I closed my eyes as I felt him draw even nearer. I was hyperaware of how close his body was to mine—his side pressing against me, his arm still across my thighs, his hand upon my leg. That awareness, combined with the passionate noises from the TV, sent chills down my spine. After what felt like an eternity, he finally touched me, but not how I had been expecting him to. His forehead touched mine and he rested his nose against mine. I could feel him breathing softly, but intensely, against me. Instinctively, I raised my chin to find his lips, a low noise escaping my throat again.

A microsecond before our mouths fully touched, when I could feel the heat of his skin, the barest brush of a lip, he glided his nose down along my cheek. I gasped at the almost-contact. He exhaled heavily down my throat, an enticing noise escaping his lips, making me shudder. He stayed there, taking two ragged breaths, while I unconsciously melted even more against his body. My knees turned even more into him; the hand on my lap dropped onto his thigh. I started to turn my head toward his mouth. He smelled so good . . .

Suddenly he grabbed my hand on his thigh and almost painfully squeezed it. He ran his lips up to my ear and roughly whispered, "Come with me."

Not sure what he was going to do, not sure what I was going to do, I stood and followed him out of the room. Matt and Griffin, who I had forgotten were even here, didn't look our way as we passed by. Surprisingly, he led me to the kitchen. I wasn't sure what he would do when we got there. I pictured him, once out of view of the guys, pulling me into him for a long, hot, passionate kiss. I pictured his hands tangling in my hair, pulling me tight to him. I pictured his entire body pressed against mine. By the time we were in the kitchen, I was breathing a little raggedly.

Kellan, however, was perfectly . . . fine. He let go of my hand as we got to the kitchen, set his beer down on the counter, and poured a glass of water. Confused, and a little annoyed at his quick change of emotion, I wondered if I had just imagined that little almost-incident in the living room. It had seemed like there was this electricity between us. He had been about to kiss me, I was sure of that. Disturbingly enough, I had been about to kiss him as well. It was . . . confusing.

He smiled warmly, like nothing weird had just happened. Handing me the glass of water, he took my beer and set it on the counter near his. I took a deep breath, calming my body. I suddenly felt very, very stupid. Of course nothing had almost happened. He was a regular guy who got turned on watching some stupid, sexy movie, like any guy would, and I had somehow turned that into him wanting me specifically. God, I must have looked like such an idiot with my eyes closed, waiting for him to kiss me. Embarrassment flashed through me and I gulped down my water, thankful for a reason to not look at him.

"Sorry about the movie choice. . . ." I looked back up when he spoke. He smiled and laughed a little. "Griffin is, well . . . Griffin." He shrugged. Completely changing the subject, he said, "You seemed upset earlier on the stairs. You want to talk about your dream?" He leaned back against the counter near the fridge and crossed his arms against his chest, looking perfectly composed and relaxed.

Still feeling foolish, I muttered, "I don't remember it . . . just that it was bad."

"Oh," he said quietly, suddenly thoughtful.

Wishing I had just stayed in bed, I set down my nearly empty glass and started to walk past him. "I'm tired. . . . Good night, Kellan."

He smiled at me as I walked past. "Good night, Kiera," he whispered.

Avoiding watching Matt, Griffin, and the seemingly endless erotic movie they were watching, I instead looked back through the living room to the rear window in the kitchen. There was enough reflection in the glass for me to clearly see Kellan. He was still leaning against the counter, but now he was slumped against it, pinching the bridge of his nose with his fingers. He looked to have a headache. I wondered about that, but hurried up the stairs, not wanting him to notice me watching him in the reflection. And I really wanted to shut out the noise of that stupid, stupid movie.

I blushed slightly when I saw Kellan the next morning, but he only smiled and offered me a cup of coffee. He made no mention of my embarrassing gaffe, and I wasn't about to bring it up either. Sitting across from him at the table, I noticed that he was wearing his Douchebags shirt again. I frowned over at him, and he paled slightly.

"What?" he asked quietly, looking a little nervous.

Not understanding his reaction, I pointed to his shirt. "You never did get me one, you know," I said, as lightly as I could manage.

He visibly relaxed. "Oh . . . you're right." He nodded at me.

Then he shrugged and, standing up, slipped the shirt off. I gaped at him as he flipped it right side out and slipped it over me. I couldn't even speak. His body drew all of my attention as he fixed the shirt around me. I couldn't even help him. He had to put my arms through the holes like I was two.

"There. You can have mine." He smiled, still standing in front of me, not bothered in the slightest that he was now half-dressed.

My face was heating up and I was sure I was bright red. "I didn't mean. . . . You didn't have to . . ." I couldn't even form a complete sentence.

He laughed softly. "Don't worry about it. I can get more. You wouldn't believe how many of those damn things Griffin made." He laughed again, then turned to leave the room. I couldn't help but gape at his muscular back as he left, broad at the shoulders, narrowing slightly at his chest, then more at the waist, naturally forcing the eye down. Kellan looked back at the entryway and caught me staring at him. He looked down and half-smiled. "I'll be right back." He looked back up at me, still smiling adorably, and I blushed deeply yet again.

Then the smell caught me. I actually closed my eyes it was so powerfully wonderful. I grabbed the bottom of the shirt and inhaled deeply. I don't know if it was his soap, his expensive shampoo, his laundry detergent, some cologne, or just his natural scent, but he always smelled so incredibly good, and now I was saturated in his smell. I was sitting there, inhaling his shirt like an idiot when he came back into the room.

He cocked his head to the side and smiled at me curiously as I dropped his shirt. I suddenly wished I had never woken up this morning. How many ways could I look like an idiot in twenty-four hours? He sat back down in his chair and finished his coffee, his shirt now a striking blue that made his eyes seem even more intensely blue. I swallowed and concentrated on drinking my coffee.

We went about our day normally. I did laundry, he did the dishes. I vacuumed, he played his guitar. But I felt embarrassed all day. Last night had been mortifying. I was planning on staying far away from him. I was planning that, but, of course, when he went to watch TV for a little bit before leaving to meet with the guys, I looked at the couch longingly. He noticed and held his arm out, patting the cushion beside his hip with his other hand. I couldn't help it. I smiled and instantly cuddled into his side, resting my head on his shoulder. I was kind of addicted to it.

The weekend went by with plenty of hand holding, cuddling on the couch, lingering hugs in the kitchen, me resting on his lap, and lying in the backyard, but no more embarrassing near-kiss incidents. Before I knew it, it was Monday morning, and school was starting the very next day.

A phone call that afternoon incited my irritation . . . and my nerves.

"Hey, babe." Hearing Denny's accent usually made me smile, but I frowned, still frustrated at his more-often-than-not short, and seemingly uninterested, phone calls. "Kiera?"

I realized I hadn't answered him yet. "Hi," I mumbled.

He sighed. "You're mad, aren't you?"

"Maybe . . ." Yes . . . yes I was.

"I'm sorry. . . . I know I've been distracted lately. It's nothing against you, I promise. I'm just so busy."

His excuses weren't helping my irritation. "Whatever, Denny."

He sighed again. "I've got time. . . . Want to tell me about school tomorrow?"

I smiled a little that he remembered, and then frowned when I remembered. I was getting anxious for the morning. "I wish you were here. . . . I'm really nervous."

He chuckled, probably remembering how I usually helped him . . . calm his nerves. "Ah, babe . . . you have no idea how much I wish I was with you right now. I miss you."

I smiled widely at that. "I miss you too . . . goofball."

He laughed genuinely. "Now tell me what you've been doing. I want to hear your voice. . . ."

I laughed and spent the next hour telling him everything I could think of. Well, I may have left out a few minor details about how close Kellan and I had become, and a certain nearly intimate moment on the couch, but I told him everything else. It wasn't as effective as the way I preferred to calm his nerves, but it did calm mine . . . a bit. I was able to get through work and get to sleep afterwards with only the tiniest knot in my stomach.

I came down to the kitchen for my coffee the next morning with a slightly larger knot in my stomach. School started in a few hours. I hated the first day at a new school more than I hated the first day at a new job. I frowned when I saw Kellan pouring his coffee. He was singing one of his songs while he did it, a small smile on his lips.

When the band played the song it was fast, but he was singing it slowly and softly, turning it into a ballad. . . . It was beautiful.

I stopped a few steps into the kitchen and leaned against the counter to listen to him. He looked over at me, still singing, and smiled wider. Maybe he noticed my melancholy, maybe he just knew me well enough by now to know that I wasn't looking forward to today, or maybe he was just bored. For whatever reason, he reached out to me and, grabbing my hand, pulled me to him. I gasped in surprise, then laughed as he put his other hand around my waist and started slow dancing with me.

He started singing the song louder and exaggerated our movements, eventually spinning me away from him and then back to him. He playfully dipped me, and I laughed again, my anxiety over school momentarily forgotten. He straightened me and slipped both arms around my waist. I sighed happily and slipped my arms around his neck, listening to the beautiful song he was softly singing.

Abruptly, he stopped singing and gazed at me. I realized I had started running my hands through the back of his hair, twirling it around my fingers. It was incredibly pleasant, but I forcefully pulled my hands down and rested them on his shoulders.

Still holding me, he quietly said, "I know you'd rather have Denny here"—I stiffened fractionally at the mention of Denny's name—"but could I take you to school on your first day?" He smiled sweetly at the end.

My heart sped a little, at his attractiveness and our closeness. Trying to look unaffected by him, I muttered, "I guess you'll do."

He laughed and squeezed me once before letting me go. "That's not something I'm used to women saying," he muttered as he grabbed a mug for me from the cupboard.

Thinking I had offended him, I quickly blurted out, "I'm sorry, I didn't mean—"

He laughed again and looked over at me while he poured my coffee. "I'm just kidding, Kiera." He watched the coffee filling my cup. "Well, kind of." He chuckled.

I blushed. "Oh . . . um . . . thank you . . . yes." I stumbled over my words and he chuckled again.

I anxiously got dressed for school and spent an inordinately long time brushing my hair and putting on my makeup. Not that I looked any better for all the effort, but it made me feel a little more put together, and hopefully that would help me get through all the embarrassing introductions ahead. Maybe I'd just hide quietly in the back all week, until I got more comfortable in my classes.

I grabbed my bag and tossed my required books, tons of pencils, and a couple notepads inside. Today I had just one class, which I was grateful for, Microeconomics. I frowned as I thought of the class. . . . That one would be Denny's favorite to talk about. In fact, I probably wouldn't be able to get him to shut up about it. I smiled. Maybe he'd call later and we could discuss it for hours . . . anything to hear his voice.

I came down when it was time to leave, and Kellan smiled when he saw me from the couch. "Ready?"

I sighed unhappily as he walked over to me. "No."

He grabbed my hand and, smiling crookedly in a way that made me nervous for a completely different reason, led me to the door. We drove to the university in silence while my stomach churned. *Really, this isn't that big of a deal*, I kept repeating to my body. . . . It refused to listen though.

Kellan's house was close to the university, so the drive didn't take long. Before I knew it, he was pulling into a parking space. My heartbeat was irrationally fast. I must have looked pale . . . or ill . . . when Kellan parked the car. He looked over at me, concerned, and then opened his door and got out. Confused, I watched him walk over to me and open my door.

I smirked at him. "I think I can handle that." I nodded at the door as I stood up.

He chuckled and grabbed my hand again. Loving the comforting warmth, I squeezed it tightly, and he smiled at me. "Come on." He indicated the intimidating brick building where my class was.

As we started walking toward it, I looked up at him curiously. "And where are you going?"

He chuckled again as he looked down at me. "I'm walking you to class . . . obviously."

I rolled my eyes, feeling stupid that he felt the need to do that. Really, I could handle this . . . embarrassment. "You don't have to. I can manage."

He squeezed my hand encouragingly. "Maybe I want to." I looked away as we approached the building, and he held the door open for me. "It's not like my mornings are earth-shatteringly busy or anything. I'd probably just be napping." He grinned wryly at me as I looked back at him and laughed.

"Why do you get up so early then?"

He laughed too as we walked down the hall—more than a few women were watching this model-worthy man walk past them. "It's not by choice . . . trust me. I would rather sleep in than function on four or five hours a night."

"Oh . . . you *should* go home and nap then," I said as we approached my classroom.

"I will." He smiled as he opened the classroom door and I wondered if he was going to walk me to my seat too. He seemed to notice my odd look and grinned. "Would you like me to walk you in?"

Releasing his hand, I pushed him back a smidge. "No," I said playfully. Walking with him did help. I was a little more relaxed. Tilting my head to the side, I watched him thoughtfully at the door for a moment. "Thank you, Kellan." I leaned in and gave him a soft kiss on the cheek.

He looked down and glanced up at me from under his eyebrows, a small smile curving his lips. "You're welcome. I'll pick you up later."

I started to protest, "You don't have to—" He cut me off with a wry look, and I closed my mouth and smiled. "Fine . . . I'll see you later."

His eyes roamed the room once before returning to me. "Have fun." Then he turned and left, and I couldn't help but watch his backside for a few moments. Unfortunately, he looked back and caught me watching him again. He smiled and waved, but I blushed horribly, feeling moronic.

Seriously, sometimes his looks were just too much. As I entered the room, I realized that I wasn't the only one who felt that way about Kellan. Most of the girls nearby were still watching the door, maybe wondering if he would return and join the class. Some of the girls were giggling and chatting with each other, pointing down the hallway. Others were pointing at me.

If I hadn't already been blushing from being caught ogling Kellan, I would have blushed at their attention. One unfortunate side effect of hanging around Kellan was that it made people wonder about me when he was gone. So much for being a wallflower in the back of the room. I hurriedly walked past the group as a couple of them were eyeing me as if they were going to ask me to join them . . . most likely to gossip about Kellan. I wasn't in the mood for awkward small talk with people I didn't know, so I found a seat near the back with only a couple of people around. A few women watched where I went, but none of them followed me.

The class was absorbing, and before I knew it, it was also over. I smiled at how pleasant the experience had been and how I really hadn't needed to worry at all. I was good at school. My sister always told me that I was book-smart, not street-smart. I wasn't quite sure if that was an insult or not, but she was right, I was much better at dealing with assignments and tests than with people. I wasn't sure what career options that left me. I was still debating a major, but I was leaning toward English. Again, I wasn't sure what kind of job that would get me. Sometimes I was jealous of how certain Denny was of his life. He had always known what he wanted to do, and he went out and did it. I still had no clue.

True to his word, Kellan was waiting for me outside the door. I smiled when I saw him, even though the attention wasn't necessary. He grabbed my hand as I walked over to him. A couple of the women who had noticed him earlier were exiting the classroom. He smiled crookedly at them, and they actually giggled. I rolled my eyes and shook my head at his unending flirtatiousness.

"Come on, Casanova," I muttered, pulling him away from the still giggling girls.

He frowned, then laughed. "How was class?"

"Wonderful!" He shook his head at my enthusiasm. Apparently he wouldn't find a lecture on economics as interesting as I did. I smiled at the thought of him sitting through the class, bored stiff. "So . . . did you nap?"

He grinned and nodded. "Yeah, a good hour. I'm solid 'til three."

I shook my head at him. "How do you do that?"

He laughed as we exited the building. "It's a gift . . . it's a curse."

He drove me to and from school for the rest of the week, which was unnecessary, since Denny had left his beloved Honda for me, but nice, since I hated driving a stick. We chatted and laughed easily. He asked about all of my classes and what I liked the best and least about each one. He insisted on walking me to my first class every morning, which was also unnecessary, but sweet. The girls would quiet at his approach and watch him, practically with drool on their chins, as he said goodbye to me every morning. And he, of course, was only too aware of their attention and would oblige them with a wink or two. He waited for me outside of class or in the parking lot after school, once with an espresso, which made me gleefully happy.

Kellan made that first week of school a pleasant transition for me, when I had been expecting the worst. I was exceedingly grateful to him for that. In fact, there was only one thing that whole week that did not make me happy . . . and it was kind of a big one. Denny.

By that weekend, my irritation at him had grown exponentially. When he'd first left, he had called me every day. Then slowly, it had turned to every couple of days. But this week, I hadn't heard from him in five days—nothing! The last conversation we'd had was the day before my school started. I really thought he would call to see how it went, but he hadn't. I left messages at his hotel, but he was rarely there because his new job kept him so busy. So late Sunday night, after throwing on my pajamas and getting all ready for bed, I decided to try calling him one last time. When I finally got through to him in his room, I was ecstatic . . . at first.

"Hey, babe." His familiar warm accent filled my heart, but he did sound very tired.

"Hey! You okay? You sound exhausted. I could call back tomorrow." I bit my lip, hoping he wouldn't ask me to do that. I leaned back against the kitchen counter and crossed my fingers.

"No, I'm glad you called. I need to talk to you." I suddenly wished he had asked me to call him back. Panicky ice filled my stomach.

"Oh?" I tried to keep my voice casual. "About what?"

He paused and my heart started pounding. "I did something. I don't think you're going to like it."

My mind instantly went through a horrible list of things that he could have possibly done that I wouldn't like. My thoughts flew once again to Kellan, and what could have happened between us while watching that stupid movie. Denny certainly would not have liked that. My throat tightened, but I managed to squeak out, "What?"

He paused for a long time and I suddenly wanted to scream at him to just tell me already! "Tuesday night, after work . . ." He paused again and my panicked mind started filling out my worst nightmare. "Mark offered me a permanent job here. . . ."

Relief washed through me; my mind had come up with something much more horrifying. "Oh, Denny, you scared—"

He cut me off. "I took it."

My mind seemed sluggish. It took me a second to comprehend what that meant. When I did, my breath stopped. "You're not coming back . . . are you?"

"It's the offer of a lifetime, Kiera. They don't offer lead positions to interns—ever." Denny's voice quavered on the phone. This was a hard thing for him to say. He so hated doing anything that might cause me pain. "Please try and understand."

"Understand? I left everything to come here for you! Now you're going to leave me here?" Tears were starting to well up in my eyes, but I forced them back. Now was not the time to lose it.

"It's just for two years. . . . When your schooling is finished, you can come join me here," he begged. "We'll be back together soon. You'll love it here too."

My heart sank farther. Two years? A few weeks without him had been brutal; how would I ever make it through two long years . . . longer than we had even been together?

"No, Denny."

He didn't respond to that right away. The silence was deafening. "What do you mean?"

"No! I want you to come back! Stay with me, take another job. You're brilliant, you'll find something!" Now I was begging him.

"This is what I want, Kiera . . ." he whispered.

"More than me?" I knew it wasn't a fair question the moment it left my lips, but rage was building inside me.

"Kiera . . ." He said my name brokenly. "You know that's not it. . . ."

"Really!" My anger was truly flaring now. "It sure feels like you're choosing your job over me, like you're leaving me." Some tiny part of my brain wanted to stop this horrid conversation, stop hurting him, but I just couldn't.

"Baby, it's just two years. I'll visit every chance I get . . ." he tried again feebly, his accent thick with emotion.

My mind fumed. Two years . . . two freaking years! Without thinking, without even bothering to talk to me about it first, he had accepted a career in a city thousands of miles away, and then he had sat on that information for days! I was stuck here in Seattle. My parents had been lenient, sort of, about the transfer, mainly because of the scholarship. They wouldn't let me transfer to yet another school in yet another state! They wouldn't pay for it, anyway, and I couldn't afford two years of school on my own. The scholarship that I had won was *my* once-in-a-lifetime. I didn't see fate lining up for me like that again.

I was stuck here until school ended . . . and he knew that.

He knew that! In my rage, my mind leapt to the likeliest conclusion—he *wanted* me to stay. He *wanted* us to be apart. He *wanted* to
leave me. He was breaking up with me. Fire burned in my belly. Well,
I wasn't about to let him do it first.

"Don't bother visiting, Denny! You've made your choice! I hope
you enjoy your *job*!" I stressed the word harshly. "I'm staying here
and you're staying there. We're done . . . goodbye."

After slamming the phone down on Denny, I unplugged it. I
didn't want him to call back. I was so angry I didn't ever want to
speak to him again. The thought of never seeing him again brought
despair so quickly behind it that I couldn't breathe. I gasped and my
head started to spin. I sank to the floor as tears flowed freely, and I
could no longer hold back the sobs.

After what seemed like hours of gut-wrenching grief, I stood.
I went to the fridge for water, but an open bottle of wine that we
had never gotten around to drinking was right there in the door. I
grabbed it instead and took a swig directly from the bottle. I knew it
was a stupid way to cope with my despair, but I needed something. I
needed a break from feelings. I would deal with them later.

Grabbing a water glass instead of a fragile wineglass, I poured as
much of the wine in it as possible and started chugging. It burned.
Wine definitely wasn't meant to be drunk that way, but I was desperate for some relief from the pain.

It only took a few moments to empty the glass and I immediately refilled it. The sobs had finally stopped, although tears still fell.
I could still see Denny's face in my mind, his beautiful, warm, brown
eyes, his goofy grin, his alluring accent, the way he was always quick
to laugh, his body, his heart. My own heart squeezed painfully and I
pulled another long drink.

This isn't real, I kept telling myself. There was no way things had
just ended, no way we were now apart. He had said I was his heart,
and you don't leave your heart behind. You can't live without your
heart.

I was just finishing the second glass and filling the third and, unfortunately, the last, when I heard the front door open.

It must have been very late, or very early, depending on how you looked at it, and Kellan was home from a night with the guys at Pete's. He strolled into the kitchen and casually tossed his keys on the counter. He paused when he noticed me standing in the room. I wasn't usually awake this late on nights I didn't work.

"Hey."

I turned toward him but never stopped drinking. At the movement, I noticed that my head was starting to swim. Good.

I studied him silently. His blue eyes had a slightly glazed look. He must have had a couple, or more than a couple, with the band. His clothes were the basic look he preferred wearing—a just tight enough T-shirt, faded blue jeans, and black work boots. Maybe it was the wine, maybe it was my grief, but tonight, he just looked extra incredible. His hair, tousled and messy, was sexy as hell. *Wow,* I thought, with the part of my brain that still could. Drinking him in was more of a distraction for me than drinking the wine.

"You okay?" He cocked his head to the side a little and looked at me quizzically. It was unbelievably attractive, and I stopped drinking for a moment.

"No." The word sounded slow to me, the wine working fast in my body. I felt steady enough to quickly add, "Denny isn't coming back . . . we're done."

Instantly, his gorgeous face filled with sympathy and he walked over to me. For a second, I thought he was going to put his arms around me. My heart started beating faster at the thought. But he leaned back against the counter instead, resting his hands behind him. I continued drinking my wine and watched him watch me.

"You want to talk about it?"

I paused. "No."

He glanced over at the empty wine bottle on the counter and up again, at the glass I was just finishing. "You want some tequila?"

For the first time in what felt like years, I smiled. "Absolutely."

He opened the cupboard above the fridge and rummaged through a stash of alcohol bottles that I didn't even know were in there. Reaching up like that caused his shirt to stretch in delightful ways, showing just a hint of the skin at his waist. The painful thoughts of Denny were slowly fading as I watched this absurdly attractive man. Damn, he was sexy.

He found what he wanted and twisted back around to me. I sighed as his shirt lowered. Sudden loneliness washed through my alcohol-soaked brain. I was alone now. I had moved all the way out here to be with Denny, and now I was completely alone. I watched Kellan's body move enticingly under his clothes as he grabbed us glasses, salt, and limes. My loneliness faded and started transforming into something else entirely.

He finished pouring, and with an alluring half-smile, he handed me my drink. "Cure for heartache, I'm told."

I reached for the glass and my fingers brushed his. That slight touch caused heat to rise up my hand and I idly thought *he* might be the better cure.

I had seen numerous people at the bar do shooters. I had done them before. But the way Kellan did it was so downright sexy, I felt a little dirty watching him. The wine surging through my system turned every move he made into something erotic. He used a finger dipped in alcohol to wet the back of his hand, then mine. He shook a little salt over them while I wondered at how my hand suddenly felt warm where his touch lingered. I watched his tongue lick his salt away, his strong jawline move, as he quickly tilted back the shot of tequila, his lips curl as he sucked on the lime. It took my breath away.

Gathering myself, I took my shot, and then the tequila hit me. Where the wine had burned, this scorched. I made a face and Kellan chuckled at me; it did delightful things to his smile.

He immediately poured another. We didn't talk. I really didn't need conversation right now, and he seemed to sense that. We silently did our second shooter and I managed to not make a face this time.

By our third shooter, my body was warm and tingly. I had trouble keeping my eyes focused, but I still watched every move Kellan made as closely as I could. If I were in his position, I would have been very uncomfortable being relentlessly stared at like that, but he acted like he didn't even notice. I remembered his "adoring" fans at the bar and thought maybe he was just used to it.

On the fourth shooter, I could tell that Kellan's eyes were even more glazed-looking. His smile was loose and easy. He slightly spilled the tequila while filling our shot glasses, and he laughed when he took his lime. I watched him sucking on it and had the craziest, most intense need to suck on it with him.

By the fifth shooter, all the despair, loneliness, and pain from earlier in the evening had completely changed into something else . . . desire. More specifically, desire for this godlike man in front of me. I remembered the electricity between us a few nights ago and, real or not, I wanted to feel that passion again.

Without thinking, I did what I had wanted to do on that very first shot. I grabbed his hand, just as he bent down to lick the salt away. I lightly pressed my tongue against the back of it, the salt pleasantly mixing with the taste of his skin. His breath caught while he watched me down my shot of tequila. I quickly set the glass down and placed the lime wedge in his partly opened mouth. I brought my lips to his. I half sucked on the lime, half pressed against his lips. Fire burned though me.

I pulled away from him slowly, taking the lime with me. His breathing was faster and a little ragged. I carefully took the lime out and set it on the counter, licking my fingers in the process. Kellan took his shot of tequila straight, his eyes never leaving mine. He roughly set down his own glass, licked his lower lip once, and grabbed my neck, pulling me back to his mouth.

Chapter 7
Mistakes

My first mistake was the bottle of wine. My second mistake was the tequila shooters. . . . But currently, only the searing throb of my headache concerned me. The light blazing brightly through the window made my eyes water, but when I closed them, the room started to spin so much that I had to stare at one spot on the ceiling and hold my head perfectly still. I groaned. God, was I still drunk?

Without moving my head, I tried to look around the unfamiliar room. Holy crap . . . . this isn't my bed! Looking down, and instantly regretting it as my head felt like it might explode and the room circled crazily, I noticed my naked body entangled in strange sheets. Holy crap . . . I'm naked!

I tried to hold my body perfectly still and think through the haze to remember last night. Oh . . . God . . . no . . . Suddenly, I knew exactly where I was. I looked over to the other side of the bed, but it was empty; Kellan was gone. My head, and now also my stomach, protested vehemently at the swift movement.

Damn, damn, damn, I thought, suddenly irritated. I pressed my fingers to my temples hard, trying to stop the merciless beating. Memories flooded my brain, like a bloody accident I didn't want to watch, but I couldn't stop myself from looking.

That unbelievable first kiss—eager, intense, and so full of passion. The hand behind my neck tightening as he pulled me closer. Another hand clutching at my lower back. Kellan slowly pressing me back into the counter and then lifting me up onto it. My legs circling around his waist. My hands tangling in his hair. His intoxicating smell, the taste of tequila on his tongue . . .

The momentary memory of tequila made my stomach lurch uneasily. Not wanting to lose my stomach in his bed, I risked the horrible swirling sensation and sat up. Waiting a second for my head to clear, and then realizing it wasn't going to, I looked around for my clothes. I could only find my tank top, hanging haphazardly from his guitar by the bed. Crap.

I slowly put it back on and stood, stumbling slightly. Seriously, shouldn't I be fine by now? I looked over at the clock . . . 2:30. Already? So much for school . . . my psych class was nearly over. I cautiously made my way to the door. My panties were lying near it. I sighed and carefully leaned over to pick them up. Quickly I pulled them back on as my stomach turned dangerously.

Somewhat dressed, I decided modesty was now the least of my problems. I had no idea where Kellan was, anyway, and I knew my stomach was no longer joking around. I ran to the bathroom and made it just in time to heave noisily into the toilet.

Leaning my head against the cool porcelain, more memories flooded my brain.

. . . Kellan's hand moving across my throat, his lips following. My head falling back, eyes closing. Breathing heavily. Moaning softly. Exhaling raggedly. Pulling his shirt off. His gloriously stunning chest. Hard muscles, soft skin. Kellan's breath coming harder as my fingers moved down his chest. Kellan groaning lightly and pulling me closer to him. His arms sweeping around me and picking me up. Moving to the stairs . . .

My stomach heaved again and sweat dewed my brow. Ugh, I hated tequila. More relentless memories . . .

. . . Stumbling to the ground drunkenly on the steps and both of

us laughing. Being sprawled across the steps, him heavily on top of me
mumbling "sorry" as he ran his tongue up my throat. Gasping as his
arousal pressed against me. Sucking his earlobe. Warm lips on mine.
Hands roughly pulling off my pants . . .

Oh, I thought distractedly, while my stomach flipped, *that's*
where my pants are.

. . . Me trying to unbutton his jeans and laughing at my numb
fingers not being able to move properly to do it. Kellan lightly suck-
ing my bottom lip. Me stroking his chest. A hand caressing my breast
under my tank top. Lightly biting his shoulder. Fingers slipping into my
underwear, circling the slick skin before pressing into me. The passion
in his eyes as he watched my breathless reaction. Begging him to take
me to his room . . .

Oh, God. I cringed. I begged him, I actually begged him . . .
someone please kill me now! And at that, my stomach heaved again.

. . . Being scooped up. My underwear being ripped off. Kellan kick-
ing off his shoes, then taking off his jeans while I laughed, since I still
couldn't do it. Him laughing with me as he pulled off my tank top. A
soft tongue dragging along my nipple, teasing, tasting. Playfully being
pushed back onto his bed. Pulling off his boxers. Taking in the sight of
his glorious, naked body. The laughter fading as things got suddenly
very intense. His eyes raking over my body, his lips on every inch of me.
My fingers on every inch of him, tracing every perfectly defined muscle.
Kissing his strong, smooth jaw . . . neck . . . throat . . . chest . . . abdomen.
The way he groaned when my tongue swirled around the tip of him . . .

Feeling slightly better with my stomach, I sat back on my heels
and made myself remember the rest.

. . . Kellan flipping me to my back and pushing smoothly inside
of me. Gasping with the pleasure of it. Our hips moving together. The
rising and falling sensations. The pleasant noises he made. The sur-
prising noises I made. The seemingly long time everything took, as our
drunken bodies absorbed every sensation. The warmth of his breath on
my neck. Grabbing his head and holding him close as we approached
the final moment—so intense, so unbelievable. Crying out in unison as

we came together. Feeling the warmth of him releasing into me. Panting breathlessly with him as our hearts slowed down. Staring into each other's eyes. Losing consciousness in his arms . . .

I stood shakily, but more securely, washed my face, and brushed my teeth. Surprised, I realized that last night with him had been . . . amazing.

I walked to my room deep in thought and stopped just inside the door, looking at the perfectly made bed. All the feelings from last night, of Denny and me ending, that I had repressed with alcohol and, yes, with Kellan, came crashing down on me. I sank to my knees and sobbed.

I don't remember when, but at some point in the day, I went downstairs and grabbed my pants from the steps. I slipped them on and stood at the bottom stair, not knowing what to do now. I was desperately thirsty and my head still throbbed, but mostly, my heart ached.

I sat on the step and hung my head in my hands. Tears came again and I had the odd desire for Kellan to come home. I just wanted my friend to put an arm around me and tell me it would be okay. That I hadn't just made a monumental mistake last night in breaking up with Denny . . . okay, two monumental mistakes. Kellan . . . I didn't know what had come over me last night. Well, tequila certainly, but was that all it was? Rita would love this bit of gossip, not that I ever intended to tell her. There had been so many warnings, and I had ignored them all. It was literally written on the wall that he was a dog who routinely slept around. And then there had been the . . . misunderstanding . . . with his ex-roommate Joey. Apparently, it *was* a pattern with him.

Great. Now, not only was I completely alone, but, like Joey, he'd probably ask me to leave. I'd be homeless too. That didn't seem quite right in my head. I had never seen him be anything but nice to people. Well, he liked to tease me relentlessly, but not in a cruel way. I couldn't see him just ruthlessly chucking me out, with nowhere to go. But he could make me so uncomfortable that I would want to leave. I wanted to leave now. . . . The thought of his surely smug, amused smile had my stomach in knots. *One more notch in his bed-post*, I thought glumly. Where was he anyway? Was seeing me so horrible to him that he was purposely keeping away?

I was such an idiot. I vowed to never drink tequila again.

Finally, I picked my wallowing body up and got the glass of water that I was so desperately craving. I ended up drinking three. I plugged the phone back in and stared at it for a good twenty minutes. I desperately wanted to call Denny, to tell him that I needed him and that I'd made a huge mistake last night—an even bigger one than Denny was aware of. I couldn't, though. My guilt was too great to talk to him. After another five minutes of blankly staring at the stupid thing, I forced myself back upstairs and into the shower, thinking I could wash away my despair. It did nothing for me, though. Afterwards, I lay down in my bed, staring at a picture of Denny and me on the nightstand, and cried yet again.

Eventually, I had to move on from my old despair into a brand-new one. I had to go to work. Numbly, I dressed, arranged my hair into a loose, messy ponytail, and threw on some makeup. I looked horrible, I felt horrible, but at least the room had stopped spinning and my stomach had stopped turning. Now if only I could do something about my heart . . .

I arrived at Pete's late—I still wasn't used to driving a stick shift and all the hills weren't helping matters—and hurried past Rita. I didn't need her inferring anything from my looks right now. My stomach was in knots as I threw my jacket in the back room. I had no idea if Kellan would come in tonight or not. Would it be weird seeing him . . . after seeing so much of him? That thought made me blush as I walked back into the bar. I swept an eye over the tables, but he wasn't there, none of the band was. I took a deep breath and forced all thoughts of Denny and Kellan to the back of my mind.

I managed to make it through half of my shift in a calm sort of numbness. I only lost it when Jenny pulled me aside and asked me what was wrong. The tears immediately started falling as I repeated the conversation Denny and I had had last night. She swiftly gave me a hug, which brought even more tears, and told me that everything would be fine, that Denny and I were perfect for each other, and that things would work out. She smiled at me so reassuringly that I felt a tiny spark of hope that maybe things would be okay. Then I remembered the second part of that evening. As Jenny gave me one final hug, I considered telling her.

"Jenny . . ."

She pulled back and looked at me sweetly, waiting. Her face was so open and honest. She was the best sort of person, and I began to feel even more horrid looking at her. She probably wouldn't understand. . . . She would look at me differently. Maybe she would even think the worst of me and stop being my friend. A part of me doubted that she would judge me that harshly, but I felt pretty harsh on myself at that minute, and didn't want to risk anyone else thinking that way about me. No, I couldn't tell anyone about Kellan.

"Thank you for listening."

"Anytime, Kiera." She smiled and hugged me again and we both continued on our shifts.

About an hour later, a sound came through the front door that made me stop breathing: Evan's big, booming laugh as he walked in the front door. Matt followed quickly behind, ducking through the door and past Evan, laughing just as much. Numbly, I watched them. Two down . . . two to go. Griffin came in a few seconds later, looking really pissed off. He glared at Evan and Matt, who were still laughing . . . apparently at him. Flipping them both off, he turned and headed for their regular table. I stared stupidly at the door while Evan and Matt, still laughing, followed Griffin.

One to go.

I kept staring at the door, but nothing happened. Shaking my head and feeling a little stupid, I realized he wasn't coming. Was he avoiding me at the bar too? Somehow, that seemed worse than him avoiding me at home. I could feel the tears re-forming.

Jenny came up to me, putting a hand on my shoulder. "You don't look so good. . . . You all right?"

I blinked back those tears. "Yeah, I'm fine." The roller coaster of recent emotions was taking its toll—I was exhausted.

Jenny seemed to see that. "Go home, Kiera."

I shook my head. I could do this. "I'm fine, Jenny . . . just a long day. I'll get through it."

She started turning me toward the back room. "Go. It's dead tonight. . . . I'll cover for you." She kept her hands on my shoulders, until I reached the hallway that led to the back.

"Jenny, really, it's not necessary."

"I know, I know . . . you're tough, you can stick it out. . . ." She smiled at me mockingly. "Just go home. . . . You can cover for me tomorrow, if you want, and I'll leave early."

I laughed a little. I was suddenly very tired and it sounded like a great idea. "Yeah . . . fine, okay."

I don't remember the drive home; one minute I was in the parking lot saying goodbye to Jenny, who said she'd check on me tomorrow, and the next I was approaching the driveway, looking over at the empty spot where Kellan's car usually rested. Still not home. That irritated me a bit, then it made me sad, then it made me even more tired. I dragged myself into the house and up into my room. Hastily, I changed into my pajamas and collapsed into bed. A few more tears leaked out before I finally faded into sleep.

Light footsteps on the stairs woke me what felt like only seconds later. Kellan must finally have come home. I looked over at the clock—11:10 p.m. Maybe he figured I was safely asleep by now and he wouldn't have to see me. I fought back the sudden tears of loneliness stinging my eyes. I should have stayed at work. . . .

Oddly, the door to my room cracked open. Great, he *was* going to ask me to leave, and he was going to do it now. Well, that was just a perfect end to my perfect day. Here, Kellan, my heart is already broken, can you please rip it into tiny shreds for me? Maybe he'd go away, wait until morning, if he thought I was sleeping. The idea gave me a sliver of hope and I held perfectly still, making sure my breathing stayed slow and even.

It wasn't going to work. Now he was sitting on the bed beside me. Jerk. He seriously couldn't wait to crush me until morning? I resisted the urge to sigh and tell him to go back to his room, that I would leave tomorrow, that I was not going to inconvenience him by staying. But I was still hoping he'd go away, so I kept up my fake sleep.

His hand rested on my shoulder and I had to strongly resist jerking my body away from his touch. "Kiera?" An all-too-familiar accent pierced my dark thoughts.

Shock opened my eyes and turned my body around to the figure sitting next to me on the bed.

"Denny . . . ?" Tears were in my eyes immediately. Was I still sleeping? Was he real?

He smiled, his warm eyes glistening as well. "Hey," he whispered.

"What . . . why . . . how . . . ?" In my confusion, I couldn't quite form a coherent question.

He put his hand on my cheek and brushed away a tear. "You're my heart," was all he said.

Sobbing, I sat up and threw my arms around his neck. "Denny . . ." I brokenly tried to speak, "I'm so sorry. . . ." In my head, I was more sorry for Kellan than for our fight, but I wasn't about to tell him that.

"Shhhh . . ." He held me close, rocking me gently and stroking my hair. "I'm here . . . it's okay."

I pulled back to look at him and saw tears on his cheeks now too. "You came back . . . for me?"

He sighed and brushed a lock of hair behind my ear. "Of course. Did you think I wouldn't? That I would let you slip away? I love you. . . ." His voice broke a little at the end.

I swallowed the lump in my throat. "Your job?"

He sighed again. "I told them no."

Sudden despair for my selfishness overwhelmed me. Two years . . . it had seemed an eternity last night, but with him now in my arms, it seemed like a ridiculously short amount of time. "I'm so sorry. I overreacted. Of course you should take the job. Call them back! Two years—it's nothing. This is your dream. . . ." Panic was leaking into my guilt.

"Kiera . . ." He stopped me. "They offered it to someone else already."

"Oh." I bit my lip. "Your internship?"

He sighed once again. "No, they gave that to someone else when I took the job."

I couldn't say anything else as the facts settled in my brain. He gave up all of it . . . for me. The dream internship, which had been our reason for moving here, the once-in-a-lifetime job that no intern had ever been offered. All of it gone, because I couldn't wait two short years, and he wouldn't let me go.

The tears of grief and guilt assaulted me again. "I'm sorry. I'm so sorry, Denny. I'm sorry. . . ." I repeated it over and over while he held me to his shoulder. When the tears over my selfishness finally subsided, the tears over being with Kellan last night during our brief time apart broke me down again.

Denny simply held me, telling me over and over that everything would be okay, that we were together and that was all that mattered. Eventually, and more to distract me than anything I think, he lightly grabbed my chin and pulled me in for a long, sweet kiss.

The warmth, the familiarity, the comfort in that kiss silenced my guilt-soaked brain for a moment. Then as his lips parted and his tongue lightly found mine, another section of my brain woke up. Desire flooded me and I kissed him eagerly. I couldn't stop the last few tears that rolled down my cheeks, though, and he tenderly brushed them away with his thumb.

He lowered me back onto the pillows and kissed my lips, my jaw, my forehead, all the while still stroking my cheek. I ran my hand through his hair, down his cheek, along his jaw—the familiar hairline soft under my fingertips—across his lips. I couldn't believe he was actually here.

I pushed the grief and guilt and horror at what I had done last night to the very back part of my mind. I would deal with it later. This moment was all I could concentrate on now. I pulled his wandering lips back to mine and kissed him fiercely. He made a pleasant noise in the back of his throat, and his breath quickened.

I pushed him back a little bit and pulled the covers away from me. He had been too far from me for too long. I needed him much closer. "Come here."

He stood up for a minute and smoothly undressed, then crawled under the covers with me and wrapped his arms around me. He nestled in to kiss my neck. "I missed you," he breathed across my skin.

My breath caught and I blinked away a quick tear. *Later,* I reprimanded myself. "I missed you, so much, Denny," I sighed, bringing him back to my mouth. It was as if his lips were oxygen and I was suffocating; I couldn't stop kissing him. It was all I wanted. All I needed were his soft lips on mine, his tongue lightly brushing mine. My mind started relaxing into him, slowly stopped thinking.

His hands pulled down my pants, slowly, gently. I sighed and kissed him harder. He slipped them off and started back up for my underwear. My mind snapped awake as I suddenly got scared that he would somehow know, that he would have some sixth sense that told him I had been unfaithful to him. But he pulled my underwear off without hesitation. His lips never left mine, his breath was still heavy. He didn't hate me. He still wanted me.

His fingers slipped inside me and my mind completely shut off. I didn't care anymore.

I took off my tank top, needing to feel all of my skin pressed against his. His lips finally left mine and trailed down my neck, down my chest. His lips teased and nibbled my breast, his fingers slid along my wet skin. I moaned his name. "Denny . . ."

He stopped swirling his tongue around my nipple and looked back up at my face. I pulled him back up to my lips. "I need you . . ." I whispered. I meant it in every way those words could be interpreted.

Gently he moved over me, and his fingers were replaced with something far more satisfying. I gasped and closed my eyes as he slid into me. A shudder passed through my body as he began to move. The ache of my loneliness over the past weeks crept up on me unexpectedly and one tear escaped my eye. "God, I missed you. . . ."

He bent over to my ear. "I love you," he whispered raggedly.

All too soon, my desire for him rose along with his. I couldn't hold back the sounds, and I didn't want to. For that perfect moment, I didn't care where I was or who else was there. I only cared that Denny was here with me, finally. We finished together. Afterwards, he held me in his arms for a long time, stroking my hair and kissing my temple, until sleep eventually took him.

I, however, was suddenly wide awake.

The room, filled only with the sound of Denny's light breathing, was suddenly suffocating to me. My guilt, my grief, that I had somehow managed to push away, were springing back. Not wanting to wake Denny, not wanting him to question my despair, I tossed my clothes back on and left the room, shutting the door as quietly as I could behind me. Not looking at Kellan's door, I made my way down the stairs. I made it all the way to the living room before the first tears started to fall.

It was seeing Denny's bags placed behind the chair, his jacket thrown over the back of it, that finally released the wall holding back my tears of guilt. I sank into the chair, nestled my head in the cool sleeve, and sobbed. What felt like hours later, I was still sitting in the chair, deep in thought and despair and guilt, when a soft knock on the door awoke me from my despondency. Wondering who could possibly be knocking at this hour, and hoping they didn't wake Denny, I brushed away my tears and quietly went over and opened the door.

A worn-looking Sam stood there, supporting a very drunk-looking Kellan. "I think this belongs to you." Not waiting for the shock to slide from my face, he stepped inside, half-dragged Kellan to the living room, and shoved him down into the chair. "There, all yours."

I stared at Kellan in disbelief. He had definitely been a touch drunk last night, but I had never seen him anywhere close to this bad before. He hunched over in the chair with his head hanging down, like he had lost the ability to sit straight.

"What happened?" I asked.

"Uh, whiskey, I'm pretty sure. I don't know, found him like this." Sam shrugged his massive shoulders.

"You found him?"

"Yeah, wasn't hard. Nearly tripped over him, sprawled on my doorstep as he was." He turned to leave, running a hand over his shaved head and then down his tired face. "Well, I got the idiot home. I've got to get some sleep. I'm beat."

"Wait! What am I supposed . . . ?" I let it trail off as Sam disappeared through the door. "Great."

I walked back to where Kellan was still collapsed on the chair, wondering what had happened to him. Probably out partying with some girls. The thought irritated me, and then I was irritated for being irritated. I smacked his thigh. "Kellan . . ."

He slowly raised his head, his eyes squinting in the soft light from the lamp. "Hey, it's my *roomie*. . . ." He stressed the last word oddly and bit his bottom lip. Drunkenly, he stood up, or attempted to, anyway. He collapsed back down in the chair, looking surprised.

I sighed and held out my hand. "Here, let me help you."

Anger flashed in his eyes as he looked up at me. "I don't need your help." He nearly spat the words.

Startled, I dropped my hand and watched him successfully stand up . . . and immediately start to tip over. I quickly helped him steady himself, putting my shoulder under his, my hand on his chest, supporting his weight . . . whether he wanted me to or not. He sagged into me a little and made no move to push me away.

He smelled horrible, like whiskey and vomit. Again, I wondered what the heck he had been doing. "Come on." I pulled him toward the stairs. Being so close to him again brought images of last night to my mind. I still wasn't sure what to feel about that, other than guilty. I pushed it further back in my head. I couldn't deal with that yet.

Somehow I managed to get him up the stairs. For every two steps he clumsily took up, he seemed to take one backward. At about the halfway point, he started to sink down, and I feared for a minute that he was going to collapse on top of me on the stairs. That brought to mind such a vivid memory that I blushed and smacked him on the chest to keep him walking forward. He didn't say anything but glanced over at me, seemingly torn between irritation and another emotion I couldn't even begin to guess.

Near the top, we crashed into the wall noisily, and I froze, looking over at my door and praying that Denny didn't wake up. Kellan followed my gaze but I couldn't see his expression because I was too busy watching the door. Not hearing any movements, I exhaled in relief and glanced up at Kellan; he was staring blankly at the floor.

I wanted to help him in some way. I thought maybe showering away the smell that permeated his body would ease his pain in the morning. Waking up wasn't going to be good anyway, but waking up that gross would be especially hard on his stomach. I dragged him to the bathroom and sat him on the toilet. He watched me quietly with unfocused eyes.

I ran the water, wondering if he would be able to do this without killing himself. I blushed suddenly, wondering if I was going to have to undress him. He took the option away from me by standing awkwardly and stepping over the tub rim into the shower—fully dressed. He slumped against the far wall and sank down into the tub, closing his eyes and letting the water drench him. The water streamed down his face. His wet hair clung to his skin. His lips were partly open, breath coming shallowly. The soaked shirt accentuated the muscles in his chest. He was gorgeous, even stumbling drunk.

I sighed again. His boots were far enough from the water that I was able to get them and his socks off before they were completely soaked. I contemplated what else to do for him. I brought my hands back to his face and ran my fingers through his hair, letting the water soak in completely. He sighed, eyes still closed. I couldn't stop the memory of clutching his hair last night. I painfully swallowed the lump in my throat.

He had gotten so still I was afraid he had passed out. Moving him on my own would be impossible. I would have to get Denny.

What if Kellan let something slip? What if he flat-out told him? I desperately did not want Denny to know. He had actually come back for me. Given up everything and returned . . . just for me. It would kill him if he found out.

I shut off the water, but Kellan didn't move. I brushed some strands of hair away from his eyes. Still no movement. "Kellan . . ." I lightly smacked his cheek. Nothing. "Kellan . . ." I smacked him a little harder. He moaned softly, and then groggily opened his eyes. He tried to focus on my face, then blinked his eyes excruciatingly slowly and shook his head a little.

"Come on." I tugged at his shoulder, wondering if I'd be able to get him back out of the shower. I had tried to make tomorrow slightly better for him, but now it didn't seem like such a great plan. Finally, my tugging got a response, and he slowly rose and exited the shower, stumbling and dripping water everywhere. I dried as much from him (and myself) as I could, and finished by scrubbing his hair a little and then running my fingers back through it. He looked a little pained when I did that, so I stopped.

I took his hand and led him back to his room. I had so many questions to ask him, but he didn't seem eager to speak. Before things had gotten . . . intense . . . between us last night, he had been respectful of my silence. I could at least do the same now.

Being in his room with him again brought back even more memories that I didn't want to have. They got especially vivid when Kellan took off his shirt. I turned and headed back to the door when he started unbuttoning his jeans. I couldn't help but watch him through a slight crack in his door, though. He started taking his jeans off, stumbling, and having a little trouble with the wet fabric. I considered going back to help him, but he finally managed on his own. Just in his boxers, he stood staring at his bed.

Suddenly, he ran his hand through his wet hair and turned to look at the door. I didn't know if saw me through the crack. I didn't think so, considering how difficult it had been for him to focus on me in the shower. I felt a little guilty watching him without him knowing, but I was just so curious about what he was doing that I couldn't stop.

His face was unreadable. He simply looked at the door, then back to his bed, then at the door again. One last time he looked at his bed, and then he seemed to lose the battle against gravity, falling heavily on top of the sheets.

I watched for a few moments longer. When his breathing grew slow and even, I figured he had finally passed out, and I crept back into his room. I paused, watching his aching perfection in slumber. Finally, I fixed the messy pile of sheets around him until he was covered. Watching over him, I had a crazy desire to kiss him. I sat on the edge of his bed, sighed softly, and leaned in to kiss his forehead. I brushed his hair back and stroked his cheek, wondering where he had gone today . . . and if he had thought about our night together at all. Should I have told him Denny came back? Would he tell Denny? Would things change?

He stirred and I pulled my hand from his cheek. His hazy eyes found mine and I froze. "Don't worry," he mumbled. "I won't tell him." Then his eyes closed and he passed out.

I sat on the edge of the bed, wondering about that. Would he really not tell him? How did he even know Denny was back? What would tomorrow be like?

Chapter 8
The Asshole

The following morning, I woke up groggy. It had been really hard to crawl back into bed with Denny, especially when, in his slumber, he had sighed happily and reached out for me. The guilt that had washed through me then had almost made me bolt from the room yet again. But I made myself close my eyes and stay there.

So, as I turned the corner to the kitchen in the morning, surprise stopped me in the doorway. Even though he'd been dead drunk the night before, Kellan had still awakened before me. But unlike every other morning since I had moved in, for the first time ever that I had seen, in fact, Kellan looked like crap. He had thrown his T-shirt from last night back on, but he was still in his boxers. His hair, while still messy and fabulous, seemed to accentuate how tired his face looked, highlighting the deep circles under his eyes and his shockingly pale skin. He was sitting hunched over with his head held in his hands at the kitchen table. He was breathing very slowly and carefully through his mouth.

"Are you okay?" I whispered.

He grimaced in pain and looked up at me. "Yes," he whispered back. He looked anything but.

"Coffee?" I barely breathed the word, to spare him a little pain.

He cringed anyway, but nodded his head. I went over to make a pot, looking at him curiously. Having just been through what he felt now, I did empathize with him, although it was his own fault for getting that ripping drunk. I tried to make as little noise as possible, but every clink, every bump, even the water running, made him wince a little. He must really be in pain.

I couldn't help but wonder who, or what, had driven him to such excess. Where had he been all day yesterday while I was suffering? I tried to run through our limited conversation last night, but he hadn't said more than a couple sentences, so I wasn't getting any clues about what he had been out doing. One comment he *had* made, however, did stand out.

Without thinking, I blurted it out at regular volume. "How did you know Denny was back?" His head sank to the table in a groan and I guiltily covered my mouth with my hand.

"Saw his coat," he mumbled.

I blinked, surprised. He hadn't seemed aware of anything last night, let alone something as small and insignificant as a jacket on the chair.

"Oh." Not knowing what else to say about that, and worried about his suddenly paler color, I asked him again, "Are you sure you're okay?"

Irritation flared in his eyes as he glanced up at me. "I'm fine," he stated coldly.

Confused, I finished making the coffee and waited at the counter while it brewed. Once it was done, I grabbed two mugs from the cupboard. Suddenly he broke the quietness. "Are you . . . okay?" he asked slowly.

I looked over at him. He had an odd look on his face as he watched me. Hoping he felt a little better, I smiled at him reassuringly. "Yes, I'm great."

A wave of nausea seemed to pass over him. He laid his arms down on the table and buried his head in them. His breathing was forced, like he was trying very hard again to keep it even. I started pouring our cups of coffee, hoping that would somehow help him.

"Put a little Jack in that." He turned slightly toward me, so I could understand him. I smirked back at him. He wasn't serious, was he? He raised his head to look at me, no humor in his eyes. "Please."

I sighed and shrugged my shoulders. "Whatever."

I scrounged as quietly as I could above the fridge for a bottle of Jack Daniel's. I set the bottle on the table in front of him. Kellan didn't move his head from his arms. Making my cream-and-sugar coffee, I left one black and set it quietly in front of him. He still didn't move. I poured just a smidge of Jack in, and then attempted to close the bottle.

Kellan coughed at me, and motioned with his fingers to pour more, his head still resting on his arms. I sighed and let an obscenely large amount go into his mug. He lifted his head a tiny bit and glanced at me. "Thank you."

I put the bottle away and joined him at the table. He took a long sip of his coffee, inhaling through his teeth a little bit afterwards. It was probably a little strong. I hoped, at the very least, it would help his head.

I sipped my coffee in silence, not knowing what to say to this man whom I had been so intimate with such a short time ago. I had a million questions, most revolving around whether or not I had meant anything to him . . . and whether our relationship was intact . . . and where the heck did he go yesterday? I finally decided that there was only one pressing issue that I needed to discuss with him now, while Denny was still upstairs.

"Kellan . . ." I really did not want to have this conversation. "The other night . . ." He watched me over his coffee. I couldn't tell what he was thinking and he said nothing.

I cleared my throat. "I just don't want a . . . misunderstanding," I finished quietly. I didn't really know what I meant by that. I didn't know how I felt about this man who had been nothing but sweet to me while Denny was away. I couldn't ponder it, though, not with Denny back. I just didn't want our friendship to change. He was . . . important to me.

He took a long draw on his coffee again before responding.

"Kiera . . . there are no misunderstandings between us." His voice was cold and flat. It gave me chills. My stomach clenched as I wondered if it was too late, if our friendship was already too changed.

We sat in silence and finished the rest of our coffees. I poured another black one for Kellan and watched, relieved, while he drank it without alcohol. A little while later, Denny came down, saying hello to Kellan and giving him a puzzled expression, since he really did look awful.

"You okay, mate?" he asked politely, while slipping an arm around my shoulder as I sat at the table. I tensed, suddenly feeling very uncomfortable with Denny and Kellan in the same room.

Kellan flinched a little. "No, actually, I'm going to go lie back down. Glad you're home, Denny." He walked by him, avoiding his eyes, and I heard him head back up the stairs.

Denny watched him leave, frowning. "God, he looks awful. Wonder what happened to him?"

"Probably some girl."

There was some irritation in my voice when I said that, and Denny looked down at me. "Everything all right between you two while I was gone?" He smiled when he said it, so I wasn't sure if he suspected anything or not.

My stomach gave me a fluttery panic attack, but I managed to smile and slip my arms around his waist. "Except for how much I missed you, everything was fine." I felt horrid. Maybe I should just tell him?

His eyes glowed with warmth and love as he looked down on me. I realized then that I couldn't tell him, even if I wanted to. I couldn't stand those eyes looking at me in any other way. He leaned down and gave me a sweet kiss. "I missed you too, but . . ."

I pulled back and looked at him cautiously. "But what?"

He sighed softly. "I don't have a job now, Kiera. We can't stay here on just your income. I need to meet some people today, see if I can't get something lined up." He shrugged and looked at me hopefully.

I bit back my irritation, remembering all that he had given up for me. Remembering how much he should be angry at me . . . if he only knew. "Right now?" I asked, hopeful that he would decide to start to-morrow, and I could have him for a full day after so much time apart. I could skip school. Heck, I could skip work to be with him today.

"I'm sorry. I need to get on this right away. I know a half-dozen people I could talk to today." He pulled me up from the chair into a hug, and I closed my eyes, wishing he would stay, but knowing he needed to leave . . . yet again.

"Fine . . ." I lifted my head up and kissed his neck. "I know you'll find something . . . being brilliant and all." I half-grinned at him. "No worries, right?"

He laughed. "Right . . . she'll be apples."

I frowned. "I've never understood that one, but . . . yeah."

He smiled as he looked down at me. "How did I get so lucky?" he asked me softly.

I couldn't stop the small tears of guilt from springing to my eyes. If he only knew . . . he wouldn't think nearly as highly of me. Taking my tears for happiness, he kissed my cheek and led me back upstairs, where he got dressed and ready to leave to try and find some work. I sat on the bed, watching him in silence. I tried not to worry about him finding something . . . and tried not to feel guilty about it either. But the guilt came anyway. Guilt over the loss of his job, guilt over Kellan, over the secrets I had to hide from Denny now. I had never had any secrets from him before. I didn't like it.

He kissed me goodbye on the bed, eager to get a jump on his hopeful day. I kissed him back and wished him good luck. I heard him walk down the stairs, heard the door close, and heard his car pull away. Loneliness swept over me. How did forty-eight hours change . . . everything? I stayed on the bed for a while considering that. Then with a sigh, I got dressed for school.

I didn't see Kellan again as I fixed my hair and makeup, grabbed my book bag and a jacket, and made my way outside. I looked over at the empty driveway. Kellan would have to pick up his car from

Sam's later, I thought idly. I looked back at the house, at the window that looked into the kitchen. Surprisingly, Kellan was standing there, watching me leave. His face was unreadable. I started to wave goodbye but he turned almost immediately and was gone. I swallowed back the sudden emotion. How badly had I messed up our friendship?

It was impossible to keep my mind on lectures. I kept drifting between happiness that Denny was back, to guilt that he'd given up so much for me, to guilt that I had been unfaithful to him, to grief at the loss of my friendship with Kellan, to irritation that I didn't seem to mean as much to Kellan as I'd thought, to irritation at myself for wanting it to mean something more to him, back to guilt that he was taking up so much of my thoughts and not Denny, which started the whole vicious cycle again. My head hurt by the end of the day.

Denny was still out job hunting when I got back home. I walked through the front door and decided that a little mindless TV might distract me from my dark thoughts. As I looked into the living room, I saw that Kellan, still in his boxers, was sprawled out on the couch. He was staring at the TV but probably not even seeing it. I debated just going upstairs and hiding until Denny got home. I shook my head, put down my bag, and hung up my jacket. As casually as I could, I walked into the room and sat down in the chair opposite the couch. Eventually things would have to get back to normal; this weirdness would have to pass, and I didn't want to prolong it by avoiding him.

He flicked his eyes to me as I sat down, and then resumed silently watching his dull TV show. Suddenly uncomfortable, and thinking that maybe this was a bad idea, I swallowed and scanned the room. The couple pieces of art that Jenny and I had picked out really had brightened up the place. Those and the few photos I had taken of all of us and scattered here and there. They made everything much cheerier. I know guys usually don't care about décor, but it had seemed sparse, even for a bachelor. Maybe he had a strict landlord. Great, maybe I'd messed up more than he let on by putting this stuff up?

Staring at a picture of the three of us, smiling and happy, back when things were simple, I asked him a question without pausing to consider it. "Who do you rent this place from?"

His voice from the couch was cold and flat. His eyes never left the TV. "I don't. It's mine."

"Oh," I said, surprised. "How did you afford—" I didn't know if that sounded rude or not, so I didn't finish my question.

He flicked another glance at me and answered, "My parents." His eyes went back to the TV. "They died in a car crash a couple years ago. Left me their . . . palace." He waved his hand to indicate the room. "Only child and all . . ." He said the last part like his parents wouldn't have left it to him, if there had been a choice.

"Oh . . . I'm so sorry."

I wished I could have rewound time a few moments and kept my big mouth shut. He still looked ill, and this conversation was probably not what he wanted right now. I was a little surprised that he had answered me, though. I looked around the room again and remembered how barren it had looked a few short weeks ago. It certainly had never given me the impression of a childhood home.

"Don't be. It happens."

He could have been talking about his pet dying, not his parents. I remembered Denny's comment about Kellan's family life. I wanted to ask him about it, but it didn't seem right, not after the night we had shared together. That had definitely been intimate, but somehow, asking him about his family felt even more intimate.

"Why do you rent the room then? I mean, if you own the house?" Why was I still having this conversation with him?

He turned his head to look at me thoughtfully. He started to say something, but abruptly shut his mouth and shook his head. Turning back to the TV, he coldly said, "The extra money comes in handy."

I didn't buy it, but I didn't press him either.

Suddenly feeling sorry that I'd ever brought up what had to be a painful topic for him, I went over to sit on the edge of the couch beside him. He looked up at me warily. "I didn't mean to pry. I'm sorry."

"Don't worry about it." He swallowed forcibly and I watched the movement of his throat.

Purely intending to give him a hug, as he seriously looked in need of one, I leaned over across his chest, bringing my hands underneath him. He radiated warmth, but he was trembling, breathing shallowly. He left his arms on the couch, not returning my hug. His body stiffened slightly. Sighing softly, I remembered how easy and comfortable touching him used to be. . . . Apparently, that was gone now too. I pulled back a little, to ask him if he needed anything.

My breath stopped when I noticed his face, his eyes. He looked pained, like I was hurting him. His eyes were gazing past my shoulder, intently focused on anything but me, and they were narrowed in anger. His breathing was shallow and fast through his open lips. I immediately let go of him.

"Kellan . . . ?"

"Excuse me . . ." he said roughly and sat up on the couch.

I grabbed his arm, not knowing what I was going to say, just not wanting him mad at me. "Wait. . . . Talk to me, please."

He slid his gaze over to mine, his eyes cold and angry. "There is nothing to say." He shook his head, irritated. "I have to go." He brushed my hand away and stood up.

"Go?" I asked quietly, staying where I was on the couch.

"I have to get my car," he said as he left the room.

"Oh . . . but—" I stopped talking as I heard his door loudly shut.

Mentally, I slapped myself. *Way to inappropriately bring up a painful subject and hurt your roommate, whom you also inappropriately had sex with just a couple of days ago. Smooth, Kiera.* Man, I was on a roll.

I stayed on the couch, watching TV but not seeing a frame of it, my mind too lost in thought. Kellan came down the stairs a while later, fully dressed and showered, his wavy hair damp and delightfully messy. His face was pale, and his eyes looked tired, but he did look slightly better. He didn't look at me, but grabbed his jacket like he was leaving.

"Kellan . . ." I said his name without thinking. For some reason, I just didn't want him to leave yet. He looked over at me. The eyes that had been so cold earlier looked a little sad now.

I stood up and walked over to him. I started blushing as I approached him, feeling incredibly stupid for our earlier conversation and for the other night. I quickly looked down, but not before I saw him frown at me. When I could see his boots, I stopped, figuring I was close enough.

Still looking down, I mumbled, "I really am sorry about your parents." I risked a look back up to his face.

He visibly relaxed. I hadn't realized he had tensed up on my approach. He looked at me thoughtfully for a second before responding. "It's okay, Kiera," he said quietly, his eyes still sad.

Are we okay? Are we friends? Do you care for me? Do I care for you? I had so many questions, but watching his sad, blue eyes watch me, I couldn't make my mouth form them. Not knowing what else to do, I leaned over and kissed his cheek. He looked away and swallowed. Then, turning from me, he headed out the door.

I went to the kitchen and watched him from the window this time. He stood on the sidewalk with his fingers on the bridge of his nose, like he had a headache again. For a moment, I wondered what he was doing, but then I remembered that his car wasn't here. Within moments, headlights splashed against the window as Griffin pulled up in his VW Vanagon, which on any other day I would have found funny. Kellan went around to the other side of the car and looked back at the window before getting inside. He startled a bit at seeing me in the window watching him. Then he stared at me with an intense expression that made my heart beat faster. Shaking his head, he turned away and got in the car. Seconds later, Griffin drove away.

Looking dejected, Denny came home about twenty minutes later. Job hunting must not have gone well. New guilt surged through me as I painfully swallowed a lump. Would this crushing guilt ever leave me? He put on his best fake smile and sat on the bathroom counter, making small talk with me as I got ready for work. He always tried to make me happy, always tried to spare me pain.

He gave me a ride to work, asking me about what I'd done while he was gone. Most of it I had already told him on our numerous phone calls, and, of course, some of it I would never tell him, but I managed to remember a few funny stories that I hadn't mentioned. We laughed as I reminisced all the way there. We were holding hands and still chuckling over some stupid comment Griffin had made one day, as he walked me into the bar.

As soon as I saw Jenny's jaw drop, I remembered just how much had changed since my half-shift last night. She composed herself and walked over to us, grinning from ear to ear.

"Denny! I'm so glad to see you." She flew into his arms to give him a huge hug.

A little surprised by her enthusiasm, he blinked and awkwardly hugged her back. I couldn't help but laugh a little. She was obviously so happy to see him, because she was happy for me—that Denny and I were back together, but Denny, not fully comprehending that, had the cutest confused look on his face.

Jenny pulled back and playfully smacked his face. "Don't ever make my girl break up with you again—she was a mess!" Then she lightly kissed his still bewildered face on the cheek and turned to give me a hug. "See . . . I told you it would work out," she whispered in my ear.

Grateful, I returned her hug. "Thank you so much, Jenny." I pulled back. "I still owe you half a shift. Don't forget, you're leaving early tonight."

She smiled at me and grabbed my arms. "I didn't." She nodded over to a handsome man at the bar. "That's my date. . . ." Denny and I both turned to look at him while she continued, "We're going to that new club in the square as soon as I get off work."

Smiling, I turned back to her. "Why don't you go now? Grab some dinner first or something. Mondays are pretty quiet . . . and I really do owe you."

She looked back at him, then at me, her beautiful face frowning a bit. "Are you sure? I don't mind staying a few hours . . . at least 'til after the dinner rush fades."

Denny perked up. "I'll help her." He smiled over at me. "I wipe down a pretty mean table."

I laughed at him and turned back to her. "See, we're good. Go . . . have fun."

She laughed and hugged me again. "Okay . . . thanks." She kissed Denny again on the cheek. "And, thank you, Denny. Good to see you again, really."

Smiling, she headed to the bar and chatted with her date, then went to the back room to change. I turned to Denny, who was smiling softly at me. "A mess, huh?" he asked quietly.

I shook my head at the memory of just what that breakup had put me through . . . and what I had stupidly done to ease the pain. "You have no idea, Denny." *And please let it stay that way. . . .*

His smile left him and he pulled me in for a hug and a tender kiss. Someone in the bar groaned dramatically and, laughing, we pulled apart. "Come on. . . ." I tugged his arm, pulling him to the back room. "We have work to do!"

The next morning, I came down to the kitchen and stopped in the entryway. Kellan was already there, of course. He was waiting for the coffeepot to finish brewing. He was leaning back against the counter, head raised to the ceiling, apparently deep in thought. He was, once again, stunningly perfect, like yesterday had never happened. His eyes slid over to mine, once he noticed my entrance. He half-smiled, but his eyes were cold, distant. Great, still awkward.

"Hey," I whispered.

"Mornin'." He nodded at me, his eyes never leaving mine.

I finally looked away from his intense stare and grabbed a mug from the cupboard. I waited in silence for the pot to finish brewing, wishing things weren't quite so weird between us, and feeling guilty that they were. Finally, the coffee was done and he poured his mug, then held the pot out to me.

"Would you like me to fill you?" The odd way he phrased it made me look up at his eyes again. They were still cold, but he was now grinning mischievously at me. It made me very uncomfortable.

"Um . . . yes." I couldn't think of any other way to answer his almost crude-sounding question.

My response made him grin wickedly. "Cream?"

I swallowed, not liking the look on his face or his odd-sounding questions. What was with him today? I would have preferred his silence. "Yes," I finally whispered.

He grinned and went to the fridge to grab some for me. I briefly considered leaving the coffee and heading back upstairs, but he was back before I could move. He held up the creamer. "Just let me know when you're satisfied." His voice was low and smooth, and still very cold.

He watched my eyes while he poured, and only a fraction of what I usually used came out before I told him to stop. He leaned in very close to me and whispered, "Are you sure you want me to stop? I thought you liked it."

I swallowed loudly and turned away from him. He let out a cold laugh while I fumbled through getting some sugar and stirring my coffee. Seriously, what the hell was with him?

His eyes never leaving me, he finally asked, "So you and Denny are . . . 'back on'?" He said the last two words rather suggestively.

I blushed. "Yes."

"Just like that . . ." He cocked his head to the side, which was usually endearing, but at the moment he looked almost threatening. "No questions asked?" I panicked a minute, wondering what he meant by that. Did he change his mind about telling Denny? I searched his cold eyes but they told me nothing. Smiling oddly, he asked, "Are you going to tell him about . . . ?" He made a crude movement with his hands and I blushed more.

"No . . . of course not." I looked away from him and then quickly back. "Are you?"

He shrugged. "No, I told you I wouldn't. It doesn't matter much to me anyway." His voice was ice; it gave me chills. "I was just curious . . ."

"Well, no, I'm not . . . and thank you for not telling him . . . I guess," I whispered. My irritation at this odd conversation suddenly flared. "What happened to you the other night?" I blurted out.

He grabbed his coffee mug and grinned wickedly, his eyes boring into mine. He took a long draw without answering. His grin was answer enough. I decided I didn't want to know what, or who, had "happened" to him. Unable to take his weirdness anymore, I turned with my coffee to head back upstairs. I could feel his eyes following me the entire way around the corner.

I tried to forget about Kellan's oddness and lose my problems in my schoolwork. I was in one of the libraries, one of the most impressive libraries I've ever seen—very Harry Potter–ish. I was getting some studying done in the hour I had between Lit and Psychology, when a familiar-looking redhead came close to my table. She frowned over at me and I frowned back, wondering why she looked so familiar. It took a second before the springy red curls registered in my head.

Candy . . . Kellan's overly eager fling. I cringed and quickly looked down as I realized just how much I had in common with her now. She walked stiffly back to a table where two of her friends were waiting. I guess Kellan had never called her; she looked pretty miffed. She pointed over at me and her friends openly gaped. I tried not to notice. I didn't see how I could be so interesting to them anyway.

Later, in Psych, both of the girls she had been talking to, girls I had never realized were even in this class, plopped down on either side of me. "Hi," the blond one cheerily said. "I'm Tina. This is Genevieve." The brunette smiled and waved.

"Hello," I said meekly, wishing to disappear.

"Our friend Candy said she saw you at school with Kellan Kyle a while ago. . . . That true?" Tina asked excitedly, barely containing her glee.

Okay, right to the point. "Umm, yeah."

She glowed and her friend giggled. "Ohhh—you know him?"

Mentally I cringed. Boy, did I ever know him! "Yes, he's my roommate."

The brunette, Genevieve, smacked my shoulder. "Shut up!"

I thought Tina might have a coronary. Gathering herself, she leaned in to me, like we were suddenly best friends "What was your name again?"

Not having said it before, I quietly answered, "Kiera. Kiera Allen."

"Kiera, so tell me, are you and Kellan like a . . . thing?" Genevieve asked suggestively.

Mentally wincing, I looked at the wall clock and cursed the professor for being late, today of all days. Without looking at her, I answered, "No. He's friends with my boyfriend." That was a mostly true statement, I guess. I didn't know what Kellan and I were . . . especially now, but we were most definitely not a "thing."

That seemed to make both of them even giddier, like my statement had completely removed me as an obstacle to them. It unnerved me, and oddly made me relax a little. I guess I should have expected his pseudostardom to follow me, but I hadn't, and I really didn't want anyone to analyze our relationship. I couldn't even do that. The less they thought about me the better.

"Damn! He's so hot!" Genevieve exclaimed. "Tell us everything—every juicy detail!"

"There's not much to tell. . . . He's just a regular guy." True, a very hot guy, who was an ass to me this morning, but a regular guy. I had no idea what else to tell them, and the juicy details that I did know, I most certainly was not about to share.

I really would rather have sat there in silence and listened to the professor, who had finally shown up and was preparing to start class, but the girls didn't seem to care if he was there or not. Not with me, a spy on their rock-god, sitting beside them. They did lower their voices, but they asked me questions throughout the whole class.

At first I just ignored them. They didn't stop. Then I tried answering some of the simple questions, hoping that would satisfy them. Does he have a girlfriend? No, I don't think so. None that I had ever seen anyway. Does he play his guitar all the time? Yes. Does he sing in the shower? Yes. I blushed a little when I answered that, and they giggled. Does he have a brother? No. I frowned a little. No, he's actually completely alone. Where do you live? Seattle. I answered that one a little sarcastically. I wasn't about to give them any more than that. Does he wear boxers or briefs? I have no idea. I did know that one, but I wasn't about to let them know that I knew. Is he hot *all* the time? Yes. I sighed, thinking about how he always looked perfect every morning, while I looked like walking death . . . well, except for that one time. The girls giggled again. Have you seen him naked? There was no way I was going to answer that, and they giggled anyway at my silence, probably taking it for a yes . . . which, of course, it was.

I looked back at the clock. Ugh, only halfway through class. I realized my mistake then. I had hoped answers to a couple innocent questions would pacify them, and they would leave me alone. But now that they had me talking, they had no intention of stopping their relentless queries. They seemed to enjoy my silence at the naked question and started turning their inquiries in that direction. Is his body amazing? No verbal response to them, but the words "beyond amazing" came to mind. Is he a good kisser? Again no response, but in my head I replayed a few and . . . yes, God yes, the boy knew how to kiss. Have I "done it" with him? Definitely no response, and I prayed for no blushing either.

I suddenly realized by the intensity of their questioning that they weren't asking for themselves. Well, I'm sure they were curious too, but they were checking me out for Candy. Gauging what my relationship to Kellan was for her. I started wondering if they were even in this class or if they had just followed me in here.

Anger flashed through me and I studiously ignored every question they asked after that . . . the small ones and especially the shockingly intimate ones that made me blush. Really, no one should ask someone they just met *that* question. Relief washed through me as the lecture finally ended and people started leaving. I hastily gathered my stuff as they threw a few final questions my way, none of which I answered.

Calmly excusing myself—well, almost calmly—I darted for the door. As I left I heard, "Hey, are you having any study sessions at your house?" followed by more giggling. Well, that was a complete waste of a class. Those weren't the sort of human sexuality questions that I wanted to be answering.

I braced myself for more obnoxious Kellan behavior the next morning, but he wasn't in the kitchen. . . . He wasn't even home. He hadn't been home when I got back from school yesterday either. Come to think of it, he hadn't been home when Denny and I went to bed. It hurt my heart a little when I walked downstairs and he wasn't there, sipping his coffee, reading the paper, and smiling warmly at me. While Denny had been away, I'd started waking up earlier than I needed to, just to see that sight every morning. That realization worried me a little, but I pushed it back. It didn't matter now. That friendship wasn't the same . . . it was practically gone. I blinked back tears as I made my own coffee.

Denny woke a while later and quickly got ready for his day of job searching. He kissed me goodbye as I got ready for my own day of school. Not that I'd expected Kellan to continue giving me a ride to school since Denny was back, or since our oddly cold conversation in the kitchen, but sadness swept through me as I waited for the bus. I missed our rides together. Maybe his coldness was a good thing. Maybe I'd gotten too attached. Now that Denny was back, it wasn't appropriate. Of course, a lot had happened with Kellan that wasn't appropriate.

Where I had barely seen him at home, I couldn't seem to escape him at the bar. It wasn't too long into my shift that evening when the foursome walked in and strolled to their table. Kellan ignored me and went straight to Rita to grab the guys some beers himself. That oddly offended me. I couldn't even wait on him now? Rita reached out and ruffled his hair while he leaned over the bar and smiled at her crookedly. That irritated me too, when I remembered that I had more in common with Rita now, as well. Ugh, that thought actually made me a little nauseous, and I had to look away from their flirting.

I walked over to where Jenny was finishing up with a customer. Pulling my head out of my own problems, I asked her about her night out. "Hey, Jenny, I never did ask you how your date went."

Jenny put her hands on her hips as she walked up to the bar. I sighed mentally as I realized where she was headed. I was sort of in the middle of a conversation with her, and I couldn't really do anything but follow her, even though Kellan was still at the bar flirting with Rita. Seriously, what were they talking about? Oh God, is that where he's been? Are they seeing each other?

"It was a disaster." Jenny was talking about her date, and I made myself focus on her and not my last horrifying thought. Jenny walked right up to Kellan's side and I stood slightly behind her, trying hard to not gaze at his perfectly sculpted back leaning over the bar. "He was so boring, Kiera. Ugh, I wanted to take a nap right in my risotto."

Kellan turned his head slightly at the mention of my name. He flicked a glance at Jenny and then a quick one back to me. Jenny looked at him briefly. "Hey, Kellan." He nodded at her politely but made no move to acknowledge me. Jenny continued with her story. "I called it a night after that and didn't even bother with going to a club."

Jenny turned and quickly told Rita her order. Rita looked a little miffed that she no longer had Kellan's attention. She grudgingly filled Jenny's order. Jenny turned to face me, while Kellan stared down at the bar, his head still cocked toward us like he was listening.

"Pretty boy, but"—Jenny pointed to her head—"not a whole lot going on upstairs."

Kellan smiled, like he was trying not to laugh at her comment. Hope sparked in me that maybe his bad mood was over, maybe he would be nice. Focusing again on Jenny, I said, "I'm sorry, Jenny. . . ." I left it at that, not knowing what else to say. I didn't have a whole lot of experience with dating.

Grabbing her drinks from Rita, she shrugged. "No biggie . . . My guy is out there somewhere." She smiled and walked back to her customers.

Feeling better about Kellan after seeing his smile, I stayed at the bar. Rita got called over to a customer on the far side and I took my chance. "Kellan," I said softly to his back.

He turned around with a smug look on his face. My heart sank a little at his near sneer. "Kiera." His voice was flat, all trace of good humor gone.

I suddenly didn't know what to say. I ended up pointing to the four beer bottles he had clutched in his fingers. "I could have gotten those for you."

He straightened from the bar and I suddenly felt very small as he towered over me. "I can manage . . . thanks." He roughly brushed past me as he headed back to the table.

I swallowed and sighed. Why did I irritate him so much? Why couldn't we still be friends? Why did I miss him so much . . . ?

Friday morning as Denny and I were snuggling on the couch, Denny sighed for the hundredth time and restlessly shifted around. His job searching wasn't going well at all. Things were full, and internships were rare anyway. He had gone out every day and night this week and had exhausted all of his resources. He started half-jokingly saying that he might need to get a job at McDonald's, just so we could pay our rent. Kellan had told him not to worry about it, which made me curious. He didn't seem to need the money, so why did he rent out his room?

Looking over at Denny, I thought for a microsecond that he could get a job at Pete's, but with Kellan being so difficult lately, so cold and callous, I decided it was probably not a good idea. Also, having the two of them in the same room together made me highly uncomfortable. Our house had been odd enough, not that Kellan had been home much. But when he was home, his cold eyes watched Denny's and my every move, every touch. I didn't need that following me to work, any more than it already did, anyway.

Things at the bar had been . . . strained. No one seemed to notice the change in his attitude toward me. I sure did, however. The guys still teased me mercilessly, only now it was Kellan, more often than not, who instigated it. He no longer stopped Griffin's crude stories upon my approach. In fact, he seemed to delight in them even more, and managed to ask just the right question just as I was coming to their table, so that I would have to hear every gory detail. "How many girls, Griff? No, I've never heard of that position. Wait, what did she do with the licorice again?"

Even worse, though, was when he would ask me my opinion on one of Griffin's little stories. I would blush horribly and dart away as quickly as I could without ever answering him. Evan would frown and tell him to be nice, while Matt would chuckle quietly. Kellan and Griffin would laugh loudly, like it was the funniest thing they'd ever seen. Their laughter would follow me all the way up to the bar, where I actually looked forward to talking to Rita instead of them.

All throughout my shift, Kellan made snide, suggestive comments. He watched me coldly and intently wherever I went. He flinched whenever I touched him—even accidentally. He made me so uncomfortable.

It made me a little sad that one stupid mistake together had changed what had been a very nice friendship. I longed for the Kellan who chatted with me over coffee, who sweetly put his arms around me, who let me rest on his shoulder, who sat with me when I cried, who had tucked me into bed. And on the rare occurrences when I could look at our drunken night together without the usual horrifying guilt, it was a pleasant memory, a fond memory, even. It hurt me that Kellan obviously didn't feel the same, that in one night I had ruined everything between us.

Mostly, though, it made me angry.

Frowning at the memories, stirring in my brain, I turned my head away from Denny on the couch so he wouldn't see my frustration. I could see now why Joey had fled. Kellan postsex was kind of—

no, he was—an ass! I didn't have the luxury of simply skipping town though. Not when I had made such a big deal out of Denny leaving, not when it would raise too many questions in Denny's eyes. I was starting to really dislike Kellan, and really miss him at the same time. I wished *he* would leave. That would greatly simplify things for me. That thought put an odd feeling in my stomach, though.

Denny noticed my frown anyway. "You all right?"

I forced a smile and shrugged. "Yeah, just worried about you." I hated lying to him. Well, it really was only a half-lie. I *was* worried about him. I was just more preoccupied with Kellan's behavior. It bothered me that Kellan concerned me more.

Denny slipped an arm around me and held me close to his shoulder. He stopped sighing. He was always trying to please me. . . . It only made me feel worse. My guilt increased tenfold every time Denny smiled at me. He tenderly kissed my head and I looked up at him. He smiled sweetly and brought a hand to my cheek, running a finger down it. "It will be okay, Kiera." His tenderness expanded my heart, and broke it at the same time.

He leaned down and softly pressed his lips to mine. Sighing, he cupped my cheek with his hand, stroking me softly with his thumb, and kissed me deeper. I relaxed into his comfort, his warmth and tenderness, and returned his deep kiss. He ran his hands down to my hips and scooted me over to his lap. I smiled, and thought how much I liked him being home with me all morning, and that I had a good hour before school started. . . .

I nestled into his lap and ran my fingers through his hair. He smiled at me between kisses. My breathing was just beginning to increase when I heard the front door open. Kellan hadn't come home again last night. In fact, he hadn't spent a night here the past two nights. I wondered who he was dating and that thought irrationally irritated me. Whoever it was, he was just now getting back. I immediately froze and looked at the door.

Kellan's eyes locked onto mine instantly. He smirked at me, his eyes suddenly mean. Then, as Denny turned to look over, his expression immediately softened. He smiled at Denny, although it did nothing to warm his eyes.

"Mornin'."

"You just gettin' home, mate?" Denny asked casually, his hands softly rubbing my thighs.

Kellan watched us for half a second, then smiled again, looking only at Denny. "Yeah, I was"—he coolly glanced over at me—"out."

Denny didn't notice the look. He simply shrugged and looked back to me. I scooted off his lap and he laughed a little at me, slipping an arm around my waist. I sat in such a way that I could see Denny and Kellan at the same time. It was odd to have both of them in my vision together. It did weird things to my stomach. Denny was still looking at me lovingly; Kellan was still watching us coolly, a slight frown on his face now. I wanted to crawl inside the couch and disappear.

Eventually, Kellan murmured something excusatory and wandered upstairs. I relaxed fractionally when I heard his door close. Denny raised an eyebrow suggestively at me and made a move like he was going to move me back on his lap, but I frowned at him. Laughing, he held me close to him until it was time for me to get ready for school.

Denny drove me to school and finally took a walk around the campus with me. I tried to be as good of a guide to him as Kellan had been to me. The memory of that day painfully squeezed my heart as I quickly pointed out the various brick buildings on our way to my psychology class. Denny, of course, wanted to talk about my Econ class and, smiling as we walked hand in hand down the concrete pathways crisscrossing the expansive lawns, I relayed as much of it as I could in the short time we had.

We entered the building and Denny was just as impressed as I had been with the beauty of the school. It was truly remarkable, like stepping back to a time where art and the detailed, intricate beauty of architecture, instead of practical form and function, were rampant.

He opened the door to my Human Sexuality class and, chuckling, said he wanted to hear all about it after school when he picked me up. Chuckling back, I leaned over and gave him a long kiss. Someone brushing past us in the door broke us apart, and I grudgingly said goodbye and went to my seat.

It was an odd class to have when my mind was so conflicted. The class had more to do with the psychological and social aspects of sexual behavior than with the mechanics of sex. The course went over cultural diversity, sexual health, abuse, and assault. It still felt very relevant to my current situation, however, and I had to force my mind away from analyzing *my* problems and back to what the professor was saying, on more than one occasion. I was a little relieved when the class was over.

I smiled at seeing Denny's old Honda in the parking lot, in the same spot he had parked it before class. He climbed out of the driver's side and walked over to me, smiling widely.

"Hey," he said as he met up with me and then, with my favorite goofy grin on his face, he picked me up and spun me around. I laughed and laced my arms around his neck. He stopped spinning and, setting me down, leaned in for a long, passionate kiss.

When I could catch my breath, I looked up at his sparkling eyes. "Someone's in a better mood."

He grinned and gave me a quick peck. "I got a phone call this afternoon—one of my contacts finally paid off." He stood up straight while I grinned back at him. "You are now looking at the newest member of SLS Advertising."

"Babe . . ." I gave him a warm hug and kissed his cheek. "That's great!" I pulled back to look him in the eye. "I knew you would find something. You are brilliant, after all."

He sighed, looking at me lovingly. "So you keep telling me." He gazed at me for a moment longer. "I love you . . . so much. I'm so sorry. . . ."

Guilt washed through me. I was an idiot and he was sorry?

"Don't. . . . it doesn't matter. Everything is back to normal now, back to how it should be." Well, nearly everything was back to normal. I smiled at him, my eyes suddenly moist. "I love you too."

We kissed tenderly for another minute on the sidewalk, while people walked back and forth around us. We ignored them all, en-joying our moment of togetherness. Finally Denny pulled back and, smiling, took my hand and drove me back home.

Denny gave me a ride to work that night as well. I was not look-ing forward to the D-Bags' performance this evening. I wasn't sure why, except I just felt like Kellan's coldness toward me was going to somehow be projected on the stage for everyone to see. Denny kissed my cheek as I made my way to the back room to set down my bag and jacket. Jenny and Kate ran into me as I was coming back out.

Kate usually worked the morning shifts. I rarely saw her and hadn't really talked with her much. She was an averagely pretty girl with long, light brown hair pulled back into a perfect ponytail, eyes so light brown they were almost ocher, and the longest, fullest lashes I had ever seen. She was tall and a little too thin, but extremely grace-ful, like she had belonged to a ballet troupe before joining the staff here at Pete's.

"Hi, Kiera!" Jenny said as she gave me a swift hug. "Kate's switch-ing to nights, since we were slammed last Friday. The guys are really pulling the people in, now that school's going again."

I smiled politely at Kate and returned Jenny's hug. "Yeah . . . I guess they are." Thinking back on last Friday, it *had* been pretty busy. I'd barely had had time that night to notice the band. I had still no-ticed Kellan though. My eyes had watched him whenever there had been a pause with the customers. So much had changed since then. Our relationship had changed so much since last weekend. I wasn't sure what to expect tonight.

The beginning of the evening went pleasantly enough. Having an extra waitress there helped. I got to spend more time flirting with Denny, who decided to stay for dinner and the show. I brought him his food and gave him a kiss. I brought him his soda and gave him a kiss. Heck, I brought him extra napkins and gave him a kiss. Jenny smiled at our cuteness. I was just glad to have him back.

But eventually, and with much fanfare, the front doors burst open and Griffin walked through, with his arms outstretched as though he were a king entering his throne room. The fans already at the bar of course went nuts and made their way over to him. He put his arms around a couple of them and headed over to his usual table, stopping on the way to steal a kiss from Kate, who quickly pushed him away, sighing and rolling her eyes. Apparently, she was used to Griffin's advances.

Matt and Evan came in much more quietly behind Griffin. Matt smiled politely and followed Griffin to their table. Evan gave Jenny a big hug and wrapped an arm around an eager girl who had kissed his cheek, then followed Matt.

My stomach clenched as I discreetly watched the door, knowing who would be coming through it next. Seconds later he appeared, and my breath caught. He was stunning. His wavy hair was perfect. His long-sleeved shirt, layered under a basic black T-shirt, emphasized his spectacular chest. His jeans, faded and frayed from years of use, clung to him enticingly. His lips were curled in a sexy half-smile and his deep blue, piercing eyes locked onto mine.

Knowing Denny was here and could be watching me, I forced my breath back and turned my eyes away. I turned to Denny, but he was clasping hands with Matt and chatting with the other guys at their table. My eyes swung back over to Kellan, who was now walking over to me, an odd look in his eyes. I debated turning and leaving, but he was in my section and I was his waitress. It would look odd if I didn't help him. I hoped he would be normal to me tonight, not his now-usual cold, jerky self.

He came right up to me. "Kiera," he said calmly.

I swallowed and made myself look him in the eye. "Yes, Kellan?"

He smiled and cocked his head to the side. "We'll have the usual." He nodded his head over to the table. "Bring one for Denny too . . . since he's a part of this."

The odd way he phrased it made me frown, but I nodded, and he turned and walked to the table with the guys. Nearly instantly, two girls were attached to his arms, running fingers through his perfectly sexy hair. I swallowed and made myself go up to the bar and get their drinks.

Rita winked conspiratorially at me when I got everyone's beers. She seemed to think she knew something. Of course, she thought I'd been jumping into bed with Kellan from the very beginning. I sighed and ignored her as I grabbed the band's drinks.

Business picked up dramatically after the guys showed up, and I no longer had time to flirt with Denny. Honestly, with Kellan there, I wouldn't have felt comfortable flirting with him anyway, especially not with them all sitting at the same table together. I did notice that Kellan sat at the opposite end of the table from Denny. Kellan faced out into the crowd, and flirted with some girls at the next table. Not even once did he look at Denny. I wasn't sure what Kellan's problem was with Denny . . . guilt, maybe?

Eventually, it was time for them to go onstage. The crowd, as usual mostly women, went nuts and crowded the front of the stage. I watched from the tables as the band started their set. They were perfect, of course. The songs were catchy, Kellan's voice was sexy, the looks he threw the crowd were downright indecent, and it wasn't long before the whole back half of the bar was dancing and carrying on, thoroughly enjoying their entertainment. I stopped watching Kellan and his . . . act . . . and turned back to the customers still seated.

The band started playing a song that I had heard but never really listened to before. Maybe it was because I was trying so hard to ignore watching Kellan that I was more intently focused on listening to him. Maybe it was because of our drunken fiasco, but the words were quite suddenly all too clear in my head. I stopped beside a table and stared up at him, my mouth dropping open. What I noticed first, oddly enough, was the look on Griffin's face, which should have been my first clue. He looked giddy . . . way too excited to play the song; obviously, he loved it. Then my eyes shifted to Kellan in disbelief.

The lyrics were all metaphors for sex, and not just any kind of sex—casual, meaningless, one-night-stand sex. The song highly implied that while the sex was great . . . I've already moved on, and I hope you remember me, because I've already forgotten you. I had heard this song before and had never interpreted it that way, until just now. Maybe I was interpreting it wrong, but with the look on Griffin's face and the steel look in Kellan's eyes, I didn't think I was.

Most shocking of all was the fact that Kellan was directing that cold stare at me. I felt like he was shouting our one night all across the bar. I couldn't move. I couldn't turn away. I was frozen with shock, and I could feel tears start to sting my eyes. Why was he being so cold, so intentionally mean? I startled at a hand slipping around my waist.

"Hey, babe," Denny whispered in my ear. "I'm getting beat. . . . I think I'll head out. Can you get a ride home?" He turned me to make me look at him and noticed my expression. "You okay?"

I swallowed and tried to fix a smile on my face, hoping no tears fell. "Yeah, I'm—" I cut off as a particularly vicious lyric cut through my head. Kellan was practically yelling the verse, "*What do you think about me now?*" The crowd went crazy over the intensity of it. Kellan's eyes were still focused in my direction.

Denny glanced over at the crowd's reaction. "Wow, that song's really good. . . . Is that a new one?"

I managed to spit out, "No, he's played it before." Forcing back my smile, I turned to him fully. "I'll get a ride with Jenny. Go home. I'm fine . . . just tired."

Smiling softly at me, he said, "Okay . . . wake me when you get home." Then he gave me a short kiss and left the bar. I wanted nothing more than to leave with him. But I couldn't, I was stuck here for a while longer, listening to Kellan torture me. . . .

The next morning, I decided it was time to get to the bottom of Kellan's oddness with me. Seriously, I could understand him feeling guilty and being odd around Denny, but why was he so mean to me?

Steeling myself to either see him or not see him, since he hadn't been home much lately, I turned the corner and found him reading the paper and drinking his coffee at the table.

He coolly glanced up at me when I entered, and my resolve wavered at seeing his dark eyes. I closed mine and took a deep breath. Giving myself a moment, I made a cup of coffee before sitting and joining him at the table.

"Mornin'," he finally said to me, not looking up from his paper.

"Kellan . . ." My mouth dried up and I had to swallow.

He looked up at me. "What?" His tone was almost harsh and I considered leaving the room again.

Don't be an idiot Kiera . . . just talk to him. After everything we had done together, I should be able to talk to him. . . . "Why are you mad at me?" I whispered, not meeting his eye.

"I'm not mad at you, Kiera. I've been exceedingly nice to you. Most women thank me for that." I could hear the smirk in his voice.

My irritation flickered, and I glared at him. "You're being an ass! Ever since . . ."

He raised his eyebrow, waiting for me to finish that thought. I didn't. Eventually he looked back down to his paper and took another drink of his coffee. "I really don't know what you mean, Kiera. . . ."

I gaped at him. Was he just going to flat-out ignore what a jerk he'd been lately? "Is it Denny? You feel guilty . . . ?"

His cold eyes flashed up to mine. "I'm not the one who cheated on him," he said, low and cold, and I flinched and bit my lip, praying for my eyes not to water.

"We used to be friends, Kellan," I whispered.

He looked down at his paper and casually tossed back at me, "Were we? I wasn't aware of that."

Feeling tears of anger starting to form, I snapped back, "Yes . . . we were, Kellan. Before we—"

He glanced up at me and cut me off. "Denny and I are friends." He looked me up and down, almost scornfully. "You and I are . . . roommates."

My anger temporarily blocked out my forming tears as I gaped at him. "You have a funny way of showing friendship then. If Denny knew what you—"

He cut me off again as he icily glared at me. "But you're not telling him, are you?" He looked back at his paper and I thought he was done speaking, when he said in a softer voice, "Besides, that's between the two of you—it had nothing to do with me. I was simply . . . there . . . for you."

I gaped at him again, not able to speak anymore. Kellan stared down at his paper for a minute, then sighed. "Are we done?" he asked, looking back up at me.

I nodded, feeling like we were done in more ways than one. He got up and left the kitchen. Moments later, I heard the door open and his car pull away. He didn't come home for the rest of the weekend.

Chapter 9
The Espresso Stand

Denny's new job was working for a small marketing company that mostly dealt with Internet clientele. It was a far cry from the prestigious internship for one of the largest advertising companies around that he had given up. His brilliance, while so welcomed and encouraged at his previous job, was almost looked down upon here. The small-minded people around him were intimidated by his ideas. They turned his job into little more than that of a glorified gofer, running their errands and stroking their egos.

He hated every minute of it. He would never flat-out tell me that, ever wanting to spare me pain or guilt, but regardless, I knew. I could see it in his eyes when he lingered in the kitchen before heading out for the day. I could see it in the slump of his shoulders when he came into the bar at night after his day was finally over. He was miserable.

One evening at Pete's, after a long day at work, Denny sat alone at a back table sipping on his beer, deep in thought. I wanted to go over and talk to him, but there was nothing left to say. I had already told him it would eventually get better, but it didn't seem to be getting any better. I had already told him I loved him eternally for coming back. That garnered a small smile, but not much more. I had even told him to quit and find work somewhere else, but there weren't any openings anywhere. He was still actively looking, but for now, if he wanted to stay in his chosen field, and if he wanted to stay in Seattle . . . he was stuck.

I sighed, watching him. I looked over at Kellan, lounging with his bandmates a few tables away from Denny. I hoped he would finally sit and talk to Denny, try to cheer him up. But Kellan was chatting with Matt and had his back to Denny. From an outside perspective it probably looked like nothing, but I knew that Kellan was still avoiding Denny. He didn't even like looking at Denny anymore, and rarely said more than a few polite words to him. I wished Kellan would just stop it and be his friend again, like he said he was. I understood his guilt—I felt it too—but enough was enough. Denny needed us right now.

A cell phone sitting beside Denny's beer rang and, sighing, he picked it up. The company had felt the need to have twenty-four-hour access to him, and had given him the phone with instructions that he could only use it to talk to them and that if it rang, he'd better answer it. The whole thing greatly irritated me. It was way beyond what an intern should have to do.

He spoke dejectedly for a few minutes, shut the phone, then stood and made his way over to me. "Hey." He tried to smile, but I could see how forced it was.

"Hi." I smiled at him reassuringly, even though I could feel the irritation in me starting to rise, at the conversation I could sense coming.

"I'm sorry," he stated abruptly. "That was Max. I have to go." Max was an irritating, shrewd little man, who seemed to enjoy nothing greater than sending Denny on pointless errands, preferably on off hours. His latest vital assignment had involved dry cleaning and Starbucks.

"Again? Denny . . ." I didn't mean to sound agitated, but I was, and it seeped into my voice. I was getting really sick and tired of the endless tasks that occupied so much of his time and thoughts and that were so beneath his brilliant mind.

"Kiera," anger flashed in his eyes, "it's my job. I have to do this."

The irritation in my voice was intentional this time. "It didn't used to be."

"No, it didn't used to be. . . ."

Guilt mixed with my anger, only increasing it. I roughly turned away from him and started picking up empty glasses from a nearby table. "Fine, see you later then."

Anger turned my thoughts dark. He was the one who had dropped everything to rush back to me. If he had given me time, I would have calmed down and we could have worked something out . . . probably. I hated feeling guilty over *his* decision. I felt guilty enough over mine . . . over Kellan.

Saying nothing else, he turned and left the bar. I watched him disappear through the double doors and started to turn back to my work when I noticed Kellan watching me. I knew he had been intently watching our conversation. *Great, more fodder for him,* I thought, my mind still in a dark place.

He slowly stood up and made his way over to me. My irritation soared even higher. Really, I was not in the mood for being attacked by him right now. He had never actually agreed that he was being mean to me, and his attitude toward me hadn't changed much since our brief conversation in the kitchen. Irritation at that conversation flashed through me yet again. Apparently, according to him, we were never even friends.

Concentrating on stacking the glasses, I decided to just ignore him.

He came up beside me, pressing his side into mine and staring down at me. The move was decidedly intimate, and a strange feeling washed through me. Even though the bar was packed, it was not *that* packed. It would look odd to someone watching for him to be standing that close to me. Instinctively, I pulled away and glared up at him. So much for ignoring him.

"Denny leave you again? I could find you another drinking buddy, if you're . . . lonely?" he asked, before grinning devilishly. "Maybe Griffin this time?"

"I don't need your crap tonight, Kellan!"

"You don't seem to be happy being with him," he responded, an oddly serious note to his tone.

"What? And I'd be happier with you?" I glared at his perfectly charming face, his sexy half-smile, and his oddly cool eyes. He didn't say anything to that, just kept that annoying, enchanting smile on his face. Suddenly I wasn't just a little angry anymore. No, I shot right past angry to thoroughly pissed off.

Leaning in close, so no one else would hear, I whispered, "You were the biggest mistake of my life, Kellan. You were right—we're not friends, never were. I wish you would just go away."

I immediately wished I could take the words back. He was being a jerk, but I didn't want to hurt him by belittling what we had shared together. And I did still think of him as a friend, even if he didn't think of me that way. His smile instantly left him. His eyes went from cool to ice cold, and he roughly brushed past me, nearly making me drop my stack of glasses.

He left shortly after that.

When I came home from my shift, Denny was waiting up for me. He was sitting on the bed, watching TV and looking very tired. His face, and the fact that he was waiting to talk to me, softened my anger at our earlier conversation and I smiled over at him. "Hey."

"I'm sorry," he said immediately, shutting off the TV. "I shouldn't snap at you. It's not your fault I'm not happy there."

I went over to sit by him on the bed. He had never admitted he hated it there before. I put my hand on his cheek. "I'm sorry too. I didn't mean to snap either. I just . . . miss you."

"I know." His accent on the word made me smile. "I miss you too. I'll do better. I promise, okay? No more grump." He smiled for the first time it what felt like weeks.

I laughed at him and softly kissed him. "Okay, I'll try to not be grumpy either, then."

The next morning, feeling better after having talked to Denny, I hoped to talk with Kellan. He was his usual self, drinking his coffee and reading the paper, but he didn't look up when I came in. Embarrassed at my outburst yesterday, I wasn't sure what to do. Quietly I made my coffee. Then I chickened out and decided to drink it upstairs. I just couldn't take the awkwardness.

But guilt stopped me before I could completely turn the corner. Not looking, I threw an "I'm sorry, Kellan" over my shoulder. I thought I heard a long sigh as I walked away, but nothing else.

Denny did seem to turn a corner. While still really unhappy about his situation, he moped a lot less, and we talked a lot more. I still didn't see nearly enough of him, and he got way too many after-hours phone calls for my taste, but I tried to not mope about that either. It was going to take both of us to make this work.

Kellan was different as well. For all the moping Denny and I were trying not to do, Kellan was making up for it. He avoided both of us for the most part. On the rare occasions we were all together, he said nothing more than a few polite words. He stopped being an ass, which I was grateful for, but his silence made my stomach feel odd. I felt something coming, I just didn't know what. It was unsettling.

One Saturday morning, Denny and Kellan were downstairs talking before I got there. I couldn't tell what they had been saying, but as I turned the corner, Kellan was smiling at Denny, who had a hand clapped on his shoulder. I had no idea what that was about, but the vision of them both together like that was both heartwarming and guilt-inducing.

Denny looked over at me when I entered the room. "Can you get someone to trade shifts with you? We're all going out tonight—mates' night out."

I tried to smile, but my stomach dropped. This was not good. "Ohhhh, that's a great idea, honey. Where are we going?"

"A friend of mine has a band playing at the Shack tonight," Kellan said quietly, looking at me for the first time in days. His look was a sad one, and my stomach hurt again.

"Okay, sounds great. I'll trade with Emily. She normally works days, but she just asked Jenny if she could work some nights. Better tips. . . ."

"Great!" Denny walked over to me and gave me a long kiss. "See, I can still be fun. No more grump, I promised." He gave me a quick hug and moved to leave the room. "I'm gonna shower, then I'll make you breakfast," he tossed over his shoulder with a quick wink.

I laughed, then looked back over at Kellan and stopped. He was looking away from us, his face pale. He didn't look good at all. "You okay?" I whispered, not really wanting to ask in case ass-Kellan popped back up again.

He looked over at me, his eyes sad but a smile on his face. "Sure. This will be . . . interesting."

Suddenly worried, I walked closer to him. "Are you sure? This doesn't have to happen. Denny and I can go alone."

His face suddenly serious, he gazed at me intently. "I'm fine, and I'd like to spend one . . . night . . . with my roommates." He turned away from me and headed upstairs through the living room. The ache in my stomach increased tenfold. He had said that oddly and it terrified me.

The night started . . . awkwardly. Kellan disappeared not long after the announcement that we were having a night out. He had left the house with an "I'll meet you guys there," and Denny and I didn't see him for the rest of the day. Really, that suited me just fine. His new sad, quiet behavior was causing my stomach to do strange, panicky things that I didn't have the heart to analyze.

Instead, I turned my attention to Denny, trying to focus on having a good time with him, like we used to have together. He seemed in a better mood than usual. Maybe he had noticed things were strained around the house with Kellan and was trying to compensate. He seemed excited for us all to go out and do something together tonight. I wasn't quite as excited, but I faked it for my man.

The day went slowly, peacefully, but eventually it was time to get ready for the evening. It was still pretty warm for this time of year, so I chose a loose, flirty black skirt and a pink button-up short-sleeved shirt with a light sweater-jacket. I left my hair loose, casual, and slightly wavy. Denny smiled at me and kissed my cheek as I put on my lipstick. He picked out my favorite blue Henley that I loved on his tan skin. Adorably, he held out a small jar of style gel and let me go crazy with his hair, shaking his head when I was satisfied with it. He was trying to please me tonight, and it was working. I was very touched by the gestures.

When we arrived at the Shack, Kellan's car was already there. We parked next to his Chevelle in a side parking lot. Making our way to the front doors, I noticed that the bar was about half the size of Pete's. I wondered where the band was going to play. Then I noticed the wide-open doors in the back of the bar and the crowd of people outside. We made our way out the back to a large, fenced beer garden. There were tables all along the sides of the fence and along the wall of the bar, with a wide-open section in front of a large stage opposite the building. A band was setting up their equipment, and Kellan was over there, talking to one of the guys. He saw us and motioned to a table along the fence that already had a pitcher of beer and three glasses.

Denny and I waved back and walked over to the table reserved for us. Denny held out my chair like we were on a first date and I smiled at him. "Thank you, sir." I teased.

"Anything for a beautiful girl." He smiled and gallantly kissed my hand.

Playing with him a little, I said in mock surprise, "Oh, are you Australian? I love Aussies."

"Ripper! Pash a bloke before joining him for a grog then, sheila?" he said back, massively over-exaggerating his accent.

I laughed at him and bent in to give him the kiss he'd asked for. "You are such a dork."

"Yeah, but you love me anyway." He kissed me back.

"Hmmm . . . yeah." I smiled, then turned when I felt eyes on my back.

Kellan was behind me, watching us blankly. I was trying to get things back to normal. I wished Kellan would at least try too. His melancholy was really starting to get to me. He sat down and poured everyone a beer, not looking at either of us.

Denny didn't seem to notice his mood. "When does your friend go on?" he asked him cheerfully.

Kellan briefly looked over at him. "Another twenty minutes or so." He took a long drink from his beer while a woman passed by and not so subtly eyed him up and down. Surprisingly, he only gave her a cursory glance, then returned his attention to his beer. In a noticeable huff, she stalked off.

The twenty minutes it took for the band to finally start felt like twenty hours. Our little trio was pretty quiet. Denny would try to start a conversation with Kellan, only to have Kellan give him one- or two-word responses. Eventually Denny stopped trying. My irritation at Kellan was growing minute by achingly long minute.

Finally the band did start to play, and Denny and I left the sulking Kellan at the table while we laughed and danced by the stage. In between twirls and dips, I cast glances at the table, only to see Kellan watching us with an unreadable expression on his face. Girls occasionally tried to get him to dance too, but he seemed to be turning everyone down. Again, my irritation with him grew. What was his problem?

During the set break we came back to the table to hastily finish our beers and relax for a few minutes. I noticed that it was starting to cool down outside, but I felt warm from dancing with Denny. Kellan sat quietly, staring at the empty glass in his hand when, suddenly, Denny's cell phone started ringing. Startled, I looked over at him as he sheepishly answered it. I hadn't realized he had brought it. I tried to not be irritated at that. It was his job, after all. He spoke for a few seconds with someone before he started saying "Hello? Hello?"

"Damn," Denny muttered as he shut the phone. "Battery died." Glancing over at me, he shook his head apologetically. "Sorry, I really need to call Max back. I'm gonna check inside, see if I can use their phone."

I smiled over at him, forcing down my irritation. Tonight was about having fun, not being bitter. "No problem, we'll be here." I nodded my head over to Kellan's chair. Kellan still wasn't looking at us. He sat awkwardly, still staring at the glass in his hands with a slight frown on his face.

Denny stood and kissed me on the cheek before turning to go back inside the bar. Kellan sighed quietly and shifted in his chair. I watched Denny disappear into the crowd and turned to look at Kellan. Sudden irritation at his odd behavior and, quite honestly, Denny's phone call, finally made me snap. "You said you were fine with this. What is with you?"

Kellan looked over at me, his blue eyes intense. "I'm having a fabulous time. What could you possibly mean?" His voice was flat, cold. I looked away and worked on keeping my breathing constant and even, my anger in check. I didn't want to ruin this night for Denny by fighting with Kellan.

"Nothing, I guess."

Kellan set his glass down and abruptly stood up. "Tell Denny that I was feeling ill. . . ." He paused as if he was going to say something more, then shook his head and only said, "I'm done." His voice was still very cold and the words came out with a finality that knotted a ball in my stomach. I suddenly felt that he wasn't just talking about tonight.

I slowly stood and looked him in the eyes. His narrowed slightly as he watched me. Without another word, he turned and headed for the gate that led to the side parking lot where we had all parked earlier in the evening. I watched him leave. Tall, lean, and muscular in just the right way, he was beyond good-looking, closer to perfection. I couldn't help the sinking feeling in my gut as I watched him open the gate. I just knew that once he closed that door, I would never see him again. Something started to break inside me as I considered that.

I should let him walk away. He was moody, always cold and silently brooding. And before that he had been a total ass, poking and prodding my relationship with Denny, making suggestive comments about our one night together and the secret we kept from everyone. Glimpses of that night passed in my head—his strong arms, his tender hands, his soft lips. I tried to think past that, to a time when he had only been a friend, a good friend. Fighting the sudden tears that stung my eyes, I darted to the gate after him.

He was halfway to his car by the time I closed the gate behind me. "Kellan!" My voice sounded too high, too panicked. *Get a grip,* I thought angrily. *Say goodbye, let him go, and get your ass back to the bar to wait for Denny.* "Please, wait."

He slowed and looked over his shoulder at me. I couldn't quite tell from the distance, but his shoulders seem to slump in a sigh. "What are you doing, Kiera?" The question seemed full of double meaning.

I caught up with him and grabbed his arm to stop him and to turn him around toward me. "Wait, please stay."

He knocked my hand away, almost angrily, and ran his fingers through his thick hair. He looked up at the sky for a brief moment before locking his eyes to mine. "I can't do this anymore."

Expecting one of his flippant, suggestive remarks, the sudden seriousness in his voice caught me off guard and turned the knot in my stomach to ice. "Can't do what . . . stay? You know Denny would want to say goodbye to you." The words sounded feeble and wrong. This had nothing to do with Denny . . . or maybe everything.

He shook his head and looked over my shoulder before again returning his gaze to mine. "I can't stay here . . . in Seattle. I'm leaving."

The tears that threatened before were now there in force. Damn, what was wrong with my body? Isn't this exactly what I'd hoped he would do? I should be slapping him on the back and saying, "Great, have a good time." Things would be so much easier here with him gone, along with his coldness, his irritating comments, the never-ending line of women fawning over him, his insanely blue eyes following me everywhere, the intimate memories that sometimes popped into my head . . .

I grabbed his arm again. He stiffened, but didn't knock me away again. "No, please, don't leave! Stay . . . stay here with . . . with us. Just don't go. . . ." My voice broke at the end and I couldn't understand why I was saying these things to him. I meant to say goodbye. Why were the words coming out so wrong?

He looked at the tears coursing down my cheeks like he was trying to solve a problem he didn't understand. "I . . . why are you . . . ? You said . . ." He swallowed and stared over my shoulder, like he couldn't bear to watch anymore. "You don't . . . you and me aren't . . . I thought you . . ." He exhaled slowly, composing himself, and looked back to my eyes. "I'm sorry. I'm sorry I've been cold, but I can't stay, Kiera. I can't watch it anymore. I *need* to leave. . . ." His voice trailed off in a whisper.

I blinked in disbelief, still waiting to wake from this weird dream. Feeling at my silence that the odd conversation was over, he started to turn away from me. Gut-wrenching panic made my body react faster than my mind could follow.

"No!" I practically yelled at him and, gripping his arm even tighter than before, I pulled him closer to me. "Please, tell me this isn't because of me, because of you and me. . . ."

"Kiera . . ."

I brought my other hand to his chest and stepped closer to him. "No, don't leave because I was stupid. You had a good thing here before I . . ."

He backed up a half step, but left my hand on his chest. "It's not . . . it's not you. You didn't do anything wrong. You belong to Denny. I never should have . . ." He sighed sadly. "You . . . you and Denny are both . . ."

I stepped closer to him again and pressed myself against him, tears still lightly falling on my cheeks. "Both what?"

He froze and let out a shaky breath. Gazing at me intently he whispered, "You're both . . . important to me."

I leaned in, bringing my head closer to his as he looked down at me, breathing slowly through his parted lips. "Important . . . how?"

He lightly shook his head and retreated another half step. "Kiera . . . let me go. You don't want this . . ." he whispered. "Go back inside, go back to Denny." He moved his hand to pull me off his arm, but I smacked it away.

The word slipped out before I could stop it. "Stay."

"Please, Kiera, go," he whispered, his beautiful eyes suddenly glistening, his perfect face torn.

"Stay . . . please. Stay with me . . . don't leave *me*," I begged quietly, my voice breaking on the last word. I didn't know what I was saying. I just couldn't bear the thought of never seeing him again.

One single tear rolled down his cheek and the thing inside me broke completely. His pain, his suffering, awakened feelings in me for him that I had never felt before. I wanted to protect him, I wanted to heal him. I would give anything to take his pain away. The coldness, the irritation, the women, Denny, right and wrong—the pain in his eyes made everything else slip away.

Softly, he still pleaded, but with me or with himself? "Don't. I don't want . . ."

Thoughtless, I placed my free hand upon his cheek and wiped the tear away with my thumb. Instantly I knew it was a mistake. The touch was far too intimate. The heat of his skin seemed to radiate all the way up my arm, igniting my whole body. His breath stopped as our eyes locked, and I knew I needed to turn and run back to the bar as fast as I could. I also knew it was too late.

"Kiera, please . . . let me go," he whispered.

I ignored him and brought my other hand to the back of his neck. I pulled him to me until my lips brushed his. I couldn't bear to look at his face, to see what he was thinking—I didn't know what I was thinking—so I tightly closed my eyes and softly pressed against him again. His body stiffened, but his lips didn't resist me.

"Don't do this . . ." he whispered, almost too softly for me to hear. I still didn't know which one of us he was talking to. I pressed harder against his lips and he made a noise, almost as if in pain. "What are you doing, Kiera?" He whispered his question again, his body still rigid.

I paused with my lips barely brushing his. "I don't know . . . just don't leave me, please don't leave me," I whispered breathlessly, keeping my eyes firmly closed, not wanting to see his reaction to my begging.

He exhaled and whispered, "Kiera . . . please . . ." Then, finally, and with a shudder passing through his entire body, he roughly pressed his lips to mine, kissing me intensely.

He brought his arms firmly around my waist and clutched me tightly against him. His lips parted and his tongue brushed mine. I made a noise at the sensation, at the taste of him, and eagerly sought him again. Through the mental fog of feeling my lips move against his and my fingers locking into his thick hair, I was vaguely aware that we were moving. He was pulling me slowly forward. I didn't know where or why, and I didn't care, as long as he didn't stop touching me. I felt him bump against something solid and took the opportunity to press him back into it, pushing myself as close to him as physically possible. His breath quickened along with mine, and he groaned as he pulled me against him.

His hands slipped under my shirt to clutch at my lower back and I sighed as his skin caressed mine. One of his hands pulled away and reached behind him, to whatever he was pressed against. I heard a click and finally cracked my eyes open, to see where we were.

He was leaning against the closed door of the espresso stand that sat in the middle of the parking lot. Somewhere in my head I had known it was nearby; I just hadn't realized we were that close to it. The hand he had removed from my back was twisted around behind him, turning the doorknob. Miraculously, the door was unlocked and easily opened. The part of me that could still perform rational thought wondered what he would have done if the door had been locked, but the majority of my brain couldn't have cared less. I just wanted to be somewhere slightly more private than this wide-open parking lot.

He pushed back from the door so he could shove it open. Our lips stopped for a moment and I risked a glance into his eyes. My breath stopped at the passion I saw in them. I couldn't think. I couldn't move. All I could do was stare into those deep blue, blazing eyes. He brought one hand around to my back and then slid both of them down. Clutching my upper thighs, he effortlessly picked me up and we backed into the dark stand.

Gently, he released me and closed the door. We stood in the dark for a moment, my arms tight around his neck, one of his hands around my waist, the other lightly pressed against the closed door. It was quiet and our breathing seemed amplified in the stillness. Something about the darkness, the feel of my body pressed against his and the intensity of our breath, snapped my brain off, and the last portion that held any rational thought left me. All that remained was passion, no, *need* . . . intense, burning need.

He moved then. Slowly, gripping me very tightly, he sank us to our knees.

My hands flew to his jacket, hastily pulling it off before attacking his shirt and almost frantically tearing the fabric off his body. My eyes had adjusted well enough to the soft light coming in through the high windows that I could see his sculpted chest. His muscles were surprisingly hard, yet his skin was astonishingly soft. Perfect. I ran my fingers down that skin, grazing my fingertips over the deep lines, while his chest rose and fell with his heavy breath. I traced every defined crease of his abdomen, lingering on the long V at the bottom. He let out a deep groan and then sucked in a quick breath. I felt my body instantly respond, felt the ache for him building, and made a pleasant noise of my own when he brought his warm mouth to my neck. His lips trailed down my skin as he slipped off my jacket and unbuttoned my shirt. I was getting overwhelmed, almost impatient, I wanted him so much. I ripped my shirt off once he undid the last button, so I could feel our skin press together.

He exhaled heavily and, raking his eyes up and down my body in a way that made me shiver, he ran a palm down my neck, down my chest, and down to my waist; my skin burned pleasurably wherever he touched me. I moaned so loudly that, if I'd have had a conscious thought left, I'd have been really embarrassed about it. He exhaled again and ran his hand right back up my skin, pausing to cup my breast and tease the nipple through the light fabric of my bra. My breath was almost a pant and I arched against his hand. I couldn't take any more of this. I needed him, and now. I found his lips again; his breath was coming as quickly as mine.

Reaching out with one arm, he lowered us both to the floor. I didn't even care that it was filthy. The aroma of coffee assaulted me. It mixed with his enticing scent in such an appealing way that I knew I would forever combine the two. I lightly raked my fingers down his back and he made a deep noise in his throat that thrilled me.

I eagerly pushed his hips away from me so I could get to his jeans. He groaned with need and inhaled through his teeth as I unbuttoned and unzipped them. I pushed them down his hips and paused a moment to take in the sight of him. He was incredibly ready for me, hard and straining against his clothes, and the knowledge that my body did that to him made me ache. I was desperately ready as well. My fingers lightly traveled down the length of him and he gently pushed his hips into me as his forehead dropped to touch mine. I curled my hand around him, through his shorts, remembering what him being inside of me felt like, needing to feel it again. His lips attacked mine as his hands suddenly got very busy, scrunching up my loose skirt and roughly pulling down my underwear. I couldn't think. I wanted him so badly it hurt.

"Oh, God . . . please, Kellan . . ." I moaned in his ear.

He quickly adjusted his clothes and pushed himself into me before my addled brain could even process what had happened. I had to lightly bite his shoulder to keep from screaming out with the pleasure of it. He buried his head in my neck and paused to catch his breath. In my impatience, I raised my hips to his and he groaned, pushing hard against me. I wanted it harder. Surprisingly, I told him so, and he roughly, and eagerly, obliged.

"God, Kiera . . ." I heard a faint, "God . . . yes," and then he muttered something else incomprehensible into my neck. His words, his tone, and his hot breath across my skin sent a shock wave through my body and I gripped him even tighter.

Scorching heat raged through me and I shook from the intensity. It was familiar, but new. It was so much different than the first time—more intense, harder and rougher, yet inexplicably sweeter, all at the same time. He plunged hard and deep, and I eagerly met him with each thrust, neither one of us caring about prolonging this— just needing to satisfy the ache that was building second by second. As every sensation in my body started rising, as I could feel the end of the crest approaching, I lost control of what very little control I had left. I couldn't hold back the sounds my body demanded I make, and it pleased me greatly that he had given up as well, his groans and cries matching my own.

In the final moment of pure ecstasy, when I could feel my body clenching around the length of him deep inside of me, my fingers once again raked down his back . . . but this time hard—very, very hard. I felt the wetness of his blood as I cut through skin, and he gasped in . . . pain? Pleasure? It only intensified the moment for me, and I let out a long cry as I rode out the warm sensation expanding deep within my core. He answered with a deep moan of his own, and clutched my thigh so hard I knew I would bruise as he drove into me a final few times with his own release.

In the very next moment, that very instant that all of the passion leached from my body, my rational brain woke up. With an icy blast that made my whole body shiver, I realized in horror what we had just done. What I had just done. I closed my eyes. It was a dream, just an intense dream. Any second, I'd wake up. Only . . . it wasn't. I brought shaking hands to my mouth and tried in vain to choke back the sobs that were now unstoppable.

Kellan looked away from me. Pulling back slightly, he fixed his jeans before sitting back on his heels. Staring at the floor, he grabbed his shirt and limply held it in his hands while his whole body shook from the cold.

My stomach clenched and I feared I might vomit as I struggled to fix my skirt and slip my underwear back up. I found my blouse and managed to slip the shirt back on, redoing the buttons with one hand while clutching my mouth closed with the other. I was afraid that if I let go, I would lose the battle with my stomach. My whole body shook with racking sobs. Other then lightly shaking, Kellan never moved, never looked up from the floor, made no attempt to help me in any way.

My mind couldn't process anything. I couldn't understand what had happened, how my body had so vehemently betrayed my mind. Why would I let him touch me that way? Why would I so eagerly touch him, want him, beg him? And, God . . . Denny . . . I couldn't even finish that thought.

Sniffling, I muttered, "Kellan . . . ?"

He looked up. Glistening, his eyes met mine, the passion that had flared in them such a short while ago now completely extinguished. "I tried to do the right thing. Why couldn't you just let me leave?" he roughly whispered.

His question fractured my heart into a thousand pieces, and the sobbing started yet again. Shaking, I grabbed my jacket from the floor, stood up, and moved toward the closed door. Kellan looked back down to the floor and made no move to stop me. I quietly opened the door and took one last look at him, still kneeling with his shirt in his hands. I suddenly noticed the thin, bright red streaks down his back, ending with fine trails of dripping blood. I gasped and made a move toward him.

"Don't," he murmured, never moving his head. "Just go. Denny has probably noticed your absence by now." His tone was flat and very cold.

In tears, I threw open the door and ran into the cool night air.

Chapter 10
Hot and Hotter

There were three things that I noticed when my mind slowly started coming to life again in the morning. The first was that my body was sore. Apparently the previous night was rougher than I had remembered. Oh, God . . . had I actually asked him to be rough with me? What the hell was that about? Unwillingly, thoughts of Kellan's hands and lips flooded my brain. I swallowed hard and forcibly changed the direction of my thoughts.

The second thing I noticed was that my stomach still felt as if I might lose whatever was left sloshing around in there. My eyes were finally dry though, I thought in relief. Convincing Denny that I went to the parking lot because I was feeling ill and I didn't want to lose my dinner in front of a crowd had been easier than I ever thought it could be.

He hadn't hesitated, never even doubted my story, just sweetly helped me into his car and took me straight home. I hadn't been able to keep from stealing a painful peek at the espresso stand as we drove by it. I couldn't help but wonder if Kellan was still in there, kneeling on the floor, waiting for the blood on his back to dry. I'd had to put a hand to my stomach then, and push down hard to stop it from rising. Denny had glanced at me, worried, and then quickly sped off. He had only asked briefly about Kellan. I told him I'd left him at the table and didn't know where he had run off to. Surprisingly, my voice had stayed even. Rough, but even. He had taken no notice of my tone. Either that, or he had brushed it off as not feeling well.

Once home, he had gently helped me change clothes and then laid me in bed. I hadn't been able to take his sweetness, the adoring way he had looked at me. I had wanted him to yell, to be cruel. I deserved that, and so much more. The tears had started anew then, so I rolled over on my side, away from him, and feigned sleep. He had lovingly kissed my shoulder before joining me in bed, and I spent the next several hours crying softly into my pillow.

I had assumed upon first waking that Kellan had gone straight from the bar to wherever he was headed. Obviously he wouldn't ever want to see me again, or ever face Denny again. Not after what he, what we, had done. Our first time had been a drunken mistake while Denny and I had been on a break, albeit a short one. This time was different. This was a clear betrayal.

This brought me startlingly to my third observation. I could hear the sounds of Denny and Kellan talking, even laughing, downstairs. I sat bolt upright in bed and listened harder. No screaming or yelling. No anger of any kind. Was he seriously having a casual Sunday morning conversation with the best friend he had just stabbed in the back?

I stood quickly and ran to the bathroom. I looked like death. My eyes were worn and bloodshot, my hair a mess of tangles. I ran a brush through my thick locks, splashed cool water on my face, and sloppily brushed my teeth. Not great, but better, and I was pretending to have just been sick, after all. I took a quick peek at my thigh, and damn if there wasn't a bruise there. I bit my lip, and my stomach churned again at the sight. Hastily adjusting my clothes, I decided to just leave my pajamas on. It wasn't unusual for me to lounge about in my sleep pants anyway, and really, I was just too morbidly curious to wait any longer.

I flew down the stairs and then nearly fell as I suddenly stopped myself at the last step. With a purposely deep inhale, I struggled to slow my too-fast lungs and surging heartbeat. Maybe Kellan was here because last night was just some horrible dream that never actually happened? If my body hadn't been bruised and delightfully sore, and if that realization hadn't turned my stomach sour, I might have believed it.

Slowly, I made my way to the kitchen and crept around the corner. Yep, there had to be some way last night was just a dream. Either that or I was dreaming now.

Denny was leaning against the counter, calmly drinking a mug of tea. He smiled over at me when he noticed my quiet entrance. "Good morning, sleepy. Feeling any better?" His charming accent was luxuriously rich this morning, but nothing inside me enjoyed it, for someone else was staring at me too.

Kellan was casually sitting at the kitchen table, one hand idly stroking his full cup of coffee, the other resting calmly in his lap. His eyes must have been in my direction since before I even entered the room, for they were instantly locked onto mine. They were a perfect tranquil blue this morning, calm and untroubled, but still oddly cold. One side of his mouth curled upwards in a slight smile that did nothing to warm his eyes.

Finally remembering that Denny had asked me a question, I quickly looked over at him and said, "Yes, much better." I sat in a chair opposite Kellan and his eyes followed me the entire way. What on earth was he thinking? Was he trying to be obvious? Did he want Denny to know? I sneaked a quick peek at Denny. He was still leaning against the counter, drinking his tea and watching the news playing on the TV in the living room. He had been awake for a while; he was showered and dressed for the day, his worn jeans hugging him perfectly, his simple gray shirt showing off every muscle. He really was quite beautiful, I thought sadly.

I sighed guiltily and looked away. Unfortunately, I had somehow forgotten that Kellan was still sitting across from me, staring, and I looked over at him. I couldn't pull away from his gaze this time. His eyes narrowed as they studied mine, his smile gone. He looked the same as last night. The exact same, I realized with a small shock. He hadn't changed clothes. He still wore his white shirt, the long sleeves pushed up to just below the elbows. He still had on the same faded blue jeans. Even his tousled hair was styled in exactly the same way it had been when my fingers had been knotted in it. He looked like he had just gotten home. I wanted to scream at him, ask him why the hell he was still here! Why was he staring holes into me with Denny standing just a few feet away?

Kellan finally looked away from me, just a half-second before Denny turned to me. I hadn't been quick enough and Denny caught me staring at Kellan, in what I had to believe looked like anger. Kellan's small smile came back just as I turned to look at Denny. Stupid, irritating smile.

"Do you want me to make you anything to eat?" Denny asked, watching to see if any signs of sickness were still with me.

"No, that's all right. I'm really not feeling up to food yet." I did still feel nauseous, just not for the reasons he imagined.

"Coffee?" He pointed to the nearly full pot next to him.

The smell hit me then, and I thought I might lose the precious control on my stomach right there. I would never be able to think of coffee the same way again, much less drink it. "No," I whispered, my face pale.

Denny didn't notice my pallor. He set down his empty mug and, straightening, walked over to me. "All right." He leaned down to kiss my forehead, and I thought I saw Kellan twitch from the corner of my eye. "Let me know when you do get hungry. I'll make you whatever you want." Denny smiled and walked by me into the living room. Lying back causally on the couch, he flipped the station over to the sports channel.

I held my breath. I wanted to go join Denny on the couch, to snuggle up in his arms and doze off while he watched TV. It sounded so warm and inviting, so comforting. But guilt kept me seated in my chair. I didn't deserve him, his warmth and caring. I deserved the cold hardness of the kitchen chair. I roughly swallowed and looked down at the table, glad that I had no more tears to spill.

Kellan softly cleared his throat. I startled. In my wallowing, I had forgotten that he was there. He briefly looked over at Denny on the couch, then met my eyes. I thought I saw a moment of pain cross his face, but it was gone before I could be sure. Not wanting to, but not being able to stop myself, I thought about last night again. I thought about the last time I had seen him, his back torn and bloody from my fingers. My eyes flicked to his shirt. I couldn't see much from this angle, but his shirt was clean as far as I could tell . . . no bloodstains anyway.

He smiled crookedly at me, his eyes warming for the first time, and I got the distinct impression he knew exactly what I was looking for. I blushed and tried to turn my head away from him, without turning it in Denny's direction.

"A little late for modesty, don't you think?" he whispered to me, still smiling that wholly irritating and fabulous half-smile.

My eyes snapped back to his, shocked again. Were we seriously going to have this conversation here? Now? I tried to gauge whether his voice had been loud enough to carry into the next room and be heard over the TV. It didn't seem possible that it had.

"Have you lost your freaking mind?" I tried to match his volume, but irritation was winning over every other emotion in my head, and the words seemed much too loud to me. "What are you doing here?" I managed much more quietly.

He cocked his head adorably to the side. "I live here . . . remember?"

I could have slapped him. I really wanted to, but the thought of inviting Denny's curiosity, and most likely his disapproval, stayed my hand. Instead, I locked my fingers together, halting the temptation. "No, you were leaving . . . remember? Big, brooding, dramatic exit . . . ringing any bells?" My irritation was apparently bringing sarcasm right along with it.

He laughed once, quietly. "Things changed. I was *very* compellingly asked to stay." He smiled wickedly and bit his lip.

My breathing stopped and I briefly closed my eyes to block out his perfect face. "No. No, there are no reasons for you to be here." I opened my eyes to find him still smiling seductively at me. He must have snapped last night; that was the only explanation for the sudden change in his behavior. I risked a glance at Denny, but he was still blissfully watching sports.

When I looked back, Kellan stopped smiling and leaned toward me intently. "I was wrong before. Maybe you do want this. It's worth it to me to stay and find out." He was whispering, but I felt like he had just shouted the words across the room.

"No!" I sputtered, for a second having no idea what else to say. Composing myself, I added, "You were right. I want Denny. I choose Denny." I pleaded with him quietly, not even daring a glance at the living room, in case Denny had heard his name being mentioned.

He smiled slightly and reached out to touch my cheek. Instinctively, I wanted to pull away, to finally reach over and slap him, but I couldn't make my body listen. Why did my body never listen to me anymore? Stupid, defiant body. Kellan's fingertips traced a line from my jaw to my lips. Instantly at his touch, I felt the fire of remembered passion shoot through me. My lips parted as his fingers glided over them, and I half closed my eyes with the pleasure of it, but I snapped them back open at the sound of his small chuckle.

"We'll see," he said casually, pulling his hand back to his lap and leaning back in his chair with a smug, triumphant look on his face. Stupid, stupid, defiant body.

"And him?" I jerked my head in Denny's direction.

His smile dropped and his eyes lowered to the table. His voice came out pained but steady. "I had a lot of time to think last night." He looked back up into my eyes. "I won't hurt him unnecessarily. I won't tell him, if you don't want me to."

"No, I don't want him to know," I whispered, glad once again that I had no tears left. "What do you mean . . . unnecessarily? What do you think we are now?"

His smile came back and he reached across the table to hold my hand. I flinched back, but he grabbed it securely and stroked my fingers. "Well . . . right now, we are friends." He eyed me up and down in a way that made me blush. "Good friends."

I gaped at him, not sure how to respond to that—then my anger flared. "You said we weren't friends. Just roommates, remember?" I couldn't quite keep the venom from my tone.

He cocked his head to the side in a distractingly attractive way. "You changed my mind. You can be very . . . persuasive." He dropped his voice seductively. "Would you like to persuade me again some-time?"

Abruptly I stood, the chair squeaking noisily against the floor as I did. Kellan calmly released my hand and watched me, while Denny called in from the living room, "You okay?"

"Yes," I called back, feeling more than a little stupid. "Just going upstairs to take a shower. I have to get ready for work . . . for Emily's shift." I had the sudden urge to wash every bit of Kellan off of me. I glanced over at Denny. He had already turned back to the TV, com-pletely oblivious to the mood in the kitchen.

"Would you like me to join you? We could continue our . . . con-versation," Kellan whispered, grinning devilishly as my heartbeat irritatingly quickened. I gave him one last glare, then strode stub-bornly from the room.

I mulled over the problem that was Kellan while I took an ob-scenely long time getting ready for my shift. What had I done? What on earth was I thinking? I should have let him leave . . . why couldn't I? Why had I been incapable of letting him slip into his car and why did I let him slip into . . .

I sighed. I really didn't want to think about *that* right now. My stomach hurt enough.

He had just said the oddest thing in the kitchen too. What was it . . . ? *"Maybe you do want this?"* This? What did he think we were . . . besides a disastrous mistake? Well, apparently we were friends now, according to him. It irritated me a little that *that* was what it took for Kellan to consider me a friend. In my head, we had been friends the entire time. And now we were *good* friends? And he might not have said it, but I sure heard it, like he had shouted it from the rooftops— good friends . . . with benefits. *Well, sorry,* I thought, as I harshly brushed my hair and threw it up in a ponytail, *we are not* that *kind of friends. Well, not again anyway.*

Denny gave me a ride to work, but was called by Max just as he was parking his car to come inside with me. Shaking his head irritably, he sighed and told me he had to go in for a few hours, but he would pick me up after my shift. I nodded and said that was fine. What I had done to him had pretty much evaporated any resentment I might have had at Max for taking away his time. What I had done to him was so much worse. I still felt ill. I clutched my stomach as I watched his taillights pull out of the parking lot. A part of me was relieved to see the lights fade away; I needed to struggle through my guilt alone.

And at Pete's on a day shift, I was pretty much alone. Not physically, of course—the place had a fairly brisk lunch crowd, but I didn't know any of these people. If Pete's was a large family, then the day shift and the night shift were distant cousins. Yeah, we saw each other on holidays, but we really didn't hang out much.

The bartender on shift was an attractive man who nodded politely at me as I entered the bar. I believed his name was . . . Troy . . . but I wasn't sure enough to call him that. No need to look like an idiot by calling someone the wrong name. "Hey" would work for now. The two other waitresses on staff were older, and had apparently been here since the beginning of time. Both had gray, fuzzy hair and called everybody "hun" or "sweetie," so I decided they wouldn't be offended if I called them that. They were really nice, though, and I felt comfortable pretty quickly.

The crowd that came in was different too. The night crowd was mostly drinkers. These people were mostly . . . eaters. I popped my head into the kitchen more times that one afternoon than I had in my entire time at Pete's. The evening kitchen was run by a shy guy named Scott. He was tall and lanky and oddly thin for a cook, but, man, could he cook! Pete's put out some of the best bar food in the area. The reason for Scott's talent in the kitchen ran the kitchen during the day—his dad, Sal. Sal was equally tall and equally thin, and was an equally (if maybe not a little better) amazing cook. He was a funny guy though, and always had a joke and a wink whenever I came in with an order.

Things were running smoothly, and I was enjoying my shift with my extended family, when I could have sworn I felt the molecules in the air thicken. I knew before I saw. I knew the very second Kellan Kyle walked into the bar.

He came up right behind me, and I didn't turn to help him. He could sit and wait like everyone else . . . preferably not in my section. He didn't though. He just continued to stand behind me as I waited at the bar for some sodas. I noticed that Troy was eyeing him with a half-smile, and that irritated me a little. Was everyone attracted to this man? Eventually, I felt a hand curl around my upper thigh . . . around my bruised upper thigh. I stiffened and turned to face him. I had planned on slapping him, but seeing him made me catch my breath and quickened my heart, and I dropped my hand.

He was freshly showered, his hair wild and messy, but still damp around the edges. He had on midnight black jeans that sharpened the contrasting redness of his perfectly tight T-shirt, a shirt that teasingly showcased every curved layer of his broad shoulders and emphasized amazing pecs that any male model would kill for. But it wasn't his smoking body that held my attention. It was the eyes. They practically . . . simmered . . . as he held my thigh. A crooked grin was fixed on his lips as he studied me.

I hastily brushed his hand from my leg, hoping that the loss of contact would calm my wildly beating heart. That might have worked, except he snatched my fingers instead. From the corner of my eye, I could see Troy watching us curiously. Well, Troy watched Kellan curiously.

"What are you doing here?" I said in a low voice, trying to separate my fingers from his.

"I was hungry. I heard the food is good here, and the staff is . . . accommodating." His grin widened as he managed to interlace our fingers together.

I gaped at his comment. "Accomm—" I couldn't even finish the word as I started blushing and stammering. He laughed once and then tucked a strand of hair that had fallen from my ponytail behind my ear. I actually closed my eyes it felt so nice, but then I immediately sprang them open and yanked my hand from his. "Then go sit down! Your waitress will be with you shortly."

He smiled and shrugged. "All right." He flicked a glance up at Troy, nodded politely at him with a small smile on his lips, and then sauntered back to his regular table. God, was there anyone the man would *not* flirt with?

I avoided it as long as I could. I helped everyone else in the bar, as Kellan watched me with a smug smile on his face, arms crossed over his chest. He was enjoying my reluctance to be near him entirely too much. More to get him out of the bar than to actually help him, or as he put it, to "accommodate him," I finally approached his table.

"What can I do for you?"

He raised an eyebrow at that and I blushed fiercely. Focusing my mind on the pad of paper in my hands, I tried to block out the intimate thought he had just successfully put in my head. Ugh, why did my brain go to such a dirty place when he was around? Why was his in such a dirty place all the time?

"I'll take a burger . . . fries . . . beer . . ." He let the tail end of that sentence trail off, like there was more to it, and I'm sure I blushed even deeper.

"Great. I'll get that started for you," I whispered.

I turned to make my hasty exit when he stopped me. "Kiera?" Reluctantly, I turned back to him. "Do you have any aspirin here?" He cringed and brought a hand to his shoulder blade. "My back is really killing me." He grinned wickedly at the end of that, and my heart stuttered.

The image of me digging my nails deep in his flesh leapt into my head so vividly that I thought I might lose the ability to keep standing. I gasped and did the girly hand-over-the-mouth thing, then turned and fled without answering him. Embarrassment flashed through me, followed by guilt, followed by . . . desire? I hurried to get his order placed, praying he would leave soon.

Finally, and after an agonizingly long lunch that would have rivaled any seven-course meal, both in length and in personal attention—not only did Hun bring him a glass of water and Sweetie refill it, since it was clear I wasn't going anywhere near his table again, but Troy personally brought him another beer, a small, shy smile on his lips as he handed it to him and a charmingly crooked grin on Kellan's as he accepted it—he stood to leave the bar. All of it made me roll my eyes. If anyone needed *less* personal attention, it was Kellan.

Coming over to me, he silently slipped a bill in my pocket. I hadn't even gone over to bring him his check. Honestly, he could probably have started a tab and had Pete send him a monthly statement, he was here so darn much. He only smiled as he paid me and then turned to leave the bar, which I swear made Troy sigh. I grabbed the bill from my pocket and started walking around the bar to the register, sighing with relief that he'd finally left, when I noticed the bill he had given me. A fifty.

A fifty? Really? Instantly irritated, I stormed out of the bar.

The harsh crunch of my footsteps on the pavement matched my annoyed mood, and courage shot through me with each step. I strode right over to where he had his hand on the handle of his black, impossibly sexy Chevelle. He either heard my approach or was expecting it, and he turned to look at me, a small smile touching the corners of his lips. That smile slipped when he noticed my expression—which was most definitely not a smile. He straightened and waited with an odd look in his eyes.

I stopped nearly toe to toe with him. "What is this?" I held up the offending bill.

The small smile reappeared on his lips. "Well, ummm . . . it's a fifty-dollar bill. You exchange it for goods and/or services."

I took a deep, calming breath. Smart-ass. How many times would I feel like slapping this man today? "I know that," I said through clenched teeth. "What is it for?"

He cocked his head and smiled fully. "It's for you . . . and my bill. Obviously."

I took another deep breath. "Why? I barely waited on you. I didn't even bring you your food." I had let Hun take care of that, faking an emergent need to use the bathroom.

He frowned slightly, leaning against his car and crossing his arms over his chest. "Sometimes a tip is just a tip, Kiera."

Yeah, right. Not with him . . . not today, not after last night. Ignoring how attractive he looked, I snapped at him, "What is it for?"

His voice oddly serious, but his face casually smiling, he said, "For everything you've done for me."

I immediately threw it back at him and stormed into the bar. He might have said it with a sweet smile on his face, but I felt the insult behind it. And it hurt that he felt the need to . . . compensate me.

Denny picked me up after work and told me about his vital assignment that couldn't wait until Monday. It involved flowers and an impossibly difficult-to-reserve restaurant for some girl that Max was currently attempting to win over. Denny looked as happy about that as I did. I faked a smile for him though, and reassured him that at least his day was over. Guilt mixed with tension as I realized that my horrid day would only continue. We were headed straight back to where Kellan was.

But he wasn't home when we got there. When he still wasn't home when it was time to get ready for bed, I started getting irritated. Was he out with the guys, or out with a girl? I pushed the irritation aside. Did it matter? It was when I was about to wash my face, and hopefully wash away my stress, when I found the paper hiding behind my cleanser. It was a note in Kellan's neat handwriting that simply read, "I meant no offense," and a twenty-dollar bill was tucked inside it.

Wow . . . a pseudo-apology. That was new.

The next morning, I was a little more rational about the tip incident. In fact, I felt sort of stupid for how I had overreacted. Maybe he had just meant to be nice with a large tip, and it was in no way a reference to our night together. It was so hard to tell with him sometimes, especially with how mean he had been after our first time sleeping together. Ugh, I hated that I now had a first time and a second time to reference. At least there would be no third. Nope, no trifecta here.

I went downstairs cautiously, wondering which Kellan I would see today. He was, as usual, already drinking his coffee at the table, smiling casually and watching me silently as I entered. I was glad for his silence, happy that he wasn't going to mention the incident yesterday either. However, he watched me in a way that made me feel completely naked. It was unnerving. It was exciting. It made me feel guilty.

He took a long drink of his coffee and I couldn't help but think of the espresso stand. My cheeks flushed and he smiled devilishly, like he knew exactly what I was thinking of. He set down his mug and calmly walked over behind me. Brushing the hair seductively off of my neck, from one shoulder all the way around to the other, he swiftly kissed the back of my neck.

"Mornin'," he whispered, directly in my ear. I shivered. Ugh, why did his touch have to do that to me? He slipped his arms around my waist and held me close to him.

"Stop it, Kellan," I whispered as I twisted sideways and gently pushed him back.

He laughed softly. "Stop what, Kiera? We used to do this all the time when Denny was gone . . . remember?" He pulled me tight again.

I sighed and pushed him back more firmly, trying to ignore how nice his arms felt around me. "Things are different now."

He pulled me tight, yet again, and breathed heavily in my ear as he whispered, "Yes . . . things are very different."

I pushed him away with weak-feeling arms. Irritation sparked in me. "You are so . . . moody. I can't keep up with you." My glare softened as I wondered if I had just incited his anger.

He only grinned crookedly at me, though. "I'm an artist . . . not moody."

"Well, then you're a moody artist. . . ." I finished my thought by muttering under my breath, "You're practically a girl."

He heard me. He abruptly turned me to face him, backed me against the counter, and pressed himself into me. I gasped as one of his hands clutched my poor bruised thigh and hitched it around his hip. His other hand ran up my back and pulled me flush against him. He breathed huskily in my ear again, "I assure you . . . I am not." His lips trailed down to my neck as I shivered again. Damn . . . no, definitely not a girl.

"Please . . . stop . . ." I managed to whisper, as I attempted another feeble try at pushing him away.

He kissed me one last time, deeply on my neck, and I worried for a second that he would leave a mark, but then he pulled away and sighed. "All right . . . but only because you begged." His voice was so smooth it was practically a purr. "I love it when you do that," he whispered, then left the room, laughing to himself.

I was luxuriating in the shower after that little encounter, trying to organize my thoughts and my emotions. The feel of Kellan pressed against me wouldn't leave my head . . . or my body, for that matter. Kissing Denny goodbye for work a few minutes ago had done horrible things to my heart. My guilt wasn't leaving me, and Kellan definitely wasn't helping with that. I sighed and tilted my head back in the water. He was so odd. The first time we'd had sex he had turned stone cold, and now he was red-hot. God, what *would* happen if we did it . . . ? No, I wasn't even going to think about that. Whatever was going on between us, *that* part of it was most definitely over! I would not betray Denny . . . again.

I was feeling a little better about the situation, when the largest spider known to mankind dropped right in front of my face. Now, I'd like to think that I am pretty practical about the rodent, insect, and arachnid world. I completely understand that they serve a purpose and that there is a place for them in the circle of life. But one dropping right in my face with, I swear to God, three-inch-long legs, brought out the girliest reaction possible—I screamed. And not just any scream, no; I screamed bloody murder.

I hopped out of the shower and immediately began doing the

icky dance. You know, the "Oh my God, I know there are about six more of those things on my body" dance. It was at that moment that Kellan burst through the bathroom door. How in the name of all that is holy did I not lock it? I froze when I saw him. He froze when he saw me . . . buck-naked.

I blushed red *everywhere* as I grabbed the closest towel I could find.

"Are you okay?" He looked around the room like there should be an axe murderer and about a gallon of blood, what with all the screaming I had done.

"Spider," I said, mortified. Could I please redo this day?

His eyes came back to me and he barely held in a laugh. He had to bite his lip and the smile that broke around it was disastrously sexy. "A spider?" he managed to say, almost evenly. "You're not . . . dying?"

I frowned as his eyes lost their smirk and trailed down my barely covered, dripping-wet body. "I think I should inspect you more thoroughly, just to make sure none are . . . on you." He took a couple steps toward me and the small bathroom suddenly felt claustrophobic.

I felt overheated and a bit faint. I beat him on the shoulder and pushed him toward the door. "No . . . get out!"

"All right." He tilted his head to the side as he turned to leave. "I'll be in my room, if you change your mind." A wicked grin and then, "Or if there are any more spiders."

As he left, I slammed the door shut and securely locked it. Okay, make that red-, red-hot. I needed to do something about this . . . but I had no idea what.

He was very sneaky about flirting with me, always finding moments when Denny was out of the room or had his back to us. The first time he had kissed my neck with Denny *in* the room, I had gasped in surprise. He had laughed once and quickly moved away as Denny looked over at me quizzically. I muttered something stupid about seeing a spider and glared over at Kellan, who laughed and raised his eyebrows at the mention of another spider. My neck burned pleasantly where he had kissed it.

More and more, I enjoyed the solitude of school. It was my only Denny- and Kellan-free zone. For a few hours, I could think about something other than the mass of confusion that was my home life. Of course, a few days later, during a psychology lecture on Sigmund Freud's views about sexual repression, the thoughts had come anyway.

I didn't know what to do. On the one hand, I had a beautiful, loving boyfriend whom I adored, whom I had moved across the country for, but, his abandoning me for a job had scarred me. I didn't like to think about it. It hadn't really been his fault that I had reacted so poorly, and he *had* changed his mind and come back to me almost instantly, and at great personal expense . . . just not quick enough. During his brief absence, Kellan had slipped in, and now he was kind of stuck there.

I sighed. I really didn't know how to feel about that. Well, besides tremendously guilty anyway. I had been warned so often about Kellan. I knew what he was like and I fell for it anyway . . . twice. I hated how weak I felt around him and how much power he had, when I had none. It was so irritating.

Of course, he had become bolder in the last few days. His touches had become much more intimate. His fingers always managed to find the scant half inch of skin that showed between my shirt and jeans when he passed me in the hall. He stroked my cheek as I opened the fridge door. His lips brushed my bare shoulder while I cooked dinner. He nibbled at my ear when Denny went outside to check the mail. He came up behind me at work and rested his hand on my backside when no one was looking.

Ugh, he was driving me crazy, and I hated every second of it. Didn't I?

I looked up. The lecture that had caused my mind to drift was over, and I really hadn't heard a word of it. I hadn't even noticed that students had started to file out and now the room was half empty. Stupid Kellan and his amazingly wonderful, stupid fingers.

Now I was going to have to go see that stupid man at the stupid bar, since my shift was starting in a couple hours. Of course he would be there, drinking with his bandmates. They had rehearsal nearly every day and almost always came into the bar either before or afterwards. And of course Kellan would not miss an opportunity to torment me while Denny was absent. He was always careful to not let anyone else witness his seduction, but I got the feeling it was easier for him when he didn't have to look Denny in the eye.

I walked into the light rain and headed for the bus stop. I was not looking forward to having to wait for the bus in this. It wasn't raining heavily, but eventually, I would get soaked. The people here didn't seem to mind getting wet. No one even bothered with an umbrella unless the rain was sheeting. Personally, I'd rather be dry, but it hadn't been raining when I left and I really didn't like walking around with an umbrella, looking like an idiot waiting for it to rain.

I decided to take the bus straight to the bar. I'd rather be early than sit around our house alone with Kellan. With Denny still at work, who knew what he would try to do with me? Not that I would let him. I'm pretty sure I wouldn't let him . . . Anyway, I could work on my Lit paper in the back room.

As I was walking, I heard someone directly behind me gasp, "Oh my God, check out that guy—he's gorgeous." Instinctively turning to look, I caught my breath. Kellan was here? Why was Kellan here? Standing outside his car, he was already partially wet, and, like the rest of the locals, he didn't seem to care. He smiled his sexy half-smile when I noticed him. I rolled my eyes and didn't even bother looking at who had made the statement. I was pretty sure it was just some random girl, drooling over his . . . perfection.

I really didn't want to get wet waiting for the bus, so I grudgingly walked over to Kellan. The rain was dampening his tousled hair and droplets were dripping onto his face. He wore his black leather jacket and leaned back against his car with his arms folded across his chest. Whoever the drooler was, she was right—he was gorgeous.

"I thought you might want a ride." He practically purred the words.

"Sure, thanks. I'm going to Pete's." I hoped I was coming off as nonchalant as I wanted to be. My heart was already racing at the idea of being in an enclosed space alone with him, but being dry was too tempting.

He smiled, like he had somehow known my answer already. He slipped behind the wheel after first opening my door with a dramatic swoosh of his arm. I was tense as we pulled away from the school, waiting for him to do . . . something. I had no idea what he would do in a situation like this, and my mind was jumbled with different possibilities. Would he pin me down on the seat and try to . . . I looked behind me at the backseat. It suddenly looked shockingly big and quite comfortable. I instantly realized that Kellan's car was his "bed away from bed" as it were. The thought made my face flush and my breath hitch.

He looked over at me and laughed a little. "You okay?"

"Yep," I lied, completely unconvincingly.

"Good." We stopped at a red light, and he looked over at me with sparkling, playful eyes while he ran a hand through his delightfully damp hair.

I realized I had started breathing a little heavily watching him. *Oh, for Pete's sake*, I thought angrily. He hadn't even touched me yet. The anticipation was starting to get to me. I wished he would just get it over with. Wait a minute . . . no. Familiar irritation flared. I didn't want him to touch me . . . right?

We started moving again, but I was staring out the window, lost in my confusion, and barely noticed. I loved Denny, so why would I ache for Kellan to touch me? That made no sense. But I couldn't ponder it any longer. Kellan had decided at long last to touch me. He simply put his hand on my knee and slid it up my inner thigh. It was enough. I closed my eyes, his touch burning through my body. I kept my eyes closed the entire way there.

We arrived at the bar all too quickly and yet . . . not quickly enough. Kellan parked the car without moving his hand from my thigh. I could feel him watching me, but I still kept my eyes closed. He slid over the seat to press against me. The heat of him, the smell of the rain on him, made my breath quicken. He shifted his hand all the way up my thigh. I gasped, my mouth dropping open in a heavy breath. I suddenly wanted much more . . . and I hated it. He ran his cheek along my jaw and I struggled to keep my head straight, to not turn into him. He kissed the corner of my jaw, then lightly trailed his tongue up to my ear while I started to tremble. He nibbled on my ear for a second before finally breathing, "Ready?"

Panic made my eyes flash open. I glanced over at him with my eyes only, my breath embarrassingly fast now. He was smiling so seductively at me that I couldn't help but turn my face to his. Inches apart now, I felt his hand run up my thigh and across my hip. Then I heard a faint click, and my seat belt gave way.

He pulled away from me and started laughing. Instantly irritated, I shoved open the door and slammed it behind me. When I looked back at his sleek-with-rain car, I could see him through the window, watching me storm off to the bar in open delight. I actually thanked the rain now, as it cooled my heated skin on the way to the double doors. Damn, he was good.

The next morning, I cornered Kellan in the kitchen as he was pouring his coffee.

"Morn—"

I immediately cut off his adorable greeting, still irritated about the car ride yesterday. "You"—I put a finger on his chest, which made him smile charmingly as he put the coffeepot back—"need to back off!"

He grabbed my hand and pulled me into an embrace. "I haven't done anything to you . . . recently," he said innocently.

I tried to push away from his embrace but he held me tight. "Uhhh . . . this?" I tried to indicate his arms around me, but couldn't move very well.

He laughed and kissed my jaw. "We do this all the time. Sometimes we do more. . . ."

Irritated, I pulled back and spat out in a horribly flustered tone, "The car?"

He laughed harder. "That was all you. You were getting all . . . excited on me, just sitting there." He squatted slightly to look me in the eye. "Was I supposed to just ignore that?" I blushed furiously; he was right. I sighed noisily and looked away from him.

He laughed softly at my reaction. "Hmmm . . . do you want me to stop?" While he spoke he ran his fingers from my hair to my cheek, down my neck, between my breasts, and down my waist to rest at my jeans. He grabbed the edge and pulled my hips toward him a little.

Instantly and annoyingly, my body reacted—my breathing increased, my heartbeat spiked and I closed my eyes, willing myself to not turn toward his lips. "Yes," I said breathlessly, wondering if I was answering his question correctly.

"You don't seem so sure—do I make you uncomfortable?" His voice was husky and enticing, and I kept my eyes closed so I wouldn't have to see his expression. His fingers were now lightly tracing my waistband, one finger on the inside, barely brushing against my skin.

"Yes." My head was spinning—what did he ask me?

He leaned over to whisper in my ear, "Do you want me inside you again?"

"Yes . . ." I blurted out my answer before the question had even registered in my head. His fingers stopped moving. My eyes snapped open at my mistake and locked onto his surprised face. "No! I meant no!" He half-smiled and looked like he was going to break out laughing at any second as he tried to keep his face composed.

Anger burned through me. *Great, now I've led him on even more and managed to make myself look like an idiot, all at the same time.* "I meant no, Kellan."

He did let one laugh escape. "Yes, I know—I know exactly what you meant."

I roughly pushed him away and went back upstairs. That had not gone well at all.

That afternoon, I had a few hours to kill after school before Denny came home from work. I was desperately tired. I hadn't been sleeping well. Denny and Kellan and guilt and passion—all of it kept spinning through my head, making sleep nearly impossible. If something didn't change soon, I was going to implode from the stress.

I was sitting in the middle of the couch staring blankly at the television, lost in deep thought, when I felt the cushion beside me compress. Knowing who it was, I instinctively tried to stand without even looking his way. He grabbed my arm and pulled me back down. I looked over at a very amused Kellan. He grinned widely at my reluctance to sit next to him. I was too tired for this right now....

Irritated at his grin, I stubbornly stayed put on the couch, crossing my arms over my chest. He softened his smile while he gazed at me, and I looked away. Feeling his arm wrap around my shoulders, I stiffened but refused to pull away. I didn't want to amuse him anymore today. This morning's embarrassment was still fresh in my head. Gently, he started pulling me down to his lap.

Shocked and angry at his crude innuendo, I jerked away and glared icily at him. He startled in surprise, furrowing his brow before relaxing and laughing at my reaction. He pointed to his lap. "Lie down—you look tired." He raised an eyebrow at me and smiled suggestively. "But if you wanted to, I wouldn't stop you."

I frowned, embarrassed at my assumption, and elbowed him in the ribs for his comment. He grunted and laughed again. "So stubborn . . ." he mocked, as he pulled me down into his lap again.

Still feeling foolish about what I had thought he had wanted me to do, I let him lay me down. He gazed at me as I flopped down onto my back. His lap was quite comfortable, and I was extremely tired. He lightly stroked my hair, instantly relaxing me.

"See . . . that wasn't so bad, was it?" His blue eyes watched me almost wistfully. He gazed at me in silence for a few minutes before he spoke again. "Can I ask you something, without you getting angry?"

I immediately tensed, but nodded. He watched his fingers running through my hair as he asked, "Was Denny the only man you'd been with?"

Irritation flashed through me. Why would he want to know that? "Kellan, I don't see how that's—"

His gaze met mine and he cut me off. "Just answer the question." His eyes were almost sad, his voice soft with some emotion.

Confused, I answered without thinking about it. "Yes . . . until you, yes. He was my first. . . ."

He nodded, considering that while continuing to stroke my hair. I felt like I should be embarrassed, answering such a personal question, but I wasn't. I suppose there wasn't much about my body that Kellan didn't either already know or couldn't correctly guess.

"Why would you want to know that?" I asked.

He stopped playing with my hair for a moment, and then he continued, smiling softly, but not speaking. He kept stroking my hair and, eventually, I relaxed again. He seemed lost in thought, just gazing at me and smiling softly. I was suddenly struck with a flood of memories of being with him innocently like this while Denny had been away. The sweetness of that time brought tears to my eyes as I gazed up at him.

He frowned slightly and wiped away a tear. "Am I hurting you?" he asked softly.

"Daily . . ." I said, equally softly.

He was silent for a few minutes, and then finally he spoke again. "I'm not trying to hurt you. I'm sorry."

Confused, I blurted out, "Then why are you? Why don't you leave me alone?"

He frowned again. "Don't you like this . . . being with me? Even . . . just a little?"

My heart hurt a little at that all-too-confusing question. Finally I decided to just tell him the truth. "Yes, I do . . . but I can't. I shouldn't. It's not right . . . to Denny."

He nodded, still frowning. "True . . ." He sighed and stopped stroking my hair. "I don't want to hurt you . . . either of you." He was silent for several minutes, looking thoughtfully at me. I couldn't speak. I could only watch him watch me. Finally he said, "I'll leave it at this. Just flirting. I'll try not to be inappropriate with you." He sighed. "Just friendly flirting, like we used to . . ."

"Kellan, I don't think we should even . . . not since that night. Not since we've . . ."

He smiled, perhaps as the memory flooded through him, like it had just flooded through me, and stroked my cheek. "I need to be close to you, Kiera. This is the best compromise I can offer you." He suddenly smiled wickedly and my heart rate spiked again at his raw sex appeal. "Or I could just take you right here on the couch." I stiffened on his lap and he sighed. "I'm joking, Kiera."

"No, no you're not, Kellan. That's the problem. If I said okay . . ."

He smiled charmingly. "I would do whatever you asked," he whispered.

I swallowed and looked away, not comfortable with this conversation. He ran a finger down my cheek, down my neck, along my collarbone and back down my waist. My breath quickened and I looked back at him sharply.

"Oops . . . sorry." He grinned sheepishly. "I *will* try . . ."

He went back to safely stroking my hair and eventually the repetitive motion lulled me to sleep. I woke hours later in my room, tucked under the covers. I prayed I was dressed and felt, much to my relief, that I was. Kellan still wanted to flirt with me, but nothing more? Was he capable of that? Was I? Was that betraying Denny . . . if it was just innocent? I wasn't sure if it was possible, but lying on the couch with Kellan had brought back so many wonderful memories of the way we used to be. If we could somehow get that back? The thought of freely touching him again gave me such a thrill, though, that it concerned me.

Denny walked into the bedroom as I was still considering Kellan and his flirting idea. I startled a bit at seeing him, still lost in my thoughts and not realizing what time it was. He looked over at me quizzically as he slipped off his shoes and stripped off his dress shirt.

"What are you doing?" he asked, with a small grin and a twinkle in his eye as he put on a more comfortable T-shirt.

Normally the sight of him changing, and the look he'd just given me, would have made me smile, but considering where my thoughts had been, I actually blushed. It was an odd reaction for me to have toward him, and he furrowed his brow as he sat on the edge of the bed.

"You okay?" He placed a hand on my forehead, then brushed aside some hair from my face. "Are you not feeling well again?"

The move was so tender that it relaxed me and I sat up in bed and slung my arms around his neck. I sighed and clung to him a little tighter than normal. He rubbed my back and held me just as tight. "I'm fine—just napping."

He pulled back to look at me lovingly and that was when I noticed how tired he looked. "Are you okay?" A slight panic went through me, but I forcefully pushed it back.

He sighed and shook his head. "Max. God, he's an idiot, Kiera. If his uncle didn't own the place, there's no way he would work there. They're doing this campaign for this retailer who—" He cut himself off and shook his head again. "Ugh, I don't even want to think about it." He ran a hand down my hair and brought me in for a sweet kiss. "I just want to think about you. . . ."

I ran a hand back through his hair as our kiss deepened a bit. He pulled back after another minute. "Are you hungry? If you want to stay and rest a while longer, I'll make us something to eat."

Smiling at his sweet offer, I ran a hand down his cheek. "No, I'll come down with you." He grabbed my hands and, smiling, helped me to my feet. I watched the darkness of his hair and the nice shape of his body as I followed him down the stairs. How could I have ever been unfaithful to him? He was amazing. I swallowed the lump in my throat and reminded myself that it wasn't going to happen again. I would never betray him again. Kellan had agreed to back off. Kellan and I were going back to our friendship. Everything would be fine.

I decided to lie on the couch, and eventually the sounds of Denny making dinner lulled me into sleep. *Great*, I thought hazily before I let go, *I'm never going to sleep tonight now.* I was woken up by a pair of soft lips. Panic shot through me. For a split second of sleep-induced delirium, I had no idea whose lips they were.

My hand automatically went to the face, however, and at feeling the light hairline, I relaxed. Denny. That's right. I had the night off from work, Denny was home from his long day, and Kellan was playing with the D-Bags at Razors. They were probably already there, relaxing before the show.

Since I'd never been one to not take advantage of alone time with him in the past, Denny was . . . um, ready for me. It felt odd to me at first, because we hadn't been together since my betrayal with Kellan, and I still felt so guilty, but after a few deep kisses on the couch and his hand slipping under my jeans, I let go of my guilt and enjoyed every inch of this beautiful, beautiful man.

The wonderful dinner he had prepared was cold by the time we got around to eating it.

Chapter 11
The Rules

I slept soundly that night, once I finally fell asleep after my multiple naps throughout the day. Apparently the stress of never knowing what Kellan was going to do to me, and the guilt that came with it, had been the cause of my insomnia. Now that I knew how he was going to touch me and how he was not going to touch me, I felt good again. Maybe we could reclaim our friendship? Maybe I could stop betraying Denny? I could never undo what we had already done to him, and I would forever carry the guilt of that, but knowing that I wouldn't be adding any more guilt made me giddy as I came down the stairs very early the next morning.

And of course, being free again with Kellan made me smile delightfully as I watched his aching perfection turn to greet me in the kitchen. His hair, loose and easy, seemed to exactly match his smile.

"Mornin'. Coffee?" He pointed at the finished pot.

Smiling widely, I went over to him and put my arms around his waist. He startled for a second and then slipped his arms around mine. He was warm and smelled amazing. Relief washed through me. It was easy to touch him like this, especially knowing that it would go no farther.

"Good morning. Yes, please." I nodded over to the coffeepot.

This would be the first cup of coffee I'd had since our tryst. I finally felt well enough to drink it again . . . and I had really missed it.

He smiled as he gazed down at me, his perfect blue eyes calm and peaceful. "You aren't going to fight me on this?" he asked, pulling me closer.

I returned his warm smile. "No . . . I missed this." He leaned in like he was going to kiss my neck and I pushed him back, frowning. "We do need ground rules though. . . ."

He chuckled. "Okay . . . fire away."

"Well, besides the obvious one, that you and I aren't ever . . ." I blushed deeply at the thought I couldn't even say, and he laughed.

"Having . . . hot . . . sweaty . . . sex?" he finished for me, raising a perfect eyebrow and saying each word slowly. "Are you sure you don't want to rethink that? We're pretty amazin—"

I looked at him sharply and cut him off, smacking him in the chest for his question. "Besides that obvious one, no more kissing . . . ever."

He frowned. "What if I just stay away from your lips? Friends kiss."

I frowned too, a sudden memory of his tongue running up my throat making me shiver. "Not like you do."

He sighed. "Fine . . . anything else?"

I smiled and stepped away from his embrace, miming a bikini top and bottom. "Off limits . . . don't touch."

He frowned again. "God, you're sucking all the fun out of our friendship." He quickly smiled after he said that. "Okay . . . any other rules I should know about?"

I stepped back into his embrace as he held his arms out to me. "This stays innocent, Kellan. If you can't do that, we end this." I searched his eyes, but he brought my head to his shoulder and hugged me.

"Okay, Kiera." He sighed. Then pushing me back, he laughed. "That goes for you too, you know." He pointed to his lips, then down to his pants. "Don't touch," he mocked. I smacked his chest. "Unless you really, really want to . . ." he added with a chuckle. I smacked his chest even harder and he laughed again and pulled me tight.

Sighing, I relaxed into his embrace, thinking I could stay all morning in his comforting arms, but then I startled at the sound of the telephone ringing. It was still awfully early. I glanced up to where Denny was still sleeping and hurried over to the phone, not wanting the sound to wake him up yet. A small river of guilt flooded through me that the reason I didn't want him awake was because I wanted to be alone with Kellan longer.

"Hello?" I answered as I bent over the counter. An amused chuckle behind me spun me around. Kellan was grinning most inappropriately at the sight of me bending over the counter. I stood up straight and put a hand on my hip, frowning at him.

"Hey, sis!" Anna's perky voice came through the phone, but I continued to frown at Kellan. He made a swift halo motion above his head—*I'll be good*—and I finally smiled.

"Hi, Anna." I leaned back on the counter, watching Kellan pour his coffee and then prepare some for me. "Isn't it a little early for phone calls?" My sister was kind of a night owl, and she usually didn't rise before noon.

"Oh, I'm just getting home and thought I'd give you a jingle before school. Did I wake you?" I frowned and looked up at the clock— 7:05 here, so Ohio would be 10:05. She just got home?

"No, I'm up." I stared at the clock, wondering what my sister had been up to.

"Good. Did I wake up Hot-Bod?" I could hear the amusement in her voice at her nickname for Kellan.

I laughed. "No, Hot-Bod is awake too." I cringed when I remembered that "Hot-Bod" was listening to the conversation, and I looked over at his highly amused face. He raised an eyebrow and mouthed the word "Hot-Bod," pointing to himself. I nodded and rolled my eyes as he softly laughed.

"Oooooohhh . . . and what were you two doing so early this morning?" she teased.

Curious what Kellan's reaction would be, I decided to play with him and my sister a little bit. "We were screwing on the table, waiting for the coffee to brew." His facial reaction matched my sister's verbal reaction so perfectly that I laughed.

"Oh my God, Kiera!" she exclaimed, while Kellan spat out his coffee and, coughing a bit, looked at me incredulously. I laughed again and had to turn away from Kellan's face when he started to grin indecently.

"Geez, Anna, I'm just joking. I would *never* touch him like that. You should hear about all the girls he's been with. Ugh, he's disgusting . . . and Denny is asleep upstairs, you know." I glanced up to where Denny was sleeping, hoping my laughing hadn't awakened him. Then I brought my gaze back down to Kellan. He was holding his coffee cup and staring oddly at the floor.

"Really? I like disgusting. Wait . . . he's back?" Anna was asking about Denny, but my focus was on Kellan and his strange expression.

"You know, a phone call to Mom or Dad here and there really won't kill you." I frowned as Kellan set down his full coffee mug and started to move toward the entryway, like he was leaving. Instantly, I realized what I, in my haste to cover with Anna, had snottily said— *"he's disgusting."*

Anna sighed. "Yeah, yeah it might. So you and Denny are okay after your extended absence from each other?"

I caught Kellan's arm as he walked by me. I *had* offended him. But surely he knew I was covering? "Everything is fine." I was speaking to both him and Anna. He looked back at me sadly as I pulled his arm around my waist. Slowly his smile returned and he held me tight, leaning us both back against the counter.

"Good . . . if it were me, I probably would have jumped in the sack with Hot-Bod while he was gone. Good thing you're not me, huh?"

I blushed at how accurate her flippant comment actually was, and Kellan eyed me curiously. "Yeah, it's a good thing you and I are nothing alike, Anna." I gazed up at his amazing blue eyes while he held me close.

"So . . . how about I come up this weekend?"

Startled, I stiffened and stared straight ahead. "No!"

Kellan tried to catch my eye, whispering, "What?"

"Oh, come on, Kiera. I'm dying to meet Hot-Bod." I avoided meeting Kellan's gaze. Things were finally comfortable between us; I didn't need my sister messing that up . . . or trying to get in his pants. I wasn't all that sure he wouldn't let her.

"He has a name, Anna," I snapped, more irritated at my last thought than at my sister's pet name.

"Fine, Kellan. God, even his name is hot." She exhaled loudly. "You can't keep him all to yourself, you know."

"I'm not!" I was really getting steamed. I finally met Kellan's worried eyes and forced myself to calm down, to relax in his embrace. I smiled and shook my head at him, trying to ease him and myself.

"Winter break, Anna . . . remember? You can come up then. I'm just too busy right now." I gazed at his calm eyes as he smiled at me. I couldn't bear the thought of them together.

"Winter break . . . but it's October?" She still sounded miffed.

"I'm busy, Anna. . . ." I said it softly, trying to pacify her.

"Ppfftt . . . one weekend won't kill you, Kiera."

I sighed, knowing that if I fought this any longer, she would get suspicious. "Fine." I frantically racked my brain, trying to think of a way to at least postpone the trip a little. Searching Kellan's achingly perfect face, the answer struck me so fast I actually said, "Oh."

"What?" my sister and Kellan asked at the same time.

I grinned and Kellan grinned with me, raising his eyebrows curiously. "Well, Anna . . . Kellan has gigs every Friday and Saturday night. He's not free until . . ." I raised my eyebrow at him and he thought for a split second, then mouthed *seventh* ". . . until the seventh. So, if you want him to come with us, you should wait to come out then."

She sighed. "Of November? That's three weeks away, Kiera. . . ."

I grinned, wanting to giggle. "I know. You're welcome to come out earlier. Kellan won't really be around, but you can hang out with Denny and me. We can go to a movie or some—"

"No, no . . . fine, I'll come out on the seventh." Then she brightened. "We'll have so much fun, Kiera!" She giggled and I wasn't sure whom she was more excited to see, me or my roommate. "Can I sleep in Kellan's room?" she asked and then giggled again.

Okay . . . roommate then. I sighed loudly. "I have to get ready for school. I'll talk to you later, Anna. Get some sleep! And take a cold shower."

She giggled again. "Bye, Kiera. See you soon!"

"Bye." I hung up the phone. "Shit."

Kellan chuckled at me and I glanced up at him. "Don't tell Griffin about that . . . please."

He shrugged and laughed some more. "What's wrong?" He smiled softly at me, still containing chuckles.

"My sister. She wants to visit." My tone was not happy.

He looked at me, confused. "Okay . . . and, you don't like her?"

I shook my head and lightly rubbed his arm. "No, no I do. I love her, dearly, but . . ." I looked away.

"But what?" He tried to meet my eyes.

I looked back at him and sighed. "You're kind of man-flavored candy to my sister," I said glumly.

He laughed. "Ahhh . . . so I'm pretty much going to be attacked, right?" He seemed really amused by that prospect. I was not.

"It's not funny, Kellan." I pouted.

He stopped laughing and gave me a warm smile. "It kind of is, Kiera."

I looked away, feeling tears start to form and not wanting him to see. He wouldn't understand. I didn't understand. I just knew how Anna would be with him, and how he would probably be with her. . . . It made me feel ill. I didn't want him touching her, but I knew I didn't have the right to ask him not to. He wasn't mine.

He hooked some hair behind my ear. "Hey . . ." He gently moved my chin to make me look at him. "What do you want me to do?" he asked softly.

I wasn't going to ask him, but it slipped out anyway. "I want you to not '*do*' her. I don't want you to even touch her." I said it rather harshly and threw him a glare.

"Okay, Kiera," he said after a minute, lightly rubbing my cheek.

"Promise me, Kellan." I stopped glaring, but gazed at him intently, my eyes brimming.

"I promise, Kiera. I won't sleep with her, okay?" He smiled at me reassuringly and I finally nodded and let him pull me in for a tight hug.

Kellan and I said our goodbyes to Denny when he left for work. Kellan was in a surprisingly good mood and clapped Denny on the back, wishing him luck with his dick of a boss. Denny thanked Kellan and gave me a swift kiss on the cheek before heading out. He seemed in a better mood, too and I was momentarily thrilled that everything between the three of us was just a bit easier. After Denny left, Kellan grabbed my hand and we cuddled on the couch to watch TV. I nearly sighed with relief, it was so wonderful to sit next to him on the couch and rest my head on his shoulder, just like I used to before things got intense between us. He put his arm around me and we enjoyed the warmth of each other for most of the morning.

I only had one class, and then I was going to study a bit before work. Kellan drove me to school, which gave me a small thrill—my old addiction was coming back full force. I thanked him, but made him stay in the car and not walk me to class. I didn't need another fifty-question session if someone else saw me with the rock star. He frowned, but stayed where I asked, and I smiled as I watched him drive away.

I never saw Tina and Genevieve in my Psych class after their grilling session that one afternoon, so I figured they had ruled me out as a potential rival for Candy. That made me smile a little, when I thought about how much of Kellan's attention I actually did have. Then I immediately frowned. Why was he so interested in plain little me? Anyway, not wanting to run into any of those three again, I tried to avoid the Harry Potter library after that. Not too long ago, I'd found a cute park nearby that was perfect for stretching out with some books. After class, I decided today was just enough of a beautiful day to study there.

I breathed in the crisp autumn air as I looked around the quaint little area. The leaves of the trees were a brilliant orange and red and quivered slightly in the soft breeze. It wouldn't be too much longer before they started to fall. I unzipped my light jacket. The weather was still unseasonably warm—I was starting to become a believer in global warming, but there was a purity and a cleanliness to the cooler air that was refreshing and cleared my head. It really was the perfect place to study a bit before work. I laid myself out on the grass and, rifling through my bag, found a bag of grapes and started popping a few.

Several groups of people were clumped around the park, enjoying the perfectly sunny day. It might be the last one we saw for a while. Some were playing catch with their dogs, some, like me, were studying, and others were enjoying a late picnic.

I noticed a group of teenage girls giggling not far from me, and I turned to look at what had their attention. A man had his back to us and his shirt off. He was doing push-ups against a park bench. I watched him idly for a minute while the girls continued murmuring. He finished and grabbed a full water bottle from the bench. Turning a little toward me, he took a drink from his bottle. His body was unbelievably perfect . . . and all too familiar. I laughed and rolled my eyes.

Of course, I thought. Of course I would pick the park where Kellan worked out after his runs. Of course he would be here now, while I was trying to study. He turned and instantly spotted me on the grass while I was still openly staring at his body. A slow, sexy smile spread on his face and he cocked his head to the side adorably as he started walking over to me, water bottle in one hand, shirt in the other. The girls he passed on the way over giggled louder at his alluring smile and turned to watch me curiously. I sat back in the grass and watched him come over, my heart beating a little faster.

He sat down in the grass next to me as I let out a loud sigh. "Can't I go anywhere without running into you?" I teased.

He laughed and extended his legs out straight, leaning back on his hands. "This is my park—you're the one stalking me." He half-smiled over at me.

I grinned and popped another grape, gazing at him. My focus started on his impossibly sexy hair, slightly damp around the edges from his workout, but eventually my gaze drifted down his perfect cheekbones, strong, smooth jaw, and down his neck to his bare, lightly damp chest. I lingered there, following every line, starting at the top and slowly mentally tracing them all the way down to the deep lines of his lower abdomen, which disappeared pleasantly into his track pants. I couldn't stop the intimate knowledge I had of touching that body from leaping into my head. I bit my lip.

"Hey." Kellan's voice snapped me out of my near trance, and I glanced back up at his amused eyes. Raising an eyebrow, he asked, "Are you objectifying me?" I blushed and looked away as he chuckled. "It's okay if you are. I was just wondering if maybe you were thinking about renegotiating our rules?" He met my eyes and grinned. "Can I kiss you yet?"

I smirked back at him, and he laughed more. Grabbing the shirt out of his hands, I threw it at him. "Put some clothes on. . . ."

He frowned at me. "I'm hot. . . ."

I smiled back. "You're indecent . . . and people are staring." I pointed over to the young girls still gawking at him.

He looked over at them, making them giggle, then shook his head as he looked down at his half-naked body and muttered, "Indecent?" He sighed. "Fine." Then he grabbed his water bottle and dumped it on his shirt before putting put his shirt back on. "There . . . better?"

I looked at him with my mouth open until I got back my control and shut it. "Yes, thank you." No, it wasn't any better. The wet shirt clung to every delightful muscle. He might as well have left it off.

I didn't want to give him the satisfaction of knowing how good he looked, though. I was pretty sure he was well aware anyway.

Sitting up, he reached into my bag and grabbed a couple of grapes. I smiled at him wryly. "Go ahead . . . help yourself."

He smiled as he popped them in his mouth. "I frequently do," he said, raising an eyebrow and grinning mischievously.

I sighed and rolled my eyes at him while he came over to sit right beside me. "And what are we studying?"

I smiled and blushed deeply as I looked over at him. "Human sexuality."

"Ahhh . . . really?" He nudged my shoulder playfully. "One of my best subjects." I cringed away from his wet, cold shirt. He laughed at my reaction, then, without warning, he tackled me, pressing his wet shirt firmly against me and laughing.

"Oh my God, Kellan! You are so cold! Get off me!" I screamed at him, and tried pushing him away, laughing so much my eyes watered. He kept on laughing and didn't move away. Grabbing my wrists so I couldn't push him off, he held me down on the grass.

Eventually our laughing slowed as we gazed at each other. He smiled adoringly at me and lowered his forehead down to mine. I suppose that wasn't specifically against my rules. We breathed softly on each other for a minute, and he moved his hands so our fingers were interlaced.

I felt like we were starting to cross a line and was about to say something, when the girls a short distance away yelled, "Kiss her!"

He pulled back and, swallowing, laughed a little. "See." He nodded his head over to the group of teenagers. "They want us to renegotiate." He grinned wickedly and I pushed him off of me.

"You." I pointed to his chest. "Go finish your run." I pointed vaguely to the direction of our house. "I do need to study . . . and you're far too distracting." I blushed and looked down.

He laughed and stood up. "Okay, have it your way then." He smiled and, turning back to the girls, shrugged at them, and winked. They giggled and then groaned as he turned to leave the park.

I rolled my eyes again and brushed off my now-dampened shirt. I zipped my jacket back up as the dampness made me shiver a bit. Well, I'm pretty sure it was the dampness.

My head drifted in and out of pleasant thoughts of Kellan's body for the rest of my study session. I found myself daydreaming and staring blankly at the same paragraph for a good ten minutes. I sighed; he was distracting even when he wasn't there. I shivered a bit, remembering his body pressed against mine, his forehead against mine, his breath against my skin. . . .

I shivered yet again and stood up. This wasn't the sort of studying I needed to be doing. I might as well go in to work. At least the bustle of activity would change the direction of my thoughts.

But being at work didn't change my thoughts at all. I found myself glancing over at the doors, waiting for the band to arrive for their performance. It seemed a little silly to me, that I was actually anxious to see him when I saw him all the time. In fact, I couldn't seem to get away from him. That thought made me smile. I think I had a goofy grin plastered on my face all night as I slyly watched the doors.

"Okay, what did he do?" Kate asked, coming up behind me a while later.

"Who?" I asked uncertainly.

"Denny. You've been grinning all night. That usually means the boyfriend did something good." She and Rita leaned across the bar expectantly. "So, spill. Flowers? Jewelry? Oh my God, did he propose?" Kate's light brown eyes sparkled at the idea. She put her head in her hands as she leaned against the bar, looking lost in that dreamy thought for a second.

I blushed deeply. Denny and I hadn't even talked about marriage yet. He was the practical type who wouldn't bring it up until he was set in his career. And he wasn't the one who was making me grin. "No, no proposals. Nothing special, I'm just happy."

Rita and Kate exchanged disappointed looks; then Kate tossed her long hair over her other shoulder. "Fine, keep your secrets." She winked as she lithely stood and went back to work.

After she left, Rita looked at me conspiratorially. "Okay . . . she's gone, you can tell me."

I blushed again. "There's really nothing to tell, Rita. Sorry, my life is pretty boring." I smiled inwardly at how untrue that was.

It wasn't too much after that when the band filtered in, and I swear my heart skipped a beat when I saw Kellan. The way my body reacted, you would think I hadn't seen him in days and not just the few hours it had been since the park. He came up to me, looking all too sexy in his black, long-sleeved shirt, layered under a light gray shirt, and asked how the rest of my studying had gone. I blushed and told him it had gone much better once he had left . . . which of course it hadn't. He smirked at me and then laughed.

After ordering his beer, he headed over to his table, where the rest of the guys were discussing something apparently really funny. I could hear their laughter from the bar. Kellan clapped Sam on the shoulder as he walked by, and I noticed that my shoulder was pleasantly warm. And then I realized that that was because he had put his hand there when he'd ordered his beer. My goofy grin stayed with me the rest of the night.

Actually, my grin stayed with me for the rest of the weekend.

Thinking about how wonderful the weekend had been had me ducking out of class a half hour early on Monday afternoon. I couldn't seem to help it. I was anxious and wanted to see Kellan. And knowing he was just sitting home alone, maybe bored, maybe thinking of me . . . ugh, it drove me crazy all through the lecture.

Our weekend had been fun and a little torturous. We had hugged in the morning over coffee and held hands when Denny was in the shower. We had all lounged around the house for most of the weekend, and whenever Denny had fallen asleep while watching TV, Kellan and I would go in the kitchen and hold each other while we talked. Denny got called out early Sunday morning by Max, and we had taken that time to snuggle on the couch. I loved it—I loved being near him. It was fun and flirty and as innocent as I could keep it, even though my heart usually started beating just a smidge faster when he was touching me.

I came into the living room and smiled at Kellan stretched out on the couch watching television, one arm on his chest, the other extended over his head. He turned to look at me when I entered the room, and my breath caught as he grinned adorably at me.

"Hey, you're back early," he said sleepily. "I was going to pick you up."

I walked over to him as he sat up and scooted back on the couch, patting the cushion between his legs. "You look tired—everything okay?" I asked, as I sat between his legs and leaned back on his chest. He played with my hair and held me tight. Flirting did have its perks.

"I'm fine . . . just a late night, didn't sleep well."

"Oh." I turned my head around to look at him with a wry grin. "Feeling guilty about something?"

He laughed a little and pulled me tighter. "About you? Every day." He sighed, then pushed me forward, away from him. I started to turn and protest, but he put his hands on my shoulders and made me face front. Then he started massaging them.

"Hmmmm . . . I could get used to this flirting thing." I relaxed into his strong hands as he moved along my shoulder blades. He laughed softly. "Did you have a bad dream?" I asked, my own head feeling dreamy.

"No . . ." he murmured. "I had a good one, actually." His voice was low and soft. I could have wrapped it around me like a blanket.

"Hmmmm . . . what about?" His fingers moved along my spine and I made a soft noise in my throat.

"You," he said idly. His fingers stayed where they were when I made the noise. He pressed slightly harder and I made a deeper noise.

"Hmmmm . . . nothing naughty, I hope. We *are* keeping this innocent, right?" His fingers moved down to my low back, pressing deep, and I exhaled loudly at the ache being released from me.

He laughed softly again. "No . . . nothing even remotely scandalous, I promise." He started bringing his hands up my back and

I made another deep noise as even more tension drained from my body; his fingers were magic.

"Hmmm . . . . good, I don't need you thinking about me that way," I mumbled.

He didn't say anything to that, just continued working his way up my pleasantly tingling back. I sighed deeply and relaxed even more into him, making even more satisfied noises. He shifted slightly behind me but said nothing further. Too relaxed to maintain a conversation, I enjoyed the comfortable silence. His fingers started back down again, reaching farther out to my rib cage. It was heaven. I practically growled in pleasure. He stopped for an extra minute anywhere I made a noise, so I started making the noises more frequently.

Eventually he made it back down to my low back, working out more toward my hips. He shifted his weight behind me again and then pulled me closer to him. Thinking he was uncomfortable, sitting sideways on the couch with me between his legs, I let him adjust me however he needed to, but he only pulled my hips back into him again. Assuming he was done, I sighed and relaxed into his chest. I was surprised at how rigid he was. I was starting to turn to face him, when his hands, which were still on my hips, slipped around in front to my thighs. He reached both of his hands down my legs and up my inner thighs, pulling tight against me at the same time. That was when I noticed that his breathing was not slow and regular like mine. . . .

I spun to face him. He was sitting very tense and straight on the couch. His eyes were closed, and his lips were partly open. His breath was noticeably faster. He swallowed and slowly opened his eyes to look at me. His gaze on mine made the tension immediately come back to my body. His eyes burned with desire. His gaze smoldered as he watched me. He brought a hand up to my cheek and, with the other one, pulled me tight to him.

I swallowed and made myself shake my head. "No . . . Kellan," I whispered, alarmed at the look on his face and proud of myself for uttering the word "no."

He closed his eyes again and gently pushed me away from him. "I'm sorry. Just give me a minute. . . ."

I moved to the other end of the couch and watched him, wondering what in the world I had done. He pulled his legs up, locked his elbows around them, and took three calming breaths. Then he slowly opened his eyes again. He still looked odd, but more controlled. He smiled, just a little.

"Sorry . . . I am trying. But, maybe next time, you could not . . . uh, make those noises?"

I blushed deeply and looked away, making him chuckle. I hadn't realized . . . maybe this wasn't such a good idea. Maybe there was no such thing as innocent flirting.

Chapter 12
Innocent

I started waking earlier and earlier. I usually was awake before Denny now, and considering how late I went to bed at night, that also usually meant I needed a nap in the afternoon after school, but I couldn't seem to help myself. The thought of Kellan awake and downstairs all alone seemed to be a natural alarm clock for me. That worried me a little, but the allure of his warm arms was too strong. I was too addicted. I couldn't stop myself from rushing downstairs to see him every morning.

One morning, while we were waiting for the coffee to finish brewing, Kellan's arms slipped around my waist and my hands folded over his. My back rested against his chest, and my head rested on his shoulder. Completely relaxed in his arms, I asked him a familiar question. "If I ask you something, will you promise not to get mad?"

I spun in his arms to face him and placed my hands on his chest. He chuckled and nodded, smiling peacefully at me. I paused, wondering if I really wanted to know the answer to my question. "Will it bother you if Denny and I sleep together?"

His face paled, but he kept his smile. "You sleep with him every night."

I jabbed him lightly in the ribs. "You know what I mean," I said, blushing.

"Will it bother me if you have sex with your boyfriend?" he asked softly.

I blushed again and nodded. He smiled softly but said nothing. "Just answer the question." I smiled and raised an eyebrow at using his phrase against him.

He laughed and looked away. Sighing, he finally answered. "Yes, yes it will bother me . . . but I understand." He turned to look at me again. "You're not mine," he said wistfully.

Sudden emotion swept through me. I felt a surge of sympathy for him and I desperately wanted to hold him tight, to stroke his cheek and kiss his lips. I pulled away from his embrace and he frowned, trying to keep me close to him. "Just a minute . . ." I whispered.

He let go and looked at me, confused. "I'm fine, Kiera."

I looked at him sadly. "*I* need a minute, Kellan."

"Oh . . ." he said softly, looking surprised.

I had to stay away from him for quite a while—the urge to kiss him was so strong. That worried me. We were staring at each other across the kitchen, leaning on our respective counters and sipping on our coffees, when I heard the shower start running. I glanced up to where the bathroom was and then back down to Kellan. He had an odd look on his face. I couldn't even begin to place it. Eventually, I finished my coffee and, putting my hand across his arm, I set down my mug. He looked down at me when I touched him, and my breath caught at the look in his eyes. Forcing it back, I gave him a quick squeeze and made my way back upstairs to where Denny was getting ready for work.

Denny smiled when he came back from his shower to find me sitting in bed. "Hey, good morning," he said warmly as he kissed my cheek.

I smiled, but I was still thinking about the conversation Kellan and I had just had downstairs. Denny sat down next to me, still just wrapped in a towel. He looked over at me with a goofy grin. That made my smile wider. Then he frowned, and I did too. "I'm probably going to be late tonight."

My heart dropped a little. "Oh . . . why?"

He sighed and stood back up to get dressed. He tossed his towel on the bed and I watched him with a small smile on my lips. Noticing my attention, he sighed again. "I wish I had more time with you," he said wistfully. I looked away and bit my lip while he laughed softly. "Max. He's got me finishing this project for him that apparently his uncle wanted today, but he was too busy with . . . um . . . paid escorts over the weekend to do it himself."

My mouth dropped open as I turned back to look at him. He had his boxers on and was pulling up some black slacks. He looked at me wryly and shook his head. "I guess I should be grateful we got the weekend together and he didn't just call me in to finish it then." He sighed and shook his head again as he buttoned his pants.

Tiny guilt washed through me at what his job now entailed and I swallowed it back. He noticed my expression and forced a smile onto his face as he grabbed a shirt from the dresser. "I'm not trying to complain, Kiera. I'm sorry."

He was sorry. I swallowed more guilt back. "No . . . you have a right to complain. Max is an ass."

He laughed and slipped on his shirt. Walking over to him, I stopped his hands from buttoning it. He smiled warmly at me as I finished with the buttons for him. When I was done, I tucked his shirt in and he smiled even wider. "I love you so much for putting up with your crappy job to stay here with me," I said to him when I was finished.

He smiled and wrapped his arms around my waist. "I would put up with much worse to stay here with you."

I knew he meant those words as endearing, but they pierced my heart. If he only knew. I was quiet while he finished dressing. I was quiet when I kissed him goodbye. I was quiet when I decided to forgo cuddling on the couch with Kellan, to get ready for school early.

The hot water cleared my head and my swirling emotions washed down the drain with the soapy water. I picked out my favorite clingy, long-sleeved blouse and khaki cargos and took time to curl my already wavy hair. I wasn't sure why . . . maybe because I had the time. Maybe because looking better had a way of making me feel better. Either way, after my relaxing shower and looking my best, which was probably just slightly past passable, really, I felt okay again.

And I was rewarded with a dazzling smile from Kellan as I made my way downstairs. That made my day a little. He seemed to be fine from our earlier conversation, as well. He grabbed my hand and my bag as he led me to his car. He begged me to let him walk me to class, so I conceded. Really, it wasn't necessary, but who was I to deny a gorgeous, begging boy? I supposed it was worth another potential quiz session to walk with him through the halls.

He lightly held my fingers as he walked me to Econ, and we talked about my parents and the last reluctant phone call I had placed to them. They weren't too happy that Denny was so busy and I was alone so much. I made the mistake of telling them that Kellan was home a lot, which had started the "Doesn't he have a job?" conversation, which led to the "He's in a band" conversation, which turned into the "I'm really not comfortable with you living with a rock star" conversation. Kellan was laughing pretty hard by the time he opened the door to my classroom. The sound of his laugh stayed with me all throughout that class.

Afterwards, Kellan met me in the hall with an extralarge espresso in his hand for me. I immediately threw my arms around his neck, careful to not spill my precious drink. "Ahhh . . . coffee! I love you!"

I froze after I realized what I'd just said, but he started laughing, and was smiling warmly at me when I pulled away. "What is it about me and coffee that drives you over the edge?" he asked playfully, biting his lip and raising his eyebrows suggestively.

I blushed and smacked his shoulder, knowing exactly what incident in a certain coffee stand he was referring to. I grabbed my cup from his hand and stormed off down the hall. He easily caught up to me, still chuckling.

I glared over at him, and he laughed even harder. "Oh, come on—that was kind of funny."

I rolled my eyes. "You're a little twisted."

"You have no idea. . . ."

I raised my eyebrow at that and he laughed again until I finally joined in with him. He grabbed my hand and interlaced our fingers as we left the building and walked casually to his car. I tried to ignore the stares he drew; none of these people knew Denny . . . right?

Denny did work late that night, and Kellan had a show at a small bar I'd never heard of, so I was alone for the evening and took advantage of the fact that I had the night off from Pete's by doing something I very rarely got to do—I went to bed early.

The next morning I woke up early, feeling rather refreshed. I was surprisingly alone in the kitchen, filling my coffee cup with creamer, and idly wondering when Kellan was going to saunter into the kitchen and slip his arms around me. It was so unusual for me to beat him downstairs. In my anticipation I could practically already smell him. Lost in warm thoughts, suddenly arms did slip around me, and I snuggled back into the embrace while stirring my coffee.

"There you are Ke—"

I immediately froze my words when lips started trailing up my neck—warm, soft lips, followed by a flick of a warm, soft tongue, and occasionally brushing against my sensitive skin, the light hair of his jawline. My heart raced. I had been about to say Kellan's name, and it wasn't Kellan embracing me.

My heart leapt into my throat, effectively cutting off all speech. Denny murmured good morning into my neck, apparently not catching my nearly disastrous mistake. My breath sped in a nervous panic as his lips trailed up my jaw. I couldn't calm down—that had been so close.

His lips ran up to my ear and sucked on an earlobe. "I missed you," he said huskily, as he pulled me tight to him. "Our bed was cold without you." His accent curled delightfully around the words.

My breath started to speed for another reason and I turned around in his arms to kiss him. His mouth eagerly met mine and I forced myself to push all thoughts of Kellan to the very back of my mind; it was surprisingly hard to do.

Abruptly Denny's lips stopped moving and, sighing, he pulled away from me. Guilt flashed through me, and again panic clenched my throat. I tried to keep my face from betraying any of my inner turmoil as he ran a few fingers down my cheek. "I wish I could stay." He sighed heavily. "Max needs me to come in early today. I have to go get ready."

Suddenly he gave me my favorite goofy grin, and I instantly started relaxing. He playfully grabbed my hand and led me from the kitchen, back up the stairs. Laughing softly as he held both of my hands and pulled me into the bathroom, I asked, "I thought you had to get ready. What exactly are we doing?"

Chuckling, he shut the bathroom door. "I *am* going to get ready." He moved past me to turn on the water for the shower. "And you're going to help me." He winked adorably at me.

"Oh, really?" I laughed, as I started to sit on the toilet to watch him.

He grabbed me just as I was sitting down, pulling me back up. "Oh yes," he said suggestively, with a glint in his eye that I knew very well.

"Oh," I said, suddenly understanding what he wanted. He made himself even clearer the next instant by stripping off my tank top. I laughed again as he kissed my neck and started pulling down my pants, underwear and all.

He pulled back and stripped off his clothes, and we gazed at each other for a moment. Love for this beautiful, wonderful man filled me, dissolving the enormous guilt built up in my heart. He smiled and tucked a lock of hair behind my ear. I put my arms around his neck and kissed him deeply.

He stuck his hand in the shower to feel the water, then scooped me up, making me laugh again as he stepped us inside. It was heaven—the water was warm, his hands were soft, his lips enticing. The water streamed off his beautiful, tanned body and I relaxed into the rightness of being with him. It felt natural and easy and good, and for just a few moments, I let myself enjoy him with no guilt and no feelings of betrayal.

I ran my fingers back through his dark hair, making sure it was completely soaked through. He smiled and closed his equally dark eyes. I grabbed our cheap all-in-one shampoo and massaged it into his hair as he sighed happily. He spun me around and moved out of the way of the warm water so he could do the same for me. I giggled and relaxed into his amazing fingers. He rinsed out my hair, kissing my forehead in the process, and then rinsed out his own while I kissed his chest and grabbed the bar of soap.

While he rinsed, I rubbed every area of his chest and abdomen with the soap, the bubbles trailing down his body suggestively. I bit my lip watching those bubbles slide down his thighs and he smiled, taking the soap from my hand and putting it back on the shelf. Then he pulled me tight to him, the soap on his body transferring to mine. He used his hands to make sure every square inch of my flesh was coated in suds, lingering on my breasts and my rigid nipples before moving around to my backside. I gasped when his hand moved between my thighs.

He smiled at me so seductively that my breath sped instantly. His lips parted as he watched my reaction to his fingers circling around my most sensitive flesh, before dipping inside me. I groaned and arched my back against him as he inserted first one, then two fingers, moving languidly inside of me for a few heavenly moments before pulling back along my wet skin teasingly. I nearly whimpered and sucked on his bottom lip as he removed his hand and carefully pushed me back against the shower wall. The water surged around us, most deflecting off his broad back, so that only a light mist sprayed on me. His body pressed firmly against mine, the soap still lingering between us making him slippery against my skin. He bent to kiss me deeply and I eagerly returned it, moaning into his mouth.

The hard length of him pressed up against my body and I tentatively reached down to curl my fingers around him. He let out a groan in my ear as my hand squeezed the base of him. I stroked my hand up and down his thickness a few times, while he panted heavily in my ear. His chest rising and falling against mine, he suddenly lifted me up against the wall slightly and then slid himself perfectly into me. He was so strong that the move was effortless for him, and surprising comfortable for me. I groaned loudly with the pleasure of it. My legs wrapped around him, pulling him even deeper inside me.

My hands moved up to grasp his neck as he used his hands to urge my hips into a euphoric rhythm against his. My head drifted into a pleasant fog as Denny became my entire world—every smell, every touch, every breath, and every movement. It was intoxicating and beautiful and heartwarming . . . and maybe, if at that moment I allowed myself to feel it, a little sad.

Within moments, his breath increased to a quick pant and he clenched my hips satisfactorily with a deep groan as he came. He never stopped his rhythm though, and moments later I arched against him and cried out as the intensity ripped through me. We both caught our breaths as the water started to cool along with us, and then he gently lowered me and moved aside so the tepid water could wash away any remaining bubbles between us.

"I love you," he said, as he shut the water off.

He stepped out of the shower and handed me a towel to dry off with. I smiled warmly at him as I stepped out of the shower to stand next to him on the fuzzy bath rug. "I love you too."

He helped dry me off a little with his towel, making me giggle, and then he dried himself off and we left our cozy, steamy little bathroom to finish getting him ready for work. It wasn't too much later that Denny, dressed in his khaki slacks and blue button-up shirt (he did look amazing in blue) with still slightly damp hair that, of course, he let me style for him, made his way down to the kitchen. I followed him in my basic jeans and blouse, my hair also damp and combed through, which Denny had lovingly done for me.

Kellan was finally downstairs, drinking his coffee and looking casually perfect, if a little pale. Denny nodded to him, smiling happily. "G'day, mate."

Kellan, although wan, managed an effortlessly casual smile. "Mornin' . . . mate."

Denny kissed me one last time, cupping my cheek. "Now I'm going to be late." He grinned at me suggestively, making me blush. "You're worth it though," he whispered.

I glanced over at Kellan. He paled a little more and continued studiously drinking his coffee, and I knew that he knew what that meant. Maybe he'd even heard us in the shower. I couldn't remember if I was quiet or not . . . probably not. Denny gave me a final hug, cheerily said goodbye, and then left for work. I stood, rather stupidly, in the middle of the room, unsure of what to do.

"I put your coffee in the microwave," Kellan whispered from the table. I looked over to his pale face, his soft eyes. "It was cold . . ." he finished.

I swallowed the lump in my throat and went over to the microwave, starting it for one minute. I turned back to Kellan while it reheated. "Kellan . . . I'm—"

"Don't," he interrupted softly, staring blankly into his cup.

I blinked. "But . . ."

He stood up and walked over to me. He stopped a ways from me and didn't touch me. "You don't owe me an explanation. . . ." He looked at the floor. "And you definitely don't owe me an apology." He looked back up at me. "So just . . . . don't say anything, please."

Guilt and sympathy for him washed through me, and I held my arms open for him. "Come here." He hesitated a moment, a torn look on his face; then he slipped his arms around my waist and buried his head in my neck. I held him tight and rubbed his back. "I'm sorry," I whispered in his ear. He might not have wanted to hear it, but I needed to say it.

He exhaled softly and nodded into my shoulder, clutching me a little tighter.

He was still pale and a little quiet when he drove me to school. Guilt surged through me. It had bothered him. I wasn't sure why; I wasn't sure what I was to him, but he had told me it would bother him, and it had. I felt bad about that. But I wasn't his. We were just friends . . . and Denny *was* my boyfriend and it was going to happen again. I watched his silent face as we drove the short distance to school. I hoped he wasn't hurt too badly.

He walked me to class again and seemed to perk up on the way there. He wanted to discuss my Lit class, and had some amusing theories on Austen's view of society . . . most of them linked with my earlier Psych lesson on sexual repression. This time, I was laughing pretty hard by the time he opened the door to the room, and I'm pretty sure my face was bright red.

I decided to skip out on Psych class. I know, not the best idea, but I was anxious to get home and spend a little free time with Kellan before work. Besides, the Psych class was more on Freud, which I just couldn't take today. When I walked through the door, I saw Kellan playing his guitar on the couch. The song was beautiful, and I smiled at him warmly as he looked over and gave me a look that quickened my heart. He stopped playing and started to set his guitar down.

"No, don't stop," I said as I walked over to sit beside him. "It's beautiful."

He looked down, smiling softly, and then shook his head. He put the guitar on my lap instead. "Here . . . try again."

I grimaced. The last time he had tried to teach me, I had been atrocious. "It's beautiful when you play it. Something seems to happen to it when I try."

He laughed and twisted me on the couch so that he could put his arms around me and his hands over mine. "You just need to hold it right," he whispered in my ear. His breath sent a shiver down my spine and I closed my eyes for a second, deeply inhaling his scent, while he adjusted our fingers on the guitar.

"Okay . . . hey." He nudged my shoulder with a short laugh when he noticed that my eyes were closed. Embarrassed, I blushed and opened my eyes and he laughed again. "Here . . . your fingers are perfect, right under mine." He lightly held my fingers in an awkward position on the neck of the guitar. "Now"—he showed me the pick in his other hand—"lightly strum it like this. . . ." He did it once. The guitar hummed beautifully.

He placed the pick in my fingers and I tried to copy his move. The sound was not a beautiful hum. It wasn't beautiful at all. He laughed and grabbed my hand, basically doing the strumming for me. With him doing all of the work, the guitar was, once again, beautiful. He idly moved our fingers across the neck, while strumming our locked hands together on the body, playing a simple rhythm. Eventually, I picked up the feel for it and relaxed into him.

He smiled and gazed at me, still playing for us without even looking. "This really isn't so hard. I learned this one when I was six." He winked at me, and I blushed again.

"Well . . . you're just more talented with your fingers," I blurted out, momentarily distracted by his easy smile.

He stopped playing and laughed. I rolled my eyes and laughed with him. "You have such a dirty mind. You and Griffin are a lot alike."

He grimaced, then laughed again. "I can't help it if I think that way around you." He gazed at me intently and then took his hands off the guitar. "You try."

I put my hands back where they had been and tried again to strum like he did. Amazingly, after the third or fourth time, it sounded okay. Looking back at him, I giggled. He smiled and nodded; then he showed me a different chord, and after a few tries I managed to make that one sound sort of decent too. After quite a few fumbled attempts, I could finally, sort of, play the song he had learned when he was just a boy.

I played for a while, him adjusting my fingers every now and then or showing me a new chord when I finally got one down. Eventually, I sagged against him and flexed my hand. He laughed and put the guitar on the ground, pulling me back into his chest and grabbing my hand to massage it. I was careful not to make any noises to distract him. It was heaven.

"You have to build up the strength for it," he murmured, as he rubbed out my aching fingers.

"Hmmmm . . ." I closed my eyes, enjoying the closeness of him.

Eventually he stopped and held me against him. I felt like I could stay there all night, warm in his arms. "Can we try something?" he asked quietly.

I stiffened automatically in his embrace, and turned to look back at him smiling at me. "What?" I asked cautiously.

He laughed at my reluctance. "It's innocent . . . I promise."

He abruptly lay back on the couch and held his arms out to me. I looked at him, confused, and then snuggled into his shoulder, nestling into the space between him and the couch. He sighed happily and wrapped his arms around me, stroking my arm lightly.

I pulled back and looked at him, still confused. "This is what you wanted to do?"

He shrugged. "Yeah, it looked . . . nice . . . when you did this with Denny. . . ."

I nodded and laid my head on his chest, fighting back the sudden guilt at the mention of Denny's name, and at the simple affection that Kellan wanted from me. I carefully put a leg over his and an arm over his chest. He sighed again and leaned his head against mine. His heartbeat was steady and strong. I felt like mine was all over the place.

"Is this okay with you?" he whispered into my hair.

I forced myself to relax. This simplicity was all he wanted, and I *was* enjoying his closeness. "Yeah . . . it's nice. Are you okay?" I absentmindedly traced a circle on his chest.

He chuckled softly. "I'm fine, Kiera." He gently rubbed my back.

I sighed and truly relaxed, clutching him tighter with my arm and my leg. He pulled me tighter in response and we simply held each other. I watched his shirt rise and fall with his even breathing. I gazed at the skin of his neck. I watched his throat move when he swallowed. I lingered over the near right angle at the corner of his strong jaw. Finally, I closed my eyes and nestled into his neck, letting the warmth of his presence wash over me.

All too soon, he stirred beneath me, and I realized that I had fallen asleep in his embrace. "Sorry . . . I didn't mean to wake you."

I sat bolt upright and stared at the front door, his familiar words stirring a memory in me. "Denny," I whispered, glancing down at his confused face.

He sat up and hooked some hair behind my ear. "You weren't asleep long. It's still early. He won't be home for an hour or so." Kellan looked away, his face thoughtful. "I wouldn't let him . . ." He looked back at me. "I won't let him see this, if you don't want him to."

I was immediately shaking my head. No, Denny wouldn't understand. I wasn't sure that I even did. Kellan nodded and stared at me intently. Needing a break from his intenseness, I spat out a question that had been jostling in my head for a while.

"Where did you go when you used to disappear? When you didn't come home all night?" I settled back into the couch sitting side by side with him. He smiled at me, but said nothing. I frowned at his reaction. "If you were . . . if you *are* seeing someone, you should just tell me." He really didn't have an obligation to tell me anything, but I was insanely curious.

He cocked his head to the side endearingly. "Is that what you think? That when I'm not with you, I'm with a woman?"

I cringed and regretted even asking him. Quietly, I made myself say, "You're *not* with me; you have every right"—I grabbed his fingers and held his hand, avoiding his gaze—"to date."

"I know," he said softly, rubbing his thumb on the back of my hand. "Would it bother you if I was seeing someone?" he asked quietly.

I swallowed and turned my head away from him, not wanting to answer. It slipped out anyway. "Yes," I whispered. He sighed, and when I looked back, he was staring at the floor. "What?" I asked cautiously.

He put an arm around my waist and pulled me close, rubbing my back. "Nothing."

"I'm not being fair, am I?" I asked, melting into his tender embrace. "I'm with Denny. You and I are . . . just friends. I can't ask you to never . . ."

He shifted uncomfortably and then chuckled. "Well, we could solve this little problem if you relaxed your rules." He grinned over at me devilishly. "Especially that first one."

I kept my face serious and he stopped laughing. Quietly, I said, "I'll understand. I won't like it, anymore than you probably like me with Denny . . . but I'll understand. Just don't hide it. Don't sneak around on me. We shouldn't have secrets. . . ."

I realized how absurd that sounded, and a part of me didn't want to know, didn't want to see it, but I didn't want to be in the dark either. I knew that we were borderline friends, occasionally drifting into something more. I realized that what we were doing—flirting, being so close all the time—was dangerous and stupid, like tempting fate. I knew it; I just couldn't stop it. I couldn't stop thinking about him, wanting to be near him, wanting to touch him, wanting to hold him. But it couldn't be anything more than that, and it wasn't right to ask him to deny himself . . . anything, for this small piece of myself that I was allowing him. That wasn't fair.

He looked at me wistfully for a full minute before finally nodding, once.

I gazed at his sad eyes. "So, where do you go?" I whispered.

His expression changed and warmed, his eyes sparkling at me. "Where do I go? Well, it depends. Sometimes it's Matt and Griffin's place, sometimes it's Evan's. Sometimes I drink myself into oblivion on Sam's doorstep." He grinned devilishly and chuckled at that.

"Oh . . ." The answer was so simple that it should have been obvious to me. I had just assumed that he had been out "sowing his wild oats," as they say. I reached up and stroked his cheek, feeling that I could finally ask him the question that I really wanted an answer to. "Where did you go after our first time? I didn't see you all day, all night? And you came home . . ." *Completely wasted,* I thought, but didn't say.

Abruptly, he stood up and held out his hand. "Come on. I'll give you a ride to Pete's."

I stood and took his hand. "Kellan, you can tell me, I won't . . ."

He smiled at me, his eyes showing no humor. "You don't want to be late."

I knew our conversation was over, and it irritated me. His avoidance also filled my stomach with dread. We shouldn't have any secrets, but apparently we did. "You don't have to give me a ride everywhere, you know." He raised an eyebrow and smirked at me. "I managed just fine without you," I pouted.

He rolled his eyes and, smiling, led me upstairs so I could get ready for work. He stayed with me at the bar for most of the evening. I chided him about missing rehearsal time with the guys, and he laughed and rolled his eyes at me again. It made me feel equally nice and equally worried, that he'd rather spend the time with me.

During one of my breaks, he attempted to teach me how to play pool better. That was pretty amusing, since our skill level was virtually the same. Honestly, I think he just liked helping me line up shots and, honestly, I liked having his body stretched across mine as he helped me. We played a quick game while I ate a small meal. Well, for anyone else it would have been a quick game. After both of us repeatedly missed shot after shot, my break was over, my meal was done, and I went back to work, leaving him to finish up the game with Griffin, to whom he lost terribly.

I stuck my head into the pool room as their game was finally finishing. Laughing that he'd predictably lost, I said, "Better keep your day job, Band Boy."

He raised an eyebrow and twisted his lips derisively. "Band Boy?" Smiling, I nodded and walked away. From behind me I heard, rather loudly, "Band Boy? Really, what are we, in the fifth grade?"

I laughed at his remark as I headed up to the bar to place an order. Jenny smiled when she joined me. "You and Kellan seem better."

I frowned at her after relaying my order to Rita, who moved to the other side of the bar to fill it. "What do you mean?" Kate joined me on my other side and gracefully sat on a stool to wait for Rita to get back.

Jenny cocked her head to the side and furrowed her brow slightly. "Well, he seemed a little cold toward you a while ago."

Kate chimed in, "Did he? What, did you use all his shampoo or something?" She sighed dreamily. "God, he's got great hair."

I laughed nervously at the both of them. "Yeah . . . just stupid roommate stuff. We're fine now." Luckily, I didn't have to elaborate, as Rita came back with my order. I left the three of them discussing the virtues of Kellan's hair as I finished up my night. I needed to be more careful around Jenny. She noticed too much.

Chapter 13
A Bad Idea

The following evening was busy for a weeknight, and Griffin was again apparently . . . bored. He had climbed on top of his usual table and was singing along loudly to the jukebox—more specifically, to Sir Mix-A-Lot's "Baby Got Back." He was making obscene gestures and gyrating his hips about in a way that was sure to give me night-mares. A few women around the table were laughing and holding out dollar bills to him. He took them gleefully and shoved them places I did not want to think about.

Evan, Matt, and Kellan had backed away from the table and were laughing hysterically at the idiot. Kellan looked over to where I was standing in the middle of the aisle watching the crude show and winked at me, still laughing. I laughed and smiled back at him.

"Get off the damn table, Griffin!" Pete had come out of the kitchen, where his office was tucked away in an old storage closet, and was scowling at the bassist.

Immediately, Griffin jumped down to the adoring harem hover-ing close to his side. "Sorry, Pete." He smiled, not looking sorry at all. Shaking his head and muttering to himself, Pete walked back into the kitchen.

I laughed even harder, until I felt something behind me. A hand had reached up the loose skirt I was wearing and grabbed my upper thigh. I squeaked and moved away. A dirty looking middle-aged man leered at me with beady brown eyes and grinned, showing a mouthful of yellowed teeth. He winked one of those tiny little eyes in a not at all charming way, while his equally scummy looking friend laughed. I quickly darted off to the safety of the bar.

I didn't recognize the men. They were not regulars, and they were not pleasant. They were also seated in such a way in my section that I had to pass by them every time I went up to the bar, and every time, the lewd man made a grab for my legs, no matter how far away I scooted. I put it off as long as I could, but inevitably the time came for me to hand them their bill. The larger man, who had felt my leg before, stood up and roughly grabbed my ass, pulling me tight against him while his other hand grabbed my breast.

Angrily, I smacked his hand away from my chest and tried to push him off of me, which only succeeded in making him laugh. He reeked of an odor I could only classify as "eau de poor life." It was an unappealing mix of stale cigarettes, three-day-old whiskey, and, I swear, manure. And that mix didn't include his breath, which made the rest of him smell downright delectable in comparison. I looked around for Sam, but then I remembered that he was off today and that Pete hadn't thought the bar was busy enough to staff another full-time bouncer. At the moment, I disagreed with him.

I wasn't sure what to do, and I didn't think I could take the guy. Abruptly, he was pulled away from me.

Evan stood behind him, with the man's arms held down to his sides. Kellan was instantly in the man's face. He looked livid. "Not a good idea." His voice was low and ice-cold.

Matt stepped up to the smaller man, who had risen to defend his friend. Griffin came up to me and casually threw an arm around my shoulders. "Yeah, this ass is ours," he said, with a big smile on his face.

The big guy angrily shook off Evan and roughly pushed Kellan back a step. "Piss off, pretty boy."

Kellan grabbed his shirt in both hands and got right back in his face. "Try it . . . please. . . ."

The man stared at Kellan, looking like he wanted to pound him into the ground. Kellan stared right back, not afraid in the least. The whole bar was quiet, watching the stare-down. Kellan finally released the big man, his hands shaking a little with restraint. "I suggest you leave now. I wouldn't come back if I were you." His voice was scarily cold.

The smaller guy grabbed his friend's shoulder. "Come on, man. She's not worth it."

Sniffing and looking Kellan up and down once, the man winked at me again, then turned to leave. Kellan relaxed and looked over at me, concern on his face. The man had almost fully turned from Kellan, when he suddenly reached into his jacket. I only saw a glint of metal and heard a flicking sound, before the man was turning swiftly around and lunging toward Kellan.

I yelled Kellan's name. Looking back to the man, he spun away from him. The knife the man had brought around just barely missed Kellan's body. Griffin immediately pulled me back from the both of them, just as I lurched forward to help. Matt pushed the smaller man away from his friend, as he looked about to join the fight. Evan made a move for the bigger man's knife hand, but Kellan was faster—he landed a hard punch along the man's jaw, sending him sprawling to the ground with a grunt. The knife clattered under a nearby table.

Kellan moved to pick the man up, but the man knew when he was beaten. He scrambled away from Kellan and, turning, stood and fled the bar, his friend quickly following. Everyone in the bar was silent for a good minute; then buzzing noises returned and people started going back to their own business.

Taking a big breath and slightly flexing his hand, Kellan looked over to me. "You okay?" He frowned.

I sighed, relaxing for the first time since the confrontation. "Yeah, thank you, Kellan . . . guys." I smiled and looked at Kellan, then Evan, and then Matt. Lastly, I looked over to Griffin beside me. "You can get your hand off my butt now, Griffin."

Kellan, looking pale, laughed softly, while Griffin pulled his hand back and held it up in the air. "Sorry." He pointed to his hand. "Mind of its own." He winked at me, and then he and a chuckling Matt went back to whatever they had been doing before the little showdown.

Evan and Kellan stayed near me. Evan gave Kellan a once-over, his face serious. "You okay, Kell? Did he get you?" I startled and looked more closely at him. Was he hurt?

Kellan cringed and, finally turning to face me, put a hand under his shirt. When he pulled it back, his fingers were smeared with blood.

"Oh, God . . ." I grabbed his hand and then lifted up his shirt. A good three-inch-long slice along his ribs showed just how close the fight had been. The cut didn't look too deep, but it was bleeding pretty well. "Kellan, you should go to the hospital."

He looked down cursorily and smirked. "He barely got me. I'm fine." He half-smiled and raised an eyebrow at me still holding his shirt up.

I dropped it and grabbed his hand again. "Come on."

Evan clapped him on the back as I led him away. With Kellen smiling and looking satisfied with himself, we worked our way to the back hallway while people occasionally stopped him, wanting to talk about it. *Men,* I thought, as I pulled him past the curious guys and practically drooling girls. I dragged him into the back room with me, grabbed a clean towel and an extralarge Band-Aid from the first-aid kit in one of the never-used lockers. I hoped it was enough, that the cut wasn't so deep that he needed stitches. Dragging him back into the hallway, I stopped outside the women's bathroom.

"You stay here." I pointed to his chest while he grinned adorably and made an X over his heart. Opening the door, I took a quick look into the stalls and, not seeing anyone, came back out into the hallway, where Kellan was patiently leaning against the wall, waiting for me. I could see the red bloodstain on his shirt now as it stuck to his wet skin. I swallowed roughly.

"This isn't necessary," he said as I grabbed his hand and led him inside the bathroom. "I'm fine," he insisted.

I scowled at his stubbornness. "Shirt off."

He grinned wickedly. "Yes, ma'am."

I rolled my eyes and tried not to notice how fabulous his body was as he stretched up to remove his shirt. He held it in one hand and waited patiently by the sink, a slight smile on his face. His cut wasn't bleeding as badly, but it still oozed a bit down his side. Butterflies danced in my stomach as I thought of what might have happened if he hadn't turned out of the way.

I turned on some cold water and soaked the towel. He inhaled a bit as I started to wipe clean the wound, which made me grin. "You're such a sadist," he muttered, and I threw him a dirty look. He gave me a delightful laugh.

"What were you thinking, going up against a guy with a knife?" I asked, trying to be gentler as I cleaned the gash. It was deeper than I'd originally thought and had started to bleed a little more when I touched it.

"Well," he inhaled again, "obviously, I didn't know he had a knife." I finished cleaning the wound on his side and pressed the towel firmly against it, making him grunt. "I wasn't about to let him keep touching you like that," he said softly, and I looked up to gaze into his sparkling blue eyes. I held the towel there for a moment while I locked gazes with him. Finally, I pulled the towel away and saw that the wound was no longer bleeding. I opened the large bandage and frowned, worried that the cut would bleed again the moment he moved. He grinned and said, "He can't touch you like that if I don't get to. It's against the rules." He chuckled and I slapped on the bandage none too gently, making him groan and flinch. Instantly I felt bad, as *I* had probably just made it bleed again.

More gently, I stroked my fingers over the bandage, flattening it out over his muscled side. "Well, it was stupid—you could have been seriously hurt, Kellan." I had to swallow the lump in my throat over that thought.

He grabbed my fingers and held my hand to his chest. "Better me than you, Kiera," he whispered. We stared into each other's eyes for a moment, then he said, "Thank you . . . for watching out for me." He stroked my fingers with his thumb. My breath caught at the look in his eye, at his bare skin under my fingertips.

I blushed and looked away. "You can put your shirt back on now."

He smiled and slid it back on. I cringed at the bloody stain in the side, the tear in the fabric; that had been much too close. Tears stung my eyes and Kellan noticed, pulling me in for a tight embrace. He inhaled a little and I relaxed my grip, realizing that I was hurting him.

"Sorry," I whispered. "You really should get that looked at."

He nodded and pulled me tighter. I sighed and relaxed into him. We were embracing like that when Jenny opened the door. "Oops . . . just checking to see how your patient was doing."

I pulled away from him. "We were just . . . he's fine," I mumbled.

Kellan laughed softly and walked past Jenny to the hallway. Stopping just past the door, he turned and looked back to me. "Thank you again, Kiera." My heart stubbornly skipped a beat. He nodded politely at Jenny. "I should probably get that knife from Griffin now."

She looked at him, puzzled. "Griffin has it?" He raised an eyebrow at her. She rolled her eyes and sighed. "Griffin . . . yeah, you should go get it." He looked back at me one last time; then, chuckling, he walked down the hall.

She looked back at me through the still open door. "Coming?"

I sighed, willing my suddenly shaking hands and surging heartbeat to calm down. "Yeah . . . I just need a minute."

I ended up taking ten.

I playfully smacked Kellan's stomach as I came up to him in the kitchen the next morning. He grunted and bent over a bit and, too late, I remembered his injury.

"Oh . . . sorry . . ." I said, a look of horror on my face.

He chuckled and pulled me in for a hug. "I'm just messing with you. It doesn't hurt that bad."

I laced my arms around his neck and frowned at him. "That's not very nice."

He grinned devilishly at me. "No . . . but I did get you to put your arms around me," he finished with a wink.

I rolled my eyes and smiled at him. "You're impossible."

"True, but you like me anyway." He pulled me tighter.

I sighed dramatically. "I have no idea why."

He grinned and cocked his head to the side, momentarily taking my breath. "So you *do* like me. I was curious. . . ."

Carefully smacking his chest, I pulled away from his embrace. "Let me see." I motioned for him to lift up his shirt.

He smirked and pulled it up. "Trying to get me naked yet again?"

I laughed in spite of myself and examined his bandage. There was some red that had seeped through; he had bled more. I frowned at him. "You were supposed to get this looked at last night." I had even made him leave the bar shortly after the incident, but apparently, he hadn't felt the need for professional help.

He shrugged.

"Well, you need a new bandage. Do you have any?" He nodded and left to go get one while I made my coffee. Just as I was taking a sip, he returned with one.

Leaning against the counter, he handed it to me. "Would you like to do the honors, since you seem to enjoy hurting me so much?"

I grinned and he shook his head, smiling. He lifted up his shirt again and made a "go ahead" motion with his hand. I carefully pulled back a corner and looked to make sure that nothing was sticking to the Band-Aid. Seeing that it was clear, I peeked up at his eyes and abruptly ripped it off him.

"Shit!" he exclaimed loudly, pulling his body away from me. Laughing, I shushed him, pointing upstairs to where Denny was still sleeping. Grimacing, he looked up, then back down to me. "Sorry, but damn it, woman . . ."

Still laughing, I smiled and shook my head. "Big baby . . ." I inspected the wound. I was no nurse, but it looked okay, not inflamed or anything. I carefully cleaned it off and smiled when no blood came out; it must have closed sometime last night. Good, he probably didn't need stitches, then.

I opened the bandage slowly, enjoying the long sigh he gave me, since he knew that this one would have to come off too. I gently pressed it against his side, laughing softly to myself. My fingers started drifting a bit from the wounded area and he chuckled quietly.

"Dang, man!" I spun toward the entryway, where Denny was standing, yawning and looking at Kellan's side. "What happened to you?"

Smoothly, Kellan dropped his shirt and leaned back against the counter. He looked casual and perfect, not in the least ruffled that Denny had just walked in on me practically stroking his chest. I backed away from him, trying to mimic his casualness.

"Some fan . . . she went nuts, wanted a piece of me . . . literally." Kellan smiled. "Luckily, Kiera here is a good nurse." He nodded over to me.

Denny smiled too. "Yeah, not the gentlest though." He smiled wider as I scowled and Kellan laughed. He walked into the kitchen, frowning at Kellan. "Is that really what happened?"

Kellan shook his head. I watched him, amazed that he could joke and be so casual with Denny, when we were being . . . well, not casual. "No, I'm kidding. Some stupid drunk last night pulled a knife on me."

"Damn." Denny walked over to me and slipped his arms around my waist, oddly making me blush. "You do his girl or something?"

I looked back at Denny. He was smiling, so I knew he was joking, but Kellan gave him an odd look before bringing back his casual smile. "Maybe. Sometimes it's hard to tell who belongs to whom." He flicked his eyes down to mine when he said that, but Denny didn't notice; he was too busy kissing my neck.

Laughing softly, Denny looked back up to Kellan and clapped him on the shoulder. "Well, I hope you got him back good." Kellan gave him a quick grin and nodded. "Good on ya. Glad you're all right, mate." Denny gave me a quick kiss on the cheek and said, "I've got time. Are you hungry?"

"Sure." He turned in for a kiss and I gave him a quick peck, sneaking a peek at Kellan, who was staring at the floor.

Denny moved to the fridge and leaned in, searching for something in the back. Kellan came up behind me, grasped my fingers with his, and pulled my hand behind me. I looked over at him, but his face was unreadable; his eyes watched Denny intently. He stroked my fingers for a second, then clenched my hand in his. He dropped my hand just as Denny popped up from the fridge.

"Aaahh, good . . . strawberry pancakes?" he asked sweetly, showing me the carton of berries he had found in the fridge.

I nodded and looked down while Kellan quietly left the kitchen. Waves of guilt washed through me and I had no idea who I felt it for—Denny or Kellan?

Jenny and Kate both approached me once I got to work that night. They wanted to hear about the knife fight yesterday, as they had both been too far away to really see it. They asked how Kellan was doing, and I blushed lightly when I told them he was fine, even a little proud of his war wound. They both shared my concern over how close that had been, and how much worse it could have been for Kellan. My heart squeezed at that and I glanced back to his table, where he was eating and waiting for the rest of his band to show up. A few girls across from him were looking like they were going to join him, but he was ignoring them, talking to Sam instead. Yeah, that had been much too close.

The three of us went back to our customers and I smiled as I glanced at Kellan again. He noticed my gaze and smiled back. My heart stuttered and I had to look away. Eventually the evening progressed, and Kellan was no longer the only D-Bag at his table. Pete caught me on my way out of the kitchen and asked me to tell Kellan that they were up. Smiling, I nodded and made my way over to his table.

Kellan smiled at my approach. He was sitting back in his chair and slightly away from the table, making his lap an almost irresistible draw. For a moment, I wanted to be like his more forward fans and plop right down for a snuggle. I imagined his arms wrapping around me. I imagined being enveloped in the smell of him. I imagined the warmth of his skin as I kissed his neck. . . .

"Kiera?" He cocked his head and looked at me curiously, and I realized my inappropriate thoughts had caused me to stare at him without saying a word.

I blushed and looked away. "You guys are up," I said to the general vicinity of the band's table.

I heard chairs squeak as the guys stood up. Matt and Evan thanked me and hopped onstage to loud fanfare. Griffin just hopped onstage. Sometimes basic niceties escaped him. I turned to watch Kellan finish his beer and then slowly stand. He stood at the table for a second, smiling at me and looking like he was waiting for something. I frowned and looked at him quizzically.

"So . . . aren't you going to wish me good luck?" he said, coming over to stand close beside me. He leaned back against the table as he waited.

I relaxed my face and then grinned at him. "You don't need my luck to do great up there."

He smiled wide and I felt a little dizzy. "True, but I like it."

I laughed and gave him a swift hug. "Well, good luck, then."

He pouted charmingly. "I generally get more than a grand-motherly hug from girls when they wish me luck." He raised an eye-brow at me suggestively.

I laughed again and smacked his shoulder. "Well, I'm not just any girl."

He smiled adoringly and shook his head. "No . . . no you're not." He turned and hopped up on the stage and I felt so dizzy again, I had to lean against the table for a second.

As usual, the band was amazing. The crowd seemed to double in size as the band played on, and I didn't have as much time as I would have liked to watch Kellan play. But in between orders, I did steal a glance or two. It thrilled me when I caught him watching me. It also concerned me a little, but I quickly pushed that to the back of my mind. I had to admit to myself, I liked his attention.

I sang along softly to the songs that I knew as I helped the many thirsty people in the bar. Near the end of their set, the band played a song that caught my attention. I hadn't heard the intense song before, but the crowd was singing along, so it must have been an old one. I glanced over at Jenny and she was singing along, too. The lyrics were intensely serious and so was Kellan's face. He almost looked mad.

"I've seen what you've done to her. . . . I know your secret. You may break her, but it won't last, you won't last. She holds herself tight, waits for the pain to be over. It won't be long now, until the angels hover."

He concentrated more on his guitar than the crowd while he played, and I couldn't help but shake the feeling that the song had nothing to do with a woman.

"You took everything, left her with nothing. She was supposed to be loved. What's wrong with you? She'll find strength, she'll be free. It won't be long . . . for her . . . for me. . . ."

I felt the sudden inexplicable need to hold him, comfort him. I watched him from the corner of my eye as I tended to my customers. Eventually the song ended, and he switched to a happy, upbeat one. All trace of the emotion in the previous song evaporated from his face, but I couldn't shake the image of his ire.

"I'm sorry, babe." Denny was looking at me dejectedly as he sat on the edge of the bed. He was removing his shoes and rubbing his feet.

"It's fine, Denny. It's just one weekend. Really, I can handle that."

"It's really just one night apart. I'll be back late the next night, probably before you get home from work." He sighed and put his feet on the carpet. "I am sorry though." He rolled his eyes. "It's ridiculous; the only reason Max is making me go to this conference instead of him is because he's flying to Vegas for a bachelor party." He shook his head, irritated. "If his uncle knew, he'd be racked off."

I shrugged. "Why don't you tell him?"

He looked at me with a wry smile and shook his head. "I really don't need to make my job any worse." I cringed a bit, remembering why he had this job in the first place and, noticing, he immediately said, "Sorry."

I shook my head, clearing away the memory. "So you're leaving Friday morning and you'll be back late Saturday, right?"

He came over to sit beside me on the bed. "Yeah. I'll miss you." He smiled at me and leaned over to kiss my neck.

My thoughts started drifting as his lips ran down my skin. I'd have an entire afternoon alone with Kellan. Maybe we could go somewhere . . . take a drive somewhere people didn't know us, where our flirting didn't have to be quite so contained behind closed doors. He had spent nearly all last weekend with Denny and me. The three of us had gone exploring downtown, Kellan showing us all of his favorite places. Kellan would squeeze my hand when Denny wasn't looking, or hold me close in a quick embrace. We would gaze at each other discreetly and we smiled . . . a lot.

Denny's lips were trailing down past my neck. It was jarring me from my pleasant memories and I pushed him away a little. "Are you hungry? I could make dinner this time." I had a feeling that wasn't what he was "hungry" for, but I really wasn't in the mood.

He frowned slightly, but pulled away. "Yeah . . . sure."

"Okay," I said cheerily, as I hopped up and kissed his forehead.

I glanced at Kellan's room as I exited our room, but he wasn't there. His band was playing tonight at a small club in Pioneer Square. I had racked my brain, wondering how I could go without making Denny suspicious. It was my night off, and I rarely got to see Kellan play anywhere but Pete's. I remembered the one time I had watched him at Razors. He had been amazing in a smaller, more intimate setting like that . . . not that he wasn't always amazing when he sang.

I sighed as I stepped off the last stair and walked through the empty living room. The house was so quiet without him. He was constantly playing or humming or singing. He filled our home with music, with his presence. It felt a little empty here with him gone. I had considered telling Denny that I was spending the evening with Jenny . . . but that would require a lot of lying. For one, Jenny was actually *at* work, and if Denny got bored and went to Pete's . . . well, that wouldn't be good.

I sighed again as I entered the kitchen and started rummaging for food. I didn't want to be a liar anyway. That wasn't me. I could wait. I would see Kellan soon. We'd have almost all this coming weekend together. I frowned a bit, as I realized that we'd also have a whole evening alone together too. I shook my head. That didn't matter. We were just friends. We weren't going any further than that.

My smile returned as I thought back over the last few days with Kellan. I found something intricate to make for dinner and let my mind wander back through the memories as I started the process of preparing our meal. Not only had our weekend been great, he had been sweet and charming the whole week too. He always took me to school and walked me to class. Women now looked at the door expectantly to see him enter with me, which made me laugh a little. He usually picked me up too, and either took me home or to Pete's, if I wanted to go in early to study. I usually didn't. I preferred to study with him on the couch, although sometimes it was just too distracting to lie on his lap and try to read *Pride and Prejudice* while he stroked my hair. I usually found myself staring into his eyes instead, making him laugh and point at the book. Then I'd hand the novel over to him and make him read it to me. He'd happily do it, his voice nearly lulling me to sleep it was so smooth and at times, I swear, purposely husky.

Denny joined me downstairs right as I finished, and we ate our dinner together at the table. He told me some more details about this conference he had to go to and I told him about my classes. We talked about my Econ class for an absurdly long amount of time—I really never needed to study for that class, since I learned more just talking it over with Denny than from reading the books or my notes. After dinner, he cleaned up while I answered the ringing phone. It was my sister, and we talked long into the night. She was excited to come up and wanted to make sure Kellan was still coming when we all went out together. I sighed and swallowed my frustrations at that—it would be fine—and then we moved on to her current flings.

I was still chatting with her on the phone when Denny came up and kissed my cheek to say good night. I don't know if I was waiting for Kellan to come home from the bar or not, but I stayed on the phone with my sister for hours after Denny went to bed. Kellan did finally come home, and I finally hung up with her, melting into his warm embrace.

"So, Denny's gone tonight?" Kellan asked, holding my hand over the kitchen table while we drank our coffee.

I eyed him suspiciously. "Yes . . . he's in Portland until tomorrow night. Why?"

He looked down, considering something, then spoke without looking back up at me. "Stay with me tonight."

"I stay here with you every night," I said, confused. We did share a house, after all.

He looked up at me, amused. "No . . . sleep with me tonight."

"Kellan! That is not going to—"

He interrupted me. "I meant literally . . . fall asleep with me on my bed." He laughed at my assumption.

I blushed and looked away, making him laugh some more. Finally my embarrassment cooled, and I looked back over to him. "I don't think that's such a good idea, Kellan."

He cocked his head and smiled brilliantly. "Why not? Completely innocent—I won't even get under the covers."

I raised an eyebrow. "Completely dressed too?" Why was I even considering this? It was not a good idea.

"Sure." He laughed again. "If that is what you'd prefer." He stroked my hand with his thumb.

I laughed, and then smiled at the thought of falling asleep in his arms. "It is." I frowned. It really wasn't a good idea though . . . too many things could go horribly wrong. "You'll let me know the moment it gets too hard."

He looked away, barely containing his laughter. Immediately, I realized how that sounded and blushed deeply. "You know what I mean," I whispered, mortified.

Laughing softly, he said, "Yes, I know what you mean . . . and yes, I will." He sighed. "You really are adorable . . . do you know that?" His face seemed sincere when he said that, so I smiled and looked away.

"Okay . . . we'll try it." I whispered, thinking this was a really bad idea.

Denny came downstairs a while later, looking freshly showered and holding one of our duffel bags. His normally warm brown eyes looked flat with sadness. He seemed reluctant to leave, and I gave him a long kiss goodbye, hoping to cheer him up a bit. He did give me a half-smile when he finally left the house. Oddly, my stomach was fine as I watched him drive off. I decided it was because he was only going to be gone for one night. It was a finite period, unlike the last time he'd left me. But then Kellan came up behind me, putting his arms around my waist as he stared out the kitchen window with me. I melted back into his embrace and wondered why I was *really* okay with Denny being gone.

Later at Pete's, I stopped wiping down a table and listened without looking to a song I'd never heard the guys play before. It was the closest thing to a love song I'd ever heard from the band. It was catchy and upbeat, with lyrics about "not being alone now" and "feeling happy when you're around." I wondered if the song was new, and my heart raced a little at the thought of Kellan writing something just for me. I was smiling contentedly as I continued wiping down the table, lost in dreamy thoughts.

"Huh." Jenny came up beside me and I startled as I looked over at her. She was watching the band curiously. I glanced over at them too, worried that maybe Kellan had looked at me inappropriately and she was suspicious. Kellan flicked a glance in our direction but was mainly smiling at the crowd of girls near him, like he usually did.

I relaxed. "What?"

Jenny turned and smiled at me. "Evan must be in love again."

"Oh . . . why?" I asked curiously.

She laughed a little and nodded her head toward the stage. "This song . . . they always play it whenever he's swooning over some girl." She looked over the crowd. "I wonder which lucky lady it is?"

My spirit deflated a bit. "Hmmm . . . don't know." Okay, so Kellan didn't write it for me. That's probably for the best anyway. I really didn't need him gushing over me. He had a hard enough time with just being attracted to me (for some odd reason), no need to throw love on top of that. We're just friends anyway. Flirty friends, who were snuggling in bed later tonight. I frowned. It really was not a good idea.

"Do you need a ride home tonight?" Jenny asked politely.

"No, Kellan's giving me a ride back." I smiled and tried hard to not look overly excited about that. "Thank you though."

"No problem." Someone paged Jenny on the other side of the bar and she politely excused herself.

I took a few more orders. A nearby couple was obviously on a first date. The man was horribly nervous, the woman cutely shy. They made me smile. While I was waiting at the bar for their drinks, Kellan's song ended and, upon hearing his speaking voice, I glanced up at the stage.

"Ladies . . ." The crowd went wild and he smiled. "And you guys, of course." A few raucous cheers in the back at that. "Thank you for coming out tonight." Kellan grinned and held up a finger. "We got one more for you; then we're baggin'." He flicked a glance at me discreetly. "Plans and all." He laughed, and some girls in the front screamed loudly.

He winked at them and, taking his shirt, used the bottom to wipe some sweat off his face; it was rather warm in the packed bar. The move exposed a good chunk of his excessively defined abs and the girls around him went nuts! The scream was so loud, I actually flinched.

From directly behind me, Rita yelled through cupped hands, "Take it off! Woooooo!"

He stopped and grinned widely at her, then over at me. The crowd screamed even louder at that prospect and Kellan laughed. He looked over at the guys beside him for a second. Griffin grinned, Matt frowned, and Evan laughed. Kellan shrugged and actually took his shirt off! I gaped at him as he casually stretched it over his head, like he was in his room alone, not up onstage, in front of a packed crowd.

The sound in the bar was deafening! The earlier loud scream paled in comparison. Rita was hollering loudly behind me, and I was a little surprised to find that Jenny and Kate had come up to the bar and were leaning back on either side of me, hollering and whistling with her.

I was still gaping openmouthed at the whole thing, when Jenny laughed at me. She nudged my shoulder. "Oh, come on. Even *you* have to admit he's hot! You're with Denny, but you're not dead." She grinned and went back to screaming.

I looked back up to the stage. Kellan had casually tucked his light T-shirt into the back of his jeans. He had his back to the crowd, his broad shoulders gleaming in the stage lights; I thanked the fates that the scratches I had left down his back had completely healed and were not noticeable. I blushed at that memory.

He was talking to Evan, who laughed, then nodded. Then Kellan spun his finger in the air twice and pointed at him and Evan started to play. I flicked a glance at Matt, who was shaking his head and smiling. He waited a few more beats, then joined in with Evan.

Kellan turned back to the mic, the crowd losing it again at his spectacularly defined chest. He took the microphone in one hand and ran his other hand through his hair, the movement pleasantly twisting his muscles. Griffin started playing and I automatically flicked a glance at him. I couldn't stop the laugh; he hadn't hesitated in taking his shirt off either. Anything Griffin could do to get naked . . .

Griffin's body was decent, his tattoos intriguing to look at, but he came nowhere near Kellan's perfection. Rita, Kate, and Jenny were all watching Kellan intently, and momentarily ignoring every cus-tomer, so I relaxed and decided it wouldn't look odd for me to watch him either. Kellan started the song low and husky. His voice sent a shiver down my back . . . well, I'm pretty sure it was his voice. The song quickly picked up in intensity. The crowd loved this song—and their half-naked rock-god—and were quickly all dancing and sing-ing along. On the chorus, Kellan would lean with the microphone over to one side and stretch out to the crowd, the move doing amaz-ing things to his body, making the crowd scream even more.

Occasionally, Kate or Jenny would holler, and they were both dancing at the bar, so I joined them and we all laughed. Pete ducked his head out from the kitchen and I thought he might get mad at Kellan for being shirtless, but he looked around the crazy-excited bar and back up to Kellan and, smiling, went back to the kitchen.

Kellan got to a section in the song where the lyrics ask the ques-tion, *"Is this all you want?"* He put a hand playfully up to his ear and the crowd went nuts again in answer. Kellan laughed through the next couple of lyrics; he was having an exceptionally good time. I laughed at his enjoyment.

My eyes naturally drifted down to the injury on his side. Even from this distance, I could see the pink line across his ribs; he would probably always have a scar there. His hand suddenly running across his lower abs and down the front of his jeans completely distracted me from that thought. It was a casual move, one he probably hadn't even thought about, but . . . damn, that was hot. He was so hot. I blushed again as more intimate memories of that fabulous body popped into my head.

He got to the last section and Matt and Griffin dropped out, so it was only Kellan and Evan. Kellan's voice was lower, the words more intense, and he locked eyes with me. *"I know there's something here. . . . I know you want more. Tell me . . . and it's yours."*

He only sang it once in that low intense voice, then Matt and Griffin joined back in and he picked up the volume, sweeping his eyes back over his adoring crowd. I sneaked a glance at Kate and

Jenny, but they were laughing and dancing and hadn't noticed that part directed solely at me. I thought for a moment about the lyrics. Maybe I should cancel tonight? It really wasn't a good idea, especially after watching his incredible body moving onstage. I laughed and bit my lip. My sister should have come out this weekend; she would have loved this. Then I was suddenly very glad she hadn't.

Finally the song ended, and Kellan took a small bow to very loud fanfare. He laughed and slipped his shirt back on—Griffin left his off. The crowd booed as their rock star covered up again, especially Rita right behind me, and Kellan laughed again and shook his head. Kate and Jenny giggled and went back to their customers. I watched Kellan for a moment longer, long enough for him to look back at me and smile breathtakingly before jumping off the stage and instantly being swarmed by fans. My heart beat double-time as I finally brought my first-daters their drinks.

At the end of my shift, I grabbed my bag from the back room and said goodbye to Kate and Jenny, who were just entering. As I walked into the main bar, I spotted Kellan sitting at a chair backwards, talking to Sam. My heart flew up into my throat; I was suddenly very nervous to be alone with this stunning man. He looked over when he noticed me and smiled warmly. His smile relaxed me enough that I was able to calmly walk to his table.

"Ready?" he asked casually, but with a huge grin on his face.

"Yep," I managed to squeak out.

He stood up, lightly chuckling, and, turning, said goodbye to Sam. Placing a hand on the small of my back, he led me to the front doors and waved goodbye to a smirking Rita.

"Good show tonight, Kellan," she said suggestively. He nodded his thanks to her and I swear I heard her mutter, "I'll think about you later."

I blushed, but Kellan either didn't hear her or was ignoring her. He grabbed my fingers once we were alone outside and led me to his car, lightly singing the song he'd just done. His a cappella version was beautiful to listen to, but I frowned at him.

He looked over at me and stopped singing, a charming smile on his face. "What?"

I put on my best pout. "Didn't we have a conversation once, about the nature of your singing?"

He laughed and tried to look innocent. "What was wrong with that?" He pointed back to the bar. "I was fully dressed for *nearly* all of the set." He scooted away as I tried to elbow him. Still laughing, he ran up to me and picked me up. I squeaked and squirmed, but he had me tight. He set me down, but kept his arms firmly around mine as we walked, locked together, over to his car across the lot. "I did that for Pete," he laughed into my ear.

I stopped walking and he ran into me. I turned my head to look at him, surprised. "Oh . . . OH!" I hadn't realized Pete would . . . enjoy seeing Kellan that way.

He looked confused for a second, then the look on my face registered with him and, dropping his arms, he backed away, clutching his stomach because he was laughing so hard. "Oh my God, Kiera! No, that's not what I meant." He wiped a tear away from his eye and sighed. "God, I can't wait to tell Griffin about that." He started laughing again.

I blushed furiously, feeling rather stupid, and getting a little irritated at his enjoyment of my misunderstanding. He noticed my expression and tried to compose himself, but then giggled again, not able to do it. "Ahhh . . . and you think *I* have a dirty mind." He chuckled as he slipped his arms around me. I frowned and he puffed out his cheeks and blew out steadily, trying to stop his laughter.

Finally able to speak normally, he said, "Didn't you hear the response when I did that? You watch, tomorrow the bar will be twice as full. He'll have to turn people away. I did it to help him, Kiera." He shrugged and rocked back and forth with me in his arms.

"Oh . . . well, I guess that makes sense. You bring in more people, he makes more money, you get more exposure, and I'm assuming more money as well. . . ."

He grinned. "Something like that."

I half-grinned at him and *his* breath actually caught. "I guess I'll just have to allow it then." Not thinking, I kissed his cheek and he immediately kissed mine back.

I blinked in surprise, but he only smirked at me. "If you get to break a rule . . . so do I." Then he winked and pushed me toward the car.

"You're awful perky tonight," I said, as we got in the car.

He gave me a wide grin. "It's not every night that I get to sleep with a beautiful woman."

I blushed, both at him calling me beautiful again, and knowing that he could pretty much have his pick of a half-dozen actually beautiful women who were probably more available than I was. What was he doing, wasting his time with me, anyway?

He started the car and then noticed my odd expression as I puzzled that out. "Hey, I said sleep, not fu—"

"Kellan!" I interrupted him, staring at him severely.

He stumbled over the word, quickly thinking up a new one. "Fu . . . or . . . ni . . . cate?" He shrugged with an *I'm innocent, don't hate me* look.

I laughed and scooted over to sit against his side in the car, putting my head on his shoulder. We were silent for a moment while he pulled out of the parking lot. Finally, I asked him a question rattling in my brain from earlier. "So . . . who is Evan in love with?"

He laughed, his face breaking into a breathtaking grin. "God, who knows, could be anybody." He looked down at me. "Why? Who told you he was?"

I frowned at his seeming lack of knowledge on the subject. "Jenny mentioned it earlier."

"Oh, I'll have to ask him." He turned and looked back at the road. "I haven't heard anything about it." I frowned as I considered that, all the way home.

I crawled into his bed fully dressed. I actually put on an extra sweater, just in case, which he found greatly amusing. Then he laid his fully dressed body down on top of the covers next to me. I felt a little stupid about the whole thing. It was odd to lie in a bed fully clothed, and even odder for him to be on the outside. I considered telling him to just get underneath as well, when he suddenly rolled to face me, putting a leg casually over mine and an arm over my stomach. I decided then that the more layers that were between us, the better. This really was not a good idea.

He reached across me and turned the lamp on his nightstand off. The instant darkness was overwhelming, and the sudden electricity in the air was immediate. All I could hear was our soft breath, and my obnoxiously loud-sounding heart. I could feel him settle down in the pillows next to me, close, his arm and leg pulling me in tight, his head right beside mine as he breathed softly in my ear. It was too much . . . too intimate. I needed a minute.

"Kellan . . ."

"Yeah?" His voice was low and husky in my ear. It sent shivers down my spine.

I resisted the urge to turn into him, to find his lips. No, not a good idea at all. "Could you please turn the light back on?"

I could feel him chuckle, but I still couldn't see him yet. I felt him reach across me again, and then the room was suddenly too bright, and I was blinking. Normalcy returned, and I no longer felt the overwhelming electricity between us that had been there, just a pleasant warmth at his nearness.

"Better?" he asked, almost playfully, as he settled back down on his pillows, snuggling up close to me again.

I stayed on my back and looked over at him as he propped himself up on an elbow to gaze at me. His eyes were a warm, tranquil deep blue, the kind of eyes you could get lost in for hours. I forced myself to focus on something else, and blurted out the first thing that popped into my head. "Who was your first time?"

He looked at me quizzically. "What? Why?"

I swallowed my embarrassment at asking him that, and as calmly as I could manage, said, "Well, you asked about Denny and me. It's only fair."

He smiled and looked down at the sheets. "I guess I did, didn't I?" He looked back up at me. "Sorry about that . . . that really wasn't any of my business."

I smiled back. "Just answer the question." I was so glad he had used that line on me since I was getting so much use out of it.

He laughed and thought for a moment. I raised my eyebrow; he had to think about it? He laughed again at my expression. "Well . . . she was a girl from the neighborhood, sixteen, I think . . . very pretty. She seemed to like me. . . ." He smiled and shrugged. "It was just a couple of times one summer."

"Oh . . . why, what happened?" I asked quietly.

He brought his hand up to run his fingers through my hair. "I got her pregnant and she had to move in with her aunt to have the baby."

I flipped over on my side to face him. "What!"

He laughed and touched his finger to my nose. "I'm just kidding, Kiera."

I pushed him back on the pillows and grunted at him. "That's not nice."

He sat back up on his elbow. "You bought it though. You must think the worst of me." He sighed softly and looked sad for half a second. "I'm not a monster, Kiera." His tone was serious.

I propped myself up on an elbow as well. "You're no angel either, Kyle." I smiled at him wryly, which made his smile return. "So, what really did happen to the girl?"

"Nothing so dramatic. She went to her school, I went to mine." He shrugged. "Different paths . . ."

I looked at him, confused. "I thought you said she was a neighbor. Why were you in different schools?"

He looked at me blankly. "We weren't in the same grade."

I tried to comprehend what that meant. "But, she was sixteen. . . . How old were you?"

He looked at me oddly. "Not sixteen . . ." he whispered.

"But—"

"You should get some sleep, Kiera . . . it's late." I could literally hear the door closing on that conversation. I was still trying to figure out the math in my head. If he wasn't in high school with her, then that made him, at the very oldest, fourteen. It hurt my heart a little.

I brought a hand out from the covers and held his with it, and his warm smile eventually returned. We both settled back on the pillows and he reached out for me, pulling me to his chest. I sighed with contentment as I listened to his steady, slow heartbeat. He really was fine with this; maybe it wasn't such a bad idea after all.

He brought both arms around me, one hand stroking my hair, the other rubbing my back. It felt warm and nice. I smiled and nestled more into his chest. I felt him kiss the top of my head. Well, I guessed that was okay, relatively safe . . . still pretty innocent. I ran my fingers along where he had been hurt on his side, and then lightly trailed them up his chest. Even with his shirt on, I could feel the lines of his defined muscles. I could also feel his heartbeat increase, and he sighed softly as he pulled me tighter to him.

I pushed up to look at him; his face was still serene, and he was watching me adoringly. "Kellan, maybe we shouldn't—"

"I'm fine, Kiera. . . . Get some sleep," he whispered, still smiling softly.

I lay back down, but nestled into his shoulder instead of his chest. I grabbed the hand that had been stroking my back and laced my fingers through his, then brought our entwined hands up to my cheek and laid my head on them. He sighed happily and kissed my head again.

"Kellan . . . ?"

"Really, I'm fine, Kiera. . . ."

I looked up at his face. "No, I was just wondering . . . why do you want to do this with me? I mean, you know it's not going anywhere—why waste your time?"

He shifted to look at me better. "No time with you is wasted, Kiera." His voice was soft, the way he said my name like a caress. "If this is all . . ." He smiled sadly and left it at that.

I couldn't stop gazing at his achingly perfect face. I started remembering every touch, every word. . . . If this was all he had with me, then he would take it. Was that what he meant? It broke my heart. He had wondered if he was hurting me—was I hurting him? Did he just want me, or did he care for me? I released our hands and reached up to stroke his cheek. He looked so sad. I hated it when he looked so sad. . . .

He suddenly leaned over and kissed the very corner of my mouth, barely brushing my bottom lip. He left his head there and breathed lightly down my neck. I was too shocked to react; my thumb was still stroking his cheek. I held my breath. He lowered his lips to my jaw and kissed me softly. Then he kissed under my jaw. His hand slipped under the covers and moved to my waist, pulling me closer to him. His breathing increased as he made a noise in his throat and trailed his lips down my neck. His hand clenched and unclenched against my skin and he stopped kissing my throat, pulling back to rest his forehead against mine. His breaths were shallow, his face looked torn; this was clearly against my rules.

"Kiera . . . ?" He struggled for control.

The look on his face, the lingering feeling of his lips on my skin, froze me. He was giving me a chance, right now, but all I could do was stare at his eyes, quickly filling with passion, his lips coming closer to mine. His gaze flicked to my eyes, my lips, then back to my eyes. He was so torn, I was mesmerized by it.

My hand still on his cheek moved over, so I could run my fingers across his amazingly soft, partially opened lips. He made a noise and closed his eyes, his breath shallow and fast. I left my fingers there across his lips and he pressed our lips together, my fingers in between, like we were kissing, without actually kissing. We were going *way* beyond innocent now. I needed to end this. I needed to get up and go to my room. This was a horrible idea. . . .

I couldn't move, though. My breath sped up in response to his. He kissed my fingers softly, his eyes still closed, his breath intense. Just a few more seconds couldn't hurt anything, I convinced myself. We weren't really doing anything that wrong. His hand from my waist came up to my wrist. He started to pull my fingers down from his lips.

"I want to feel you. . . ."

He got them partway down, and fully pressed against my upper lip. That's when I woke up. I pushed him as far away from me as possible and scrambled out of the bed. He sat up, breathless, and I was startled to realize I was breathless as well.

"Kiera, I'm so sorry. I won't . . ." He swallowed a couple of times to try and control his breathing.

"No, Kellan . . . this was a really bad idea. I'm going to go to my room." I pointed at him. "Alone."

He started to get up. "Wait . . . I'm fine, just give me a minute. It will pass. . . ."

I put both arms up. "No . . . please stay here. I can't . . . I can't do this. That was too close, Kellan. This is too hard." I backed up to the door.

"Wait, Kiera . . . I'll do better. Don't . . . don't end this. . . ." His eyes were instantly so sad that I paused.

"I need to be alone tonight. We'll talk tomorrow, okay?"

He nodded and said nothing further, so I turned and left. Mentally I berated myself. What did I think was going to happen? That was a really stupid idea . . . this whole thing was a bad idea. As nice as it might feel, it wasn't not fair to all three of us.

I stared at my ceiling for most of the night, wondering what he was thinking about, what he was doing, if he was sleeping, if I could just crawl back into bed with him, if I should . . . When I did fall asleep, I dreamed about him in vivid, glorious detail. In my dream, I did not get out of his bed. In my dream, we did very little actual sleeping.

He knocked on my door early the next morning and opened it when I answered him. He walked into my room and sat on the edge of the bed. He was in different clothes, dressed and perfect for the day already. "Mornin'," he said quietly. "Are you still mad at me?"

"No . . ." Having him on my bed was too much. The memory of

last night, and my vivid dream, still had me weak in the knees. "You shouldn't be in here, Kellan. It's disrespectful to Denny."

He chuckled and looked away. "You think, of all the things we've done together, that me sitting on his bed is what he would find the most offensive?" He looked back to me as I glared icily at him. "Sorry . . . okay." He backed off with his hands held up and stopped in the doorway. "Better?"

I sat up in the bed, feeling stupid. He was right of course, but still . . . "Yes, thank you."

He sighed and I looked up at him, still standing in the doorway. "I can't talk to you from here," he said quietly, holding his hand out for me.

Sighing, I walked over and took it. He smiled and led me downstairs. On the way, he spoke softly. "I am sorry about last night. You were right, that wasn't a good idea. I did try though." He looked over at me hopefully, like he should get a reward for at least trying.

I sighed again as I looked over at him. "This isn't a game, Kellan."

He stopped on the bottom step and turned to face me on the step above. "I know that, Kiera." His tone and look were more serious.

I laced my arms around his neck and he relaxed. "Then don't take it that far again." I wasn't ready for this to end either. "Innocent, remember."

He smiled and lifted me down to the bottom of the stairs, to stand beside him. "Innocent, right. I can do that."

Still smiling, he grabbed my hand and led me to the kitchen. Mentally I sighed. This wasn't a good plan. I was being an idiot.

Chapter 14
Tipping Point

We decided to spend our free Saturday together taking an Amtrak up north. I'd never been on a train before and it made me a little nervous at first, until Kellan held my hand. Then I relaxed against him in the seat and we watched the world speed by with the rocking motion of the train. It was an amazing view, what with the snowcapped mountains in the distance and the greenness of the abundant evergreens whizzing by. I loved it here. I'd only been here a few months, but I already loved this state. We got out at a small, touristy town and walked around hand in hand. Without the fear of someone we knew watching us, we were much closer, and a lot less careful, than we usually were with each other.

We stopped often to look out over the river surging beside us or to look into a quaint shop as we walked by it, and he would hold me tight against his chest. I would turn into him and delight in his warmth and tenderness. Something had changed between us (again) after last night in his bed. I wasn't sure what it was exactly, just that our gazes were longer, and our touches were, while he was careful to not break any more of my rules, a little more intimate. Lines were starting to blur. It bothered me. It excited me.

Eventually, we made our way back down south so I could go to work. I sighed as Seattle came back into view. It had been so freeing to be with him openly, with no fear of being caught. I had enjoyed our little outing . . . and I knew it probably wouldn't happen again for a long time. I looked up at his face as he gazed out the window. He had a slight frown on his full lips and I wondered if he was thinking the same thing that I was. I watched the sunlight bounce off his eyes, altering the deep blue color to a lighter shade. I smiled at how amazingly beautiful his eyes were. He looked down at me then, and smiled in return. The urge to kiss him overcame me, and I had to look straight ahead and close my eyes.

"You okay?" he asked.

"Motion sickness . . . it will pass. I just need a minute." I wasn't sure why I lied to him. He would have understood if I had told him the truth. Well, honestly he would have understood too much, and I wasn't positive that, after last night, he wouldn't press his advantage instead of giving me space. And at the moment, I just needed a little space.

I had to keep my eyes closed until the train completely stopped. Honestly, it was just ridiculous how attracted to him I was. Once we were situated, he drove me straight to Pete's. He stayed at the bar with me until the D-Bags arrived, and they started their set. Kellan had been right about his previous night's "performance"—the place was buzzing, and I was flitting from person to person all night long. By the end of the evening, I was exhausted. I got a ride home with Jenny, instead of Kellan, which I think, based on the frown he gave me when I told him, may have hurt his feelings a little. But Denny would be home, and even though he'd probably be sleeping, I didn't want Kellan and me to arrive home together. After our amazing weekend, I felt like it would be a neon sign of what had passed between us, and I couldn't risk that. I hoped Kellan wasn't too hurt.

Denny was home when I got there. Kellan was not, which made me frown as I walked up the stairs. Denny was sitting up in bed, watching TV like he'd been waiting for me. "Hey, babe," he said warmly, his accent rich in his tiredness, as he held his arms open for me.

I ignored the pit in my stomach that my free time with Kellan was now over (and where was he anyway?), and, swallowing a sigh, I crawled on top of the bed to snuggle in Denny's arms. He rubbed my back and told me about his trip. I fell asleep against his chest, fully dressed, while he talked about his conference and his jerk of a boss. As sleep swam over me, I thought I heard him say my name in a questioning tone, but I was too exhausted from my weekend to resist the pull, and I succumbed to it. I hoped Denny wasn't too hurt by that.

A couple of days later, Kellan and I were spending some free time together after school, before I had to go into work. We sat close together on the grass in a secluded area of what we now considered "our" park near the school. We met here frequently between classes, or sometimes afterwards. We'd stay in his car and listen to the radio if it was raining, or grab a blanket from his trunk and sit out on the grass if it was nice. Today, it was sunny, but it was cold, and our park was mostly empty. Kellan and I sat close together on his blanket atop the crisp lawn, huddled in our jackets after just having finished our espressos, enjoying the chilly day and each other's warm presence.

Kellan played with my fingers, a small smile on his lips. Curiosity overcame my common sense and I quietly asked him, "That song the other weekend, the kind of intense one . . . it's not really about a woman, is it?" He looked up at me, surprised. "Denny," I explained. "He told me what happened, while he was staying with your family. The song was about you, wasn't it? You and your dad?"

Kellan nodded and looked out over the quiet park, remaining silent.

"Do you want to talk about it?" I asked timidly.

Still looking away from me, he quietly said, "No."

My heart broke at the haunted look in his eyes. I hated myself for what I was about to say, but I so desperately wanted him to open up to me. "Will you anyway?"

He sniffed, then looked down at the grass. He picked up a blade and twirled it idly in his fingers. Slowly, he turned to face me. I tensed, wondering if he would be angry. As his eyes met mine, however, all I saw were years of sadness. "There's nothing to talk about, Kiera." His voice was soft but full of emotion. "If Denny told you what he saw, what he did for me, then you know as much as anyone."

Not quite willing to let it go, I said, "Not as much as you." He watched me silently, his eyes begging me to not ask anything else. I did anyway, hating myself for it. "Did he hit you often?"

Not looking away from my eyes, he swallowed and nodded his head once.

"Very badly?" *As if just a small hit wasn't bad enough,* I thought, irritated at my own question. He was motionless for so long, that I thought he wasn't going to answer me, but then he nodded his head slightly, just once.

"Since you were little?" A single nod again, his eyes glistening now.

I swallowed, willing myself to stop asking him painful questions that he obviously did not want to answer. "Didn't your mom ever try to stop him . . . help you?"

He shook his head no, a tear rolling down his cheek.

My eyes watered, the tears threatening to spill. *Please stop this,* I begged myself. *You're hurting him.* "Did it end when Denny left?" I whispered, hating myself even more.

He swallowed and shook his head no again. "It got worse . . . so much worse," he whispered, finally speaking. Another tear fell from his eye, sparkling in the sunlight.

Wondering how a parent could possibly do that to a child, how a mother could possibly allow it—not give her own life to protect her only son, I inadvertently whispered, "Why?"

With dead eyes, Kellan whispered, "You'd have to ask them."

Tears spilled down my cheeks now, and he watched them fall. I put my arms around his neck and pulled him in for a tight hug. "I'm so sorry, Kellan," I whispered in his ear, as he loosely put his arms around me.

"It's okay, Kiera," he said brokenly. "It was years ago. They haven't hurt me in a long time."

By his reaction, I didn't think that was true. I held him close, feeling his body shake against mine. His cheeks were wet when I did pull back. I wiped them dry and held his face in my hands, gazing at him, and trying to picture how awful his childhood had been, trying to imagine his pain. I couldn't, though. My own childhood had been happy and full of wonderful memories. My parents were overprotective, yes, but warm and loving people.

He gazed back at me sadly, a new tear spilling from his eye and rolling down his cheek. I leaned over and kissed the tear away. As I was pulling back, he turned his head and our lips brushed together.

Overwhelmed with sympathy for his pain, intoxicated by his sudden nearness, I left his lips on mine. My hands were still on his cheeks, we were still sitting close together on the grass, and our closed lips were pressed together, but neither one of us was moving. I wasn't even sure we were breathing. We must have looked very odd, if anyone had been there to look our way.

Eventually, he inhaled through his lips, causing them to slightly part against mine. My response was involuntary, instinctual, and immediate—I kissed him. I moved my lips against his, feeling his warmth, his softness, his breath.

He didn't hesitate. He immediately returned my kiss, moved his lips tenderly against mine. His passion quickly overcame him however, and he grabbed my neck, pulling me in for a deep kiss. His tongue flashed against mine, just once. I groaned with how good it felt, how much I wanted it, but I forced myself to push him away. I made myself not be angry. I had started this one.

He immediately started apologizing. "I'm sorry. I'm so sorry. I thought . . . I thought you changed your mind." His eyes looked fearful.

"No . . . that was my fault." Things were picking up between us; lines were blurring faster and faster. Even now, watching his anxious face, my heart was beating harder, my lips burned with the memory of his. "I'm sorry, Kellan. This isn't working."

He leaned toward me and grabbed my arm. "No, please. I'll do better, I'll be stronger. Please don't end this. Please don't leave me. . . ."

I bit my lip, my heart in pain over his aching words, his frantic face. "Kellan . . ."

"Please." His eyes searched my face. I wanted to reach out and kiss him again, anything to take his pain away.

"This isn't fair." A tear fell down my cheek, and I stopped him from brushing it away. "This isn't fair to Denny. This isn't fair to you." I felt a sob rising. "I'm being cruel to you."

He sat up on his knees and grabbed both of my hands in his. "No . . . no you're not. You're giving me more than . . . Just don't stop this."

I gazed at him, dumbfounded. "What *is* this to you, Kellan?"

He looked down and didn't answer my question. "Please . . ."

Finally, his voice and face caved me in. I couldn't take causing him pain. "Okay . . . okay, Kellan."

He looked up and smiled charmingly at me. I sat up on my knees and laced my arms around his neck, pulling him in for a tight embrace, hoping that I knew what I was doing.

I pushed all thoughts of the park from my mind while I went about my shift at Pete's. Well, I pushed the kiss out of my mind, although my lips still tingled pleasantly, which concerned me. But no, I wasn't going to think about that.

I couldn't quite push back the horrid conversation we'd had though. My selfish need to know everything about him had opened up some of his old wounds. I watched him throughout my shift, wondering if he was truly okay. He seemed to be fine, laughing with his bandmates, sipping on a beer, one foot propped up on his knee. Same old relaxed Kellan. I frowned, wondering how much of his casualness was real, and how much was a conditioned response to a lifetime of pain.

I thought about that as I watched him approach the bar to talk to Sam. He leaned back and Rita slipped him another beer. He glanced back at her and smiled warmly, with a nod of his head. Sam left after a minute and Kellan stayed, quietly sipping his beer at the bar. He casually leaned against it and looked over at me when I approached to give Rita a quick order.

"So, where are we taking your sister this Saturday?" He leaned back farther onto his elbows, which did wonderful things to his chest and just barely exposed the skin above his waistband. I had the sudden desire to run my fingers down his shirt and feel that bare skin. Rita eyed him hungrily as she took her sweet time making my drinks, her thoughts seemingly in line with mine, from the look on her overtanned face. I hated that look on her.

Rita's face, combined with talk of my sister's approaching visit, spoiled the pleasant vision of him in front of me. "I have no idea," I said grumpily. Truly I'd forgotten her visitation weekend was already upon me. My mind had been a little . . . preoccupied lately.

Kellan laughed at my expression. "It will be fine, Kiera. We'll have fun, I promise." I raised an eyebrow at him and frowned. "Not that much fun . . . I swear." He smirked at me playfully.

Griffin suddenly came up behind me and put his arms around my waist. I elbowed him hard in the ribs, making him grunt and Kellan laugh. "God, Kiera . . . where's the love?" Griffin asked indignantly. I rolled my eyes and ignored him.

"Griff, what's a good club around here?" Kellan asked him. My eyes flashed over to him, alarmed. Griffin's idea of a good club was probably not the same as mine.

"Ooooohhhh . . . we going clubbing?" He sat down on a stool next to Kellan, an eager look on his face. His pale eyes practically sparkled with anticipation. He tucked his hair behind his ears. "There's this strip club in Vancouver, that does this thing with a—"

"No, no." Kellan quickly, and thankfully, interrupted him. "Not us." He indicated Griffin and himself and then pointed over to me. "Kiera's sister is coming up. We need a *dance* club to take her to."

Griffin smiled and nodded at me approvingly. "Sister action . . . nice!"

"Griff . . ."

Griffin turned back to Kellan and simply said, "Spanks."

Kellan seemed to know what he was talking about. He nodded and looked at me thoughtfully. "Yeah, that would work." He turned back to Griffin and smacked him on the arm. "Thanks."

Griffin grinned ear to ear. "When are we going?"

I started to sputter in protest, but Kellan smoothly smiled and said, "Bye, Griffin." Griffin pouted, but did walk away.

I started getting an uneasy feeling in my stomach as I watched Griffin walk over to a girl and slip his hand up her skirt, earning him a smack on the arm. I didn't think I wanted to go anywhere he thought was fun. And Spanks sounded particularly . . . not fun.

"Spanks? I'm not going to some sex club," I said quietly, blushing a bit as I met Kellan's amused eye.

He laughed and shook his head at me. "I love where your mind automatically goes sometimes." He laughed again. "It's just a club." I eyed him warily and he made an X over his heart. "I promise."

He laughed again and for a moment, I could only stare at his attractive smile. Rita smacked my arm, apparently having been trying to get my attention. "Here . . . your order's up." She looked at Kellan while I blushed, grabbed my tray, and hurried back to work.

He could be so distracting for me. I needed to watch that.

The next few days after the park flew by smoothly, and, thankfully, with no more over-the-line incidents, but the feel of Kellan's lips on mine still wouldn't leave me. I needed to watch that too. This was getting really stupid. I was being stupid. I should end this. But he was so . . . I sighed. I couldn't end it yet. I liked it too much. My addiction was too strong.

Like most evenings, I tried not to watch Kellan as I went about my duties, and like most evenings, I couldn't help but sneak a peek now and then. Tonight, he was casually sitting back in his chair, spinning a bottle in his hands. Matt was telling him something and Kellan was laughing with him. His loose, carefree smile was amazing. He really was achingly handsome. A few women around him were working up the nerve to talk to him, and I wondered idly which one would. Would he be interested? Flirt back? He really had toned down the flirting with the barflies since our . . . flirting . . . had started. That thought worried me some. He should flirt. He should have more than what little I gave him. That thought broke my heart, though.

I realized I was frowning at him at the exact same time he looked over at me. I tried to fix my face, but he'd already seen. He slowly got up and walked over to where I was wiping off a table. The women, who had looked about ready to finally make their move, seemed highly disappointed.

He walked up close to me in the packed bar. "Hey." He put his hand close to mine on the table, letting our fingers touch.

"Hi." I looked up at him shyly, wishing I could put an arm around him. I settled for standing and stepping closer to him, so that our bodies were touching.

He smiled down at me, his finger lightly stroking my pant leg as I stood uncharacteristically close to him. "You looked like you were thinking of something . . . unpleasant. Anything you want to talk about?" His eyes suddenly seemed almost sad and almost . . . hopeful. It was strange. I had no idea what to make of it.

I started to reply to him when Griffin came up to us from the bar, clapping Kellan on the shoulder. Kellan immediately stepped away from me.

"Oh, man, you have got to see this little hottie at the bar." He bit his knuckle. "She totally wants me. . . . Think I could nail her in the back room?" He seemed to ponder that for a moment, while I made a disgusted face and glanced over at her. She was pretty, but she seemed to be staring more at Kellan than Griffin.

Griffin seemed to notice this too. "Oh fuck, man! Did you already bang her? God, I hate getting your seconds. They never shut up about—" He didn't have a chance to explain what women never shut up about, as Kellan smacked him hard in the chest.

"Griff!"

"Dude, what?" Griffin looked confused.

Kellan flung his hands in my direction. Irritation flashed in me.

Had he been with that woman? Then guilt filled me. We were just friends, I didn't own him. What did it matter?

"Oh, hey, Kiera." Griffin said it like he hadn't noticed me until just then, and like he hadn't said anything even remotely crude or offensive, which in his mind, he probably hadn't. He clapped Kellan on the shoulder again and turned to walk back to the woman, apparently going to give it a shot anyway.

Kellan actually looked sheepish. Not saying anything else, he turned and walked back to his table.

I spent the rest of my shift wondering if Kellan had been with that girl. Wondering if I was just another in a long line of girls. Wondering what women never shut up about. Wondering at Kellan's silence after Griffin left. Wondering about the weird look on his face before Griffin even showed up. Wondering if I was being a complete moron by letting our flirtations continue. Wondering why the whole night left an icy pit in my stomach. Wondering why I spent so much time wondering about Kellan . . .

Feeling odd at the end of the night, I had Jenny give me a ride home instead of Kellan, who had of course sweetly offered to stay until I was done working. He had yawned a couple of times as he left the bar, though, quickly glancing at me with a small smile before flitting outside, so I figured he'd be asleep by the time I got home. I was pretty surprised when Kellan swiftly pulled me into his bedroom as I walked by the open door. He'd apparently stayed up to see me.

He quietly closed the door and playfully backed me into it, in one smooth move. Then, with a hand pressed against the door on each side of my body, he leaned into me until our lips were just inches apart. He held that position, mouth slightly parted, breathing softly into my face.

"Sorry about Griffin," he whispered. "He can be . . . kind of, well, an ass." He smiled breathtakingly.

I couldn't speak. I couldn't think to answer him. I wanted to ask about the girl, but aching froze my body. I couldn't even move my arms to push him away. I was trapped against the door, held in place by his sensual body, and my body had shifted into overdrive. I was overdosing on my addiction. He was too close . . . much too close. I needed a minute. I just couldn't find the words to say it.

"What were you thinking about earlier?" he obliviously whispered, still inches from my face.

I tried to speak, to tell him to back off, to give me space so I could think again, but I was frozen, speechless. He was so close . . . he smelled so good. My breath quickened and he noticed.

"Kiera, what are you thinking about, right now?" His breath, so light against my skin, made me shudder. "Kiera?"

He eyed me up and down and then pressed his body firmly to mine. I gasped, but the words still didn't come out. His hands ran down my shoulders and then my waist, to rest at my hips. His lips parted and his breathing sped up as he watched my eyes with an increasing passion. My lips parted as I struggled to slow my own breathing. I needed to stop this, I needed to speak . . .

"Kiera . . . say something." His words exactly echoed my thoughts.

His eyes seemed to struggle with something for just a fraction of a second. Then he lowered his forehead to mine, breathing softly but intensely on me. He pressed one knee between mine, closing every gap between us. A moan stubbornly escaped my lips, but still no words were forming. Making a noise deep in his throat, he bit his lip and started running both hands up under my shirt. This wasn't innocent flirting anymore. This wasn't innocent at all.

"Please . . . say something. Do you . . . ? Do you want me to—"

Abruptly, he roughly exhaled and bent his head slightly, to run his tongue along the inside of my upper lip. He slid his fingers up over my bra, then around to my back. I sighed raggedly and closed my eyes. Making another deep noise, he kissed my upper lip, slipping his tongue into my mouth. I shuddered and gasped, and he lost all control. He brought a hand to my neck and, exhaling roughly again, kissed me fully, pulling me into him.

His lips fully around mine, acted like an adrenaline shot straight to my heart; I was finally free to move again. Panting, I roughly shoved him away from me. This was way beyond my rules and it definitely wasn't innocent anymore. It was also too late. Whatever this was now—I wanted more.

He held up both hands up, like I might hit him. "I'm sorry. I thought . . ." he whispered.

I walked right over to him and put one hand on his chest and the other on his neck, pulling him close to me. He stopped talking, stopped breathing. He even retreated half a step, confused, before I forced him closer to me again. I breathed against him heavily, biting my lip. I watched his eyes go from panic, to confusion, to smoldering. Good, he wanted me. I felt powerful as I watched his mouth part, his breath starting again and increasing to match mine. I knew I could push him back on the bed and do whatever I wanted to him.

I ran my hands down his incredibly hard chest and pulled on the belt loops of his jeans, until our hips touched. "Kiera . . . ?" he asked raggedly, glancing once to my bedroom, where Denny was sleeping. His hands were still up in the air slightly, like he was surrendering to me.

My resolve wavered at the questioning tone in his voice. Our "innocent" flirting had been steadily escalating, and I was at the breaking point. I was either going to take him right now, and betray Denny, asleep in the very next room, or I was going to finally end this.

I summoned every ounce of willpower I had, and breathed huskily into his mouth. "Don't touch me again. I'm not yours." Then I shoved him hard onto the bed and fled the room, before I changed my mind.

Denny reached out for me when I finally crawled into bed a few moments later. He sleepily tried to pull me closer to him, and I stiffened and roughly pulled away, not wanting his closeness, not wanting anyone's. At least, that's what I kept telling myself.

"Hey . . . are you all right?" he whispered groggily in the dark.

"I'm fine." I hoped my voice was smooth. It felt shaky to me.

"Okay," he said, as he moved over to kiss my neck. I stiffened again and turned my head away from him. "Kiera . . ." he said huskily, his fingers trailing up my body, his leg wrapping around mine, his lips moving up to my ear.

I recognized his tone, I recognized his movements. I knew what he wanted from me, and I just . . . couldn't. My mind was spinning. Thoughts of Kellan and how close we'd just about come to . . . How much I still wanted him to . . . I just couldn't be with Denny right now. Denny wasn't whom my body was aching for.

"I'm really tired, Denny. Just go back to sleep, please." I tried to keep my voice soft and sleeplike, not irritated and riled up, like I truly felt.

He sighed and slumped against me. His fingers stopped moving across my body and rested on my belly. I closed my eyes and hoped I could fall asleep quickly, before my willpower faded and I ran back to Kellan's room.

Denny breathed softly on my neck and I thought he had fallen asleep again, but then he shifted his weight suggestively and moved his hand up under my tank top, pulling me tight against him. I shifted irritably under his clinginess. "Denny, I'm serious . . . not tonight."

He sighed and flopped over onto his back. "Where have I heard that one before?" he muttered, irritated.

Annoyed, I snapped, "What?"

He looked over at me and sighed. "Nothing."

Still annoyed, I didn't let him drop it. I probably should have. "No . . . if you have something to say to me, then say it." I propped up on an elbow and glared at him.

He glared back. "Nothing . . . it's just . . ." He looked away. "Don't you realize how long it's been since we've . . . ?" He looked back to me and shrugged sheepishly.

I bit back my angry retort and tried to think about how long it actually had been. I couldn't remember. . . .

Denny understood my blank look. "You can't even remember, can you?" He looked away again, irritated. "It was the shower, Kiera.

We don't usually go . . ." He looked back to me and stopped where he had been going, while I felt my face heat. "It's not that it's been a while. We've gone longer . . . and that doesn't matter to me." His eyes searched my face. "It's that you don't even seem to care. You don't seem to miss me at all."

He looked up at the ceiling. "I thought when I got back from Portland, things would be different." He glanced over at me. "Honestly, I thought you'd attack me when I got home. But you didn't . . . you haven't. You've been so . . . I don't know, distant."

His irritation left him and he gazed at me wistfully, running his fingers down my arm. "I miss you." His accent curled around the words.

Instantly, remorse took me over and I snuggled close, trying to kiss him, hold him, make love to him . . . but he pushed me away. Surprised, I could only stare blankly at him.

"No." He shook his head, his irritation back. "I don't want you to have sex with me because you feel guilty. I want you to"—he searched my face again—"want me."

"Denny, I do. I . . . I just . . ." I had no idea how to explain what I had been feeling lately. I hadn't realized we'd gone a while without. . . . I hadn't realized I'd been cold or distant to him. I *had* been preoccupied, and I hadn't realized he'd noticed. And I couldn't tell him why. I couldn't tell him *who* was occupying my thoughts.

I sat up on my outstretched arm and stared down at him. "I'm sorry."

He stared at me a moment and then sighed and patted the bed under his shoulder. I snuggled up against him and breathed in his rich scent, trying to calm my mind and my heart. "I love you, Kiera," he whispered, and kissed my head.

I nodded and nestled into his chest, wrapping my arms and legs around his body. A tear rolled off my nose to drip onto his shirt. "I love you too, Denny." I squeezed him tighter, praying that things got better between us. I was right to finally end things with Kellan. I was finally making the right choice.

But even so, and I think, just to torment myself, I dreamed about Kellan that night. That is, when I finally did drift off to sleep in my conflicted pool of emotions. I dreamed that I had stayed with him, that I had ripped off his clothes, shoved him onto his bed, and taken him. It was a great dream . . . it was a horrible dream.

Kellan met me in the entryway of the kitchen the next morning and immediately put his hand on my arm. "Kiera, I'm sorry. I went too far. I'll be good."

I brushed him off. I should have stayed in bed with Denny, but I needed to get this over with. Kellan needed to know . . . and accept that this was finally over. "No, Kellan. We went way past innocent flirting a long time ago. We can't go back to that time. We're not those people anymore. It was a stupid idea to try."

"But . . . don't end this, please." He cringed and searched my face.

"I have to, Kellan. Denny knows something's not right. I don't think he suspects what . . . or you . . . but he knows I've been distracted." I bit my lip and looked down. "Denny and I haven't . . . done anything . . . in a long time and he's hurt. I'm hurting him," I whispered.

Kellan looked down too. "You don't have to. I've never asked you to not . . . be with him. I know you two are going to . . ." He shifted uncomfortably. "I told you, I understand."

"I know, Kellan, but I've been so preoccupied, wrapped up in you. . . ." I sighed heavily. "I'm ignoring him."

Immediately, he grabbed my arms and pulled me close to him. His eyes searched mine almost frantically. "You're wrapped up in me. What does that say, Kiera? You want to be with me. You want to be more than friends. Some part of you wants me too."

I closed my eyes and tried to block out his pleading face. "Please, Kellan, you're tearing me in two. I can't . . . I can't do this anymore." I tried to steady my breathing. I tried to keep the tears from stinging my eyes. I had to keep them firmly closed. If I opened them, if I saw his perfect face, his pleading eyes, I would surely cave again.

"Kiera, look at me . . . please." His voice wavered on the end, and I had to squeeze my eyes even tighter together.

"No, I can't, okay? This isn't right, it doesn't feel right. You don't feel right. Just don't, please don't touch me anymore."

"Kiera, I know you don't really feel that way." He pulled me in tight and whispered huskily in my ear. "I know you feel something here. . . ."

I opened my eyes, but kept my gaze on his chest as I firmly pushed him back from me. I needed him to leave me alone, and I was going to have to hurt him to do it. "No. I don't want you. I want to be with him. I'm in love with *him*." I looked up to his eyes and instantly wished I hadn't. He was hurt. His eyes were filling with pain. I almost caved, but I needed to end this. I made myself say it . . . and hated myself for it. "I'm attracted to you . . . but I feel nothing for you, Kellan."

He immediately dropped his arms and left, without saying another word.

I didn't see him for the rest of the day. I didn't see him at work. I didn't see him when I came home from work. In fact, I didn't see him until the next morning. Relief and guilt flashed through me when I finally did see him. Relief that he wasn't hiding anymore, and guilt that I had hurt him enough that he'd felt the need to hide from me.

He was sitting at the table, sipping his coffee, when I came into the kitchen. He looked tired. Perfect . . . but tired. He glanced over at me, but said nothing as I sat across from him. I wondered if he'd be cool toward me again, like he had been so long ago.

"Hey," I said softly.

The very edge of his lips curled up. "Hey," he whispered.

Well, at least he was talking to me. I resisted the urge to lace my fingers in his as he set down his coffee mug. We had been so close to each other for so long, that it was more natural for me to touch him than to not touch him. His fingers twitched on the table and he moved them underneath it. I searched his eyes, wondering if he was struggling not to touch me as well.

A sudden tension filled the room, with our joint effort of no contact, and I blurted out, "My sister is coming in tomorrow. Denny and I are going to pick her up from the airport in the morning."

"Oh . . . right," he said quietly. "I can crash at Matt's. She can stay in my room."

"No . . . you don't have to do that. It's not necessary." Sadness swept through me. "Kellan, I hate how we left things."

He tilted his head to the side and stared blankly at the table. "Yeah . . . me too."

I again resisted the urge to touch him, to cup his cheek. "I don't want this . . . weirdness . . . between us. Can we . . . can we still be friends? Truly, just friends?"

He looked up at me and smirked. "Are you really giving me the 'let's be friends' speech?"

I grinned at him. "Yeah . . . I guess I am."

His expression turned very serious and my stomach flared painfully. I suddenly didn't want to hear his answer to my question, so I interrupted him when he looked about to speak. "I should probably warn you about my sister."

He blinked and looked at me, confused. Then his face relaxed and he smiled softly. "I remember . . . man-flavored candy." He pointed at himself.

"No . . . I mean yes, but that's not what I was thinking of."

"Oh?" he said curiously.

I looked away, a little embarrassed. "She's kind of . . . well . . ." I sighed. "She's very beautiful." And flirtatious, confident, alluring, interesting . . . `

"I figured she was," he said simply, and my eyes snapped back to his. He quietly added, "She's related to you . . . right?"

Him comparing me to my sister was beyond ridiculous, but then, he hadn't seen her yet. I sighed. He really shouldn't look at me that way. "Kellan . . ."

"I know," he mumbled. "Friends."

The look on his face made me ache with sympathy. "Are you still coming with us to the club?"

He looked away. "You still want me to?"

I clasped my hands together, to not reach out to him. "Yes, of course. We're still friends, Kellan, and my sister expects . . ." I let my voice trail off.

He looked back at me and seemed to understand where I had been going with that. "Right, we wouldn't want her asking the wrong questions." His voice had a hard edge to it.

"Kellan—"

"I'll be there, Kiera." He finished the rest of his coffee and stood up.

"Thank you," I whispered. As he started to leave, a sudden panic swept through me. "Kellan!" My soft voice had an edge to it as well, and he stopped at the entryway to look back at me. "Remember your promise." I couldn't quite keep the heat out of my tone.

He looked at me thoughtfully for a second, and I wondered if he would snap at me. His eyes seemed to get even more tired, however, and, shaking his head, he quietly said, "I haven't forgotten anything, Kiera."

Chapter 15
Clubbing

"Oh . . . holy . . . fuck!" Griffin muttered as he smacked Matt, who happened to be sitting next to him at their table, across the chest. "Dude, I'm in love. Look at that piece of ass!"

Knowing Griffin's *types*, I studiously ignored him while I handed the guys their beers. I glanced at Kellan from the corner of my eye the whole time. He was glancing at me from the corner of his too. He looked . . . resigned. I had worried about how Kellan would be toward me today, after our conversation this morning in the kitchen. But he had given me a ride to school like normal, picked me up like normal, and driven me to work, all just like normal . . . if a little more quietly. I had told him it wasn't necessary, and he had given me the look. You know, the look that clearly says, *Don't be ridiculous, of course I'll still take you where you need to go . . . since we're friends and all.* Well, that's what the look had said to me anyway.

I was wondering what he was thinking about when I noticed Griffin grin stupidly and sit up a little in his chair. I looked over at him curiously when suddenly hands covered my eyes.

"Guess who?"

I pulled down the hands and spun around. "Anna?" I pulled my sister in for a hug. "Oh my God! We were supposed to pick you up from the airport tomorrow. What are you doing here?"

She looked at me briefly, then her eyes drifted over to Kellan, sitting casually at the table near her, watching us. "I couldn't wait . . . hopped an earlier flight."

Ignoring who her gaze was focused on, and Griffin's impatient cough—he obviously wanted an introduction—I stepped back to look at her. My crazy, impulsive sister—she looked exactly the same. We had nearly identical heart-shaped faces with high cheekbones and our mom's perky nose, but that was where the similarities stopped. She was tall, almost as tall as Denny actually, and she emphasized that with slinky black high heels. She was voluptuous, where I was more . . . athletic, and she also emphasized that with an absurdly tight red dress. Inwardly I sighed; she looked like she had just walked off a runway, not an airplane.

Her lips were perfectly full and painted a bright red, the same shade as her dress. Her eyes were a deep, constant green, where my hazel ones seemed to continually change color. Where my dark brown hair was wavy and unmanageable, hers, so dark brown in color it was almost black, was so luxuriously shiny that it rippled like water when she moved. Currently, she had half of it effortlessly pulled up in a clip. The hair that loosely spilled around her shoulders was streaked with red as bright as her dress.

I picked up a strand of the bright red locks. Well, not everything about my sister was the same. "This is new. I like it." I smiled at her.

She shrugged, still gazing at Kellan, who was annoyingly gazing right back at her. "I dated a hairdresser"—she turned to look at me with a charming grin on her face—"for like, an hour." I heard Griffin groan indecently behind me.

I sighed inwardly again. My sister was adventurous and provocative. She was everything I was not. She was the one that my parents could never seem to mention without adding glowing adjectives like "beautiful", "gorgeous," and "stunning," although the end of their sentences usually involved the phrase "What did she do now?" She was much too attractive and alluring, and now I had to introduce her to my equally attractive and alluring roommate.

"Guys, this is my sister—"

"Anna," she interrupted, holding her hand out to Kellan warmly. My sister was anything but shy.

"Kellan," he responded politely, shaking her hand for an annoyingly long time.

Griffin abruptly stood up and took her hand away from Kellan. Mentally, I actually thanked him. "Griffin . . . hey." My sister giggled attractively and said hello.

Matt and Evan politely introduced themselves, while I felt a little stupid, realizing that she didn't need me here to make introductions for her. She was doing just fine on her own. Kellan watched me curiously as I blushed. Anna smiled and said hello to Matt and Evan, perfectly at ease with this group of good-looking guys that she'd just met.

Griffin grabbed a chair, forcefully taking it from a nearby customer, and plopped it down at the end of the table near him. He patted the seat and Anna smiled and thanked him. Then she scooted the chair to the other side of the table to sit beside Kellan. Matt and Evan both chuckled quietly. Griffin and I scowled in exactly the same way, but my sister didn't notice. Her attention was all on Kellan as she moved the chair so that it touched his. She gracefully sat down and, smiling charmingly, leaned against his side. He irritatingly grinned back at her.

I hated this already. She had been here a whole of maybe ten minutes and I was already wishing she would leave. I felt a little guilty about that. I did love my sister. I just didn't want to see her all over Kellan. We may have ended our . . . flirtations, but, well . . . it bothered me. He had better honor his promise.

"Well, I've got to get back to work. I'll bring you a drink, Anna."

"Okay." She never looked back at me. "Oh, some guy named Sam put my jacket and bags in the back room."

I sighed at what my sister could get men to do for her. "Okay, I'll call Denny. He can give you a ride home."

She looked back at me and winked. "I think I can manage." She looked back to Kellan. "So . . . you're a singer, huh?" She eyed him up and down. "What else can you do?" She let out a husky laugh while Kellan grinned again.

I hurriedly walked away. Like it or not, I *was* calling Denny, and he was giving her a ride to our house. I quickly phoned him and explained what had happened. He laughed at my sister's exuberance and said he could swing by in a couple hours. He had to finish up a project for Max first. I was pretty sure his "project" was something ridiculously not-important for late on a Friday evening. Filing or something.

My sister was invested in a conversation with Kellan when I came back with a vodka-cran, her preferred drink. They were chatting easily while Griffin tried to interject as much as possible. She looked over and thanked me for the drink, then immediately looked back at Kellan while I frowned. Kellan peered up at me from the corner of his eye. He seemed amused that I was *not* amused.

Throughout my shift, I watched Anna flirt with Kellan. He didn't seem to encourage her advances or make any advances of his own, but he didn't discourage her advances either. While they talked, she brushed hair from his forehead, touched his shoulder, grazed her arm against his leg. She was subtle, but also not subtle. He would say something amusing to her and she would laugh, tilting her head to the side. Then she'd seductively bite her lip and run a finger lightly along her low neckline while continuing her throaty chuckle. Griffin was as irritated at that display as I was. I never thought I'd feel the same way as Griffin about anything.

When I came up a bit later to tell the band they were set to go on, Anna had her hand brazenly high on Kellan's inner thigh, and he seemed perfectly fine with that.

"Time's up, Kellan." The words came out harshly, and my sister looked at me oddly. I fixed my face into what I thought was a passable smile and explained to her. "They need to go onstage and play now." Kellan smiled at my forced tone, highly amused.

"Oh . . . great!" my sister beamed, and I wished Denny would hurry up and get here already.

As the D-Bags climbed up onstage, my sister forcefully made her way through the quickly swarming crowd to a place directly in front of Kellan's microphone. He irritatingly smiled down at her while the guys got set up. I frowned but couldn't watch anymore, as customers started demanding my attention. Where the heck was Denny?

Denny finally arrived at the bar halfway through the guys' set. Anna had been enjoying the show a little too much for my taste, and Kellan had his bedroom eyes on her—and the half-dozen women around her—for most of it. I was not in a good mood when Denny finally walked through the doors.

"Where have you been?" I snipped.

Denny looked at me oddly and ran a hand through his dark hair. "I told you, I had to finish work first." He glanced over to where Anna was reaching up to Kellan, and Kellan was annoyingly reaching back toward her. "She seems to be enjoying herself anyway." He laughed once and smirked.

I closed my eyes and swallowed my irritation. Reopening them, I caught him watching me curiously. "Why don't you take her home now? Her stuff is in the back room."

Still looking at me with a curious expression, he shrugged his shoulders and said, "Okay." He relaxed his expression then and slid his arms around my waist. "I missed you." His eyes sparkled as a warm smile crossed his face.

I relaxed and smiled back at him. "I missed you too." I kissed him softly. He pulled me tight and started to deepen the kiss. I pulled away. "I'm sorry, we're really busy. Can you please take her home now? I'm sure she's tired after her trip." I shrugged lamely as I stepped away from his embrace.

Denny looked back to the stage, where Anna was jumping around with the girls around her, clamoring for the rock-god before them. "Yeah, she looks . . . wiped." He grinned back at me but I frowned in response. He sighed. "Okay. I'll put her stuff in the car, then drag her home."

I smiled and kissed him softly again. "Thank you."

He went to the back and got her things, then came back inside and attempted to fight his way through the thickening crowd. Once he got to her, I watched him place a hand on her shoulder. My sister looked over at him, and then, smiling widely, flung herself into his arms. I couldn't help the chuckle that came out at the look on Denny's face. He seemed a little unsure whether it was okay to hug this beautiful woman (who was clinging to every part of him) back. I smiled at his faithfulness . . . which, of course, made me frown, as I glanced up to Kellan on the stage. He was watching Anna and Denny with an amused grin. Suddenly his eyes flicked up to mine, and I was trapped by his deep blue depths and alluring voice.

I was held in his gaze and unable to look away when I suddenly felt a light hand on my shoulder. I startled and looked over at Denny. He'd apparently walked back from the stage in the time I had been entranced by Kellan.

"Sorry, she won't leave with me." He shrugged, like he wasn't too surprised by that.

"She what?" I took a couple of calming breaths and hoped that Denny hadn't noticed what had held my attention for so long.

"She wants to listen to the rest of the set." He shrugged again. "Do you want me to stay? Give you guys a ride home?" He tucked a lock of hair that had fallen from my ponytail behind my ear.

I sighed, irritated and relieved. "Yeah . . . thank you." At least she wouldn't be riding home with Kellan.

Of course, I had forgotten how tenacious my sister could be when she wanted something . . . and apparently, she wanted Kellan. No big surprise there. I had been pretty sure that she would want him once she got around to him. He was kind of hard to resist. I sighed as I watched her slide casually into his car at the end of the night. Denny chuckled as he watched her as well. I had been too busy finishing up work to stop her from leaving the bar with Kellan. They were just getting into his car when I finally walked out the door with Denny. What had they been doing for so long out here? Irritation flared in me again as their car pulled out of the lot. Kellan had better drive her straight home.

Fortunately for him . . . he did. His Chevelle was in the driveway when we pulled up beside it. I quickly walked through the front door and found them sitting on the couch together, bent over in conversation. What were they always talking about? They both looked over at me as I walked into the living room. Irritation flashed through me yet again at the sight of Anna's hand all the way up his thigh. Really, why couldn't she keep her hands to herself?

Denny walked in a moment later and slipped his arms around me.

"So . . ." Anna smiled alluringly at Kellan, "where am I sleeping tonight?"

Kellan half-smiled at her and started to reply, when I butted in. "You're sleeping with me, Anna." I looked over at Denny, while Anna frowned and Kellan stifled a laugh. "Do you mind sleeping on the couch?"

Denny twisted his lips unhappily. "The couch?" He looked at the ragged, lumpy couch even more unhappily. "Really?"

My eyes surely as cool as my voice, I said, "Well, if you prefer, you can sleep with Kellan." My tone indicated that that was his only other option. Anna was sleeping with me, where I could make sure she stayed there, all night long.

Denny raised an eyebrow at me, while Kellan laughed and said, "I'm just warning you now—I kick."

"Couch it is," Denny grumbled, and went upstairs to get a blanket.

Anna brightened. "You know, I could sleep with—"

I grabbed her hand and pulled her off the couch. "Come on." I pulled her up the stairs with me, leaving an entirely too-amused Kellan watching me herd her away from him.

I didn't sleep a wink. My sister had gotten ready for bed after me, and as I couldn't exactly justify standing in the hallway, watching over her like some overprotective father keeping an eye on his daughter's virtue, I had to lie in bed and grit my teeth while I listened as carefully as I could. I could have sworn that at some point I heard Kellan's laughter, and it took everything I had to not rush out there and drag her to bed, kicking and screaming.

Eventually, she entered the dark room and snuggled down on Denny's side, cheerily saying good night to me. I ignored it, feigning sleep. I'm not sure why. Needless to say, sleep was impossible. I was hyperaware of every movement she made. Was she twisting in her sleep, or was she shifting to get up and have a secret rendezvous with Kellan in his room while everyone slept? It drove me crazy all night long and I didn't know how I was going to get through another night of this. Maybe I'd make Kellan go to Matt's after all.

But morning finally did come, and hearing Kellan's door open, since I was wide awake, I followed shortly after and joined him downstairs for coffee. I paused at the bottom step to glance at Denny, lying on the couch. He was sound asleep, but he really didn't look very comfortable. I felt a twinge of guilt that I'd made him sleep there. Oh well, I could make it up to him later.

Kellan didn't seem surprised to see me, as I rounded the corner into the kitchen. He gave me a knowing smile as he looked over at me, pouring some fresh water into the coffeepot as he did. "Mornin'. Sleep okay?" The amusement in his question was all too clear to me.

"I slept fine." Yeah, right. "You?"

Starting the machine, he turned to lean back on the counter. "Like a baby."

I gritted my teeth and forced a smiled as I sat at the table and waited for the coffee to brew.

"Your sister is . . . interesting," he said after a minute.

I frowned up at him but said nothing, wondering if he was going to elaborate on that. He didn't. I flushed deeply and he watched my reaction curiously. "Yes . . . she is." I didn't elaborate either.

The coffee finished brewing and he prepared our two cups. We sat and drank them in silence . . . and not a completely comfortable silence either. Well, he looked completely comfortable, and disastrously perfect, but I was agitated . . . and agitated at being agitated. I really needed to calm down.

After finishing my coffee, I leaned against the archway and stared at Denny's sleeping form on the couch in a near trance. I came out of it when my sister came into the kitchen, wearing a Douchebags T-shirt . . . and nothing else. I mentally thanked fate that Kellan had disappeared back up to his room shortly after finishing his coffee. She was entirely too attractive for just having woken up.

"Where did you get that?" I said, astonished. It had taken weeks for Kellan to . . . well, literally give me the one off his back. Did she just bat her stupidly long eyelashes at him, and he stripped for her too? I felt oddly betrayed by that.

"Griffin . . . after the show. He's got a box full of them in his van. Do you want one?" She smiled sweetly at me, and I instantly felt guilty for thinking badly of her.

"No . . . I have one." One that still smelled amazingly like Kellan, so I never actually wore it—not that I was ever going to mention that to her. "You should put some more clothes on, though. Denny will be awake soon." It really wasn't Denny that I was worried about staring at her in that all too alluring outfit.

"Oh, sorry, sure thing. So . . . is Kellan awake?" she asked, almost demurely.

I sighed. "Yes, I think he went back to his room."

"Oh." She smiled and looked up at the ceiling, to where his room was. "Did he mention me at all?"

I hated that I suddenly felt like I was playing matchmaker, but I told her the truth anyway. "Yeah, he said you were interesting."

She frowned slightly. "Hmmm . . . That's not exactly what I'm used to hearing. I suppose it could be worse though." She smiled and turned to head back upstairs. "I'll just have to step up my game plan." She winked and left the room.

I sat heavily at the table and sighed again. Was it Sunday yet?

Anna wanted to do a little shopping while she was in town, so we borrowed Denny's car and she drove us to Bellevue Square, since she was a much better stick-shift driver than I was. We were walking through Macy's when she found this tiny black dress and decided to try it on for tonight. Of course, it looked amazing on her. It was a simple tank-top dress, but it hugged every inch of her perfectly . . . and it was really, really short. I could never pull off an outfit like that. I'd feel too self-conscious about the world seeing my underwear to even try. My sister looked completely comfortable as she spun around in the dressing room though. She could have been wearing her favorite comfy sweats with how breezy she looked.

On our way to check out, we wandered through the cologne section. I stopped when I found the scent Denny liked to wear. Grabbing a tester, I inhaled it deeply—it immediately brought him to mind. My sister rolled her eyes but smiled at me as she started grabbing a few testers and sniffing them.

"What cologne does Kellan wear?" she asked as she sniffed bottle after bottle, a slight frown on her face.

I froze at the mention of his name. Why would she think I knew that? "I don't know . . . why?" I had actually wondered that myself.

She smiled widely as she looked over at me. "He smells amazing. Haven't you ever noticed that?"

I had. "No."

She snorted, which on her was oddly endearing. "Kiera, I know you're gloriously content with Denny"—she gave me a dry look— "but for the sake of all womankind . . . when life throws yumminess in your lap"—she smiled widely again and grabbed a bottle, inhaling it—"take a whiff." Putting the bottle back, she laughed and grinned devilishly, in a way that reminded me painfully of Kellan. "And if necessary . . . a lick or two."

I grimaced. If she only knew how much I had already done . . . of both.

We finished up our shopping trip with my sister finding the perfect pair of flirty high heels and a delicate-looking silver necklace. I sighed mentally. She was going to look amazing. . . . She already did, just wearing jeans and a tight blouse. I didn't have the money to splurge on clothes right now, so I was going to have to dig through my closet for something decent to wear. It really didn't matter. I wouldn't be able to hold a candle to her anyway. And I didn't have to, I reminded myself. Denny loved *me,* and that was what mattered. Denny, not . . .

I didn't even let myself finish that thought.

We ate a light dinner and she gabbed about the various men she had been "seeing" since dumping Phil quite harshly, from the way she told the story. I momentarily felt bad for Phil. She had probably torn apart his heart and not even realized it. I felt oddly, and sympathetically, connected to him.

After our meal, we shopped a few more stores, my sister picking up a few more items, and then we made our way home to get ready for our . . . evening.

Anna quickly and easily slipped into her new outfit, hustling downstairs while I still rummaged around for something to wear. Denny offered suggestions, until I glared viciously at him. He stopped after that, shaking his head as he buttoned up his shirt. I watched him for a moment, a little annoyed at how easy it is to dress when you're a guy. His white shirt fit his body perfectly and he wore it untucked over his favorite faded blue jeans. He looked great. If I had been in a different mood, I would have stopped him from buttoning his shirt up and slipped it back off of him.

But I wasn't—I was irritated. Finally, I found something and halfheartedly slipped it on.

I came downstairs moments later, and stopped dead in my tracks on the bottom step. My sister and Kellan were sitting on the couch. Kellan was sitting on the very edge of the cushion, elbows on his knees, and my sister was straddled behind him, kneeling on the cushions, with her body pressed firmly against him. Her skimpy black tank-top dress was so short that her entire thigh was exposed, and she seemed not to care at all. Kellan either, for that matter. She was playing with his hair while he idly watched TV. Irritation made me frown.

Anna looked over at me and smiled. "Hey . . . you look great!" Staring at her beauty, I felt anything but great—passable, more likely. Kellan looked over as well and gave me a small, approving smile.

"You're beautiful," Denny purred into my ear, coming down the stairs behind me. He kissed my neck and I relaxed a bit. I *was* glad he liked the outfit that I'd had such a hard time picking. I knew I couldn't compete with my sister, so eventually, I had just decided to dress for comfort. I had picked out my chunky black shoes, black low-rise jeans and a red, low-cut, slinky tank top number; clubs got hot pretty quickly. My hair was already pulled up in a low ponytail. I was ready for the heat I knew was coming.

"She's not going to do that to me, is she?" Denny asked, coming over to stand beside me, and staring at Anna and Kellan on the couch with a small frown on his face. I finally got past my irritation at how they were sitting and looked more closely at what they were doing. Anna wasn't just playing with his hair, she was styling it.

Denny and I walked into the living room. Denny took a seat in the chair and, patting his lap, encouraged me to sit on top of him. After a quick glance at Kellan, I did. "What are you doing, Anna?" I asked, trying to sound nonchalant.

She smiled brightly at me. "Doesn't he have the best fuck-me hair! Don't you just want to . . . ?" She grabbed a section on either side of his head and lightly tugged, making Kellan flinch, and then grin. "Uh!" she growled suggestively.

I blushed deeply, knowing exactly what she meant, and said absolutely nothing.

Anna went back to styling his hair, while Kellan smiled softly and looked down. "He's letting me clubify it. He's going to be the hottest thing in there." She looked over at Denny. "No offense or anything."

Denny laughed at her. "None taken, Anna."

"Oh," I said quietly, thinking his hair was fabulous before Anna got to it. But watching her work . . . he was oddly hotter. She was taking some of the longer pieces and shaping them with pomade, to define his shaggy mess into random, chunky, spike-like pieces around his head.

The effect was incredibly sexy and as he watched me watch him, I started blushing and had to look away. A flash of jealousy went through me that she was doing something so intimate for him, followed quickly by a flash of longing that I forcefully pushed aside.

"What do you think?" Kellan asked.

"Uhhh . . . looks great, man," Denny said, laughing a little.

"Oh, you just don't understand girls, Denny. They'll go nuts for this. Right, Kiera?" Anna said spunkily.

Kellan chuckled softly, and I blushed even deeper. "Yeah, sure, Anna. He'll be—"

"Man-candy?" Kellan finished, highly amused, his eyes never leaving mine.

"Oohhh . . . I like that!" Anna exclaimed, slipping her arms around his neck, apparently finished. I bristled at her closeness to him.

"Are we ready to go?" I spat out, a little too intently.

Kellan nodded and stood up, and I finally noticed what he was wearing. He was in head-to-toe black—black boots, black jeans and a fitted, black, short-sleeved, button-up shirt. Combined with his now impossibly sexy, spiky hair, I had to close my eyes and take a minute at his attractiveness.

Tonight was going to be . . . interesting.

We arrived at the club named Spanks that Griffin had recommended to Kellan. Knowing Griffin and his . . . tastes, I was really unsure about walking into this place. Kellan assured us that it was just a normal club with a weird name and that the music was good. Of course, Kellan would find it only too amusing to convince us all to go to some S&M club. Come to think of it, Anna would find that amusing too. In some ways, they were too perfectly matched. That thought saddened me a little.

The music was pleasantly loud, even from the outside. Denny grabbed my hand and, grinning, helped me from his car. Kellan had driven his own car. Anna had, predictably, darted into his car before I could say anything. He'd managed to find a spot a few spaces away from us, and Kellan helped Anna get out of his car too. Looking like supermodels, they walked over to Denny and me.

My sister adjusted her ridiculously short dress and checked her slinky black high heels before giving me a quick hug. I couldn't help the jealousy that sprang through me at her beauty. Her lips were bright red again, her green eyes popping out gloriously from her expertly done mascara, and her shiny hair was curled into perfect, large rolls that bounced effortlessly when she moved, the red streaks peeking out through the bottom layers enticingly. If Kellan's perfection could be somehow morphed into a woman . . . it would be my sister. For a split second, I couldn't help the thought that if she and Kellan had children, they would be breathtaking. That thought instantly irritated me.

Anna grabbed Kellan's hand and led him to the front door. He smiled and put his arm around her shoulders. Denny put his arm around me as we followed them across the lot. I was grateful for that. I was suddenly very cold.

The burly man attending the rope to the packed club took one look at Kellan and Anna approaching him and instantly raised the rope for them. Well, of course. The superhot people didn't need to wait in line. Kellan paused at the rope and waited for Denny and me, the less-hot people, to make sure we got inside too.

Spanks really was just a cleverly weird name to draw people in. The inside was, thankfully, a typical generic club. Some couches here and there, long tables with bar stools, some mildly interesting art thrown on the walls, a long bar taking up the far wall across from the entrance, and, slightly around a corner, the crowd of moving bodies on the dance floor—which was massive. The music was pleasantly deafening. I was glad for it, and for the confusing mass of bodies. I was ready to disappear.

Denny, Anna, and I found a free spot at one of the long tables while Kellan braved the four-person-deep mob waiting for drinks at the bar. He was back in record time, though, and I couldn't help but notice the female bartender giving him disgustingly inappropriate looks. It irritated me.

Kellan handed everyone a shot of . . . something. I sniffed it and immediately made a face. I snapped my eyes up to where he was grinning at me with an eyebrow raised. Tequila? He had actually brought us all tequila? He set down a container of limes and some salt while I looked at him incredulously. Everyone around me set up their shot, no one else having a problem with Kellan's drink choice. I braced myself and prepared mine as well.

Kellan laughed softly, which thankfully got swallowed up in the noise, and no one but me noticed. He dipped his finger in the tequila to wet the back of his hand, and the memory of him doing that on our first night together suddenly overcame me so fast that I had to close my eyes and breathe deep.

"You okay?" Denny leaned over and said in my ear.

I opened my eyes and looked over at his concerned face. "Yeah . . ." I glared over at Kellan. "I'm just not a big fan of tequila."

Kellan smiled wider. "Really? You struck me as the type that would . . . love it."

My sister butted in as Kellan laughed again and I frowned. "Well, I love it. . . . Cheers!"

Kellan raised an eyebrow and his glass and toasted Anna; they did their shots together. They both laughed as they sucked on their limes. Denny raised his glass and I stubbornly raised mine, and we toasted and did our shots together. Feeling a little snotty, I took Denny's lime . . . from his mouth, lingering for a long kiss.

While kissing a surprised but willing Denny, I heard my sister yell, "Wooo . . . there's my girl!"

Pulling back, I risked a glance at Kellan. He no longer looked amused. He clenched his jaw. Then, half-grinning sexily, he looked over at Anna and extended a hand out to her. "Want to?" He nodded over to the dance floor, and she eagerly nodded her head. They disappeared into the crowd, his hand on her lower back . . . her extreme lower back. He glanced back at me once, an odd glint in his eye, as they were swallowed by the throng.

I swallowed my ire and focused on my own date.

"They make a good couple," Denny said, also watching them leave.

I swallowed again and forcibly shoved all irritation aside, making myself relax completely for the first time in what felt like forever. Denny was looking at me adoringly, a big goofy grin on his beautiful face. He nodded over to the dance floor, and I eagerly nodded back.

"Dancing" was a loose term in a club this full. It was more like tightly packed, rhythmic moving. Denny grabbed my hand so we wouldn't get separated in the massive swarm, then pulled us to a more central location. It was already getting warm and I was glad for my breezy outfit choice. I had no idea what the song playing was, and I didn't care. The beat was heavy and drowned out every thought in my cramped head.

Denny grabbed my waist and we moved closely together. I laughed and threw my arms around his neck. Sometimes I forgot just how attractive Denny was. He had the first three buttons undone on his shirt and his skin showed through enticingly. His hair was perfectly piecey and fabulously styled, and I ran my fingers back through the short layers near his neck, making him smile.

The women around us sure hadn't missed him. As we had moved into place, they barely registered me before turning to look at him with open interest on their faces. Denny took no notice of them. He never did. His eyes were purely for me. He leaned in close to kiss me, his warm eyes sparkling. I ran a finger along the wonderfully light hair following his jawline and sighed happily, letting the music, and his body, carry away my troubles.

We never saw Kellan and Anna again. I made myself not wonder about where they'd taken off to in the club, and about how provocatively they must be grinding together. I made myself not think about them possibly having abandoned us here to find a more intimate setting. Eventually, I managed to block out everything in my head, and loud music, gyrating bodies, and thumping bass were all I cared about. That and having Denny close to me. My bliss lasted for what felt like hours.

The heat was building, as close to the center of the mob as we were. Denny made a drinking motion with his hand, since hearing someone in this noise was virtually impossible, indicating that he was ready for the next round. I playfully pushed him away and shook my head, not ready to give up my music-induced sanctuary. I gave him a swift kiss and pointed to the ground, to let him know I would stay in this spot.

He fought his way back through the crowd, the women watching him as he passed. I sighed and shook my head as he rounded the corner to the bar. Yes, my man was beautiful, and completely unaware of it. I closed my eyes and focused on the music, happy and content. Mindless.

I froze when a strong, familiar hand came up behind me and floated up under my slinky shirt, to rest on my bare stomach. My eyes flashed open, but I didn't need to turn and look. I knew his touch only too well, instantly recognized the fire burning in my belly. In my happiness, I had almost forgotten Kellan was still here. Had he been watching? I was beyond shocked that he would make a move after we'd ended things, and with Denny and Anna here? He pulled me back into his hip and we suggestively moved together with the music. What had been fun and innocent with Denny was now so much more intense. I felt naked.

The heat in the room seemed to double. I could feel a bead of sweat form between my shoulder blades and start to roll down the exposed skin of my back. His free hand brushed aside a few strands of hair on my neck that had fallen from where the rest was pulled back, sending electricity shooting through my spine. He bent down and slowly brushed the bead of sweat away with his tongue, following the salty trail up past my shoulder blades to the back of my neck, biting the skin very, very softly. I inhaled sharply; my vision swam. Damn . . .

Apparently, since we had completely ended things, all innocent pretensions went out the window. Not good. I needed to stop this.

Against my will, though, I closed my eyes again and melted into him. One of my hands rested on his hand over my stomach, the other wrapped around behind him, to rest on his hip. My breathing sped as I rested my head back against his chest. His hand on my stomach moved down fractionally, his thumb resting on the button of my jeans. It was enough to make me gasp and I interlaced our fingers and clenched his hand. I wanted to run, I wanted to claw my way through the crowd and find Denny, return to my sanctuary, get away from the scorching sensation Kellan drove throughout my body. But that was in my mind. My body shivered, my hand on his hip ran down the front of his thigh, and my head . . . slowly turned around toward him.

His other hand grabbed my chin, and roughly pulled my lips to his. I moaned, the sound lost in the driving music. Weeks of escalating flirting, tempting each other with our touching, our bodies, and our lips, but never caving to the wanton desire between us, had left me craving him more than I had realized. I couldn't press against his lips hard enough, my whole body burned with the need of it. I couldn't even think of stopping him now.

His lips parted and his tongue touched the roof of my mouth. Fire erupted throughout my whole body. I lost even more of the fragile hold on my control. I spun in his hands, turning to face him, and pressed myself completely into his embrace, never breaking the connection of our lips, never opening my eyes. My heart racing even harder, I threw my hands up and knotted them in the back of his thick hair. His hands ran up my bare back, under my shirt, and pulled me even closer. We were already both panting in between the brief breaks in our lips.

The heat, the throbbing music, his strong hands, his fast breath, his scent, his taste, his soft lips and exploring tongue—all of it was driving me insane. One of his hands ran down my backside, and he grabbed my upper thigh, pulling my leg slightly up his hip. From that position, it was painfully obvious how much Kellan wanted me. I groaned, wanting him right that minute as well. My eyes opened and I pulled away from his lips, resting my head against his and panting softly. My hands automatically started unbuttoning his shirt, uncharacteristically not caring where we were. His eyes burned, watching me intently.

Some of the women around us had noticed Kellan and were

watching him lasciviously. So far, no one seemed to care how intimate we had become, or were about to become. He closed his eyes and roughly exhaled when I was halfway done with his shirt. He gripped my body tight and crushed his lips back down to mine. We couldn't stay here like this for much longer. It was like I was a different person, being absorbed into his passion. I didn't know what to do, didn't know how to stop myself from making this far too graphic for such a public place. I wanted him to take me somewhere . . . anywhere.

I had two buttons left on his shirt, when he suddenly, roughly, pushed me away from him. Then he turned to melt into the crowd, his face breathless but unreadable. I panted, confused, and attempted to catch my breath.

That was when I felt Denny grab my hand and pull me into him. I hadn't noticed his return. Did he see anything? Did I look different to him? I searched his eyes, but they only looked happy to see me. He must have written off the sweat and breathlessness to the dancing.

Then I did something that would later haunt me. I pressed into Denny, grabbing his face roughly in my hands and kissing him—hard. Excitement coursed through my body, as, in my mind's eye, I pictured being with Kellan again. Denny reacted with surprise for half a second, then returned my kiss eagerly. Disgusted with myself, I could not stop kissing him, wanting him, needing him—knowing all too well, that, while Denny was with me physically, he was not whom I was ravishing. From somewhere in the club, I could feel eyes burning into me.

"Take me home," I moaned into Denny's ear.

Much, much later, I sat up in bed, naked, and glanced over at Denny's sleeping form next to me. Guilt washed through me. If he ever knew what I had just done . . . who I had just mentally replaced him with . . . I tried to swallow, but my throat was too dry. Suddenly desperately thirsty, I grabbed the first piece of clothing I could find, and stood to put it on. Denny's button-up shirt was closest to my side of the bed. It smelled wonderfully of him as I slipped it on.

Wanting the clean, cold water from the fridge, I made my way to the stairs. I paused for only the slightest fraction of a second as I passed Kellan's door. A small part of me hoped he somehow hadn't just heard that. I couldn't imagine what he would think while listening to Denny and me. I hadn't exactly been quiet. Picturing Kellan in my head like that had made me lose all control. I frowned, not liking that thought at all.

I made my way into the kitchen, thinking about Kellan, about what had happened at the club, how intense it had gotten between us, how much I had wanted him, how much he had wanted me. Things were getting dangerous between us. I wasn't sure what to do.

I glanced out the window and stopped. His car wasn't there. Kellan still wasn't home? I went back to the living room. Anna wasn't there? Oh God, they were still out together . . . alone. I instantly thought of a half-dozen places, and positions, that they could be in. The thought made me feel ill, and then I felt guilty. I settled on angry. Whatever was going on between Kellan and me, he had promised—promised!—that he wouldn't sleep with Anna.

No longer thirsty, I turned around and went back to bed.

Chapter 16
Rain

I heard Kellan's car in the driveway around lunchtime. It didn't turn off, and, after a door opened and closed, he sped off again. A few moments later, Anna entered through the front door, dressed in her clothes from last night. She looked happy and extremely satisfied.

I bit back my anger as she sat down on the couch beside me. It wasn't her fault that she had fallen for Kellan's allure. No, all of my anger was reserved for him. . . . He had promised. "Good night last night?" I asked flatly.

She flopped back on the couch and, smiling widely, laid her head back on the cushions. "Oh . . . God, you have no idea."

Actually, I did.

"Kellan took us to Matt and Griffin's place and—"

I really didn't want to hear about it. "Ugh, please don't tell me."

She frowned and looked over at me; she did enjoy a good sex story. "Fine." She grinned again and leaned over at me. "You and Denny took off in a hurry." She raised an eyebrow suggestively. "Kellan said you guys needed alone time." She giggled. "How was your night?"

Guilt, anger, and embarrassment coursed through me. Kellan told her we needed *alone time*? "I don't want to talk about that either, Anna," I said quietly.

She flopped back on the couch and sulked. "Fine." She looked over at me. "Can I just tell you this one thing—"

"No!"

She sighed loudly. "Fine." We were both silent for a while. "You okay, sis?" She frowned at me.

I laid my head back on the cushion and tried to ease my expression. "Yeah . . . just tired, didn't sleep much." I instantly regretted saying that.

She grinned knowingly. "Ahhh, yeah! That's my girl!"

Denny made the three of us lunch, and Anna looked at him approvingly. I guess being handy in the kitchen bought Denny bonus points with her. She bit her lip several times during our meal, and I knew she was holding back the little story that she was dying to tell me. I prayed she would keep her mouth firmly shut—I didn't want to hear it. I was pretty positive it would kill me if I did hear about it. The mental play-by-play that I had supplied myself with was bad enough.

I kept my eyes on Denny, instead, as I ate the cashew chicken salad he'd made for us. It was incredibly good; he really was quite handy in the kitchen. He smiled warmly at me, his deep brown eyes calm and peaceful. Last night had been . . . intense . . . between us. I cringed mentally, knowing that it was a different memory for me than for him. For him, it had probably just been us reconnecting after a too-long separation. For me, it was . . . not that simple.

Anna and Denny supplied ninety percent of the conversation as I quietly watched them. My own thoughts were too conflicted to speak in coherent sentences. After a long afternoon of watching the two of them have the breezy conversations that I wished I could have with my charming sister, it was time to pack up her things and get her to the airport.

Anna gave me a warm goodbye hug. "Thanks for letting me finally visit." She smiled coyly. "It was . . . fun." I cringed in my head but outwardly smiled. "Next time we'll do more together, just the two of us . . . okay?" She smiled sweetly at me and I hugged her again.

"Yeah, okay, Anna."

She pulled back and looked at me intently. Speaking quickly, she added, "Please tell Kellan thank you for me." She grabbed my arm and, still speaking fast, so that I wouldn't stop her, she excitedly said, "I know you don't want to hear about it, but, God, last night was so unexpectedly amazing! Like, the-best-night-of-my-life amazing." She smiled brilliantly.

"Oh," was all I could squeak out.

"Oh . . . yeah." She giggled and bit her lip. "The best . . . multiples . . . if you know what I mean."

I did . . . and I really wished I didn't.

She sighed. "Oh, God, I wish I could stay. . . ."

God, I wished she would hurry and leave.

They announced that her flight was boarding and she looked over at the gate, then back to me. "I'll miss you." She hugged me again then pulled back, smiling. "I'll come back soon." She kissed my cheek. "Love you."

"Love you too . . ."

Anna walked over to Denny, who was standing a little ways away from us, giving us space. She threw her arms around his neck and kissed his cheek. "I'll miss you too." She grabbed his bottom before she walked away. "Stud," she muttered, making Denny, and me, blush.

Then my crazy, impulsive sister boarded her plane and went back home to Ohio, unknowingly leaving my world a little more tangled than she had found it.

Kellan still wasn't home when we got back from the airport. In fact, I didn't see Kellan at all that night. I didn't see him until late in the evening the following night, when he and the D-Bags strolled into Pete's while I was working. I glanced over at him cautiously as he entered. I had no idea what to expect from him. He was wearing different clothes than the night of the club, a thin gray T-shirt that hugged his muscles distractingly under his black leather jacket, and his favorite faded jeans. He looked freshly showered, his chunky, al-luring spikes gone, so he had gone home at some point. He looked

no

over my way and gave me a tiny smile and a nod. Well, he wasn't ignoring me then.

I wasn't sure if I wasn't ignoring *him* however—the jerk had promised! The more I thought about that, and the more vivid the horrid pictures became in my mind, the more I ignored him. I rarely went to the guys' table. Evan eventually flagged me down and, without asking what they wanted, I just brought them beers. It was all they ever ordered anyway. I said nothing as I set the beers down. I listened to nothing as I set the beers down. I did my best to mentally escape my body. I didn't want to deal with Kellan.

He did not feel the same. After a bit of my silent waitressing, he cornered me in the hallway when I was coming back from the bathrooms. Seeing him at the end of the hall, I considered hiding out in the back room. I quickly dismissed that thought, though, since the lock on the door was broken and if he really wanted to talk to me, and he appeared to want to do just that, then he would simply follow me. And being alone in a room with him was something I wanted to avoid. I tried to brush past him, but he roughly grabbed my elbow as I walked by.

"Kiera . . ."

With narrowed eyes, I looked up at his handsome face. That made my eyes narrow even more. That stupidly perfect face, with those startlingly inhuman, deep blue eyes, eyes that dropped panties everywhere . . . including mine. It pissed me off! I jerked my arm away from him and said nothing.

"We should talk. . . ."

"Nothing to talk about, Kellan!" I snipped.

"I disagree," he said quietly, a slight frown on his lips.

"Well . . . you can apparently *do* whatever you want." I didn't even try to keep the sneer from my voice.

"What's that supposed to mean?" His eyes narrowed as his tone sharpened.

"It means we have nothing to talk about," I said, finally brushing past him and storming off.

I ended up working later than I had expected to, and with my head in an angry, distracted fog all night, I hadn't bothered to line up a ride home. In fact, by the time I started thinking about it, almost everyone was already gone. Jenny had the night off. Kate got a ride with her boyfriend. Sam and Rita left not long after her, while I was distracted with calling a taxi for a drunken customer. Evan was currently strolling out with a cute blonde. Matt had left hours ago. And Kellan, not that I would allow him to be an option, was leaning against a table with an amused grin on his face, watching me look for a ride home. I could see the light rain splashing on the sidewalk when Evan walked out the door. This was not good. Maybe I should call Denny. It was so late though. Maybe one of the regulars?

I noticed Griffin was still here, and happened to be alone tonight. Maybe . . . Ugh, that option really wasn't great either . . . but he was better than Kellan and better than walking in the rain. Hopeful, I approached him. I could see Kellan's grin widen at my choice.

"Hi, Griffin," I tried casually.

He was suspicious. I usually was neither nice to him nor casual with him. "Yeah? What do you want?" Getting an idea that I probably didn't want to hear, he raised a pale eyebrow at me and smiled in a way that made my skin crawl.

Ignoring my instincts, I nicely said, "I was hoping maybe you could give me a ride home."

He grinned. "Well, Kiera . . . I never thought you'd ask." He eyed me up and down. "I'd love to give you a ride . . . all the way home."

Smirking, I flatly said, "I literally meant a car ride to my house, Griffin."

He frowned. "No sex?"

Shaking my head vigorously, I said, "No."

He sniffed. "Well then . . . no. Get your no-sex ride with Kyle." And with that, he turned and left. Kellan was laughing softly now. I looked around, but everyone else had gone. Pete was still in his office, maybe he would . . .

"Would you like me to give you a ride?" Kellan asked softly.

Angrily shaking my head at his perfect face, I hurried to the front doors. I crossed my arms over my chest, bracing myself for the rain, and walked outside. He didn't follow me, which gave me an odd sort of angry-sad-relieved feeling. The rain wasn't heavy, but it was cold. In my hurry to get away from Kellan, I had forgotten to grab my bag and my jacket. I regretted that haste now, as a few steps through the empty parking lot found me shivering, droplets running down my face. I sighed and considered going back for my stuff, but then stubbornly decided I did not want to see Kellan anymore tonight. I was achingly furious over him and my sister—the bastard had promised!

I made it one block from the bar when mentally I was done with the rain that was starting to take a turn for the worse. I started wondering just how many blocks away our house was. It wasn't long in the car . . . but walking? Shivering uncontrollably, I thought maybe I should find a phone and call Denny. I was looking around for a phone booth or an open store when I noticed a slow-moving car approaching me. Panic started to flare. This really wasn't the greatest neighborhood. Being alone out here in the middle of the night, getting soaked, I suddenly felt very vulnerable.

The car pulled up beside where I was walking on the sidewalk and matched my pace. I suddenly felt even more vulnerable, staring over at the familiar black Chevelle. Of course he would come find me. Kellan leaned across his seat and rolled down the window. Looking at me incredulously, he shook his head.

"Get in the car, Kiera."

I glared over at him. "No, Kellan." Being alone in a small space was not a good idea after our intense moment at the club, especially given how angry I was with him.

He sighed and looked up at the ceiling of his car. Bringing his eyes to mine again, he said with forced patience, "It's pouring. Get in the car."

Feeling stubborn, I glared at him again. "No."

"I'm just going to follow you like this all the way home." He raised his eyebrows and smirked at me.

I stopped walking. "Go home, Kellan. I'll be fine."

He stopped the car too. "You're not walking all the way home by yourself. It's not safe."

It's safer than a car ride with you, I thought irritably. "I'll be fine." I started walking again.

With an exasperated sigh, he took off and peeled around the corner. I thought that was the end of it, but he stopped right around the corner and I saw him getting out of the car. I stopped walking again. *Damn it . . . why doesn't he just leave me alone?*

He had his leather jacket on, but by the time he made it over to where I was still standing, he was quite wet. The rain was dripping through his hair, which hung down over his face and around his eyes and darkened the exposed portion of his light shirt. It suddenly reminded me of the fully clothed shower he had taken so long ago. My breath quickened at his attractiveness. This was definitely not good. My irritation grew. I did not need this right now.

"Get in the damn car, Kiera." He was getting irritated too.

"No!" I pushed him back, away from me.

He grabbed my arm and started dragging me to the car. "No, Kellan . . . stop it!" I tried to pull my arm free, but he was stronger. He pulled me over to the passenger's side. Watching the rain running down the back of his neck made me shiver more than the cold . . . which made me mad. I did not need this—I did not *want* to want him! Becoming enraged, I yanked my arm away, right as he opened the door. I started to walk off, but he reached around behind me and picked me up. I tried kicking and squirming, but he had me tight. He set me next to the opened door, trapping me there with his body.

"Stop it, Kiera—just get in the goddamn car!"

His body, wet and pressing against mine, drove me over the edge. I was so angry at him for the club, for my sister, for Denny, for everything he made me feel . . . for simply existing at all. However, I was also more turned on than I had ever been in my life. I angrily threw both my hands into his wet hair and yanked him close to me, my lips stopping a hairbreadth from his. My eyes glared daggers, my breath came in angry pants as I held our faces close together. Hungrily, I pressed against his lips, cool from the rain. Then . . . I slapped him.

He roughly pushed me back onto the cold car; I barely felt the chill in my rage. Shock passed over his face for a second, then he matched my glare with his own. Good, he was mad too. I could hear the rain pound around us, splashing on the metal roof, the leather seats. He grabbed my waist and bent my body, forcing me into the seat. All I could see were his angry, passionate eyes, so dark blue they were almost black.

I felt the edge of the seat beneath me, but he scooted me up toward the middle, getting in behind me. He released his grip on my waist so he could turn around and slam the door. Freed from his intense glare, I started to scoot up the bench seat away from him, thinking I could get out the other side, wanting to flee again. He turned back around to me and, pulling my legs, dragged me closer. Then he moved over me, forcing me to lie down on the seat. Angrily, I pushed against his chest, but he didn't move away.

"Get off me," I panted, while he stared down at me intently.

"No." His eyes looked furious and confused.

I grabbed his neck and forcefully pulled him closer instead. "I hate you . . ." I seethed.

His hands forced my legs on either side of his hips and he pressed himself against me hard, before I could even react. Even through jeans, the intensity of the move, the feel of him, of how turned on he was as well, made me gasp, made my breath heavier.

"That's not hate you feel. . . ." His voice had a hard edge to it. Enraged, I stared at him icily. He smiled wickedly, breathing heavier as well, his eyes showing no humor. "And that's not friendship either."

"Stop it. . . ." I squirmed under him, trying to move away, but he grabbed my hips and held me in place. He did it again, pulling against my body for leverage. I groaned and started to drop my head back. He grabbed my cheek and made me look back into his eyes.

"This was supposed to be innocent, Kellan!" I spat at him.

"We were never innocent, Kiera. How naïve are you?" he said in the same tone, moving against me again.

"God, I hate you . . ." I whispered, tears of rage stinging my eyes. Equally enraged, he stared right back at me. "No, you don't. . . ."

He did it again, not quite as slow this time, biting his lip and making a noise that sent electricity through me. I could barely catch my breath. Water dripped from his hair onto my wet cheeks, the smell of the rain mixing with his scent intoxicatingly. A tear rolled down my cheek, merging with the rain dropping from his hair. "Yes I do. . . . I hate you . . ." I whispered again between pants.

He pushed against me again and groaned, cringing at the intensity of it. Fire burned in his eyes. "No . . . you want me . . ." he panted back at me, his eyes narrowing. "I saw you. I felt you . . . at the club, you wanted me." He brought his mouth right over mine, almost touching, breathing heavy into me. It was maddening. All I could see, all I could feel, and now all I could breathe, was him. It excited me, it angered me.

"God, Kiera . . . you were undressing me." He smiled wickedly. "You wanted me, right there in front of everyone." He ran his tongue along my jaw to my ear. "God, I wanted you too. . . ."

I tangled my fingers in his wet hair, yanking him away. He inhaled sharply, but only moved against me again. "No, I chose Denny." My eyes rolled back as he did it again. "I went home with him. . . ." I snapped my eyes back to his, anger flashing through me. "Who did you choose?"

He stopped moving his hips for a moment and stared cruelly at me. "What?" he said flatly.

"My sister, you asshole! How could you sleep with her? You promised me!" I smacked him in the chest, hard.

His eyes narrowed dangerously. "You can't be mad at me for that. You left to go screw *him*! You left me there . . . ready, wanting you . . . with her." He smirked and ran his hands along my hips suggestively. "And she was all too willing. It was so easy to take her . . . to slip inside her," he whispered intensely.

I bristled at that and tried to smack him away, but he held me down tight. "You son of a bitch."

He gave me a wicked grin. "I know who I screwed, but tell me"—barely able to keep speaking through his anger, he lowered his head to my ear and panted breathlessly—"who did you fuck that night?" He pushed hard against me as he said that. The intensity of the movement, the crudeness of his question, electrified me, made me groan, suck in a quick breath through my teeth.

"Was he better . . . as me?" He looked back into my eyes, dropped his lips to just touching mine, and flicked his tongue along my lip. "There is no substitute for the real thing. I'll be even better. . . ."

"I hate what you do to me." I hated that he knew what I had done to Denny. I hated that he was right—it had been the best I'd ever had with Denny. I really hated that I knew he was right—he would be so much better. . . .

He watched my eyes intensely. "You love what I do to you." He ran his tongue up my throat, licking the rain from my still-damp skin. I shivered. "You ache for it," he whispered. "It's me you want, not him," he persisted.

I ran my fingers through his hair as he moved against me again. I started bringing my hips up to meet his. It intensified it for both of us and he groaned at the exact same time, and in the exact same way that I did. The windows steamed up with our heavy breathing. God, I hated him. God, I wanted him.

I pulled his jacket off his shoulders, telling myself that I only wanted him to be as cold and miserable as I was. He tore it the rest of the way off, an eager look in his eyes, and tossed it in the backseat. Fire burned through me at the feel of his perfect chest so close to mine. An angry fire, like molten lava.

I tried to bring him to my lips, he pulled back. That made me mad. I tried to touch his open mouth with my tongue, he pulled back. That pissed me off, and I ran my nails down his back, hard. He made an odd aroused-pained sound and dropped his head to my shoulder, digging his hips into me even harder. I cried out and grabbed his back jeans pockets, pulling him tighter to me, curling my legs around his hips.

"No, I want him . . ." I moaned, as I clutched him to me.

"No, you want me . . ." he muttered into my neck.

"No, he would never touch my sister," I spat. "You promised, you promised, Kellan!" My anger at that resurfaced, and I tried to push him away again, tried to squirm out from under him.

"That's already done with. I can't change it." He grabbed my hands and pinned them on either side of my head, digging his hips into me again. I gasped and made a noise deep in my throat. "But this . . . Stop fighting, Kiera. Just say you want this. Tell me you want me . . . like I want you." He brought his mouth to hover over mine again, his eyes blazed. "I already know you do. . . ."

He kissed me then, finally. . . .

I groaned into his mouth and took him eagerly. He released my hands and I tangled them back in his hair. He kissed me deeply, passionately. His hands twisted back in my wet hair, pulling the elastic band out. His hips continued rocking into mine.

"No . . ." I ran my hands down his back, "I hate"—I grabbed his hips and pulled him into me—"you." We kissed hard and heavy for an eternity. Between pants, I continued spewing how much I hated him. Around my lips, he kept telling me I didn't.

"This is wrong," I moaned, my hands running up under his shirt to feel his fabulously hard body.

His hands ran everywhere along my body—my hair, my face, my breasts, my hips. "I know . . ." he breathed, "but, God, you feel so good."

The continuous grinding motion was escalating, I either needed something more . . . or I needed it to stop. Then, as if reading my thoughts, he stopped kissing me and pulled back. Panting with need, he dropped his hands to my jeans. *No . . . yes . . . no,* I thought frantically, not able to decipher my own rapidly swinging emotions. He began to unbutton them, staring at me intently, angrily—just as I was staring at him. There was so much heat between us, I thought for sure we would both ignite.

On the last of the four buttons, I grabbed his wrists and brought his hands up over my head and against the door, holding him against me. I wrapped my fingers around his tightly and he groaned as our bodies pressed together again. "Stop it, Kiera," he snarled. "I need you. Let me do this. I can make you forget him. I can make you forget *you.*"

I shuddered, knowing he was absolutely right.

He pulled a hand free from my weaker grasp and trailed it down my chest, back to my jeans, his lips on my neck with an intense fervor. "God, I want inside you . . ." he growled intensely in my ear.

Electricity shot through me as my entire body reacted to his words; my body desperately wanted that too. My head, however, could not get the image of him being this intimate with my sister out of it. "Stop it, Kellan!" I hissed at him.

"Why?" he hissed back, his lips brushing my neck giving me chills. "It's what you want . . . what you beg for!" he growled, slipping his hand into my jeans, on the outside of my underwear.

The closeness was too much. His touch promised me unimaginable pleasure. I moaned loudly and closed my eyes. Quickly reopening them, I grabbed his neck and brought his face right to mine. I was so angry. . . . His heavy breath was ragged, and he inhaled through his teeth and groaned. God, he was just as turned on as I was.

"No . . . I don't want you to." I was saying no, but his finger was tracing the edge of my underwear along my thigh, and my voice broke halfway through. It sounded like anything but a refusal. I removed my hand from his neck, to try and move his fingers away from me, knowing that if he actually touched me, well, game over, but he was stronger, and his fingers stayed temptingly close.

"I can feel how much you do want me to, Kiera." His eyes burned with a deep, smoldering desire as he watched me. I could see how difficult this was for him, how much more he wanted. He groaned heavily, his face a mixture of painful need and lingering anger. It was the hottest thing I'd ever seen. "I want you . . . *now*. I can't take any more," he said breathlessly, and ripped free his other hand that I was still holding, bringing them both to my jeans. He quickly started tugging the wet fabric down. "God, Kiera. I need this. . . ."

"Wait! Kellan . . . stop! I . . . I need a minute. Please . . . I just need a minute. . . ."

Our old code phrase for "I'm way too riled up, please step back" seemed to penetrate through his passion. He stopped his hands. He stared at me with those intensely smoldering eyes and my breath caught at his gorgeousness. I made myself say it again, with great effort.

"I need a minute." I panted the words.

He stared at me for a second longer. "Shit!" he exclaimed suddenly. I flinched but said nothing. I couldn't get another word out anyway.

He sat up, his eyes still wild with passion, and ran his hand through his damp hair. He swallowed roughly and glared over at me, his breath heavy and ragged. "Shit!" he said again, hitting the door behind him angrily.

Watching him warily, I buttoned my jeans and sat up, trying to slow my breathing and my heartbeat.

"You . . . are . . ." He immediately shut his mouth and shook his head. Before I could respond, he opened the door and stepped out into the freezing, pouring rain. I peered out the open car door to watch him, feeling really stupid and quite unsure what to do.

"Fuck!" he yelled as he kicked the car tire. The rain was sheeting now, and it ran down him, quickly resoaking his hair and soaking his body. He kicked the tire a few more times, shouting other obscenities. I gaped at his tantrum. Finally he walked away from the car and, clenching his fists, yelled loudly to the empty street, "FUUUUCK!!"

Panting in a mix of passion and rage, he put his hands over his face and then ran them back through his hair. He left them tangled there and tilted his head up to the sky, closing his eyes and letting the rain completely soak him, cool him. Slowly, his breath became more even, and he let his arms fall to his sides, palms up, welcoming the rain.

He stayed that way for an achingly long time. I watched him from the relative warmth and dryness of the car. He was breathtakingly handsome—his wet hair slicked back from his fingers, his face relaxed and tilted up to the sky, his eyes closed, his lips parted, his even breath sending droplets of water away from him, rain streaming down his face, water running down his bare arms to his upturned hands, his light shirt clinging to every muscle of his unbelievable body, his jeans soaked and clinging to his legs. He was beyond perfection. He was also starting to shake from the cold.

"Kellan?" I called out over the sound of the rain.

He didn't answer me. He didn't move other than to raise a hand toward me, one finger up—he was taking a minute.

"It's freezing . . . please come back to the car," I pleaded.

He slowly shook his head no.

I wasn't sure what he was doing, but I was sure he was going to freeze to death out there. "I'm sorry, please come back."

He clenched his jaw and shook his head no again. Still angry then.

I sighed. "Damn it," I muttered and, bracing myself, I went back out into the downpour.

He opened his eyes and looked at me with a furrowed brow as I approached. Still very angry then. "Get back in the car, Kiera." He bit off each word, the passion in his eyes replaced with coldness as icy as the rain.

I swallowed under his intense gaze. "Not without you." He couldn't just stay out here in this. His whole body was shaking uncontrollably from the cold now.

"Get in the damn car! For once, just listen to me!" he yelled at me.

I took a step back from his outburst, and then my temper flared. "No! Talk to me. Don't hide out here, talk to me!" I was getting soaked now too, in the freezing rain, but I didn't care.

He took an angry step toward me. "What do you want me to say?" he yelled.

"Why won't you leave me alone? Tell me that! I told you before that it was over, that I wanted Denny. But you still torment me. . . ." My voice cracked with anger.

"Torment you? You're the one who"—He stopped talking and looked away from me.

"The one who what?" I yelled back.

I should have left him alone. I never should have pushed his buttons. . . .

Abruptly, he snapped his eyes back to mine. They blazed in fury and he smiled coldly. "Do you really want to know what I'm thinking right now?" He took another step, and I involuntarily took a step back. "I'm thinking . . . that you . . . are a fucking tease, and I should have just fucked you anyway!" I gaped at him, my face pale, as he took another angry step to stand right in front of me. "I should fuck you right now, like the whore you really—"

He didn't finish saying the words before I slapped him hard across the face. Any sympathy I ever felt for him immediately vanished. Any tender emotion that I ever felt for him immediately vanished. Any friendship I felt for him immediately vanished. I wanted him to vanish. Tears sprang to my eyes.

Really pissed off now, he pushed me roughly back into the car. "You started this. All of this! Where did you think our 'innocent' flirting was heading? How long did you think you could lead me on?" Roughly, he grabbed my arm. "Do I still . . . torment you? Do you still want me?"

The tears streaming down my face were lost in the downpour of rain. I yelled, "No . . . now I really do hate you!"

"Good! Then get in the fucking car!" he yelled and shoved me in through the open door.

I fumbled my way into the seat, starting to cry, and he slammed the door shut behind me. I flinched at the angry noise. I wanted to go home. I wanted the safety and comfort of Denny. I never wanted to see Kellan again.

He paced for a long time outside, probably trying to calm down, while I cried on the inside, watching him and wanting to be far away from him. Then he stalked over to the driver's side and slid into the seat, slamming his door behind him. "Damn it!" he said suddenly, slamming his hand on the steering wheel. "Damn it, damn it, damn it, Kiera." He slammed his hands repeatedly on the wheel and I flinched away from him.

He sank his head down to the wheel and left it there. "Damn it, I never should have stayed here . . ." he muttered. He raised his head and pinched the bridge of his nose with his fingers. I was extremely wet, but he was drenched; water dripped off him everywhere. He sniffed and shook with the cold, his lips were nearly blue, and his face was very pale.

I turned away from him, still crying miserably, as he finally started the car. We waited in awkward silence as he blasted the heat. We sat in that silence for a second, then he sniffed and quietly said, "I'm sorry, Kiera. I shouldn't have said that to you. None of that should have happened."

I could only cry in response.

He sighed, then reached behind him and grabbed my jacket from the backseat. I took a look and saw my bag back there too; he had picked them up for me. I swallowed a lump in my throat as he handed me the jacket in silence. I slipped it on, grateful, but equally silent. Without either of us saying another word, he drove us home.

Pulling up to the driveway and shutting off the car, he immediately exited into the still pouring rain and went inside the house, leaving me alone, staring after him. Swallowing again, I went inside and up the stairs. I stopped at his door. He was in there—I could see the wet footprints in the carpet. I hated him. I looked over at my door, where Denny was waiting for me, most likely asleep, then back to Kellan's door. I wished Denny and I were back in Ohio, back safely with my parents. Then in the silence, I heard a sound I'd never expected to hear—ever. I took a deep breath, opened Kellan's door, and closed it soundlessly behind me.

Kellan was sitting in the middle of his bed, getting water everywhere, his shoes getting the sheets filthy. His arms were locked firmly around his legs and his head was slung down between his knees. His whole body shook . . . but not from the cold. He shook because he was crying.

He said nothing as I sat down next to his dripping body; he didn't look at me, and he didn't stop crying either. Emotions flooded through me—hate, guilt, grief . . . even desire. I settled on sympathy, and put an arm around his shoulders. A sob escaped him and, turning into me, he slipped his arms around my waist and laid his head on my lap. He completely lost it. He clutched at me like I might vanish at any moment. He sobbed so hard he could barely breathe.

I leaned over him, stroking his hair and rubbing his back, as new tears sprang to my eyes. The hurt of his words evaporated in my mind at his pain. Guilt at what I had driven him to flooded through me. He was right . . . in a crude, vulgar way. I *was* a tease. I *did* lead him on. I continually brought him to the brink, then left him for another. I had hurt him. I *was* hurting him. He'd blown up at me, and I had kind of deserved it . . . and he hated himself for it.

He was shaking uncontrollably. His chill was seeping into me, so some of his trembling must have been because he was soaked through. I reached behind me, and he clutched me tighter, like he was afraid I was leaving. Grabbing the edge of a blanket nearly falling off his messy bed, I pulled it up and wrapped it around the both of us. I laid myself over his back, slipping my arms around him. My body eventually started to warm, in turn warming his body, and his shaking slowed.

After what felt like an eternity, his sobs eased to gentle crying, and then that eased as well. I continued to silently hold him to me, surprised to realize that I was lightly rocking him, like he was a child. After a moment, his arms around me loosened, his breath became smooth and regular, and I realized that, also like a child, he had cried himself to sleep, on my legs.

My heart ached with so many emotions, I couldn't keep track of them all. I tried to forget our horrid night, but it started replaying itself in my mind. I shook my head to clear the bad memories, and softly kissed his hair, running my hand down his back. Gently, I shifted out from under him. He stirred, but didn't wake up. As I pulled away from him, he instinctively reached out for me, grabbing my legs again and holding me tight, still asleep. That stirred my heart again, and swallowing, I gently released his hold on me. He cringed and said, "No," and for a moment, I thought he was awake, but after another minute of watching him, he didn't move again or speak again.

I sighed and ran a hand through his hair. Tears sprang, yet again, and I desperately needed out of that room. I fixed the blanket around him so he would stay warm, and then slipped from his room and into mine.

Chapter 17
Like It Should Be

The next morning, Kellan came into the kitchen after me. He was wearing the same clothes, and his hair was styled back from how it had dried overnight. His eyes were dreadfully tired and still a little red. He had cried an awful lot last night. I looked over at him uncertainly. He stopped in the doorway and paused, looking at me equally uncertain. Finally, he sighed and came up to the coffeepot, where I was standing, waiting for it to finish brewing.

He held his hands up in front of him. "Truce?"

I nodded slowly. "Truce."

He leaned back against the counter, putting his hands behind him. "Thank you . . . for staying with me last night," he whispered, staring at the floor.

"Kellan—"

He interrupted me. "I shouldn't have said what I did, that's not who you are. I'm sorry if I scared you. I was so angry, but I wouldn't ever hurt you, Kiera . . . not intentionally." He met my gaze, his voice was calm, but his eyes looked worried. "I was way out of line. I never should have put you in that position. You're not . . . You are in no way a . . ." he looked away, embarrassed, ". . . a whore," he finished softly.

"Kellan—"

He interrupted me again. "I never would have . . ." He sighed and in a barely audible whisper, he said, "I wouldn't ever force you, Kiera. That's not . . . I'm not . . ." He froze and stopped talking, looking at the ground again.

"I know you wouldn't." I suddenly didn't know what else to say. I was equally responsible, and I felt horrible for my part in what had happened. "I'm sorry. You were right. I . . . I led you on." I lightly grabbed his cheek and forced him to look at me fully. His gorgeous face was horribly sad and equally remorseful. "I'm sorry for all of it, Kellan." His pained eyes broke my heart.

He looked at me oddly. "No . . . I was just mad. *I* was wrong. You didn't do anything. You don't need to apologize for—"

I cut him off. "Yes, I do." I lowered my already low voice. "We both know I did just as much as you. I went just as far as you did."

He frowned slightly. "You clearly told me no . . . repeatedly. I didn't listen . . . repeatedly." He sighed again and pulled my hand away from his cheek. "I was horrible. I went too far, much too far." He ran a hand down his face. "I'm . . . I'm so sorry."

"Kellan . . . no, I wasn't being clear. I sent mixed signals." My words might have been telling him no, but my body certainly had been telling him something else. How could he feel responsible for that?

His voice heated. "'No' is clear, Kiera. 'Stop' is pretty damn clear."

"You're not a monster, Kellan. You never would have—"

He cut me off again. "I'm no angel either, Kiera . . . remember? And you have no idea what I'm capable of," he finished quietly, eyeing me warily.

I didn't know what he meant by that, but I refused to believe that he would ever, that he *could* ever . . . force me. "We both messed up, Kellan," I said, reaching out for his cheek again. "But you would never force yourself on me."

He watched me with a torn look on his face, and then he pulled me to his chest in a tight embrace. I threw my arms around his neck and, for just a moment, let myself believe that it was months ago, and we were just two friends giving one another a moment's comfort.

But . . . we weren't. Our friendship had flamed into passion, and, once ignited, that burn was impossible to turn back down.

"You were right. We have to end this, Kiera."

He took a hand and brushed aside a tear on one side of my face, then the other; I hadn't even realized I was crying. Then he cupped my face, stroking my cheek with his thumb. It was such a tender gesture that my heart sped, but I knew he was right. I had known it a while ago.

"I know."

I closed my eyes and more tears dropped to my cheeks. His lips softly brushed mine. I half-sobbed and pulled him harder against me. He kissed me back, but not in the way I expected. It was so different, soft and tender, in a way our kisses had never been before. It terrified *and* thrilled me. His thumb continued to stroke my cheek softly.

He kissed me tenderly for a minute more, then, sighing, he pulled away. He moved his hand from my cheek and ran his fingers through my hair and down my back. "You were right. You made your choice." He pulled me close to him, almost touching my lips. "I still want you," he growled intensely, then his voice softened, and he pulled away again. "But not while you're his. Not like this, not like last night." He said it wistfully, his eyes looking even more tired.

"This"—he lightly ran a finger down my lips, as more tears fell on my cheeks—"is over." He exhaled heavily, his own eyes glistening. "I don't seem to be very good at leaving you alone." He dropped his hand from my lips and swallowed. "I won't let last night happen again. I won't touch you again. This time . . . I promise." His tone rang with finality.

Then, smiling sadly, he turned to leave. He stopped and paused at the doorway, turning to face me again. "You and Denny are good together. You should stay with him." He looked down and tapped the doorway with his hand a couple times, and then, nodding his head, he looked back up at my face, a tear dropping to his cheek. "I'll make this right. It will be like it should be."

Then he turned and left. I watched him leave, confused, tears dripping from my eyes. Once I couldn't hear him anymore, I sighed and put my head in my hands. Wasn't this exactly what I had wanted? Why did I feel so sad, then, like I had suddenly just lost everything?

Kellan stayed true to his word—he never again made any inappropriate moves toward me. In fact, he tried never to touch me. He stayed as far from me in a room as possible, without being obvious about it. He would make sure we never brushed against each other, and he would even apologize whenever we accidentally did touch each other. He still watched my every move though. I could always feel his intense eyes on me. In some ways, I would have preferred his touch to the intensity of those stares.

I tried to focus on school, but my heart was only half in it. The lectures, while still interesting and thought provoking, weren't as captivating as they-once were, and my mind drifted on more than one occasion. I tried to focus more on Denny. He had perked up some since our evening at the club, which made me feel horribly guilty, but he was still miserably trudging through his work day. I listened as he went on and on about Max and the meaningless tasks he had him doing, but in all honesty, I wasn't really hearing a word of it. My mind continually drifted. I tried to focus on Jenny and Kate, on being closer friends with them. We sometimes met for coffee before work, and they would chat about the guys they were seeing. Not really having a whole lot to add to that conversation, I would listen halfheartedly, and my mind would drift . . . to Kellan.

I even tried to focus on my family, on calling them more often. My mom picked up on my mood, and immediately wanted me to come home and see her. My dad blamed Denny for breaking my heart when he left, which I assured him he hadn't. If anything, I broke his, when I dumped him for ditching me, even though that had never been his intention. And my sister . . . well, I couldn't even talk to her yet. I wasn't mad at her or anything. I'd even grudgingly forgiven Kellan in my head. Well, maybe not forgiven him, but I

320   S. C. Stephens

had forced the memory to the very back corner of my mind. But I couldn't speak to Anna yet. I couldn't even bear to hear his name pass her lips. Not yet . . . or ever.

As the days went by, I found myself missing Kellan—missing his touch, missing our quiet conversations as we cuddled in the kitchen over coffee, missing his laugh as he would relay a funny story while driving me all over town. I began to wonder if we should try again. Maybe this time, we could find a way to make it work. . . .

"Kellan," I said softly, as he walked by me one morning when I came down for coffee. "Please don't leave. We should be able to be alone together."

He paused and looked back at me, his blue eyes sad. "It's better if we're not, Kiera. It's safer."

I frowned. "Safer? You say that like we're time bombs or something."

He half-smiled and raised his eyebrows. "Aren't we?" His smile dropped and he suddenly looked exhausted. "Look what happened. I'll never forgive myself for talking to you like that."

I blushed at the horrible memory and looked down. "Don't. You were right. Horribly rude, but right." I peeked up at him under my eyebrows.

He cringed and took a step toward me. "Kiera, you're not—"

I cut him off, not wanting to start that horrid conversation again. "Can't we have just some of our friendship back? Can't we talk?" I made a move toward him, until we were only a step apart. "Can't we ever touch?"

Kellan immediately took two steps back and swallowed, shaking his head. "No, Kiera. You were right. We can't go back to that. It was stupid to even try."

I felt tears stinging. I missed how it used to be so much. "But I want to. I want to touch you, just hold you . . . no more." I was in withdrawal from my addiction. I wanted his warm arms to slip around me. I wanted to put my head on his shoulder. It was all I wanted.

His tired eyes closed, and he took a deep breath before opening them. "You shouldn't. You should only hold Denny. He's a good guy for you. . . . I'm not."

"You're a good guy too." I couldn't stop the thought of him sobbing in my arms. I'd never seen someone more remorseful.

"I'm really not," he whispered, as he walked out of the room.

Kellan's words echoed through my head as I sat with Denny while he got ready for work. He cheerily gave me a kiss as he slipped on his shirt. I wanted to cringe away from him, and then felt guilty for feeling that. It wasn't Denny's fault that I was miserable. Aside from how much time he had to commit to his job, which I constantly reminded myself was not his fault either, Denny hadn't done anything wrong since he'd come back to me. He was warm, sweet, funny, charming, and constantly trying to make me happy. His moods were near-constant, his love and loyalty never wavering. I was always sure how he felt about me . . . unlike Kellan. So why did I feel such loss over losing Kellan? And can you lose something that was never yours to begin with? I debated that as Denny sat beside me and gave me a soft kiss.

"Hey, I was thinking . . ."

I startled as I realized that Denny was speaking to me. "What?" I asked, forcing my mind back to the present.

He half-grinned. "You're not quite awake yet, are you?" He shook his head as he slipped his shoes on. "It can wait—why don't you go back to sleep." He looked over and smiled warmly. "You don't have to get up with me every morning, you know. I know you come in late." He leaned over and kissed me again. "You need your sleep too."

I cringed, knowing that Denny wasn't really the reason I woke up early every morning. Wanting to fight off painful thoughts that I shouldn't have been having in the first place, I made Denny continue on his original train of thought. "No, go ahead, I'm awake. . . . What were you thinking?"

He tied his shoes and then sat on the bed with his elbows on his knees. He looked over at me a little sheepishly and ran a hand along his jaw. Insanely curious over what was making him so uncomfortable, and a little worried about what he knew that would make him look that way, I hesitantly asked, "What is it?"

Not noticing the reluctance in my question, he shyly said, "Have you thought about your winter break next month?"

I instantly relaxed. "No, not really. I guess I figured we'd go home Christmas Eve and stay for the weekend." I looked over at him, concerned. "Can you not get the time off?"

He grinned widely at me. "I actually demanded the whole week off."

I eyed him warily. Denny wasn't the demanding type. "You demanded?" I cocked an eyebrow at him.

He laughed at my expression. "Okay . . . apparently the office shuts down that week. Nobody works it . . . not even Max." He grinned sheepishly again. "So I'm truly free for a week . . . and . . ." He looked down and laced his fingers together. "I'd like to take you home."

I blinked, confused. Wasn't that what I had just said? "Okay, I kind of figured . . ."

He looked over at me, his face serious. "My home, Kiera . . . Australia. I'd like you to meet my parents."

I looked down, surprised. "Oh." I had always wanted to meet them, even though that thought terrified me. But so much had changed since then. They would know. Somehow, the parental sixth sense would kick in, and with just a glance, they would declare me a harlot and denounce me in front of him. I just knew it. I couldn't go. Denny wouldn't understand that though.

"But Christmas, Denny? I've never missed one with my family." I sighed brokenly, from my previous thought and the thought of the holidays away from my loved ones. "Couldn't we go another time?"

He sighed and I looked back to where he was studying his hands. "I don't know when that will be, Kiera. Who knows when I'll be free from Max again?" He sighed a second time, and ran a hand through his hair before turning his head to look at me. "Will you just think about it?"

I could only nod. Great, one more thing for me to think about. As if my mind wasn't full enough. Denny looked at me thoughtfully, then stood and finished getting ready. I was still sitting on the bed, thinking, when he kissed me goodbye.

A big chunk of me was worried about what his parents would think of me, but watching Kellan at work that night brought a different heartbreak closer to the surface. I would miss him . . . horrifically. Watching him sit at his table with his friends, watching me, I thought maybe I should just talk to him about it. But I didn't. I knew what his answer would be anyway—go with Denny, the time apart will be good for us, you should be with him, he's the guy for you, etc. etc. etc. Most of it was what my head was already telling me, but my heart? We could possibly stretch Denny's time off to almost two weeks with the weekends, and two weeks away from Kellan's piercing blue eyes . . . well, just the thought made my addictive withdrawals go into hyperdrive.

A couple days after Denny's proposition, I awoke from a deep sleep, feeling confused. I felt odd, and I didn't know why. I must have been dreaming again. I had dreamt about the last painful kiss I had shared with Kellan all week. Our amazingly tender kiss, I had never wanted it to end. But then afterwards, there was the sadness in his eyes, that final devastating tear on his cheek as he left the room, and his ominous last words. I sighed softly, conflicted.

Light fingers trailed down my hair, my back. I cringed a bit. I always felt so guilty when Denny touched me while I was thinking about Kellan, and lately, I was usually thinking about Kellan. I was still turning over the thought of leaving with Denny or not. Even if we didn't end up going to Australia, we'd still go home to my parents' place, and Anna would be there. It was an almost lose-lose situation for me. I was either going to another country, to face people who would surely see straight to the heart of my deception toward their son, or I was going to face Anna, who wouldn't be able to contain the horrid affair she'd had with Kellan for an entire week. That brought me full circle to the fact that, either way, I was going to have to leave

Kellan for a time. And God, was I going to miss him, even if we had ended things. . . .

"Mornin'." A familiar nonaccented voice pierced my heart.

Instantly snapping out of my thoughts, I spun around to come face-to-face with a very sexy, very satisfied-looking Kellan, staring right back at me. I instantly became more aware of my surroundings. I glanced down to the strange sheet barely covering my naked chest, barely above Kellan's naked waist. I glanced around the room . . . his room. My heart raced as I watched the late-morning light filter through the window.

"Oh, God . . ." I whispered, as he casually brought a hand to my cheek and pulled me in for a kiss.

He laughed, deep in his throat. "No . . . just me," he teased, kissing me softly.

I pushed him back, all too aware of his naked chest under my fingertips, the rest of his bare body just inches from mine. "What happened? I don't remember. Why are we . . . ? Did we . . . ?" Great, now I wasn't forming complete thoughts.

Kellan pulled farther back, looking confused. "Are you okay?" He grinned mischievously. "I know this morning was pretty intense, but did I break you or something?" He winked at me and went in for another kiss.

Panic swept through me. "Oh, God, we did. Kellan, we ended this. We aren't . . . We can't . . ."

"Kiera, you're starting to freak me out." His brow scrunched together in concern.

"Just tell me what's going on!" My voice was a little too high and loud. I quieted it with great effort. "Where's Denny?"

"He's at work, Kiera. We always do this when he's at work." He propped himself on his elbow and looked at me, frowning. "You really don't remember this?"

"No . . ." I whispered. "What do you mean . . . 'always'?"

He leaned over me, lightly stroking my cheek with his finger. "Kiera, Denny leaves for work, we come in here, we have"—he bit his lip and smiled seductively—"hot . . . sweaty . . . sex . . . before you have to leave for school." He ran his fingers back through my hair. "Sometimes, like today, you skip school and stay in bed with me for most of the day." He kissed me gently, tenderly. "We've been doing this for weeks. How can you forget something like that?"

I stared at him, shocked. "But . . . but, no. After the fight in the car, we ended things. You ended things. You promised. . . ."

He smiled wryly. "I also said I wasn't good at staying away from you. We're meant to be, Kiera. We need each other. Staying away was impossible. It's been so much better since we gave in." He kissed me again, slowly, even more tenderly. "I'll show you. . . ."

Confusion overwhelmed me, froze me. I had no memory of anything intimate, other than our last painful embrace in the kitchen. Wouldn't I remember sleeping with him every day? Was he drugging me or something?

I could no longer ponder it, as he kissed me lovingly and cupped my cheek in his hand. I relaxed into it. I returned his kiss fully, eagerly. I did miss this. He leaned over me, forcing me to my back, and slid his hand down my neck, my chest, my waist. My breath quickened, my heart raced.

He smiled and kissed my cheek, my jaw, my neck. "See . . . you do remember. . . ."

I closed my eyes, trying to have some recollection of how I got here. He moved on top of me, his knee sliding between mine. He brought his lips back to my mouth and his kiss intensified. I gasped at the sensations running through my body. I didn't know how to stop this. I didn't know if I should. I considered caving, and giving in to something I was apparently frequently giving in to anyway, when suddenly, the door burst open.

Denny stood there, watching us in horror, his eyes enraged. "Kiera?"

I sat up quickly and pushed a very calm Kellan off of me. "Denny . . . wait, I can explain." I had no idea how to explain any of this.

He strode over to the bed, eyes wild with fury. "Explain?" He leaned over me. "There is no need for you to explain that you're a whore! I can clearly see that for myself!"

I started to sob. Kellan slowly sat up on the bed and looked at me with amusement.

Denny grabbed my arm and shook it. "Kiera?" His voice was gentle and tender, but his eyes were still enraged. He did it again and I gaped at him in confusion. His soft voice in no way matched his enraged face. "Kiera?"

I woke up with a start. It was night. I was in my pajamas. I was in my room . . . and Denny was calmly lying beside me in bed, lightly shaking my arm. "You're having a nightmare, it's all right." His accent was warm and comforting.

I blinked back tears. Oh thank God . . . just a dream. Suddenly, I blinked back tears of sadness. Just a dream . . .

"You want to talk about it?" he asked sleepily.

I shook my head. "I don't . . . I don't remember." I looked over at him cautiously. "Did I say anything?"

He shook his head. "No . . . you were just whimpering, shaking. You looked scared."

Relief washed through me. "Oh." I sat up on the bed, and he started to rise with me. "No, go back to bed. I'm just going to get some water."

He nodded and slumped back down, closing his eyes. I leaned over and kissed his forehead, making him smile, and then I stood and quietly made my way out the door. That had been one hell of an intense dream. I couldn't even look at Kellan's door as I walked past it. What had brought that on? I wasn't sure, and that worried me . . .

I quietly walked into the kitchen, still thinking about the dream, and stopped dead in my tracks in the doorway. Kellan was in there and surprisingly, not alone. He was pushing a tall, leggy brunette up against the fridge. One bare, feminine leg was wrapped around one of his and Kellan's hand was sliding up her short skirt. They were voraciously kissing, the woman completely lost in her thrill of being with him. He was more aware; he glanced over at me as I entered the room.

Shock passed over his face for a second, as the woman turned her attentions to his neck, his jaw, his ear. Her hand stroked down his chest, coming to rest on his jeans. Her hand slid firmly down and back up the front of his jeans and she moaned loudly. My stomach rose and I wanted to leave the room, but I couldn't stop staring at them.

Composing himself, Kellan turned to the woman. She tried to kiss him, but he deftly pulled away from her. "Sweetheart . . ." he cooed at her. She gazed at him adoringly, biting her lip. "Could you wait upstairs for me? I need to speak with my roommate."

She never once even looked at me. She never took her eyes off of him, only nodded and gasped as he leaned in to kiss her deeply again. She looked about ready to lose herself in him again, but he pulled away from her and firmly led her to the entryway. "The one on the right. I'll be up in a second," he cooed again. She giggled, practically fleeing the room to get to his bed.

I felt like throwing up. I considered bending over the sink and just letting it happen right there. Kellan paused for a moment at the entryway, his back to me. "Do you think Denny would be intrigued or upset if she opened the wrong door?" he said casually over his shoulder.

I gaped at him, speechless. He finally turned to look at me, an odd look in his eyes for half a second, before calmness settled in his features. He took a few steps toward me. I felt like backing away, but I held my ground. "You said before that you wanted to know when I was . . . seeing someone. Well . . . I guess I'm seeing someone."

I still couldn't find any words in me, so he continued. "I'm going to date. I told you I wouldn't keep it a secret from you, so . . ." He paused for a deep breath. "I'm going upstairs now, and—"

I made a face that could only have looked like horror and disgust, and he immediately stopped explaining just what he was going to do. I had pretty much figured that out anyway.

"I said I wouldn't hide it. I'm not. Full disclosure, right?"

Irritation flashed through me. I hadn't exactly wanted him bringing home strange women for me to listen to through our very thin walls when we had talked about this. I guess I had just meant that if he found someone he liked, and dated her for months and months, then maybe, they could go to a hotel room far, far away from me and I would . . . understand. I suppose that scenario had been a bit unrealistic.

"Do you even know her name?" I whispered heatedly.

He stared blankly at me for a second before answering. "No, I don't need to, Kiera," he whispered. I gave him a cold, icy look. He returned it as he snapped, "Don't judge me . . . and I won't judge you." With that, he turned and left the room.

My thirst completely gone, I practically ran back up the stairs once I could move again. The laughter and erotic noises that later came from his room turned my stomach for the rest of the night. . . .

The next morning, I stayed in bed and waited for Denny to wake up. The image of that woman's hands running up and down Kellan's jeans wouldn't leave me, the sounds still echoed in my head. I swallowed back tears at the memory of hearing them last night; she had not been quiet. I had heard her leave in the middle of the night (apparently, sleepovers were not encouraged), but I had no desire to be alone with Kellan this morning. I wasn't sure what was more surreal to me, my odd dream of us together, or seeing him with that woman. Was that really what he considered dating?

Denny woke up a while later and smiled over at me still in bed with him; I usually ducked out while he was still sleeping. He reached over to me and started kissing my neck. I stiffened, and he stopped with a sigh. I was not in the mood right now. I waited patiently for him to sit up, stretch, and stand, and then I sat up and walked over to him, smiling as best as I could.

"Are you all right? You look tired," he asked, sweetly running his hand through my hair.

I nodded and tried to brighten my smile. "I just didn't sleep well. . . . I'm fine."

We both got dressed and ready for our days. I took as long as I could, without making Denny late, and he watched me get ready with a soft smile on his lips; always patient, always willing to spend a little time with me where he could. I swallowed the lump in my throat from that thought, and took his hand. We went downstairs to the kitchen together. Kellan was awake, of course, and was watching TV in the living room. Upon hearing us, he shut the TV off and walked into the room. Denny smiled at him while I rolled my eyes and stifled a sigh.

Kellan greeted us, then, looking at me oddly, asked Denny, "I was thinking of having a couple of friends over tonight. Would you guys be okay with that?"

Denny answered for us. "Sure, mate, whatever . . . it's your place." Denny smiled and clapped him on the shoulder, as he went to the fridge to make a quick breakfast for us.

Kellan glanced over to where I was silently standing by the table. "Are you okay . . . with that?"

I blushed and looked down, catching the pause in his question, and what he was really asking me. "Sure . . . whatever." Looking back on that later, I probably should have been honest and said no.

My head was in a fog the remainder of the day. All throughout school, and all throughout my shift at work, my mind kept flipping between our last tender kiss in the kitchen, my dream of having an affair with him, and his leggy brunette pressed against the fridge.

In the middle of my shift at Pete's, the D-Bags rolled in, but Kellan wasn't with them. He must have already been at home, entertaining. If he wasn't having the band over, I wasn't sure who I was going to find at our house. The anticipation tied my stomach into painful knots. I honestly had no idea what to expect. I had no idea what Kellan had meant by "a couple friends."

I was handing the band their beers, when Evan noticed my fog. "You okay, Kiera? You seem kind of out of it?" he asked politely.

Griffin was not so polite. "Yeah, you raggin' or something?"

Matt smacked him across the chest, in a move so similar to what Kellan would have done that I had to swallow. "No, I'm fine . . . just tired." I looked at them thoughtfully for a second, then blurted out, "Are you guys going to Kellan's thing at our house?"

Matt looked over from Griffin, surprised. "Kellan's having a party?"

I frowned. "He didn't tell you?"

Griffin looked affronted. "We do have lives outside of Kellan Kyle, you know."

I blushed and Evan quickly answered, "No. I'm not going, anyway. I have a date." He winked at me, his warm brown eyes sparkling at the prospect of a new love.

Matt shook his head too, running a hand back through his spiky hair. "No, I don't feel like hanging out with Kellan's groupies tonight." He looked over at Griffin. "You?"

Griffin, surprisingly, scowled. "Hell, no! Fuck Kellan and his stupid-ass parties."

Matt laughed at him. "Dude, are you still mad about that? That was forever ago."

He crossed his arms over his chest, pouting like a five-year-old, and glared at Matt. "I clearly called dibs."

Evan sighed. "You can't call dibs on a human being, Griffin."

Griffin shot him a look, while I blushed deeply, realizing what they were talking about. "Yes, yes you can . . . and I did, and he clearly heard me. He even said, 'Whatever, Griffin,' in total agreement. But who did that fucker take to his room later?" He angrily pointed to his chest. "My chick!"

Matt laughed again. "Since when is 'whatever' total agreement?" He laughed some more and Evan joined him.

Griffin took a swig of the beer I had just handed him. "Dude, it's not cool to kype another man's dibs. I'm not playing on his home turf anymore." He sulked in his chair while Matt laughed hysterically.

Evan chuckled and said, "Right . . . . that's why Kellan got the girl, home field advantage."

Griffin exhaled loudly and then scowled at the both of them. "Shut it . . . fuckers." Then he chugged his beer.

Sorry I even brought it up, I quickly left the table. Now I was really dreading going home.

Jenny gave me a ride that night after my shift. "Want to come in?" I suddenly asked Jenny, as she pulled up to the extrapacked street and driveway. "Kellan's having a . . . thing." I shrugged. I just had a feeling I would need her support tonight, even if she didn't realize it.

"Oh . . . sure, I can come in for a little bit." She smiled, and, managing to squeeze in behind Denny's car, parked hers, and we made our way to the front door.

I held my breath as I opened it. The first thing I noticed was Denny and Kellan on the couch, chatting and laughing easily. I walked into the entryway, set my bag down, and hung up my jacket, feeling more relaxed. It was wonderful to see them happy together again. It felt like ages ago that they had really talked to each other. As I started walking toward them, however, my mood suddenly shifted. A dark-haired, dark-skinned, and outrageously beautiful girl plopped right down onto Kellan's lap and kissed him. He laughed and kissed her back. Denny smiled and looked away from them and over to me. He smiled warmly at me and waved, but then he frowned. I realized I was scowling at Kellan and his hussy, and attempted to fix my face.

"Wow . . . do you know all these people?" Jenny asked, as she moved up beside me.

It was only then that I realized there were a good dozen people in the living room, with more voices drifting over from the kitchen. *A few friends, huh?* I looked over at her. "No."

She waved at Denny sitting on the couch and laughed a bit. "Well, Kellan sure seems to know them."

Grudgingly, I looked back to the couch. Kellan was still intently kissing the girl, his hand running up her thigh. I turned away from the sight, when flashes of his tongue in her mouth made my stomach rise and fire burn through me. I slid my eyes over to Denny, who was still watching me curiously. He stood and walked over to us as we entered the living room.

"Hey, Jenny," he said politely to her. Then he turned to me. "You okay? I know there's kind of a lot of people here. Kellan said we only had to tell him, and he would kick them out." He smiled at me and pulled me in for a hug.

I managed a weak smile as I hugged him back. Over his shoulder, I could see Kellan. He'd stopped making out, and was now running his fingers through the dark-haired girl's locks, while talking to a strawberry-blond girl in the spot Denny had just left. To my surprise, he leaned over and gave the blonde a soft kiss; the woman on his lap didn't seem to care in the least.

"No . . . it's fine. I do need a drink though." I hoped there wasn't too much venom in my voice. My anger was starting to simmer, which I didn't quite understand.

"Sure, come on." He pulled me through the crowd, while Jenny followed in our wake.

Denny grabbed a beer from an open pack on the counter and handed it to me. I thanked him and quickly opened it, taking a swig. Really, I needed to relax. So what if Kellan was . . . spreading himself around? No great shock there. I already knew he was like that.

Forcing myself to get through the next couple of hours without making an embarrassing, and question-inducing, scene, I sat in an empty chair at the table and concentrated on making polite conversation with Jenny and Denny. I watched the half-dozen strangers around us. I was a little surprised that the band hadn't shown up here anyway. Surely they would have enjoyed something like this? But the group, ninety percent of which was women, was full of people I hadn't seen before. Actually, now that I was watching them more closely, a couple did look vaguely familiar . . . fans, maybe?

I was listening to Denny talk to one of the few guys in the room and watching the crowd, when I turned to people-watch in the living room. A break in the bodies gave me a view of Kellan. He was dancing with the strawberry blonde while the dark-haired woman watched them from the couch. My jaw dropped in remembered surprise. He was dancing with her exactly the way he had danced with me at the club. He was behind her, his arm around her waist, hand resting on her jeans, pulling her into his hips, and they were moving together in a way that made me blush. Smiling, he lowered his head to her ear and whispered something to her, making her bite her lip and sag against him. Our intimate moment being used on another made me curiously furious.

Still smiling, he glanced up and, for the first time, caught my eye. His smile slipped for half a second and he gave me an odd, almost sad, look. Then the smile was back and his eyes warmed. He nodded politely to me, and turned his attention to the dark-haired woman, who had come up behind him and was pressing against his back. He grinned widely at her and, leaning back, kissed her deeply. I turned away, sickened.

Jenny, who had been watching me watch him, noticed. "Are you okay?" She glanced at Kellan dancing with his two floozies, then back to me. She whispered, "Is that bothering you?"

Panicked, I wasn't sure how to explain why it made me angry. I shook my head and looked down at my bottle. "No, no of course not. It's just . . . it's gross." I looked back up at her, trying to look prudish. "Two women . . . really? That's just asking for trouble."

She laughed a little and looked over at him. "Yeah . . . I suppose it is." She shook her head, like it didn't really matter to her. "Well, he says he's careful, so I guess whatever floats your boat, right?"

That surprised me a little. "You asked him about . . . that?"

She laughed again. "Noooooo . . . Kellan's love life is *not* something I want to talk with him about." She laughed again at my confused face. "Evan asked him once and I overheard his answer. Evan . . . he's always looking out for Kellan." She smiled at the thought.

"Oh," I said quietly. I couldn't help but think of the times that Kellan and I had been together. He hadn't been careful at all. The first time we were too drunk to think about being safe. The second time we were . . . overcome . . . by it. Every time was so intense that safety kind of went out the window. It hurt me a little that he hadn't cared enough to be safe with me. That thought increased my anger at how many girls he *was* being "safe" with.

I kept my head down and purposefully stayed away from the living room for the rest of the party. Not too much later, people started heading out; it was pretty late for a weeknight. Jenny gave me a hug and said she'd call me tomorrow. I watched her give Denny a hug and, looking into the living room, smile at Kellan and wave goodbye to him. I resisted the urge to see if Kellan's harlots had left yet. Eventually, everyone else filed out.

After everyone had left the kitchen, Denny yawned and looked over at me. "Ready for bed?"

I stood and stretched. "Yeah." Instinctively, I stretched to my side and glanced into the living room. I stopped moving. The two girls were both still there. In fact, they were the only two "friends" still there with Kellan. They were sitting on the couch, on either side of him, and both had their hands on his chest. The dark-haired girl was kissing his neck, while the blonde entertained his lips. She pulled back breathlessly and Kellan smiled over at the other girl. The dark-haired girl stopped sucking on his neck and looked up at the blonde, and then she leaned over and kissed the blonde, while Kellan bit his lip and watched them with hungry eyes.

I forced my gaze away and back to Denny, my stomach full of fire. Denny was grinning like an idiot at them, which increased my anger. "Come on." I grabbed his hand and pulled him roughly through the kitchen and up the stairs. He laughed at my reaction, and pulled me in for a kiss as we reached our bed. I moodily pushed him down and changed into my pajamas. The thought of what was going on downstairs burned me with the intensity of my anger.

Denny noticed my mood. "What, Kiera?"

"Nothing," I spat back at him.

"Hey . . . are you mad at me?"

I spun around to face him. "I don't know. You seemed to really enjoy seeing that. Should we invite the girls up here when Kellan's done with them . . . into our bed?" I knew he wouldn't do anything with any of them, but I was really mad, and I needed an outlet.

He blanched. "No, babe. I wouldn't touch them. That's not me, you know that."

"Oh? And what were you doing at this little orgy before I got here? Did you sneak a couple up here for a quickie?"

He looked at me with blank shock. "I sat on the couch and talked to Kellan. That's all, Kiera." His voice got a little irritated. "I didn't *do* anything."

"Whatever." I angrily got into bed, shoving him out of my way, and pulled the covers around me. "I have a headache. I just want to go to sleep now."

He sighed. "Kiera . . ."

"Good night, Denny."

He rolled over to his side, then undressed and crawled under the covers with me. "Okay . . . good night." He tenderly kissed my head and I pulled away a bit. I knew I wasn't being fair. Denny hadn't done anything wrong, but my anger was swelling, not decreasing. My imagination was going crazy, picturing Kellan with his whores. Denny sighed and rolled over.

I lay there, fuming and listening for sounds from downstairs. Eventually, Denny's breathing slowed and evened. . . . He was asleep. A little while later, light laughter and footsteps, three sets of them, made their way upstairs, and I heard Kellan's door lightly close and music being turned on.

I sat up. I couldn't take it. I couldn't listen to it. I hurried as quietly as I could out of the room and down the stairs. I considered leaving . . . but had no idea where to go, or how to explain that to Denny in the morning. Instead, I went to the kitchen and poured a glass of water. I gulped it, leaning against the counter, begging my body to calm down. Kellan had every right. . . .

My head was down, both hands on the counter and tears starting to form, when I felt a body join me in the kitchen. I couldn't turn to look. Either way, I was screwed. Denny wouldn't understand my being so upset. Kellan . . . well, I just didn't want him to see how much he bothered me.

"Kiera?" Kellan's voice broke through my dark thoughts.

Of course. Of course it would be him. "What, Kellan?"

"Are you okay?" His voice was soft, concerned.

Angry, I spun to face him, and stopped and stared. He was half-naked, bare-chested with his jeans unbuttoned. His hair looked freshly played with and distractingly sexy. I swallowed the lump in my throat at his gorgeousness, and the thought of whom he was half-dressed for. "What are you doing down here? Shouldn't you be . . . entertaining?" I could feel the tears in my eyes. I prayed for them not to spill.

He smiled shyly. "The girls wanted . . ." He pointed to the fridge, then opened it and grabbed a can of whipped cream. He shrugged and left it at that.

I rolled my eyes and let out a loud exhale. Of course the hussies would want to make it as horrifying as possible for me. I closed my eyes and prayed that he would just leave me alone and go back to his porn set.

"Kiera . . ." He said my name so tenderly that I opened my eyes. He smiled sadly at me. "This is who I am. Before you got here . . . this is me." He pointed upstairs to where Denny was sleeping. "That, that is you. This is how it's supposed to be. . . ."

He moved toward me like he was going to hug me or kiss my forehead, but at the last minute he seemed to change his mind and, turning, he started to leave the room. At the doorway, he turned and softly said, "Goodnight, Kiera."

He left then, without waiting for a response from me, and the tears brimming in my eyes finally fell. I spent that night on the couch, with the television turned up as loudly as I thought was possible without waking Denny.

Chapter 18
Man Whore

A few sleepless nights later, I came down the stairs in the morning with Denny. Lately, I always waited until Denny was ready for the day before I got my coffee. Denny insisted I could sleep in, that I didn't need to get up with him, but, honestly, weeks of getting up early to spend a little time with Kellan in the mornings had started a pattern in me that I couldn't quite shake.

The fact that Kellan had disrupted my physiology irritated me, but upon entering the kitchen with Denny, seeing Kellan irritated me even more. It wasn't his stupidly perfect blue eyes that turned to look at us when we entered, it wasn't his stupidly perfect tousled hair, casual and messy, it wasn't his stupidly perfect chiseled body, and it wasn't the stupidly perfect crooked smile that he was giving us. It was his stupid shirt!

He was relaxing against the counter, waiting for the coffee to brew with both hands behind him, making the bold lettering on his red T-shirt stick out all the more. It very simply read: "Will sing for sex." It looked odd on him. It was something more in line with what Griffin would wear, which gave me a sneaking suspicion about where he'd gotten it. It was blatant. It was crude. It was pissing me off!

Denny cracked a smile when he saw it. "Ace! Do you—"

I immediately cut him off. "If you even ask him for one of those, you will be sleeping on the couch for a month." My tone was a little more seething than perhaps a crude T-shirt warranted, but I couldn't help it.

Denny found my reaction humorous, however. He grinned goofily and cocked his head. "I wasn't going to, babe." He gave me a swift kiss on the cheek and went over to Kellan, slapping him on the shoulder before grabbing mugs for my coffee and his tea from the cupboard. Glancing back at where I was still glaring at him, he chuckled and said, "You know I can't sing anyway."

Kellan, who had been silently watching the exchange with an amused grin on his face, sniggered and struggled to contain his laughter.

Steamed at both of them now, I frowned and icily said, "I'll be upstairs when the coffee's done." I turned and stormed out, their no-longer-containable laughter following me up the stairs. Men!

Hours later, I was at work and still mired in irritation over the whole morning, when I was interrupted by a sweet voice. "You're doing it again, Kiera." Jenny leaned over a table and smiled at me.

"What?" I said, shaking my head a little to come out of my trance.

I was having trouble focusing. Kellan was doing something that he had never, in all the months Denny and I had lived with him, done. He was, as he put it, dating. Kellan had brought a different girl home every night, and every night, I had to listen to his "date" through our thin walls. I would have to use the term "date" loosely, as these women seemed very little interested in Kellan as a person. They were more enamored with his small slice of fame, and of course, how fabulously he was shaped. The same woman never entered our doors more than once, and there seemed to be a never-ending line of them. It made me ill. Sleep was impossible. Eventually, I passed out from exhaustion each night. But it, and the constant angry fire in my belly, was taking its toll.

"You're glaring at Kellan again. You guys fighting or something?" She eyed me curiously.

I startled, realizing that I had been glaring at him openly for the last several minutes while I had been lost in thought. I hoped no one else had noticed that. I struggled to fix my face into a genuine smile. "No, we're fine . . . perfect."

"You're not still mad about the women at the party, are you?" Fire wrenched my gut as she brought up that horrible memory. I wanted to bend over and clench my stomach, it hurt so badly. But I stood there and took it, trying to maintain my fake smile. "You know, that's just how he is. Always has been, always will be." She shrugged her shoulders.

"No . . . I don't care *what* he does." I stressed the word "what" more than would pass for casualness, and Jenny noticed. She started to say something, and I blurted out the first thing in my head to stop her. "Have you and Kellan ever . . . ?" I stopped my tongue when I realized where my question was heading. I really did not want to know that.

She understood though and, grinning, she shook her head. "No, no way." She glanced over at him at his table. He had some adorably cute little Asian girl sitting on the edge of it and was whispering to her in between nibbling on her ear, much to the girl's delight. Kellan had worn that damn shirt to the bar and it had been effective. Earlier, he'd had a small group of adoring women clustered around him at his table and had obliged them with a few verses. He seemed to have narrowed his choice down to one. My face heated, knowing I would see—or hear—her later.

Jenny looked back at me, still smiling. "Not for his lack of trying though."

I blinked, surprised, and then realized I shouldn't be. Jenny was a beautiful girl. "He hit on you?"

She nodded, coming around to my side of the table. "Hmmmm . . . relentlessly, for the first week I worked here." She crossed her arms over her chest and stood beside me, watching him with his bimbo. "One day, I just had to tell him flat out, no, but we could be friends, if he stopped trying to get into my pants." She laughed and looked over at me. "He found that pretty hilarious and he stopped, and we've been fine ever since."

I struggled to keep the incredulity from my face. She turned him down . . . repeatedly? I had been so bad at it that it was a wonder to me that someone could. "Why didn't you . . . ?"

She looked at me thoughtfully. "I knew what he was like, even from the beginning. I'm not interested in a one-nighter, and I don't think he's capable of anything more." She shook her head. "At least, not yet. Maybe one day he'll grow up, but"—she shrugged again—"it wasn't worth it for me."

I blushed and looked away, feeling really stupid. She was right. That was what Kellan was—a seducer. But he wasn't relationship material. Never had been, never would be. I sadly watched him with his woman. Jenny looked over at me curiously.

"Why do you ask, Kiera?"

I realized I didn't have a good reason to ask her about Kellan. "No reason. Just curious, I guess."

She stared at me intently for a second, and I wondered how to walk away without offending her. "Did he . . . did he hit on you?"

I blanched and struggled to maintain my composure. "No, no, of course not." That was pretty true . . . well, maybe half the time anyway.

She didn't buy my answer. "If you need to talk to me, Kiera, about anything, you can. I would understand."

I nodded and grinned, like I hadn't a care in the world. "I know. Thank you, Jenny. I better get back to work, I see some thirsty people." I tried to laugh, but it came out dead and hollow.

She watched me leave, clearly suspicious, and then she turned and looked at Kellan, equally suspicious. God, they were friends. . . . Would she talk to him? Would he tell her anything?

While at first, I had never seen him do anything other than flirt with women, and even that had tapered off while we were . . . flirting now I was seeing way more than I ever wanted to. It seemed to be everywhere. I couldn't escape it. If I had the night off he would bring a woman home, and I'd have to endure the sound of them kissing in the kitchen before they disappeared upstairs. On nights I worked, he would usually already be . . . deeply involved in his date by the time I trudged upstairs. And these women were not concerned in the least that Kellan had roommates. In fact, I don't think they were even concerned that he had neighbors. Maybe they were operating under the false assumption that Kellan gave out awards for who could be the loudest . . . who was the most enthusiastic . . . who could say "Oh, God!" the most. Then again, maybe the jerk actually did give out prizes.

And I was getting sick and tired of hearing Kellan's name being called out. I mean, really . . . he was aware of his own name. Actually, the *only* name he was probably aware of in the whole room was his own.

I couldn't even escape it at work. He always seemed to be tucked away somewhere, shoving his tongue down someone's throat. One time, I had even watched him try and help a girl play pool, which made me laugh smugly, since I knew he was a worthless pool player. But watching him bend someone else over the table . . . yeah, that had hurt a little. Watching their joint shot miss horribly and watching her immediately spin in his arms to practically molest him . . . that had hurt a lot.

By the time he was up to the fifth "date" in a row, in just that week alone, I finally lost it. Trying to ignore the laughter and intimate noises drifting across the hall, I angrily shifted in bed.

"Denny!" I snapped.

He shifted over to look at me and took his eyes off the uncomfortably loud TV he was trying a little too intently to watch. "What?"

I glared at him. "This is beyond ridiculous! Do something! I need some freaking sleep!" And for Kellan to not be a man whore! Our last kiss in the kitchen had been so amazingly soft and tender, but now it seemed as phony as the overeager noises coming from his room.

Denny looked alarmed and slightly embarrassed. "What do you want me to do? Knock on his door and ask him to keep it down?"

Yes! That was exactly what I wanted him to do—maybe he could even throw the hussy out! "I don't know. . . . Do something!"

"You know, he does have to put up with us." He laughed. "Maybe this is payback."

I looked away before my suddenly hurt eyes could betray me. It was something all right, just not what Denny thought.

Denny considered something for a moment. "It's a little weird. Kellan has never had issues with women, but when we moved in, he sure seemed to go through a dry spell." He shook his head. "Well, apparently everything is back to normal." He looked down at me sheepishly. "Not that I condone that. It's just, well . . . Kellan is, you know, Kellan." He shrugged.

More miffed than I should have been at that statement, I snapped at Denny, "What do you mean, 'never had issues with women'? You knew him for one year in high school, and he was what . . . a freshman, sophomore? How active could he have possibly been back then?"

Looking a little curious at my reaction, he shrugged. "Well, let's just say that Kellan got an . . . early start." He laughed at a memory. "This one time, when his parents were gone, he brought home these twins—" He stopped relaying the story at the icy daggers I was glaring into him.

"Not for me. They disappeared into his room. I didn't see a thing. I didn't touch them . . . promise." He smiled sheepishly and said nothing further.

My icy stare didn't stop. I had not thought *he* had touched them. That was not what had me pissed off. So why was I so angry? So Kellan had always been a slut. The way he was with women, was that any great shock? He wasn't mine, I wasn't his. I really needed to let this go. . . .

I fought back sudden tears and tried desperately to keep my voice even. "Just talk to him, please."

He looked at me intently for a second, before finally saying, "No."

My icy daggers returned. "Why not?"

Still looking at me thoughtfully, he calmly replied, "I'm sorry, but you're overreacting."

I sat up on my elbows, getting irritated at him. He didn't usually deny me anything. "Overreacting!"

Denny sat up straighter too. "I hate having to tell you no, Kiera, you know that, but . . . the fact is, this is his place and if he wants to . . . entertain nightly, then he has every right to. He's letting us stay here for next to nothing. This is the best we can do right now. I'm sorry, but you're just going to have to ignore it."

His tone, although pleasantly accented, offered no rebuttal. He was not going to budge on this. It was not a tone I was used to hearing from him. I didn't like it.

"Fine," I said heatedly, flopping back down to my pillows.

He sank back on to one elbow, tilting his head to the side, watching me. Suggestively, he ran a few fingers down my arm. "You know . . . we could try and drown them out?"

Absolutely not in the mood, I smacked him in the chest with my pillow and flopped over on my side, away from him. He sighed irritably and shifted to look back at the TV, turning up the already too loud volume just a tad, as the noises across the hall miraculously increased. "Fine . . . can I finish watching my show then?"

"Whatever." I bit my lip and prayed for sleep to take me.

A few days after that, still nothing had changed. Denny really wasn't going to talk to Kellan about something he deemed none of our business. I disagreed, but I couldn't really explain why to him. I was getting beyond irritated. *I* was about to "speak" with Kellan about it . . . and I wouldn't be nearly as diplomatic as Denny.

After kissing Denny goodbye, a brief peck that I didn't even bother to get out of bed for, and that, although endearing, clearly said, "I'm not happy with you, buddy," I dressed and went to the bathroom to get ready for my day. I looked horrid. There were deep circles under my eyes from lack of sleep, and my hair was a mass of snarls from tossing and turning. Kellan's newest behavior was going to drive me straight to the loony bin. I ripped through my hair angrily, picturing Kellan's perfect face in every snarl.

Sooner than I would have liked, I saw his actual face . . . and it was more perfect than in my imagination, which, at the moment, I deeply resented.

"Mornin'."

I said nothing, his sparkling eyes, charming greeting, and perfectly wild, messy hair instantly irritating me. I silently vowed to not utter a word to him today. If I had to hear . . . too much . . . from him, then he could hear absolutely nothing from me.

"Kiera?"

Stubbornly, I grabbed a coffee cup and began pouring some, ignoring his smooth voice, ignoring how amazing he smelled, even from a distance.

"Are you . . . mad at me?" His voice seemed amused by that idea.

Breaking my vow of silence, I glared over at him. "No." Well, that didn't last long.

"Good, because you shouldn't be." His smile faltered while he spoke.

"Well, I'm not. . . ." I knew my tone was snotty, but I couldn't seem to help it. If he *was* going to hear me this morning, then at the very least, I could make it an unpleasant sound. "Why shouldn't I be?"

"We *both* ended things, when it started getting . . . out of hand." He cocked his head to the side and narrowed his eyes.

"I know that. I was there." There was definitely some ice in my voice, and he frowned at hearing it.

"I'm only doing what you asked. You *wanted* to know if I was seeing someone." His tone was starting to get snotty as well. He was not happy with my attitude this morning.

That was fine with me. I wasn't happy with his . . . behavior. "I didn't want secrets between us . . . but"—I angrily shook my head as I glared at him—"I didn't want to see it!"

His eyes cooled as they narrowed even more. "Where would you have me . . . ?" He stopped and took a calming breath. "I have to see it . . . hear it. You're not exactly quiet either. Do you think I like that? That I've ever liked . . ." He took another deep breath and stood up while my face heated in embarrassment. "I try and understand. You could do the same." And not looking at me again, he left the room.

I took the bus to school, as I had ever since Kellan started his . . . dates. Really? He wanted me to understand? Was I just supposed to be okay with his . . . whoring all over town? Yes, he had to listen to me be with my *boyfriend,* but . . . well, I'm not sure how that relates, but what Denny and I had—have—is vastly different than just screwing for the sake of screwing. It was sickening. I hated every second of every day.

I sighed as I walked through the campus to my class, the chill in the air causing the other students around me to hurry toward the warmer buildings. I also missed Kellan every day. Even now . . . I missed him. My withdrawal was no less painful simply because I was angry at him. If anything, it was worse. Being . . . replaced . . . made it worse. I sighed again as I entered the building where my Lit class was, and immediately froze. Standing just down the hall was a familiar head of springy red curls. Curls that I didn't want to see any closer, curls that were walking my way, curls that, even from a distance, looked agitated.

Candy stopped directly in front of me as I tried to step away from the doors. "Are you Kellan's girlfriend?"

Well, abrupt then. No formal how-do-you-do? I've never even been introduced to this girl.

I sighed and stepped around her to walk toward my class. She followed close beside me, her hair flaming as red as her mood. "No . . . I already told your spies that months ago. He's just a roommate."

"Well, people keep telling me that they've seen the two of you together all over campus . . . all over each other." Her tone was annoyingly snotty.

By people, I assumed she meant her two friends. I blushed, knowing that we had been a little casual at school . . . although we were hardly "all over each other." I picked up my step, hoping I could lose her inside the classroom. She easily matched my pace and glared at me icily, clearly expecting an explanation.

"Well, I don't know what to tell you. I have a boyfriend and it is *not* Kellan." A boyfriend that I was determined to remain faithful to. A boyfriend who did not drop his pants for every willing woman who walked by. Irritation knotted my stomach, and I blurted out something I really shouldn't have. "If you really want to hook up with him so bad, you should just go to Pete's Bar. He's always there."

She stopped following me, just as I reached the door to my sanctuary. "Maybe I will," she replied, rather haughtily, as I walked through the door.

Well, that's just great. . . .

As if to further accentuate how sucky my day was, the stupid bus broke down on the way home. They made us wait on the bus until a new one came to pick us up. They wouldn't even let us out to walk if we so chose. Personally, I think the bus driver was having just as crabby of a day as I was, and was exerting his power over us helpless life forms. Of course, some of the more aggressive people simply pushed their way off the bus, but I wasn't that forward of a person, and the bus driver scared me a little bit, so I just stayed put and grumbled a lot.

I had already stayed late at school, studying—and avoiding home, if I were honest with myself—so now I was running really late for work. I should have gone straight there, but my original hope had been to get home in time to take a refreshing shower. It had been a long, emotional day.

Kellan's car was in the driveway as I hurried past it to the front door. I hated to ask him to do anything, and I really didn't need another awkward car ride, but maybe he could help me out and take me to Pete's? My shift started in ten minutes. If I had to take yet another bus, I was going to be so incredibly late. . . .

I swiftly went to my room and set down my bag. Pulling off my blouse, I grabbed my Pete's T-shirt from the floor, where I had tossed it last night after my shift. Quickly, I put it on, then scrounged around the room for an elastic band. Finding one in between the bed and the nightstand, I hastily began pulling my hair into a low ponytail. I put my jacket back on, grabbed my bag again, and made my way to the hallway.

I was just wondering where Kellan might be, when I heard soft music from his room and I noticed that his door was cracked open. Only thinking that I was massively late and needed his help, I went to the door and automatically put my hand on it, opening it slightly wider. I froze in shock when I peered through the crack in the door. My stomach clenched and threatened to rise. My mind wouldn't register what I was witnessing.

Kellan was sitting on the edge of his bed. His head was down, his eyes were closed, he was biting his bottom lip, and his hand was clutching the sheets. My mind resisted, but the rest of the picture snapped painfully into focus. A woman with loose blond curls was kneeling on the floor in front of him, her head in his lap. Looking at the picture as a whole, there was no mistaking what she was doing.

Wholly absorbed in what they were clearly enjoying, I don't think they were even aware of me standing at the partially open door. I felt ill. I wanted more than anything to run as far away as I could, before I lost my stomach right there. I couldn't move though, couldn't stop staring in horror.

The woman must have finally felt another presence in the room. She started to raise herself off of him. Kellan was not so aware—either that, or he didn't care. His lips parted, his breath noticeably faster, and, with a slight cringe on his face, he automatically moved his hand to firmly hold her in place. The woman went nuts; she immensely enjoyed that. I, however, felt the acid in my stomach starting to rise.

Finally able to move, I ran from the room and down the stairs. Only thinking of escape, my fight-or-flight response in full alert, I hastily grabbed Kellan's car keys from where he had tossed them on the entryway table. I slammed the front door shut behind me—if he hadn't been aware I was home before, he was now!

I flipped through the keys as I rushed to his car, and stopped on the one for the ignition. He never locked his . . . *baby*, so I opened the door and slipped inside, immediately starting it. A perverse thrill went through me as the car growled to life, knowing that he would hear it and instantly recognize what I had done. I watched the door for half a second, but he didn't rush out. I threw it in reverse and peeled out in my haste to get away from him. I watched the house through the rearview mirror, but the front door never opened. Perhaps he was too busy enjoying his "date" to care about his car.

I broke a half-dozen traffic laws getting to work on time, but I did. I smiled when I parked the car in the lot at Pete's. It was really fun to drive, and I loved the thrill that Kellan was going to be so angry about his precious car being gone. Good. I shouldn't be the only one angry in the house. Grinning wickedly, I turned his radio to a station that was playing what sounded like polka music and cranked the volume before I shut the car off. It was a childish prank, I know, but it made me feel better, and I was grinning from ear to ear as I walked through the parking lot.

"Hey, you're peppy tonight," Jenny exclaimed as I bounced through the front door, still a little high from my carjacking.

"Yeah? No particular reason . . ." I grinned at her as I shoved his keys into my front jeans pocket.

Throughout my shift, though, my joyride high faded, and sadness over the scene I had unintentionally witnessed took over. It was one thing to hear one of Kellan's dates, it was quite another to see one. I was feeling pretty melancholy when the doors to Pete's angrily burst open, about an hour later.

I cringed and looked over to the door. Kellan was striding through, looking decidedly more put together than I had last seen him. He also looked pissed off. His fiery blue eyes locked onto mine instantly. Matt came in closely behind him and attempted to place a hand on his shoulder. Kellan snapped his head around to him, pulling back his body, and said something heated. Matt immediately held his hands up in the air, apparently backing off.

My heart started racing and panicking. I backed up a couple

steps. Taking his car had not been a good idea. What was I thinking? Should I just toss him the keys and make a run for it? Irritation
flashed through me and I took a deep breath. No! He would never
physically hurt me. If the jerk wants his keys . . . let him come over
and get them.

He strode over to my location. The people between us quickly
scooted out of his way at the look on his face. His blazing eyes
narrowed in anger, his lips compressed into a thin line, his hands
clenched into fists, his chest noticeably rising and falling—he was
strikingly attractive angry.

He walked right up to me and simply held his hand out.

Expecting a more flagrant reaction, I snottily said, "What?"

"Keys," he seethed.

"What keys?" I wasn't sure why I was goading him. Maybe the
sight I had witnessed had finally unhinged me?

He took a deep calming breath. "Kiera . . . my car is right over
there." He pointed to where it was in the lot outside. "I heard you
take it—"

"If you heard me take it, why didn't you try to stop me?" I
quipped.

"I was—"

I pushed a finger into his chest, cutting him off. "You were"—I
raised my fingers into air quotation marks—"on a date."

His face noticeably paled. Apparently, he hadn't realized I had
seen that. Scowling, his color returned. "So? That gives you the right
to steal my car?"

He was right, of course, not that I would ever admit that to him.
"I borrowed. Friends borrow, right?" I asked haughtily.

He took another deep breath and then shoved his hand into my
front jeans pocket.

"Hey!" I tried to beat him away, but he already had them.

Holding them up in front of me, he seethed, "We're not friends,
Kiera. We never were." Then he turned and stalked out of the bar.

My face heated at his hurtful words and, turning, I fled to the hallway, then to the safety of the bathroom. I collapsed against the wall, breathing heavily through my mouth, trying not to cry. I felt pale, I felt faint. My heart felt torn to pieces.

The sound of the door opening entered my awareness, as I sat there inhaling and exhaling forcibly.

"Kiera . . . ?" Jenny's soft voice asked. I couldn't answer her. I could only stare up at her blankly. She walked over and knelt down beside me. "What was that about? You okay?"

I weakly shook my head. Then I started to sob, racking, tortured sobs. She immediately sat by my side, gently putting her arm around my shoulders. "Kiera, what's wrong?"

In between sobs, I managed to choke out, "I made a horrible mistake. . . ."

She stroked my hair and pulled me tight. "What is it?"

Suddenly, I didn't just want to tell her about taking the car—I wanted to tell her everything. I choked up; how could I tell her? She would hate me, she wouldn't understand. . . .

She looked over at me. "You can tell me, Kiera. I won't say anything to Denny, if you don't want him to know."

My sobs eased as I blinked at her in surprise. Did she already know? It came out before I could stop it. "I slept with Kellan." I held my breath, shocked at myself.

She sighed. "I was afraid of that." She hugged me with both arms. "It will be okay. Tell me what happened."

I was so shocked, I could only ask, "You knew?"

She leaned back against the wall, putting her hand on her lap. "I suspected." She stared at her hand quietly for a second, twirling a ring on her finger. "I've seen things, Kiera. Looks you would give him, when you thought no one was watching. Smiles he would give you. I've seen him touch you in discreet ways, like he didn't want anyone to notice. I've seen your face when he sings. Your reaction to him at his party . . . I've wondered for a while."

I closed my eyes. She really had seen way too much. Had anyone else?

Quietly she asked, "When did it happen?"

The sobs started again and finally through my sobs, I opened up to her and told her everything. It was such a relief to finally talk about it with someone. She listened in silence, occasionally nodding, smiling, or looking sympathetic. I told her about the first innocent touches. Our drunken first time while Denny was gone. His coldness afterwards. My panicked reaction to him almost leaving, which led to our second time. Our not-so-innocent flirtations. The club, although, I left out what I did to Denny, and what Kellan did with my sister—I just couldn't talk about that yet. The fight in the car, which made her gasp and say, "He said what!" My jealousy over his women . . . the last one that was still burning through my mind. His last hurtful comment . . .

Jenny drew me tight to her, both arms around me. "God, Kiera . . . I'm so sorry. I knew he was like that with women. Maybe I should have warned you earlier? He's just *that* kind of guy."

I sagged against her, tired from the emotional night, and she held me until my sniffles stopped. "What are you going to do now?" she asked, pulling away.

"Besides kill him?" I wasn't sure if I was joking or not. "I don't know . . . what can I do? I love Denny. I don't want him to ever know, I don't want to hurt him. But Kellan . . . I can't stand the women, it kills me. I feel—"

"Do you love Kellan?" she asked.

"No!"

"Are you sure, Kiera? If you weren't angry, what would your answer be?" I didn't answer her. I couldn't, I wasn't sure. Sometimes I felt . . . something for him.

Without warning, the bathroom door swung open. Kate stood in the doorway, looking down at us on the floor. "Oh, hey . . . there you are. It's getting crazy out there. Are you guys coming back . . . please?"

Jenny piped up. "Yeah, we're coming. Just give us another couple minutes."

Kate gave me a sympathetic look as a few tears escaped my eyes and I hurriedly wiped them away. "Oh, okay . . . no problem." She smiled sweetly at me, then left the room.

"Thank you, Jenny." I looked over at her, grateful for her listening to me without judging me.

More tears dropped on my cheeks and she wiped them away. "It will be okay, Kiera. Have faith."

I was pretty quiet for the rest of my shift, and absorbed myself in helping to solve my customers' simple problems. That helped. By closing time, I at least no longer felt like sobbing. I also didn't feel like going home. I didn't know if Kellan had had enough . . . dating for one day. Who knows, maybe he ran out of milk and went to the store, only to pick up another hussy there. I was pretty sure that for people who looked like him, those kinds of things were stocked items, tucked right in between the deli meats and the day-old-bread rack. Yes, I'll take a pound of ham, and the busty brunette.

I sighed and approached the bar, where Kate and Jenny were talking to Rita. Pete had ducked out early. He usually was the very last one to leave, probably hours after the rest of us, but tonight, he'd grabbed his coat right at closing and told Rita to lock up. She was taking advantage of his absence by pouring drinks for us girls. She set a shot of something dark in front of me as I came over to stand beside Jenny. I sighed again. At least it wasn't tequila.

"Okay, ladies," she said, holding her glass high, "one for the road." We all raised ours, clinking them together, and then downed them quickly. Kate and Jenny giggled as I made a horrid face. Whatever it had been, it burned. Rita made no face at all and began pouring us all another. "Okay, one more."

Kate and Jenny made a face at each other, but let her pour one more. I didn't care, I wasn't driving, and it had been one heck of a long day. I glanced over at Jenny, who smiled reassuringly, her pale blue eyes sparkling warmly at me. She truly was the nicest person. She offered me a ride home every night, and even though I felt bad about accepting, she wouldn't take no for an answer if I had no one else to take me. She insisted that she drove past my street anyway, so it really was no big deal. That made me feel a little better about the whole thing.

Rita finished pouring everyone's second shot and looked at each of us with a sneaky half-grin. "If you had one night . . . with any man . . . no strings attached, no complications . . . who would it be?" She looked at me pointedly. "And you can't pick your own boyfriend."

She looked at each of us while Kate and Jenny started giggling again. Thinking of my answer, even though I really didn't want to, I started blushing. Rita sighed. "Okay, well it's an easy one for me . . . Kellan." She sighed dreamily while I paled. "God, I'd do that boy again in a heartbeat. . . ."

Kate giggled and then gave me an odd look. I wondered for a split second if she suspected what Jenny had suspected, and paled even more. She daintily shook her head and shrugged. "Kellan . . . definitely."

She and Rita shared a knowing glance and turned to stare at me, waiting for my answer. My throat went dry and I felt ill. I tried to think of someone else, anyone else . . . someone innocuous, but my mind went completely blank, and only one name was shouting through my head. And it was the one name I dared not utter . . . not here.

Jenny popped up beside me. "Denny," she said cheerily.

Kate and Rita both turned to stare at her, then at me, and then back to her, like she had just committed the act she had spoken of. I could have kissed her. With one simple word, she had shifted all of the focus off of me and my stupid answer, which was of course also Kellan. They were still staring at her in disbelief—well, Kate's look was of disbelief. Rita looked more amused and possibly impressed, while I forced a fake frown.

"Cheers," Jenny said in her still bubbly voice, and we all did our second shot, everyone forgetting that I never actually answered Rita's stupid question. "Ready to go, Kiera?" she calmly asked.

"Yeah," I said in a displeased voice, even though I wanted to hug her.

Rita laughed, while Kate gave me a quick consolatory hug. Out the door and out of earshot, I thanked Jenny profusely.

I came downstairs a few heartbeats before Denny the next morning. Our house had been quiet last night. Apparently once a day *was* enough for Kellan. Well, at least he had his limits. The quiet hadn't helped the hurt in my heart, though. I frowned when I saw him sitting at the table with an elbow propped on it and his fingers tangled in his hair. He was staring at the table and looked deep in thought. He glanced over at me when he noticed my entrance and opened his mouth like he was going to say something. He immediately shut his mouth when Denny followed me a few seconds later.

His latest hurtful comment stung my brain and, feeling a little snotty, I turned to face Denny. "I know you're dressed already"—I ran a hand down his shirt and rested my fingers on his belt—"but do you want to run up and take a shower?" I angled my face so that Kellan could see me raise my eyebrows suggestively and bite my lip.

I flicked a glance at Kellan while Denny chuckled. Kellan didn't look happy as he concentrated a little too hard on the tabletop. Good.

Denny kissed me softly. "I wish I could, babe, but I can't be late today. Max is on a rampage with the holiday coming."

"Oh." I exaggerated my disappointment. "It could be a quick shower?" I bit my lip again and flicked another glance at Kellan. His jaw clenched and I resisted the urge to smile.

Denny grinned wider. "I really can't. Tonight though, okay?" He whispered that last part, but I was completely sure Kellan heard him.

I kissed him deeply, running my hands over every inch of his body. Denny seemed a little surprised at my enthusiasm, but kissed me back eagerly. I watched Kellan from the corner of my eye as we kissed. He stood and, not looking at me, sniffed once and stalked into the living room. I pulled away from Denny, smiling warmly at him as I heard Kellan's door close . . . loudly. Inwardly, my smile was vindictive. Two could play at this game.

Chapter 19
You're Mine

The Thanksgiving holiday came and went, with Denny making a truly fabulous meal and Kellan ducking out with a "Have a nice dinner," not even bothering to join us for it. We didn't see him again for the rest of the evening. Denny had made a small turkey with some glaze he saw on a cooking show, cranberry stuffing, and mashed potatoes. I made the salad . . . which was all he would let me help with. I sat on the counter and kept him company throughout the day while he cooked, though. He smiled a lot and kissed me a lot, and seemed genuinely happy. I tried to match his good spirits. I tried to not worry about where Kellan had taken off to . . . and who he might possibly be with.

While Denny cleaned up after dinner (really, how great of a boyfriend was he?), I called my family, wishing them lots of love . . . and avoiding any direct conversation with my sister. I still couldn't deal with that yet. I knew it was ridiculous. Eventually I would have to speak to her again, but not now, not when things were so odd between Kellan and me. My parents wanted to know if I was coming up for Christmas. They had already bought our tickets—hint, hint—and had my room all ready for the both of us. That surprised me a lot. They had never let us both stay under their roof before. They must really have missed me. With a heavy heart, I told them that

Denny wanted me to go home with him, and I hadn't decided yet. And knowing Denny, he had probably already bought those tickets as well . . . just in case.

They were clearly upset at hearing that, and although the conversation drifted to other things, I knew what they would all be discussing over the next several days. It hurt my heart as I hung up the phone with them. I hadn't answered Denny either on what I wanted to do, and he had asked me again on several occasions. I still didn't know. I didn't know which path to choose, whom to hurt . . . I hated these kinds of decisions. There was no winning, and someone would be hurt, either my parents or Denny. And then Kellan . . . Although his latest cruelty toward me was sure making the thought of leaving him easier, that still hurt my heart too.

My irritation toward him was escalating just as surely as our flirting had been escalating none too long ago. Just a few weeks ago, Kellan and I had been nearly inseparable, but now he was "inseparable" with nearly half of Seattle . . . and Candy. She had taken me up on my stupid suggestion, and shortly after Thanksgiving she'd showed up at Pete's. Recognizing her, and throwing me a look that clearly said, "I know you recognize her too," Kellan stayed attached at the hip with her all evening. And by all evening . . . I mean *all* evening. I had to listen to her "appreciation" of Kellan's talent over and over through our agonizingly thin walls.

Her smug look when I ran into her in the halls Monday morning was what finally broke me, I think. That one look screamed at me, "I just took what I know you secretly want—and I loved every damn second of it."

I was done. That very evening, I finally snapped.

Pete and I'm assuming either Griffin or Kellan had decided to make Monday night ladies' night, with $2 shots 'til midnight. As a result, the bar was jam-packed full of college-age women getting drunker by the minute. The band was there, of course, and having a wondrous time with their expanded, inebriated harem.

Kellan was being . . . blatant. Some pixie-haired harlot was nestled provocatively in his lap, sucking on his neck. He was immensely enjoying it, stroking her thigh. None of the other guys paid them any attention; they all had women of their own. She pointed suggestively to the back room. Kellan smiled and shook his head at her. Well, of course not. Why would he want the hussy now, when he could take her home and march her upstairs later, driving me crazy all night long? The thought incensed me. Why did this bother me so much?

I was angrily scrubbing a clean table when I noticed him walking by me. Too late, the words slipped out. "Wanna try keeping it in your pants, Kyle?"

He had walked a few steps past me before what I had just stupidly said registered in his mind. He turned around, his eyes suddenly intensely angry. "That's rich." He laughed once, rather haughtily, I thought.

"What?" I said flatly.

He walked over to where I was standing at the empty table and leaned in close, pressing his body against mine. He grabbed my arm and pulled me tight against him. My heart sped at his touch. It had been a long time since he had actually touched me, and the unexpectedness caught my breath.

He leaned even closer, to whisper in my ear, "Is the woman with the live-in boyfriend, the one whom *I've* had sex with on not fewer than two occasions, really lecturing me on abstinence?"

My face heated in anger. I glared daggers at him and tried to pull away, but he firmly held my arm and the table behind me allowed no escape. His sudden anger not quite finished, he put his lips directly on my ear. "If you actually marry him, will I still get to fuck you?"

The following incident became known as "the slap heard round the bar."

Acting on its own, my hand came around and smacked his face shockingly hard, ten times harder than I had ever hit him. He staggered back slightly and inhaled a sharp breath. Red marks appeared on his skin instantly where my hand had connected with him. He looked completely stunned.

"You stupid son of a bitch!" I yelled at him, momentarily forgetting that we were in a jam-packed bar full of witnesses.

Despite how badly my hand was stinging, it felt good to release my long-pent-up frustrations. I brought my hand around for another hit, but he caught my wrist and twisted it painfully. His eyes snapped to mine. They were filled with an anger to match my own. I struggled in his painful, tight grasp, desperate to hit him again . . . wanting so much to hurt him.

"What the hell, Kiera? What the fucking hell!" he yelled back.

He grabbed my other hand so I couldn't hit him, so I made a move with my knee, hoping to drop him. He saw it coming though and shoved me to the side, away from him. My hand throbbed as blood finally rushed back into it. My pent-up anger beyond reasoning, I immediately sprang back and leapt at him again. A strong set of arms around my waist held me back and, irritated and confused, I struggled against them.

"Calm down, Kiera." Evan's gentle voice broke through my fog of anger.

He was holding me from behind and pulling me away from Kellan. Sam had his hand on Kellan's chest. Kellan was seething in anger, glaring viciously at me. Matt and Griffin had moved behind Kellan. Matt looked concerned, Griffin looked wildly amused. Jenny was in between Kellan and me, both arms outstretched like somehow her tiny body could keep us apart if we were going to attack each other again. Aside from Griffin's chuckling, the entire bar was deathly quiet. Sam looked unsure what to do. Normally he would just kick the troublemakers out, but we both worked here . . . and were friends.

Eventually, it was Jenny who, looking around at the bar full of bystanders, grabbed Kellan's hand and then mine. Furrowing her brow and not directly looking at either of us, she muttered, "Come on," and dragged us to the back room. Kellan and I studiously ignored each other, and the mass of people, as we allowed Jenny to pull us along. I noticed Evan nod his head at Matt, who nodded back, and forcibly made a very disgruntled Griffin stay where he was. Then Evan followed closely behind us.

Once in the hallway, Evan passed our unhappy trio and opened the door to the back room to usher us all inside. Taking a final look up and down the hallway, he closed the door behind us and stood in front of it, keeping us in the room and also keeping any curious bar patrons out. He crossed his tattooed arms across his chest as he barred the door with the still broken lock, and a pair of flames lined up perfectly on his forearms. My mood matched those flames.

"Okay," Jenny said, releasing our hands. "What's up?"

"She—"

"He—"

Kellan and I both started speaking at the same time and Jenny, still standing between us, held up her hands. "One at a time."

"We don't need a mediator, Jenny," Kellan snapped, turning his glare to her.

Not intimidated by his fierce look, she calmly said, "No? Well, I think you do." She pointed back to the bar. "Half the people in there think you do." She eyed him up and down warily. "I happen to know a thing or two about your fights. I'm not leaving you alone with her."

Kellan gaped at her, then looked over her shoulder to glare at me. "You told her . . . she knows?" I shrugged and cast a glance at Evan. He still looked confused, and concerned. "Everything?" Kellan asked, still stunned.

I shrugged again.

Kellan grunted and ran a hand through his hair. "Well . . . isn't that interesting. And here I thought we weren't talking about it." He looked over at Evan. "Well, since the cat's out of the bag, why don't we all get on the same page?" He dramatically flung his hands out to me, while keeping his focus on Evan. "I fucked Kiera . . . even though you warned me not to. Then, for good measure, I did it again!"

Everyone said something at once. Jenny scolded Kellan for his language, Evan cursed at him, and I yelled at him to shut up. Kellan glared at everyone and added, "Oh . . . and I called her a whore!"

360 S. C. Stephens

"You're such a prick!" I said, looking away from him. Tears of rage stung my eyes and my face heated from embarrassment. Evan hadn't known any of that. He really didn't need to know either.

Kellan looked incredulous as I glanced back at him. "A prick? I'm a prick?" He angrily took a step toward me, and Jenny put a hand on his chest. "You're the one who hit me!" He gestured to his face, where red streaks were still visible. "Again!"

Evan butted in, looking peeved at Kellan. "Jesus, man. What were you thinking . . . or were you?"

Kellan's angry eyes snapped to him. "She begged me; I'm only human."

I made an affronted noise, unable to speak coherently. Did the whole room need to know such intimate details? I was astonished at how he was making me sound . . . like he was some innocent and I had seduced him. Yeah, right!

His eyes flashed back to me. "You begged me, Kiera! Both times, remember?" He irritably gestured at me, and Jenny pushed him back. "All I did was what you asked. That's all I've ever done—what you've asked!" He held his hands out to the side, looking exasperated.

That loosened my tongue, as anger and embarrassment shot through me. He rarely did anything I "asked." I had a long list in my head, but foremost in my mind was the word he had spoken, just moments ago. "I didn't ask to be called a whore!"

He stepped toward me and Jenny put two hands on his chest. "And I didn't ask to be hit again! Quit fucking hitting me!"

Jenny muttered, "Watch your language," which Kellan ignored.

Evan told him to "calm down," which Kellan also ignored.

"You did ask for it, prick!" No woman would have let the things he had spat at me slide. He had practically engraved me an invitation. "Since we're *sharing*"—I angrily emphasized the word—"why don't you tell them what you said to me!" I stepped toward him and Jenny put one of her hands on my shoulder. The only thing keeping our anger apart was this pretty little blond girl.

"If you'd given me two seconds, I was going to apologize for that.

But you know what . . . now I don't!" He shrugged and shook his head. "I'm not sorry I said it." He angrily pointed at me. "You were out of line! You just don't like that I'm dating!"

My eyes blazed with fury. "Dating? Screwing everything that walks isn't dating, Kellan! You don't even bother learning their names. That's not okay!" I shook my head. "You are a dog!" I growled.

Evan butted in again before Kellan could respond. "She has a point, Kellan."

"What?" Kellan and I both gaped at him. "You got something else to say to me, Evan?" Kellan snapped at him, backing away from Jenny, who lowered her hand from his chest.

Evan's normally jovial face darkened. "Maybe I do. Maybe she's right. And maybe, just maybe, you know it too." Kellan blanched but said nothing. "Why don't you tell her why you're so . . . free . . . with yourself? She might understand."

Kellan got really pissed and took a step toward Evan. "What the fuck do you know about it!"

Evan suddenly looked sympathetic, and quietly replied, "More than you think I do, Kellan."

Kellan stopped moving, his face paled. "Back off, Evan. . . . I'm not asking. Back the fuck off." His voice was low and icy cold, he really wasn't joking.

"Kellan . . . . language," Jenny scolded him again.

At the same time, I snapped, "What are you talking about?" I was highly irritated at their confusing exchange.

Kellan ignored both of us and gave Evan an icy glare. Evan stared back, then resignedly sighed, "Whatever, man . . . your call."

Kellan sniffed. "Damn right it is." He pointed at all of us. "How I date is none of your concern. If I want to screw this whole bar, you all—"

"You practically have!" I shouted, cutting him off.

"No! I screwed you!" he shouted back, and in the sudden quiet that followed the statement, I heard Evan curse again and Jenny softly sigh. "And you feel bad about cheating on Denny." He leaned in over

Jenny's head, and she brought her hand back to his chest and pushed against him. "You feel guilty about having an affair, but you—"

I interrupted him. "We are *not* having an affair! We made a mistake, twice—that's it!"

He exhaled in a rush. "Oh, come on, Kiera! God, you *are* naïve. We may have only had sex twice, but we've most definitely been having an affair the entire time!"

"That makes no sense!" I yelled back at him.

"Really? Then why did you so desperately want to hide it from Denny, huh? If it really was all so harmless and innocent, then why weren't we open about our . . . relationship . . . to anyone?" He raised his arm to the door, to indicate the outside world.

He was right. We only let others see a fraction of how close we really were with each other. I couldn't answer him. "I . . . I . . ."

"Why can't we even touch anymore?" My breath stopped. I didn't like his question or the huskiness of his voice. "What happens to you when I touch you, Kiera?" His tone, almost a low growl, was getting as suggestive as his words, and Jenny took a step away from him, dropping her hand from his chest again.

He ran a hand down his shirt, as he answered his own question. "Your pulse races, your breath quickens." He bit his lip and started simulating heavy breathing, keeping his eyes locked on mine. "Your body trembles, your lips part, your eyes burn." He closed his eyes and exhaled with a soft groan, then reopened his eyes and suggestively inhaled through his teeth. With a purposely strained voice, he continued antagonizing me. "Your body aches . . . everywhere."

He closed his eyes again and exactly mimicked a low moan that I had made with him on several occasions. He tangled a hand back through his own hair, in a way that I had done time and again, and ran his other hand back up his chest, in a way that was only too familiar to me. He had a decidedly intimate look on his face, and the overall effect was so shockingly erotic, and familiar, that I blushed deeply. He swallowed and made a horribly enticing noise as he let his mouth fall open in a pant. "Oh . . . God . . . please . . ." he mimicked in a low groan, as his hands started running down his body, toward his jeans. . . .

"Enough!" I spat out. Thoroughly embarrassed, I glanced at Jenny. She looked as pale as I was red. She glanced back at me and her hand on my shoulder became sympathetic, rather than restraining. From the door, I heard Evan mutter, "Jesus, Kellan."

Kellan's angry eyes flashed open and he snapped, "That's what I thought! Does that sound innocent to you?" He looked around the room. "To any of you?" He glared at me again. "You made your choice, remember? Denny. We ended . . . this." He indicated himself and me. "You had no feelings for me. You didn't want to be with me, but now you don't want anyone else to be with me, right?" He shook his head. "Is that what you want? For me to be completely alone?" His voice broke on the end of that sentence in his anger.

My face, still red with embarrassment, heated in rage. "I never said that. I said if you were to see someone, I would understand . . . but God, Kellan, Evan's right, show some restraint!" Silence filled the room, with everyone glaring at everyone else. Finally, I couldn't take it anymore. "Are you trying to hurt me? Do you have something to prove?"

He eyed me up and down. "To you . . . ? No . . . nothing!"

He backed away from Jenny a little and I pushed into her. She brought both her hands to my shoulders, to hold me back. "You're not trying to purposely hurt me?" I snarled at him.

"No." He ran his hand through his hair again, and shook his head.

I actually saw red I was so infuriated with him. Of course he was trying to hurt me! Why else would he be whoring himself all over town? Why else would he have broken his promise? "Then what about my sister?"

He groaned and looked up at the ceiling. "God, not that again."

Evan took a step to help Jenny, who was beginning to struggle with me; I was really pissed off and pushing against her. Jenny looked over at Evan and, not saying anything, shook her head. He stayed where he was by the door.

"Yes! That! Again! You promised!" I yelled, pointing at him.

"Obviously, I lied, Kiera!" he yelled back. "If you haven't noticed, I do that! And what does it matter anyway? *She* wanted me, you didn't. What do you care if I—"

"Because you're mine!" I yelled back at him, quite unintentionally. Of course, he wasn't actually mine. . . .

The immediate silence after that was deafening. Kellan's face paled and then slowly got very, very angry. "No, no I'm not! THAT'S THE WHOLE FUCKING POINT!"

"Kellan!" Jenny scolded him again, and he finally glared at her.

My face heated even more in embarrassment at my unthinking declaration. "Is that why you did it? Is that why you slept with her, you son of a bitch! To prove a point?" My voice cracked in my anger.

Jenny finally interrupted. "He didn't, Kiera," she calmly stated.

Kellan gave her an icy glare. "Jenny!"

"What?" I asked her, and she dropped her hands from my shoulders.

Ignoring Kellan's cold stare, she again, very calmly, said, "Kellan wasn't the one who slept with her."

Kellan took a menacing step toward Jenny, and Evan took a step toward Kellan. Glancing up at Evan, Kellan stopped. "This doesn't concern you, Jenny, butt out!" he snapped.

Slightly irritated with him now, she coolly met his gaze. "Now it does! Why are you lying to her, Kellan? Tell her the truth! For once, tell her the truth."

He shut his mouth and clenched his jaw. Evan scowled at him and Jenny frowned. Not able to stand it any longer, I shouted, "Will someone please tell me . . . something?"

Jenny looked back at me. "Don't you ever listen to Griffin?" she asked softly.

Irritated, Kellan said, "No, she avoids conversations with him, if she can help it." Quieter, he added, "I counted on that."

I furrowed my brow, confused. "Wait . . . Griffin? My sister slept with Griffin?"

Jenny nodded, rolling her eyes. "He hasn't shut up about it, Kiera. He keeps telling everyone—'Best 'O' of my life!'" She made a disgusted face.

Kellan clenched his jaw again. "That's enough, Jenny."

I stared at her, disbelieving, and then looked over at Evan. He shrugged, nodded, and looked curiously at Kellan. So did Jenny. And then so did I.

"You lied to me?" I whispered.

He shrugged noncommittally. "You assumed. I simply . . . encouraged that thought."

Anger flashed through me. "You lied to me!" I yelled.

"I told you, I do that!" he snapped back.

"Why?" I demanded.

Kellan looked away from all of us and didn't answer.

"Answer her, Kellan," Jenny said. He looked back to her, and she raised an eyebrow at him. Kellan frowned, but remained silent.

Memories flooded me. "The whole fight in the car . . . the rain . . . all of that started, because I was so angry about you and her. Why would you let me think—"

He glared over at me. "Why did you automatically assume—"

"She told me. Well, she made it sound like . . ." I closed my eyes. I hadn't wanted to hear it. I had never let her fully explain what had happened that night. All she had said about Kellan was that she wanted me to thank him for her. I had assumed she wanted me to thank him for . . . that. Maybe she had just meant for showing her a good time, for dancing with her all night, for taking her to Griffin's house, for giving her a ride home, or . . . God, it could have been anything really.

Reopening my eyes, I looked at him and softened my gaze and my voice. "I'm sorry I assumed . . . but why would you let me think that for so long?"

His gaze and voice softened too. "I wanted to hurt you. . . ."

"Why?" I whispered and took a step toward him. Jenny, seeing us both calmer, let me pass. Kellan looked away and didn't answer. I walked over to him and put a hand on his cheek. He closed his eyes at my touch. "Why, Kellan?"

Without opening his eyes, he whispered, "Because you hurt me . . . so many times. I wanted to hurt you back."

My anger extinguished. Kellan, his anger sapped as well, slowly opened his eyes, pain clearly visible in his features. He stared back at me silently. Somewhere in the back of my head, I heard Jenny walk over to Evan and tell him that they should give us a moment. Then I heard the door open and close, and Kellan and I were alone.

"I never wanted to hurt you, Kellan . . . either of you." The silence of the space reverberated back to me and I sank to my knees, right there in the middle of the room. The roller coaster of emotions was wearing me down—the guilt, the excitement, the pain, the thrill, and the anger. I could barely remember how perfect I had thought things were in the beginning, before I had ruined everything.

Kellan knelt down on the ground across from me and took my hands in his. "It doesn't matter now, Kiera. Things are how they're supposed to be. You're with Denny and I'm . . . I'm . . ." He swallowed.

I just so missed how things used to be, how sweet our relationship used to be, before Kellan got cold, then hot, then . . . whatever it was he was being now. It slipped out before I could think about it. "I miss you," I whispered to him.

His breath caught and I heard him swallow loudly. "Kiera . . ."

The tears started coming and I just wanted my friend back. Surprisingly, Kellan pulled me into an embrace, like he used to so long ago. I clutched him tight, needing his nearness. He stroked my back while I started sobbing into his shoulder. I just wanted to stop feeling so much. My head was spinning with guilt and anger and heat and pain.

He mumbled something into my shoulder that almost sounded like, "I'm sorry, baby." My heart sped at the thought of those tender words coming from him.

He sat back on his heels, keeping me tight to him, so that I was sitting on his lap, my knees on either side of him. He started stroking my hair and I started relaxing into him. He held me that way for a long time. My tears slowly stopped, and I turned my head to look at him.

Surprisingly, his eyes were closed and his head was down. He looked sad. I tried to move off of him, but, keeping his eyes closed, he pulled me tighter to him. "No, please . . . stay," he whispered.

Instantly, I was aware of how dangerous our position was. But for our breathing, how silent the room was, how tight he embraced me, how long it had been since we had really held each other. He slowly opened his eyes and turned to look at me, and I could see that he was aware of the danger too. His lips parted, his breath quickened. I could see the wistful pain of wanting me in his eyes. Kellan was right—there was a reason we should never touch.

Thinking only of telling him that I couldn't do this anymore to Denny, I whispered, "I miss you, so much." That wasn't what I had been going to say at all. What was wrong with me?

He closed his eyes and lowered his forehead to rest on mine. I could clearly see how difficult I was making this for him, and I really didn't mean to. . . .

"Kiera, I can't. . . ." He swallowed again. "This is wrong, you're not mine."

I thrilled at the word "mine" coming from his lips, and hated myself for it. Mentally agreeing with him, I whispered, "I *am* yours." Wait, no that's not what I meant to say either. . . .

He made an odd noise and drew a ragged breath. "Are you . . . ?" He whispered so softly, I barely heard him. He looked up at me and the passion was burning in his eyes again. "I want you so much. . . ."

I felt such sorrow for the loss of the easy friendship we once had, such guilt over what I constantly did to betray Denny, and such a painful need being in Kellan's arms . . . and the latter was winning. I had missed him so much, and now that he was with me, I suddenly didn't want him to leave me ever again.

"I want you too," I whispered, and for the first time, it was what I meant to say.

He rolled then, so that I was lying on the floor and he was pressing into me. Breathing softly, he paused, almost touching my lips. He held himself there and I could see the struggle in his eyes. He wasn't sure if I really wanted this.

Before I knew what I was saying, it all spilled out in a rush. "I've missed you so much. I've wanted to touch you for so long. I've wanted to hold you for so long. I've wanted you for so long. I do need you, Kellan . . . I always have."

He still held himself, hovering over my lips, his eyes frantically searching my face, looking for a lie in my words. "I won't . . . I won't be led on again, Kiera. I would rather end this than be hurt by you again. I can't. . . ."

I searched myself for the truth . . . but all I could find in my body was an aching loneliness for him. I couldn't take another day of him being with another woman. I couldn't handle another second of his lips on anyone's but mine. I wasn't even thinking about what that meant for Denny and me. I was only thinking that I needed Kellan to be mine . . . only mine.

I gently grabbed his face with my hands. "Don't leave me. You are mine . . . and I'm yours. I want you . . . and you can have me. Just stop being with all those—"

He pulled away from me. "No. I won't be with you because you're jealous."

I brought his face close to mine again, and borrowed one of his moves that so long ago had driven me mad. I lightly slid my tongue under and along his upper lip. It had the same effect on him that it had on me. He closed his eyes and shuddered, inhaling quickly.

"Kiera . . . no. Don't do this to me again. . . ."

I paused. "I'm not, Kellan. I'm sorry I pushed you away before, but I'm not saying no anymore."

I brought my tongue back to his intoxicatingly delicious skin. I only made it halfway along his lip, when he brought his mouth down to mine. He paused while kissing me and pulled back, his breath shallow and fast. He stared at me, suddenly looking very nervous.

"I'm in love with you," he whispered, searching my eyes. He looked very pale and very scared, and a little . . . hopeful.

"Kellan, I . . ." I didn't know what to say. My eyes were starting to tear up again.

He didn't let me even attempt to finish. He brought a hand up to stroke my cheek and kissed me again, but tenderly, sweetly, the kiss was full of emotion. "I'm so in love with you, Kiera. I've missed you so much. I'm so sorry. I'm sorry I say awful things to you. I'm sorry I lied about your sister. . . . I never touched her. I promised you I wouldn't. I couldn't let you know . . . how much I adore you . . . how much you hurt me."

It was as if finally telling me what he really felt released all the rest of his bottled-up emotions, and he couldn't stop himself.

He spoke rapidly in between his tender kisses. "I love you. I'm sorry. I'm so sorry. The women . . . I was so scared to touch you. You didn't want me. . . . I couldn't take the pain. I tried to get over you. Every time with them, I was with you. I'm so sorry. . . . I love you."

Tears flowed freely down my cheeks as I listened in shocked silence. His heartfelt words, his tender lips, it made me even weaker, made my heart race.

His lips never stopped moving over mine, his words never stopped flowing between them. "Forgive me . . . please. I tried to forget you. It didn't work. . . . I just wanted you more. God, I've missed you. I'm sorry I hurt you. I've never wanted anyone like I want you. Every girl is you to me. You're all I see . . . you're all I want. I want you so much. I want you forever. Forgive me. . . . I love you so much."

I still couldn't process what he was saying, the look of fear and hope in his eyes. It made me want him even more, though. It made my breath heavy and ragged. His kiss picked up intensity in response. "God, I love you. I need you. Forgive me. Stay with me. Say you need me too. . . . Say you want me too. Please . . . be mine."

He instantly stopped kissing me and froze, staring at me terrified again, like he finally just realized exactly what he had been saying. "Kiera . . . ?" His voice was shaky. His eyes glistened while he searched mine.

I realized that I hadn't said anything in a really long time. He had been pouring his heart out to me, and I hadn't said a word. Of course, he really hadn't left me an opportunity to speak, but from the terror in his eyes, I don't think he realized that. All he could see were my tears and my silence.

Emotion locked up my throat and I closed my eyes, giving myself a minute to absorb everything. He loved me? He adored me? He loved me? He wanted me . . . forever? He loved me? He wanted me to be with him? He loved me? Feelings for him that I had struggled so hard to push back flooded through me. Everything we had gone through—every tear, every joy, every jealousy—had he loved me the whole time?

I felt him pull away from me, and I realized I was still lying silent with my eyes closed. I opened them and looked up to his sad, terrified face. I grabbed his arm and stopped him from moving away from me. He met my gaze, the tear in his eye finally rolling down his face. I brushed it away with my thumb and cupped his cheek. I pulled him closer and tenderly kissed him.

"Kiera . . ." he muttered between my lips, pulling away slightly.

I swallowed the lump in my throat. "You were always right— we're not friends. We're so much more. I want to be with *you*, Kellan. I want to be yours. I *am* yours." It was all I felt in that moment, all I could think to say. In that instant, he was my entire world. Nothing else even existed to me besides him, and I didn't want to resist him anymore. I was tired of fighting this. I wanted to be his . . . in every way.

He rolled back on top of me and brought his mouth back to mine. He let out a soft exhale and kissed me deeply, as if we hadn't kissed in years. The passion I felt coming from him was almost overwhelming, his whole body trembled with it. He shifted his weight and pushed against me, making a noise deep in his throat that thrilled me.

I ran my hands down his back and he shuddered. I felt the edge of his shirt and, grabbing it, ran my fingers up his bare skin, taking the shirt with me. Gently I pulled it off of him, gazing at his amazing perfection for a second, before his lips came back down to mine.

He shifted his weight again and brought his hands slowly down my neck, across my chest, and up under my shirt. His hands were shaking as he pushed my shirt up and pulled it off me. His body was still shaking as he kissed me. He was holding back, I realized, forcing himself to go slowly, forcing himself to remain in control, in case I changed my mind. The thought of how much he wanted me, and how unsure he was of me, filled my body with fire.

I ran my hands back down his bare back, feeling every muscle, every defined line. He lightly groaned as I brought my hands around to his chest and ran my fingers along the faint scar on his ribs, the scar he had gotten because of me . . . because he loved me. His lips never leaving mine, his hands brushed over my shoulders, down my arms, over my bra, down to my waist. I sighed at how good it felt to feel his touch again; it had been so achingly long. He shifted again and his shaking hands lowered to my jeans. His fingers played with the waistband on them, almost considering if he should . . .

I pulled away from his lips and whispered in his ear, "I'm yours . . . don't stop." I shifted my weight under him suggestively.

Exhaling and relaxing, Kellan listened to me, he didn't stop. He started unbuttoning my jeans and, biting my lip, I moved to unbutton his. He pulled back to watch me intently. He stopped shaking. He seemed to finally believe that I wasn't going to stop this. I finished undoing his jeans as he was starting to pull mine down. Gazing at me with such love in his face, he softly said, "Kiera, I love you," and started kissing my neck.

His face, his words, hit me with such intensity that I stopped breathing. Suddenly this felt wrong, dirty. It didn't match his tender words, and I couldn't go through with it. "Kellan, wait . . . just a min—" I said tentatively.

"Kiera . . ." He stopped tugging at my jeans and groaned heavily. His entire body sagged against mine, his head resting on my shoulder. "Oh . . . my . . . God. Are you serious?" He rocked his head back and forth on my shoulder. "Please don't do this again. I can't take it."

"No, I'm not . . . but—"

"But?" He pulled back to look at me breathlessly, his blue eyes blazing with desire and, now, irritation. "You do realize that if you keep doing this to my body, I will never be able to have children?" he snipped.

I laughed at his unintentionally amusing remark. He pulled back more and frowned at me. "I'm glad you find that funny. . . ."

Still chuckling, I ran a finger down his cheek, eventually making him smile. "If we are going to do this . . . if I'm going to be with you"—I looked around at the dirty floor we were lying on—"it's not going to be on the floor in the back room of Pete's."

He frowned, then immediately reversed it and softly kissed me. "Now you object to being with me on a dirty floor?" he whispered.

I laughed again at his reference to our tryst in the coffee stand, and at hearing his humor return. It had been a long time since I had heard that too.

He kissed me again, then, pulling back, forced a frown on his face. "Did you . . . did you just get me to pour my heart out to you . . . so you could get me naked again?" He raised an eyebrow at me charmingly.

I laughed again and gently grabbed his face in my hands. "God, I missed you. I missed that."

"Missed what?" he asked quietly, gazing back at me and softly stroking my bare stomach.

"You . . . your humor, your smile, your touch, your . . . everything." I gazed back at him warmly.

His face got serious. "I missed you so much, Kiera."

I nodded, swallowing the emotion in my throat, and he kissed me again. Suddenly, he pulled back and, eyeing me half-naked beneath him, bit his lip and raised an eyebrow. "You know . . . there are other options for this room besides the floor."

"Really?" I asked, enjoying his playfulness.

"Yeah . . ." He looked around the room, smiling. "Table . . . chair . . . shelf . . ." He looked down at me, his grin suddenly devilish. "Wall?"

I laughed and stroked my hand down his chest, marveling at how quickly my emotions around Kellan could change. Here we'd just been at each other's throats, and now we were intimately joking around. "Just kiss me." I shook my head at him.

"Yes, ma'am." He smiled and started kissing me deeply. "Tease," he muttered, moving his lips to my neck.

"Whore," I muttered back, grinning and kissing the cheek I had ruthlessly slapped earlier. He laughed huskily in response and moved his lips to the base of my throat.

A persistent soft knock drifted through the room, but Kellan and I both ignored it.

"Hmmm . . ." I closed my eyes as he lightly ran his tongue up my throat. God, I loved that.

He was bringing his tongue up and over my chin when the annoying knocking that we had both been ignoring suddenly became a door swinging open. I gasped and tilted my head up, my heart racing. Kellan raised his head to look at the door.

"Jesus, Evan . . . you scared the shit out of me!" Kellan said, laughing.

I didn't feel like laughing. This was not how I wanted someone to walk in on me. To his credit, Evan was covering his eyes. He immediately closed the door behind him and looked away. "Uh, sorry, man. I know you two are . . . uh, I need to talk to you, Kellan."

Evan seemed really embarrassed, but he couldn't be any more embarrassed than me. Kellan lay over me, protectively shielding me from Evan's view, not that he was looking in our direction. "Your timing kind of stinks, man." He frowned at him.

Unintentionally, Evan flicked a glance at us and immediately looked away again. I clutched Kellan tighter, wanting to be anywhere but here. "Sorry . . . but you're going to thank my timing in about ten seconds."

Kellan smiled widely. "Really, Evan, can't this wait, like ten—" I nudged his ribs and he looked down at me, then back up at him. "Twenty minutes?" I giggled.

"Denny's here," Evan stated.

I stopped giggling. "What?" I asked quietly.

Kellan sat up, straddling me. "Shit." He handed me my shirt and I quickly slipped it on. He stayed on my lap, thinking.

Evan finally looked over at us without looking away. "Unless you want tonight to get . . . even more interesting, Kiera needs to leave, and you need to stay and talk to me."

Kellan started nodding and, finding his shirt, slipped it back on. "Thank you . . . ." he said, looking back up at Evan.

Evan half-smiled. "See . . . I knew you'd thank me."

I felt ice-cold as Kellan finally got off my lap and helped me get up. We adjusted our clothes and I started having trouble breathing. Kellan put a hand on my shoulder. "It's fine . . . it will be fine."

Panic flared through me. "But the whole bar . . . they all saw that, they'll be talking. He'll know something."

Kellan shook his head. "He'll know we had a fight . . . that's it." He looked over at Evan, who looked impatient for me to leave. "You should go, before he comes back here looking for you."

"Okay . . ."

"Kiera . . ." He grabbed my arm as I turned to leave, then he pulled me in for one long, last kiss.

I was breathless when I went out into the hallway.

Chapter 20
Confessions

Luckily, the hallway was empty. I quickly ducked into the ladies' room, which was also empty. The panic abated and I sank to the floor and put my head on my arms. That had been too close. What if that had been Denny and not Evan? My stomach clenched at the thought. If I was going to leave Denny, it wasn't going to be with him finding out like that.

Was I really going to leave Denny for Kellan? I loved Denny, I didn't want to leave him . . . but . . . Kellan's arms had felt so good around me again. I knew that I wasn't going to say no to him anymore. I needed him too much. Maybe it could work with both of them? I smiled and held my fingers to my lips, remembering Kellan's tender kiss. Did Kellan really love me? Did I love him? That thought thrilled and terrified me. Could I really handle having an irrefutable affair? Could Kellan? Could Denny?

Opening the door, I peered down the hall. Still empty . . . good. I glanced over at the mirror and decided I didn't look like I had almost been with Kellan . . . again . . . and, sighing, turned and left the small room.

My eyes instinctively went over to the band's table as I reentered the bar. I frowned. No Kellan. Was he still in the back room with Evan? I couldn't worry about it, as I was getting icy stares from several customers, who looked none too happy about my prolonged absence. Also, Denny was approaching me, a little cautiously.

I hoped for a moment that maybe no one had told Denny anything yet, but over the low rumble of voices in the bar, I heard Griffin loudly yell, "Yeah, Kiera, woooo—nice bitch slap!" I saw Matt smack him hard in the chest, and heard him mutter, "What? Fucker probably deserved it."

I closed my eyes and cursed the stupid, loudmouthed ass. Seriously, what did my sister see in him?

"Kiera?" Denny's soft accent made me open my eyes. "Everything okay? The whole bar has been going on and on about you hitting Kellan?" His brow was scrunched in concern, his eyes reflecting the same.

Walking by him, I grabbed his hand and made my way to the bar, stalling for time. What do I tell him? Kellan never told me what to say. My earlier irritation at Griffin actually sparked an idea, and without carefully thinking it over, I spit out, "The jerk slept with Anna when she was here, then never called her again . . . broke her heart."

Denny stopped walking alongside me and I stopped walking . . . and breathing. "Oh," was all he said. His brow didn't soften though, and I had no idea if he believed me or not.

"I couldn't take him using her like that, and then . . . all the women he's been bringing home. It was just so disrespectful to her. And tonight he was practically getting a lap dance, and I guess I just lost it. I . . . defended her honor, in a way."

"Oh," he said again, then his brow softened and he smiled softly. "Why didn't you tell me that earlier? I would have talked to him about that."

I relaxed and started breathing regularly again. "I . . . I told her I wouldn't tell anybody."

"Really?" he asked, suddenly curious. "The way she was hanging all over him, I figured she'd spray-paint it on the walls." He shrugged. "Your sister is quite the character." He leaned over and kissed my cheek. "Can you please let me do the fighting from now on?"

I giggled nervously and squeezed his hand tighter. Was he really going to buy that? "Yeah, yeah, no problem." I gave him a swift kiss. "My customers probably aren't happy with me. I should get back to work."

Denny laughed. "They probably loved dinner with a show. Speaking of dinner . . . I'm starving. I think I'll grab something here." He laughed again and hugged me tight. "I love you, Kiera." He was still chuckling as he made his way to a table . . . the band's table.

I felt like I might be sick.

I didn't know what Evan was talking to Kellan about in the back room, but he was in there for over an hour. When they did eventually come out, Kellan kept his head down and quite sheepishly left the bar. He never so much as glanced at me. I was offended by that at first, but as I noticed the gossiping whispers around me, I decided that if we'd just had the major fight that the bar patrons thought we had—and I suppose, in a way we had—then his reaction was probably the correct one.

Kellan stayed away the remainder of the night. Luckily, Denny accepted my version of the story and didn't ask the band about it. When I gave him his dinner later, they were all happily chatting about some game that was on last night. Denny smiled at me and leaned in for a kiss, which I immediately gave him. I couldn't help but look at Evan when I did that, the compromising position that he had walked in on still blazing in my mind. Apparently, it was in his as well. He glanced over at me too, and blushed a little bit. I avoided looking at him for the rest of the evening.

Denny left shortly after his dinner, and I had to endure a few more hours of huddled whispers that quickly silenced at my approach as I finished out my shift. I hoped none of them were piecing things together too accurately. I didn't need anyone letting something slip to Denny.

Jenny offered me a ride home. I thanked her for always doing that, and also for her help with Kellan earlier. We were walking across the lot to her car when I stopped in my tracks, my heart suddenly in my throat. Jenny noticed and stared over at what had my rapt attention. Kellan's car was parked across the street and he was outside of it, leaning against the door with his arms crossed on his chest. A smile spread over his face when he saw me notice him.

My heartbeat doubled at seeing him. Jenny sighed, and I looked over at her pleadingly. "All right . . . go. If anyone asks, I'll say we went for a late coffee and lost track of time or something."

I grinned and hugged her tight. "Thank you, Jenny."

She grabbed my arm as I started to leave. "I'm only doing this once, Kiera." She shook her head, her pale blue eyes narrowing a bit. "I won't be involved in hiding an affair."

I swallowed and nodded, feeling horribly guilty. "I'm so sorry. I never should have dragged you into all of this."

She looked at me thoughtfully as she released my arm. "You should pick one, Kiera. Pick one, and release the other. You can't keep them both."

I nodded and swallowed the painful lump in my throat at that thought. I watched Jenny for a second as she waved briefly at Kellan and then made her way to her car. Then I nearly sprinted across the street to him.

He smiled warmly at my approach and, taking my hand, led me to the other side of the car, where he sweetly helped me inside. I was glad to see his departure from the bar was just an act, and he didn't seem to have any problems being around me. As I watched him cross the front of the car, our horrid fight much earlier in the evening started replaying itself in my head, and a certain section of it just wasn't leaving me.

I forced a frown on my face as he slid into the car, closing the door gently behind him. Kellan eyed me curiously. "What? I haven't been around you for hours." He smiled wryly. "What could I have possibly done?" he purred.

Keeping my face frozen in disapproval, I stated, "I've been dwelling on something you did earlier . . . for hours."

He cocked his head charmingly to the side. "I did quite a bit . . . can you be more specific?"

The corners of my mouth started to rise, and then true irritation made me scowl. "Oh . . . God . . . please." I smacked him on the arm. "How could you mock me like that in front of Evan and Jenny?" I smacked him repeatedly on the arm. "That was so embarrassing!"

He leaned away from me and laughed. "Ow! Sorry." He smiled wickedly. "I was making a point."

I smacked him a final time. "I think you made it, asshole!"

He laughed again. "I think I'm a bad influence—you're starting to swear as much as I do."

I smirked at him and snuggled up close to his side. He looked down at me. "You can mimic me sometime if you like." He seemed entirely too excited by that prospect, and I couldn't help but laugh at him.

I blushed, remembering his . . . performance. "You were quite good at . . . that."

He laughed again. "Not my first time."

I gaped in disbelief at his answer, and he chuckled at the look on my face. Then suddenly, he got an odd glint in his eyes. It made my heart quicken. "Hmmm . . ." He cocked his head to the side and smiled crookedly. "You are right . . . that wasn't very fair of me." He grinned fully and my heart skipped a beat. "Here, I'll do me. . . ."

I was about to protest that it wasn't nearly the same thing, the two of us locked in a car with only me to hear him, when he snuck his arms around me and held me tight against his body, bringing his lips directly to my ear.

My argument left me. My conscious thought left me.

Increasing his breath in my ear, he lightly groaned. I shut my eyes, my own breath increasing. The warm air passing his lips tickled my neck, giving me shivers as he let those soft lips brush my ear.

"Oh . . ." He elongated the word enticingly, then inhaled noisily. I was shocked at my body's reaction—electricity shot through me instantly.

"God . . ." He strained his voice intimately and ran his hand up my thigh. I shifted on the seat, my breath embarrassingly fast.

"Yes . . ." He whispered the word, and added a noise on the end that made me lose all pretense of control.

I spun to face him, grabbing his neck and pulling him into me, kissing him hard. Excitement and surprise coursed through me as our kiss deepened. He smelled so good . . . he tasted so good . . . he would feel so good. Maybe a car wasn't as bad as a dirty floor?

Abruptly, he pulled away from me. "Can we do something?" he calmly asked, his eyes sparkling playfully.

"Yes . . ." I practically moaned the word. God, he could do anything he wanted to me. . . .

He pulled back a little farther and grinned. "Do you need a minute?" The smile on his face turned a little smug, and he laughed as I smacked him on the arm again.

He started the car as I frowned at him, my face heating embarrassingly. Damn . . . he was good. "What did you have in mind?" I said a little grumpily.

He laughed at my look and shook his head a little. "Sorry, I didn't mean to get you all . . . riled up." I raised an eyebrow at him and he laughed again. "Okay . . . yeah, maybe I did." He winked and I blushed even more. "But right now, I want to show you something." He smiled breathtakingly at me and I could only nod as we pulled away from the street.

I sighed contently and relaxed into him, his arm slung over my shoulders holding me tight. I was gazing into his amazing eyes, watching the streetlights alter the color, when I noticed that we were driving toward Seattle Center.

"Where are you taking me?" I asked him curiously.

"Well, I did promise you that we'd go up the Space Needle."

"Kellan . . . it's two in the morning, it's closed."

He smiled at me. "It's okay . . . I know people." He winked.

We parked and, like the first time we came here, he grabbed my hand. A man who obviously worked there met us and let us in. I looked up at Kellan, curious. The man had been expecting us. What had Kellan been up to this evening? He handed the man more than a few large bills, and, smiling, the man led us to the elevators at the Needle. As the doors closed in front of us, I leaned over and whispered to Kellan, "How much did you give him?"

He smiled and whispered back, "Don't worry about it. The house wasn't the only thing my parents left me."

He winked at me and I was going to ask him another question, but the elevator was rising. Through the front of the glass doors I could see the city quickly dropping below us. I gasped and pressed against the far wall. Heights weren't my favorite, and the elevator suddenly felt tiny and very breakable.

Noticing my pallor, Kellan turned my chin so I was looking at him. "You're completely safe, Kiera," he said; then he kissed me gently and I completely forgot about the fragile-looking elevator.

We arrived at the top, just as my hands were coming up to tangle in his hair, his arms slipping around my waist, our kiss now quite intense. The man Kellan knew cleared his throat, quite loudly, and we both looked over at him. I blushed and Kellan laughed.

"I guess we're here," he chuckled, leading me out of the elevator.

He patted the man on the back and, grabbing both of my hands, walked backwards, toward the edge of the inside observatory overlooking the city. It was dark in the building, since it was closed. Only a couple of emergency lights were on, and they did little to illuminate the room. But it seemed every light was on outside, and the city glowed beneath us.

"Kellan . . . wow . . . it's beautiful," I said softly, stopping to look out over all the sparkling lights.

"Yes, it is," he said, just as softly, but he was leaning against the railing with his back to the view, staring at me, not the city below us. "Come here." He held his arms out to me.

We were on the inside of the Needle, and a safe distance from the edge, so I felt okay enough to walk over to his embrace and lean against the railing with him. He turned his head to look outside at the city, but now all I could see was him. I studied his features in the half-light; he was more breathtaking than the view. I couldn't see why this perfect creature was enamored with me.

"Why me?" I whispered to him.

He turned to look back at me and, as expected, my breath caught when he smiled. "You have no idea how attractive you are to me. I kind of like that." He cocked his head to the side as he watched my cheeks fill with color. He was thoughtful for a second, then added quietly, "It was you and Denny . . . your relationship."

I ran my fingers through his hair above his ear and frowned. "What do you mean?" He looked back over the city but didn't say anything. I grabbed his cheek and made him look back at me. "What do you mean, Kellan?" I repeated.

He sighed and looked down. "I can't explain this properly, without . . . without clarifying something Evan said."

I frowned again and thought back over our earlier fight. It seemed a lifetime ago, so much had changed. "When you told him, quite rudely, by the way, to back off?"

He looked like he'd rather not talk about it. "Yeah."

"I don't understand—what does that have to do with me?"

He smiled and shook his head. "Nothing . . . everything."

I half-smiled at him. "Eventually you're going to start making sense, right?"

He laughed and looked over the city again. "Yeah . . . just give me a minute."

I embraced him tightly, putting my head on his shoulder. He could have all the time in the world, if I could keep holding him like this. The city twinkled mesmerizingly and I deeply inhaled his intoxicating scent as I snuggled further into his leather jacket.

He held me back just as tightly, rubbing my back with one hand, the other hand holding the back of my head. Finally, he slowly said, "You and Evan were right about the women. I've been . . . using them . . . for years."

I pulled back a little to look at him. "For years? Not just because of me?" I felt oddly hurt by that.

He tucked some hair behind my ear. "No . . . although that certainly made it worse."

I frowned, slightly uncomfortable by the conversation. "You shouldn't use people, Kellan . . . for any reason."

He raised an eyebrow at me and smiled. "You didn't use me, to block out Denny our first time?" I looked away. Of course I had used him. He grabbed my chin and made me look back at him. "It's okay, Kiera. I suspected that." He sighed and looked out over the water on our other side. "It didn't stop me from believing we might have had a chance, though. I spent that whole damn day wandering around the city, trying to figure out how to tell you . . . how much I loved you, without sounding like an idiot."

"Kellan . . ." I had always wondered where he went that day.

He looked back at me. "God . . . when you went right back to him, like we were nothing at all, that killed me. I knew it. . . ." He shook his head, almost angrily. "The minute I finally came home, and heard you two upstairs, I knew we didn't have a chance."

I blinked in surprise. "You heard us?" I was confused. Kellan had come home much later . . . and drunker.

He looked down, like he hadn't meant to mention that. "Oh . . . yeah. I came back and heard you guys in your room, getting . . . reacquainted. That . . . pretty much sucked. I grabbed a fifth, headed to Sam's, and, well, you know how that turned out."

An odd guilt washed through me. "Kellan, God, I'm sorry. I didn't know."

He faced me again. "You didn't do anything wrong, Kiera. . . ." He looked away for a second. "I was such a dick to you afterwards. I'm sorry about that." He grinned sheepishly at me and I grimaced at the memory; he had been a jerk. "I'm sorry, I tend to lose the filter on my mouth when I'm angry . . . and no one seems to be able to make me angrier than you." He smiled apologetically at me.

I laughed once and raised an eyebrow at him. "I've noticed that."
I thought back over some of our more colorful fights. He laughed
softly and guilt washed through me. "You were always right though.
And I did kind of deserve your . . . harshness."

He stopped laughing and grabbed my cheek. "No, you didn't.
You never deserved the things I said to you."

"I was horribly . . . misleading to you."

"You didn't know I loved you," he said softly, stroking my cheek.

I looked up into his loving blue eyes and knew I didn't deserve
his kindness. "I knew you cared for me. I was . . . callous."

He half-smiled and kissed me. "True," he whispered. "But we
seem to have gotten off track." He smiled warmly, changing where
our conversation had been going. "I believe we were talking about
my messed-up psyche."

I laughed and looked over his shoulder, shaking off my bad
mood. "Right, your . . . whoring."

He laughed. "Ouch." I laughed and ran a hand over his chest
while he gazed at me for a moment. "I suppose I should start with the
whole tortured-childhood speech."

"We've already talked about that, you don't have to bring it up
again." I gazed at him sadly, not wanting him to reopen that painful
subject unnecessarily.

"Kiera . . . we only scratched the very tip of that very deep wound,"
he said softly. "There is so much more that I don't talk about . . . to
anyone."

"You don't have to tell me, Kellan. I don't want to hurt you by—"

He looked past me, his eyes haunted. "I want to . . . in a weird way.
I want you to understand. I want you to know me." Feeling melancholy
sweep over him, I met his eye and suggestively raised an eyebrow at that.
It worked, he laughed. "Not just . . . biblically," he muttered playfully.

I twirled my fingers around the hair brushing his neck. "Okay,
if you want to . . . I'll listen to whatever you want to tell me, and I'll
respect anything you don't want to tell me." I smiled encouragingly,
hoping this wasn't going to hurt him even more.

But he surprised me by laughing. "You're going to find it funny."

I froze and gaped at him. Nothing about his childhood that he had told me so far was even remotely funny. "I don't see how that's possible," I whispered, searching his eyes.

He sighed. "Well, okay, maybe not funny . . . coincidental, then." He half-smiled at me sadly as I scrunched my face in confusion. "It seems that my mother was . . . enamored with my father's best friend."

My face paled. *Coincidental indeed.* Kellan smiled at my reaction and continued. "So when dear old Dad had to leave town for several months . . . some family emergency thing back east," he shook his head, "you can imagine his surprise, when he came back home to find his blushing bride pregnant."

My mouth dropped open and Kellan grinned sarcastically. "Surprise, honey."

"What did your dad do?" I asked quietly.

"Ahhh . . ." He nodded his head, looking away, and his smile left him. "Well, here is the part where my mother showed her true brilliance." He looked over at me, as I looked at him, confused again. His gaze intensely serious, he calmly said, "She told him that she was raped while he was gone . . . and he believed her."

My face felt like it had just lost all the color from it as I stared at him, disbelieving his completely true story. What kind of person would do that?

His face paled too, as he softly said, "He looked at me as the seed of a monster from day one. He hated me before I was even born."

His eyes watered, but no tears fell. I kissed his cheek, wishing I could do more. "I'm so sorry, Kellan." He nodded and continued gazing at me thoughtfully. "Why would your mom do that?"

He shrugged. "She didn't want to lose everything, I guess." He laughed once, humorlessly. "Once she played that card though, man, she committed to it. There's even a police report somewhere, blaming some generic white guy." He laughed humorlessly again. "My birth certificate even says 'John Doe' under the 'father.' Dad wouldn't claim me." He whispered that last part.

"God, Kellan . . ." A tear dripped down my cheek. "And they told you all this?"

He looked out over the water. "Repeatedly. It was practically my bedtime story. Good night, boy . . . by the way, you ruined our lives."

Another tear dripped down my cheek. "How do you know about your . . . about the best friend?"

Kellan looked back at me and sighed. "Mom. She told me the truth." He brushed a tear off my cheek. "I guess my . . . sperm donor dad . . . bagged out when she told him she was pregnant. She never saw him again. It broke her heart . . . and she hated me for it." He cocked his head as he watched the horror on my face. "I think she hated me even more than Dad did," he whispered.

More tears fell as I hugged him and kissed his cheek again. He hugged me back loosely. "You never told your father the truth? Maybe he would have been—"

He cut me off. "He would never have believed me over her, Kiera. He hated me. I only would have gotten brutally hurt, and I generally tried to avoid that." I pulled back to look at him, and brushed some hair off of his forehead while he continued. "He had to have known anyway."

I blinked, surprised. "Why?"

He half-smiled sadly again. "I look just like Dad's best friend . . . spitting image. Who knows, maybe that's why he really hated me . . . Mom too."

Anger welled in me over these people who had grudgingly raised him. "You were innocent. It wasn't your fault." I couldn't stop my seething tone.

He ran both hands down my hair to my cheeks. "I know that, Kiera." He kissed me. "I've never told anyone that before. Not Evan, not Denny . . . no one."

I was moved that he would confide something so personal to me, but I didn't really understand what this had to do with all the women . . . and me? "Why did you tell me?" I asked softly, hoping that didn't sound rude.

He only gave me a warm smile though. "I want you to under-stand." He looked down and quietly said, "Can you imagine, grow-ing up in a home filled with such loathing?" He looked back up at me with a sad smile and ran a finger down my cheek again. "No, I'd imagine you were surrounded by love. . . ."

Not being able to stand his painful smile, I leaned in and kissed him. He lovingly smiled back at me, and then stood up straight and took my hand. "Come on." He nodded toward the railing and we started walking along it, looking out over more of the beautiful city. My eyes were mainly on his, though, as he blankly stared out the windows. He was obviously still in thought. There was more he wanted to tell me.

After a few silent paces, he finally did. "I was quiet as a child. I kept to myself. I had no real friends to speak of." He smiled wryly. "I had my guitar—that was my closest relationship." He shook his head and laughed once. "God, I was pathetic."

I squeezed his hand and stopped walking, grabbing his cheek with my other to make him look at me. "Kellan you were not—"

"No, I was, Kiera," he interrupted, kissing my hand after remov-ing it from his cheek. Starting to walk again, he said, "Let me clar-ify . . . I was pathetically lonely." He smiled down on me as I frowned. "And then . . . quite by accident on my part, I assure you"—he looked thoughtfully out the windows, now almost completely showing a view of the dark Sound—"I discovered something that made me feel, for the first time ever . . . wanted, cared for . . . almost . . . loved." He said the last part quietly.

"Sex?" I whispered.

"Hmmm . . ." He nodded in agreement. "Sex. I was young that first time"—he grinned and shook his head—"which you've prob-ably already pieced together." I blushed a little at that remembered conversation on his bed. "Probably way too young, but I didn't know it wasn't . . . okay. It just felt like someone finally cared. I started . . ." He looked away from me. "I started repeating that feeling as often as I could. Even back then, it was shockingly easy for me. There was always someone, and I didn't care who, who would want to be with me. I kind of got obsessed with it . . . with feeling that connection. Who knows, maybe I still—"

He stopped walking and looked back at me, a worried expression suddenly on his face. "Do you think less of me?"

I didn't see how he could be blamed for seeking out any kind of love, living the life forced upon him. I put my hand on his arm. "Kellan, I couldn't possibly think any less of you."

He laughed and I realized how bad that statement sounded. I looked away, embarrassed. "You know what I mean."

He laughed softly. "You really are truly adorable."

"How old were you?" I asked, mainly to cover my embarrassment.

He sighed and then admitted, "I was twelve. In her defense, I told her I was fourteen. She bought that. I don't think she really cared though."

I looked back at him, my mouth open again. I forced myself to shut it and smile at him. The thought of how desperately he must have wanted some tenderness brought tears to my eyes. He searched my face, a slight crease of worry on his perfect brow. Needing to comfort him, I leaned over and tenderly gave him a brief kiss. He smiled and relaxed, gazing at me for a few quiet minutes.

"So, you use women to feel . . . love?" I asked quietly.

He looked down, embarrassed again. "I didn't realize it at the time. I really didn't even think about it, until you. I couldn't figure out why you were so different to me. I know now that it's not right. . . ." He looked back up at me. "But it was something. It made me feel less . . . lonely." I felt another of my tears drop at that, and he brushed it away. "Anyway . . . what no one seems to consider is the fact that they use me too. They don't care about me." We started walking again and he looked out over the sparkling city, showing itself again on the other side of the water.

I searched his thoughtful face and couldn't help the wave of guilt that I had also, at one point, used him. But surely, not every encounter he'd had had been an empty one. "You've never been in love?" I asked timidly.

He looked back at me with a half-smile that doubled my heartbeat. "Until you . . . no. And no one has loved me either."

Continuing to watch him as we walked in silence, I tried to see how this impossibly gorgeous man in front of me could never have felt real love. That made no sense. Surely, this beautiful, talented, funny, seductive, and just . . . amazing . . . man had known love before.

"Surely, some girl—"

"No," he cut me off. "Just sex . . . never love."

"A high school sweetheart?"

"No. I tended to . . . associate . . . with older women. They weren't really looking for . . . love." He smiled wryly, and I wasn't sure I wanted to know what he meant by that.

"Some . . . naïve waitress?"

He smiled at me. "Again, before you . . . no, no one who cared for me."

"Oh . . . well, one of your fans then," I said meekly. I knew from experience just how much he had been "loved" by them.

He laughed genuinely. "Definitely no, that is the fakest sex of them all. They could care less who I actually am. They're not even with me, when they're . . . with me. They're with this rock-star image that they have of me, but that's not . . . that's not who I am. Well, it's not all I am."

I smiled and kissed him softly on his jaw. No, he was so much more. . . .

Pulling back, I hesitantly asked, "Roommates?" I also knew full well that I wasn't the only one he'd bedded. I wasn't sure if I wanted to hear about him and . . . Joey, but I was curious.

He looked over at me with the corner of his eye and smiled sheepishly. "I really wish Griffin hadn't mentioned that one. You must have thought I was horrible. Sometimes I don't know why you ever touched me at all." I frowned and tried to shake my head, but he sighed and started explaining. "No, there was never anything between Joey and me but sex." He looked up, like he was trying to think of how to put it for me. "Joey . . . liked being worshipped. When it was clear to her that her body wasn't my only . . . temple . . . well, she was also overly dramatic." He grimaced and shrugged. "She ran off in a huff, with boy-toy number . . . three, I think."

He stopped walking again and turned to look at me, grabbing both of my hands in his. "I know I've overdone it with women, but I've never felt for anyone what I feel for you. And I've never felt from anyone what I am feeling from you now," he whispered.

I swallowed the emotion in my throat and kissed him softly again. Pulling back, I gazed into his love-filled eyes. "So, Denny and me . . . our relationship?" I asked, starting to get lost in his amazing blue depths.

"Right . . . that." We continued walking along the circular railing and he lightly swung my hand, as he regained his original train of thought. "Well, I guess at first I was just intrigued by it. I'd never seen anything like that. So warm and tender and . . . real. And the fact that you moved across the country to be with this guy . . . I can't think of anyone who would do that for me. The people that I know don't have relationships like that, and my parents certainly never . . ."

"Right . . ." I said, watching his face momentarily darken.

He bit his lip and looked out the windows. "Living with you, watching you with Denny, day after day . . . I started to want what the two of you had. I stopped"—he looked over at me and grinned—"as you put it, whoring." I smiled and he laughed, then frowned. "But unfortunately, I started to care for you. I didn't understand it at first. I just knew it was wrong to think about you like that. You were clearly Denny's. People's relationships haven't always . . . mattered to me, but Denny means a lot to me. That year he stayed with us . . . that was the best year of my life." He smiled warmly at me and whispered, "Well, maybe until this year."

I smiled back at him and kissed him on the corner of his jaw. It gave me a small thrill of delight. It was so wonderful to be able to kiss him freely, whenever I wanted to. I squeezed his hand and cuddled into his side as I looked out over the skyline.

"When I fell in love with you . . . it was like nothing I'd ever known before. It was nearly instant. I think I started falling for you the moment you shook my hand." He chuckled at the memory and playfully nudged my shoulder while I blushed. "It was so powerful. I knew it was wrong, but it was addicting." He stopped walking and spun me out away from him, then quickly drew me back in, slipping his arms around my waist and holding me tight. "You are so addicting to me." He kissed me softly.

He smiled at me, his eyes filled with love. "Sometimes, it felt like you cared for me too, and then everything in the world was perfect." He frowned. "But most of the time, you wanted him, and a part of me wanted to die." He paused, watching my startled reaction to that. "I tried so hard to stay away from you, but I kept making excuses to touch you, to hold you," he smiled coyly and looked away, "to nearly kiss you while watching porn. God, you have no idea how difficult that was to turn away from you."

I giggled in remembered embarrassment.

He closed his eyes and shook his head. "That first time, I held you for hours afterwards . . . just feeling your warmth, your breath on my skin." He opened his eyes and looked at my again-startled face. "You said my name once while you slept. That made me feel . . . well, it was almost as good as the sex." He grinned devilishly and I laughed, feeling my face heat.

He sighed and looked away from me. "I wish I had been strong enough to stay . . . but I wasn't. I chickened out. I couldn't tell you what I had just figured out." He looked back to me with wistful eyes. "That I desperately loved you."

I curled my fingers through the back of his hair, wishing I had something profound to say. "Kellan . . . I . . ."

He continued, not letting me finish the thought that I didn't have anyway. "I wanted to leave when you went back to him. After having you . . . it was so hard to watch you with him. To watch you love him how I wanted you to love me. It made me so angry. I'm so sorry."

I felt my eyes water as I remembered that time, and hugged him tight against me. I hadn't known. I had assumed I was just another conquest to him. I had hurt him . . . deeply. "I'm the one who's sorry, Kellan. . . ." My voice trailed off.

He sighed and, smiling, looked down. "And then, when I finally got the strength to leave . . . you asked me to stay, and I got my hopes up. I started to believe that maybe . . . at the very least, you cared for me." He looked at me crookedly for a second. "You seemed to really want me to stay."

My face heated in embarrassment at just how "badly" I had wanted him to stay. He smiled at my reaction and then his face smoothed into seriousness. "You probably didn't hear me, but I told you I loved you that night. I couldn't seem to stop it from slipping out."

"Kellan, I—"

He interrupted me. "Then you cried for Denny, and I wanted to die again." I felt more tears drip down my cheeks at hurting him, yet again. He watched my tears thoughtfully. "That night was so . . . intense for me. I wanted so badly to hold you after, but you were so upset . . . you looked ill." He swallowed a lump in his throat. "I made you feel ill. You hated what we had done, and it had meant so much to me." He peered at me from the corner of his eye, as he nearly looked away. "I hated you after that," he whispered.

More tears fell on my cheeks, and I sniffled a bit. He sighed and fully looked away. "I almost left that night. I wanted to. . . ." He turned to look back at me, and softly grabbed my cheeks with his hands. His expression softened and his eyes gazed into mine adoringly. I felt my tears dry, as I watched his perfect face stare at me. "I couldn't leave you. I remembered the look on your face when I told you I was leaving. No one's looked at me that way before. No one's ever cried for me before. No one's asked me to stay before . . . no one. I convinced myself that you cared for me." He shook his head and smiled. "I knew then that I would stay with you . . . even if it killed me."

He pulled me to him for a deep kiss. I eagerly kissed him back, wanting to make up for hurting him, in some small way. When I was nearly breathless, he pulled away. Grabbing my hand, he started walking again.

He looked over to me as we walked stories above the peaceful-looking city below. "I am sorry about being so . . . amorous with you. I never wanted to hurt you. I simply . . . wanted you." He smiled crookedly at me, making me miss a step. He laughed softly and continued. "When you asked, I did try to keep it . . . well, you had to know on some level that we were never innocent, right?" He looked over at me with an eyebrow raised, and I grudgingly nodded. He smiled. "Well, I tried to keep it less . . . sinful . . . then."

He glared down at me. "You made that shockingly hard to do."

"Me?" I asked, confused. He was the absurdly sensual one.

Kellan shook his head in mock exasperation. "Yes, you. If you weren't dressed provocatively, or throwing yourself at me provocatively, or"—he grinned at me indecently—"making very provocative noises . . ." I blushed and he laughed. "If you weren't doing all that, then you were simply just too adorable to resist." He glared at me again. "I am only a man after all."

I shook my head at him. I hadn't done any of those things . . . well, except for the unfortunate-noises part. "You're absurd, Kellan." I rolled my eyes and he laughed charmingly.

"Again . . . you don't realize how attractive you are to me." He grinned mischievously. "After all this time, I would think that was painfully obvious," he murmured, and I playfully elbowed him. He laughed, then more seriously said, "I am sorry I took it too far." I looked up into his suddenly sad-again eyes as we continued walking. "I should have let you end it. You were right to stop it. Everything that happened later was my fault. I should have let you go. I just, couldn't. . . ."

"Kellan, no it—"

He interrupted me again. "The club, that was . . . intense. I wanted you so bad, and you wanted me, too. I considered pulling you into a bathroom and taking you right there. I think you might have even let me?" He looked down at me, and I could only nod speechlessly;

he could have taken me anywhere. He started to smile, but frowned instead. "I saw Denny coming. I couldn't do it. I pushed you away, praying desperately that you would tell him you wanted me. That you would choose to leave with me. You . . . didn't, and it killed me."

I stopped walking again and he took a step, then slowly turned to look back at me. He looked hurt again. I stepped up to him and put a hand on his cheek. How badly had I repeatedly hurt him? I felt horrible inside.

He gazed at me, lost in the memory. "I couldn't even come home. I took your sister to Griffin's. I think I bored her. I wasn't much fun, moping on the couch all night like I did. Eventually, she gave up on me and turned her attention to Griffin." He shrugged. "And, well, you know how that ended."

I swallowed roughly. I had assumed so much that was not true about that night.

"I was . . . I *am* really freaked out about what happened . . . in the car," he said quietly. "What I said. What I did. I didn't know you thought I slept with Anna until that moment, and I was so angry at you for . . . Denny, I let you believe it. I . . . embellished it." He looked down, embarrassed. "Being angry with you almost made me want you even more."

I had to swallow three times before I could speak. "Kellan . . . you have no idea how difficult that was for me. How hard that was to ask you to stop, when my whole body was begging for you not to." I stroked his cheek and considered kissing him. He swallowed roughly.

"You have no idea how hard it was to stop myself. I wasn't lying, about what I had been thinking." I swallowed nosily at the look on his face, and remembered what he had crassly said to me. He intensely watched my face. "Do you think less of me now?"

Stubbornly, I shook my head and he sighed and looked away. "I'm so sorry I yelled at you, Kiera." His eyes glistened as he faced me again, and I ran my hand back through his hair.

Swallowing loudly, I found my voice again. "I know you are sorry . . . I remember."

"Ah, yes, me sobbing like a baby . . . not my finest hour." He tried to look away again, but I brought my hand back to his cheek and made him look at me.

"I disagree. If you hadn't, if I hadn't seen that remorse, I probably would never have spoken to you again."

"It wasn't just remorse. True, I felt horrible for speaking to you like that . . . but mostly, I was sure that I had just completely severed the only loving relationship I've ever had. I knew I'd lost you. I knew you were completely Denny's then. I saw it in your eyes, and I knew I'd never have a chance with you—none." A tear did finally escape his eye then, and I brushed it aside with my thumb. "I never expected you to . . . comfort . . . me. No one's ever done that . . . ever. You don't know how much that meant to me."

He swallowed roughly again, and again I thought to kiss him, but he pulled back a little and stared at me intently. "I was so scared to be near you after that. I allowed myself one last goodbye with you in the kitchen, but I didn't want to touch you anymore." He scanned my eyes, like he was searching for forgiveness in them. "I'm sorry that I hurt you, but I needed to be distracted from you, to make sure I never took things so far again." He pulled my hand off his cheek and looked away, out over the city again. The lights sparkled in his still overly moist eyes. "I'm so sorry about all the women, Kiera. I never should have hurt you like that. I didn't want to. . . . Well, maybe a part of me did. I just—"

I interrupted him. "You don't . . . you already apologized for that, Kellan."

"I know." He looked back to me, another tear threatening to spill. "I just really feel like I messed up. But you didn't want me, not in the same way that I wanted you . . . and I couldn't bring myself to leave you anymore. I did the only thing I knew, that I've ever known, for blocking out the pain." He shook his head remorsefully, and the tear fell down his cheek. "To feel . . . wanted," he whispered.

"Women," I stated, watching pain flash through his features.

"Yeah." His face looked bleak and desolate, like he had just confessed to multiple murders rather than to being a single guy who slept around with perfectly willing women.

"Lots and lots of women." I added a note of sarcasm, hoping to lighten his mood.

"Yeah . . . I'm sorry." He did fractionally raise his lips in a smile.

"It's okay. Well, it's not okay, you still shouldn't use people . . . but I think I understand."

He looked up at me from under his eyebrows, an adorable expression of hope on his face. I couldn't resist anymore. I leaned up and kissed him for a moment.

"So . . . ?" he asked, pulling away all too soon.

"What?" I asked, confused and mildly irritated. I wasn't done kissing him. I didn't think I'd ever be done kissing him.

He half-smiled in a charming way. "Was I right? Did you use me?"

"Kellan . . ." Guilt flashed through me, and I looked away.

His smile left him and he very seriously said, "It's okay if you did, Kiera. I just . . . I would like to know."

I sighed. "I have always felt . . . something for you, but . . . yes, the first time I did use you, and I'm so sorry, that was incredibly wrong of me. If I'd have known that you loved me, I never would have—"

"It's okay, Kiera."

"No, it's not," I whispered, and then softly added, "The second time, I didn't. That had nothing to do with Denny. That was about us. That was real. Every touch after that was real."

"That's surprisingly good to hear," he whispered, not looking at me, but smiling softly, and then suddenly he frowned. "You should be with Denny . . . not me. He's a good man."

"You're a good man too," I said, searching his perfect but still frowning face.

He shook his head, and I ran my fingers through his hair and sighed. "Don't let our relationship make you think that you're a bad person. You and I are . . . complicated."

"Complicated . . ." he repeated, cupping my cheek and running his thumb along my cheekbone. "I suppose we are." He dropped his hand. "That's my fault—"

"Don't, Kellan. I'm just as culpable as you. I've made mistakes—"

"But" he started to interrupt.

"No, we both messed this up, Kellan. It takes two to . . . you know. I wanted you just as badly as you wanted me. I needed you as much. I wanted to be near you just as much. I wanted to touch you as much. I care for you. . . ." I couldn't quite finish that thought, and I let it hang in the air between us, unfinished.

Tears welled in his eyes again. "I've never been very clear with you. Maybe, if I had just told you that I loved you from the beginning? I'm so sorry, Kiera. I hurt you so many times. There's so much I wish I could take back. I—"

I stopped him with a deep kiss. I understood better now. It still hurt, but I could see just how badly I had hurt him as well. He did the only thing he knew how to do to cope with his pain. Right or wrong, it was all he knew. He brought his hand to my cheek again and returned my kiss just as deeply, both of us forgetting, for a moment, our emotional conversation.

After an eternity that was entirely too short, he pulled back and quietly said, "We should get going."

"Wait, you brought me all the way up to this highly romantic . . . vacant . . . spot, and all you wanted to do was talk?" I raised an eyebrow at him suggestively.

He grinned and shook his head. "My, my—look how I've corrupted you."

I smirked and laughed.

"Come on, I'll take us home." He started leading me to the elevators while I pouted. Noticing my expression, he said, "Kiera, it's getting late . . . well, early, and you don't want to be late from your ball." He frowned as he looked at me. "It's not your carriage that will turn into a pumpkin."

I rolled my eyes at his analogy, but he was right, I did need to get home. I pushed aside my disappointment, and my surprise that I actually was disappointed. I had kind of expected . . . I blushed, and didn't bother finishing that thought.

We finished our circular walk back to the elevators, and I took one last look at the spectacular city below us and the spectacular man before me. I smiled as he pushed the button and we waited for the doors to open.

"Fine. Your loss, though." I pulled him through the now-open elevator door by his T-shirt. "I've been told that we're amazing," I teased. He grinned wickedly and pulled me in for a deep kiss, as the doors closed behind us and we descended.

On our way out of the Needle, he looked over to me with a somber expression. I looked back at him curiously, and butterflies tickled my stomach. He stopped as we stepped up to his car and cocked his head to the side as he regarded me.

"There is one more thing I wanted to talk to you about."

The butterflies tickling my stomach were doing somersaults now. "What?" The word was barely more than a whisper.

Abruptly, his grim expression changed to a wry grin and a cocked eyebrow. "I can't believe you stole my car . . . really?"

I laughed at my remembered joyride—then I remembered why I had taken it, and gave him a sour face. "You kind of deserved it at the time." I poked him in the chest. "You're lucky it came back to you in one piece."

He frowned as he opened my door. "Hmmmm . . . in the future, could you just slap me again, and leave my baby alone?"

I grabbed his chin as I put my foot in the car. "In the future, could you not go on anymore 'dates'?"

His look was somber again, until he grinned and lightly kissed me. "Yes, ma'am." He shook his head at me as I sat down. I smiled to myself as he closed the door and walked around to his side of the car.

I snuggled into his shoulder as we silently drove home. The comfort of our silence was as palpable to me as the warmth of his skin as he held my hand in his. It was only now, freely touching him, freely giving myself over to him, that I could fully comprehend how much I had missed him. How severe my addiction had been. I smiled inwardly at the memory of him saying that I was his addiction. It pleased me tremendously that we felt the same draw toward each other. Although I still didn't see what he saw in me.

Even after we pulled into the driveway and he turned the engine off, we stayed locked together in the car, my head on his shoulder, and his arm around my waist, pulling me in tight. Neither one of us wanted to face the cold reality of life outside this cozy vehicle.

Kissing my head, Kellan broke our comfortable silence. "I dream about you sometimes . . . about what it would have been like if Denny hadn't come back, if you were mine. Holding your hand, walking into the bar with you on my arm . . . not having to hide anything anymore. Telling the world that I love you."

I smiled and looked up at him. "You mentioned that you dreamed about me once. You never said about what though." I kissed his cheek and smiled warmly at him. "I dream about you too sometimes." I immediately blushed, remembering some of my steamier dreams of him.

"Really? Huh, we're kind of pathetic, aren't we?" He laughed, then, noticing my blush, he half-smiled adorably at me. "And what are your dreams about?"

I giggled like an idiot. "Honestly, I mostly dream about sleeping with you."

He laughed for a good minute, while I blushed and laughed with him. "God . . . is that all I am to you?" he teased, grabbing my hand and lacing our fingers together.

I stopped laughing and gazed at him. "No . . . no, you're so much more." My tone got serious on me.

He nodded, not laughing anymore as well. "Good, because you mean everything to me."

Feelings for him flooded through me, and I snuggled closer and clutched his hand tightly in mine. I never wanted to leave this car.

I never wanted Kellan to leave this car. But I knew we couldn't stay like this forever.

Kellan broke through my thoughts, with a question I didn't want him to ask. "What did you tell Denny?"

I cringed a bit, knowing my lie probably wasn't as good as what he would have come up with. And the thought of him being the better liar didn't entirely thrill me. "That you slept with my sister and broke her heart. That's believable. Everyone saw you at the bar together. Denny seemed to buy it."

Kellan was looking at me with his brow furrowed. "That won't work, Kiera," he said slowly.

My heart rate started increasing. "Yes, it will. I'll talk to Anna; she'll back me up. I've had to lie for her before. I won't tell her why, of course . . . and Denny probably will never ask her about it anyway."

His brow still furrowed, he shook his head. "I wasn't thinking of your sister. That's not why that won't work."

I looked at him, confused, until a sudden realization hit me. "Oh God . . . Griffin."

His brow furrowed more and he nodded. "Yeah . . . Griffin. He really does tell everyone." His brow relaxed and he looked at me amused. "I don't know how you managed to miss that. You've gotten good at tuning him out." His amusement didn't last long, and he frowned. "When Denny hears that it isn't true . . ."

"What was I supposed to tell him, Kellan? I had to come up with something." I looked down at my hands. "You know, it's possible that you both—"

"No." I looked back up to where he was smiling warmly at me. "It's not possible." His frown returned. "Griffin is very . . . specific . . . about what he tells people. It's not just that he slept with her. It's that he slept with her, and I didn't, like he stole her away from me or something. He's got this weird competitive thing—"

I cut him off. "I've noticed that." I sighed and laid my head back on the seat. "God, I didn't even think about that."

Kellan sighed. "I can't guarantee you anything, but I could try talk-

ing to Griffin. Maybe get him to alter the story. I'll probably have to
threaten to kick him out of the band. Actually, I may just do that anyway."

"No!" I exclaimed, a little loudly, and I slapped a hand over my
mouth and looked fearfully at the door.

Kellan looked at me oddly. "You want me to keep him in the
band?"

I looked at him wryly, a faint smile coming to my lips, until I remembered my real objection. "No, I don't want him to know—ever!
He won't stay silent about that. He'd tell everyone, in horrifying detail. He'd tell Denny! Please, don't ever—"

"Okay." He put his hands on my shoulders as I was starting to
panic. "It's okay. I won't tell him anything, Kiera." I breathed out in
relief and he sighed again. "It wouldn't matter, anyway. He's told too
many people already." He looked at me sadly as he brushed a lock of
hair behind my ear. "I'm sorry, but Denny will find out that you lied
to him . . . and then he'll start to wonder why."

I gazed up at him, swallowing roughly. "And then what? After he
knows I lied, how long do you think we have?" I asked quietly.

"How long before Denny figures out that we've slept together?"
He grabbed my hand and interlaced our fingers. "Well, if you stay out
here with me all night, he'll probably have it figured out by morning."
He chuckled and rested his cheek against my head. Sighing, he said,
"I don't know, Kiera. A few hours, maybe? A couple of days at the
most."

I pulled back and looked up at him, alarmed. "Hours? But . . . he
has no real proof. He couldn't possibly think . . ."

"Kiera . . ." He released my hand and stroked my cheek. "He has
all the proof he needs, right here." He brushed a lock of hair behind
my ear again.

"What do we do, Kellan?" I whispered, suddenly afraid that
Denny could somehow hear us, all the way out here in the car.

He looked at me thoughtfully for a moment. "I can start the car,
and we can be in Oregon before the sun comes up."

Run away? He wants to run away with me? My insides tightened. I could imagine it—running off into the night with him and never looking back. Giving up school, work, friends, everything . . . everything but leaving Denny. A sharp pain wrenched through me, and I thought I might get sick, right there in the car. The thought of never seeing him again, of never seeing those warm, brown eyes sparkling at me . . .

"Hey." Kellan's hand stroked my hair. "Breathe, Kiera, it's okay. . . . Breathe." He cupped my cheek as I struggled to do what he asked. "Look at me. Breathe."

I stared into his deep blue eyes and focused only on my breathing. I hadn't realized I was starting to hyperventilate. I shook my head as tears started to fall. "Not like that. He's too much a part of me. I need time. I can't talk about this yet." He nodded, and his eyes started to glisten. "I'm so sorry, Kellan."

"Don't be . . ." he whispered. "Don't be sorry for loving someone." He pulled me into his shoulder and kissed the top of my head. "Don't worry, Kiera. I'll think of something. I'll fix this, I promise."

Chapter 21
I Love You

He held me in his arms in his chilly car, our breath making small clouds of steam, but neither of us was willing to leave the safety and solitude of that vehicle. Eventually the first morning rays did poke through the sky. There was a fog in the air that hovered just above the pavement, making the entire world seem ethereal and dreamlike. I wanted this moment to be a dream, one I would never have to wake up from, but those golden morning rays brought more than just light to my world, they brought reality as well.

"You should go inside," he whispered, hugging me tight.

I pulled back and looked at him. "What about you? Aren't you coming?" I tried to keep the panic from my voice when I said that.

He looked at me calmly. "There's something I need to do first."

"What?"

He smiled but didn't answer my question. "Go on . . . it will be okay." He placed a soft kiss on my lips and then leaned way over me to unlatch the door. As I got out, he whispered, "I love you," then he slid over to my side and tilted his head up, wanting me to kiss him again.

I nodded and bent down to press my lips to his, unable to speak through the lump in my throat. Then he slid back over, started the car, and pulled away. I brushed a couple of tears off my cheeks.

Denny was sound asleep when I came into our room. Guilt

flooded through me as I grabbed a change of clothes and quietly went to the bathroom to freshen up. I glanced at Kellan's door as I finished, and had an odd desire to lie on his bed. I didn't. That would be a little unexplainable if Denny woke up and found me there. I made my way downstairs to make some coffee and sat at the table, processing everything that had happened in the past several hours. What a difference one day can make. I sipped my coffee and stared at the empty chair where Kellan usually sat. Where was he? Why wouldn't he want to spend today with me?

Denny tenderly kissed me goodbye when he came down a while later, all ready for his normal day of work. Guilt washed through me again as his lips brushed mine. I had an odd feeling of betrayal flash through me, and not betrayal for being with Kellan, no, betrayal for being with Denny. I'd felt guilty before, but nothing quite as strong as pure betrayal. It took me by surprise, but I firmly pushed it back. I couldn't think about that yet. For right now, Denny was my boy-friend, but, I supposed . . . Kellan was too.

What do I do? This decision suddenly overwhelmed my now simple-seeming question of where to spend winter break. Couldn't I just go back to worrying about that instead?

I lay down on the couch to ponder it . . . and didn't wake up until it was time to catch the bus for work. Oops, so much for school today. I needed to be more careful, or I was going to lose my precious scholarship. Luckily, I was still very good at schoolwork, even if I was slacking off on attendance.

Jenny pulled me aside as I came into Pete's a while later. "So, you and Kellan . . . ?"

I smiled and wiped away a sudden tear. He hadn't come home in time to give me a ride to work, and I already missed him. "He's in love with me, Jenny . . . deeply in love." To-the-bottom-of-his-soul deep. "I've never felt this for anyone" deep. It was overwhelming to think about.

She hugged me. "I'm glad he told you—you should know the truth. You should make an informed decision."

I pulled back and stared at her, terrified. "What do I do? I love Denny. I can't bear hurting him. I can't bear hurting Kellan either. I don't know what to do."

She sighed and patted my arm. "I can't tell you that, Kiera. You have to figure it out on your own." She looked over at some customers just sitting down in her section and made a step toward them before stopping and looking back at me. "You do have to choose though." She smiled reassuringly and patted my back as she walked away.

Kellan didn't come in that night. He didn't come home that night. That was when worry settled in on me. When that cycle repeated the next night, that was when panic settled in on me. When the cycle repeated yet again the next night, that was when despair settled in on me.

Four achingly long days went by without a trace of him . . .

Every morning, I came downstairs, expecting to find Kellan sitting at the table, looking flawless and drinking his coffee, greeting me with a sexy half-smile and a "Mornin'." But every morning, he wasn't there, and tears filled my eyes at his absence. Before school, I would grab his band's T-shirt (that I still never wore) and hold it tight to me, breathing in his scent, wondering where he was and what he was doing. Every night that I worked, I waited impatiently for the band to stroll in, and every night, Matt and Griffin would walk in, disagreeing about something, but never with Kellan. At night, I would get up after Denny fell asleep and lie on Kellan's empty bed, clutching his pillow.

Panic flared in me. Did he leave? Was that his solution? To just skip town and run away without me? I couldn't even ask the band where he was. I couldn't form the words around them, and they never talked about him . . . not once. I felt empty without him.

Every day, I sank more and more into a depression. I was cooler to Denny. He tried to cheer me up, but it didn't work. He tried to get me to talk to him, but that didn't work either. He tried to kiss me, and I'd turn away after a brief obligatory peck. Eventually my mood seeped into him, and he stopped trying to please me. There was no point to trying anyway. Nothing was going to please me. Denny never directly asked the reason for my mood though . . . not once. It was almost like he was afraid to ask, which was good, because I was afraid of him asking.

It was a dreary Friday morning when I glumly kissed Denny goodbye before work. My kiss was automatic and had no feeling behind it. He looked at me sadly and swallowed. I tensed, waiting for the questioning words that would slice me open.

"Kiera . . . I . . . I love you." He tenderly ran a finger down my cheek, and I could see his eyes glisten. I knew he felt our distance. I felt it too.

"I love you too, Denny," I whispered, begging my eyes to not well up. He leaned in and kissed me tenderly, running his fingers back through my hair.

I brought my hands along his jaw, trying to ignore my disappointment that his had light stubble, and wasn't smooth like Kellan's. I ran my hands through his hair, trying not to care that his was shorter, and I couldn't curl it around my fingers like Kellan's. I intensified our kiss, willing my breath to quicken, willing for his lips, so different from Kellan's, to thrill me, willing our old passion to spark. It didn't.

He pulled away after a moment, his breath as slow and relaxed as mine. "I have to go . . . I'm sorry." His sad eyes watched me for a second, and then he turned and left. I couldn't hold back the few tears that spilt down my cheeks. Was it too late for us?

Kellan had been gone for so long, my need for him was so great, my grief so strong, that it felt like a hole had been punched straight through my stomach. I knew it was wrong. I knew it was choking the life out of Denny's and my relationship. I just didn't know how to stop it. He had just left . . . disappeared. I'd had no time to prepare, no final goodbye . . . no closure. It was killing me.

I sullenly made my way upstairs to the bathroom to get ready for school. My world might have been ending, but life drudgingly continued. I dressed. I brushed my hair. I put on makeup. I did all the things expected of me to look normal for a normal day of school . . .

and I hated every second of it. I wanted to curl up on my bed and sob for hours. Sob over missing Kellan. Sob over what Denny and I had become. I exhaled loudly and swallowed back the threatening tears.

Yes, he was gone. *Deal with it,* I berated myself. He was right to leave. Eventually things will get easier. Maybe Denny will never ask . . . if Kellan never comes back.

I slowly opened the door with that painful thought in my head, and then stopped breathing. Kellan was just climbing up the top step, his eyes on the floor. He looked up when he heard the door and slowly smiled a heart-stopping half-grin. He was spectacular. Nearly a week without seeing him had softened my memory of just how attractive he was. His hair, wavy and wild, was just begging for my fingers to run through it. The enticing way his long-sleeved T-shirt clung to his body was just asking for my fingers to trace every amazing line. His smooth, strong jaw was an open invitation for my lips, and his full lips, curled in a smile, were still keeping my breath at bay. But most amazing of all were his impossibly deep blue eyes, glowing with love and adoration . . . for me.

"Mornin'," he said softly, in his typical greeting.

I ran over to him as he started walking toward me, and threw my arms around him. I buried my head in the crook of his neck and let the tears I had been holding back flow. "I thought you left," I managed between sobs, while he pulled me tight against him. "I thought I'd never see you again."

He rubbed my back while I cried. "I'm sorry, Kiera. I didn't mean to hurt you. I needed . . . to take care of something," he whispered comfortingly.

Pulling back, I smacked him in the chest. "Don't ever do that again!" He smiled and put a hand on my cheek. "Don't leave me like that. . . ." I let the thought trail off as I gazed at his suddenly pained eyes.

"I wouldn't, Kiera. I wouldn't just . . . disappear," he said, stroking my cheek.

Without thinking of the consequences, I blurted out what I had been holding back for so long. "I love you." His eyes watered instantly. He closed them, and twin tears ran down his cheeks. I brushed them away with my fingertips. He probably had never heard anyone say that . . . and truly mean it. And I did. With every part of my soul, I meant it. "I love you . . . so much."

He opened his eyes, more tears falling. "Thank you. You don't know how much I've wanted . . . How long I've waited . . ."

He couldn't finish his thought, as I leaned in and kissed him warmly, tenderly. He immediately returned my soft kiss, bringing his other hand up to cup my other cheek. Still tenderly kissing him, I pulled him gently by his neck into his bedroom. Our lips barely pausing, we undressed each other silently. As I stood naked before him, he pulled back to look at me, his eyes overflowing with warmth and love.

"You are so beautiful," he whispered, running his hand through my hair.

He brought his lips back to my smiling ones and gently eased me down to his bed. We explored each other's bodies in unhurried and unpressured ways, like we'd never been together before. There were no walls between us, no barriers to hold us back. We both finally knew how the other felt. We both knew that, this time, this was about love.

We took our time, our fingers and lips tracing and teasing, and discovering new ways to touch the other. I listened to the sounds he made when I kissed him in the soft spot below his ear, when my fingers moved over the scar along his ribs. The delightful groan he made when my tongue trailed along the deep V of his abdomen. He studied the noises I made as he kissed my collarbone, as he gently tugged at a nipple with his teeth. My cries as he ran his tongue over my sensitive flesh, tasting what he was about to be taking.

When we could both endure no more, he moved over me and slowly adjusted my thigh up his hip. His gaze lingered along my skin, following the lines and curves, followed shortly after by his hand. When his eyes met mine again, they were filled with such love and passion that I had to painfully bite my lip. Not out of desire, although

I surely felt that, too, but to assure myself that this moment was no vivid dream. That this perfection before me was real . . . and mine.

Never taking his glorious eyes from mine, he slid into me, almost painfully slowly. We both closed our eyes, overwhelmed by the magnitude of emotion and sensation at finally being together again. I reopened my eyes first and lightly grabbed his cheek.

"I love you," I whispered.

He opened his eyes to gaze at me again. "I love you so much," he whispered back.

And then we did something that we had never done before, something that maybe Kellan had never done before—we made love. It wasn't a drunken rollick. It wasn't burning passion and hot, fiery need. It was so much more. He clenched my hand the entire time, as we experienced something wondrous and intense together. He whispered how much he loved me, when he could speak through the emotion of it. I whispered it to him, whenever I could. There was no doubt, there was no fear, and there was no guilt. Our hips rocked together and apart in perfect unison, speeding and slowing at the same precise moment, like we were one person and not two. And even though I could tell he was ready before me, he held off his climax until we could come together. When we did, it was glorious and intense and perfect. He cried out my name and I found myself responding with his.

Afterwards, he pulled me to his chest, his whole body shaking. I listened to his heartbeat gently slow in rhythm with mine as a few tears rolled down my cheek. Not tears of guilt this time, but tears of joy for the immense love I felt for him, mixed with tears of sorrow that our time together wouldn't last, that we had only a few more precious moments together. He knew it too. Looking up at his face, I saw the exact same look of joy and sorrow reflected in his glistening eyes.

"I love you," he said quietly.

"I love you too," I said right back, kissing him softly.

He closed his eyes and a tear escaped, trickling down his cheek. I wiped it away. "What are you thinking about?" I asked timidly.

"Nothing," he replied, keeping his eyes closed.

I lifted my head higher to look at him more closely. He opened his eyes and gazed back at me. "I'm trying to not think about anything," he said softly. "It hurts too much when I think. . . ."

I bit my lip and nodded, very sorry that I had even asked. "I love you," I said again.

He nodded sadly. "Just not enough . . . not enough to leave him?"

I closed my eyes and choked back a sob. I had hoped he wouldn't ask me that . . . wouldn't *ever* ask me that. He ran his hand down my hair. "It's okay, Kiera. I shouldn't have said that."

"Kellan, I'm so sorry . . ." I started to say, but he put a finger on my lips.

"Not today." He smiled warmly and pulled me in for a kiss. "Not today . . . okay?"

I nodded, then kissed him back. I pulled away after a moment. "Do you think . . . ? If we had never, that first time . . . would the three of us just be close friends?"

He smiled as he interpreted what I was trying to say. "If you and I had never gotten drunk and had sex, would we all be living happily ever after right now?" I nodded and he thought for a second, tucking a lock of hair behind my ear. "No . . . you and I were always more than just friends. " He stroked my cheek lovingly with his thumb. "One way or another, we would have ended up right here anyway."

I nodded and looked down at his chest beneath me. He stroked my arm for a while, watching me, and then softly asked, "Do you regret it?"

I looked back up at his pained eyes. "I regret being horrible to Denny." He nodded and looked away from me. I gently placed a hand on his cheek and forced him to look at me again. "I don't regret a single second that I spent with you." I smiled wryly at him. "No time spent with you is wasted." He smiled at his line repeated back to him and pulled me in for a kiss that quickly became deeper and deeper.

I didn't go to school that day. I didn't leave his bed that day. I couldn't—there was nowhere else I needed to be.

Kellan said goodbye to me an hour before Denny was to be home from work. My eyes instantly watered, and he cupped both of my cheeks in his hands and kissed my eyelids.

"I'll be at Pete's tonight. I'll see you there, okay?"

I nodded wordlessly, and he gave me a final tender kiss before walking out the door. My heart ached as I watched him leave. Our afternoon together had been . . . beyond words. My heart was more torn than ever. Jenny's words came back to me: "*You should pick one. You can't keep them both.*" I just didn't know how to let either one go.

Denny came home a bit earlier than usual, looking very tired. He came over to where I was sitting on the couch, staring blankly at a show on TV. He sat down beside me and I looked over to his sad, beautiful face. I instantly felt a wave of guilt. It overcame me, and I broke down in sobs.

He put his arms around me. "Come here." He lay down on the couch with me sideways, facing each other, his arms around me, clutching me tight. My head on his chest, my hands clutching his shirt, I sobbed until I could barely breathe. "It's okay, Kiera. Whatever it is, it's okay." His voice was shaky, his accent thick with emotion, and I knew he was close to tears. He choked as he whispered, "Baby . . . you're my heart." My sobs gained in strength. I knew I was hurting him, but I couldn't stop, the tears were relentless.

Eventually they subsided, and I felt the pull of slumber as he held me close and rubbed my back. He pulled away and stared at my half-open, tired eyes. "Kiera . . . ?" Panic and fear sent my eyes flying wide open. Was this it? Was he finally going to ask me about Kellan? I couldn't speak to answer him.

"Do you . . . ?" He closed his mouth for a second and looked away. Looking pained, he started again. "Do you . . . want a ride to work? You're going to be late." He looked back at me and I visibly relaxed.

I still couldn't speak. I only nodded.

"Okay." He stood up and held out his hand. "Let's go then."

We were silent on the ride over. Denny didn't ask me about
my breakdown, and I didn't volunteer any information. There was
nothing I could share with him anyway. There were so many secrets
between us now, it was hard remembering a time when things had
been simple and easy, when it had felt like pure puppy love. I suppose
all love eventually comes back down to earth.

Denny decided to stay for a while at the bar. He kept looking
over at me, like he was expecting me to lose it again. My reaction
earlier had brought out the caretaker in him, and I quickly realized
that he was going to watch over me all night . . . while Kellan was
here. I sighed as I went about my duties. I should have swallowed
back my grief. I shouldn't have let Denny see that. He didn't need
to, and I couldn't explain why I had completely broken down. It was
cruel to him, to keep him in the dark. And I had been cruel enough
to him while Kellan was away—constantly pushing him back from
me, constantly withdrawing into my hard shell of loneliness.

Kellan came in a bit before his band, and Denny met him at the
door. Kellan smoothly gave him a guy hug, and they seemed to casually chat on their way to the guy's usual table. But I caught a glimpse
Kellan directed at me, when Denny turned his head to check out a
loud sound on the other side of the bar. The look of wistful passion in
Kellan's eyes in that one brief glance almost had me running across
the room to throw myself in his arms. I didn't, though. I had at least
enough willpower to not do that.

Once there, they sat next to each other, bent over in what looked
to be a serious conversation. My heart sped a little at what they might
be talking about. Then Kellan nodded and Denny clapped a hand on
his shoulder. I understood. Denny was talking to him about my sister. My heart warmed as I thought of that. Kellan hadn't touched my
sister. He had been faithful to me. Well, okay, he hadn't exactly been
faithful, he *had* done about half of Seattle while he was "getting over
me," but she was the one he had promised me about . . . and he had
kept that promise . . . and it warmed my heart.

It was a little surprising to watch the two of them converse throughout the night. Not just that Kellan could be so carefree with the man whose girlfriend he had just bedded . . . repeatedly. No, it was that their friendship didn't seem to suffer one tiny bit after the fight Kellan and I had had—the slap incident. I was sure Denny had chided him about it, and I was equally sure that Kellan had taken it stoically and completely backed up my story. But neither one seemed to let the incident interfere with their easy friendship. I swallowed, knowing that my choice, the one Jenny was correct in telling me I had to make, most definitely would affect their friendship. I would be the one to break them apart. That thought killed me a little.

The rest of the band finally did show up and Kellan quite skillfully kept Griffin away from Denny for the remainder of the evening. The two friends drank their beers, played some pool, and chatted with Matt. Evan seemed a little uncomfortable about the whole thing and mainly spent the night flirting with a group of nearby fans. Kellan and Denny kept up their night of bonding until, eventually, the guys went onstage to play.

For the remainder of my shift, I endured wistful glances from Kellan and concerned glances from Denny, who apparently still thought I was going to break down again. Did I still look sad? Denny stayed until the final moment of my shift, and dutifully gave me a ride home. Kellan was still there, chatting (a little animatedly) with Jenny, when Denny and I left. I hoped she was being nice to him.

I thought about Kellan's wistful, passionate glances all the way up the stairs. I thought about his warm hands as I got undressed. I thought about his hard body as I put my pajamas on. I thought about his intoxicating smell as I brushed my teeth. I thought about his insanely wonderful hair, and how amazing it felt wrapped in my fingers, as I slipped under the covers with Denny. But what kept me awake, and in a state of anxious longing, were his lips, repeating over and over that he loved me.

I stayed in my room much longer than most women in my position would have—well, that's what I convinced myself of, anyway—but eventually, the draw of my addiction was too strong and I slipped out of my bed. Denny didn't move. He was sound asleep as I quietly shut our door. I opened Kellan's, and he sat up on his elbows at the sound. Moonlight filtered through his window and I could see his perfect face watching me curiously. No trace of exhaustion was in his liquid blue eyes. He hadn't been able to sleep either.

That thought thrilled me, emboldened me. I slid into his bed and under his covers, and immediately wrapped my legs around his. Lacing my arms around his neck, I threw all of my body weight on his chest, knocking him back down to the pillows.

"Am I dreaming?" he whispered, before my lips lowered to his. He ran his hands up my back and tangled his fingers in my hair. He pulled me into him even tighter, deepening our kiss. "I missed you," he muttered around my lips.

"I missed you too . . ." I muttered back, "so much."

I kissed him for as long as I could before my breath started to increase too much, and then I pulled away. I stripped off my tank top and he eyed me, running a hand gently down my chest. With a heavy, reluctant sigh, he said, "What are you doing, Kiera?"

I pressed myself against him and kissed his neck softly in answer. He glanced up at the door. "Kiera, Denny is right—"

"I love you," I interrupted him, "and I missed you. Make love to me." I gazed lovingly at his impossibly glorious face, then pulled off the rest of my clothes.

"Kiera . . ."

I kissed him again and pressed my naked body against the entire length of his. He groaned softly, and eagerly returned my affections. I ran my hands down the length of his incredible body and started to tug at his boxers.

"I love you. . . . Make love to me," I whispered again in his ear.

His breath quicker, passion in his eyes, he glanced back at the door again and then at me. "Are you sur—"

"I'm sure," I interrupted breathlessly, and then kissed him hungrily.

Our kiss was deepening when he abruptly pulled away from my lips. "Wait . . ." He looked at me wistfully. "I can't."

Surprised, I said, "Oh . . . well, I can . . ." I timidly ran my hand down inside his shorts. He felt fine to me . . . more than fine actually.

"Ah," he groaned, "you're killing me, Kiera." He pulled my hand away and quietly laughed once. "That's not what I meant. I can . . . obviously, but"—he looked at me intently—"I don't think we should."

"But, this afternoon? That was . . . Didn't you . . . ? I . . . Don't you want me?" I asked, confused, and a little hurt.

"Of course, of course I do." He eyed me, looked down at himself pointedly, and then looked back to me. "You should know that." I blushed as he continued. "This afternoon was the most . . . I've never had anything like that. I didn't even know it could be like that, which, for me, is saying a lot." He grinned sheepishly and I smiled at him.

"Don't you want that again?" I asked stroking his cheek.

"More than anything," he whispered huskily.

"Then take me. . . ." I kissed him breathlessly.

He groaned softly. "God, Kiera. Why do you make everything so . . . ?"

"Hard?" I whispered, then blushed again, as he laughed quietly. "I love you, Kellan. I feel like time is slipping away from us." I searched his eyes. "I don't want to miss a minute."

He sighed softly and I smiled, knowing I had just won. "For the record, this is a really bad idea. . . ." I smiled wider and kissed him as he rolled over on top of me. "You will be the death of me," he muttered, as I finally pulled off his shorts.

Making love to Kellan soundlessly was extremely difficult. It involved a lot of skin clutching—actually, we clutched each other so hard, I was pretty sure we'd both have bruises—and well-timed deep kisses, holding our mouths together to contain the intensity of it. At one point, near the end, Kellan had to clamp his hand over my mouth. The slowness and restraint required in our conscious attempt at quietness seemed to make everything more intense, and the experience lasted longer than I ever would have believed possible. That was fine by me. It could have lasted forever. . . .

Afterwards, we lay facing each other with our bodies pressed close together. Every breath he took pushed against my body, and every breath I took pressed against his. We didn't speak. We simply gazed at each other. He stroked my hair and occasionally gave me a soft kiss. I ran a finger along his cheek, then his jaw, and then his lips, feeling lost in his tranquil blue eyes. We stayed nearly motionless, completely silent, and soul-baringly naked with each other, until Kellan finally sighed.

"You should go back to your room," he whispered.

"No." I didn't want to move away from his warmth.

"It's nearly morning, Kiera."

I glanced over at the clock and startled when I realized he was right, it was nearly dawn. I stubbornly clutched him tighter.

He kissed me. "Wait in bed an hour, then come downstairs and have coffee with me, like we always used to." He kissed me again, then gently pushed me away from him. I pouted as he started handing me my clothes. I refused to move and, shaking his head at me, he began dressing me. When he finished, he made me sit up, then stand up. "Kiera . . ." He stroked my cheek. "You have to go . . . before it's too late. We got lucky—don't push it."

He kissed my nose, and I resignedly sighed, ignoring his double entendre. "Okay, fine. I'll see you in an hour then." I couldn't stop myself from one last lingering gaze down his naked body, then, sighing again, I left his room.

I stealthily crept back to my room and closed the door behind me. Denny didn't move, he was still deeply asleep, rolled on his side away from me, in his typical slumber. I watched him sleep in oblivious peacefulness for a moment, before I crawled into bed with him. I turned on my side to face him and gazed at his T-shirt rising and falling with his even breath. I didn't feel like crying, as I had earlier. Guilt still washed through me, but it wasn't nearly as bad as before. This was getting easier. . . . I hated that it was. I lightly ran my fingers through the shorter hair near his neck, and he sighed contentedly. I swallowed the sudden lump in my throat and slipped my arms around him, snuggling firmly into his back. He stirred and interlocked our fingers, then fell back asleep. I kissed the back of his neck and rested my head against his shoulder. And then the tears did come.

This was easier . . . but it wasn't easy.

Chapter 22
Choices

Kellan looked different when I made my way downstairs in the morning. Not physically. Physically, he was still achingly perfect. Well, maybe his deep blue eyes were more tired than usual, but neither one of us had slept at all last night. No, he looked different emotionally. He didn't look up when I entered the room. He gave me no cheery greeting, just kept staring blankly into his coffee mug, seemingly lost in thought.

I walked over to him and grabbed his still full cup, setting it on the counter and breaking his focus. He turned his head and looked at me wistfully. Then he lightly kissed me and slipped his arms around my waist. I laced my arms around his neck and laid my head on his shoulder, pulling him into a tight embrace.

"I can't believe I'm going to say this," he whispered, and I automatically tensed. "Last night can't happen again, Kiera."

I pulled back and looked at him, hurt, confused, and a little scared.

He looked over the emotions on my face and sighed. "I love you, and you understand what that phrase means to me. I don't say it . . . to anyone . . . ever." Gently removing my arm from around his neck, he grabbed my hand and laced our fingers together. "There was a time when I would have been fine with this. I would have taken any part of you that you wanted to give to me and found a way to deal with the rest. . . ."

He ran our laced fingers over my cheek. My face softened at his words, but I was still confused and scared. He sighed as he looked me over. "I want to be the kind of man you deserve to have." I started to interrupt him, and he put our fingers over my lips. "I want to be honorable—"

"You are," I interrupted, pulling our fingers from my lips. "You are a good man, Kellan."

"I want to be the better man, Kiera . . . and I'm not." He sighed again and looked up to where Denny was still sleeping, then back down to me. "Last night wasn't the honorable thing to do, Kiera . . . not under Denny's nose like that."

I frowned and felt tears of guilt and shame sting my eyes. He recognized my look and instantly understood. "No . . . I didn't mean, you're not . . . I wasn't trying to insult you, Kiera." He held me close as a couple of tears escaped my eyes.

"Then what are you trying to say, Kellan?"

He closed his eyes and took a deep breath. "I want you to leave him . . . and stay with me." He slowly opened his eyes. They were suddenly very fearful.

I gaped at him, at a complete loss for words. Was he giving me an ultimatum? Making me finally choose?

"I'm sorry. I was going to be stoic, and say nothing for as long as you wanted me, but then we made love . . . and I've, I've never had that . . . and I just can't go back to being who I was before. I want you and only you and I can't bear the thought of sharing you. I'm sorry." He looked down sadly. "I want to be with you the right way—in the open. I want to walk into Pete's with you on my arm. I want to kiss you every time I see you, no matter who's looking. I want to make love to you without fear of someone finding out. I want to fall asleep with you in my arms every night. I don't want to feel guilty about something that makes me feel so . . . whole. I'm sorry, Kiera, but I'm asking you to choose."

I continued to gape at him as tears rolled down my cheeks. The picture he painted was so wonderful. I could see it—a future with him, a life with him. A part of me, a large part of me, wanted that. But the rest of me saw warm, sparkling brown eyes and a goofy grin. "You're asking me to destroy him, Kellan."

He closed his eyes and swallowed. "I know," he whispered. When he reopened his eyes, they were glistening. "I know. I just . . . I can't share you. The thought of you with him, it kills me, now more than it ever did before. I need you. All of you."

Panic flared through me at the thought of losing one of them. "What if I don't choose you, Kellan? What will you do?"

He looked away, a tear rolling down his cheek. "I'll leave, Kiera. I'll leave, and you and Denny can have your happily-ever-after." He looked back at me. "You wouldn't even need to tell him about me. Eventually, the two of you . . ." His voice broke and another tear fell on his cheek. "The two of you would get married, and have children, and have a great life."

I fought back a sob. "And you? What happens to you in that scenario?"

"I . . . get by. And I miss you, every day," he whispered.

Finally a sob did break free, and to reassure myself that he was still here in front of me, that the horror he had described hadn't yet happened, I grabbed his face and intensely kissed him. I felt more of his tears land on my skin as he returned my kiss just as intensely. We broke apart, breathless, and rested our foreheads together as our tears continued to fall.

"Kiera . . . we could be amazing together," he whispered.

"I need more time, Kellan . . . please," I whispered back.

He kissed me softly. "Okay, Kiera. I can give you time, but not forever." He kissed me again and I finally felt my heart start to slow to normal, the ice in my belly melting. "I don't want to hang around the house with him today. I'm going over to Evan's."

I clutched at him, my heart racing again. Seeing my panic, he soothingly said, "I'll see you at Pete's tonight. I'll be there." He kissed me again, and started to pull away from me.

"Wait . . . now? You're leaving now?" I asked in a near whine.

He ran his hands down my hair, then brought them to my cheeks. "Spend the day with Denny. Think about what I said. Maybe you'll be able to . . ."

Decide? Decide which heart I would break? I didn't see how I could ever decide that.

He didn't finish his thought. He simply brought his lips to mine and kissed me for what felt like hours, but when he pulled away, it suddenly felt like mere seconds. Smiling wistfully at me, he turned and left the room, and then, a few moments later, the house. I turned to stare at his full cup of coffee on the counter and wondered what I was going to do.

In the end, I laid myself down on the couch and sobbed until sleep took me.

Hours later, I woke up feeling completely unrefreshed. Kellan's words tumbled through my mind as I went into the kitchen to reheat the coffee he had made earlier . . . before he'd abruptly left.

I looked up from pouring the coffee into my mug when I heard Denny enter the room. My heartbeat doubled at the look on his face. I had never seen such a look on his face before. He was grief-strcken—tortured and defeated. His normally sparkling brown eyes were dead and flat. He was dressed and freshly showered, but it did nothing to make him look well and rested. He looked like he hadn't slept in weeks. Then he closed his eyes, took a deep breath, and, smiling halfheartedly, entered the room.

I froze at the counter watching him. What made him so sad? Did he know that I wasn't with him last night? Did he know where I went? Were Kellan and I not as quiet as I thought? He walked over to me and almost reached out to me before he stopped himself. There was an odd feeling in the room. My breath started increasing in my nervousness. I knew it was odd for me not to ask him what was wrong—his crushed look would have never gone unquestioned by me before—but I just couldn't get enough air to speak. And I was terrified to ask him.

Finally, he spoke. "You disappeared on me," he whispered.

My heartbeat tripled, my vision swam. Oh, God, I was going to pass out right here in front of him. "What?" I unintentionally squeaked out.

"This morning." He nodded over to the couch. "I came down earlier, and you were sleeping on the couch. I didn't want to wake you. . . ."

My heartbeat slowed fractionally. "Oh."

His crushed look returned, as he reached out for my hand. "Did I . . . do something, Kiera?"

I immediately started shaking my head and had to swallow twice before I could speak. "No . . . no, of course not."

"Really? Because I feel like there's this wall between us. We used to talk about everything. I knew almost every single thought in your head, and now I have no clue what you're thinking half the time."

I swallowed back the tears again.

"Will you talk to me?" His sad brown eyes searched my face for a moment, and then he gently pulled my arm, leading me into the living room. I begged myself not to start sobbing again, like yesterday.

We sat down close beside each other on the couch. He leaned over, his knees on his elbows. Then, running a hand halfway through his hair, he looked over to me. "Are you happy here?" he asked, his accent thick with controlled emotion.

I shook my head no but said, "Yes." His face looked just as confused as I felt by my odd answer.

"Is it Kellan?" he whispered, and I felt my stomach lurch like I might be sick. Was he finally asking me? I knew my face was a white as a ghost, and I felt like any second I might hyperventilate again.

"Does his lifestyle bother you that much? Do you not like being here with him as a roommate anymore?"

I relaxed. He wasn't asking me about an affair—he was asking me about Kellan's women. That was the last thing Denny knew of that had made me unhappy, that slap in the bar, but so much had changed since then. Kellan loved me, deeply loved me. And I . . .

"No, he's fine. I barely see him, anyway," I said quietly, my thoughts still spinning.

"No, he hasn't been around lately, has he?" He looked at me oddly when he said that, and I cringed that I had placed that realization in his head. I waited for the next question that could only rationally come: Were you desperately sad all week because he was gone? Did you have a breakdown yesterday because he came back? Because you made love to him . . . and then felt guilty in my arms?

The question he did ask, though, hurt worse than any of my imagined questions. "Is it me, then? Are you not happy with me?" he asked so quietly, I barely heard him.

I threw my arms around him and tried to choke back a sob. "No, I love you." My voice broke, anyway. "I'm happy with you." *Don't ask any more questions. Don't find out what I've done. Don't leave me. . . .*

He returned my hug, clutching me to him as if I were pulling away instead of pressing against him. "Then move to Brisbane with me."

I pulled back and gazed, confused, at his still flat eyes. "What?"

"When your school ends . . . come to Australia with me." He almost frantically searched my face, trying to gauge my reaction.

I blinked at him in disbelief. We had never talked about moving to his homeland, merely visiting over winter break. "Why?"

"I've made some phone calls. There's a really great job waiting for me there . . . whenever I want it. We could move there. It's near my parents. They would love having us close." His accent started thickening as he talked about his family and his home.

"It's so far away, Denny. . . ." Physically, about as far away from Kellan as he could get me. "What about . . . my family?"

"We'll visit as often as you want, Kiera. Holidays. Vacations. Whatever you want, whenever you want." He softly stroked my cheek as he spoke. I could hear the slight desperation in his tone. He really wanted this.

"Australia? I didn't know you wanted to go back there."

"It's a great offer. . . ." He looked down at the floor, before looking back up to me. "We could get married there," he whispered.

My heart started pounding. We had never talked about marriage before either. I couldn't say anything. A million thoughts went
through my head at the same time, some about a life here with Kellan, some about a life thousands of miles away with Denny. He ran
his hand through my hair as I stared at his beautiful, sad, face.

"We could be happy . . . there." He swallowed. "I could be a great
husband to you. Maybe someday, a father .. ." His voice trailed off
as my eyes started to water. I could see the picture he was painting,
too . . . and it was just as wonderful as Kellan's. I didn't know how to
choose. He stroked my cheek again and brought me in for a tender
kiss. I closed my eyes, melted into his touch, and considered his pro-
posal . . . both of them.

He brought both of his hands to my cheeks and kissed me deeply.
I returned it just as deeply. Abruptly, he stood, then leaned over
and picked me up. He had no problems carrying me—he was very
strong—and he kissed me the entire time it took to carry me upstairs
to our room. I purposely kept my eyes closed as we passed Kellan's.

For the first time ever in our relationship, being with Denny
was . . . odd. There was a frenzied desperation to our lovemaking that
had never been there before. It was heartfelt, it was heartbreaking. It
was extreme joy, it was bone-crushing grief. It was fiery-hot, it was
icy-cold. It was true love sprouting . . . it was true love dying. It was like
we were both trying to hold onto something that was slipping through
our fingers, and we didn't understand why. I understood more than he
did, of course, but just barely. I would never fully understand how I
could have ever strayed from such a warm, sensitive, and caring soul.

Afterwards, he stroked my hair as I nestled into his shoulder.
Guilt washed through me. This would kill Kellan. He had to have
known when he left this morning, that there was at least a possibility
Denny would want to . . .

That thought made me feel worse. Then I felt guilty for not completely loving being with Denny. I angrily brushed aside a tear. I was
tired of feeling guilty. Kellan was right: one way or another, I needed
to make a choice.

"Are you all right, Kiera?"

I closed my eyes and tensed; was he finally asking me? "Yes."

He kissed my head. "You've been so sad, and yesterday you seemed so . . ."

I sighed. He *was* going to ask. "Just a bad day—no big deal."

"Oh." I could tell from his timbre that he didn't believe me. "Do you want to talk about it?" His accent was getting thicker; it usually did when he was getting emotional. I needed to end this conversation.

I looked up at him and forced a smile. "No . . . I want to go to Australia with you." I hated to say it, but I needed more time.

He smiled widely and kissed me, all traces of our conversation forgotten.

Denny drove me to work that evening and decided to stay for the night. He had an odd happiness about him, which only made me feel worse. I had given him hope for us . . . and it could possibly be a false hope. I wasn't sure yet.

I set Denny up with some food and a beer at the band's table. My stomach was already tense at the idea of Kellan and Denny sitting down together. All too soon, the band strolled into the bar. Evan and Matt came in together. Evan spotted Denny at their table and eyed me curiously, making me look down and blush. I missed seeing Griffin's entrance, but I heard it. He yelled upon entering the bar, "The stud is here—this party can start now!"

I rolled my eyes and looked over right as Kellan came walking through the door. I held my breath at seeing him. He still stopped my heart with his perfection. He ran his hand through his perfectly messy hair as his absurdly blue eyes locked onto mine. I mouthed a "hi" and he half-grinned at me sexily and nodded his head. He started to walk toward me, until I slightly shook my head. He cocked his head, confused, and then, following my line of sight as I looked back at their table, he understood. His smile left and his eyes darkened. He looked back at me wistfully and then turned to join the guys at his table.

I watched Kellan discreetly as I went about my night. It was difficult to do. I wanted to go over and hold him, kiss him, snuggle in his
lap . . . but I couldn't. Even if Denny were not sitting directly across
the table from him, I couldn't. We didn't have that type of relationship, and that was what he wanted from me. He didn't want to hide
anymore. I didn't either, but . . . I shifted my focus to Denny at the
table. I didn't want to hurt him. I couldn't. I loved him too.

Denny was smiling, happier than I'd seen him in days. My melancholy during Kellan's absence had affected him more than I had
realized. He was excited that we had a future planned now. He was
currently engaged in a conversation with Matt, so I shifted my focus
back to Kellan.

Kellan glanced over at me, making eye contact for just a fraction
of a second, then looking pointedly at the hallway for only the brief-
est moment. Anyone looking at him wouldn't have thought twice
about the movement, he was simply scanning the room. But I knew
better—he wanted to talk to me. He calmly finished his beer, then
got up and made his way to the hallway. Denny watched him leave
for half a second, then turned back to his conversation with Matt.

I swiftly walked over to Jenny. I didn't have much time. "Jenny,
can you—"

She looked at the guys' table, and, noticing Kellan's absence, immediately said, "I'm not lying for you, Kiera."

I shook my head. "No, I'm not asking you to. Just . . . come find
me, if Denny asks . . . anything."

She sighed resignedly. "Fine . . . make it a quickie."

I smirked at her and then smiled. "Thank you."

She nodded and went back to her work. Then, making sure no
one, particularly Denny, noticed, I followed Kellan to the hallway.
My heartbeat increased when I saw him. He was leaning against the
wall in the space between the two bathrooms—his foot against the
wall, his hands in his pockets, his head turned in my direction. He
smiled softly at me when he saw me, and I smiled back. He reached
out for my hand as I approached, and, with the other, opened the

women's bathroom door. I noticed an "Out of Order" sign from the back room taped on the door.

I pointed at it. "Did you . . . ?"

He smiled and led me inside. Then his smile left him. "Are you going to Australia with Denny?" he asked me, as soon as the door swung closed.

My stomach clenched. "What? Where did you hear that?"

"Denny . . . he's telling everyone, Kiera. What did you tell him?" His blue eyes bored into mine.

I closed my eyes and leaned against the wall. "I'm sorry. He was asking the wrong questions. I just needed time." I opened my eyes, feeling very stupid.

"So you told him you would leave the country with him? Kiera, God!" He ran a hand through his hair, then pinched his nose with his fingers. "Can't you ever stop and think before you just spit things out!"

"I know it was stupid, but in the moment, it seemed like the right thing to say," I mumbled feebly.

"God, Kiera . . . did you agree to marry him too?" he asked sarcastically. I didn't say anything, and the sudden silence spoke volumes. Kellan raised his eyebrows at the stillness crashing around us. "Did he . . . did he ask you?"

"I didn't say yes," I whispered.

"But you didn't say no," he whispered back, dropping his hand from his face.

Seeing his hurt, I tried to explain. "He never really asked. He just said that when we were there . . . we could . . . like, eventually, years from now . . ."

He swallowed and looked at me warily. "Are you . . . considering it?"

I took a step toward him. "I need time, Kellan."

"Did you sleep with him?" he whispered.

I stopped moving and blinked rapidly several times. "Kellan . . . don't ask that."

He nodded and looked away, scowling. "So, until you decide,

S. C. Stephens

how exactly does this work? Should Denny and I draw up a schedule?" He looked back at me, his face and voice suddenly heated. "Do
I get you during the week, and he gets weekends, or should we just
do the week-on, week-off thing? Or how about we all fuck together?
Would you prefer that?" he snapped.

I calmly walked over to him and put a hand on his cheek. "Kellan . . . filter."

He blinked at me, then smiled sheepishly. "Right . . . sorry. I'm
just . . . I'm not okay with this, Kiera."

I kissed him softly and a tear fell from my eye. "I'm not either,
Kellan. I don't want this anymore. I don't want to feel guilty. I don't
want to lie. I don't want to hurt people. I just don't know how to
choose."

He gazed at me silently for an achingly long time and then whispered, "Can I plead my case?" He gently grabbed my head in his
hands and gave me a heart-stopping kiss.

A light knocking filtered through the door. "Guys? It's me . . .
Jenny." We both ignored her, as Kellan's "case" got more intense. She
slowly swung open the door and we still didn't stop kissing. He even
exhaled softly and kissed me deeper.

Jenny sounded a bit . . . uncomfortable. "Uh . . . Kiera, sorry, but
you wanted me to find you?"

I nodded around Kellan's lips and ran my fingers through his
hair, while he smiled through his kisses. "Uh, okay . . . can you guys
stop doing that?" She sounded a little irritated now.

Kellan mumbled a "no" and I laughed once, the sound lost in his
mouth. Jenny sighed. "Okay, then. Well, two things actually. One,
Kellan, you're up."

Kellan raised his hand to her, thumb up, but never stopped voraciously kissing me. I was pretty sure Jenny was seeing way more
of Kellan's tongue than she probably wanted to, since when I smiled
and laughed at his movement, he ran it across the roof of my mouth
before closing his lips around mine.

Jenny sighed again. "Second, Denny talked to Griffin."

Kellan and I broke apart at the same time and looked at her. "What?" we both said together, our momentary good humor gone.

Jenny shrugged, looking apologetic. "I tried to sideline Griffin, but Denny was talking about you having a hard time leaving your family." She gave me an icy look. Apparently she didn't like what I had done either. "Denny casually mentioned Anna, so, naturally, Griffin told him every gory detail of their time together while she was here." She made a face, like she had repeatedly heard every detail. My own face paled.

"Denny, of course, brought up Kellan and Anna, and the fight between you and Kellan in the bar." She shook her head. "Griffin got all bent out of shape. He vehemently denied that Kellan had ever slept with her. That he actually took Anna out from under Kellan, and that"—she glanced at Kellan, who looked equally as pale as I did—"Kellan was a prick for trying to . . . and I'm quoting here . . . 'nab his score.'" She made another face, then looked at me sympathetically. "I'm sorry, Kiera . . . but Denny knows that you lied."

I clutched at Kellan, not wanting to hear any of this. "Thank you, Jenny," Kellan said calmly.

"Yeah . . . I'm sorry." She smiled sadly, then turned and left us alone in the room.

My breathing became labored as I clutched Kellan's shoulders. "What do we do?" I searched his face, hoping to find an answer there. My mind started spinning as Kellan silently watched me. "Okay . . . it's not so bad. I'll just tell him that you lied to me . . . and Anna lied to me . . . and . . ." I looked away, thinking through the various lies to tell Denny.

"Kiera . . . that won't work. He'll just be even more suspicious, if you start saying that everyone else is lying. No lies will work, baby."

I looked up at him when he called me that, a small smile on my lips as his tender word fractionally lifted my spirits. It didn't last though. I immediately frowned. "Then what do we do?"

He sighed and ran a finger down my cheek. "We do the only thing we can. I go onstage, and you go back to work."

"Kellan . . ." That wasn't going to solve anything.

"It will be fine, Kiera. I need to go. I need to talk to Evan before we start." Then he kissed me softly on the forehead and left me alone in the room, my head still spinning. Things were starting to crash down around me. I put a hand on my stomach and struggled to maintain my breath.

Kellan was near the stage, having a deep conversation with Evan, when I reentered the bar. Evan did not look happy about whatever Kellan was telling him. Evan flicked a glance at me, then, scowling, looked back at Kellan, who never turned to look at me. Eventually Kellan said something that, from his stance, looked like an order. Evan finally seemed to accept it, and with one last flick of a glance at Denny, he hopped onstage.

The rest of the guys followed shortly after. Kellan ran his hand through his hair and, glancing at Denny, who happened to also look back at him with an odd expression on his face, hopped on the stage as well. The crowd went nuts for their stars, but I didn't hear any of it. I was too busy wondering what all that had been about.

I was making my way back to my section to start helping customers, when I met Denny's eye. He was still sitting at the band's table, which was now filling up with female fans, and he was openly scowling at me. My breath caught. He knew I'd lied. He was thinking, right now, about why. I intentionally kept my eyes from the stage. I tried to smile at Denny, but only managed a feeble grin. He didn't smile back. His eyes narrowed and I forcefully pulled my gaze away.

Mentally, I thanked the packed bar of thirsty customers for giving me an excuse to not have to go near his table for a while. The band's music started playing, but I never glanced back to the stage. I may have pulled my gaze from Denny, but I could feel Denny's gaze burning into me.

Toward the end of the night, I started relaxing. Not that my stomach wasn't churning and my head wasn't spinning, but Denny never approached me. I eventually had to go to his table, to serve some of the females, and he only ordered another beer from me. He asked me nothing. But his eyes said everything—he was suspicious, highly suspicious.

Later, Kellan announced that they had one more song . . . and it was a new one. It started with just Matt and Evan, then a few beats later Griffin came in, and Kellan started singing. His voice was low and husky. The lyrics were sad, and I discreetly watched him for a moment before I turned to help a customer.

"Hi, what can I—?" I couldn't finish my question. A phrase Kellan had just sung seeped into my brain and froze me in place, blocking out all other thoughts.

"You're everything that I need, but I'm nothing that you need. I failed you, I betrayed you, over and over, but you'll be all right . . . when he holds you tight."

My jaw dropped as I stared back up at the stage. This was a new song he'd been working on . . . and it was about him . . . and me.

"Miss? I said we'll . . ." I ignored the customer. Kellan's voice had picked up strength, and it was all I could focus on.

"It's better to never say goodbye, to just move on, to end the lie."

But he *was* saying goodbye . . . in song . . . in front of the entire bar, in front of Denny. Kellan wasn't looking my way. He was staring out over the crowd, not noticing any of them, focusing solely on the words.

I stood where I was, completely in shock, at the table of a customer who was still trying to get my attention. I was only a few feet away from Denny, and he had to be watching me stare at Kellan on stage, terror in my eyes and my mouth open in disbelief. Evan hadn't wanted him to sing this, most likely because Denny was here. What was Kellan thinking?

On the second verse, I stopped caring who was watching as tears filled my eyes. I couldn't possibly have stopped the reaction as Kellan's voice burned through me.

"We had what we had, we did what we did . . . and it was amazing, something I'll never forget. It will hurt me, it will hurt you too. But everything ends, so save your tears. This won't break you. With him by

your side, you'll be just fine. But I promise you . . . my love for you will never die."

His words were beautiful and heartbreaking. He was saying goodbye, for real this time. On the second "*I failed you, I betrayed you, over and over . . .*" I felt the tears spill down my cheeks.

Finally, Kellan looked straight at me. He locked his intense gaze to mine and repeated the chorus, "*It's better to never say goodbye, to just move on, to end the lie.*" I could see a tear, which he completely ignored, fall on his cheek. His voice held steady and strong. I felt my breath choke. I felt pain rip through my stomach. I felt my heart seize, and I felt the few tears that had escaped turn into streams running down my face.

"Miss . . . ?"

Vague voices buzzed around me, but Kellan's words were piercing straight through me . . . and they weren't stopping. The next line, "*Every single day I'll keep you with me, no matter how far from me you are,*" followed immediately by another "goodbye" section, had me clutching my gut and holding a hand to my mouth, desperately trying to hold in a sob.

As the music and Kellan's voice picked up even more, I felt a hand on my shoulder. "Not here, Kiera," Jenny's soft voice whispered in my ear.

I couldn't even break myself away from staring at Kellan to look at her. Another tear fell down his cheek as he stared at me, unabashed. I didn't know who was watching us. I didn't know if Denny was watching us. Kellan's face was all I could see, his heart-wrenching words all I could hear. A sob broke free.

Jenny started tugging at my arm. I stubbornly resisted her. "Not here, Kiera. Denny's watching . . . not here."

I stopped resisting and let her pull me into the kitchen as Kellan sang the last few bars, "*I promise you . . . my love for you will never die.*" His heartbreaking eyes watched me leave. His voice cracked just once, as I disappeared through the kitchen doors with Jenny. Immediately I started sobbing, and Jenny put her arms around me.

"It's okay, Kiera. It will be okay. Have faith." She repeated it over and over while she rubbed my back, and I sobbed mercilessly on her shoulder.

He was leaving. . . .

When my crying spell was over, Jenny fixed my face and brought me a drink. . . . It was not water. I sat up at the bar and downed it. Kellan watched me wistfully from the edge of the stage. I desperately wanted to run over to him, to throw my arms around his neck and kiss him, to beg him not to leave. I couldn't do anything, though, not with Denny still here watching. For the first time in my life, I wished Denny would leave.

Denny approached Kellan after his set and asked him a serious-looking question. Kellan flicked a glance over to me, and I felt my heart skip a beat. Then Kellan smiled casually and shook his head, clapping Denny on the shoulder. With a blank face, Denny watched Kellan shove his guitar back in his case and quickly leave the bar, risking one final glance at me as he opened the doors. I watched his fingers go to the bridge of his nose as he walked through them.

Denny sat and solemnly waited at the table until my shift was over. When I grabbed my things, he finally approached me. Ice flooded my veins, but he said nothing. He simply held out his hand and we walked in silence out of the bar.

Kellan was already home when Denny and I got there. His light was off when I slyly glanced at his room as we walked by, but I could hear soft music playing and knew he was awake. Denny undressed silently, occasionally giving me odd, sad glances. He hadn't asked about catching me in my lie. He hadn't asked about my meltdown during Kellan's last song. But combined with my melancholy all week, Kellan's sudden reappearance last night at the bar, and the heartfelt glances Kellan and I gave each other at the end of the night, I could feel the unasked questions in Denny's uneasy eyes. I was ter-rified for the questions I felt coming closer each minute.

I changed into my pajamas, equally silent, and then softly ex-cused myself to the bathroom. Denny slipped under the covers and watched me leave. I left the door open, hoping to ease any suspicions he might have. That didn't stop me from glancing longingly at Kellan's door. He was leaving and I couldn't bear it. I had to find a way to stop him . . . somehow.

I took my time in the bathroom. I let the cold water drench my face repeatedly, hoping to wash away my fears. Kellan was leaving, Denny was horribly suspicious—my world was crashing inward.

Taking a last, deep breath that did nothing to calm me, I opened the door and walked back to Denny. He was still awake, still watching the door, waiting for me to return to him. I searched his eyes for a moment, wondering what he thought, what he felt . . . how much he was hurting. Why he didn't ask me . . . anything.

He held his arms out for me, and I crawled into them, grateful for at least some comfort from the continual assault on my emotions. It wasn't what I wanted though. His arms weren't the ones I was craving. That thought made my throat tight, and I was glad Denny wasn't talking. I closed my eyes and waited.

Each second felt like minutes, each minute felt like hours. I strained my hearing to listen to Denny's breathing. Was it slow and steady? Was he asleep? Then he would shift and sigh, and I knew he was still awake. I feigned sleep the best I could, hoping he would relax and give in to slumber. I felt frustrated tears building, but I shoved them back. I wanted out of this room, but I needed to be patient.

To pass the time, I imagined what Kellan was doing over in his room. I couldn't hear his music anymore. Was he asleep? Was he awake, staring at his ceiling, wondering if I was asleep in Denny's arms? Was he wishing he had never said anything this morning? Was he waiting for me to crawl into bed with him? Was he planning his departure?

Eventually Denny's breathing became slow and regular in true slumber. I opened my eyes and cautiously raised my head to look at him. His beautiful face was calm and peaceful for the first time since he'd caught the lie. I sighed softly, then carefully moved his arm off of me. Still asleep, he rolled over to his normal sleeping side, away from me. I waited for an achingly long time, just to be sure, and then I quietly got up. I ran through a list of excuses in my head, just in case Denny looked over at me leaving, but he didn't, and I soundlessly slipped out the door.

My heart was thudding as I opened Kellan's. I was suddenly really nervous. . . .

Kellan was sitting on the edge of the bed, away from the door with his back to me, when I quietly entered his room. He was still dressed and was intently looking at something in his hand. He was lost in thought, and didn't hear me approach him.

"Kellan?" I whispered.

He startled and clenched his hand, hiding whatever he had been looking at. He turned to look at me, and, at the same time, shoved his hand under the mattress. "What are you doing here? We talked about this. You shouldn't be here." His face was pale and he looked dreadfully sad.

"How could you do that?"

"What?" he asked, looking both tired and confused.

"Sing that song to me . . . in front of everyone. You killed me." My voice broke, and I sat heavily on the edge of the bed.

He looked away from me. "It's what needs to happen, Kiera."

"You wrote that days ago . . . when you were gone?"

He didn't answer me for several seconds. "Yes. I know where this is going, Kiera. I know who you'll choose, who you've always chosen."

Suddenly not knowing what else to say, I blurted out, "Sleep with me tonight." My voice was thick with my churning emotions.

"Kiera, we can't. . . ." He looked over at me wistfully.

"No . . . literally. Just hold me, please."

He sighed and then laid back on his bed, holding his arms open for me. I snuggled into his side, wrapping my leg around his, my arm over his chest, and nestling my head in his shoulder. I breathed in his dizzyingly amazing scent, and raptured in his warmth and comfort. The overwhelming joy of being close to him brought with it the heartbreaking sadness that he was leaving me.

I sniffled back a tear and he held me tighter. I felt him sigh brokenly beneath me, and I knew he was on the verge of tears, the same as me. It slipped out in my grief. "Don't leave me."

He exhaled brokenly and clutched at me, kissing my head. "Kiera . . ." he whispered.

I looked up into his torn face, his eyes shining with tears waiting to spill. Mine already were. "Please stay . . . stay with me. Don't go."

He closed his eyes, squeezing out the tears. "It's the right thing to do, Kiera."

"Baby, we're finally together, don't end this."

His eyes opened at my tender word, and he lovingly ran a finger down my cheek. "That's just it. We're not together. . . ."

"Don't say that. We are. I just need time . . . and I need you to stay. I can't bear the thought of you leaving." I kissed him deeply, bringing my hands to his cheeks.

He pulled away. "You won't leave him, Kiera, and I can't share you. Where does that leave us? He's going to figure it out if I stay. That leaves us with one option. . . . I go." He swallowed back his emotions as another tear fell on his cheek. "I wish things were different. I wish I'd known you first. I wish I was your first. I wish you would choose me—"

"I do!" I blurted out.

We both froze and stared at each other. Another tear dripped from his eye, as he stared at me with a look of such pain and hope that I instantly regretted coming into his room. My panic at the thought of him leaving again had made me blurt out something that I knew would make him stay . . . and I did want him to stay. I desperately wanted him to stay. I wanted to walk into Pete's on his arm. I wanted to kiss him every time I saw him. I wanted to make love without worry. I wanted to sleep in his arms every single night. . . .

Oh, God, I suddenly realized. I wanted to be . . . with him.

"I do choose you, Kellan," I said again, surprised at my decision, but happy I had finally made one. He was looking at me like any second I might light him on fire. "Do you understand me?" I whispered, getting concerned at his odd reaction.

Finally, he rolled over and pressed into me, grabbing my face and kissing me intensely. I could barely breathe through his enthusiasm. I ran my fingers through his hair and clutched him tight to me. His hands started pulling at my clothes. He pulled off my tank top, but before I could ask a question, his lips were back on mine. He pulled off his shirt, and again his lips were back on mine before I could speak. He deftly slipped off my pants and was working on his jeans, when I finally pushed him away.

Breathless, I gaped at him. "What happened to your . . . rules?"

"I never was good at following rules." He smiled and moved in to kiss me. "And I never could say no to your begging anyway . . ." he finished softly, kissing my neck.

He slipped off his jeans and kissed me again. "Wait . . ." I pushed him back again. "I thought you didn't want to do this"—I looked over at the door—"here."

He slid his hand into my underwear and I gasped. "If I'm yours, and you're mine . . . then I will take you, wherever and whenever I can," he growled in my ear, his intensity making me moan.

"I love you, Kellan," I whispered, bringing his face back to mine.

"I love you, Kiera. I will make you so happy," he whispered seriously.

I bit my lip and started pulling off his boxers. "Yes, I know you will."

Chapter 23
Consequences

I shifted on his bed for the hundredth time. Kellan's arm was around me and he was sleeping soundly, his cheek resting on his other arm, his face turned toward me. All the doubt and worry had been erased from his perfect features. I wasn't quite so sure they were erased from mine. I'd finally chosen, and in the heat of the moment, I'd chosen Kellan. It all still felt a little surreal to me. I snuggled into Kellan's side and he sighed contentedly. I tried to imagine being with him like this every night, having the open relationship with him that he wanted—that *we* wanted. It had been such a taboo idea for so long that I couldn't quite envision it at the moment.

I shifted again on the bed. There was one final hurdle to tackle before I could really picture going forward with Kellan . . . and it was one that was tearing my heart apart. Denny. I should get up now and sneak back into our room. I shouldn't risk him finding out this way. I shouldn't have risked making love to Kellan last night . . . again. I just, I seemed to not always have the best judgment when it came to that amazing man. But Kellan was right, it was a bad idea. Denny should never catch the two of us being intimate like that. I remembered his reaction in my dream. I couldn't even begin to imagine his real reaction if he walked in on us. Especially now that he knew I had lied, now that he was suspicious.

I should tell him. I should finally tell him . . . everything. I just had no idea how.

Sighing, I lifted Kellan's arm off of me. He mumbled something in his sleep and started to reach out for me again. I smiled and, brushing a lock of hair off his forehead, kissing him softly. I grabbed my hastily flung clothes and slipped them back on; then I opened his door and, with a final glance at his peaceful body, the sheet half-heartedly draped over his physical perfection, I shut it and headed back to my room.

I slipped into my bed as stealthily as I could. Denny didn't stir when I carefully lay down next to him, and I didn't look at him this time. I kept my back to him and carefully breathed in and out. I waited for him to move, for him to roll me over and demand to know where I'd been. He didn't. He slept as soundly as Kellan had been sleeping. Eventually, exhaustion took me and I gave in to slumber, intimate thoughts of Kellan on my mind.

I awoke a short while later from a particularly good dream, anxious to see Kellan again. Denny was still sleeping, but I was positive Kellan would not be. I quickly darted to the bathroom to freshen up, and then quietly dashed downstairs. As predicted, Kellan was leaning against the counter, a fresh pot of coffee brewing behind him, smiling over at me, looking completely perfect, dressed in my favorite bright blue shirt that made his eyes seem inhumanly blue.

"Morn—"

He didn't get a chance to finish his greeting before my lips were locked on his and my hands were twisted in that fabulous hair. He returned my kiss eagerly, his hands cupping my cheeks. Between our lips, I muttered, "I missed you."

"I missed you too," he muttered back. "I hated waking up with you gone."

You would think we hadn't seen each other in days, instead of hours. I luxuriated in the smell of him, the feel of him, the taste of him. I reveled in his warmth, in his tender hands traveling down my shoulders, in the feel of his hair between my fingertips and his tongue brushing against mine. I never wanted him to stop kissing me. That was when he suddenly pulled away from me, taking a few steps toward the table.

"We should talk about Denny, Kiera. . . ."

Just then, Denny walked into the kitchen. "What about me?" he asked curtly.

Kellan and I had luckily been a few paces apart when Denny had unexpectedly appeared in the entryway, but my heart shifted instantly into triple time. Kellan was more composed, and smoothly said, "I was just asking Kiera if you would be interested in hangin' with me and the guys today. There's this thing at EMP—"

Denny cut him off while I gaped at him. Did he just come up with that on the fly, or was that really his plan for today? "No, *we'll* stay here."

I didn't miss Denny's inflection on the word "we'll," and neither did Kellan. His face paler, he said, "Okay . . . come by if you change your mind. We'll be there all day." An odd tension built up in the kitchen and Kellan finally broke the silence. "I'd better go . . . pick up the guys." And with a final meaningful glance at me behind Denny's back, he left the two of us alone, in the suddenly too quiet kitchen.

A few moments later, I heard the door close. Kellan's car growled to life and drove away. And just like that, he was gone, and my heart dropped a little. By his final look, I knew he was giving me time to "talk" to Denny, and I wasn't ready yet. I wasn't even sure if I could do it. I mean, how do you tear someone that you still care for to pieces? And I did . . . even throughout everything, I still loved him. Love doesn't exactly come with an off switch.

I spent the bulk of the afternoon lying on the couch, sleeping . . . or pretending to, while Denny watched over me from the chair, the TV playing in the background purely a distraction for the over-whelming silence between us. I wasn't ready to destroy him yet. I wasn't sure if I would ever be ready for that. I didn't know how to tell someone who had been everything to me for so long that it was over.

I could feel his dark eyes resting on me all day . . . thinking.

Denny was brilliant. The only reason he hadn't put it all together yet was pure devotion to me. He refused to see my flaws and he hated to cause me pain. Acknowledging my betrayal would force him to do both.

He might have been avoiding the words, but I saw it in his eyes—the fear, the doubt. I knew that eventually he would gather the courage to ask me that dreaded question: Are you in love with someone else?

Every look he gave me, every time he touched me, every conversation he started with me, I was sure he was going to ask me. Ask me if I was leaving him. Ask me if I was in love with Kellan. I tensed in anticipation every time. I didn't know what I would say if he did ask.

But the questions never came. . . .

He never once asked me about the lie he had caught me in last night. He never once asked me for the real reason for the awful slap I had given Kellan. The few times we did speak that horridly long afternoon, he seemed to purposefully avoid any topic of conversation that might lead to Kellan.

By the end of the day, his expression was darker, his mood introspective. Eventually all conversation dried up, and I began avoiding his dark, accusatory glances.

Kellan did eventually come back, late, hours after the sun set on our chilly little home. He walked into the kitchen and saw Denny and me finishing a silent dinner. Kellan glanced over to me, probably wondering if I had talked to him at all. I could only shake my head nearly imperceptibly, no. He understood. His face was torn, and I thought he might turn around and leave again, but, calming himself, he put his keys on the counter and grabbed a beer from the fridge. His disheartened eyes haunted me, though, and I couldn't help but stare at him, even though I knew Denny was intently watching me. I so wanted to go over to him and explain, but I knew I couldn't.

His eyes not leaving mine, Denny spoke over to Kellan, "Hey, mate. I think we should all go out. How about the Shack? We could go dancing again?" His accent inflected oddly on the word "dancing." My heart jumped. Why would he want to go back there? I forced my eyes back to my plate.

I could hear Kellan shifting uncomfortably. "Yeah . . . sure," he said quietly.

My heart started to race and I kept my head down, concentrating on my food and my breathing. This was not good . . . not good at all.

Kellan turned and took his beer to his room. Denny and I finished our awkward meal in silence, his eyes never straying far from mine. Finishing before him, I mumbled something about getting ready and stumbled upstairs to prepare for a night that I felt would be as horrific as the last time we had all gone there together.

Kellan's door was closed as I passed it, and I briefly wondered if I should pop in and explain why I had chickened out about talking to Denny today. I couldn't, though. I wasn't ready for that conversation, either. I sighed and went to the bathroom to rearrange my hair, redo my makeup—anything to stop my mind from spinning.

Finally, during the car ride over, Denny broke his hours of long silence. "Have you decided what you want to do for winter break?" he asked, an oddly flat tone in his accented voice. He looked over to me and his expression softened for the first time all day, moisture glistening in his eyes. "I'd really like to take you home with me . . . over the holidays. Will you think about it, Kiera?" His voice wavered a bit on my name.

I clearly heard the real question he was asking me: *Will you choose me?* I could only nod at him, moisture stinging my own eyes as well. I turned to look out the window at the city flying by me. That was how my insides felt, that I was flying toward something, and it was too late to stop it.

Denny and I beat Kellan there. He seemed to be delaying the inevitable weirdness. I wished I could. Denny pulled us straight through the bar, to the doors leading to the beer garden in back. I noticed a sign on the door as he opened it: "Winter Fest—Beat the Chill." Apparently we were celebrating the iciness in the air.

Even though the weather was really too chilly to just sit around and drink beer, there were a lot of people outside, and Denny led me to the same table where we had sat the last fateful time we were here. I had no idea if he did that deliberately or not. My eyes flicked back to the gate, back to the espresso stand. Did he know about that night? I tried to force my stomach to stop turning. He ordered drinks for the three of us and we sipped our beers in silence, Denny looking thoughtful.

My breath inadvertently caught when Kellan walked out of the bar. I hadn't meant for it to happen. I prayed Denny didn't see it happen. He was just so . . . breathtaking. He walked smoothly to our table, his eyes oddly at peace. He even smiled over at Denny while he took a seat by me. My heart sped a little, partly from nerves, partly from his nearness.

The bar was busy. Loud music came from speakers all around the beer garden, and several people were out on the makeshift dance floor having a good time in the approaching-frigid air. I hoped Denny wasn't serious about the dancing, I didn't think I could fake that right now, not with the way my heart and stomach were flopping around. I watched the drunken people warming their bodies with physical movement and started to shiver a bit from the cold. Again, I wondered why Denny sat us out here, and not inside the warm bar. I put my cold hands in my lap, resisting the instinct to reach under the table and grab Kellan's.

I don't know how long we sat there in silence, Kellan and I watching the crowd, but studiously ignoring each other, Denny watching me intently, but eventually, Denny's work phone rang. Startled, I looked over at him while he smoothly picked it up. He spoke a few sentences, then closed it. Sighing, he looked over to me.

"I'm sorry. They need me to come in." Looking over me to Kellan, he said, "Can you take her home? I have to go." Kellan simply nodded and Denny stood to leave. I was too shocked by the turn of events to speak properly. Denny leaned down to me. "Will you think about what I asked?" he said quietly. I mumbled an okay and, grabbing my cheeks in both hands, he kissed me so deeply that I groaned and instinctively brought my hands up to his neck. My heart raced and I was slightly breathless as he pulled away.

Kellan shifted noisily in his chair and, for a second, I had a horrifying image of Kellan starting something with *Denny*. He cleared his throat and shifted in his chair again as Denny said goodbye to both of us and, turning, left the bar. I watched him leave, my heart still racing. His beautiful face turned once at the door, to give me a final glance goodbye. He nodded a little and smiled fractionally when he saw me still watching him, and then he entered the bar to leave out the front doors.

I numbly turned my head to look over at Kellan. Would he be mad at me for that? Would he be mad at me for not talking to Denny today? Surely he could understand how hard this was for me. Meeting his gaze however, I only saw love in his eyes.

He grabbed my hand under the table and started talking, as if we had been on a date the entire evening and my boyfriend had not just thoroughly kissed me and left the bar.

"I was wondering . . . since you probably don't want to take me home to your parents yet . . ." He paused and looked at me meaningfully. "Which I completely understand." He smiled. "Maybe you'd like to spend winter break with me here? Or we could go up to Whistler? Canada is beautiful and—" He stopped and looked at me curiously. "Do you ski?" He shook his head, not waiting for a response from me, which was good, since I couldn't form words yet. "Well, if not . . . we don't have to leave our room." He grinned wickedly at me.

I was staring at his blue eyes and I was hearing his words . . . but I wasn't seeing him, and I wasn't absorbing what he was saying, other than that he wanted to spend winter break with me. Unknowingly, he was asking me the same thing Denny just had. Kellan continued going on and on about what we could do in Canada and I tuned him out.

My mind started thinking about what Denny had asked in the car. Denny wanted to take me home with him to meet his parents before we moved over there. Only that wasn't the plan anymore. We would be over by then, we would be over soon, and he would go home alone. I swallowed painfully and my mind tortured me by allowing every memory I had of him to flood through me.

I remembered our first meeting. He had been smiling at all the students as they walked in, and my breath caught when I saw him. I looked down when his smile turned to me. The professor had him pass out some papers to the class, and as I was sitting on the edge of the row, he handed me a large stack to pass down to the others.

"Hello. Enjoying the class so far?" he said quietly, and the surprise over hearing his delightful accent, and, honestly, having his attractive face so close to mine, had caused me to clumsily drop the entire stack of papers to the floor.

"I'm so sorry," I said, as I knelt down beside him to help him pick them up. My face was surely bright red.

"It's okay," he said sweetly. When we were all finished, he stuck his hand out. "My name's Denny Harris."

I shook his hand. "Kiera . . . Allen," I mumbled.

He helped me stand up and carefully rehanded me the stack. "It's nice to meet you, Kiera." He had said it warmly, and even now I remembered the thrill of hearing his accent curl around my name that first time. I hadn't been able to take my eyes off of him after that day. I'd had to work extra hard paying attention in that class.

I remembered our first date. He had asked me one afternoon in the quad. I had been completely surprised and definitely eager. I tried to keep a smooth face, though, as I'd casually said "sure." He picked me up that night and we went to a very nice restaurant overlooking the river. He suggested something good to eat but let me make my own choice. He never even let me see the bill, and we had an amazingly easy conversation all throughout dinner. Afterwards he held my hand, and we walked down the sidewalk talking casually, neither one of us wanting the evening to end. When it did end, he walked me to my door and gave me the softest, sweetest kiss that anyone had ever given me. I think I fell for him on that night.

My awareness jerked back to the present when Kellan asked me a question, and I didn't respond right away. I finally heard the question on his second attempt. "Kiera . . . did I lose you?" I blushed, realizing I had no idea what he'd been talking about. He was still sweetly stroking my hand with his thumb, but was looking at me with a concerned expression. "Are you all right? Do you want to go home?"

I nodded, still feeling unable to speak. We stood and he led me with a hand comfortingly on my back to the side exit in the gate. Immediately upon seeing the parking lot, I looked for Denny's car. It was gone . . . he was really gone. Unintentionally, I glanced over to the fateful espresso stand. Kellan noticed my gaze and, squeezing my hand, looked down on me, smiling softly as the gate closed behind us. But seeing the stand didn't take my mind back to Kellan and our night of tortured bliss. It took me back to a simpler, purer time . . . with Denny.

I remembered our first time together . . . my first time ever. We had been dating for two months. For a guy in his early twenties, that was an eternity, but he never pushed me. We would kiss and do . . . other things . . . for as long as I wanted, but the second I pushed him away, he happily retreated. He never once made me feel guilty about it, which had only made me want him more. He knew it was my first time and he made it special for me. He rented a cabin and we spent a long winter weekend there. Our first time had been the stuff of movie magic—warm fireplace, soft blankets, and quiet music. He took his time with me, making sure I was completely comfortable with every step . . . which I was. He had been so amazingly gentle and tender, it hadn't even hurt. Afterwards, he'd held me tight to his chest, and told me for the first time, that he loved me and I, of course, started to cry and told him that I loved him too . . . which promptly led to our second time.

Back in the real world, Kellan was leading me to his car. He was still talking softly to me. His topic had changed to what we could do this summer. "After high school, I hitchhiked down the Oregon coast. That's actually how I met Evan. Anyway, we should go, you would love it. There are these caves . . ."

I tuned him out. Step after step was barraging me with more heartfelt memories of Denny.

We took two steps toward the car—memories of birthdays, the latest being my twenty-first, when he had taken me to a local bar and sweetly held my hair back when I got very, very ill. Memories of Christmases past, at my parents' house, snuggled on his lap watching my family exchange gifts. Memories of a dozen red roses given to me on Valentine's Day . . . and my birthday . . . and our anniversary, all with the sweetest goofy grin on his face.

Another step—memories of getting food poisoning and having him wipe my forehead with a cold rag and bring me water. Memories of him trying out new recipes on me, most of them really good, a couple astoundingly bad. Memories of snuggling in his bed and watching a movie. Memories of studying together for school . . . and making out instead.

Another few steps—more current memories of traveling across the country in his beat-up car, tossing fries at each other, playing the license plate alphabet game for hours, singing along with the radio and thoroughly enjoying the twangy country songs through the Midwest, taking a quick dip in an ice-cold river to freshen up, making love in his car at an empty rest stop.

One more step—walking along the pier, falling asleep with him on the couch, dancing together at the bar, him sappily calling me his heart. . . .

Another step—the soft hair along his jawline, his warm brown eyes, running my fingers through his dark hair, his soft lips, his alluring accent, his gentle words, his goofy grin, his good humor, his good nature, his good soul. . . .

He was my comfort. He was my solace. Nearly everything I had faced in my young life, I had gotten through because of him, because he was always there for me with soft words and a tender heart. Would I have that with Kellan? I remembered all of our heated fights, the words we used to hurt each other. Denny and I rarely said unkind things to one another . . . but with Kellan . . .

What would happen in a relationship with him? Surely, we'd eventually have disagreements and they might be very vocal. I thought back over the course of our entire relationship and what flooded my brain was an image of a roller coaster—up and down, up and down—flying from one extreme to the next. Was that what being with him would be like? Always shifting from high to low, low to high? Could I live a life happily that way?

I liked constant. I liked safe. It was one of the reasons Denny and I clicked so well. He was a cooling lake: supportive, refreshing, and, most of all, never changing. Kellan . . . Kellan was fire: passionate, emotional, and searing to the core. But fire didn't last . . . passion eventually fades . . . and then what? Kellan had so many options available to him. Surely one day, when that passion had faded, and no matter how much he loved me, he would cave to one of the beautiful women always flocking to him. I mean, gorgeous girls were constantly throwing themselves at him. I wasn't physically special, even if he insisted I was beautiful. And he was talented—he could really make it big one day. Then what? The number of women already flocking would quadruple. How could he possibly resist them all . . . forever? That would never happen with Denny, of that I was sure, but with Kellan . . . I knew he would hate himself, but it seemed . . . possible.

I stopped walking. I yanked my hand away from Kellan and he stopped walking too. I couldn't do it. I couldn't leave the man who had been my life for so long that I couldn't even contemplate my life without him in it. At least . . . I couldn't yet. I needed more time. I needed to be sure that Kellan and I had something that could work, before I threw away a promising future with a good man that I did love deeply.

Kellan took a step and then turned to face me. His face was gorgeous in the moonlight, composed and yet, at the same time, achingly sad. His eyes nearly broke my heart, and I had to look away. It wasn't just that they suddenly glistened too much, the deep blue crystallizing into what could very easily become tears. It was the calm resignation in them that tore my heart.

He regarded my expression for a minute and then, quietly, he said, "I did lose you . . . didn't I?" I looked up at his calm face, surprised. Had he known me better than I knew myself? Had he known that I would do this to him, all along?

"Kellan, I . . . I can't do this . . . not yet. I can't leave him. I need more time. . . ."

His calm face broke with a touch of anger behind his eyes. "Time? Kiera . . . nothing is going to change here. What good is time to you?" He shook his head and nodded it in the direction of our home. "Now that he knows you lied, time will only hurt him more." He meant my indecision would hurt Denny, but as his eyes glistened even more, I was sure he was also talking about himself.

"Kellan, I'm so sorry . . . please don't hate me," I whispered, my own eyes brimming as well.

He ran both hands back through his hair and left them in the tangled mess for a moment before bringing them back to his sides. "No, Kiera . . . no." His voice was quiet with restraint, and a shot of fear went right through me.

"What do you mean? No, you don't hate me or no . . . you do?" My voice broke on the end, and I swallowed painfully.

Seeing my pained face, he brought a hand up to my cheek. In a tight voice, he softly said, "No, I can't give you any more time. I can't do this. It's killing me. . . ."

I shook my head as tears finally dropped to my cheeks. "Please, Kellan, don't make me—"

"Ugh . . . Kiera." He bought his other hand to my other cheek and gripped me harshly, cutting off my objection. "Choose right now. Don't even think, just choose. Me . . . or him? " His thumbs brushed aside tears that were spilling over them. "Me or him, Kiera?"

Thoughtless, I blurted out, "Him."

The very air around us seemed to vibrate with the sudden silence between us. He stopped breathing and his eyes widened in shock. I stopped breathing and my eyes widened in shock. Oh, God . . . why would I say that? Was that . . . was that what I wanted? It was too late to rethink my hasty choice. It was too late to take the word back. I watched as a tear dropped heavily to Kellan's cheek. That single tear seemed to solidify my word. The damage was done. I couldn't go back now if I wanted to.

"Oh," he finally whispered.

He started to remove his hands and back away from me, and I clutched him tight and tried to pull him closer. "No, Kellan . . . wait. I didn't mean—"

He narrowed his eyes. "Yes, you did. That was your instinct. That was your first thought . . . and first thoughts are usually the correct ones." His tone got a little icy, and then he closed his eyes and swallowed. "That's what's really in your heart. He's what's in your heart. . . ."

I grabbed his hands and held them tight in front of us, as he took a few calming breaths. I could see the struggle on his face to control his anger, and I feebly flipped through my head to come up with something to repair the damage I'd just carelessly caused. I had nothing. No burst of genius on how to fix this.

When his face was calmer, he opened his eyes and my heart broke at the sadness in them. "I told you I would walk away, if that was your choice . . . and I will. I won't make trouble for you."

His gaze sad but achingly full of love, he quietly added, "I always knew where your heart really was anyway. I never should have asked you to make a choice . . . there never was a choice to make. Last night, I did hope that . . ." He sighed and looked down to the pavement. "I should have left ages ago. I was just . . . being selfish."

I gaped at him, disbelieving. He thought he was being selfish? Here, *I* was the one literally shuffling between the beds of two men, and *he* was selfish? "I think I give new meaning to the word, Kellan."

He smiled a little when he looked back up at me, and then his face got serious again. "You were scared, Kiera. I understand that. You're scared to let go . . . I am too. But everything will be fine." Almost as if to convince himself, he repeated, "We will be fine." He spoke so quietly that I could barely hear him over the loud music drifting over the fence from the beer garden.

He swept me into his arms for a tight embrace. I threw my arms around his neck and curled one hand through his wonderfully thick hair. I inhaled the scent of his skin mixed with his leather jacket, savoring every second with him. His arms pulled me in so tight that I could barely breathe. I didn't care, he could have compressed me into his body and I wouldn't have cared. I ached for his closeness so badly. My mind was still spinning over my shifting choice. I wasn't sure what I wanted, but maybe Kellan was right . . . maybe first thoughts were the correct ones.

In a voice thick with emotion, he whispered in my ear, "Don't ever tell Denny about us. He won't leave you. You can stay at my place for as long as you like. You can even rent out my room if you want. I don't care."

I pulled back to look at him, tears streaming mercilessly down my face now. He answered my unasked question, another tear shimmering down his cheek in the moonlight as well. "I have to leave now, Kiera . . . while I can." He brushed multiple tears away from my cheeks. "I'll call Jenny and have her come get you. She'll take you to him. She'll help you."

"Who will help you?" I whispered, searching his achingly perfect face in the silver light. I knew how much he cared now. I knew what I meant to him, and how extremely difficult leaving me was for him. I knew how hard it was for me, and I felt like dying.

Swallowing, he ignored my question. "You and Denny can go to Australia and be married. You can have a long, happy life together, the way it was supposed to be." His voice cracked on the end and another tear rolled down his cheek. "I promise I won't interfere."

I wasn't letting it go, though. "What about you? You'll be alone. . . ." I needed to know he would be okay.

He smiled sadly. "Kiera . . . it was always supposed to be that way too."

I stared at his liquid blue eyes. I placed a hand on his cheek and held back a sob. He was willing to give up everything he had ever wanted in this world—a real, deep, to-the-bottom-of-his-soul love, without a fight, to save Denny's and my relationship. His good heart broke mine. "I told you you were a good man," I whispered.

"I think Denny would disagree," he whispered back.

I threw my arms tightly around his neck again as a hauntingly slow beat drifted over the fence and pounded through my body. I ran my fingers back through his hair and choked back another sob as he rested his forehead against mine.

"God, I'm going to miss you. . . ." His voice cracked at the end and he swallowed loudly.

It was too much, it was too hard. I couldn't breathe. I couldn't let him slip away. I loved him too much. This was too hard. This felt wrong . . . all of this just felt wrong. I couldn't let him go. . . .

"Kellan, please don't—"

He immediately cut me off. "Don't, Kiera. Don't ask me that. It has to happen this way. We need to stop this cycle, and we both seem incapable of staying away from each other . . . so one of us needs to leave." He let out a heavy breath and spoke quickly, rocking his head back and forth against mine with his eyes tightly closed. "This is the way Denny doesn't get hurt. If I'm gone, he may not question your lie. But if you ask me to stay . . . I will, and he'll eventually find out, and we'll destroy him. I know you don't want that. I don't either, baby." He almost seemed to be willing himself to say the words that he clearly didn't want to say.

Pain rocketed through my body and I couldn't stop the sob. "But it hurts so much. . . ."

He kissed me softly. "I know, baby . . . I know. We have to let it hurt. I need to leave, for good this time. If he's what you want, then we need to end this. It's the only way."

He kissed me again and then pulled back to look at me. His eyes were as wet and pained as mine must have been. He reached a hand into his jacket pocket and grabbed something. Holding his fist out to me, he gently pried open my hand with his other one. Very slowly, he opened his fist and placed something in my palm.

Through my blurry vision, I looked at what he'd given me. It was a very delicate silver chain. Attached to the chain was a silver guitar, and in the center of the guitar was a round diamond that had to be at least a carat. It was simple and stunning—perfect, just like him. I inhaled sharply and couldn't speak. My hand started to shake.

"You don't have to wear it . . . I'll understand. I just wanted you to have something to remember me by." He cocked his head to the side and gazed at my tear-streaked face. "I didn't want you to forget me. I'll never forget you."

I looked at him, barely able to speak through the pain. "Forget you?" The very idea was ludicrous. As if he wasn't seared into the very fabric of my soul. "I could never . . ." I grabbed his face in my hands, the necklace still laced in my fingers. "I love you . . . forever."

He brought his lips to mine, kissing me deeply. The music behind us swelled along with my heart. Again, I doubted that I could do this, that I could let him leave me. It still felt so wrong. His leaving, after everything we'd gone through, felt completely wrong. How would I survive this? Surely the withdrawals of a permanent separation would break me into pieces. I missed him already, even with his lips pressed firmly to mine, I longed for him.

We savored every second that we had together. I felt like the pain would bring me to my knees. A sob broke through my lips, and he clutched me tighter to his chest. He placed a hand on my cheek and, a second later, a sob broke through his lips, and I deepened our heartbreaking final kiss. This was wrong. I couldn't watch him walk away from me. I needed to speak, find some magic words to get him to stay with me . . . I just didn't know how. I knew my life would never be the same once this kiss ended. I never wanted it to end. . . .

But of course, nothing lasts forever.

The sound of the gate behind me smashing forcefully closed forever changed the way I would remember this last tender moment with Kellan.

Terrified, I immediately broke contact and stared at Kellan's wide eyes. He was looking past me, at the figure at the gate, but I could not make myself turn to look. I didn't need to look anyway. There was only one person on this earth who could have caused the intense look of fear, sorrow, and guilt on Kellan's face. My whole body started shaking.

"I'm so sorry, Kiera," Kellan whispered to me, never once taking his eyes from the gate.

Denny had just entered our small circle of private hell and there was no going back for him, for any of us.

"Kiera . . . ? Kellan . . ." My name came out like a question, Kellan's like a curse. Denny moved closer to where Kellan and I were quickly stepping away from each other. His face was confused and, at the same time, livid. He had seen that all too tender moment.

"Denny . . ." I tried to come up with something, but I couldn't. I suddenly realized that Denny had lied; he had never been called away. He had orchestrated this, tested us. . . . We had failed.

He ignored me and glared at Kellan. "What the hell is going on?"

I ran through some excuses that Kellan could make in my head, but my mouth dropped open in shock as Kellan simply told Denny the truth. "I kissed her. I was saying goodbye. . . . I'm leaving."

I fought back my despair at that statement, as I watched anger flare in Denny's dark eyes. "You kissed her?" I thought for a moment that he would leave it at that, but then he blurted out, "Did you fuck her?"

Shock again flared through me at Denny's conclusion to Kellan's simple statement. He *had* known, or at least suspected. I looked over at Kellan, silently pleading with him to lie.

He didn't.

"Yes," he whispered, cringing a little at Denny's crudeness.

Denny's mouth dropped wide open as he glared at Kellan. Both men seemed to have forgotten that I was even there. "When?" he whispered harshly.

Kellan sighed. "The first time was the night you broke up."

Denny's eyebrows rose, along with his voice. "The first time? How many *times* were there?" I closed my eyes, hoping this was just a nightmare.

Kellan answered very calmly. "Only twice . . ."

My eyes flashed open at his statement. Why would he lie about that? But at a meaningful look from him, I understood. Our last few days together had in no way constituted what Denny had crudely asked him. It wasn't a lie, simply . . . a half-truth. Even in my horror over the situation, my heart warmed a little at his omission.

Kellan calmly finished his thought, looking back toward Denny. "But I wanted her . . . every day."

The small warmth in my heart froze and my heart squeezed painfully. My breath completely stopped. What was he doing? Why would he tell Denny that? *I must be dreaming.* This couldn't be real. It wasn't real.

It happened so fast that I didn't have time to comprehend it. Denny's fist flew around and connected with Kellan's jaw, the blow staggering him backwards. Recovering slowly, Kellan stood straight and faced Denny again, blood trickling down his cut lip.

"I won't fight you, Denny. I'm so sorry, but we never wanted to hurt you. We fought against . . . We tried so hard to resist this . . . pull . . . we feel toward each other." Kellan's face cringed as he spoke, his emotional pain worse than his physical one.

"You tried? You tried to not fuck her?" Denny yelled, and hit him again.

My mind wanted me to scream at Denny to stop. My body wanted me to pull him away. Aside from shaking with fear and an aching coldness that pierced me to my very bones, I couldn't move. Shock froze me in place. Gaping like an idiot, I stood there silently.

"I gave up everything for her!" Denny struck him repeatedly. Kellan did nothing to block the blows, and made no attempt to fight Denny back. In fact, after every hit he turned to face Denny, intentionally or unintentionally giving him the best possible angle every time. Blood oozed from cuts on his cheek, his lip, and over his eye. "You promised me you wouldn't touch her!"

"I'm sorry, Denny," Kellan muttered between hits, barely audible to me, and probably completely inaudible to Denny in his rage.

I wanted Denny to yell at me, to blame me, to hit me, to at least look at me as being equally responsible for this mess, but all his rage was focused on Kellan. I had stopped existing to him. Inside I was sobbing, screaming for it to end. But I just stood there silently.

Eventually Kellan's strength wore out, and he fell to his knees in a pant, his blue shirt stained with his blood. "I trusted you!" Denny screamed at him, as a particularly brutal knee to Kellan's chin knocked him to his back.

My mind couldn't comprehend it. I started rejecting this reality. I was dreaming, that had to be it. This was just a nightmare, my worst nightmare. Soon I would wake up. But still, like I was stuck in quicksand, I just stood there silently.

Denny now began kicking him repeatedly with his heavy boots, screaming obscenities with every blow. A vicious kick landed on Kellan's arm, causing a sickening snap that I heard even in my stupor. Kellan cried out in pain, but Denny didn't stop. "You said you were my brother!"

My stomach rose. My body shivered uncontrollably. Tears flowed down my cheeks. Reality was shifting to me. Was I going mad? Was that why I couldn't move, couldn't shout for help? I desperately wanted to pull Denny away, hit him if I had to, but, listening in horror, I still just stood there silently.

Another swift kick to Kellan's side, and another audible crack as a rib or two broke. Kellan again cried out in agony, spat out blood, but did nothing to defend his body, said nothing to defend his actions, only endlessly repeated, "I won't fight you. . . . I won't hurt you. . . . I'm sorry, Denny. . . ."

If my sanity was slipping, Denny's was completely gone. He was a completely different person, viciously beating the life from Kellan's weakening body. Denny was beyond angry, beyond enraged. He was screaming ruthlessly at Kellan, a stream of vile things that I had never heard him utter. He seemed to have completely forgotten I was there, frozen in shock and horror as I was.

"Your word is worthless! *You* are worthless!"

Kellan cringed and turned his head away from those hurtful words, and I had the horrid feeling that it was not the first time he'd heard them. It wasn't the first time he'd been called worthless. "I'm sorry, Denny."

Denny didn't care about his apologies and was still kicking him viciously. "She is *not* one of your whores!"

Denny paused, panting in his fervor. Kellan weakly raised himself up on one elbow, his body crumpled and bruised in pain, blood stringing from his mouth and freely flowing from a cut above his eye and cheek. He looked up to meet Denny's enraged eyes and I watched Kellan's face twist with pain.

Kellan's next words filled me with an endless warmth and a bottomless fear. "I'm sorry I hurt you, Denny, but I love her," he panted. His eyes drifted back to mine and contentment filled them. He seemed at peace with the fact that he'd finally done it. He'd finally openly declared his feelings for me to his best friend, his brother.

Smiling warmly at me, he also added something onto his declaration that managed to push his friend over the breaking point. "And she loves me too."

I could literally see Denny snap. Glaring wildly at Kellan, he shifted his weight and aligned his foot for what I could clearly see would be a disastrous blow to Kellan's head. Besides panting in pain, his eyes still fixed on mine, Kellan didn't move. Watching me, he wasn't paying attention to what Denny was about to do. His inhumanly blue eyes took me in, absorbing me like he was memorizing me. It was going to be the last thing he ever did.

Without any conscious thought, I screamed, "*No!*" Finally able to move, I dove to the ground to shield Kellan. The surely fatal blow meant for him connected with my temple instead. I thought I heard Kellan shout my name, and then the whole world went black.

Chapter 24

Guilt and Regret

I became aware of sounds first—an insistent beeping near my ear that wasn't stopping, and soft male voices echoing in my head, as if they were speaking through a tunnel. I tried to focus on those voices, to bring them closer to me so I could understand what they were saying. Bits and pieces fell to my ears, but not enough to make any sense.

". . . now . . . leave . . . she'll . . . hurt . . . sorry . . . her . . . kill . . . you know . . ."

A light chuckle filled the room and I thought it sounded familiar, but nothing in my mind or body really felt familiar at the moment. My head felt light and airy, like a balloon tethered to my body. Then I moved it, and a sharp pain screamed at me to not do that again. I listened and stayed still until that airy feeling returned to me. A dull ache in my head registered my body's relief at my decision.

As I was wondering why my head hurt so much, memories started flooding my brain. Horrid memories that I wished I could block out, that I wished had fallen out of my head when the pain had entered it. Memories of my painful goodbye with Kellan. Memories of Denny's face when he discovered us. Memories of Denny beating up Kellan, taking out all of his frustrations on him, trying to kill him. His foot lining up for a devastating blow to Kellan's waiting head . . .

"No!"

My memory of the attack invoked the action of what I'd foolishly done to stop it. I sat upright in bed as I yelled, "No!" and immediately fell back in a heap against the pillow, tenderly clutching my head and gasping at the level of pain searing my body.

Denny's concerned face filled my hazy eyes. He stroked his thumbs across my cheekbones and turned behind him to mutter something to someone else in the room. A response was muttered back and I heard footsteps walking away as the pain in my head subsided to a throbbing ache. Denny turned back to me and continued stroking my cheeks, drying away some tears that had reached his fingers.

"Shhhh, Kiera. You're okay. It's okay . . . . relax."

I realized I was clutching the front of his T-shirt with a death-like grip and forced myself to calm down. My eyes went in and out of focus and I blinked heavily several times to try and see him more clearly.

"Denny?" My voice was scratchy, my throat raw and aching from thirst. "Where am I? What happened?"

Denny exhaled and rested his forehead gently against mine. "What happened? What happened is I thought I'd lost you. I thought I'd killed you. I can't believe what I . . ." His accent sounded strained to me, like it did sometimes when he was upset or emotional. He exhaled heavily and swallowed before giving me a chaste kiss on the forehead. Pulling back, his dark eyes looked moist. "You're at the hospital, Kiera. You've been in and out of it for a couple days now. It was touch and go for a while there. We were very lucky—there was bruising, but very little bleeding. You'll be okay."

I reached up and felt the side of my head carefully. Denny's fingers brushed mine as we both felt the tender area above my right ear. "They almost had to relieve the pressure with surgery, but they were finally able to get you back with medicine . . ." he murmured, as he rubbed his thumb against the back of my hand. My stomach twisted at the thought of a piece of my skull almost being removed. Thank

God they didn't have to do that. I closed my eyes and dropped my hand, clutching Denny's tightly.

"Good . . . she's awake. Probably in a good dose of pain too." A cheerful, plump nurse with a smile about five miles long walked through my door. I cringed at her loud, peppy voice and tried to slip on a smile. It felt a little weak to me. "My name is Susie and I'll be taking good care of you today." With an air of authority she shooed Denny off the bed, even though I tried to keep him there, and shot clear liquid into an IV attached to me. That was when I noticed the needle in my hand and again felt my stomach twist. She checked on my vital signs and seemed pleased with them. "Do you need any-thing, sweetie?"

"Water . . ." I croaked out.

She patted my leg. "Of course. I'll be right back."

She turned to leave, and my more-focused eyes followed her cat-covered scrubs out the door. Denny sat down on the other side of my bed and grabbed my non-IV-needled hand, but I barely no-ticed. I barely noticed anything anymore, and not because the pain meds were kicking in. No, that only cleared the ache in my head. My heart . . . ? That was suddenly throbbing. The beeping beside me sped up as well.

As I watched the nurse leave, my eyes had drifted across the per-son who had gone out to find her. A person who was still standing beside the door, leaning against the wall, keeping his distance from me and from Denny. A person whose left arm was casted from the wrist to the elbow and whose face was a mosaic coloring from yellow to near black . . . and still completely perfect.

He smiled at me when our eyes met, and I involuntarily clutched Denny's hand. Denny noticed my rapt attention and looked over to Kellan leaning against the wall. I couldn't understand what both of them were doing in my room . . . and not trying to kill each other. They looked at each other and then Kellan nodded to Denny and, throwing me a final smile, turned and left the room.

I wanted to shout at him to stay, to talk to me, to tell me what he was thinking, what he was feeling, but Denny cleared his throat. I looked back to him, confusion clear in my eyes. Denny smiled warmly at me and my confusion leapt even higher.

"You're not angry?" was all I could find to say.

He looked down for a moment, and I saw his jaw clench under the light hair there, hair that was a bit longer and stragglier than he usually kept it, like he hadn't left my side long enough to see to himself. He looked back up to me and I watched his eyes shift through multiple emotions before he relaxed his features and seemed to settle on one.

"Yes . . . I'm angry. But . . . almost killing you, well, that sort of put things in perspective." He raised one corner of his lips in a sad smile, and then dropped them to a frown. "I don't know what I would have done if you hadn't made it." He ran a hand down his face. "I don't know how I would have gotten through that. That would have destroyed me. . . ."

I brought my IV hand to his face; it felt heavy and solid, like the rest of my body was starting to feel. He looked back at me as my fingers ran across his jaw. He sighed and gave me a slight smile. "I wish you'd just told me, Kiera . . . from the beginning."

I withdrew my hand that suddenly felt overly hot. My heart started thumping and I begged it to calm down, as the monitor with the insistent beeping beside me picked up its pace to match it. He noticed my reaction and sighed. "It would have been hard . . . but so much better than how I found out."

He dropped his head and ran a hand through his hair; I noticed that his knuckles were still raw and red from attacking Kellan. "Of course . . . I should have talked to you when I suspected. I never should have set you up like that. I was just hoping . . . I just so wanted to be wrong."

He raised his head, and his eyes suddenly looked exhausted, like he hadn't really slept in days. "I never thought you'd hurt me, Kiera." He cocked his head as I bit my lip to not cry. "Not you . . ." He spoke so softly, I had to lean in to hear him. "I thought Kellan might try for you. I even made him promise not to touch you when I left. But I never really thought you'd . . ." He looked away from me and a bitter note that I was not used to hearing from him entered his accent. "How could you do that to me?"

He looked back to me and I opened my mouth to try and speak. Before any rational speech came out, the nurse came back and merrily handed me a Styrofoam cup, one bead of water hanging off the end of its straw. I couldn't take my eyes off that drop of water, and immediately slurped down the drink when she handed it to me. I think I mumbled some sort of thank-you before she cheerfully walked away.

Denny waited patiently for me to gulp down half the water. Finally, I removed the straw and looked down at the cup in my hands, no longer able to meet his sad eyes. "Where do we go from here?" I quietly asked, terrified of his answer. With shaking fingers, I put the cup down on a table beside my bed.

He leaned in and gently kissed my uninjured temple. "We go nowhere, Kiera," he whispered in my ear before pulling away from me.

Tears immediately sprang to my eyes as I looked over his sad but calm face. "But I was leaving him. I love you."

He tilted his head and ran the back of his finger down my cheek. "I know . . . and I love you. But I don't think we love each other in the same way. And . . . I think keeping you near me would destroy me. Look at what it almost made me do to you and Kellan. Look what I *did* do to you and Kellan." He looked back down to the pillows. "I'll never forgive myself for any of that . . . but it could have been so much worse, and I think it would be, if we stayed together."

The tears spilled down my cheeks now and when he looked back at me, similar tears were on his. "Stayed together? We're not together?"

He swallowed roughly and wiped some of my tears away. "No, Kiera . . . we're not. If you think about it, really think about it, we haven't been together for a while." I started to shake my head but he kept going with his awful truths. "No . . . there's no point in trying to deny it. It's right there, Kiera. Somewhere along the way, you and I started drifting. Even when we've been together, we haven't . . . connected, like we used to. I don't know if it's only because of Kellan, or if this was just going to happen with us anyway. Maybe he just sped up something that was already coming."

I shook my head again, but I couldn't deny what he was saying. The only thing echoing in my head was "he's right," and I couldn't say that to him. I couldn't confirm what was surely going to be the end of us.

He smiled slightly at my feeble attempt to disagree with him. "I think in the end, you would have stayed with me, out of obligation . . . or maybe comfort. Maybe I was safe to you, and you needed to feel that." He rubbed my cheek again. "I know how scared you get of the unknown. To you . . . I must be kind of a security blanket."

More tears rolled down my cheeks and I wanted to both agree and disagree, but I had no idea what the right response was. Which one was worse? He seemed to understand my confusion. "Do you see now how that doesn't work for me? I don't want to be someone's safety net. I don't want to be there simply because the idea of me being gone is too . . . scary."

He placed his hand upon my chest, over my heart. "I want to be someone's everything. I want fire and passion, and love that's returned, equally. I want to be someone's heart." He removed his hand and stared at it. Holding back a sob at the immense loss I felt when his hand pulled away, I stared at it too. "Even if it means breaking my own," he whispered, his accent thick.

With a voice tight with ready to explode with emotion, I managed to squeak out, "What are you saying, Denny?"

He sniffed and a couple tears fell from his heavily glistening eyes. "I took the Australia job. I'm going back home in a couple of weeks, once I know you're going to be okay. I'm going back home alone, Kiera."

Then I couldn't control it anymore. Then I did sob. Then I let

every emotion I had about Denny and our darkening relationship
seep through me, and I knew . . . I knew that he was right. He should
leave. He should find happiness with someone, since he'd never truly
find it with me. Not with the turn our relationship had taken. Not with
how I'd betrayed him. Not with the fact that, even while I was listening
to Denny say goodbye, I was wondering where Kellan had gone.

Denny's arms carefully came around me and he swept me up
into a tight hug. He cried against me, as I cried against him. He
promised that he still loved me and that he'd stay in touch. I'd never
lose his friendship, we had too much history for that, but he couldn't
be near me. Not as long as I loved someone else. I wanted to assure
him that I didn't. I wanted to tell him that I only loved him, and I
only wanted to be with him. But it was a lie, and I was done lying, to
others and to myself.

I don't know how long he held me. It felt like days. When he
pulled away, I tried to hold him tight, but the pain meds had kicked
in enough that I was too weak and sleepy to really have much hold
on him. It was sort of symbolic, and I hated that. He kissed my head
as my fingers drifted weakly down his skin.

"I'll be back to check on you tomorrow, okay?" I nodded and he
kissed me one last time before turning and leaving.

I watched him stop at the doorway and talk to someone standing where I couldn't see. He looked back to me and then back to the
person. He spoke a few soft words and then reached his hand out.
He looked to be apologizing. I scrunched my brows, confused, and
wondered if the meds were making me loopy as well as tired. Denny
gave me a final smile then, and turned away from the person he'd
been talking to.

I watched him disappear and my chest seized at the vision of
him leaving. I knew this was just the first of many painful breaks he
and I would have, the last and most painful being the final one, when
I'd have to watch him leave on a plane again, but permanently this
time. I closed my eyes, grateful for a moment that he hadn't done
something so stupid that that future would be closed to him. If any-

thing, at least Denny would have a great job that he could find solace in. And I knew that eventually he'd find a great woman too. God, I hated that thought. But he was right, I'd been holding onto him for the wrong reasons.

A light touch along my cheek roused me from my troubling thoughts. Thinking Denny had returned, my breath caught when I saw Kellan's deep blue eyes gazing at me. His face was a mess—his lip was cut but pink from healing; his cheek had a pink line across it with a nasty bluish yellow bruise surrounding it and a couple of thin strips of surgical tape holding the healing skin together. His right eye had a taped, healing cut above it as well, and his left eye was so bruised, it was almost black. Between all that and his casted arm, and I'm sure a few taped-together ribs, he looked like he'd been put through the wringer . . . twice.

But my heart still skipped a beat at the sight of him. Literally, I heard it on the annoying monitor beside me. His smile was warm and soft as he sat in the spot Denny had just vacated. I realized then that he'd been outside the room the whole time, and he'd talked to Denny as Denny had left. I wondered if he'd heard our talk, if he knew that Denny had broken it off with me.

"Are you okay?" he asked, his voice low and husky, warm with concern.

"I guess," I mumbled. "The pain meds kicked in, and I feel like I weigh a thousand pounds, but I guess I'm going to be fine."

He smiled a little more and shook his head. "That's not what I meant. Believe me, I've talked to about every nurse in here, I know your situation . . . but are you okay?" His eyes flicked over to the door and I knew that he did indeed know about Denny. He might have been listening, maybe not, but nevertheless, he knew.

A tear rolled down my cheek as I looked up at him. "Ask me again in a couple days."

He nodded and bent down to softly kiss my lips. The stupid monitor beside me increased a tad and Kellan looked over at it and laughed quietly. "I suppose I shouldn't do that."

As he pulled away, I grabbed his cheek and ran a finger along the bruise under his eye. "Are you okay?"

He grabbed my hand and pulled it away from his face. "I'll be fine, Kiera. Don't worry about that right now. I'm just so glad that you're . . . that you're not . . ." He swallowed and looked unable to say anything more than that.

He held my hand in both of his, and I stroked the skin of his wrist, where it disappeared under his cast. "You and Denny were both here?"

"Of course. We both care about you, Kiera."

I shook my head. "No, I mean, you were both here in the same room, talking calmly when I woke up. You weren't trying to kill each together?"

He smiled wryly and looked away from me. "Once was enough." He looked back to me. "You've been out of it for a couple days. Denny and I . . . have had several talks." He started to bite his lip and then stopped when that seemed to hurt him. "Those first few talks weren't so . . . calm." He reached up to stroke some of the hair away from my face. "Our concern for you eventually tempered those conversations, and we talked about what to do, instead of what was done."

I started to say something, but Kellan beat me to it. "He told me he took the job in Australia, and when I asked if he'd take you with him . . . he told me no." He stroked my cheek as more tears flowed down them.

"You knew he was going to break up with me today?"

He nodded, and his eyes looked very sad. "I knew he was going to do it soon. When you woke up and he looked at me . . . I figured he wanted to do it as soon as possible." He looked away from me and his voice got very quiet. "Rip off the Band-Aid. . . ."

His eyes turned speculative as he examined a spot on the floor for a long time. I started to reach for his face again, when he spoke, eyes still on the floor. "What are your plans now, Kiera?"

I startled and dropped my hand. My head suddenly felt like the blow was nothing, my heart was hurting more than that wound ever would. "My plans? I don't . . . I don't know. School . . . work . . ."

You. I wanted to say it, but I knew how horrible it would sound.

He seemed to hear it anyway, and when his eyes turned back to mine, there was a coldness in the blue depths. A coldness I'd seen many times before when I'd hurt him. "And me? Do we just pick up where we left off? Before you left me . . . again . . . for him?"

I shut my eyes and willed my body back to unconsciousness. Like always, my body didn't listen. "Kellan . . ."

"I can't do this anymore, Kiera."

I opened my eyes at the heartbreak in his voice. His eyes were watering now as he gazed at me. "I was going to let you walk away that night. I told you I'd let you go, if that was what you wanted, and when you said . . ."

He closed his eyes and sighed. "After that, I couldn't even find it in me to lie to Denny when he found us." He opened his eyes and looked down at our hands, his thumb still stroking my skin. "I knew he'd attack me when he heard the truth . . . but I couldn't fight him back. I'd hurt him so badly, I couldn't find it in me to hurt him physically."

I wanted to hold him so much it hurt worse than my head. "What we did to him . . ." Kellan shook his head, his eyes still unfocused as he remembered that night. "He's the nicest guy I've ever known, the closest thing to real family I've ever had, and we turned him into my . . ." His eyes closed for a moment as pain flashed over his features.

"I think a part of me wanted him to hurt me. . . ." His voice was soft and spoke volumes of where his head had been that night, his guilt and his pain. His eyes came back to mine. "Because of you, because you always chose him. You never really wanted me, and you're all I've ever . . ."

He swallowed and looked away. "So . . . now that he's left *you,* now that the choice isn't yours, do I get you?" He looked back to me and the fury was there again. "Am I your consolation prize?"

My mouth dropped wide open as I gaped at him. Consolation prize? Hardly. He was never second place, I was just scared. Oh, God, I was just scared. . . .

I tried to open my mouth to speak, to tell him that everything I did was out of fear. That I pushed him away so many times because the level of love between us was terrifying to me, trusting him was terrifying, letting go of Denny's comfort was terrifying. I couldn't though. My heavy lips couldn't form the words. I didn't know how to tell him that I was wrong . . . that we never should have said goodbye in that parking lot.

He nodded as he took in my silence. "That's what I thought." He sighed and dropped his head again. "Kiera . . . I wish . . ." He raised his head and looked at me, the anger earlier in his eyes replaced with sadness. "I've decided to stay in Seattle." He closed his eyes and shook his head. "You wouldn't believe how much crap Evan gave me for almost leaving the band." He opened his eyes and searched my face, his eyes lingering on the tender spot by my ear. "I never even thought about my band in this whole mess. I hurt them when they found out I was planning on ditching town." He shook his head sadly and sighed while I struggled with something compelling to say.

Eventually, he sighed softly again and whispered, "I'm sorry." He leaned down again to brush our lips together. Exhaling, he kissed along my cheek to my ear. The monitor betrayed my body's reaction to his nearness, to the smell of him, the feel of him, and he sighed as he kissed the soft spot below my ear. Pulling back some, he rested his head against mine. "I'm so sorry, Kiera. I love you . . . but I can't do this. I need you to move out."

Before I could react to that, before I could sob and tell him no, that I wanted to stay, I wanted to stay and try and work things out, he stood and left the room without a backwards glance.

For the second time that day, my heart broke, and I cried so hard, I lulled myself back to sleep.

When I woke up later it was dark outside and my small room was a pale, peaceful green under the softly lit lights. A painting on the wall depicted geese in a V formation, flying south for the winter maybe, and a whiteboard next to it let me know that my night nurse's name was Cindy. I attempted to stretch my body and got both pleasant relief from my well-rested muscles and a dull ache from my head. I finished the cup of now-lukewarm water on the table beside me and tried to stand. My muscles at first refused to cooperate. I was stiff and sore from being in the same position for so long, but eventually I won out and, ignoring the protest in my brain, stood, unplugged the beeping machine tracking my heartbeat, and made my way to the bathroom, dragging the IV bag attached to its movable stand with me.

Once in the bathroom, I was sorry I'd moved. I looked atrocious. My wavy hair was a mess of curls and snarls, and the right side of my face from my eyebrow to my cheekbone was a horrid black-and-blue color. My eyes were bloodshot from what felt like days of crying, and my face had a permanent look of desolation.

I'd done it. I'd successfully pushed away two wonderful men. My desire to hurt neither of them had ended up hurting them both. I'd pushed Denny into doing something that was so out of character for him, I could barely contemplate it. The look on his face as he'd struck Kellan repeatedly . . . I'd never have guessed that side of him was in there, buried deep, waiting to explode one day. I suppose we all have our buttons, our triggers that, pushed hard enough, will make even the calmest person flip.

And Kellan, always the passionate one . . . if I hadn't beaten him down so much, he would have reacted much differently to Denny's outburst. Possibly he'd have fought back. Possibly with an even worse outcome. But it all came down to me . . . me and my multiple poor decisions and indecisiveness.

I used the bathroom as quickly as a sore person could and shuffled back to my bed. Curling into a ball, I wondered what I was going to do now. I didn't come up with anything. My eyes slowly closed from pain and exhaustion and I fell back asleep.

I woke briefly during the night when the nurse—Cindy, I'm assuming, since I was too groggy with sleep to ask—checked my vitals and reattached me to my annoying beeping machine. I didn't fully wake until the next morning, when the bright and cheery Susie returned.

"Here she is, sweetie. Oh, and she's awake too. Great!" She came over to check my vitals and handed me some pills for the pain, which was a bit better today. I barely registered the plump, merry woman, though, since my eyes were mainly focused on the beautiful vision of a woman beside her.

"Hey, sis," Anna whispered as she sat at the foot of the bed. Her long hair was back to its traditional near-black, shiny luxuriousness, and she had it pulled into an adorably high ponytail. The sweater she wore was royal blue and tight enough to reveal all of her marvelous curves. For once, I didn't care how plain I looked beside her. I only cared that someone I loved was here with me.

My eyes watered as the nurse went about her business. I thought I heard her murmur something about "lunch is in an hour and you should try eating today," before she shuffled out the door. My mind momentarily registered that it was almost lunchtime already and then focused back on Anna, still gazing at me with perfectly green, but sad, eyes.

Just when I was about to ask her what she was doing here, she spoke. "Those boys really did a number on you, didn't they?" I cringed, knowing she must know everything then. She shook her head and then, with a sigh, stood and wrapped me in a hug. "Really, Kiera . . . what were you thinking? Getting involved in a fight?"

I choked back a sob and muttered, "I wasn't . . . obviously."

She held me for a moment, and then crawled into the bed beside me, snuggling up to the side of me that wasn't attached to an IV. She held my hand tightly in hers and put her head on my shoulder. "Well, I'm here to do the thinking for you from now on," she muttered into my shoulder. I smiled at her comment, relaxing into her warmth.

"I love you, sis, and I'm so glad you're here . . . but what are you doing here?" I hoped that didn't sound ungrateful. I really was thrilled to see her.

She pulled back to look at me. "Denny. He called after the . . . accident." Her eyes narrowed as she looked me over. "You're lucky he got me and not Mom or Dad. Your broken butt would be on a plane back home by now."

I cringed again at that thought. No, it was probably better if my parents never knew about this. "Well, don't you have a job or something back there?"

She cocked an eyebrow at me. "Trying to get rid of me?" I was already shaking my head no, and clutching her arm to keep her near me, when she chuckled. "No . . . I've been between jobs. Honestly, I think Mom will be glad to have me off her couch for a while, and what better place to find work than way out west with my self-destructive sister?"

She beamed at me, as what she was saying registered in my slow head. "Wait . . . you're staying in Seattle?"

She shrugged and put her head back on my shoulder. "I *was* just going to make sure your stupid ass was okay, but then I heard that you needed a place to stay and thought maybe I could find a job out here and we could be roommates. At least until your school is over with." She looked up at me with a stunningly beautiful and playful expression. "Do you think Hooters is hiring? I bet the guys there tip crazy good."

I rolled my eyes at my capricious sister, and then narrowed them at her. "How did you know I needed a place to live? Kellan only told me that yesterday. . . ."

Her face went blank and she sort of looked like a deer in headlights, a painfully attractive deer in headlights. "Shit. I wasn't supposed to mention that. Damn, he's gonna be pissed." She shrugged again. "Oh well." She sat back on the pillow and I turned to look at her better, curious over what she was talking about.

"I ran into Kellan downstairs. He told me what was going on. He told me that he asked you to leave." She raised her eyebrow again. "He looks like shit, by the way. Hot shit, but shit nonetheless. Denny really did that to him?"

I was nodding at her without really thinking about it. "Kellan is still here . . . at the hospital?" I kind of figured he'd written me off and gone home to dwell with a bottle of Jack and maybe even a girl . . . or two.

She sighed and tucked some hair behind my ear, her fingers staying on the gross bruise I knew covered part of my face. "He's crazy in love with you, Kiera. He won't leave the hospital. He wanders around downstairs, drinking coffee and waiting to hear if your condition has changed." She removed her hand and tucked it under her cheek on the pillow. "Some of the nurses here were even talking about him when I came up. Apparently, he's charmed quite a few and they tell him things about you when he comes up here every once in a while." She rolled her eyes. "There's some serious crushing going on in that nurses' station."

I blushed at that and turned to stare at the ceiling. I tried to picture where he might be in the hospital, feel his warmth, even through our distance. All I could feel was the dull ache in my head and the greater ache in my heart. "He's not coming back in here . . . is he?"

Anna sighed heavily and I turned again to look at her with glistening eyes. "No," she whispered. "He said it's too hard. He needs space." She scrunched her brow in a too-cute expression of confusion. "He said he needed a minute." She shrugged, like she didn't understand that.

I closed my eyes. I did. Our code . . . He needed a break . . . from me. How badly had I hurt him this time? Bad enough for him to finally stay away . . . sort of. Even though I was chilled with loneliness at forcing two men away from me, it warmed me that he still cared enough to stay somewhat close to me.

I opened my eyes at my sister's voice. It was completely serious for once. "Really, what were you thinking, Kiera . . . carrying on with two men?" Her voice lost its seriousness for a second as her lips twisted in a wry smile. "Did you learn nothing from the John and Ty fiasco?"

I smiled at her brief love triangle and then frowned, remembering my own. "I certainly never planned it, Anna. I just . . . I got . . ." I sighed heavily and felt tears sting my eyes. ". . . overwhelmed."

She held me close and kissed my head. "You're such an idiot, Kiera." I pulled back to look at her, irritation clear on my face, and she gave me an amused grin. "Don't shoot the messenger. You've got to know how badly you messed things up." She touched my head for emphasis.

Humility tumbled through me and I shut my eyes again. "I know . . . I'm an idiot."

She hugged me as my tears started to spill over my cheeks. "Well, you're still my little sister, and I still love you." She sighed as I cried on her shoulder. "I always told you to stick to books and not people. People just aren't your thing."

Says the Queen of Broken Hearts, I thought, a little unfairly.

Almost as if she heard my thoughts, she pulled away to look at me. "I'm not saying I'm a role model or anything, but at least I never promise the guys . . . anything. And you promised them both, didn't you?"

I nodded and brought my hands to my face as a sob of guilt and grief filled me. She held me and rubbed my back. "It's okay . . . it will be okay. You're just young. You're young and inexperienced, and Kellan is hotter than all fuck."

I stiffened a bit and looked up at her, shaking my head. She interpreted for me. "I know . . . it was more than that. I have noticed his softer side. I have noticed the melancholy, the pain he tries to hide, the intensity in his music. I'm guessing he's pretty deep. I'm guessing he's pretty emotional, and I'm guessing he was pretty damn hard to resist."

I sighed and slumped against her, happy that at least she understood that it had nothing to do with his looks . . . not really. She rubbed my back and again whispered that everything would be okay. We were silent for a long time, until she finally sighed and pulled away from me. "You must have hated me when I came to visit." She shook her head on the pillow. "Me all over Kellan like that."

I opened my mouth and, remembering that horrid visit when I'd assumed the worst about her and Kellan, I had to try again to speak when nothing came out the first time. "No," I finally whispered. "I never hated you. I hated him." She looked at me funny, and I continued on with my explanation. "He led me to believe that the two of you slept together."

Her eyes widened then looked a little fiery. "He what?" Her tone relaxed along with her face. "Wait . . . is that why you avoided talking to me for so long? God, I thought I'd offended you by grabbing Denny's butt at the airport."

I giggled at her and felt relieved that I could still laugh about certain things. "No, that was funny." I sighed as I watched her emerald eyes stare back at me. "Don't be mad at Kellan. He was hurt and angry and wanting to torture me. You were just the easiest way. I didn't know you slept with Griffin until much later." I pulled back and narrowed my eyes at her. "Griffin . . . *really*?"

She bit her lip and squealed a little. "God, do I finally get to tell you that story. You know I've been dying, right?" I blushed three shades of red, as she proceeded to tell me everything . . . and, God, I mean *everything* that they had done that night. My stomach hurt a little bit at the end, but I managed a weak smile. She sighed and cuddled into me. After a moment, she said, "You know I'd never have even touched Kellan if you'd have told me what was going on . . . right?"

I sighed and hugged her back. "I know. . . . You understand why I couldn't say anything?"

She shook her head. "No . . . well, maybe." She kissed my head. "I love you, Kiera."

She cuddled with me until my lunch came, and then she perked up and started going on about wanting to find a job and an apartment for us, something cute with a view of the water. I sighed as I started in on my bland Jell-O. Of anyone in Seattle, my sister would be able to get both a job and an apartment by sundown. She kissed my head and told me she'd be back when she had good news. Truly, I expected her back anytime.

I slept more after lunch, woke when the nurse checked on me, then fell back asleep. I wasn't sure if sleepiness was a side effect of the accident, the meds they had me on, or the overwhelming fact that I didn't want to deal with my life right now.

But life wasn't quite leaving me alone. Denny came back that evening, and he smiled briefly when he saw I looked a little better—well, more aware, anyway.

"Hey." He leaned down like he was going to kiss my lips, and then he seemed to remember why he shouldn't and kissed my forehead instead. Habits . . . they can be so hard to break.

He sat in a chair next to the bed, and not beside me this time. I got the feeling he was distancing himself, preparing himself for the final break that we both knew was coming. His eyes lingered on the bruise on my face, while we spoke of semi-important things—he had put in his notice at the job he hated, his parents were thrilled that he was coming home, sad that I wasn't coming with him, and he was leaving his car for me since he couldn't afford to ship it.

That last piece of information startled me, and he looked over my quickly tearing-up face. "I know you'll take good care of it, Kiera." His accent was warm and soft, and for a moment, just a moment, I missed him while he was still sitting there.

I wanted to speak of the important things—the accident, the guilt I knew he felt whenever he looked at me, the guilt I felt whenever I looked at him, the love I still felt between us, even if it was a different kind of love now, the affair . . .

I didn't though. I was too tired, too weak, and I just couldn't handle another heartbreaking conversation while hooked up to that damn beeping monitor that was slowly driving me to madness. Instead, we left things only on the semi-important topics. I told him about Anna dropping everything to move out here with me and that, right now, she was job and apartment hunting. He seemed to agree with me that she'd find something in no time.

His eyebrows lifted when I talked about moving in with Anna, and I could tell he wanted to ask about Kellan. Whatever they had discussed, Kellan must not have told him, or known himself at the time, that he'd be asking me to leave. That he'd be breaking up with me too. Denny didn't ask though. Maybe he was too afraid of my answer. Maybe he'd be too tempted to stay if I told him Kellan and I really weren't anything anymore. Then again, maybe he just didn't care enough to make himself ask.

Denny stayed with me until Anna came back later in the evening. She gave him a reserved hug, which confused me at first. Anna was usually more exorbitant in her affections. But when she glanced at my face, I understood. He'd hurt me and that lowered him quite a few pegs in her eyes. I should talk with her about that, since technically he hadn't been trying to hurt me, and he really couldn't be blamed for my stupid actions. Like she said, I was the idiot.

Turning to me, she practically glowed when she spoke of our new apartment and her new job . . . at Hooters. I sighed and listened to her go over the steal she got on the place because the old guy wouldn't stop staring at her rack, and she promised him a free plate of hot wings whenever he popped into the restaurant. That pretty much sealed the deal for him. Again, what my sister could get men to do for her.

Denny quietly said goodbye to us both and kissed my forehead again before leaving, his eyes never straying from the injured side of my face. As he was at the doorway and I felt that familiar squeeze in my heart, I heard my sister say, "Wait." She stepped outside with him. I didn't know what they talked about, but they were out there a good twenty minutes. When she came back, my sister only smiled when I asked. Curious, but tired, I let it go. Maybe they had worked out their differences and she'd be nicer to him from now on. My injuries really weren't his fault.

My sister stayed for hours longer and then, because she was looking antsy, I told her it was okay if she wanted to go . . . socialize. She grinned devilishly and told me she'd be back tomorrow afternoon. I was pretty sure a visit with Griffin was in her future. I'm glad he appealed to her in some odd way, but I really didn't get it. And now I had a horridly descriptive visual to go with the image in my head.

She did come back the next afternoon, and told me all about their impossibly long night. If I had to give Griffin anything, it was that he had . . . stamina. After a while, other friends came in to visit. Matt and Evan stopped in and each gave me brief hugs. They seemed a little uncomfortable but wanted to be supportive with an appearance. Evan looked particularly guilty, like he felt he should have been there, or told Denny earlier or something. As he was leaving, I assured him that he did nothing wrong. He did what Kellan and I had asked, and we didn't hold him responsible for anything. He nodded and a big grin lit his happy, teddy-bear face as he scooped me into as much of a bear hug as he could, whispering that he was glad I was all right.

Jenny and Kate came in together before their shifts and Jenny's eyes teared up as she looked over my still-bruised face. She hugged me tight and repeated over and over that she was so glad I was okay, that everyone at work was glad I was okay, and that everybody was anxiously waiting for me to return to the bar.

I pulled away from her hug and watched another tear drop down her cheek. "Jenny . . . I can't go back to Pete's."

Her blue eyes widened at that. "But . . . why not, Kiera?"

My eyes moistened now. "I can't . . . I can't be around . . . him."

The room got really quiet, as everyone in there understood who I meant. Kate and Jenny shared a look between themselves, and I wondered if Kellan was still here and if Kate and Jenny had run into him downstairs like my sister had. By the look in Kate's eyes and the frown on Jenny's face, I figured they had.

Jenny's lack of any further argument only confirmed that suspicion for me. "Where will you go?"

I shook my head as tears finally spilled down my cheeks. "I don't know. Do you know anyone who needs a semi-good waitress?"

She smiled sadly and hugged me. "You're better than semi-good. I'll ask around. It won't be the same without you, Kiera . . . it just won't."

Feeling unworthy of her praise, I could only nod and hug her back. She pulled back to look at me and, wiping her tears, said, "Well, it's not like we're not going to be friends anymore, just because we don't work together, right?"

I nodded and wiped away my own tears. "Absolutely."

Griffin came in a bit after Jenny and Kate left, which surprised me. Of course, I think he was there more to pick up Anna than anything else. He did give me a hug . . . and copped a feel, but I actually appreciated the sentiment, if not the delivery. Smacking his ass, my sister mock scolded him for the feel-up. He feigned innocence and pulled her into a stomach-churning French kiss. Playfully holding each other, they said their goodbyes and went off to, as Griffin put it, "christen the new apartment." I prayed they stayed out of whatever room was being allocated to me.

After they left, my doctor gave me a once-over and, feeling satisfied with my condition, had the nurses turn off that damn machine and unplug me from the IV. As I ate a lifeless dinner, I wished I felt as put back together as the doctor had tried to convince me I was. After my meal, once Susie checked on me again and then left me alone, the silence of the room pressed in heavily.

The space was fully lit, but the darkness of the winter night outside seemed to seep in through the wide window, almost as if that blackness was stealing my warmth and my light. I stared at those cheer-stealing windows for what had to be hours, watching the darkness thicken and deepen. I shivered and pulled the covers tighter around me. I felt very cold and alone. Guilt and remorse pressed around me, squeezing to a point at the soft spot in my head. Just as I was wondering how I'd make it through like this, a soft accent spoke to me from the doorway.

"Hey. How are you?"

I peeled my eyes from the window and brushed a tear that I hadn't realized had fallen off my cheek. I looked over at Denny leaning against my doorframe. His arms were crossed over his chest and his foot was propped up, like he'd been watching me for a while. He smiled softly at me, a smaller version of his goofy grin that usually lit my heart. Today . . . today, though, it made the tears flow harder.

He instantly made a move toward me and then stopped half-way to my bed, a torn look on his face. He looked back to the door and, through my tears, I saw a hazy figure step back from the opening. I couldn't make out the body through my watery vision, but I knew who it was. I knew Kellan had come back up here and was making himself stay away from me. Like before, we were back to a no-touching policy. Only now it was worse, now we had a no-visual policy too.

A sob broke free from me and that seemed to firm up Denny's mind. He crossed the few feet to my bed and sat beside me, picking up my hand and holding it in his. It was a simple touch, and far more friendlike than I was used to getting from him when I was upset, but I knew that was all he'd allow himself to give me. I squeezed his hand, taking what comfort from him that I could.

"Don't cry, Kiera . . . it's okay."

I sniffled and worked to calm down, hating the fact that this beautiful man beside me was comforting *me* . . . even though he was the one I'd broken. It seemed unfair. He should yell and be angry, call me a whore and storm out, never to look on me again. But . . . that wasn't Denny. He was warm and caring and kind, almost to a fault. And by the way his eyes never strayed far from my injury, I knew that a large part of his continual presence here was due to the fact that he felt such enormous guilt over hurting me.

I swallowed back the tears as we silently watched each other. Warmth from his hand in mine calmed me, and I eventually looked at him without sobbing. He smiled again, once my tears dried up.

"I saw your new place," he said quietly. "I think you'll like it. Your sister has good taste."

I cocked my head at him. "You saw it?" He nodded and I held his hand tighter. "What did you and Anna talk about yesterday?"

Denny looked down and shook his head. "She's a little angry with me"—he looked up—"for hurting you." His eyes looked haunted for a moment, and drifted to my injury before he continued. "She cussed me out good." He raised his eyebrow at me. "She's got quite a mouth on her sometimes." I smiled at that and he smiled back in a genuine way that made his eyes come alive more than I'd seen in a while.

"Anyway, once she was satisfied, she asked for my help in moving your stuff. I needed to move mine too, so"—he shrugged—"I told her I'd help. We got all of it done tonight, and Anna got some furniture from Griffin, Kate, Jenny . . . well, anybody who had anything, really." He almost timidly ran a hand out to tuck a lock of hair behind my ear. "You're all set to go."

I tried to see the good in that as I tried to smile, but all I felt was an ache at being removed from a home that, until things got messy, had been nothing but a joy to me. Denny seemed to understand my melancholy and gently stroked my cheek once, before removing his hand and placing it back in his lap.

"What about you? Where are you staying, while you're . . . here?" I asked, my voice shaking a bit at the end.

"I've been staying with Sam. He's been really kind to me. I've been crashing on his couch for a few days now." He ran a hand through his hair and grinned at me crookedly. "I couldn't stay there with Kellan. My patience with him only goes so far."

"Why are you guys . . . ?" I let my question trail off, not wanting to incite his anger about the affair. Not that it probably wasn't always there, just under the surface.

He didn't let it drop though. "Why are we what? Not killing each other? Not screaming, yelling, carrying on? Why are we civil?"

I shrugged and cringed. He looked at me a moment and I thought I saw anger in his eyes, but I couldn't be sure. When he spoke again, his voice was controlled but his accent was thick. "I could have killed you that night . . . and I don't even want to think about that nightmare. But . . . even with what I did do, things should be so much worse for me than they are. And Kellan is the reason they're not."

I cocked my head, completely confused. "I don't . . ."

He sighed and his face softened. "You know, I never thought much about moving in with him. About how appealing women thought he was. Even back at school, he could just look at a girl and she'd . . ." He sighed again, while I felt my face heat a bit. "I never even considered how tempting he might be . . . to you. I just never thought that would matter, because what we had was so . . ." He closed his eyes as tears instantly filled mine again. At that moment, I completely hated myself for what I'd done to him. I started to reach my free hand out to touch his cheek, but stopped, and let it fall back to my lap when he opened his eyes. Calmly, he kept my gaze. "Once I figured it out . . . I knew I'd never be able to compete with him."

I blinked at what he said and furrowed my brow. Compete with Kellan? He never had to. I'd always wanted him. Well, maybe a part of me didn't? He noticed my confused look. "When I started piecing things together—looks I'd seen, touches I'd ignored, how distant you'd become, how forlorn you were when *he* wasn't around—I knew I'd lose you, if I hadn't already. I knew I didn't stand a chance against"—he rolled his eyes and shook his head, looking down at the sheets on my bed—"quite possibly the most attractive man in the Pacific Northwest."

"Denny . . . I—"

He cut me off. "I was so angry at *him* for that." He looked up at me and then back down at his hands, still holding one of mine. "Like I knew you wouldn't be able to resist his charm, so it was up to him . . . and he failed." I started to look down, right as his eyes looked up, and we met in the middle. "I think that's why I asked him to stay away from you at the airport. I didn't think you'd stray, not really. . . . I trusted you, but only if he kept his distance." He shrugged. "He gets every girl he goes after, and I knew he'd get you, if he really tried, and I just couldn't compete with that."

"It wasn't like that, Denny." I wanted to argue against it more, but there just wasn't much to say. I couldn't exactly tell Denny that I'd started nearly everything that had happened with Kellan and me. That Kellan hadn't deserved his rage, because I'd initiated the contact with him . . . and he'd already been in love. Whatever good intentions I'd started out with when Denny had left, somewhere along the line, *I* had strayed, even before the actual . . . straying.

And even worse, I'd fallen in love too. I wasn't even sure when I had fallen for Kellan anymore. It might have been that first awkward meeting in the hallway, it might have been the first time I cried in his arms, it might have been him telling me I was beautiful, or it might have even been the first time I heard him sing that deeply moving song that still touched me. All I knew for sure was that I did. I fell madly in love, and that ache added to my current one as I watched Denny's eyes gloss over with unconcealable pain.

"When I saw the two of you in the parking lot . . . actually saw the passion between you . . . I hated him so much. I hated what he took from me. I wanted to end him, for treating you like one of his groupies." He shook his head and cut me off when I tried to object. "It never occurred to me that he was in love. It never occurred to me that you were in love. It never occurred to me to blame you at all. I had you on this pedestal. . . ."

I nodded and looked down, the tears stinging my eyes, threatening to spill. I wasn't worthy of being on a pedestal, and from the look I'd seen in his eye when he said that . . . I thought maybe he now agreed. Quietly, and feeling very foolish, I confirmed that he should view me differently. "We were. We were in love . . . and we both never wanted to hurt you."

He sighed and lowered his head. "I know. I think I know that now." He rubbed his fingers down the side of my hand, tracing patterns in the skin subconsciously while he thought. Finally, he spoke again. "The fight . . . it was like . . ." He looked back up at me. "It felt like I was outside of myself, watching a really horrid movie that I couldn't shut off. I don't even really remember all of what I said or did. It was like I walked away from my body for a second."

I nodded and looked away, hating what I'd driven him to. At the sound of his strained accent, I turned back to look at him. "All I felt was hate. All I could see was red." His eyes searched mine as he spoke, occasionally drifting to the injury he never let himself forget about. "I couldn't control anything my body was doing. I just wanted to hurt him." He sighed again and looked at the ceiling. "I think I may have gone insane."

He closed his eyes and shook his head. "I could have lost everything . . . *everything.*" He reopened his eyes and I frowned at the sorrow on his face. "Kellan is the reason I'm not in cuffs for assault right now."

My mouth dropped open and my brow scrunched together so hard it hurt my head. His dark eyes looked over my confused face. "I beat the shit out of him, Kiera. I knocked you unconscious. I could have kill—I could have seriously hurt you, both of you. People go to jail for that kind of stuff. But I'm not. I'm leaving the country soon, and the only reason I can do that . . . is because Kellan covered for me."

I shook my head. "I don't understand."

He smiled softly and his face relaxed. "I know." His fingers in my hand started stroking my skin, and I relaxed as his anger seemed to fade. "When you went down, once we knew you were still breathing, still alive," he shrugged, "he made me leave."

"Leave?"

Denny nodded and smiled ruefully. "I didn't want to. I wanted to help you. I wanted to do something, anything. He yelled some . . . not pleasant things at me, and told me that I'd be hauled off if I didn't leave." Denny's eyes drifted to the dark windows, and they seemed to darken in kind, like he was absorbing that blackness into himself. "You were so pale . . . so tiny . . . barely breathing. He held you so tight, and I wanted to be the one . . ." He exhaled and closed his eyes.

"He convinced me that I had to leave and call for help, and then when the paramedics got there, he would tell them both of you were mugged. That they beat him up and when you went to help him, they attacked you." Denny sighed and brought his eyes back to my wide-open ones. "He even gave me his wallet, to make it look more real." He shook his head and looked back to the windows. "Everyone bought it. I showed up later at the hospital, and no one even questioned me."

He looked back to me and his eyes held immense grief and guilt. "It's like I got away with it . . . with hurting you and him . . . because of him." He looked down and a tear dropped to my sheet. I automatically brushed his cheek dry and he looked back up to me. "It kind of kills me."

I shook my head. "No . . . don't feel that way. He was right. You've been punished enough for our mistakes. You shouldn't lose everything because we drove you to . . . to . . ." My tears welled up again and I couldn't contain it, or the need to embrace him. I threw my arms around him and he stiffened, but finally relaxed and hugged me back. "I'm so sorry, Denny."

He exhaled brokenly and rubbed my back. "I know, Kiera." He clutched me to him tightly, and I felt his body start to shake. "I'm sorry too. I'm so sorry."

He let me hold him for most of that night, in fact nearly all of it. Somewhere, in between our repeated mutual apologies, we fell asleep holding each other, and by morning I felt certain that while we would never be what we once were to each other, we would always be connected in some way. And I found immense comfort in that.

Chapter 25
Goodbyes

The following morning, I was cleared to leave. My sister was delighted at the news and actually kissed the doctor on the cheek when he told her. As she was wearing her Hooters outfit—tighter-than-tight orange shorts and a much too opaque, white logoed tank top—the doctor blushed furiously and quickly fled the room. My sister giggled and helped me dress and brush out my bed-tangled hair.

I watched the doors while we waited for the okay to leave. I wasn't sure who I was hoping would come to see me off—Denny or Kellan. I hadn't seen Kellan again, and when I asked my sister, she would only frown softly and say that he was "around." I remembered that he hadn't wanted her to mention to me that he was hanging around the hospital, and wondered if he'd found out about her slip-up.

I'd hurt him enough that he couldn't make himself even see me, but not so much that he could leave me completely alone. I had no idea what that meant. He said he still loved me and I certainly still loved him. Even now, even after my mistake in the parking lot, after Denny's awful discovery and the fight that still woke me up screaming sometimes, I loved him . . . and missed him. But I understood his need to be away from me, to finally let me go.

Jenny came in while we waited and sat on the bed with me, occasionally stroking my arm or tucking some hair behind my ear, revealing my yellowing bruise. She told Anna and me stories of the bar and the crazy things some of the customers had done. She started to tell a story about Evan and Matt ganging up on Griffin, but stopped shortly after mentioning their names. I didn't know if that was because she thought I didn't want to hear about men so close to Kellan, or if it was because Kellan was in the story too. I couldn't bring myself to ask her.

Anna grabbed the reins of the conversation once Griffin's name was halfheartedly mentioned, and by the end of her story, even sweet, "whatever floats your boat" Jenny was bright red. Anna was laughing about that as Denny walked through the door.

He waved a greeting to the room and I startled at seeing him during the day . . . and in casual clothes. When I asked him if he should be at work, he shrugged and said that he took the day off to help me get settled. He raised his eyebrows at my expression and dryly said, "What are they gonna do, fire me?"

I smiled and thanked him, and the four of us chatted amicably until I was discharged.

Two hours later, I was staring out at a view of Lake Union from the two-bedroom apartment my sister had managed to find and acquire in one afternoon. Granted, the apartment was tiny. The kitchen had space for the stove, refrigerator, and a dishwasher. A slab of Formica above it constituted the counter. The two bedrooms were on opposite ends of a short hall. I had to smile that my sister's had the full-length closet, while mine was only half the size. My room had a futon and a dresser and my sister's had a mattress on a low bed frame with a nightstand. The bathroom was the shower-only kind, and was already overflowing with my sister's beauty products. The living room and dining room were combined, and a rickety folding table indicated where we'd be eating. The remainder of the space was filled with an ancient-looking orange couch and a chair that I knew, from experience, was the single most comfortable chair in the world. My heart seized as I ran a hand along the back of it. It was Kellan's . . . and it was the only semi-decent piece of furniture he owned.

THOUGHTLESS

As Denny curiously watched me, I brushed my fingers over my cheeks, swallowed repeatedly, and sat on the ugly orange couch. Denny made up a small lunch with some groceries he'd picked up for me, Anna left for her job, and Jenny sat by me on the couch, turning on some soaps on the tiny television tucked in the corner. I half-watched TV with her, half-ate the sandwich Denny made for me, and cast several looks at the comfortable chair . . . that no one was sitting in.

The following week, while I recovered and adapted to my new home and my sister's fanciful presence, things adjusted into a new routine. Jenny would come and visit in the afternoons, sometimes with Kate, and try to get me out of the apartment and back to work at Pete's. I'd shake my head at both suggestions and stay buried in warm blankets on the growing-on-me ugly couch.

My sister would head off to work, telling me that they were looking for another girl, and sisters would be a huge tip-maker. I blushed at just the thought of wearing those tight shorts. Then she'd come back later in the evening with an obscenely large wad of cash from those tips . . . and sometimes with Griffin's hands firmly attached to that absurdly tight uniform. On those nights, I wished our apartment was a little bigger, or soundproof.

And Denny stopped by every night after he got off work. I marveled at first that he was still so attentive, after everything I'd done to him. But I did notice the emotions he didn't want me to see—the tightness around his eyes when he looked at Kellan's chair, the sadness in his features when he looked over my body, and the guilt he'd swallow back when he looked at my bruise.

His voice also betrayed the casualness of his actions. He'd harden up whenever we talked about our history. I tried not to bring it up very often. He'd crack and have to swallow and restart if we talked about *that* night, about the fight; I tried to do that even less. And he'd refuse to talk at all about Kellan, only saying that he rarely saw him, but when he did things were "cordial." In fact, the only time his voice warmed and his accent thickened in an excited way was when he spoke of going home, of starting his new job and seeing his family.

I was equally delighted and scared of that prospect that was looming larger every day. It seemed to grow larger and larger every time he visited. As I got better, he got more and more anxious to be gone. By the end of the week, we talked less and less about "us," and he talked more and more about his job. It was no surprise to me when he told me he'd moved up his flight a few days early. It was no surprise, but it still hurt tremendously.

A few days later found me driving him to the airport in his Honda, wanting that final goodbye, that closure. I walked with him through the sea of holiday travelers and held his hand. Surprisingly, he let me; he usually tried to keep our physical contact minimal. I thought maybe he was savoring every last minute as well.

When we finally arrived at his gate, I froze and my mouth dropped open in complete shock. Sitting on a chair and staring at his cast, which was completely covered in writing and drawings, was Kellan. He looked up as we approached and my heart sped up. He looked better since I'd last seen him at the hospital; only a bluish bruise at the base of his eye and a couple of pink scratches marred his perfection, or perhaps they amplified it. Whatever the case . . . he was stunning.

He stood as Denny slowly walked over to him. Denny reflexively clutched my hand tighter for a second, and then he dropped it completely. I struggled to keep Denny's slow pace over to where Kellan waited, my eyes never leaving Kellan's face.

His deep blue eyes, however, were locked only on Denny's. He seemed to be purposely avoiding looking at me. I didn't know if he did that for Denny's benefit . . . or his own.

Kellan held his hand out to Denny in a symbol of friendship. His eyes studied Denny's face as Denny regarded the offered hand. With a small sigh, that to me echoed loudly throughout the noisy, crowd-filled room, Denny grabbed his hand and firmly shook it. The corners of Kellan's lips curled up in a tiny smile, and he nodded briefly at Denny.

"Denny . . . man, I'm . . ." He trailed off, words failing him, as his eyes drifted to their still shaking hands.

Denny released his hand and brought his to his hip. "Yeah . . . I know, Kellan. That doesn't mean we're okay . . . but I know." His voice was tight, his accent thick, and tears stung my eyes watching the two once-close friends struggle to find words to give each other.

"If you ever need anything . . . I'm . . . I'm here." Kellan's eyes moistened as he said that, but they remained fixed on Denny's face.

Denny nodded and clenched his jaw. Several emotions seemed to sweep through his features before he finally sighed and looked away. "You've done enough, Kellan."

My heart squeezed painfully at the infinite ways that one sentence could be interpreted. In one line, Denny had pretty much summed up everything between them—the good, as well as the bad. It tore my heart, and warmed it at the same time.

I felt a tear roll down my cheek, but I was watching Kellan too intently to do anything about it. I was sure he was going to crack. I was sure he was going to sob and beg Denny's forgiveness, on his hands and knees if he had to, but then a ghost of a smile touched his lips and he roughly swallowed, forcing back the tears encroaching on his eyes. It seemed that Kellan had decided to take the good in that sentence and leave the rest behind.

Kellan clapped Denny's shoulder affectionately. "Take care . . . mate." He said it warmly and with no trace of an implied accent; Kellan was one of the few people I'd met who never tried to sound like Denny. With Kellan, it somehow seemed a level of respect that he never tried to copy Denny.

Denny seemed to understand that and, while maybe not exactly reciprocating feelings of respect for Kellan, he did clap him warmly on the shoulder. "You too . . . mate."

Then Kellan gave him a swift hug and walked away from us. The urge to reach out and grab his shirt, to make him look at me, talk to me, was so great . . . but I couldn't make a scene with Kellan while saying goodbye to Denny, not after everything we'd put him through.

So I balled my hands into fists to stop the strong desire sweeping through me, and I silently watched Kellan leave. Just as the crowd was swallowing him up, he turned to look back at us. Our eyes finally met for the first time in so long that an actual ache ripped through my body at the all too brief connection. I watched his mouth drop open and his face contort in pain and I knew he'd felt the same agony rip through him. He wanted me . . . he still wanted me, but I'd hurt him too greatly.

His hand came to the bridge of his nose as he turned back around. The crowd immediately obliterated any sign of him. I closed my eyes, and when I reopened them, Denny was watching me with an expression on his face like he finally understood something. I didn't know what he'd seen in that one painful glance, but he'd definitely seen it. With a shake of his head and a suddenly sympathetic look, he put his arm around my shoulder and pulled me to him, in an almost consolatory way.

I laid my head on his shoulder and, as one, we turned to face the windows, to watch his plane gleam in the sun. "I'll miss you, Denny," I finally whispered, once I could speak again.

His arm squeezed me tighter. "I'll miss you too, Kiera. Even with everything, I'll still miss you." He paused, then whispered, "Do you think . . . ?" I pulled my head up to look at him, as he turned his head to look down at me. "Do you think, if I had never taken the job in Tucson, you and Kellan never would have . . . ?" He looked down at the ground and bunched his brows. "Did I throw you to him?"

I shook my head and rested it on his shoulder. "I don't know, Denny, but I think that, one way or another, Kellan and I would have . . ." I looked up at him and stopped talking. I couldn't finish that sentence, not directly to him, not with his dark brown eyes looking back into mine so painfully.

"I'll always love you, you know," he said thickly.

I nodded and swallowed. "And I'll always love you . . . always."

He smiled softly and tucked a lock of hair behind my ear, his fingers starting to brush my cheek. With a look of great internal debate, he finally bent down and gave me a tender kiss on the lips. It lasted longer than a friendly kiss would, shorter than a romantic kiss would. Somewhere in the middle, just like us.

When he pulled away, he kissed my bruised face once before I laid my head back on his shoulder. I squeezed his free hand while his other held my body close to his, and we waited. Waited for them to announce his departure. Waited for our separation to be permanent. Waited for our deep, but broken, connection to be physically severed.

Eventually it did happen, and with a long sigh he pulled away from me. After grabbing his bag from where he'd dropped it when he'd taken Kellan's hand, he kissed my head in farewell. I clutched his hand and held on to him until the last possible second. The very tips of our fingers were the last pieces of our bodies to stop touching each other. I felt something leave me when the contact stopped. Something warm and safe, and at one point in my life, something that had been everything to me. He held my watery eye contact with his own until he disappeared around the corner, and I knew that those warm, deep brown eyes and that charming goofy grin were finally lost forever to me.

My body shut down. I felt it going. I felt my legs leaden and my knees buckle, and my head fade to a hazy gray-black. My legs hit the floor with a thud that I was sure shook the bolted seats in front of me, and, just as I waited for my still tender head to smack painfully onto one of those seats, warm hands cradled me.

I recognized the scent first, the unmistakably delicious odor of leather and earth and man that was Kellan Kyle. I didn't know how he was with me, and I couldn't see him yet through my foggy vision, but I felt him and knew it was his arms that held me.

He lowered my head carefully to his knees as he huddled on the floor beside me. One hand stroked my back, while the other felt my face, making sure I was okay. "Kiera?" His voice still sounded distant, even though I knew he was right beside me.

My vision started clearing and his faded jeans came into focus. I weakly lifted my head and attempted to understand what was happening. His eyes softened as he gazed down at me, his casted hand rubbing my back, his fingers on my face lovingly tracing me. Instantly I realized I'd fainted, and he'd been watching me, always watching me, and had saved me from a world of pain. Then I remembered our distance, and my ache and overwhelming grief at watching Denny leave. I sat up and threw myself into his arms, straddling his knees on the floor and tangling my arms around his neck, never wanting to let go. He stiffened and convulsed like I'd hurt him, but eventually he brought his arms around my back and held me tight to him, rocking us gently on the floor and murmuring that it would be okay.

The roar of the airplane's engines brought our attention back to the ache forefront in our minds, and we both turned to look at the window and watch the huge plane begin to taxi away from us. We both watched it silently, tears streaming down my face and soft sobs escaping my lips. Kellan continued to rub my back and rested his head against mine, occasionally bringing his lips to my hair. I clutched at him fiercely and when the plane left my sight, I dropped my head to his shoulder and sobbed mercilessly.

He let me hold him until my pain eased, if not stopped. When I was hiccupping and attempting to breathe with some normalcy, he gently but firmly pushed me off his lap. I tried to stay, embarrassingly clutching at his clothes, but he was persistent and eventually he released himself from under me and stood.

His face was resolute as he stood in front of me. I had to look down. I had to stare at the floor. For a brief moment, I'd thought we'd reconnected in our mutual grief, but I must have been wrong. His face didn't look like he was welcoming me back to him. His face looked like he was about to say goodbye again. I didn't want to hear it.

A hand reached out and gently touched the top of my head as I stared at my knees on the floor. I tentatively looked up into Kellan's amazingly perfect, bruised face. A soft smile played on his lips and his eyes had warmed a bit, although the sadness never really left them.

"Can you drive?" he asked in a low voice.

Grief threatened to wrench through me again at the thought of driving home alone and sitting in my empty apartment alone. I wanted to tell him no, that I needed him , that I needed to stay with him, and we needed to find a way back to each other, back from my mistake. But I couldn't. I nodded my head yes, and prepared myself for the one thing that had always terrified me . . . being alone.

He nodded and held his hand out to me to help me stand. I took it and clutched his warmth tightly as he pulled me up. I stumbled a bit and put my hand on his chest to steady myself. I felt a bandage under my fingertips and he flinched in pain. My hand was resting on his pecs, not his ribs, so I wasn't sure why that hurt him. Maybe his injuries were worse than I knew. Maybe he just didn't like me touching him.

He removed my hand, but continued holding my fingers. We faced each other, both hands clasped together and standing close, but an almost insurmountable distance was between us.

I'd chosen him and then left him. How would he ever forgive me?

"I'm so sorry, Kellan—I was wrong." I didn't offer any more explanation than that. I couldn't, since my throat closed up completely and speech just wasn't possible.

His eyes misted over and he nodded. Did he understand what I meant? That I meant I was wrong for leaving him . . . not wrong for loving him? I couldn't explain, and he didn't ask. He bent his head down to me and I instinctively raised my chin. Our lips met in the middle—soft and passionate, pulling apart before fully sinking into the feeling of being together. Dozens of tiny, hungry, not nearly long enough kisses that spiked my heart rate.

Finally, he forced himself to stop. He pulled away before it got to be too much and we both caved to the underlying sexual tension that was always between us. He dropped my hands and took a reluctant step back from me. "I'm sorry too, Kiera. I'll see you . . . around."

Then he turned and left me, breathless, spinning with confusion and grief, and . . . alone. His final words echoed in my ears and I felt one hundred percent positive that he hadn't meant them. I felt positive that I'd just seen the last of Kellan Kyle.

Somehow I made it home. Somehow I managed to not break down while driving and smack right into the back of someone in my teary haze. No, I saved all of my tears for the heart-shaped pillow my sister had scrounged somewhere for me. I drenched that thing, and then mercifully fell asleep.

My world felt a little lighter when I woke the next day. Maybe it was because my head felt better and the bruising was switching colors, indicating that some healing was going on somewhere in my body. Or maybe it was because the final painful break with Denny had been made, and I didn't have to be anxious about it anymore. It was done—we were done—and even though those words hurt my heart, I felt okay.

Showering and getting dressed brought even more relief, and, as I looked over my beaten skull, I wondered where my life would go from here. Certainly I needed to find a job. And I definitely needed to catch up on schoolwork. Winter break had already hit while I'd been recovering, but a few phone calls from my doctor, and me, and surprisingly Denny, had gotten me an extension on the classes I was behind in. And if I poured myself into school, I was confident I'd be caught up before next quarter.

I clenched my jaw and decided that was what I'd do. I might have lost my job, my boyfriend, and my lover, but if I focused hard enough, I could possibly keep my precious scholarship. And if I did that . . . maybe, just maybe, my heart would heal as slowly and assuredly as my head.

Denny called me two days later, right before my sister and I were about to fly home for Christmas. My parents had the tickets they'd gotten for Denny and me switched over to my sister and me. They seemed genuinely sorry when I'd told them that things hadn't worked out with Denny. They'd also grilled me for two hours on when I was coming back to Ohio University.

Denny told me all about his new job and his upcoming plans

with his family. He seemed genuinely happy, and his good spirits lifted mine. Of course, his voice did break when he wished me a Merry Christmas, followed immediately by, "I love you." It seemed to slip out of his mouth without him thinking about it, and a silence hovered in the air between us as I wondered what to say to that. In the end, I told him that I loved him too. And I did. There would always be a level of love between us.

The next day, my sister and I braved going home for the holidays. She artfully covered the slight yellowing of my bruise with makeup and vowed that she wouldn't mention the accident to Mom or Dad; they'd never let me come back to Seattle.

Before I left my bedroom, I rifled through my dresser for the hundredth time, looking for the necklace that Kellan had given me. Every day I wanted to wear it, wear a piece of him with me, since I hadn't seen him in so long, but I hadn't been able to find it since the night he'd given it to me. A part of me feared that it had been lost or stolen in the fiasco. A part of me feared that Kellan had decided to take it back. That would almost be the worst scenario. It would be like he was taking back his heart.

I still couldn't find it and had to leave the city without my symbolic representation of him . . . and it cut deep to do so.

Being home with my family was odd. It was warm and welcoming, and a barrage of childhood memories hit me, but it didn't feel like "home" anymore. It felt like I was walking into a best friend's house, or an aunt's house. Somewhere comfortable and familiar, but still a little foreign. It had the overall vibe of childhood safety, but I felt no desire to stay and wrap myself in that feeling. I wanted to be home . . . my home.

We stayed a couple of days after the holidays and then, my sister even itchier than me, we said tearful goodbyes to our parents at the airport. My mother was a blubbering mess as she watched her two girls depart, and I momentarily felt bad that my heart was anchored so far away from them. I'd told myself that I'd just fallen hopelessly in love with the city . . . but a tiny part of my brain that I forcefully ignored knew that wasn't it. A place was just a place. And it wasn't the city that made my heart pulse and my breath quicken. It wasn't the city that drove me to distraction and left me sobbing in the still of the night.

After my frantic catch-up on schoolwork over the holiday break, and wistfully watching my sister duck out on New Year's Eve for a special D-Bag performance that twisted my heart into knots, I focused on the second-most-important thing I needed to get squared away—a job. What I ended up getting early on in the New Year was a waitressing job at a popular little diner in Pioneer Square, where Jenny's roommate, Rachel, worked. The place was famous for its all-night breakfast, I guess, and drew quite a crowd of college kids. It was hopping busy on my first night there, but Rachel gleefully showed me the ropes.

Rachel was an interesting mix of Asian and Latin with latte skin, mocha hair, and a smile that charmed quite a few frat boys out of some large bills. She was as sweet as Jenny, but quiet like me. She didn't ask about my injury and, even though she had to know about the whole torrid love triangle (being Jenny's roommate and all), she never once commented on my romances. Her quiet was soothing.

I fell into my new job easily enough. Along with great managers and amusing cooks, the tips were good there, the other waitresses welcoming, and the regulars patient. It didn't take me too long to feel moderately comfortable in my new home.

Of course, I missed Pete's like crazy. I missed the smell of the bar. I missed Scott in the kitchen, even though I didn't really spend too much time with him. I missed talking and laughing with Jenny and Kate. I missed dancing to the music from the jukebox. I even missed horny Rita and her never-ending stories that made me blush all over. But of course, what I missed the most about Pete's was the entertainment.

I saw Griffin repeatedly, as he came over often to "entertain" my sister. Actually, I saw way more of him than I ever wanted to see. In fact, I now know that he has a piercing in a spot that I'd never imagine a guy voluntarily asking someone to push a needle through. I considered scrubbing out my eyes after that little naked encounter in the hallway one evening.

Matt would occasionally stop by with him, and we'd chat quietly. I'd ask how the band was doing, and he'd start talking about instruments and gear and songs and melodies and shows that went really well and a few places that he'd managed to line up gigs, and on and on about the business end of it. Not exactly what I wanted to hear about, but I nodded and politely listened to him, watching his pale eyes sparkle as he talked about the love of his life. I was glad after talking to him that Kellan hadn't left Seattle. Matt would be crushed if their little band broke up. He really believed that they had a shot at going big one day. Thinking over their performances, with a painful tug in my heart, I agreed. With Kellan as their front man . . . they could go all the way.

Sometimes Matt and my sister would talk about Kellan, but they stopped when I entered the room. One such conversation left an icy pit in my stomach. I'd just quietly cracked open the front door and heard them talking in the kitchen. I heard Matt's soft voice finishing telling her, ". . . right over his heart. Romantic, huh?"

"What's romantic?" I muttered as I walked into the room, thinking they were surely talking about Griffin, although, I couldn't imagine what he'd do that was "romantic." I had grabbed a glass and started filling it with water when I finally noticed the awkward silence suddenly in the room.

Pausing, I noticed my sister staring at the floor, biting her lip. Matt looked out into the living room, like he really wanted to be over there. That was when I understood that they weren't talking about Griffin. They were talking about Kellan.

"What's romantic?" I said automatically, even as my stomach clenched. Had he moved on?

Anna and Matt looked briefly at each other for a second before simultaneously saying, "Nothing." I set down the glass and left the room. Whatever romantic gesture he'd made, I didn't want to hear about it anyway. I didn't want to think about who he was with now, about who he was "dating." Whatever romantic thing he had done for a girl—some girl who wasn't me—I didn't want to *ever* hear about it.

Surprisingly, I ran into Evan at school. Aside from work, school was really the only place I went. I spent every free moment there studying and, quite honestly, busying my head to stop the gnawing ache in my heart. I'd been coming out of one of the impressive brick buildings, lost in painful thoughts I shouldn't have been thinking anyway, when I'd nearly run right into him. His warm, brown eyes had widened and glowed at seeing me. Then he lifted me into a massive bear hug, and I giggled until he let go.

Apparently, Evan was a big fan of people-watching on the campus. He loved hanging around the school and had even made Kellan take the freshman tour with him nearly a half dozen times a couple of years ago. With a small grin, Evan confessed to me that he'd had a huge crush on the girl giving the tour at the time. Surprise flashed through me, as I realized that that was how Kellan knew so much about the campus. He had certainly been with girls here, but the majority of his intimate knowledge was because of Evan dragging him on the same tour that I'd dragged him on.

That thought made my eyes water, and Evan's happy face looked me over with a trace of concern in it. "Are you alright, Kiera?" I tried to nod and that only made my eyes water more. Evan sighed and brought me back in for another hug. "He misses you," he whispered.

I startled and pulled away at that. Evan shrugged. "He acts like he doesn't . . . but I can tell. He's not Kellan. He's moody and writes a lot, and snaps at people, and drinks a lot, and . . ." He stopped talking and cocked his head. "Okay, well, maybe he's still Kellan." He grinned as I managed a half-laugh. "But he really misses you. You should see what he—"

He stopped talking again and bit his lip. "Anyway, just know that he hasn't moved on or anything." A tear fell on my cheek as I wondered if that was true, or if Evan was just trying to make me feel better. He tenderly brushed the tear away. "Sorry, maybe I shouldn't have said anything."

I shook my head and swallowed. "No, it's okay. No one will really talk about him in front of me, like I'm porcelain or something. It's good to hear about him. I miss him too."

He cocked his head at me, and his brown eyes turned unusually serious. "He told me how much he loved you. How much you meant to him." Another tear threatened to fall, and I brushed my lid to halt it. Evan blushed as I sniffled. "That night . . . that I kinda . . . walked in on you. I really didn't see anything," he quickly added. I blushed in kind, and he looked at the pavement for a moment.

"He told me once about his childhood . . . about his parents' abuse." My mouth dropped open as I gaped at him. I got the impression that Kellan didn't talk about that with anyone. Evan seemed to understand my expression and smiled grimly. "I figured he told you. With me . . . he was really drunk. I don't think he even remembers telling me. It was right after they died . . . when he saw the house." He raised an eyebrow at me. "You know that's not his childhood home, right?"

I frowned and shook my head. I hadn't known that. Evan nodded and sniffed. "Yeah, we were playing bars in L.A., once we got together with Matt and Griffin. Doing pretty good too, made a name for ourselves down there. Then . . . well, I still remember the day his aunt called and told him that they'd both been killed. He dropped everything and drove up here that night. We followed him, of course."

Evan looked down at the pavement and shook his head. "I don't think he ever really understood why we did that, why we moved here with him. I don't think he grasped that we believed in him and loved him, like family. I still don't think he grasps that. I think that's why he thought he could ditch town without telling us." He shook his head again. "He said he thought we wouldn't care, that we'd just replace him." I cringed that Kellan had been going to bail on them because of me. I was a little surprised that Kellan thought he was so easy to replace. That word sounded so wrong in reference to him.

After a silent moment, Evan looked back up at me with an eyebrow raised. "Of course, his version of family is a little . . . skewed." I nodded at that, and thought over just how twisted Kellan's version of love had been for most of his life. Evan cleared his throat and continued. "Anyway, they left him everything they had, even the house. He seemed really surprised that they would do that, but he was even more surprised when he saw the house . . . and realized they'd moved."

Evan looked out over the campus, his eyes speculative and sad for his friend. "They never even bothered to tell him that they'd sold the home he'd grown up in. That they'd moved across town. And then . . . he found out that they'd tossed out all of his stuff. And I mean, everything. There wasn't a single trace of him in that house, not even a picture. I think that's why he tossed out everything of theirs."

My breath caught as I realized that was why Kellan's house was so barren when we first moved in. It wasn't just that he didn't care about decorations, which I was pretty sure he didn't. It was mainly because he had inherited a home that was completely foreign to him, and then, out of anger or resentment, or maybe both, he'd tossed everything of his parents . . . everything. He'd left no trace of them in his life, really he'd left no trace of *any* life in his life, until I'd come in and thrust mine upon him. His never-ending pain made my heart thud loudly in my chest as I ached with sympathy for him.

Evan sniffed again as he looked back to me. Another tear rolled down my cheek. I was too stunned from his revelation to wipe it away. "They were real bastards, but . . . their death still really affected him. He got really ripped and told me about what they used to do to him. Some of his stories . . ." Evan closed his eyes and shook his head, a light shudder running through him.

I closed my eyes as well as I thought over all the conversations I'd had with Kellan about his childhood. He'd never gone into specifics with me about just what his father used to do to him. From the look on Evan's face, I guessed he'd gone into some pretty horrific details, and it had really affected Evan. I was both grateful I didn't know, and curious to know, those details.

When Evan reopened his eyes, they shone with compassion for his friend. "He must not have grown up around a whole lot of love. I kind of think that's why he screwed around so much. I know that sounds weird, but . . . he's always seemed a little different in the way he went after women." He scrunched his brows as he unknowingly correctly analyzed his bandmate. "He's not just a hornball like Griffin. He was almost . . . desperate . . . to connect with someone. Like he really wanted to love somebody—he just didn't know how."

He shrugged and laughed. "That sounds weird, I know. I'm no psychologist or anything. Anyway, I think that's what he saw in you . . . why he risked it. I think I understand what you meant to him." He put his hand on my shoulder. "What you *mean* to him."

I brought a hand to my mouth and held in a cry. I was sure Evan didn't know everything about Kellan's upbringing, but he understood a lot more than Kellan probably realized he did. He smiled sadly at my reaction and shrugged again. "I'm not trying to hurt you or anything. I guess I just wanted you to know that he still thinks about you."

With tears freely flowing down my cheeks, we said our goodbyes and he walked away, waving. I couldn't tell Evan that, even though I knew I'd meant something to Kellan at one point, and maybe he did still think about me . . . I also knew from Matt's slip-up that he was trying to get with other people. I liked to think that it was hard for him, that he was forcing himself to do it, but Kellan had every right to try and move on from me. I'd hurt him so badly. But I couldn't mention that to Evan. That part of Kellan's life, I did not want to talk about . . . with anyone.

And even though I missed my D-Bags, I was a little glad that I didn't see them more often. It hurt too much. And of course, the one I really wanted to see stayed completely hidden away from me . . . and I let him, even though it kind of killed me.

Chapter 26
Love and Loneliness

It was March, and the air was still crisp with the last edge of winter lacing it, but a smell of renewal was in the air too. The cherry blossoms at the university were in full bloom, and the quad was bursting with blushing pink flowers that lifted my leaden heart whenever I walked through it.

It had been a hard winter for me. Being alone wasn't something I enjoyed, and I'd had to endure a lot of alone time lately. My sister was a social butterfly and had quickly amassed a bevy of beautiful Hooters girls to party with. I'd heard they were in line to be in the "Girls of Hooters" calendar next year.

Jenny tried to take me out on occasion, but we had different schedules, and lining up a night when we were both off work and I wasn't doing something for school was tricky. We did manage to see a movie every now and then, or grab some coffee before her shift, but it wasn't nearly as often as I would have liked.

School kept me busy, work kept me busy, and even staying in contact with Denny kept me busy. Since our time zones were so far apart, it gave "phone tag" a whole new meaning. But my heart couldn't be kept busy enough to not miss Kellan. That just wasn't possible.

I might have been forced through a three-month rehab with our self-imposed separation, but my underlying addiction was still there, and it beat and coursed deep throughout my veins. I could almost hear his name with my heartbeat and I berated myself for my stupid mistake every day. How could I have been so scared and foolish, to push away such a wonderful man?

My sister inadvertently brought that ache right to the surface one night. She was in the bathroom, getting ready to hit a club with some friends. She was drying her silky hair, head bent over, letting the dryer give her already perfect locks extra volume. I walked by just as she flipped up and fluffed out her tresses. She was wearing a backless triangle top that was going to be much too cold for outside, but that wasn't what got my attention. It was the sparkle at her neck.

I stopped in the doorway. My mouth dropped open and my eyes watered. "Where did you get that?" I could barely even form the words.

She looked at me, confused for a minute, and then noticed my eyes locked onto the necklace around her throat. "Oh, this?" She shrugged and the necklace slid up and down her creamy skin. "It was stuck in with my stuff. I'm not sure where it came from. It's pretty though, huh?"

I couldn't speak again, as I stared in disbelief at the silver guitar necklace that Kellan had lovingly said goodbye to me with. The large diamond twinkled in the bathroom lights and my tearful vision amplified the sparkle until a rainbow streaked across my eyes.

My sister seemed to notice that I was starting to break down. "Oh, God . . . is this yours, Kiera?"

I blinked and my vision cleared as tears dropped down my cheeks. I watched her hastily reach behind her neck to unclasp it. "I didn't know. I'm sorry." Her fingers practically flung it at me as she held it away from her.

"It's okay," I mumbled. "I just thought I'd lost it." Or Kellan had removed it.

She nodded and pulled me into a tight hug, lacing the necklace around me, since I still seemed reluctant to touch it. As she clasped it around my neck, she whispered, "Did Kellan give this to you?"

As she pulled away, I nodded, more tears dripping down my cheeks. "The night . . . he was leaving, the night we got caught." I ran my fingers down the silver piece and it seemed both burning and cooling to my touch.

My sister watched my face a minute and then ran a hand through my hair. "Why don't you go see him, Kiera? He's always at Pete's, and he still looks so . . ."

I shook my head and didn't let her finish. "I only ever hurt him. He wanted this . . . he wanted space." I looked up at her and exhaled brokenly. "I'm trying to do what's best for him . . . for once. Besides, I'm sure he's moved on by now."

She smiled sadly as she tucked a strand of my hair behind my ear. "You're an idiot, Kiera," she said softly, but warmly.

I smiled sadly back at her. "I know."

She shook her head and seemed to swallow back an emotion. "Well, why don't you come out with us girls, then?" She shook her hips alluringly. "Go dancing with me."

I sighed, remembering the last time I went dancing with Anna. "I don't think so. I'm just gonna stay here, crash on the couch."

She twisted her lips as she leaned into the bathroom mirror to start doing her makeup. "Oh good . . . something new," she muttered sarcastically.

I rolled my eyes at her and walked away. "Have fun . . . and wear a coat."

"Sure thing, Mom," she shouted back playfully as I walked down the hallway to the living room.

It was raining outside, and I watched the slanting drops hit the window and roll down it like tears. The rain always reminded me of Kellan—him standing in it, letting it soak every part of him. Angry and hurt, and trying to stay away from me so he didn't lash out at me. Crazy in love with me, even when I turned him away for someone else. I couldn't even imagine what that must have felt like for him.

How could I see him . . . after everything I'd done to him? My chest hurt, though. I was tired of being alone. I was tired of trying to stay busy so he wouldn't enter my head—he did anyway. And mostly, I was tired of the hazy version of him in my memory. More than anything else, I wanted the sharp, crystal-clear and perfect version of him right in front of me.

Without thinking about it, I sat in his chair. I didn't ever sit there. It was too hard, being on something that had belonged to him. I sank into the cushions and laid my head back. I imagined it was his chest I was leaning against, and a soft smile came to my lips. I touched the lost-but-found-again necklace and closed my eyes. I could see him more clearly this way. I could almost even smell him.

I turned my face farther into the fabrics and startled when I realized that I *could* smell him. My hand clenched the cushion near my head and brought it to me. It didn't smell like the overwhelmingly wonderful scent that lingered on his skin, but it had the faint smell of him that lingered in his house. It smelled like his home, and to me, that smell was more binding than the childhood feeling I'd gotten at my parents' house.

He was my home . . . and I missed him terribly.

Anna came out of the bathroom as I was inhaling the chair and, feeling stupid, I dropped my hands to my lap and looked out the window again. "Are you okay, Kiera?" she asked quietly.

"I'll be fine, Anna."

She bit her perfect red lip and looked like she wanted to talk about something. Then she shook her head and asked, "Do you mind if I borrow the car, since you're staying here?"

"No . . . go ahead." I often let her take it when I didn't need it, and aside from work and school, I rarely needed it.

She sighed and, coming over to me, softly kissed my head. "Don't mope all night."

I smiled up at her warmly. "Sure thing, Mom."

She laughed charmingly and grabbed the keys off the counter in the kitchen. Quickly saying good night, she left without taking a coat. Shaking my head at her, I traced the fabric of the chair under my fingers and wondered what to do.

I briefly considered calling Denny. Brisbane was seventeen hours ahead of Seattle, and he would be in the middle of his Saturday afternoon. He would probably answer at this hour, but I was reluctant to talk to him. Not that I had any qualms about calling him; we talked frequently and had moved into a "friendly exes" stage. No, what made me hesitate was the fact that last month he'd told me that he'd asked a girl out on a date. At first I'd been hurt, then surprised that he'd mention such a personal fact to me, but I'd settled on happy. He should date. He should be happy. He was too wonderful to be anything else.

The next few phone calls from him included brief snippets about her and, as of last week, they were still together and doing well. I knew that was a good thing, and a part of me was thrilled for him, but I was feeling really lonely tonight and I didn't want the happy tone of his voice reminding me just how unhappy I was. Besides, he really shouldn't be getting calls on the weekend from his ex if he was seeing someone new. And he was probably with her right now, playing in the ocean or lying on the beach. I briefly wondered if they were kissing, right at this moment. Then I wondered if they were sleeping together. My stomach clinched, and I forced myself to not think about it. It didn't matter if they were—we'd let each other go in that respect. Of course, that didn't mean I liked the thought.

I ended up curling up on Kellan's chair with a warm blanket and watching a sad movie—one where the hero dies and everyone is broken, but endures the grief to make his sacrifice mean something. I was blubbering long before the actual death scene.

My eyes were red and raw and my nose was dripping like a faucet when the door to my apartment suddenly banged open. I spun my head to look at the door, alarmed, and then brought my brows together in confusion when I saw my sister standing there.

"Anna . . . are you okay?" She strode over to me and, without a word, yanked me off the chair. "Anna! What are you . . . ?"

The words halted as she pulled me forcefully to the bathroom. She cleaned me up, slapped on some lipstick, and brushed my hair, while I sputtered questions and tried to hold her back. My sister didn't give up easily though, and she had me cleaned up and was shoving me toward the front door before I even really knew what was going on.

I realized as she opened the door that she was absconding with me. I muttered no, and braced myself on the doorframe. She sighed and I looked back at her, irritated. She leaned into me and very intently said, "You need to see something."

That confused me so much that I dropped my hands. She successfully shoved me out of the door. She dragged me to Denny's Honda as I sulked and pouted. I didn't want to go dancing with her. I wanted to go back to my cave of perpetual mourning and finish my sad movie. At least that movie made my life seem cheery in comparison.

She sat me in the car and harshly pointed at me to stay put. I sighed and sank back into the familiar seat, sort of wishing the car still felt like Denny, and sort of glad nearly all trace of him was gone from the vehicle. It was now littered with lip gloss, empty shoe boxes, and a spare Hooters uniform.

I crossed my arms over my chest and pouted while my sister got in and drove us away. She didn't take any of the roads that would take us toward the Square, where most of the clubs were, and I started wondering where we were going. When we got onto a road that was so familiar it made my chest hurt, I started panicking. I knew exactly where she was taking me on this Friday night.

"No, Anna . . . please. I don't want to go there. I can't see him, I can't listen to him." I clutched at her arm and tried to physically turn the wheel, but she batted me away effortlessly.

"Calm down, Kiera. Remember . . . I'm doing the thinking for you now, and there is something that you need to witness. Something I should have showed you a while ago. Something that even *I* hope to someday . . ." Her voice trailed off as she stared out the window, almost longingly.

The look on her face was so odd, I forgot my protests. They swelled up again in my chest as we pulled into the parking lot of Pete's. She shut the car off and I stared at the familiar black Chevelle. My heart was thudding in my chest.

"I'm scared," I whispered into the silence of the car.

She grabbed my hand and squeezed it. "I'm here with you, Kiera."

I looked over at her perfectly beautiful face and smiled at the love I saw there. I nodded and jarringly opened the door to step out. She was at my side again almost instantly and, holding my hand tight, she walked me through the inviting double doors.

I didn't know what to expect. A part of me thought everything would somehow have changed in my absence, like maybe every wall would be black now, and the cheery lighting would be dull and dingy gray. But I was startled when I stepped through the doors, and saw that everything was exactly the same . . . even the people.

Rita did a double take when she noticed me, then gave me a suggestive wink and smiled devilishly. Apparently she knew about the affair, and since I'd joined her "I've had sex with Kellan Kyle" club, we were now bonded. Kate waved to me from where she was waiting for a drink at the counter, her perfect ponytail bouncing in her happiness. And Jenny was almost instantly in front of me, squeezing me tight and laughing about how good it was to see me out and about . . . and here. She glanced at the stage when she said that, and I shut my eyes to not look. I couldn't stop hearing though. His voice shot right through my core.

Jenny leaned into my ear when she noticed my reaction, and said over the music, "It will be okay, Kiera . . . have faith." I opened my eyes and stared at her smiling warmly at me. I felt my sister pulling my hand and Jenny, seemingly understanding what Anna was doing, grabbed my other hand. They both started weaving me into the massive crowd that packed Pete's on the weekends, when the band played. I instinctively tugged against them.

Insistently they dragged me forward, all the way forward. We pushed through the crowd and I kept my eyes focused on my feet, not wanting to look at him yet. It had been so long. . . . It had been even longer since I'd heard his voice, though, and it traveled all the way from my ears, down my spine, to the very bottom of my toes.

My breath hitched as the next song started while we inched through the packed bar. It was slow and haunting and dripping with emotion. His voice had an ache to it that seared me. I glanced slyly at the people we were passing, and watched them sing along to the song with solemn faces. They knew it, so it wasn't new. Still not looking at the stage, I let his timbre affect every cell in my body. He was sing-ing about that night in the parking lot, I suddenly realized. He sang of needing me and feeling ashamed for it. He sang of trying to leave me and it breaking him. He sang about crying, as we gave each other our final kiss. . . . Then, the lyrics turned to what he was feeling now.

That's when I looked up at him.

His eyes were closed. He hadn't noticed me approaching him yet. After not seeing him for months, his perfection was almost too much to take in all at once, like I'd go blind if I didn't absorb him in segments. Just the jeans—those perfectly fitted faded jeans that looked a little more worn than usual. Just the basic T-shirt that he preferred to wear—not decorated, not elaborate—simple, black, and perfectly sculpted to him. Just the delightfully toned arms, the left one completely healed and no longer casted, slinking down to strong hands that clutched the microphone while he sang. Just the impos-sibly sexy and wild hair, a little longer than I remembered it, but still a tousled mess, hinting at multiple past intimacies that rang loudly in my head, and in my body. Just that movie star jaw, that for the first time had light stubble along it, like he'd given up on the task of stay-ing groomed—it only highlighted that strong right angle and made him even more impossibly attractive, crazy as that sounds. Just the full lips, holding no trace of the sexy grin he usually sang with. Just the slope of his nose. Just the perfect cheekbones. Just the long eye-lashes of his closed lids, hiding the amazing blueness behind them.

I had to take everything about him in separately at first; he was just too perfect to take in all at once. When I could handle it, I finally noted the fact that the perfection was unmarred. His face was perfectly healed, and no sign of the physical trauma he'd endured was with him. But looking at that face as a whole was affecting me in an unexpected way. My breath came in stuttered pulls and my heart squeezed painfully, as Jenny and Anna drew me toward him relentlessly.

His eyes were still closed and his body rocked gently to the music, but his face was almost . . . desolate. His words matched his face, as he sang about how each day was a struggle, and never seeing my face caused him physical pain. He sang that my face was his light, and he felt drenched in darkness without it. Tears fell freely after I heard that line.

Jenny and Anna successfully pulled me right to a spot in front of him. Some rabid fans didn't like that, but my sister was not one to be messed with, and after some flowery words from her, they left us alone. I barely noticed, as I stared up at his godlike perfection.

Eyes still closed, he sang of being beside me, even if I couldn't see or hear him. He sang of being scared of never again feeling me, never again feeling what we had. A long instrumental section followed his last verse and, eyes still closed, he rocked his head back and forth, biting his lip. Some girls around me screamed at that, but it was clear to me that he wasn't trying to seduce anyone. He was in pain. I wondered if thoughts of me, of our time together, were flashing before his eyes, like they were flashing before mine.

I wanted to reach my hand out to him, but he was too far away to touch, and Jenny and Anna still had a hold of me, maybe fearing I would bolt. I couldn't move now, though. Not when he was filling my eyes, my ears, and my heart. I could only stare at him, enraptured.

I didn't even notice the other members of the band, and I didn't know if they noticed me. I barely noticed the crowd anymore as I watched him, and after another minute, I barely even noticed the feeling of Jenny's and my sister's eyes boring into me. Eventually I couldn't even feel their hands anymore, and I didn't even have it in me to wonder if they'd finally let go.

When the instrumental section came to a close, he finally re-opened his inhumanly beautiful eyes. He happened to be looking down at me, and my face was the first thing he took in when he opened them. I felt the shock run through his body, even from where I was standing. The deep blue eyes widened and instantly glassed over. His mouth fell open and his body stopped moving. He seemed to be completely thrown, like he'd woken up in a different universe. His eyes locked onto mine, as tears flowed down my cheeks.

He sang the next lyrics with his brows scrunched, like he was sure he was dreaming. The rest of the band was quiet on this section, and his voice rang clearly through the bar, through my soul. He repeated the line about me being his light, a look of reverence on his face. His voice drifted off along with the music, but his look of awe never left him.

I didn't know how to respond, other than with tears. I wiped a few away as I realized that my hands were indeed free. I could understand what Anna had wanted me to see now. That was the most beautiful, heartbreaking thing I'd ever heard, more intense and emotional than anything I'd ever heard him sing. My whole body was buzzing with the need to comfort him. But we were still just staring at each other, him on the stage, and me on the floor in front of it.

The fans stirred with an uneasy energy, as the guys waited for Kellan to signal the next song. He didn't. An unnatural silence filled the bar as we continued our silent stare-down. From the corner of my eye, I saw Matt lean toward Kellan, lightly smack his arm, and whisper something. Kellan didn't react, just kept staring at me with his mouth slightly open. I was positive several fans were staring and wondering about me, as I had his rapt attention, but for once, I didn't care. My only focus was him.

Eventually, Evan's voice broke through the sound system. "Hey, everybody. We're gonna take a breather. Until then . . . Griffin's buying a round for everyone!" The bar erupted in whooping, as something streaked behind Kellan to where Evan was sitting at his drums. Laughter broke out around me and I barely heard it.

The crowd dispersed a little bit, as three of the D-Bags hopped off the stage and melted into it. Kellan still didn't move though. His brow creased as he regarded me intently. Nerves shot through me. Why wasn't he jumping down and scooping me into his arms? His song made it seem like he ached for me . . . but his actions?

I took a step toward him, determined to be closer, even if I had to jump up on the stage with him. He looked away, out over the thinning crowd, and I watched several emotions pass over his face. It was almost like reading a book: confusion, joy, anger, sorrow, bliss, and then confusion again. Looking down briefly, he sniffed once and then carefully lowered himself to stand before me. My body hummed with the restraint to not touch him. He stepped closer to me and our hands in front of our bodies lightly brushed together. It sent fire through me, and he inhaled sharply.

Looking torn, he gently reached up and stroked a tear off my face with a knuckle. I closed my eyes, and a small sob escaped me at the contact. I couldn't even care that I probably looked horrid, my eyes tired and bloodshot from sleepless nights, my hair an unruly mess, even though my sister had attempted to fix it, and still dressed in my "moping" clothes—ratty lounge pants and a torn, long sleeved T-shirt. None of that mattered . . . because he was touching me, and it affected me just as it had always affected me. He cupped my cheek and stepped closer to me, our bodies touching now. I brought a hand to his chest and exhaled with relief that his heart was hammering as hard as mine. He was feeling this too.

Then some of the fans around us seemed to think we weren't having a moment, and that they had every right to intrude. I opened my eyes as some girls jostled me. Kellan put an arm around me to steady me, and stepped us away from the swarm a couple of spaces. Most of the girls acknowledged the retreat and left him alone. A particularly drunk blonde saw it as an opening instead. She aggressively walked up to him and grabbed his face like she was going to kiss him. Anger flared in me but before I could even react to her, he leaned back and removed her hands from his face. Then he harshly pushed the eager woman away from him.

I turned to stare at him, and he looked down at me. I'd never seen him push anyone away, and definitely never that rudely. The girl did not appreciate it. From the corner of my eye, I noticed the woman narrow hers in drunken anger and swing her hand back for a maneuver that I knew all too well. My hand automatically reached up and grabbed her wrist, right before her hand made contact with his cheek. Kellan startled and looked back at her, seeming to finally understand that he'd just about been slapped again.

The woman's mouth dropped open and she looked me over with a comically surprised face. I thought she might fight me, but her cheeks suddenly flamed bright red, and she yanked her hand out of my grasp. Looking thoroughly embarrassed about what she'd almost done, she sheepishly backed off and disappeared into the crowd.

I felt Kellan chuckle beside me and I looked back at his small smile and warm eyes. The expression had been gone for so long from my life that I felt an actual pang looking at it. I smiled in kind and his eyes warmed even more. He nodded over at where the girl had disappeared to. "No one gets to smack me but you?" he asked playfully.

"Damn straight," I said, blushing furiously at my curse. He chuckled again and adorably shook his head. Bringing seriousness back to my voice, I quietly said, "Can we go somewhere without so many . . . admirers?"

Seriousness marked his face, too, and he slinked down to grab my hand. He deftly led us through the remaining fans, and pulled us into the hallway. Nerves flashed through me as I started wondering if he'd pull me into the back room. Too many memories were in there. It was too secluded, too quiet. There was too much heat between us. Too much could happen in that room, and we had too many things to talk over.

Maybe he felt my reluctance, maybe he understood that we needed to talk, maybe he'd never intended to lead me in there—whatever his reason, he stopped in the hallway, well before the door, and I leaned against the wall in relief and confusion.

He stood in front of me, his hands loose at his sides and his eyes traveling the length of me. I felt heated under his intense gaze.

Eventually his eyes stopped on my necklace—his necklace—and with shaking fingers, he reached out to touch it. One of his fingers brushed my skin as he felt the cool metal, and I closed my eyes.

"You're wearing it. I didn't think you would," he muttered.

I opened my eyes and sighed as his deep blue ones locked onto mine. It had been so long. . . .

"Of course, Kellan." I put my hand over his on my necklace and was struck with how much that tiny contact affected me. "Of course," I repeated.

I tried to lace our fingers together, but he pulled his hand back and looked down the hallway. A few people were loitering around back here, coming in and out of the bathrooms, but it was relatively quiet and peaceful. He shook his head slightly, before returning his gaze to mine.

"Why are you here, Kiera?"

His question broke my heart. Did he really not want to ever see me again? Confused, I blurted out, "My sister." He nodded, like that filled in all the blanks for him, and twisted his body like he was going to walk away. I grabbed his arm and roughly pulled him back to me. "You . . . for you."

My voice was a little panicked when I said that, and his eyes narrowed a bit as he looked me over. "For me? You chose him, Kiera. Push came to shove—you chose him."

I shook my head and pulled his arm closer, his body taking a step nearer as well. "No . . . I didn't. Not at the end, I didn't."

His brows scrunched together. "I heard you, Kiera. I was there, I heard you clearly—"

I cut him off. "No . . . I was just scared." I pulled him even closer and put my other hand on his chest. "I was scared, Kellan. You're . . . you're so . . ." I suddenly didn't know how to explain it to him, and I fumbled around for words.

He stepped closer to me and suddenly our hips were touching. "I'm what?" he whispered.

The fire at his nearness flew through me, and I stopped trying to think about what to say and just let whatever wanted to come out, come out. "I've never felt such passion, like I feel when I'm with you. I've never felt this heat." My hand rubbed his chest and then pushed up to his face. His eyes watched me intensely, his lips parted as he breathed shallowly. "You were right, I was scared to let go . . . but I was scared to let go of *him* to be with you, not the other way around. He was comfortable and safe and you . . . I got scared that the heat would burn out . . . and you'd leave me for someone better . . . and then I'd have nothing. That I'd throw Denny away for a hot romance that would be over before I knew it, and I'd be alone. Flash fire."

His head lowered as his body pressed closer to me—our chests were touching as well now. "Is that what you think we had? Flash fire? Did you think I'd just throw you away if that fire died?" He said "if," like the very idea was ridiculous to him.

He rested his head against mine and one of his legs shifted in between mine. My breath picked up and then nearly stopped at his next words. "You're . . . the only woman I've ever loved . . . ever. You thought I'd toss that out? Do you really think anyone in this world compares to you in my eyes?"

"I get that now, but I panicked. I was scared. . . ." My chin lifted until our parted lips brushed together.

He pulled back and took a step away from me. My hand clenched his arm to keep him from leaving. He looked down and then back up to me, his eyes struggling with wanting me and not wanting me. "You don't think this scares me, Kiera?" He shook his head. "Do you think loving you has ever been easy for me . . . or even sometimes pleasant?"

I looked down at his words and swallowed loudly. I supposed loving me hadn't always been a picnic for him. His next words confirmed that. "You have put me through hell so many times that I almost think I'm crazy for even talking to you right now."

A tear dripped down my cheek and I shifted my body to leave. He grabbed my shoulders and held me against the wall. I looked up at him, and another tear hit my cheek. His thumb came up to tenderly wipe it away, and then both hands held my face and kept me looking at him. "I know what we have is intense. I know it's terrifying. I feel that too, believe me. But it's real, Kiera." His hand ghosted from his chest to mine, and then back again. "This is real and it's deep, and it wouldn't have just . . . burned out. I'm done with meaningless encounters. You're everything I want. I'd never have strayed from you."

I brought my hands up to hold his face, to pull him into me, but he stepped back again before I could reach him. His eyes filled with an almost unbearable sadness as he gazed at me, a foot apart now. "I still can't be with you, though. How can I ever trust that . . . ?" his eyes drifted to the floor, and his voice quieted to barely reach me above the din of the hallway, "that you won't leave *me* one day? As much as I miss you, that thought keeps me away."

I took a step toward him and reached out for his hands. "Kellan, I'm so—"

He looked up at me and cut me off. "You left me for him, Kiera, even if it was just some knee-jerk reaction, because the thought of us terrified you." His brows scrunched together unhappily as he said those words. "You still were going to leave me for him. How do I know that won't happen again?"

"It won't . . . I won't ever leave you. I'm done being apart from you. I'm done denying what we have. I'm done being scared." My tone came out surprisingly calm, and I was a little startled to realize that my nerves were calm, too. I truly meant what I'd just said, maybe more than I'd ever meant anything I'd said to him.

He shook his head sadly. "I'm not, Kiera. I still need that minute. . . ."

I put my hand on his stomach and he looked down at it, but left it there. I murmured, "Do you still love me?" My breath stopped as I waited for his answer. I hoped from his expression and his song that he did, but I needed to hear him acknowledge it.

He sighed and looked over my face. Slowly, he nodded. "You would never believe how much."

I stepped closer to him and ran my hand up to his chest; he closed his eyes at the contact. My fingers ran over his heart, and his hand came up to hold my fingers there. "I never left you. . . . I kept you with me, here." I thought he was being symbolic with that phrase, until I remembered Matt talking to Anna in the kitchen. He'd said, ". . . right over his heart . . ." I'd assumed at the time that Kellan had done something romantic for another woman, but what if he'd . . .

I moved my fingers to the collar of his shirt and pulled it down. He sighed softly, but dropped his hand and didn't stop me as I stretched the fabric. I wasn't sure what I was looking for, but then I saw the black markings on his once-pristine skin. Confused, I pulled the shirt down farther. That was when my mouth dropped open in shock. He'd told me once that he couldn't think of anything he'd want permanently etched into his skin, and here I was, staring at my own name in beautifully scripted letters, right above his heart. He literally had kept me with him. My own heart cracked into pieces, as I traced the large swirling letters.

"Kellan . . ." My voice choked up, and I had to swallow.

He moved his hand onto mine and pulled my fingers away from his skin, hiding his tattoo again. Interlacing our fingers, he brought them back to his chest and then rested his forehead against mine. "So . . . yes, yes I do still love you. I never stopped. But . . . Kiera . . ."

"Have you been with anyone else?" I whispered it, not sure if I really wanted to know or not.

He pulled back fractionally, and looked at me like I'd just asked him something he couldn't even contemplate. "No . . . I haven't wanted . . ." He shook his head. "Have you?" he whispered.

I bit my lip and shook my head as well. "No. I just . . . I just want you. We're meant to be, Kellan. We need each other."

We both stepped together at the same time, until every inch of us was touching, head to foot. His other hand traveled to my hip as mine slipped around his waist. Without a thought, we both pulled each other even closer. My eyes kept drifting down to his lips and I made myself lift them back to his eyes. He was also staring at my mouth, and when he brought his tongue over his lower lip, followed by his teeth slowly dragging across them, my eyes quickly darted back down and I gave up trying not to stare.

"Kiera," he started again, as his head angled down to me and mine angled up to him. "I thought I could leave you. I thought distance would make this go away, and it'd get easier, but it hasn't." He shook his head as I started to get lost in the overwhelmingly wonderful smell of him that was enveloping me. "Being apart from you is killing me. I feel lost without you."

"I do too," I murmured.

He exhaled brokenly. Our mouths were only inches apart. Our fingers against his chest disentangled and I ran mine up over his shoulder. He dragged his slowly down my necklace again. He whispered, "I've thought about you every day." I inhaled sharply as the very tips of his fingers traveled down my chest and over my bra. "I've dreamt about you every night." The pads of his fingers trailed along my ribs, as mine reached around his neck to twirl around the hair at the back of his head. We both kept drawing each other nearer while he talked, still attracted to each other, almost subconsciously.

"But . . . I don't know how to let you back in." His hand on my hip moved up my back and mine followed suit down his back. His eyes, flashing over my face, reflected nervousness, anxiety, fear, even. He looked the opposite of how I felt. His lips drifted even closer, until I could practically feel the heat coming off of them. My heartbeat spiked and I closed my eyes when he whispered, "I don't know how to keep you out, either."

Just then, he was pushed from behind. For a fraction of a second, I thought I heard my sister's throaty chuckle, but I couldn't focus long enough to be sure. My rational thoughts were suddenly obliterated. Whoever had pushed him into me had closed the distance for us, and Kellan's lips were now firmly on mine. We froze for a good ten seconds, and then stopped denying what we both wanted and began to move together simultaneously—light, lingering, soft kisses that seared my lips and quickened my breath. I offered no resistance and completely gave myself over to him. I was his anyway. . . .

"Oh, God," he whispered along my lips, "I've missed . . ." He pressed harder against me and I moaned slightly under his touch. "I can't . . ." His hand ran back up my chest to clutch at my neck. "I don't . . ." Our lips parted and his tongue lightly slid into me, barely touching mine. "I want . . ." He groaned deep in his chest and I found myself matching his sound. "Oh, God . . . Kiera."

Both of his hands drifted to my face, gently stroking back my now freely flowing tears before clutching me firmly. He pulled back to look in my eyes. With a heavy breath, I returned his intense gaze. His eyes were smoldering in a way that made me weak. "You wreck me," he growled, crashing his lips back down to mine.

It was like someone had flipped a switch on us both. He pushed us back into the wall, his body hard on mine. My hands flew up into his hair, while his drifted over my chest and down to my hips. I was pretty sure we were going way beyond simple PDA now, and even though I knew some people were still lingering in this hallway, quite possibly my sister among them, with Kellan's hands, body, and tongue on mine, I just couldn't care enough to be embarrassed.

I savored his heat, his passion, the roughness of his stubble on my sensitive skin, and the occasional noises that he made that were so suggestive and alluring. I brought him closer to me and wished we were alone in that back room. As his hands reached around behind me, playing with the indentation of my lower back that he seemed to have such a thing for, I suddenly realized that this was what I'd wanted to avoid happening when he first brought me back here. Not that I didn't want physical contact with him, every part of me did, it was just . . . this wasn't what we needed right now.

Physical contact had never been our problem. It was the slowing things down, having an actual relationship that had panicked me into making a foolish mistake. Firmly, but gently, I pushed his shoulders away from me. With confused, blazing eyes, he let me. Hurt almost immediately entered those eyes, as some realization passed through him. I was sure it wasn't what had passed through me, so I quickly said, "I want you. I choose you. It will be different this time, everything will be different. I want to make this work with you."

He relaxed and looked at my lips and then my eyes and then back to my lips. "How do we do that? This is what we do . . . back and forth, back and forth. You want me, you want him. You love me, you love him. You like me, you hate me, you want me, you don't want me, you love me . . . you leave me. There's so much that went wrong before. . . ."

I brought a hand to his cheek and he looked up at me. I could see it then—the confusion, the lingering anger, the rejection, the pain and, underneath it all, a deep insecurity. He felt so conflicted all the time. He doubted himself. He doubted his goodness . . . all because of me, because of our twisted relationship. I was tired of bringing such turmoil into his life. I was tired of "wrecking" him. I wanted to be good to him. I wanted to bring him joy. I wanted us to have a future together. But, regardless of his assurance, we really would burn out at this pace.

"Kellan, I'm naïve and insecure. You're a . . . moody artist." His lip twitched at that and, smiling softly, I continued. "Our history is a mess of twisted emotions, jealousies, and complications, and we've both tormented and hurt each other . . . and others. We've both made mistakes . . . so many mistakes." I leaned back from him and smiled wider. "So how about we slow down? How about we just . . . date . . . and see how it goes?"

He looked at me blankly for a long moment, and then a devilish look passed over his face. It was a look that had been absent from my sight for so long that it hurt my heart in the best possible way to see it. I blushed, and my whole body felt five times hotter when I remembered what Kellan considered "dating."

I looked down, embarrassed. "I meant . . . actual dating, Kellan. The old-fashioned kind."

I looked up at his light chuckling. His smile softened to a calm, peaceful one, as he warmly said, "You really are the most adorable person. You have no idea how much I've missed that."

My smile matched his, as I stroked the rough stubble on his face. "So . . . will you date me?" I added a slight suggestive tone and he raised an eyebrow at hearing it.

His smile widened playfully. "I'd love to . . . date you." His look turned more serious. "We'll try . . . we'll try to stop hurting each other. We'll take this easy. We'll go slowly."

I could only nod in response.

In a way that I'd never thought possible with Kellan, we went exceedingly slow. I stayed with my sister at our apartment. Anna delighted over and over in telling people that she had literally "shoved" us back together. Kellan stayed alone in his house, never having gotten another roommate. Our first official date was that Sunday night, when we both had the evening off. We went out to dinner. He held my hand when he met me at my door and, at the end of the evening, kissed my cheek when he took me home. It was such a chaste evening it nearly shocked me. But even though the physical contact was restrained, our other emotions were running rampant. There was a lot of eye-gazing and dopey smiles from the both of us.

Next, he took me dancing again. My sister—who took great joy in repeatedly smacking Kellan on the back of his head for lying about the two of them sleeping together, and I always let her, a grin plastered on my face each time—Jenny; her roommate, Rachel; and, of course, the other band members came out with us . . . kind of a group-date thing.

I smiled as I watched shy Matt flush with color as his pale eyes took in the exotic beauty of quiet Rachel. They spent most of the night together, getting to know each other in a secluded corner in the back. The rest of us stayed close together on the packed floor, dancing mainly as one large group. Kellan did nothing more suggestive than slow dance with his arms around my waist, his fingers along the ridge of my lower back. I smiled at his restraint and carefully put my head on his shoulder, determined to match his level.

With lazy, satisfied eyes, I watched Anna and Griffin being too obscene for words on the floor and quickly shifted my focus to where Evan and Jenny appeared to be having a moment. I nudged Kellan's shoulder and, smiling, he looked down at me. I flicked my head to where they were slow dancing with their heads together, Jenny gazing up at Evan dreamily, Evan playing with a long piece of her golden hair. Kellan looked back at me and shrugged, a wide smile breaking over his gorgeous face. I couldn't bring my attention back to Jenny after that moment, as his perfect eyes trapped me.

He didn't kiss me until our third date, to see a romantic comedy that he protested loudly that he didn't want to see. But it being a standard dating rite of passage, I made him go. I did notice tears in his eyes at the end. He walked me to my door afterwards and politely asked if he could. I smiled at his attempt to be a modest gentleman and told him yes. He attempted a brief peck of a kiss, and I grabbed his neck and pulled him in for a kiss that left us both gasping for air. Hey, impulse control was not always my strength with Kellan, and, as my sister had accurately pointed out, he is hotter than all . . . well, you know.

He'd meet me at school sometimes, and we'd talk over my new classes. I unfortunately had a class with Candy now, and while at first that had hurt and irritated me, now that Kellan and I were making a go of an actual relationship, I found that I didn't care one iota about her. Well, I might have enjoyed the flash of jealousy on her face when I gave him a kiss at the door, but that was about all I felt toward her. Kellan completely ignored her.

We'd frequently have lunch in our park as the days warmed up. Kellan wasn't the world's greatest cook or anything, and honestly, neither was I, but he'd make us sandwiches and we'd eat them under a large tree, our backs to the bark, our legs entwined, comfortable, relaxed, and feeling like we'd always been together this way.

I eventually put in my notice at my new job and got back my old shift at Pete's. Emily from the day crew had taken over for me, and she was more than willing to switch back to her old time slot. She made it sound like she just couldn't handle the drunken idiots on the packed weekend nights, but I got the impression it was just *one* drunken idiot who had swayed her. A drunken idiot that was still having frequent sleepovers with my sister, although they didn't seem to be too strict on the whole "monogamy" thing. My sister would occasionally have other houseguests, while Griffin never stopped his tales of sordid conquests, tales that I tried very hard not to hear. Whatever they had, it was at least a mutual arrangement.

It had been long enough that the bar was no longer buzzing with gossip over the messy love triangle, although I did get quite a few inquisitive stares my first few days back. Most of the people seemed to believe that Kellan's and my injuries really were sustained by a group of punks robbing us, but a few people gave me appraising looks, and I wondered if they hadn't figured out the truth.

The affair, however, wasn't hidden well at all. With Denny leaving the country and me leaving the bar, added to Kellan's snappy, moody behavior while I was gone, it didn't take a genius to fill in the blanks, and most of the regulars had it figured out right away. The ones that still hadn't realized what had been going on figured it out on the night that I showed up at Pete's, and Kellan and I . . . worked things out . . . in the hallway. And if that wasn't clear enough—and I think the only one who still didn't get it at that point was Griffin—Kellan kissing me every time he sauntered into the bar was a dead giveaway.

Once the stares and whispers died down, being back at Pete's was healing to me, especially listening to the band again. Kellan always sang the emotional song directly to me, and it always brought me to tears. If words could be caresses, then he was making love to me every time he sang it. Several girls in the front of the packed crowd would swoon when he sang that one, probably picturing themselves as the object of his affection. Occasionally, some would get too eager with him after the show, and I'd smile as he gently pushed them back or stopped their lips from attacking his body. It did make a flash of jealousy go through me, but his heart was mine, and I didn't doubt that. How could I, after he'd branded himself?

And, oh the tattoo . . . I stared at it frequently. Once our relationship progressed to the stage of him taking his shirt off, it stayed there for quite a while, and I traced the letters often, as we kissed on his couch. I told him that I could get one of his name, but he insisted that wearing his necklace, which I never took off, was enough, and that my "virgin" skin was perfect as it was. I blushed fiercely at that, but I couldn't get over staring at what he'd done while we'd been apart. Because of his history, I'd assumed he'd found comfort in an assortment of eager girls, but he hadn't. He'd found comfort in me, in my name across his skin. I couldn't ignore the aching beauty in that.

He told me that he'd gotten it the night before we'd seen Denny off at the airport. He'd decided to do it the day Denny and Anna had moved all of my stuff out of his house, as a way to keep me close to him, because he always did need to be near me. I'd never have imagined that my name could be so beautiful, but there were few things in the world as wonderful to me as that black ink swirled on his chest. Well, maybe his smile . . . or his hair . . . or his adoring eyes . . . or his heart . . .

He confessed to me one evening that he still kept in contact with Denny. That shook me. I sort of thought their last words had been at the airport. He told me that after Denny went back home he'd called Denny's parents daily. Eventually his persistence paid off and he'd gotten through to Denny. They didn't have much to say to each other in the beginning, but Kellan kept trying. Truly, their relationship didn't advance much, until Kellan confessed that he and I weren't a couple.

Denny had never straight-out asked me about Kellan, and I had never volunteered, not wanting to mention such a painful topic when we were trying to be friendly with each other. He'd assumed that we'd jumped into coupledom the moment he'd left. He was shocked when Kellan had told him that that wasn't the case. And most shocking of all . . . he'd called Kellan an idiot for letting me walk away. My jaw dropped when Kellan relayed that piece of information.

When I talked to Denny a few days later, he confirmed it. He said that after everything that had happened, it seemed like a waste if we didn't end up together. I laughed at him and told him he was too good of a person. He agreed and laughed with me. He was happy. His job was going great, and he was already in line for a promotion. His relationship was also going strong and "Abby" was quickly becoming more than just a casual girlfriend to him. I ached at that for a few moments, and then was immensely happy for him. He deserved it.

My own relationship was progressing wonderfully as well. Kellan actually *could* do the great-boyfriend thing, and he seemed to delight in the fact that we were taking things painfully slowly. In fact, he seemed to make a point of riling me up to the edge of bursting and then calmly saying we needed to slow things down. The boy always was a tease. But his eyes were, more often than not, carefree and untroubled, and his grin was loose and easy.

That's not to say that everything in our relationship was smooth and untroubled. It wasn't. We did on occasion have . . . disagreements. They were generally started by some woman that Kellan had slept with at some point. One even knocked on his door, wearing a long coat that she left unbuttoned, revealing her skimpy underwear set that made me furiously blush. I'd been visiting before my shift when the vixen had shown up. He'd quickly ushered her out, but a tiny part of me couldn't help but wonder what he'd have done if I hadn't been there, and if half-naked women showing up on his door was a common event. I didn't doubt his love, but I'm only human, a human who frequently felt horribly plain next to her Adonis of a boyfriend, and the woman had been extremely beautiful . . . and extremely well endowed.

And that was only one instance. There were others. Girls he'd been with would walk up to him at the bar, or even sometimes at my school, and try to restart their "relationship." He always turned them down, assuring me that they meant nothing, and he generally didn't even remember their names, which did not make me feel any better, but the insecurities were there in me, and it hurt. Our "talks" usually brought up his insecurities as well, about me not being over Denny, and really wanting to be with him. Kellan still felt like he was second place. I repeatedly told him he was not.

We tried to reassure each other that we were in this together, and we were being faithful to each other, but knowing that the person you're with has cheated on a loved one before lends itself to additional insecurities, even if you were the person that they'd cheated with. And each of us had to deal with our history, with the knowledge that we'd been intimate with other people while being in love with each other. The memories of hearing, and in that one instance with Kellan, seeing, those intimacies, were hard to overcome sometimes.

Kellan even yelled at me once, for sleeping with Denny after our long, passionate afternoon of being together. He'd felt betrayed by that, and he confessed how much that had hurt, how much that had to do with his decision to leave that fateful night. He'd hidden a lot of how much it had bothered him when I was with Denny, and it had really affected him after I slept with Denny right after our seemingly perfect day together. He was quite vocal in proclaiming his pain. But then, almost instantly, he felt bad for yelling and sank his head in his hands. He resisted at first, but eventually, he let me put my arms around him, muttering repeated apologies in his ear while he shed a few tears.

We'd both wounded each other so deeply. But we made a point of never letting one of us sulk in pain or anger. We talked things out, even if that meant having a two-hour powwow in the parking lot at Pete's one night, after I tearfully, and quite inadvertently, brought up his threesome, which he countered with a tale of watching me flee the club with Denny, knowing exactly where our night was headed and who was really in my mind. But we did eventually work it out, and continued to work it out.

It took some time, but we eventually found a balance between friendship, love, and fire. Kellan hugged me whenever he walked into Pete's and kissed me thoroughly after every show, which embarrassed and delighted me. He stayed close without smothering, and he gave me space without distancing.

Jenny told me repeatedly that we were good together and that she'd never seen Kellan with anyone the way he was with me. I took that to heart, since she'd known him for a while, bad behavior and all. She was still constantly surprised that he was capable of being a one-woman man. She also stepped up her flirtations with Evan, and I was mildly surprised when I caught them full-on making out in the back room one night. Evan blushed as deeply as I had when he'd caught me. Jenny, however, laughed just like Kellan had laughed. Embarrassed, but smiling widely at their budding relationship, I quickly shut the door and ran to go tell Kellan the scoop. He shook his head and, laughing, told me that Matt was still having a quiet relationship with Rachel. It would seem the D-Bags were starting to settle down.

As Kellan gave me a sweet kiss, my sister, watching us at the corner of the guys' table, said she was jealous of our closeness, while giving an oblivious Griffin a pointed glance that he completely ignored. I couldn't help but wonder if my sister would eventually tame *that* D-Bag—maybe they'd tame each other. As Griffin had his hands on some other girl's ass the next night, and my sister brought home (I swear) a Calvin Klein model, I thought, maybe not.

I didn't care. I had my man and he had me. It took an additional three months, but eventually, he did have *all* of me. Our first time being together as legitimate boyfriend and girlfriend was coincidentally a year to the day that I had seen Kellan singing at Pete's for the first time. We took our time, savoring every moment and every sensation.

He sang my song softly to me as he undressed us, his voice low, husky, and full of emotion. I fought back tears the entire time. When the part where the long instrumental section came up, and his ministrations to my body got more . . . intense, the rest of the song was quickly forgotten, and it became very clear that six months of separation and restraint had done nothing to squelch our fire. If anything, the wait had made it better—it meant more. It meant everything.

Our reconnection was intense and deeply emotional, like much of our relationship had been. He muttered things to me while we made love—how beautiful he thought I was, how much he'd missed me, how much he needed me, how empty he'd been, how much he loved me. I couldn't even speak to tell him I felt the exact same way. I was too overcome by the emotion in his voice. Then he said something that tore me.

"Don't leave. . . . I don't want to be alone." He had actual tears in his eyes as he looked down on me. "I don't want to be alone anymore." Even through the intensity of everything else I was feeling, I could sense the waves of loneliness coming off of him.

I grabbed his face, our movements never stopping. "I'm not. I won't . . . ever . . ." I kissed him fiercely to reassure him, and he twisted us so that we were still facing each other but lying sideways on the bed—still connected, still moving together, still making love to each other.

His eyes watered to near overflowing and he closed them, his hand moving from our hips to trail up the side of my body, pulling me even closer to him, like he couldn't get near enough. "I don't want to be without you," he whispered.

"I'm right here, Kellan." I grabbed his hand and put it over my racing heart. "I'm with you . . . I'm right here." My eyes watered now too, and I closed them as emotion flooded me.

I kissed him again and he left his hand over my heart, almost as if he was afraid that if he removed it, I suddenly wouldn't be real anymore. I moved my hand over his heart, right over his tattoo, and we both felt the pulsing life of each other. I opened my eyes and studied his face between tender kisses. He relaxed a bit as my kiss and heartbeat eased his ache, but he left his eyes closed.

I got lost in the moment, watching him, watching the emotion and the pleasure, and even moments of pain shift through his features. His steady rhythm started increasing, along with his breath, and I kissed him softly as low groans he made quickened my own breath. I knew he was getting close, but I was so mesmerized by watching him that I'd almost stopped paying attention to the amazing things going on in my body. I couldn't concentrate on anything but the look on his face and the ache in his voice.

Just when I knew he was on the edge, he opened his eyes and cupped my cheek with the hand that had been resting on my heart. "Please," he whispered intently. "I'm so close, Kiera." He inhaled through his teeth and groaned softly. "I don't want . . . I don't want to do this alone." His eyes still glistened, like any minute a heavy tear would drop, and my own eyes moistened again in response.

"I'm right here, Kellan. You're not alone . . . you're not alone anymore."

I stopped focusing on what I was doing to him and started focusing on what he was doing to me. That tiny mental shift was all I needed to fall right off the edge. I gripped him tight and held absolutely nothing back from him, letting him know exactly how deep in this I was with him, and he fell right off that edge with me. Then, as we both fell, our eyes locked and we simultaneously stopped breathing, stopped vocalizing, and, silently, experienced something deeply profound . . . together.

Our lips found each other's as the fire raged through each of us— hard at first, deep and intense kisses, and then tapering off to light, barely brushing each other caresses, as the fire in us dulled to glowing embers, waiting to flare up again when the moment was right.

He readjusted our bodies, but kept us facing each other, his arms wrapped around me and holding me tight. With another soft kiss, he murmured, "Thank you," and I blushed horribly, but clutched him tight. He dropped his head to the crook of my neck and, rocking against my skin, softly said, "I'm sorry."

I pulled back and he reluctantly lifted his head to look at me. He looked satisfied, but a little embarrassed too. "I didn't mean to . . . practically become a girl." He shook his head and looked down while a soft laugh escaped me, at the memory of once accusing him of being just that.

I brought a hand to his cheek and he looked back up at me. "Can I assure you that you're not?" He smiled softly at the comment.

His smile flipped to a small frown and he looked down again. "It's just been a while, and there was a time when I thought we'd never be . . ." He shrugged as he struggled for words. "I guess I just got a little . . . overwhelmed by it, and I'm sorry." He looked up, and an adorably cute grimace was on his face. "I didn't mean to freak out. That was . . . embarrassing."

"There is nothing about you to be embarrassed about." A small, devilish smile lifted his lips, and I blushed as the way he'd taken my words sank in. With a small laugh, I ran my hand back through his hair and kissed him for a long moment. Pulling back, I ran my fingers down his cheek and, in as comforting a voice as I could muster, said, "You don't have to ever feel sorry with me for that . . . for saying what you really feel . . . or fear."

I shifted us, so I was on my back and he was mostly on top of me, our legs warmly tangling together. I cupped his face in both of my hands while he smiled contentedly above me. "Don't ever hold anything back from me. I want to know . . . I want to know what you're feeling, even if you think I don't, even if you have trouble saying it." His eyes drifted away from mine and I gently moved his head, until he looked at me again. "I love you. I'm not going anywhere."

He nodded and sank down to lie on top of me, his arms tucked under me, his forehead resting against my neck. I sighed and began repeatedly running my fingers back through his hair, occasionally turning to kiss his head, making him sigh and hold me tighter. And so, our first night sleeping together, in the figurative and literal sense of the word, ended with me holding and comforting *him*. And I found something deep and emotionally binding in that. As my fingers brushing through his hair eventually soothed him into sleep, his hold on me never slackened, and I realized that it never would. The love we felt for each other, while definitely never planned or expected, as I suppose most love isn't, had irrevocably seared us both . . . to the core. It wouldn't fade. It wouldn't shift to another. It probably wouldn't always be easy . . . but it would always be . . . always. And as sleep drifted over me, true peace followed right behind it.

Read on for a sizzling sneak peek of

Effortless

Chapter 1
MY BOYFRIEND,
THE ROCK STAR

According to the Channel Four weatherman, it was the hottest summer on record in Seattle. Since I'd only been there a little over a year, I took the kind man's word for it. As I was jostled, smashed into, and bumped up against, I felt the afternoon heat in the clammy skin of every person who touched me. It was revolting to have strangers rubbing up against my body. It was even more revolting when some of those people decided that being crammed together like sardines gave them the freedom to invade my personal space. I'd smacked more hands off my butt in that one afternoon than in the entire time I'd worked at Pete's Bar.

Sweat poured down the back of my T-shirt, and I momentarily cursed my fashion choice. As I glanced up at the cloudless, azure sky, the midday sun hit me square in the eye, blinding me. I rolled up the short sleeves of my midnight black shirt, then went to work tying a knot above my belly button, just like Mary Ann from *Gilligan's Island*.

But then I smiled, remembering why I was wearing it and what I was doing in this crowd of sweaty bodies. As I stared past the few rows of glistening people in front of me to an empty stage, I was overcome with nervous energy. Not for me. No, all my nerves were for my boyfriend. Today was his and his band's big day. In anticipation, I bounced on my feet as I waited for him to bound up onto that stage.

I knew he was going to rush to that microphone at any moment, and the waiting crowd was going to let out an ear-splitting scream.

I couldn't wait.

Hands next to me grabbed my bare arms. "Can you believe it, Kiera? Our boys are playing Bumbershoot!"

I looked over at my best friend, my coworker and my confidante, Jenny. Her face wasn't pouring with sweat like mine; she looked gloriously dewy. The spark of excitement lighting up her eyes was identical to mine, though. Her boyfriend was also playing at the Seattle music festival for the first time.

Squealing in my growing eagerness, I clutched her arms in return. "I know! I can't believe Matt actually booked them here." I shook my head, impressed that my boyfriend was performing in the same venue that Bob Dylan would be playing at later tonight. Hole and Mary J. Blige were scheduled to perform in the next couple of days.

Jenny looked over when some stranger collided into her; he seemed completely stoned. Glancing back at me, her blond ponytail lightly flicking my face, she shrugged. "Evan says he worked really hard to get them this spot. And it's prime! Saturday afternoon on a perfect summer's day, smashed right in between two great acts. It doesn't get any better than that."

She tilted her head up to the sky. The sun's rays glinted off the white lettering on her matching black T-shirt, a T-shirt glorifying the full name of our favorite band—Douchebags—although they shortened it to D-Bags, for marketing purposes.

I nodded when her face returned to mine. "Oh, I know, Kellan said he—"

A sudden eruption of sound disrupted my conversation and my eyes automatically darted to the stage. Smiling broadly, I watched what had the raucous crowd's complete attention. Our D-Bags had finally decided to grace the crowd with their presence.

The assemblage before the outdoor stage started jumping and hollering as Matt and Griffin hopped onstage. Matt was his normal, contained self, acknowledging the fan fest with a small smile and a slight wave. He quietly walked to his microphone and strapped on his guitar. I hollered for him, but the cacophony of noise drowned out my voice, and the guitarist didn't hear me. His light blue eyes scanned the crowd nervously as he adjusted the strap on his shoulder.

On the opposite end of the spectrum, Griffin, Matt's attention-seeking horn dog of a cousin, ran up and down the stage, smacking people's hands and pumping his fist in the air. His pale eyes scanned the crowd, and although I wasn't yelling for him, he actually heard me. Spotting Jenny and I back a ways from the front, he pointed at us. Then he lifted his fingers up to his mouth in a V shape and did suggestive things with his tongue that made my cheeks flame hotter than the steamy sunshine I was standing in. I immediately averted my eyes.

Several people around Jenny and I laughed and looked at us. My embarrassment tripled. Jenny saucily exclaimed, "Ewww, Griffin!" then started laughing with the crowd. I shook my head, wishing my sister, Anna, wasn't at her photo shoot for the Hooters calendar today so she could maybe attempt to keep her pseudo-boyfriend in line.

Evan entered during the middle of that display and, seeing Griffin sexually harass us, looked over our way. He smiled and waved, blowing a kiss to Jenny. She snatched it in the air and blew one back. His smile expanded, but once he acknowledged us, he twisted to take in the scene, and his dark eyes seemed awed by what he saw. I laughed at the look, happy that the good-spirited man was taking a second to enjoy his success.

Then the screams grew so loud my ears started ringing. I actually cringed in pain. The girls beside me, looking all of fourteen, started clutching each other and chanting, "Oh my God, there he is. Oh my God, he's so hot. Oh my God, oh my God, oh my God!"

I grinned and shook my head, amused at how my rocker boyfriend could affect people. Of course, I completely understood. Lord knows he had completely affected me in the beginning. Still did. Just watching him confidently strut onto the stage, the stage he owned with every fiber of his being, my body tingled for him.

Kellan slowly walked toward his microphone. Or perhaps it was a regular pace and my mind was operating in slow motion. For whatever reason, it seemed to take him forever to get to his destination. He raised one hand, waving to the electrified crowd clamoring for him, and he ran the other back through his thick, bed-head hair. The heat and sweat made the sandy-brown mess stick out even more haphazardly; he looked completely edible.

I bit my lip as he sauntered to his microphone stand. He scanned the crowd as he adjusted the height of the stand. I knew from experience just what the front row was feeling as those midnight blue bedroom eyes washed over them. Kellan had a way of looking at you that made you feel like no one else existed in the world, even if a crowd was around you. Add that to the sexy half-smile on his face, and you got a man who could ignite you with just a glance. He was igniting me now, and he hadn't even spotted me yet.

As his face turned away, hopefully searching for me out in the masses, I studied his jaw line—strong, masculine, so freakin' sexy it hurt. The girls behind me obviously thought so too. From among the shrieking, I clearly heard, "That is going home with me tonight," and, "God, that man is completely fuckable." I resisted the urge to turn and tell them that he was mine and instead focused my gaze on him. I knew I shouldn't be jealous or irritated by his fans, but their remarks were a lot less cute than the previous comments from the pubescent girls.

As Kellan's eyes finished inspecting the first half of the crowd, they shifted over my way. Like magic, he spotted us instantly. Jenny waved, then whistled with her fingers in her mouth. I flushed and smiled as those amazingly intense eyes locked on mine. He nodded at me and mouthed, "I love you."

The idiotic girls behind me started moaning that he'd said it to them. I again ignored my desire to tell them that he was mine. It wouldn't change their feelings toward him one tiny little bit, and it would only create endless questions about our personal life. Questions I did not want to discuss with complete and total strangers. I'd put up with enough of that at school before Kellan and I had even started dating.

Instead, I discreetly mouthed that I love him too and gave him a couple of thumbs up. He laughed at my move and shook his head in amusement, clearly confident that he'd completely kick ass onstage. And he would. If anything, Kellan had spent his whole life preparing himself for this moment by playing small bars and clubs in L.A. and Seattle.

Slinging a guitar over his shoulder, he wrapped his hand around the microphone. The screams intensified when it became obvious that he was going to speak. Over the sound system, I heard his warm laugh, then, "Hello, Seattle!" The girls around me jumped and screamed his name. I laughed and tried to move away from some of the more excitable girls, but with nowhere to go, I only ended up colliding into a couple of guys in front of me.

I was muttering apologies when they glared back at me as Kellan's voice hit me again. "We're the D-Bags . . . in case you didn't know"—he paused for another long screaming session— "and we've got something for you . . . if you want it."

He raised an eyebrow and gave some of the women in the front row a look that was a little lascivious for my taste. But I knew it was an act. While his face clearly said, *Screw me later,* that wasn't what was in his heart. I was in his heart. Heck, I was tattooed over his heart. Well, my name was, anyway. I smiled, enjoying the fact that not a single woman here was aware of his hidden art. Well, besides Jenny.

He held up a finger to quiet the crowd. They surprisingly responded. "Do you want it?" he asked suggestively.